Carl Hiaasen was born and raised in Florida. His previous novels are *Tourist Season*, *Double Whammy*, *Skin Tight*, *Native Tongue*, *Strip Tease*, *Stormy Weather* and *Lucky You*, which together have been translated into twenty languages. Since 1979 he has worked at the *Miami Herald* as a magazine writer, investigative reporter and metropolitan columnist.

CARL HIAASEN

SICK PUPPY

AND

SKIN TIGHT

PAN BOOKS

Sick Puppy first published 1999 by Alfred A. Knopf,
a division of Random House, Inc., New York,
and simultaneously in Canada by Random House of Canada Limited, Toronto.
First published in Great Britain in 2001 by Pan Books
Skin Tight first published 1989 by G.P. Putnam's Sons, Inc., New York.
First published in Great Britain 1990 by Macmillan.
First published by Pan Books 1991

This omnibus edition published 2004 by Pan Books
an imprint of Pan Macmillan Ltd
Pan Macmillan, 20 New Wharf Road, London N1 9RR
Basingstoke and Oxford
Associated companies throughout the world
www.panmacmillan.com

ISBN 0 330 43272 9

A CIP catalogue record for this book is available from
the British Library.

Typeset by Intype London Ltd
Printed and bound in Great Britain by
Mackays of Chatham plc, Chatham, Kent

SICK PUPPY

~ FOR FENIA, ~

Η ΜΟΝΑΔΙΚΗ ΜΟΥ ΑΓΑΠΗ

ONE

On the morning of April 24, an hour past dawn, a man named Palmer Stoat shot a rare African black rhinoceros. He fired from a distance of thirteen yards and used a Winchester .458, which knocked him flat on his back. The rhinoceros wheeled, as if to charge, before snorting twice and sagging to its knees. Its head came to rest under a spread of palmettos.

Palmer Stoat instructed his guide, a former feed salesman named Durgess, to unpack the camera.

"Let's first make sure she's dead," Durgess said.

"Are you kidding? You see that shot?"

Durgess took the Winchester from his client. He approached the lifeless mass and poked it in the rump with the rifle barrel.

Stoat grinned as he dusted off his mail-order khakis. "Hey, Bungalow Bill, look what I killed!"

While Durgess assembled the video equipment, Stoat inspected his newest trophy, which had cost him thirty thousand dollars, not including ammo and gratuities. When he moved the palmetto fronds away from the rhino's face, he noticed something wrong.

"You ready?" Durgess was wiping down the lens of the video camera.

"Hey, look here." Stoat pointed accusingly.

"I'm lookin'."

"Care to explain?"

"Explain what? That's a horn," said Durgess.

Stoat gave a yank. It broke off in his hands.

Durgess said, "Now see what you done."

"It's fake, Jethro." Angrily Stoat thrust the molded plastic cone at Durgess.

"The other one's real," Durgess said defensively.

"The other one's a nub!"

"Look, it wasn't my idea."

"You glued a phony horn on my thirty-thousand-dollar rhinoceros. Is that about right?"

Nervously Durgess cracked his knuckles.

"What'd you guys do with the real one?" Stoat demanded.

"Sold it. We cut it off and sold it."

"Perfect."

"They's worth a fortune in Asia. Supposably some kinda magic dick medicine. They say it gives you a boner lasts two days." Durgess shrugged skeptically. "Anyhow, it's serious bucks, Mr. Stoat. That's the program for all our rhinos. Some Chinaman over Panama City buys up the horns."

"You bastards are gypping me."

"Nossir. A jenna-wine African rhinoceros is what the catalog says, and that's what you got."

For a closer look, Stoat knelt in the scrub. The rhino's cranial horn had been taken off cleanly with a saw, leaving an oval abrasion. There the plastic replacement had been attached with white gummy industrial adhesive. A foot or so up the snout was the animal's secondary horn, the caudal, real enough but unimpressive; squat and wart-like in profile.

"The whole idea," Stoat said irritably to Durgess, "was a head mount for my den."

"And that's a helluva head, Mr. Stoat, you gotta admit."

"Except for one tiny detail."

Stoat tossed the fake horn at Durgess. Durgess let it drop to the ground, now sodden with rhino fluids. He said, "I got a taxidermy man does fiberglass on the side, he'll fix you up a new one. Nobody'll know the difference, sir. It'll look just like the real deal."

"Fiberglass."

"Yessir," Durgess said.

"Hello, why not chrome—ever thought of that? Rip the hood ornament off a Cadillac or maybe a 450-SL. Glue it to the tip of that sucker's nose."

Durgess gave Stoat a sullen look. Stoat took the Winchester from the guide and slung it over his shoulder. "Anything else I should know about this animal?"

"Nossir." There was no point telling Stoat that his trophy rhinoceros also had suffered from cataracts on both eyes, which accounted for its lack of alarm at the approach of heavily armed humans. In addition, the animal had spent its entire life as tame as a hamster, the featured attraction of an Arizona roadside zoo.

Stoat said, "Put the camera away. I don't want anybody to see the damn thing like this. You'll get with that fiberglass man right away?"

"First thing tomorrow," Durgess promised.

Palmer Stoat was feeling better. He rubbed a hand across the rhino's bristly plated hide and said, "What a magnificent creature."

Durgess thought: If only I had ten bucks for every time I've heard that line.

Stoat produced two thick cigars and offered one to his faithful guide. "Cohibas," Stoat said, "the genuine article." Theatrically he fired up.

Durgess declined. He grimaced at the acrid comingling of fumes, stogie and rhino piss.

Stoat said, "Tell me something, little bwana."

Oh blow me, Durgess almost said.

"How old you figure this animal to be?"

"I ain't too sure."

Stoat said, "She looks to be in her prime."

"Yeah, she does," said Durgess, thinking: Blind, tame, fat and half senile—a regular killing machine, all right.

Palmer Stoat continued to admire the carcass, as he felt this was expected of a triumphant hunter. In truth, it was himself he was admiring, as both he and Durgess knew. Stoat patted the flank of the carcass and said to his guide: "Come on, man. I'll buy you a beer."

"Sounds good." Durgess took a portable two-way radio from a pocket of his safari jacket. "First lemme call Asa to bring the flatbed."

Palmer Stoat had more than enough money to go to Africa, but he didn't have the time. That's why he did his big-game hunting at local safari ranches, some legal and some not. This one, located near Ocala, Florida, was called the Wilderness Veldt Plantation. Officially it was a "private game preserve"; unofficially it was a place where rich people went to shoot exotic wild animals. Palmer Stoat had been there twice before, once for a water buffalo and once for a lion. From Fort Lauderdale it wasn't a bad drive, a shade over four hours. The hunts were staged early in the morning, so usually he was home in time for dinner.

As soon as he made the interstate, Stoat got on the phone. He had three cellular lines to his Range Rover, as his professional services were in high demand.

He called Desie and told her about the kill. "It was classic," he said, smacking on the cigar.

"How so?" his wife asked.

"Just being out there in the bush. The sunrise. The mist. The twigs crackling under your boots. I wish you'd come along sometime."

"What did she do?" his wife asked. "When you blasted her, I mean."

"Well—"

"Did she charge?"

"No, Des. Everything was over in a second. It was a clean shot."

Desirata was Palmer Stoat's third wife. She was thirty-two years old, an avid tennis player and an occasional liberal. Stoat's buddies once called her a bunny hugger because she wasn't a fan of blood sports. It all depends on whose blood you're talking about, Stoat had said with a taut laugh.

"I suppose you took video," Desie said to her husband. "Your first endangered species and all."

"As a matter of fact, no. No video."

"Oh, Dick's office called."

Stoat rolled down the window and flicked the ash off his Cuban. "When?"

"Four times," Desie said. "Starting at seven-thirty."

"Next time let the machine pick up."

"I was awake anyway."

Stoat said, "Who in Dick's office?"

"Some woman."

That really narrows it down, Stoat thought. Dick Artemus was the governor of Florida, and he liked to hire women.

Desie said, "Should I make dinner?"

"No, let's you and I go out. To celebrate, OK?"

"Great. I'll wear something dead."

"You're a riot, Des."

Palmer Stoat phoned Tallahassee and left a message on the voice mail of Lisa June Peterson, an aide to the governor. Many of Dick Artemus's staff members went by three names, a vestige of their college sorority days at FSU. So far, none of them had consented to have sex with Palmer Stoat, but it was still early in the new administration. Eventually they would come to see how clever, powerful and charismatic Stoat was; one of the two or three top lobbyists in the state. Only in politics would a job like that get you laid; no normal women were impressed by what Stoat did for a living, or even much interested in it.

In Wildwood he got on the turnpike and soon afterward stopped at the Okahumpka Service Plaza for a late lunch: Three hamburgers all the way, two bags of french fries and a jumbo vanilla shake. He drove one-handed, stuffing his cheeks. The digital Motorola started ringing, and Stoat checked the caller ID. Hastily he touched the OFF button. The man on the other end was a Miami commissioner, and Stoat had a firm rule against speaking directly with Miami commissioners—those who weren't already under indictment were under investigation, and all telephone lines into City Hall had long ago been tapped. The last thing Palmer Stoat needed was another trip to the grand jury. Who had time for such nonsense?

Somewhere north of Yeehaw Junction, a dirty black pickup truck appeared in the Rover's rear window. The truck came up fast and then settled in, three car lengths behind Stoat's bumper. Stoat was gnawing on fries and gabbing on the phone, so he didn't pay serious attention until an hour or so later, when he noticed the truck was still behind him. Weird, he thought. Southbound traffic was light—why didn't the idiot pass? Stoat punched the Rover up past ninety, but the truck stayed close. Gradually Stoat eased off the accelerator until he coasted down to forty-five; the black pickup remained right there, three lengths behind, as if connected by a tow bar.

Like most affluent white people who owned sport-utility vehicles, Palmer Stoat lived in constant fear of a carjacking. He had been led to understand that luxury 4↔4s were the chariots of choice for ruthless black and Latin drug gangs; in such circles a Range Rover was said to be more desirable than a Ferrari. Glare on the truck's windshield made it impossible for Stoat to ascertain the ethnicity of the tailgater, but why take a chance? Stoat groped in the console for the Glock semiautomatic that he'd been given as a Christmas gift by the president of the state Police Benevolent Association. Stoat placed the pistol on his lap. Ahead loomed a slow-moving Airstream travel trailer, as wide as a Mississippi barge and just about as nimble. Stoat accelerated around it and cut back sharply, putting the camper rig between him and the pickup truck. He decided to get off the turnpike at the next exit, to see what the tailgater would do.

The Airstream followed Stoat off the ramp; then came the dirty black pickup. Stoat stiffened at the wheel. The clerk at the tollbooth glanced at the gun between his legs but made no mention of it.

"I'm being followed," Stoat informed her.

"That'll be eight dollars and seventy cents," said the clerk.

"Call the Highway Patrol."

"Yessir. Eight-seventy, please."

"Didn't you hear me?" Stoat asked. He handed the clerk a fifty-dollar bill.

"Have you got something a little smaller?"

"Yeah. Your brain stem," Stoat said. "Now, keep the change and call the goddamn Highway Patrol. There's some lunatic tailgater following me."

The clerk ignored the insult and looked toward the vehicles stacking up behind the Range Rover.

In a low voice, Stoat said: "It's the black pickup truck behind the travel trailer."

"What pickup truck?" asked the clerk.

Palmer Stoat placed the Glock on the dashboard and stepped out of the Rover so he could peek around the Airstream. The next car in line was a station wagon with a square-dance pennant attached to the antenna. The tailgater was gone. "Sonofabitch," Stoat muttered.

The driver of the camper honked. So did another motorist, farther down the line. Stoat got back in the Range Rover. The tollbooth clerk handed him change for the fifty. Dryly she said, "You still want me to call the Highway Patrol?"

"No, thanks."

"How about the CIA?"

Stoat smirked. The little smart-ass didn't know who she was dealing with. "Congratulations, young lady," he told her. "You're about to enter the cold cruel world of the unemployed." Tomorrow he would speak to a man in Tallahassee, and it would be done.

Palmer Stoat found an Exxon station, gassed up, took a leak and then headed back toward the turnpike. All the way to Lauderdale he kept checking his rearview—it was mind-boggling how many people owned black pickups. Had the whole damn world gone redneck? Stoat's nerves were whacked by the time he got home.

They had brought their idea for Shearwater Island to Governor Dick Artemus in glitzy bits and pieces, and he'd liked what he'd heard so far.

A planned seaside community. Beach and boardwalks between the condominium towers. Public parks, kayak tours and a nature trail. Two championship golf courses. A clay pigeon shooting range. A yacht harbor, airstrip and heliport.

But Dick Artemus could not locate Shearwater Island on the wall map of Florida in his office.

That's because it's not called Shearwater Island yet, explained Lisa June Peterson. It's called Toad Island, and it's right there on the Gulf, near the mouth of the Suwannee.

"Have I been there before?" Dick Artemus asked.

"Probably not."

"What does 'Shearwater' mean?"

"It's the name of a bird," Lisa June Peterson said.

"Do they live on the island?" asked the governor. "Is that going to be a problem?"

Lisa June Peterson, having already researched the question, reported that shearwaters were migratory seabirds that preferred the Atlantic coastline.

"But there are other kinds of birds on the island," she added.

"Like what?" Dick Artemus frowned. "Eagles? Don't tell me there's goddamn bald eagles on this island, because that means we got a federal scenario."

"They're doing the survey this week."

"Who!"

"A biological survey. Clapley's people," Lisa June Peterson said. Robert Clapley was the developer who wanted to rename Toad Island and subdivide it. He had contributed most generously to Dick Artemus's gubernatorial campaign.

"There's no votes in bulldozing eagle nests," the governor remarked gravely. "Can we all agree on that?"

"Mr. Clapley is taking every reasonable precaution."

"So what else, Lisa? In fifty words or less." Dick Artemus was famous for his insectine attention span.

His assistant said: "The transportation budget includes funding for a new bridge from the mainland. It passed the Senate, but now Willie Vasquez-Washington is being a prick."

Willie Vasquez-Washington was vice chairman of the House Appropriations Committee. He and the governor had tangled before.

"What's he want this time?" Dick Artemus said.

"We're not sure."

"You reach out to Palmer?"

"We keep missing each other."

"And I suppose this thing won't fly, this Shearwater Island," the governor said, "without a brand-new bridge."

"The one they've got is sixty years old and wooden," Lisa June Peterson said. "It won't hold a cement truck is what Roothaus says." Roger Roothaus was president of the engineering firm that wanted the contract for designing the new bridge to Toad Island. He, too, had contributed generously to Dick Artemus's gubernatorial campaign. In fact, almost everyone who stood to profit from the development of Shearwater Island had donated money to the governor's election. This, Dick Artemus took for granted.

"So get Palmer to fix the bridge problem," he said.

"Right."

"Anything else?"

"Nothing major. We're anticipating some local opposition," said Lisa June Peterson.

The governor groaned. "People *live* on this island? Christ, nobody told me that."

"Two hundred. Two fifty max."

"Shit," said Dick Artemus.

"They're circulating a petition."

"I guess that means they're not golfers."

"Evidently not," said Lisa June Peterson.

Dick Artemus rose and pulled on his coat. "I'm late, Lisa June. Would you relate all this to Mr. Stoat?"

"As soon as possible," she said.

Twilly had spent the day in Gainesville at the University of Florida veterinary college, reputedly one of the best in the country. Many famous nature parks and zoos, including the one at Walt Disney World, sent their dead animals there to be necropsied. Twilly had gone to deliver a red-shouldered hawk that appeared to have been shot. The bird had fallen on a remote patch of beach at a place called Madeira Bay, in Everglades National Park. Twilly had bubble-wrapped the broken body and placed it on dry ice in a cooler. He'd made the drive from Flamingo to Gainesville in less than seven hours. He hoped the bullet had remained in the bird, because the bullet was a key to resolving the crime.

Which wasn't exactly the same thing as solving it. Knowing the caliber of the weapon would have been useful: something to file away in case the shooter returned to the park and was foolish enough to let himself get stalked, captured and lashed naked for a month to a mangrove tree.

Twilly Spree wasn't a park ranger or a wildlife biologist or even an amateur bird-watcher. He was an unemployed twenty-six-year-old college dropout with a brief but spectacular history of psychological problems. Not incidentally, he also had inherited millions of dollars.

At the veterinary school, Twilly found a young doctor who agreed to do a postmortem on the hawk, which had in fact succumbed to a single gunshot wound. Unfortunately the slug had passed cleanly through the bird's breast, leaving no fragments, no clues, only blood-crusted feathers. Twilly thanked the young doctor for trying. He filled out a form for the U.S. government stating where he had found the dead hawk, and under what circumstances. At the bottom of the paper he signed his name as "Thomas Stearns Eliot, Jr." Then Twilly got in his black pickup truck and drove south.

He intended to return directly to the Everglades, where he had been living in a pup tent with a three-legged bobcat.

On the turnpike somewhere south of Kissimmee, Twilly came up behind a pearl-colored Range Rover. Normally he wouldn't have paid attention to the style of the vehicle, but this one had a vanity plate that said in green capital letters: COJONES. As Twilly swung into the passing lane, a Burger King hamburger carton flew out the driver's window of the Rover. Next came an empty cup and then a wadded paper napkin, followed by another hamburger carton.

Twilly put a heel on the brake, steered his truck to the shoulder of the highway and waited for a gap in traffic. Then he sprinted into the road and picked up the litter, piece by piece, depositing it in the cab of his truck. Afterward it took him only a few miles to catch up with the pig in the Range Rover; Twilly got behind him and camped there, contemplating his options. He thought about what his therapists would recommend, what his former teachers would say, what his mother would suggest. They were indisputably mature and sensible people, but their advice often proved useless to Twilly Spree. He remained baffled by their outlook on the world, as they were baffled by his.

All Twilly could see of the litterbug was the man's shoulders and the top of his head. To Twilly, it seemed like an exceptionally large head, but possibly this was an illusion caused by the cowboy-style hat. Twilly doubted that an authentic cowboy would be caught dead in a pearl-colored, fifty-thousand-dollar, foreign-made SUV with vanity tags that celebrated the size of his testicles, in *español*. Nor, Twilly thought, would a true cowboy ever toss hamburger wrappers out the window. No, that would be the work of a garden-variety asshole . . . .

Suddenly the Range Rover cut ahead of a slow-moving travel camper, then vectored sharply off the highway at the Yeehaw Junction exit. Twilly followed toward the toll plaza before switching to the exact-change lane, and scooting past. Then he drove across State Road 60 to I-95 and headed at imprudent speeds toward Fort Pierce, where he again hooked up with the turnpike southbound. He parked in the shade of an overpass, raised the hood of the pickup and waited. Twenty minutes later the Rover sped by, and Twilly resumed the pursuit. This time he stayed farther back. He still had no plan but at least he had a clearly defined mission. When the litterbug flicked a cigar butt out the window, Twilly didn't bother to stop. Biodegradable, he thought. Onward and upward.

TWO

After three glasses of wine, Desie could no longer pretend to be following her husband's account of the canned rhinoceros hunt. Across the table she appraised Palmer Stoat as if he were a mime. His fingers danced and his mouth moved, but nothing he said reached her ears. She observed him in two dimensions, as if he were an image on a television screen: an animated middle-aged man with a slight paunch, thin blond hair, reddish eyebrows, pale skin, upcurled lips and vermilion-splotched cheeks (from too much sun or too much alcohol). Palmer had a soft neck but a strong chiseled chin, the surgical scars invisible in the low light. His teeth were straight and polished, but his smile had a twist of permanent skepticism. To Desie, her husband's nose had always appeared too small for his face; a little girl's nose, really, although he insisted it was the one he'd been born with. His blue eyes also seemed tiny, though quick and bright with self-confidence. His face was, in the way of prosperous ex-jocks, roundish and pre-jowly and companionable. Desie wouldn't have called Stoat a hunk but he was attractive in that gregarious southern frat-boy manner, and he had overwhelmed her with favors and flattery and constant attention. Later she realized that the inexhaustible energy with which

Palmer had pursued their courtship was less a display of ardor than an ingrained relentlessness; it was how he went after anything he wanted. They dated for four weeks and then got married on the island of Tortola. Desie supposed she had been in a fog, and now the fog was beginning to lift. What in the world had she done? She pushed the awful question out of her mind, and when she did she was able to hear Palmer's voice again.

"Some creepo was tailing me," he was saying, "for like a hundred miles."

"Why?"

Her husband snorted. "To rob my lily-white ass, that's why."

"This was a black guy?" Desie asked.

"Or a Cuban. I couldn't see which," Stoat said, "but I tell you what, sweets, I was ready for the sonofabitch. Señor Glock was in my lap, locked and loaded."

"On the turnpike, Palmer?"

"He would have been one stone-dead mother."

"Just like your rhino," Desie said. "By the way, are you getting her stuffed like the others?"

"Mounted," Stoat corrected. "And just the head."

"Lovely. We can hang it over the bed."

"Speaking of which, guess what they're doing with rhinoceros horns."

"Who's they?" Desie asked.

"Asians and such."

Desie knew, but she let Palmer tell the story. He concluded with Durgess's fanciful rumor of two-day erections.

"Can you imagine!" Stoat hooted.

Desie shook her head. "Who'd even want one of those?"

"Maybe *you* might, someday." He winked.

Desie glanced around for the waiter. Where was dinner? How could it take so long to boil pasta?

Stoat poured himself another glass of wine. "Rhino horns, Holy Christ on a ten-speed. What next, huh?"

"That's why poachers are killing them off," his wife said.

"Yeah?"

"That's why they're almost extinct. God, Palmer, where have you been?"

"Working for a living. So you can sit home, paint your toenails and learn all about endangered species on the Discovery Channel."

Desie said, "Try the *New York Times*."

"Well, pardon me." Stoat sniffed sarcastically. "I read the newspaper today, oh boy."

This was one of her husband's most annoying habits, dropping the lyrics of old rock songs into everyday conversation. Palmer thought it clever, and perhaps it wouldn't have bothered Desie so much if occasionally he got the words right, but he never did. Though Desie was much younger, she was familiar with the work of Dylan and the Beatles and the Stones, and so on. In college she had worked two summers at a Sam Goody outlet.

To change the subject, she said: "So what did Dick Artemus want?"

"A new bridge." Stoat took a sideways bite from a sourdough roll. "No big deal."

"A bridge to what?"

"Some nowhere bird island over on the Gulf. How about passing the butter?"

Desie said, "Why would the governor want a bridge to nowhere?"

Her husband chuckled, spraying crumbs. "Why does the governor want *anything*? It's not for me to question, darling. I just take the calls and work my magic."

"A day in the life," said Desie.

"You got it."

Once, as a condition of a probation, Twilly Spree had been ordered to attend a course on "anger management." The class was made up of men and women who had been arrested for outbursts of violence, mostly in domestic situations. There were husbands who'd clobbered their wives, wives who'd clobbered their husbands, and even one grandmother who had clobbered her sixty-two-year-old son for blaspheming during Thanksgiving supper. Others of Twilly's classmates had been in bar fights, gambling frays and bleacher brawls at Miami Dolphins games. Three had shot guns at strangers during traffic altercations and, of those, two had been wounded by return fire. Then there was Twilly.

The instructor of the anger-management course presented himself as a trained psychotherapist. Dr. Boston was his name. On the first day he asked everyone in class to compose a short essay titled "What Makes Me Really, Really Mad." While the students wrote, Dr. Boston went through the stack of manila file folders that had been sent to him by the court. After reading the file of Twilly Spree, Dr. Boston set it aside on a corner of the desk. "Mr. Spree," he said in a level tone.

"We're going to take turns sharing our stories. Would you mind going first?"

Twilly stood up and said: "I'm not done with my assignment."

"You may finish it later."

"It's a question of focus, sir. I'm in the middle of a sentence."

Dr. Boston paused. Inadvertently he flicked his eyes to Twilly's folder. "All right, let's compromise. You go ahead and finish the sentence, and then you can address the class."

Twilly sat down and ended the passage with the words *ankle-deep in the blood of fools!* After a moment's thought, he changed it to *ankle-deep in the evanescing blood of fools!*

He stuck the pencil behind one ear and rose.

Dr. Boston said: "Done? Good. Now please share your story with the rest of us."

"That'll take some time, the whole story will."

"Mr. Spree, just tell us why you're here."

"I blew up my uncle's bank."

Twilly's classmates straightened and turned in their seats.

"A branch," Twilly added, "not the main office."

Dr. Boston said, "Why do you think you did it?"

"Well, I'd found out some things."

"About your uncle."

"About a loan he'd made. A very large loan to some very rotten people."

"Did you try discussing it with your uncle?" asked Dr. Boston.

"About the loan? Several times. He wasn't particularly interested."

"And that made you angry?"

"No, discouraged." Twilly squinted his eyes and locked his hands around the back of his neck. "Disappointed, frustrated, insulted, ashamed—"

"But isn't it fair to say you were angry, too? Wouldn't a person need to be pretty angry to blow up a bank building?"

"No. A person would need to be resolved. That I was."

Dr. Boston felt the amused gaze of the other students, who were awaiting his reaction. He said, "I believe what I'm hearing is some denial. What do the rest of you think?"

Twilly cut in: "I'm not denying anything. I purchased the dynamite. I cut the fuses. I take full responsibility."

Another student asked: "Did anybody get kilt?"

"Of course not," Twilly snapped. "I did it on a Sunday, when the bank was closed. That's my point— if I was really pissed, I would've done it on a Monday morning, and I would've made damn sure my uncle was inside at the time."

Several other probationers nodded in agreement. Dr. Boston said: "Mr. Spree, a person can be very mad without pitching a fit or flying off the handle. Anger is one of those complicated emotions that can be close to the surface or buried deeply, so deeply we often don't recognize it for what it is. What I'm suggesting is that at some subconscious level you must've been extremely angry with your uncle, and probably for reasons that had nothing to do with his banking practices."

Twilly frowned. "You're saying that's not enough?"

"I'm saying—"

"Loaning fourteen million dollars to a rock-mining

company that's digging craters in the Amazon River basin. What more did I need?"

Dr. Boston said, "It sounds like you might've had a difficult relationship with your uncle."

"I barely know the man. He lives in Chicago. That's where the bank is."

"How about when you were a boy?"

"Once he took me to a football game."

"Ah. Did something happen that day?"

"Yeah," said Twilly. "One team scored more points than the other team, and then we went home."

Now the class was snickering and it was Dr. Boston's turn to manage his anger.

"Look, it's simple," Twilly said. "I blew up the building to help him grow a conscience, OK? To make him think about the greedy wrongheaded direction his life was heading. I put it all in a letter."

"Yes, the letter's in the file," said Dr. Boston. "But I noticed you didn't sign your name to it."

Twilly spread his hands. "Do I look like an idiot? It's against the law, blowing up financial institutions."

"And just about anything else."

"So I've been advised," Twilly muttered.

"But, still, at a subconscious level—"

"I don't have a subconscious, Doctor. That's what I'm trying to explain. Everything that happens in my brain happens right on the surface, like a stove, where I can see it and feel it and taste the heat." Twilly sat down and began massaging his temples with his fingertips.

Dr. Boston said, "That would make you biologically unique in the species, Mr. Spree, not having a subconscious. Don't you dream in your sleep?"

"Never."

"Seriously."

"Seriously," Twilly said.

"Never once?"

"Not ever in my whole life."

Another probationer waved a hand. "C'mon, man, you never had no nightmares?"

"Nope," Twilly said. "I can't dream. Maybe if I could I wouldn't be here now."

He licked the tip of his pencil and resumed work on the essay, which he submitted to Dr. Boston after class. Dr. Boston did not acknowledge reading Twilly's composition, but the next morning and every morning for the following four weeks, an armed campus security guard was posted in the rear of the classroom. Dr. Boston never again called on Twilly Spree to speak. At the end of the term, Twilly received a notarized certificate saying he'd successfully completed anger-management counseling, and was sent back to his probation officer, who commended him on his progress.

If only they could see me now, Twilly thought. Preparing for a hijack.

First he'd followed the litterbug home, to one of those exclusive islands off Las Olas Boulevard, near the beach. Nice spread the guy had: old two-story Spanish stucco with barrel-tile shingles and vines crawling the walls. The house was on a cul-de-sac, leaving Twilly no safe cover for lurking in his dirty black pickup. So he found a nearby construction site—a mansion going up. The architecture was pre-*Scarface* Medellin, all sharp angles and marble facings and smoked glass. Twilly's truck blended in nicely among the backhoes and cement mixers. Through the twilight he strolled back toward the litterbug's home, where he melted into a hedge of thick ficus to wait. Parked in the driveway next to the Range Rover was a Beemer convertible, top down, which Twilly surmised would belong to the wife, girl-friend or boyfriend. Twilly had a notion that made him smile.

An hour later the litterbug came out the front door. He stood in the amber light under the stucco arch and fired up a cigar. Moments later a woman emerged from the house, slowly backing out and pulling the door shut behind her; bending forward at the waist, as if saying good-bye to a small child or perhaps a dog. As the litterbug and his female companion crossed the driveway, Twilly saw her fanning the air in an exagger-ated way, indicating she didn't much care for cigar smoke. This brought another smile to Twilly's face as he slipped from the hedge and hustled back to his truck. They'll be taking the ragtop, he thought. So she can breathe.

Twilly followed the couple to an Italian restaurant on an unscenic stretch of Federal Highway, not far from the seaport. It was a magnificent choice for what Twilly had in mind. Litterbug parked the convertible in true dickhead style, diagonally across two spaces. The strategy was to protect one's expensive luxury import from scratches and dings by preventing common folks from parking next to it. Twilly was elated to witness this selfish stunt. He waited ten minutes after the cigar-smoking man and cigar-hating woman had entered the restaurant, to make sure they'd been seated. Then he sped off on his quest.

Her stage name was Tia and she was already up on their table, already twirling her mail-order ponytail and peeling off her lacy top when the stink hit her like a blast furnace. Damn, she thought, did a sewer pipe break?

And the three guys all grins and high fives, wearing matching dark blue coveralls with filthy sleeves; laughing and smoking and sipping their six-dollar beers and going Tee-uh, izzat how you say it? Kinda name is Tee-uh? And all three of them waving fifties, for God's sake; stinking like buzzard puke and singsonging her name, her stage name, and slipping brand-new fifty-dollar bills into her G-string. So now Tia had a major decision to make, a choice between the unbelievable gutter-rot stench and the unbelievably easy money. And what she did was concentrate mightily on breathing through her mouth, so that after a while the reek didn't seem so unbearable and the truth was, hey, they were nice-enough guys. Regular working stiffs. They even apologized for stinking up the joint. After a few table dances they asked Tia to sit and join them because they had the wildest story for her to hear. Tia said OK, just a minute, and hurried to the dressing room. In her locker she found a handkerchief, upon which she sprinkled expensive Paris perfume, another unwanted gift from another smitten customer. She returned to the table to find an open bottle of the club's priciest champagne, which was almost potable. The crew in the dirty blue coveralls was making a sloppy toast to somebody; clinking their glasses and imploring Tia to sit down, c'mon, sit. Have some bubbly. They couldn't wait to tell her what had happened, all three chattering simultaneously, raising their voices, trying to take charge of the storytelling. Tia, holding the scented hankie under her nose, found herself authentically entertained and of course not believing a word they said, except for the part about their occupations, which they could hardly embellish, given the odor.

How come you don't believe we got our load hijacked! one of them exclaimed.

Because it's ridiculous, said Tia.

Really it was more of a trade, said one of his pals. The young man give us three grand cash and the use of his pickup and told us to meet back here in a hour.

Tia flared her eyebrows. This total stranger, he hands you three thousand bucks and drives off in a—

All fifties, one of the men said, waving a handful of bills. A grand each!

Tia, giggling through the handkerchief: You guys are seriously fulla shit.

No, ma'am, we ain't. We might smell like we are, but we ain't.

The one waving the fattest wad was talking loudest. What we told you, he said, that's the honest-to-God truth of how we come to be here tonight, watchin' you dance. And if you don't believe it, Miz Tee-uh, just come out back to the parkin' lot in about fifteen minutes when the boy gets back.

Maybe I will, said Tia.

But by then she was busy entertaining a table of

cable-TV executives, so she missed seeing Twilly Spree drive up to the neon-lit strip club in a full-sized county garbage truck. When Twilly got out, one of the men in blue coveralls tossed him the keys to the black pickup.

"You guys go through all that dough I gave you?" Twilly asked amiably.

"No, but just about."

"And it was worth every dollar, I bet."

"Oh yeah."

Twilly shook hands with each of the men and said good-bye.

"Wait, son, come on inside and have just one beer. We got a lady wants to meet you."

"Rain check," said Twilly.

"No, but see, she don't believe us. She thinks we robbed the bingo hall or somethin'. That's how come you gotta come inside just for a minute, to tell her it's no bullshit, you paid us three grand to rent out the shitwagon."

Twilly smiled. "I don't know what you're talking about."

"Hey, man, where's the load? The truck, it looks empty."

"That's right," Twilly said. "There's nothing to haul to the dump. You guys can go straight on home tonight."

"But what happened to it?"

"Best you don't know."

"Oh Lord," one of the garbagemen muttered to his pals. "This is a crazy-ass boy. He's gone done some crazy-ass thing."

"No," Twilly said, "I believe you'd approve. I really

26

do." Then he drove off, thinking how wrong Dr. Boston had been. Anger wasn't such a complicated emotion.

Palmer Stoat ordered an antipasto salad, garlic rolls, fettuccine Alfredo, a side of meatballs, and before long Desie had to look away, for fear of being sick. He was perspiring, that's how hard he went at the food; droplets of sweat streaking both sides of his jawline. Desie was ashamed of herself for feeling so revulsed; this was her husband, after all. It wasn't as if his personality had transformed after they got married. He was the same man in all respects, two years later. Desie felt guilty about marrying him, guilty about having second thoughts, guilty about the rhinoceros he'd shot dead that morning.

"From here to the salad bar," Stoat was telling her. "That's how close she was."

"And for that you needed a scope?"

"Better safe than sorry. That's Durgess's motto."

Stoat ordered tortoni for dessert. He used a fork to probe the ice cream for fragments of almonds, which he raked into a tidy pattern along the perimeter of the plate. Watching the fastidious ritual plunged Desie deeper into melancholy. Later, while Palmer reviewed the bill, she excused herself and went to the rest room, where she dampened a paper towel to wipe off her lipstick and makeup. She had no idea why, but it made her feel much better. By the time she finished, her husband was gone from the restaurant.

Desie walked outside and was nearly poleaxed by the smell. She cupped her hands to her mouth and looked around for Palmer. He was in the parking lot, beneath a streetlight. As Desie approached him, the odor got worse, and soon she saw why: a sour mound of garbage ten feet high. Desie estimated it to weigh several tons. Palmer Stoat stood at the base of the fetid hill, his eyes fixed lugubriously on the peak.

"Where's the car?" Desie asked with a cough.

Palmer's arms flopped at his sides. He began squeaking like a lost kitten.

"Don't tell me." She struggled not to gag on the stink. "Dammit, Palmer. My Beemer!"

Haltingly he began to circle the rancid dune. He raised an arm, pointing in outraged stupefaction. A cloud of flies buzzed about his face, but he made no effort to shoo them away.

"Goddammit," Desie cried. "Didn't I tell you to put the top up? Didn't I?"

THREE

Twilly made it back to the Italian restaurant in time for the show. Under the amused supervision of several police officers, a detachment of workers with rakes and shovels had begun the unsavory task of digging out the BMW. This Twilly watched through field glasses from high in a nearby pine tree. There was no sign of the press, which was a shame—here was a story made for TV. Over the rhythmic crunch of digging, Litterbug's voice could be heard admonishing the sanitation workers to be careful, goddamn you, don't scratch the paint! Twilly found it comical, considering the likely extent of the Beemer's contamination. He imagined virgin leather upholstery ripening under an ambrosial lode of orange rinds, cottage cheese, Heineken bottles, coffee grounds, eggshells, crumpled wads of Kleenex, potato skins, sanitary napkins, pizza crust, fish heads, spare ribs, leaky toothpaste tubes, bacon grease, coagulated gravy, cat litter and chicken necks. Twilly wished he could infiltrate the cleanup crew, to see the ghastly sight up close.

Litterbug's wife/girlfriend could be observed pacing, arms folded, beneath a flickering streetlight. Twilly couldn't make out her expression, but the clip in her step suggested impatience. He wondered if she truly cared about the BMW; in any event, the insurance company would buy her a new one. Twilly also thought about the sanitation workers, being called out so late on such a strange job. He had a feeling they might be enjoying themselves, exhuming a fancy red sports car from a heap of refuse, but still he hoped they were getting overtime.

It was quite an extensive operation, and Twilly wondered why he wasn't feeling a commensurate sense of satisfaction. The answer came with a sour jolt as he studied the litterbug through the binoculars; watched the man unwrap a piece of candy—probably an after-dinner mint from the restaurant—then crumple the wrapper and drop it nonchalantly to the ground. The dumb fuckwad didn't get it! Didn't make the link between his piggish misbehavior on the turnpike and the malicious defilement of his automobile. He probably figured it was the random mischief of vandals; a prank.

I should've left a message, Twilly thought glumly. I should've made it crystal clear. He muttered a curse and climbed cautiously through the darkness down the trunk of the tree. By the time he reached the parking lot, the excavation of the car was complete. Litterbug and his wife/girlfriend could be seen leaving in a taxi. The soiled BMW was being hooked to a tow truck, whose burly driver wore a baby-blue hospital mask and joked with the sanitation crew, which was shoveling the last dregs into a Dumpster.

Twilly asked one of the cops what had happened to the red convertible.

"Somebody emptied a garbage truck on it," the officer reported with a harsh chuckle.

"Jesus," said Twilly. "Why?"

"Who the fuck knows. It's the sick society we live in."

Twilly said: "I saw all these police cars, I was afraid there was a murder."

"Naw, just some big shot left his ragtop down in the wrong neighborhood."

"He famous or something?"

"I never heard of him before tonight," said the cop, "but obviously he's got some juice. Otherwise I wouldn't be here, I'd be home in my underwear watching basketball. Stand back now."

The tow-truck driver was maneuvering out of the parking lot, the cop waving directions. Twilly knew better than to press for the litterbug's name; he didn't need it anyway. He approached one of the sanitation workers and asked if the Beemer was totaled.

"Yeah, and it ain't right. A sweet car like this."

Twilly said, "Completely ruined, huh?"

"You can't never get the interior clean, not after somethin' such as this. We're talkin' about a minimum—I'm guessin' now—four tons of raw garbage." The man stopped working and rested his weight on the stem of the shovel. "I mean, hell, an expensive car like that—why trash it when you can just steal the damn thing? Any fool leaves the convertible top down deserves to lose his wheels. But this? This is evil shit, you ask me. Taking this much trouble to destroy a perfectly splendid vehicle. Deeply evil shit."

"Sick world," Twilly Spree said, in his own defense.

He was born in Key West, where his father had gone to sell commercial waterfront. Little Phil Spree was a real-estate specialist. If a property wasn't on the sea or the Gulf, Little Phil wasn't interested. He would buy and sell beach until there was no more beach to buy or sell, then pack up the family and move to another town where, Little Phil typically would exult, "the coast is clear!" Florida has thirteen hundred miles of shoreline, and young Twilly got to savor plenty of it. His mother, who kept out of direct sunlight, wasn't crazy about the tropics. But Little Phil was making excellent money, so Amy Spree basically stayed indoors for eighteen years, tended to her complexion and endeavored to occupy herself with hobbies. She grew bonsai trees. She started writing a romance novel. She learned to play the clarinet. She took up yoga, modern dance and strong martinis. Meanwhile Twilly ran wild, literally. Every free moment was spent outdoors. His parents couldn't imagine what he was up to.

When Twilly was four, Little Phil briefly moved the family to Marco Island, which was famous for its white dune-fringed beaches. The sand was spangled with ornate tropical seashells, which Twilly collected and organized in shoe boxes. Usually he was accompanied by a sitter, hired by his mother to make sure he didn't wander into the Gulf of Mexico and drown. Years later, at age fourteen, Twilly hot-wired a friend's station wagon and drove back to Marco, in order to prowl the shore for shells. He arrived late at night in a howling downpour, and fell asleep in the car. When he awoke at dawn, he comprehended for the first time what his old man did for a living. The island had sprouted skyline; a concrete picket of towering hotels and high-rise condominiums. Waterfront, of course. Twilly fixed his eyes downward and marched the beach, his shoe box under one arm. He hoped he was seeing a mirage, a trick of the fog and clouds, but when he glanced up, the hotels and condos were still there, looming larger than before. As the sun began to rise, the buildings cast tombstone shadows across the sand. Soon Twilly found himself standing in a vast block of shade—shade, on an open beach under a bright clear sky! He sunk to his knees and punched the hard-packed sand with both fists until his knuckles were skinned.

A woman tourist came up to Twilly and told him to stop carrying on, as he was upsetting her children. The woman wore a stretch two-piece swimsuit and spoke with a New England accent. Her toenails were colored magenta and her nose was buttered with zinc oxide and in one hand she brandished an Arthur Hailey paperback. Twilly howled and resumed pummeling the beach. The woman glowered over the rims of her sunglasses. "Young man," she said, "where is your mother?"

Whereupon Twilly whirled and chomped down on her bare foot and didn't let go until a beefy hotel security man came and pried him off. Little Phil arrived later that day with lawyers and a checkbook. On the trip home Twilly had nothing to say to his father. At bedtime Amy Spree went to her son's room and found him mounting a gaily painted human toenail in his seashell display. The next morning she took him to a psychologist for the first time. Twilly was given a battery of tests, none of which pointed toward violent sociopathy. Though Amy Spree was relieved, her husband remained skeptical. "The boy's not right," he would say. Or: "The boy's not all there." Or sometimes: "The boy's playing on the wrong team."

Eventually Twilly tried to talk to his father about Marco Island and other heartaches. He reminded him that Florida for eons had been underwater and was steadily sinking again, the sea and the Gulf rising each year to reclaim the precious shoreline that Little Phil and others were so avidly selling off. So what? Little Phil replied. That's why people got flood insurance. Twilly said, No, Dad, you don't understand. And Little Phil said, Yeah, well, maybe I don't understand geology so good but I understand sales and I understand commissions. And if this goddamn place starts sinking to where I can see it with my own eyes, then me, you and your mother are packin' up and moving to Southern California, where a man can still make a dandy living off oceanfront.

And Twilly said, Forget I even mentioned it.

On the eve of Twilly's eighteenth birthday, Little Phil drove him to a banker's office in Tampa, where it was explained to Twilly that he was about to inherit approximately $5 million from a man he had met only once, Little Phil's father, the late Big Phil. Big Phil Spree made his fortune off copper mines in Montana, and had retired at age sixty to travel the world and play golf. Not long afterward he dropped dead in a sand trap on the sixteenth hole at Spyglass. His will left a third of his money to Little Phil, a third in trust to his only grandchild, Twilly, and a third to the National Rifle Association.

As they walked out of the bank, Little Phil threw an arm around his much taller son and said: "That's a shitload of dough for a young fellow to handle. But I believe I know what your grandfather would have wanted you to do with it."

"Let me guess. Oceanfront?"

"You're a smart one," said Little Phil, beaming.

Twilly shook free. "Mutual funds," he announced.

"What?" Little Phil was aghast.

"Yep."

"Where'd you hear about such nonsense?"

"I read."

"Look around, boy. Hasn't real estate done right by us?" Little Phil rattled off all the fine things in their life, from the swimming pool to the ski boat to the summer time-share in Vermont.

Twilly said: "Blood money."

"Uh?"

"What Grandfather left me is mine, and I'll do what I please with it. That'll be no-load mutuals."

Little Phil grabbed his shoulder. "Lemme see if I understand. I'm offering you a half partnership in a two-hundred-and-twenty-room Ramada at Daytona, *beachside*, but you'd rather stick the cash on that insane roulette wheel otherwise known as the New York Stock Exchange?"

"Yep," said Twilly.

"Well, I always knew you were playing for the wrong team. This ices it," said his father. "Did I mention the motel comes with a liquor license?"

A few months later Little Phil ran off to Santa Monica with a secretary from a title-insurance company. Despite her son's unease in structured settings, Twilly's mother beseeched him to enroll at Florida State University, in the state capital of Tallahassee. There Twilly majored in English for three semesters before dropping out and moving in with a poetry professor, who was finishing a doctorate on T. S. Eliot. She was a dynamic and intelligent woman who took a fervid interest in her new boyfriend, particularly his inheritance. She encouraged him to use the fortune to do good and noble deeds, beginning with the purchase of a snazzy new 280-Z for her garage. Eventually Twilly was spiffed up and presented to the dean of the English department, who proposed the funding of a resident Poet's Chair to be named in honor of Twilly's late grandfather, a man who wouldn't have known W. H. Auden from Dr. Seuss.

Twilly said sure, what the hell, but the gift was never made; not because Twilly welched but because in the interim he was arrested for assault and battery on a state legislator. The man, a Democrat from Sarasota County, had been written up in the news for blocking clean-water reforms while at the same time accepting illicit campaign donations from a cattle ranch that was flushing raw manure into an estuary. Twilly had spotted the legislator in a restaurant and followed him to the rest room. There Twilly shoved him into a stall and lectured him for forty minutes on the immorality of water pollution. In fear the legislator feigned contrition, but Twilly saw through the act. Calmly he unzipped his jeans, pissed prodigiously on the man's Bally loafers and said: "There, that's what your pals on the ranch are doing to Black Drum Bay. How do you like it?"

When a sanitized version of the incident hit the press, the dean of the English department decided it would set a poor precedent to accept grant money from a deranged felon, and broke off contact with Twilly Spree. That was fine with Twilly, for although he enjoyed a good poem, he felt subversion was a worthier cause. It was a view that only hardened as he grew older and met more people like his father.

*

"Dick says you're the man." Robert Clapley raised his bourbon and gave a nod.

"Dick exaggerates," said Palmer Stoat, well practiced at false modesty.

They were having a late lunch at a walnut-paneled country club in a suburb of Tampa. The governor had set it up.

"Dick's not the only one," Clapley said, "to sing your praises."

"That's very flattering."

"He explained the situation?"

"In a general way," Stoat said. "You need a new bridge."

"Yes, sir. The funding's there, in the Senate bill."

"But you've got a problem in the House."

"I do," Clapley said. "A man named Willie Vasquez-Washington."

Palmer Stoat smiled.

"Have you got any earthly idea," said Clapley, "what he's after?"

"I can find out with a phone call."

"Which will cost me how much?" Clapley asked dryly.

"The call? Nothing. Getting your problem fixed, that'll be a hundred grand. Fifty up front."

"Really. And how much kicks back to your friend Willie?"

Stoat looked surprised. "Not a dime, Bob. May I call you Bob? Willie doesn't need your money, he's got other action—probably some goodies he wants hidden in the budget. We'll work things out, don't worry."

"That's what lobbyists do?"

"Right. That's what you're paying for."

"So the hundred grand. . . ."

"My fee," Stoat said, "and it's a bargain."

"You know, I gave a sweet shitload of money to Dick's campaign. I've never done anything like that before."

"Get used to it, Bob."

Robert Clapley was new to Florida, and new to the land-development business. Palmer Stoat gave him a short course on the politics; most of the cash flying around Tallahassee could be traced to men in Clapley's line of work.

He said, "I tried to reach out to Willie myself."

"Big mistake."

"Well, Mr. Stoat, that's why I'm here. Dick says you're the man." Clapley took out a checkbook and a fountain pen. "I'm curious—is Vasquez-Washington a shine or a spic or what exactly?"

"A little pinch of everything, according to Willie. Calls himself the Rainbow Brother."

"You two get along?" Clapley handed the $50,000 check to Stoat.

"Bob, I get along with everybody. I'm the most likable motherfucker you'll ever meet. Hey, do you hunt?"

"Anything that moves."

"Then I know just the place for you," said Stoat. "They've got every critter known to man."

"How about big cats? I made space for a hide on the wall of my library," Clapley said. "Something spotted would go best with the upholstery. Like maybe a cheetah."

"Name your species, Bob. This place, it's like where Noah parked the ark. They got it all."

Robert Clapley ordered another round of drinks. The waitress brought their rib eyes, and the two men ate in agreeable silence. After a time Clapley said, "I notice you don't ask many questions."

Stoat glanced up from his plate. "I don't *have* many questions." He was chewing as he spoke.

"Don't you want to know what I did before I became a land developer?"

"Not really."

"I was in the import-export business. Electronics."

"Electronics," said Stoat, playing along. Clapley was thirty-five years old and had Yuppie ex-smuggler written all over him. The gold, the deepwater tan, the diamond ear stud, the two-hundred-dollar haircut.

"But everybody said real estate's the smart way to go," Clapley went on, "so a couple years ago I started buying up Toad Island and here we are."

Stoat said, "You're going to lose the 'Toad' part, I hope. Switch to some tropical moth or something."

"A bird. Shearwater. The Shearwater Island Company."

"I like it. Very classy-sounding. And the governor says it's going to be gorgeous. Another Hilton Head, he says."

"It can't lose," said Robert Clapley, "as long as I get my bridge."

"Consider it done, Bob."

"Oh, I will."

Palmer Stoat drained his bourbon and said, "Hey, I finally thought of a question."

Clapley seemed pleased. "Fire away, Mr. Stoat."

"Are you gonna finish that baked potato?"

*

That same afternoon, a man named Steven Brinkman was summoned to a cluttered double-wide trailer on Toad Island. Brinkman was a biologist, fresh out of Cornell graduate school, who had been hired as an "environmental specialist" at $41,000 a year by the prestigious engineering firm of Roothaus and Son, designers of highways, bridges, golf communities, office towers, shopping malls, factories and residential subdivisions. Roothaus and Son had been recruited by Robert Clapley to the Shearwater Island project, for which a crucial step was the timely completion of a comprehensive biological survey. Without such a document, the development would be bogged down indefinitely in red tape, at great expense to Clapley.

Brinkman's task was to make a list of species that lived on the small barrier island: plants, insects, birds, amphibians, reptiles and mammals. The job could not be sloppy or hurried, because the government would be doing its own survey, for comparison. Steven Brinkman, in fact, once had been offered a position of staff biologist with the U.S. Army Corps of Engineers, but had chosen the private sector for its higher salaries and broader opportunities for advancement. That was the upside. The downside was having to answer to soulless cretins such as Karl Krimmler, the project supervisor, who would have been rapturous to hear there was no wildlife whatsoever on Toad Island. In nature Krimmler saw neither art nor mystery, only bureaucratic obstacles. A flight of swallowtail butterflies or the chirp of a squirrel could send him into a black funk that lasted for days.

Now Krimmler wedged a phone at one ear and fanned himself with Brinkman's list. Krimmler was an

engineer, not a biologist, and he reported directly to
Roger Roothaus. It was Roothaus to whom Krimmler
was now speaking on the phone.

"Gators?" Krimmler relayed the query to Brinkman.
Brinkman shook his head.

"Bald eagles? *Any* kind of eagles?"

Brinkman said no. Into the phone Krimmler said:
"He's sure. No eagles. You want me to read you what
he's got? Yeah. No. OK, lemme ask."

To Brinkman then Krimmler explained: "All we're
really worried about is endangereds."

"I haven't found any yet."

"You're positive? We don't want any surprises—six
months from now, some fucking red-bellied caterpillar
turns out to be the last of its race. That we don't need."

Steven Brinkman said: "So far, I haven't found a
single endangered species."

To Krimmler this was the happiest of news, and
with a satisfied tone he repeated it into the phone. He
chuckled at Roothaus's reply, saying, "I know, I know.
It's too damn good to be true. But the young man tells
me he's sure."

"So far," Brinkman interjected tentatively, "none so
far." There was always a chance of the odd burrowing
owl or gopher tortoise.

Krimmler glanced up. "Mr. Roothaus wants to know
if you've found anything weird. Anything we need to
take care of before the eco-pinheads from Fish and
Wildlife show up."

Brinkman took a deep breath. It didn't take much to
set Krimmler off.

"Well, there's this." The biologist held out his right
hand.

Krimmler peered. "The hell is it?" Then, into the phone: "Hold on, Rog."

"It's a toad," Brinkman said.

"Gee, and here I thought it was a baby unicorn. I *know* it's a toad, OK? I know what a goddamn toad looks like. The question is, what kind of goddamn toad, Mr. Brinkman?"

"It's doctor. *Doctor* Brinkman." Some things you couldn't let slide, even at forty-one grand a year.

Krimmler glared. He cupped a hand over the receiver and whispered, "I'm waiting."

"*Bufo quercicus.*"

"Now in English."

"It's an oak toad."

"And?"

"The smallest toad native to North America."

"That I can believe," Krimmler said. "But it's not on the endangered list?"

"No, sir."

"The 'threatened' list?"

"No."

"Any other goddamn lists?"

"None that I'm aware of."

"Then what's the problem?" Into the phone he said, "Hey, Roger, young Dr. Brinkman brought me an adorable baby frog. . . . Well, that's what I'm trying to find out."

Brinkman said, "There's no problem, really, with the oak toads. It's just they're all over the place, by the hundreds. I've never seen so many."

"That would probably explain the name of the island."

"It would," Brinkman said, sheepishly.

42

The toad in his palm was smaller than a quarter. Its coloration was a mottled gray and brown, with a vertical orange stripe bisecting its back. The toad blinked its shiny eyes and began to squirm. Gently, Brinkman closed his fingers around it.

Krimmler said, "Take your little pal outside before he pees on this fine linoleum. I'll be with you in a second."

Brinkman shut the door behind him. The sun was so bright it made his eyes water. He knelt and placed the diminutive toad on the ground. Immediately it hopped off, into the shade of the trailer.

Five minutes later, Krimmler came down the steps. "Mr. Roothaus says you're doing a super job. He's a little concerned about those toads, though."

"They're completely harmless," Brinkman said.

"Not necessarily. These days it wouldn't take much to stir up another snail-darter scenario. I mean, if some tree-hugger type really wanted to throw a wrench in this project."

Brinkman said, "I told you, they're not endangered. They don't even take a cute picture."

Krimmler shrugged. "Still and all, we can't be too careful. Where exactly did you find these toads, Dr. Brinkman?"

"All over the island, like I said."

"Uplands or wetlands?"

"Uplands, mostly," said Brinkman.

"Excellent."

"In the flatwood and shrub. There's so many, you'll never catch them all."

"You're absolutely right," Krimmler said. "That's why we're going to bury 'em instead."

FOUR

On the drive to the airport, the man tossed from the Range Rover a styrofoam coffee cup and the cellophane wrapper from a Little Debbie's cinnamon-raisin roll. This happened at eighty miles an hour in breakneck traffic on the interstate, so Twilly was unable to pull over and retrieve the trash. By now he had ditched his dirty black pickup and rented a generic maroon Chevrolet Corsica, of which there were no fewer than half a million on the highways of South Florida during tourist season. Twilly enjoyed feeling inconspicuous behind the wheel; for the sake of appearances, he even spread a road map upside down across his lap. He followed the litterbug all the way to the airport parking garage and, by foot, into the terminal. Twilly shouldn't have been surprised to see the man greeted affectionately at the Delta gate by a top-heavy blond woman with a Gucci overnighter, but Twilly *was* surprised, and a bit pissed off. Why, he didn't know. He drove back to the litterbug's house and waited for the wife/girlfriend to make a move. She came out wearing a short tennis ensemble and carrying not one but three over-sized rackets. Twilly watched her slide into a black BMW that her husband/boyfriend must have leased to replace—temporarily, Twilly felt certain—the ruined red one.

After she was gone, Twilly slipped through the hedgerow into the backyard and scoped out the window jambs, which were wired for an alarm. He wasn't concerned. Based on his observations of Litterbug and wife/girlfriend, Twilly had a hunch the alarm wasn't set. And, sure enough, neither of them had remembered to lock the laundry-room door, which Twilly nudged open. No sirens, beeps or whistles went off. Twilly stepped inside and listened for a maid or a cook or a nanny. Through a doorway he could see into the kitchen. While there was no sign of movement, Twilly thought he heard breathing.

"Hello?" he called. He had a story ready—county code inspector, checking for hurricane shutters. Saw the door ajar, got worried, et cetera. For the occasion Twilly had worn a thin plain necktie and a white short-sleeved shirt.

"Hello!" he said again, louder.

An enormous jet-black dog trotted around the corner and clamped onto his right calf. It was a Labrador retriever, the largest Twilly had ever seen, with a face as broad as a bear's. Twilly was annoyed with himself for failing to anticipate an oversized house pet, because it fit Litterbug's profile.

He remained motionless and unflinching in the dog's grip. "Bad dog," he said, vainly hoping the animal would be intimidated by his composure. "No!" was Twilly's next try. "Bad boy! Bad boy!" Never before had he been attacked by a dog that didn't growl or even snarl. He took the Labrador by its silky ears. "You made your point. Now let go!"

The dog glanced up with no discernible hostility. Twilly expected to feel more pain, but the Lab actually wasn't biting down very hard; instead it held on with an impassive stubbornness, as if Twilly's hide were a favored old sock.

I haven't got time for games, Twilly thought. Bending over the dog, he locked both arms around its barrel-sized midsection and hoisted it clear off the tile. He suspended the dog in an upside-down hug—its ears slack, hind legs straight in the air—until it let go. When he put the dog down, it seemed more dizzy than enraged. Twilly stroked the crown of its head. Immediately the Lab thumped its tail and rolled over. In the refrigerator Twilly found some cold cuts, which he placed on a platter on the kitchen floor.

Then he went prowling through the house. From a stack of unopened mail in the front hall he determined that the litterbug's name was Palmer Stoat, and that the woman was his wife, Desirata. Twilly moved to the master bedroom, to get a better sense of the relationship. The Stoats had a four-poster bed with a frilly gossamer canopy, which Twilly found excessive. On one nightstand were a novel by Anne Tyler and a stack of magazines: *Town & Country, Gourmet, Vanity Fair* and *Spin*. Twilly concluded that this was Mrs. Stoat's side of the bed. In the top drawer of the nightstand were a half-smoked joint, a tube of Vaseline, a pack of plastic hair clips, and a squeeze bottle of expensive skin moisturizer. On the other nightstand Twilly saw no reading material of any type, a fact that jibed with his impressions of the litterbug. Neatly arranged inside the drawer were a battery-operated nose-hair clipper, a loaded .38-caliber revolver, a Polaroid camera and a stack of snapshots that appeared to have been taken by Palmer Stoat while he was having sex with his wife. Twilly found it significant that in all the photographs Stoat had one-handedly aimed the lens at his own naked body, and that the most to be seen of the wife was an upraised knee or the pale hemisphere of a buttock or a tangle of auburn hair.

From the bedroom Twilly went to the den, a tabernacle of dead wildlife. The longest wall had been set aside for stuffed animal heads: a Cape buffalo, a bighorn sheep, a mule deer, a bull elk, a timber wolf and a Canadian lynx. Another wall had been dedicated to mounted game fish: a tarpon, a striped marlin, a peacock bass, a cobia and a bonefish scarcely bigger than a banana. Centered on the oak floor was the maned hide of an African lion—utterly pathetic, to Twilly's eye, the whole white-hunter motif.

He placed himself at Stoat's desk, which was strikingly uncluttered. Two photographs stood in identical silver frames; one on the left side, the other on the right side. One picture was of Desirata, waving from the bow of a sailboat. She wore an electric pink swimsuit and her face looked sunburned. The water in the background was too bright and clear to be in Florida; Twilly guessed it was the Bahamas or someplace down in the Caribbean. The other picture on the desk was of the big Labrador retriever in a droopy red Santa cap. The dog's forbearing expression made Twilly laugh out loud.

He listened to Stoat's telephone messages on the answering machine, and jotted some notes. Then he got up to inspect a third wall of the den, a burnished floor-to-ceiling bookcase that was, predictably, devoid of books. Twilly found three thin volumes of golfing wisdom, and a glossy coffee-table opus commemorating the first and last World Series championship of the Florida Marlins baseball franchise. That was it—Palmer Stoat's whole library; not even the obligatory leather-bound set of Faulkner or Steinbeck for decoration. Exquisite tropical mahogany had been used to craft the bookshelves, which Stoat had filled with, of all things, cigar boxes—empty cigar boxes, presumably displayed in a way that would impress other smokers. Montecristo #1, Cohiba, Empress of Cuba Robusto, Don Mateo, Partagas, Licenciados, H. Upmann, Bauzá—Twilly knew nothing about the pedigree of tobacco products, but he realized that for Stoat the empty boxes were trophies, like the stuffed animal heads. Prominently displayed on its own shelf was more proof of the man's fixation: a framed mock cover of *Cigar Aficionado* magazine featuring a nine-by-twelve photograph of Stoat wearing a white tuxedo and puffing a large potent-looking stogie. The dummy caption said "Man of the Year."

Twilly heard a noise at the door and spun around— the Labrador, done with his snack. Twilly said, "Hey, bruiser, come here." The dog gazed around the den at the dead fish and dead mammals, then walked off. Twilly sympathized. A rolling library ladder provided convenient access to the taxidermy. Twilly glided from one mount to the next, using his pocketknife to pry out the glass eyeballs, which he arranged with pupils skyward in a perfect pentagram on Palmer Stoat's desk blotter.

*

"What is it you want, Willie?"

Palmer Stoat had waited until they reached the back nine before bracing the cagey vice chairman of the House Appropriations Committee.

And Representative Willie Vasquez-Washington replied: "What kind of fool question is that?" He was looking at a four-footer for a double bogey. "Makes you think I want something?"

Stoat shrugged. "Take your time, Willie. I'm on the clock." But he was thinking how he'd undercharged Robert Clapley for the job, because one hundred grand was seeming more and more like a dirt-cheap fee for spending a whole wretched day on the golf course with Willie Vasquez-Washington.

Who, after missing his putt, now asked Palmer Stoat: "Is this about that damn bridge?"

Stoat turned away and rolled his eyes.

"What's the name of that island again?"

"What's the fucking difference, Willie?"

"The governor told me but I forgot."

They rode the cart to the eleventh tee. Stoat hit first, slicing his drive deep into the pines. Willie Vasquez-Washington sculled his shot fifty yards down the right side of the fairway.

What is it you want?

Sometimes Stoat was too direct, Willie thought. The question had sounded so common and venal, the way it came out.

"It's not about wanting, Palmer, it's about needing. There's a neighborhood in my district that needs a community center. A nice auditorium, you know. Day-care facilities. A decent gym for midnight basketball."

"How much?" Stoat asked.

"Nine million, give or take. It was all there in the House version," said Willie Vasquez-Washington, "but for some reason the funding got nuked in the Senate. I think it was those Panhandle Crackers again."

Stoat said, "A community center is a fine idea. Something for the kids."

"Exactly. Something for the kids."

And also something for Willie's wife, who would be appointed executive director of the center at an annual salary of $49,500, plus major-medical and the use of a station wagon. And another something for Willie's best friend, who owned the company that would get the $200,000 dry-walling contract for the new building. And another something for the husband of Willie's campaign manager, whose company would be supplying twenty-four-hour security guards for the center. And, last but not least, something for Willie's deadbeat younger brother, who happened to own a bankrupt grocery store on the southwest corner of the proposed site for the community center, a grocery store that would need to be condemned and purchased by the state, for at least five or six times what Willie's brother had paid for it.

None of this would be laid out explicitly for Palmer Stoat, because it wasn't necessary. He didn't need or want the sticky details. He assumed that somebody near and dear to Willie Vasquez-Washington stood to profit from the construction of a new $9 million community center, and he would have been flabbergasted to learn otherwise. Pork was the essential nutrient of politics. Somebody *always* made money, even from the most noble-sounding of tax-supported endeavors. Willie

Vasquez-Washington and his pals would get their new community center, and the governor and his pals would get their new bridge to Shearwater Island. A slam dunk, Palmer Stoat believed. He would arrange for Willie's project to be inserted into the next draft of the Senate budget, and from there it would easily pass out of conference committee and go to the governor's desk. And, his private concern for the Shearwater development notwithstanding, Governor Dick Artemus would never in a million years veto the funding for a community center in a poor minority neighborhood, particularly when the elected representative from that district could claim—as Willie Vasquez-Washington had at various times—to be part Afro-American, part Hispanic, part Haitian, part Chinese, and even part Miccosukee. Nobody ever pressed Willie for documentation of his richly textured heritage. Nobody wanted to be the one to ask.

"I'll fix everything tomorrow," Stoat assured Willie Vasquez-Washington. "Listen, I'm kind of late for a meeting at the capitol."

"What're you talkin' about, 'late'? We got eight holes to play." Willie was gesticulating with a three iron. "You can't quit in the middle of a fairway. Specially when I'm down twenty-six bucks!"

"Keep the money, Willie, and the cart, too. I'll walk back." Stoat hung his golf bag over one shoulder and took a beer from the cooler. He gave a genial but firm wave to the vice chairman of the House Appropriations Committee, then began the trudge to the clubhouse.

"Hey, Palmer! One more thing!" Willie Vasquez-Washington called out.

Stoat turned and cupped a hand to his ear. Willie

motioned him closer. Stoat cursed sharply under his breath and walked back.

"It's about the name," said Willie, dropping his voice.

"What about it?"

"Didn't you see the name? In the House budget item."

Palmer Stoat said, "I don't read the House budget word for word, Willie. I don't read the Miami phone book word for word, either. So help me out here, OK?"

"The name should be the same in the Senate version. That's all I'm saying."

Stoat had an urge to snatch Willie's three iron and wrap it around his blotched sweaty neck. "What name," he said thinly, "would you like me to put in the Senate bill?"

"The Willie Vasquez-Washington Community Outreach Center."

"Done," said Stoat. Once again he turned for the clubhouse.

"Shouldn't you maybe write it down?"

"No, I'll remember." Stoat thinking: Community *Outreach* Center? Willie's not reaching out, he's just reaching.

"Hey, Palmer, what about your new bridge?"

"I'll fax you the draft language. And it's not *my* bridge." Stoat was moving away briskly now; long purposeful strides.

"What I meant, is it gonna be named after somebody in particular?" Willie called after him. "You want, I could name it after the governor. Or maybe even you!"

"No thanks!" Palmer Stoat shouted pleasantly, but he kept his back to the man and continued walking.

"Maggot," he grumbled. "Another greedy little maggot on the make."

The human population of Toad Island was 217 and in decline. Repeated efforts had been made to develop the place, and many of its remaining inhabitants were casualties of those doomed enterprises. The unofficial mayor was Nils Fishback, former landscape architect of an ambitious project that had promised three high-rise beachfront condominiums, a total of 660 units, called the Towers of Tarpon Island. (Everyone who sought to develop Toad Island renamed it as the first order of business. In addition to Tarpon Island, it had been incorporated fleetingly as Snook Island, Dolphin Island, Blue Heron Island, White Heron Island, Little Spoonbill Island, Big Spoonbill Island, Sandpiper Key, Sandpiper Cay, Sandpiper Isle and Sandpiper Shoals. The circumstances of failure varied from one busted scheme to the next, but a cheerlessly detailed history was available for scrutiny in the bankruptcy files of the federal courthouse at Gainesville.)

Resistance to the latest Toad Island makeover came from a small core of embittered landholders masquerading as environmentalists. In protest they had begun circulating an impassioned, Thoreau-quoting petition, the true purpose of which was not to protect pristine shores from despoliation but to extort more money from the builders. Among the private-property owners it was strongly felt that Robert Clapley was being stingy about buying them out, and that he could easily afford to overpay for their property, just as previous developers had overpaid previous Toad Island inhabitants. The petition strategy had worked well before, stirring up legitimate conservation organizations and luring big-city editorial writers and columnists to Toad Island's cause. Lacerated by headlines, the developers usually caved in and doubled their offers. There was no reason to believe Clapley wouldn't do the same, to expedite groundbreaking on his luxury-resort community.

Fame and seniority handed Nils Fishback the lead role in the anti-Shearwater Island petition drive. He'd bought thirty-three lots there, having invested his life savings—unwisely, it had turned out—during the euphoric first gush of hype for what was then Tarpon Island. It had been Fishback's fantasy to escape Miami and retire to a placid Gulf Coast paradise, surrounded by water. He planned to keep four of the most scenic lots and, using his landscaping earnings from the high-rise project, build a grand plantation-style estate house for himself and his wife. Unfortunately for the Fishbacks, the Towers of Tarpon Island went belly-up shortly after the first slab was poured, due to the unexpected incarceration of its principal backers, two young gentlemen cousins from Barranquilla. At that point, Fishback had decorated only the sixty-by-sixty-foot parcel upon which the Towers of Tarpon Island sales kiosk had been assembled—an admittedly modest landscaping chore, but one for which Nils Fishback nonetheless expected compensation. He was not paid, nor were any of the other subcontractors. Worse: After eight years and three more failed Toad Island ventures, Fishback remained stuck with seventeen barren lots of the original thirty-three. His dream home had never advanced beyond blue-prints; Fishback lived alone in the abandoned Tarpon Island sales hut, one of the few company assets in which the U.S. Drug Enforcement Administration showed no interest.

Fishback's wife long ago had given up hope and bolted for the mainland, leaving him with an unhealthy amount of solitude and free time. He went through a stretch of hard drinking, during which he regularly neglected to shave, bathe, floss or change clothes. He commonly passed out for days on the beach, and his skin became as brown and crinkled as a walnut. One morning, while drunkenly urinating off the old wooden bridge, Nils Fishback was approached by an impressionable young feature writer for a St. Petersburg newspaper. The following week, a long story appeared under a headline christening him "The Mayor of Toad Island." Although Fishback could not recall giving the interview, or any of the wild lies he told, he embraced his colorful new title with zest. He grew out his beard and bleached it snowy white, and took to going shirtless and barefoot and sporting bright bandannas. Deftly, Fishback recreated himself as a crusty and reclusive defender of Nature who had settled on the island purely for its grandeur, not to make a real-estate killing. He happily posed for photographers, pretending to smooch one of the tiny striped oak toads that had given the place its name. Fishback was always good for a wistful quote or bittersweet adage about the demise of old Florida. For that reason he had been sought out over the years by the *Washington Post, Newsweek*, CNBC and the Turner networks, not to mention local media outlets. In this manner, he had evolved into a regional celebrity eccentric.

In truth, Nils Fishback didn't give a damn what happened to Toad Island or the squirmy creatures that lived there. The most breathtakingly beautiful sight he could imagine in all God's kingdom would be a cashier's check from Robert Clapley's company for the sum of $510,000, which was Fishback's preposterous asking price for his seventeen orphan lots. He would, of course, ecstatically accept half as much and be gone from Toad Island before sunset. He feigned horror when Clapley's crew started bulldozing the toad habitat, but Nils Fishback was secretly delighted. He had never been fond of the toads, especially during mating season when their high-pitched stridulations rang all night long in his skull. Second, and more important, Clapley's mechanized assault on the petite amphibians was potent public-relations ammunition for the petition drive—the man was a monster, was he not? Smushing innocent creatures by the thousands. Fishback kept a Rolodex of media contacts, for precisely such occasions. He would personally lead the TV crews across the old bridge and down the beach road to the site of the massacre, and show them where to set up their cameras. The Shearwater Island Company couldn't afford such gruesome publicity! Nils Fishback would warn Robert Clapley an hour or so in advance, giving him just enough time to call the bank and get a check cut for the escrow deposit on Fishback's property.

The only question in Fishback's mind was when to pick up the phone. If he waited too long, the toad massacre would be over and there'd be nothing left for the TV people to film. On the other hand, if he intervened too swiftly, the toad infestation would remain substantially undiminished, with the spring breeding season only weeks away.

Fishback stood up and dusted off the seat of his

tattered cutoffs. He jerked two beers from the cooler; one he opened, the other he tucked under an arm. Then he ambled down the hill into the trees, where one of the big yellow bulldozers was being refueled. Fishback handed the unopened beer to the driver and said, "How long you boys gonna be at it?"

The driver grunted. "Years, pop. Get used to it."

"No," Fishback said, "I mean this part here." He waved a hand, as bony and gnarled as driftwood. "Buryin' all these damn toads."

The driver's gaze narrowed. "What're you talkin' about?"

"Check out your boots, jocko. That's toad guts, if I'm not mistaken."

The driver stepped back, wiping his soles across the pine needles. "You're fuckin' nuts," he said to the old man.

Fishback sighed impatiently. "Fine. There's no happy hoppers around here. Not one. So just tell me how long it'll take."

The bulldozer driver glanced appreciatively at the cold beer in his hand. Hell, he thought, the old fart seems harmless enough. Probably just the racket he cares about.

"One week," the driver said to Fishback. "That's what the work order says."

"Perfect." Fishback pointed into the woods. "There's a freshwater pond a quarter mile or so down that path. Be a good place to dump some dirt. I mean lotsa dirt."

"Yeah?" The driver sounded interested.

Nils Fishback offered a conspiratorial wink. "Oh yeah," he said. "We're talking Toad Central, partner."

FIVE

In the week that followed, a conference committee of the Florida Legislature agreed to appropriate $9.2 million for a neighborhood development project in southwest Miami called the Willie Vasquez-Washington Community Outreach Center. The same committee approved $27.7 million in transportation funds toward the design and construction of an elevated four-lane concrete bridge to replace the creaky two-lane wooden span that connected Toad Island to the mainland. Governor Dick Artemus declared his strong support for both projects, and praised lawmakers for their "bipartisan commitment to progress."

A few days later, as the last of the oak toads were being plowed under, Nils Fishback and twenty-two other signatories of the anti-Shearwater Island petition met with Robert Clapley and his attorneys in a private dining salon at a fashionable Cuban restaurant in Ybor City. A deal was reached in which Clapley would purchase Fishback's seventeen vacant lots for $19,000 each, which was $16,500 more than Fishback originally had paid for them. The other Toad Island "protesters" received, and eagerly accepted, comparable offers. They were flown home on a Gulfstream jet, and the next morning Nils Fishback called a press conference at the

58

foot of the old wooden bridge. With a handful of local reporters present, "the mayor" announced he was terminating the petition drive because the Shearwater Island Company had "caved in to virtually all our demands." Wielding a sheath of legal-sized papers, Fishback revealed that Robert Clapley had promised in writing to preserve the natural character of the barrier island, and had agreed to provide on-site biologists, botanists and hydrologists to supervise all phases of construction. In addition, Clapley had endorsed an ambitious mitigation program that required replanting three acres of new trees for each acre sacrificed to development. What Nils Fishback didn't tell the press was that Clapley legally was not compelled to revegetate Toad Island itself, and that the new trees could be put anywhere else in Florida—including faraway Putnam County, where Clapley happened to own nine hundred acres of fresh-cut timberland that needed replanting.

The architect of the mitigation scam was none other than Palmer Stoat, who'd had a very productive week. The governor's cronies would be getting their new bridge, Willie Vasquez-Washington would be getting his new community center, and that impertinent tollbooth clerk in Yeehaw Junction would be getting a pink slip. Palmer Stoat flew home from Tallahassee and drove directly to Swain's, his favorite local cigar bar, to celebrate. Here he felt vigorous and important among the ruddy young lawyers and money managers and gallery owners and former pro athletes. Stoat enjoyed watching them instruct their new girlfriends how to clip the nub oh-so-carefully off a bootleg Bolivar—the Yuppie foreplay of the nineties. Stoat resented that his wife wouldn't set foot in Swain's, because she would've looked spectacular sitting there, scissor-legged and preening in one of her tight black cocktail dresses. But Desie claimed to be nauseated by cigars. She nagged him mercilessly for smoking in the house—a vile and toxic habit, she called it. Yet she'd fire up a doobie every time they made love—and did Palmer complain? No, ma'am. Whatever gets you past the night, he'd say cheerfully. And then Desie would say, Just for once shut up, wouldya? And that's the only way she'd do it, with him completely silent in the saddle. The Polaroid routine she'd tolerate, but the moment Palmer blurted a single word, the sex was over. That was Desie's ironclad rule. So he had learned to keep his mouth shut for fifteen or twenty minutes in the bedroom, maybe twice a week. Palmer could handle that. Hell, they were all a little crazy, right? And besides, there were others—the ones up at the capitol, especially—who'd let him talk all he wanted, from start to finish. Like he was calling the Preakness.

The bartender delivered a fresh brandy.

"Where'd this come from?" Stoat asked.

"From the gentleman at the end of the bar."

That was one thing about cigar joints, the customers were all "gentlemen" and "ladies."

"Which one?" said Stoat.

"In the sunglasses."

Young guy in a tropical-print shirt; parrots and palm fronds. Stoat couldn't place the face. Deeply tanned, with long sun-bleached hair and a two-day stubble. Probably an off-duty deckhand from Bahia Mar or Pier 66, Stoat thought, somebody he'd met on a party yacht.

Stoat raised the brandy and mouthed a thank-you. The boat guy in the sunglasses acknowledged with a wry nod. Stoat turned his attention to an effervescent brunette who wasn't smoking a seven-inch Cuban knockoff so much as fellating it. And while the woman would hardly be mistaken for a serious cigar connoisseur, her husky giggle indicated an enthusiasm to learn. Stoat was about to introduce himself when the bartender touched his sleeve and passed him a folded cocktail napkin. "The young gentleman in the sunglasses," the bartender said, "he left this for you."

Palmer Stoat opened the note:

Mr. Yee called from Panama City about your "vitamins." Also, Jorge from Ocean BMW—they'll have another ragtop by Monday. This time be more careful where you park it!

Stoat's hands were shaky when he put down the napkin. He scanned the bar: no sign of the boat guy. Stoat flipped open his cell phone, dialed the nonlisted number to his den, and punched in the numeric code of his answering machine. The first two messages, recorded on the same morning he'd flown to Tallahassee, were exactly as described in the boat guy's note. Mr. Yee—Durgess's elusive rhino-horn connection—had finally returned Stoat's call. (Without Desie's knowledge, Stoat intended to score some of that magic erection powder; he was scheming some wild recreation for his next business trip.) And the second phone message on the machine was indeed from the BMW salesman, a young go-getter named Jorge Hernandez.

Spooky, Stoat thought. Either the boat guy pirated my phone code or he's been snooping inside my house. Stoat laid a twenty on the bar and raced home. Once inside the front door, he sidestepped the dog and hurried to his den. The room did not appear ransacked, and none of the personal items on his desk had been taken or moved out of place.

Then Palmer Stoat noticed the polished glass eyeballs, arranged in a pentagram star. The geometry was so flawless that it appealed in an occult way to Stoat's obsession with neatness and order. (The inverse manifestation of this fetish was a compulsion to jettison all traces of potential untidiness—every scrap of trash, waste or rubbish—with no regard for the consequences. It's what made Stoat the impenitent litterbug he was.)

So he did not disturb the mystery pentagram. Slowly he raised his face to look at the walls; at the stuffed lynx, the timber wolf, the mule deer, the bighorn ram, the elk, the marlin, the tarpon, the peacock bass. Stoat stared at all of them, but they weren't staring back.

Twilly Spree had a habit of falling in love with any woman who was nice enough to sleep with him. One was named Mae, and she was ten years older. She had straight straw-blond hair, and caramel freckles from her cheeks to her ankles. Her family was wealthy, and she showed an endearing lack of interest in Twilly's inheritance. He likely would have married her, except for the fact she was already married to a businessman in Singapore. Mae filed for divorce three days after meeting Twilly, but the lawyers said it would take years for her to get free, since her spouse avoided the United States and therefore could not be served with papers. Having nothing else to do, Twilly got on a plane and flew to Singapore and met briefly with Mae's husband, who quickly arranged for Twilly to be beaten up, arrested in a brothel and deported. After Twilly was returned to Florida, he said in all innocence to Mae: "What'd you ever see in a creep like that?"

Mae and Twilly lived together five months. She said she wanted him to help her become a free spirit. Twilly had heard the same line from other girlfriends. Without him asking, Mae gave up her bridge league and her Wednesday pedicures and took up the mandolin and bromeliads. Mae's father became concerned and flew down from Sag Harbor to check Twilly out. Mae's father was a retired executive from the Ford Motor Company, and was almost single-handedly responsible for ruining the Mustang. To test Twilly's character, he invited him to a skeet range and placed a 12-gauge Remington in his hands. Twilly knocked down everything they tossed up. Mae's father said, Sure, but can you hunt? He took Twilly to a quail plantation in Alabama, and Twilly shot the first four birds they jumped. Then Twilly set the gun in the grass and said, That's plenty. Mae's father said, What the hell's the matter with you, we're just getting warmed up.

And Twilly said, I can't eat more than four birds so what's the point?

The point, thundered Mae's father, isn't the eating. It's the sport of it!

Is that so? Twilly said.

To shoot something fast and beautiful out of the sky, Mae's father told him. That's the essence of it!

Now I see, said Twilly.

And that evening, as Mae's father's chartered King Air took off from a rural Montgomery airport, somebody hiding in the trees with a semi-automatic rifle neatly stitched an X pattern in one wing, rupturing a fuel bladder and forcing the plane to turn back for an emergency landing. The sniper was never found, but Mae's father went on a minor rampage to the authorities. And while he ultimately failed in his efforts to see Twilly Spree prosecuted, he succeeded in convincing his daughter that she had taken up with a homicidal madman. For a while Twilly missed Mae's company, but he took satisfaction in knowing he'd made his point emphatically with her father, that the man definitely got the connection between his own vanities and the Swiss-cheese holes that appeared in his airplane.

And, really, that was the most Twilly ever hoped for, that the bastards would get the message. Most of them did.

But not the litterbug. Twilly decided he'd been too subtle with Palmer Stoat; the man needed things spelled out plainly, possibly more than once. For days Twilly tailed him, and wherever Stoat went, he continued to toss garbage out the car window. Twilly was weary of picking up after him.

One afternoon Stoat and his wife returned from a senator's wedding in Jacksonville and found a note under a windshield wiper of the Range Rover. The note said: "Quit trashing the planet, fuckwad." Stoat gave a puzzled shrug and showed Desie. Then he crumpled the note and dropped it on the pavement of the parking garage.

When Stoat sat down in his sport-utility vehicle, he was aghast to find it full of dung beetles. One pullulating mass covered the tops of his shoes, while a second wave advanced up the steering column. Massing on the dashboard was a third platoon, shiny brown shells clacking together like ball bearings.

Despite appearances, dung beetles actually are harmless, providing a unique and invaluable service at the cellar of the food chain; that is, the prodigious consumption of animal waste. Worshiped by ancient Egyptians, the insects are almost as dearly regarded by modern cattle ranchers. In all there are more than seven thousand known species of dung beetles, without which the earth would literally smother in excrement. This true fact would not have been properly appreciated by Palmer Stoat, who couldn't tell a ladybug from a cockroach (which is what he feared had infested his Range Rover). He yelped and slapped at his thighs and burst from the vehicle as if shot from a cannon.

Desie, who had been standing in wait for her husband to unlock the passenger door, observed his athletic exit with high interest. In a flash she produced her cellular phone, but Palmer whisked it from her hand. No cops! he exclaimed. I don't want to read about this in the newspapers. Desie wondered what made him think such nonsense would rate press attention.

On his own phone Palmer Stoat summoned an exterminator, who used a canister-styled vacuum to remove the bugs from the Range Rover—a total approaching three thousand, had anyone endeavored to count them. To Desie, they sounded like pebbles being sucked through the hose. After consulting an illustrated field guide, the exterminator correctly identified the intruders.

"A what?" Desie asked.

"Dung beetle. A common bovine dung beetle."

"Let me guess," Desie said dryly, "how they get their name."

"Yes, it's true," the exterminator acknowledged.

Stoat scowled. "What're you saying? You saying they eat *shit*?"

And still he missed the whole damn point.

The very next afternoon, on his way to the driving range, Stoat tossed a Kentucky Fried Chicken box. At the time, he was stopped for the drawbridge on the Seventeenth Street Causeway in Fort Lauderdale. Stoat casually leaned across the front seat and heaved the chicken box through the passenger window and over the bridge railing. Waiting three cars back in traffic, Twilly Spree watched the whole thing; saw the cardboard box and fluttering napkin and gnawed-on drumsticks and coleslaw cup tumble downward, plopping into the Intracoastal Waterway. That's when Twilly realized that Palmer Stoat was either unfathomably arrogant or unfathomably dim, and in either case was in need of special instruction.

On the morning of May 2, the maid walked into the bedroom and announced that Boodle, the dog, was missing.

"Oh, that's not possible," said Stoat.

Desie pulled on some clothes and tennis shoes and hurried out to search the neighborhood. She was sobbing when she returned, and said to her husband: "This is all your fault."

He tried to hug her but she shook him off. "Honey, please," he said. "Settle down."

"Somebody took him—"

"You don't know that."

"—and it's all your fault."

"Desie, now."

It *was* his fault that she was so jittery. In retrospect, he shouldn't have shown her what had been done to the trophy heads in the den. Yet at the time Stoat was half-wondering if the furtive vandal might be Desie herself; maybe she'd gone postal on him. She definitely was no fan of his big-game hobby—he remembered the grief she'd given him about the rhinoceros kill. And, in truth, it wasn't difficult to envision his wife perched on the library ladder and using one of the sterling lobster forks—a wedding gift from the pari-mutuel industry— to meticulously remove the simulated eyeballs from his hunting trophies.

But Desie couldn't have been the one who had done it. Palmer Stoat knew by her reaction to the macabre pentagram on the desk and the wall of eyeless animal faces. Desie had paled and run from the room. Later she implored her husband to hire some security guards to watch the house; she didn't feel safe there anymore. Stoat said, Don't worry, it's just some local weirdos. Kids from the neighborhood breaking in for kicks, he told her. But privately he suspected that both the glass eyeball episode and the desecration of the BMW were connected to his lobbying business; some disgruntled, semi-twisted shithead of a client . . . or possibly even a jealous competitor. So Stoat had the locks on the house changed, got all new phone numbers, and found an electronics dweeb who came through and swept the place for listening devices. For good measure, he also polygraphed the maid, the gardener and the part-time cook. Desie made her husband promise to set the alarm system every night from then on, and he had done so faithfully. . . .

With the exception of the previous night, when he'd gone to a Republican fund-raiser and gotten so plastered that a cab had to carry him home. The time was 3:00 a.m., an hour at which Stoat could barely identify his own house, much less fit the new key in the door; typing a nonsequential five-digit code on the alarm panel required infinitely too much dexterity.

Still, he couldn't believe somebody had snuck in behind him and grabbed the Labrador. For one thing, Boodle was a hefty load—128 pounds. He had been trained at no small expense to sit, fetch, shake, lie down, heel, and not lope off with strangers. To forcibly abduct the dog, Stoat surmised, would have required more than one able-bodied man.

Then Desie reminded him that Boodle wasn't functioning at full strength. Days earlier he had been rushed into emergency surgery after slurping five of the glass eyeballs from Stoat's desktop. Stoat didn't notice the eyes were missing until the taxidermy man came to repair the mounts. Soon afterward Boodle grew listless and stopped eating. An X ray at the veterinarian's office revealed the glass orbs, lodged in a cluster at the anterior end of the Lab's stomach. Four of them were removed easily during a laparotomy, but the fifth squirted into the intestinal tract, out of the surgeon's reach. Another operation would be needed if Boodle didn't pass the lost eyeball soon. In the meantime the dog remained lethargic, loaded up on heavy antibiotics.

"He's gonna die if we don't get him back," Desie said morosely.

"We'll find him, don't worry." Stoat promised to print up flyers and pass them around the neighborhood.

"And offer a reward," Desie said.

"Of course."

"I mean a *decent* reward, Palmer."

"He'll be fine, sweetie. The maid probably didn't shut the door tight and he just nosed his way out. He's done that before, remember? And he'll be back when he's feeling better and gets hungry, that's my prediction."

Desie said, "Thank you, Dr. Doolittle." She was still annoyed because Palmer had asked the veterinarian to return the glass eyes Boodle had swallowed, so that they could be polished and re-glued into the dead animal heads.

"For God's sake, get some new ones," Desie had beseeched her husband.

"Hell no," he'd said. "This way'll make a better story, you gotta admit."

Of the surgically retrieved eyeballs, one each belonged to the Canadian lynx, the striped marlin, the elk and the mule deer. The still-missing orb had come from the Cape buffalo, Stoat's largest trophy head, so he was especially eager to get it back.

Her own eyes glistening, Desie stalked up to her husband and said: "If that poor dog dies somewhere out there, I'll never forgive you."

"I'm telling you, nobody stole Boodle—"

"Doesn't matter, Palmer. It's your dumb hobby, your dumb dead animals with their dumb fake eyeballs. So it's your damn fault if something happens to that sweet puppy."

As soon as Desie had left the den, Stoat phoned a commercial printer and ordered five hundred flyers

bearing a photograph of Boodle, and an offer of
$10,000 cash to anyone with information leading to his
recovery. Stoat wasn't worried, because he was reasonably sure that none of his enemies, no matter how
callous, would go so far as to snatch his pet dog.

The world is a sick place, Stoat thought, but not *that*
sick.

Twilly Spree had followed the litterbug's taxi from the
party to the house. He parked at the end of the block
and watched Palmer Stoat stagger up the driveway. By
the time Stoat had inserted the key, Twilly was waiting
thirty feet away, behind the trunk of a Malaysian palm.
Not only did Stoat neglect to lock the front door behind
him, he didn't even shut it halfway. He was still in the
hall bathroom, fumbling with his zipper and teetering
in front of the toilet, when Twilly walked into the house
and removed the dog.

With the Labrador slung fireman-style across his
shoulders, Twilly jogged all the way back to the car.
The dog didn't try to bite him, and never once even
barked. That was encouraging; the big guy was getting
the right vibrations. The smart ones'll do that, Twilly
thought.

Even after they got to the motel, the Lab stayed quiet.
He drank some cold water from the bathtub faucet but
ignored a perfectly scrumptious rawhide chew toy.

"What's the matter, sport?" Twilly asked. It was true
he often spoke to animals. He didn't see why not. Even
the bobcat with which he'd shared a tent in the swamp.
Don't bite me, you little bastard is what Twilly had
advised.

The dog settled in at his feet. Twilly patted its glossy rump and said, "Everything's going to be all right, buddy." He couldn't bring himself to address the animal by the name on its tag—Boodle. It was a quaint synonym for *bribe*, Palmer Stoat at his wittiest.

"From now on," Twilly said to the dog, "you're McGuinn."

The Lab raised its head, which seemed as wide as an anvil.

"After a great guitar player," Twilly explained. The dog uncurled and stretched out on his side. That's when Twilly noticed the tape and bandage. He knelt beside the dog and gingerly peeled the dressing from a shaved patch of belly. Beneath the gauze was a fresh surgical incision, in which Twilly counted twelve steel staples. He pressed the tape back in place and lightly stroked the dog's ribs. It let out one of those heavy sighs that Labs do, but didn't appear to be in pain.

Twilly worried about the wound, wondered what could have gone haywire on such a strapping critter— the gallbladder? Do dogs even *have* gallbladders? I know they get arthritis and heart disease and autoimmune disorders and cancers—for sure, they get cancer. All this was going through Twilly's mind; a juicer commercial on the television and Twilly hunched with his elbows on his knees, on the corner of the bed, with McGuinn snoozing on the burnt-orange shag.

That dog, it had the softest breathing for an animal that size. Twilly had to bend close to hear it, the breathing like a baby's in a crib.

And Twilly thinking: This poor fella's probably on some heavy-duty dope to get past the surgery. That would explain why he'd come along so meekly. And the longer Twilly thought about it, the more certain he became about what to do next: Return to Palmer Stoat's house and find the dog's medicine. Risky—insanely risky—but Twilly had no choice. He wanted nothing bad to happen to McGuinn, who was an innocent.

Master Palmer, though, was something else.

He got fooled. He went back the next night, arriving at the same moment Stoat was driving away, the silhouette of a woman visible beside him in the Range Rover. Twilly assumed it was the wife, assumed the two of them were going to a late dinner.

But it turned out to be one of the maids riding off with the litterbug; he was giving her a lift home. And so Twilly made a mistake that changed everything.

Ever since his previous incursion, the Stoats had been more scrupulous about setting the house alarm. But Twilly decided to hell with it—he'd bust in and grab the dog's pills and run. He'd be in and out and on the road in a minute flat.

The kitchen door was a breeze; a screwdriver did the job and, surprisingly, no alarm sounded. Twilly flipped on the lights and began searching. The kitchen was spacious, newly refurbished in a desert-Southwest motif with earth-tone cabinets and all-stainless appliances. This is what guys like Palmer Stoat do for their new young wives, Twilly thought; kitchens and jewelry are pretty much the upper reach of their imaginations.

He found the dog's medicines on the counter next to the coffee machine: two small prescription bottles and a tube of ointment, all antibiotics, which Twilly put in his pocket. The Lab's leash hung from a hook near the door, so Twilly grabbed that, too. For the daring raid he awarded himself a cold Sam Adams from the refrigerator. When he turned around, there stood Desirata Stoat with the chrome-plated .38 from the bedroom.

"You're the one who stole our dog," she said.

"That's correct."

"Where is he?"

"Safe and sound."

"I said *where*." She cocked the hammer.

"Shoot me, you'll never see McGuinn again."

"Who?"

"That's his new name."

Twilly told Mrs. Stoat he hadn't known about the dog's surgery—not an apology but an explanation for why he was there. "I came back for his medicine. By the way, what happened to him?"

The litterbug's wife said, "You wouldn't believe it if I told you. Put your hands on top of your head."

"I'm sorry, Mrs. Stoat, but that's not how it goes in real life." Twilly took a minute to polish off the beer. "You recycle?" he asked.

Desie motioned toward a closet. Inside was a plastic crate, where Twilly deposited the empty bottle. Then he turned around and calmly snatched the revolver away from the litterbug's wife. He shook out the bullets and put them in the same pocket as the dog's medicine. The gun he placed in a silverware drawer.

Mrs. Stoat lowered her chin and muttered something inaudible. She wore no shoes and a long white T-shirt and pearl earrings, and that was about it. Her arms were as tanned as her legs.

"You're the sicko who put the bugs in my husband's truck?"

"Beetles. Yes."

"And left those nasty notes? And pulled the eyes out of all the animal heads?"

"Correct." Twilly saw no point in mentioning the attack on her red Beemer.

Desie said, "Those were terrible things to do."

"Pretty childish," Twilly conceded.

"What's the matter with you anyway?"

"Evidently I'm working through some anger. How's Palmer holding up?"

"Just fine. He took the maid home and went over to Swain's for a cocktail."

"Ah, the cigar bar." That had been Twilly Spree's original target for the insect infestation, until he'd hit a technical snag in the ventilation system. Also, he had received conflicting scientific opinions about whether dung beetles would actually eat a cured leaf of Cuban tobacco.

"What's your name?" Desie asked.

Twilly laughed and rolled his eyes.

"OK," she said, "you're kidnapping our dog?"

"Your husband's dog."

"I want to come."

Of course Twilly chuckled. She couldn't be serious.

"I need to know what this is all about," she said, "because I don't believe it's money."

"Please."

"I believe it's about Palmer."

"Nice meeting you, Mrs. Stoat."

"It's Desie." She followed Twilly out to the rental car and hopped in. He told her to get out but she refused, pulling her knees to her chin and wrapping both arms around her legs.

"I'll scream bloody murder. *Worse* than bloody murder," she warned.

Twilly sat down heavily behind the wheel. What a twist of rancid luck that Stoat's wife would turn out to be a head case. A light flicked on in the house across the street. Desie saw it, too, and Twilly expected her to start hollering.

Instead she said: "Here's the situation. Lately I've been having doubts about everything. I need to get away."

"Take a cruise."

"You don't understand."

"The dog'll be fine. You've got my word."

"I'm talking about Palmer," she said. "Me and Palmer."

Twilly was stumped. He couldn't think of anything else to do but drive.

"I'm not very proud of myself," she was saying, "but I married the man, basically, for security. Which is a nice way of saying I married him for the dough. Maybe I didn't realize that at the time, or maybe I did."

"Desie?"

"What."

"Do I look like Montel Williams?"

"I'm sorry—God, you're right. Listen to me go on."

Twilly found his way to the interstate. He was worried about McGuinn. He wondered how often the dog needed the pills, wondering if it was time for a walk.

"I'll let you see the dog, Mrs. Stoat, just so you know he's all right. Then I'm taking you back home."

"Don't," Desie said. "Please."

"And here's what I want you to tell your husband—"

"There's a cop."

"Yes, I see him."

"You're doing seventy."

"Sixty-six. Now here's what you tell Palmer: 'A dangerous drug-crazed outlaw has kidnapped your beloved pet, and he won't give him back until you do exactly what he says.' Can you handle that?"

Desie stared in a distracted way out the window.

Twilly said: "Are you listening? I want you to tell your husband I'm a violent bipolar sociopathic lunatic. Tell him I'm capable of anything."

"But you're not."

He was tempted to recite a complete list of personal felonies, but he thought it might freak her into jumping from the car. "I blew up my uncle's bank," he volunteered.

"What for?"

"Does it matter? A bombing is a bombing."

Desie said, "You'll have to do better than that. I still don't believe you're nuts."

Twilly sighed. "What do you and Palmer talk about—politics? Television? Repression in Tibet?"

"Shopping." Desie spoke with no trace of shame or irony. "He's got a keen interest in automobiles and fine clothes. Though I suppose that doesn't count for much in your social circle."

"I have no social circle."

"And he also plays a little golf," Desie said, "when he's not hunting."

"You play golf, too?"

"Exactly twice in my life. We're members at Otter Glen."

"How nice for you," Twilly said. "Ever see any otters out there?"

"Nope."

"Ever wonder why?"

"Not really," Desirata Stoat said.

Back in the motel room, McGuinn-Boodle was happy to see her. Twilly tried to play vet but the dog kept spitting out the pills. It turned into quite a comic scene. Finally Desie shooed Twilly aside and took over. She slipped one of the big white tablets under McGuinn's tongue while she massaged his throat. Serenely the Labrador swallowed the pill. When Twilly tried to duplicate Desie's technique, the pill came shooting out at him.

She said, "I'd say that clinches it."

"No, you *cannot* come along."

"But I'm the only one who can give him the medicine. Yesterday he nearly took off Palmer's thumb."

"I'll get the hang of it," Twilly said.

After Desie got the dog to gulp the second pill, she asked Twilly about the new name.

"After a musician I'm fond of. Roger McGuinn."

She said, "You're way too young to be fond of Roger McGuinn."

"You know about him?" Twilly was thrilled.

"Sure. Maestro of the twelve-string. 'Eight Miles High,' 'Mr. Spaceman,' and so on."

"Fantastic!" Twilly said. "And how old are *you*?"

"Old enough." Desie gave him the knowing older-woman smile. She didn't mention her summer stints at Sam Goody's.

Twilly noticed she was stroking McGuinn with one hand and twisting the tail of her T-shirt with the other. Finally she got around to the big question.

"Tell me exactly what you want from my husband."

"I want him to clean up his act."

"Do what?"

"He's a loathsome pig. Everywhere he goes he leaves a trail of litter."

Desie said, "That's it?"

"I want him to get the message, that's all. I want to see shame in his eyes. Beyond that, hell, I don't know." Twilly tugged a thin blanket off the bed and tossed it to her. "Cover up, Desie. I can see your butt."

She said, "You're aiming low, Mr. Spaceman."

"How do you mean?"

"You know who my husband is? You have any idea what he does for a living?"

"No," Twilly said, "but the governor's office was on his answer machine the other night."

"Exactly, there you go—the governor himself. Probably calling about that ridiculous bridge."

"What bridge?" asked Twilly.

Desie got cross-legged on the floor, with the blanket across her lap. "Let me tell you some stories," she said, "about Palmer Stoat."

"No, ma'am, I'm taking you home."

But he didn't.

SIX

Twilly drove all night with the woman and the dog. They arrived at Toad Island shortly before dawn. Twilly parked on the beach and rolled down the windows.

"What are we doing here?" Desie said.

Twilly closed his eyes. He didn't open them again until he heard gulls piping and felt the sun on his neck. The Gulf was lead gray and slick. In the distance he saw Desie strolling the white ribbon of sand, the hulking black McGuinn at her side; above them were seabirds, carping. Twilly got out and stretched. He shed his clothes and plunged into the chilly water and swam out two hundred yards. From there he had a mariner's perspective of the island, its modest breadth and altitude and scraggled green ripeness, as it might have appeared long ago. Of course Twilly understood the terrible significance of a new bridge. He could almost hear his father's voice, rising giddily at the prospects. That this scrubby shoal had been targeted for development wasn't at all shocking to Twilly. The only genuine surprise was that somebody hadn't fucked it up sooner.

He breaststroked to shore. He stepped into his jeans and sat, dripping, on the hood of the rental car. When Desie returned, she said: "Boodle wanted to jump in and swim. That means he's feeling better."

Twilly gave her a reproachful look.

"McGuinn, I mean," she said. "So, is this what you expected to find?"

"It's nice."

"You think Governor Dick owns this whole island?"

"If not him, then some of his pals."

"How many people," Desie said, "you figure they want to cram out here? All total."

"I don't know. Couple thousand at least."

"That explains why they need a bigger bridge."

"Oh yes. Trucks, bulldozers, backhoes, cement mixers, cranes, gasoline tankers, cars and bingo buses." Twilly blinked up at the clouds. "I'm just guessing, Mrs. Stoat. I'm just going by history."

Desie said, "McGuinn found a man passed out on the beach. He didn't look too good."

"The unconscious seldom do."

"Not a bum. A regular-looking guy."

Twilly said, "I guess you want me to go have a look. Is that the idea?"

He slid off the car and headed down the shore. Desie whistled for the dog, and off they went. The passed-out man was in the same position in which she'd found him—flat on his back, pale hands interlocked in funereal calm across his chest. The man's mouth hung open and he was snorting like a broken diesel. A gleaming stellate dollop of seagull shit decorated his forehead; one eye was nearly swollen shut, and on the same cheek was a nasty sand-crusted laceration. Nearby lay a shoe and an empty vodka bottle.

Tail swishing, McGuinn inspected the passed-out man while Twilly Spree shook him by the shoulder.

The man woke up hacking. He whispered "No" when Twilly asked if he needed an ambulance.

When Desie knelt beside him, he said, "I got drunk and fell off a bulldozer."

"That's a good one."

"I wish it weren't true." The man wiped his sleeve across the poop on his forehead. He grimaced when McGuinn wet-nosed the swollen side of his face.

"What's your name?" Desie asked.

"Brinkman." With Twilly's assistance, the man sat up. "Dr. Steven Brinkman," he said.

"What kind of doctor?"

Brinkman finally noticed what Desie was wearing—the long T-shirt and pearl earrings and nothing else—and became visibly flustered. The big Labrador retriever was also making him jumpy, snuffling in his most personal crevices.

"Are you an M.D.?" Desie said.

"Uh, no. What I am—I'm a field biologist."

Twilly stiffened. "What're you doing out here on the island?"

"This is where I work."

"For who?" Twilly demanded. "The Army Corps? Fish and Wildlife?"

Brinkman said, "Not exactly."

Twilly took him by the arm, hauled him to his feet and marched him up a grassy dune. "You and I need to talk."

Dr. Brinkman was not the only one who'd had a rough night. Palmer Stoat had relaxed to sloppy excess at Swain's bar, then wound up at a small party in the owner's private salon with two bottles of Dom, a box of H. Upmann's straight off a boat from Varadero, and a call girl who made Stoat show his voter's card, because she only did registered Republicans. Stoat was so bewitched by the woman's ideological fervency that he couldn't properly concentrate on the sex. Eventually the halting encounter dissolved into a philosophical colloquy that lasted into the wee hours and left Stoat more exhausted than a routine night of illicit intercourse. He crept home with a monstrous headache and collapsed in one of the guest rooms, so as not to alert Desirata, whom he presumed to be slumbering alone in the marital bed.

Stoat slept past noon and woke up to a grim hangover and a silent house. Spears of sunlight slanted harshly through the Bahamas shutters. Stoat buried his face in a pillow and thought again of the voluble prostitute at Swain's. To meet someone with genuine political ideals was a rarity in Stoat's line of work; as a lobbyist he had long ago concluded there was no difference in how Democrats and Republicans conducted the business of government. The game stayed the same: It was always about favors and friends, and who controlled the dough. Party labels were merely a way to keep track of the teams; issues were mostly smoke and vaudeville. Nobody believed in anything except hanging on to power, whatever it took. So, at election time, Palmer Stoat always advised his clients to hedge generously by donating large sums to all sides. The strategy was as immensely pragmatic as it was cynical. Stoat himself was registered independent, but he hadn't stepped inside a voting booth in fourteen years. He couldn't take the concept seriously; he knew too much.

Yet it was refreshing to hear the call girl go on so earnestly about the failure of affirmative action and the merit of prayer in public schools and the dangerous liberal assault on the Second Amendment. None of those subjects affected Palmer Stoat's life to the point that he'd formed actual opinions, but it was entertaining to meet someone who had, someone with no covert political agenda.

If only he'd been able to screw her, Erika the call girl. Or was it Estelle? Brightly Stoat thought: Now there's a candidate for an evening of fine wine and rhino powder. He reminded himself to reach out once more to the mysterious Mr. Yee in Panama City.

The ring of the telephone cleaved Stoat's cranium like a cutlass, and he lunged for the receiver. The sound of his wife's voice befuddled him. Maybe he was in the wrong house! If so, how had Desie found him?

"I didn't want you to worry," she was saying on the other end.

"Right." Stoat bolted upright and looked around the room, which he was relieved to recognize.

"I can explain," Desie was saying, an odd jittery edge in her tone.

"OK."

"But not right now," she said.

"Fine."

"Aren't you going to ask if I'm all right?"

"Yes, sweetie. I've been, huh, out of my mind wondering where you went."

An unreadable pause on the other end. Then, too sweetly, Desie saying, "Palmer?"

"Yes, hon."

"You didn't even know I was gone, did you?"

"Sure I did. It's just . . . see, I got home late and crashed in one of the guest bedrooms—"

"Sixteen hours."

"—so I wouldn't wake you up."

"Sixteen bloody hours!"

Stoat said, "What?"

"That's how long it's been."

"Christ. Where? Tell me what happened."

"You just got up, didn't you? Unbelievable." Now Desie sounded disgusted. "You were so smashed, you never bothered to check in the bedroom."

"Desie, I'll come get you right now. Tell me where."

But when she told him, he thought she was joking.

"An Amoco station in Bronson? Where the hell's Bronson?"

"Not far from Gainesville," Desie said. "That's where you should send the plane to pick me up."

"Now hold on—"

"It doesn't need to be, like, a jet. I'm sure one of your rich big-shot clients has something they can loan out. Did I mention I was kidnapped?"

Stoat felt bilious and fevered. Bobbling the phone, he sagged back on the pillows.

"It *was* a kidnapping, sort of," Desie was saying. "It's a long freaky story, Palmer."

"OK."

"But I did find Boodle."

"Hey, that's great." Stoat had almost forgotten about the missing dog. "How's the big guy doin'?"

"Fine. But there's a slight problem."

Stoat grunted. "Why am I not surprised."

Desie said, "I'll tell you everything when I see you."

"In Bronson," Stoat said weakly.

"No, Gainesville. Remember?"

"Right. Where I send the private plane."

Once they got some black coffee into Dr. Brinkman, he was able to pull himself together for a short tour of soon-to-be Shearwater Island.

Here's where the yacht harbor will be dredged. There's where the golf courses go. That's being cleared for the airstrip. And, everywhere else: homesites.

"Houses?" Desie asked.

"Very expensive houses," Brinkman said. "But also condominiums and town homes and even some year-round rentals. Duplexes and triplexes."

Twilly pulled off the road into the shade of some pine trees. "What's the tallest building they've got in the plans?" he asked Brinkman.

"Sixteen stories. There'll be one at each end of the island."

"Assholes," Twilly muttered.

Desie remarked on the multitude of peeling, bleached-out signs advertising other past projects. Brinkman said they'd all gone bust.

"But these new fellows have serious capital and serious financing," he added. "This time I think it's a done deal."

"Provided they get their bridge," said Twilly.

"Obviously."

"And your job here," Desie said to the biologist, "is what exactly?"

Brinkman told them about the field survey. "Basically a complete inventory," he explained, "of every living plant, animal and insect species on the island."

"Wow," said Desie.

Twilly snickered contemptuously. "Fuck 'wow.' Dr. Steve, please tell Mrs. Stoat why she shouldn't be so impressed."

"Well, because. . . ." Brinkman looked uncomfortable. "Because it's fairly routine, a survey like this. More bureaucracy than science, if you want the truth. Sure, it makes us appear responsible and concerned, but the purpose isn't to figure out what trees and animals to save. The purpose is to make sure the developers don't run into a snail-darter type of crisis."

Desie looked to Twilly for elaboration.

"Endangered species," he told her. "That would be a showstopper, am I right, Dr. Steve? Shut down the whole works."

Brinkman nodded emphatically.

"And I'm guessing," Twilly continued, "that you finished your field study this week, and didn't come across anything like a snail darter or a spotted owl on this entire island. Nothing so rare that it would get in the way of the building permits. And I'm also guessing that's why you went out and got plastered last night, because you'd secretly been hoping to come across something, anything, to block this project—even an endangered gnat. Because you're probably a decent human being at heart, and you know exactly what's going to happen out here once these bastards get rolling."

In a voice raw with sadness, Brinkman said, "It's already started."

Then he took them into the upland woods to see what had become of the oak toads. Right away McGuinn started digging.

"Make him stop," Brinkman implored.

Desie hooked the dog to his leash and tugged him along. Twilly Spree walked ahead, kicking at the fresh-churned dirt, following the checkerboard tread marks of a large earth-moving machine. When they reached the area where the bulldozers were parked, Brinkman pointed and said: "That's the one I fell from. I was trying to get the darn thing started."

"What for?" Desie asked.

"I was drunk."

"That, we've established."

"I had a notion to destroy Mr. Clapley's billboard."

Twilly said, "He's the main guy?"

"Mr. Shearwater Island himself," said Brinkman. "Robert Clapley. I've never met the man, but he put up a huge sales sign. You must've seen it when you came across the old bridge. I suppose I was wondering what it might look like, that goddamn billboard, all busted to splinters."

Twilly said, "I could be persuaded to wonder the same thing."

"What about the frogs?" Desie asked. McGuinn was on the prowl again, jerking her around like a puppet.

"Toads." Steven Brinkman made a sweeping motion with one arm. "They buried them."

"Nice," said Twilly.

"Because Clapley's people got it into their heads that they might be a problem later on, when the crews started clearing the island. They were afraid somebody like the Sierra Club would make a stink with the newspapers, because the toads were so small and there were so many. So Clapley's people decided to bulldoze 'em in advance, to play it safe."

Desie was watching Twilly closely. She said: "He's making this up, right?"

"I wish."

She said, "No, it's too awful."

"Well," said Brinkman, "you didn't hear it from me. We never spoke, OK?" He turned his back on them and slowly made his way into the pines. He walked with his head down, pausing every few steps as if he was searching for something.

Twilly said to Desie: "I've seen enough."

"You think he was on the level? I say he's still drunk."

"Turn the dog loose."

"I will not."

He pried the leash from her fist and unclipped it from McGuinn's collar. The Lab bounded to a hillock of freshly turned soil and began digging exuberantly, his shiny black rump waggling high. After a minute or so, Twilly told Desie to call him back. Twilly went over to the place where McGuinn had been digging and, with the toe of a shoe, finished the hole. Then he reached down and picked up a pearly gelatinous clot of mushed toads.

"Come here, Mrs. Stoat."

"No, I don't think so."

"You wanted proof, didn't you?"

But she was already running, McGuinn at her heels.

Later, in the car, Twilly told Desie it was time for her to go home. She wasn't prepared to argue. He dropped her at a gas station in Bronson and gave her two fifties for breakfast and clothes and a cab ride to Gainesville. So she wouldn't be walking around half-naked, Twilly purchased a plastic raincoat from a vending machine. The raincoat was bright yellow and folded into a kit no larger than a pack of Camels. Desie unwrapped it and, without a word, slipped it on.

Twilly walked her to the telephone booth and put a quarter in her right hand. He said, "I'll be on my way now."

"Can't I say good-bye to Bood—I mean, McGuinn?"

"You two already said your good-byes."

"Now, remember the trick I showed you to give him his pills. The roast-beef trick. He's partial to rare."

"We'll manage," Twilly said.

"And keep him out of the water until those stitches are healed."

"Don't worry," he said.

Desie caught her reflection in the cracked glass door of the phone booth. With a frail laugh, she said, "God, I'm a mess. I look like a drowned canary." She was stalling because she couldn't make sense of her feelings; because she didn't want to go home to her wealthy powerful husband. She wanted to stay with the edgy young criminal who had broken into her home and abducted her pet dog. Well, of course she did. Wouldn't any normal, settled, well-adjusted wife feel the same way?

"You're serious about this?" she said to Twilly.

He was incredulous at the question. "You saw what I saw. Hell yes, I'm serious."

"But you'll go to jail."

"That all depends."

Desie said, "I don't even know your name."

Twilly smiled. "Yes, you do. It's printed on the car-rental receipt, the one you swiped out of the glove compartment last night in Fort Pierce."

She reddened. "Oops."

As Twilly turned away, Desie reached for his arm. She said, "Before I go home, I want to be sure. That was no joke back there? They deliberately buried all those harmless little—"

"Yeah, they did."

"God. What kind of people would do something like that?"

"Ask your husband," said Twilly, pulling free.

SEVEN

The airplane was a twin-engine Beech. When Desie stepped aboard, the pilot asked, "Where's your friend?"

Desie was flustered; she thought he meant the kidnapper.

"The dog," said the pilot. "Mr. Stoat said you were traveling with a dog."

"He was mistaken. I'm alone."

The plane took off and banked to the west. Desie expected it to turn southbound, but it didn't. Squinting into the sun, she leaned forward and tried to raise her voice above the engines.

"Where are you going?"

"One more stop," the pilot said over his shoulder. "Panama City."

"What for?" Desie asked, but he didn't hear her.

It was a choppy and uncomfortable flight, more than an hour, and Desie was steaming by the time they got there. Palmer should have come up on the plane to pick her up; that's what a husband ought to do when his wife is freed from a kidnapping. At the least, he should have directed the pilot to bring her straight home, instead of making her sit through a bumpy add-on leg. Desie assumed Palmer was taking advantage of the plane's availability to pick up one of his big-shot cronies, thereby saving a few bucks on a separate charter. She wondered who'd be riding with her on the return trip to Lauderdale, and hoped it wasn't some asshole mayor or senator. Some of Palmer's lobbying clients were tolerable in small doses, but Desie couldn't stand the politicians with whom her husband avidly fraternized. Even Dick Artemus, the undeniably charismatic governor, had managed to repulse Desie with a distasteful ethnic joke within moments of being introduced; Desie had been poised to launch a margarita in his face when Palmer intervened, steering her to a neutral corner.

But no other passenger boarded the Beechcraft in Panama City. The pilot stepped off briefly and returned carrying a Nike shoe box, which he asked Desie to hold during the flight.

"What's inside?" she said.

"I don't know, ma'am, but Mr. Stoat said to take special care with it. He said it's real valuable."

Through the window Desie saw a gray Cadillac parked on the tarmac near the Butler Aviation Terminal. Standing by the driver's side of the car was a middle-aged Asian man in a raspberry-colored golf shirt and shiny brown slacks. The man was counting through a stack of cash, which he placed into a billfold. Once the plane began to taxi, the Asian man glanced up and waved, presumably at the pilot.

Desie waited until they were airborne before opening the shoe box. Inside was an opaque Tupperware container filled with a fine light-colored powder. Desie would have guessed it was cake mix, except for the odd musky smell. She snapped the lid on the container and set it back in the box and began to wonder, irritably, if her husband had gone into the narcotics business.

Palmer Stoat didn't fly to Gainesville to meet Desie because Robert Clapley unexpectedly had phoned to congratulate him for icing the funds to build the new Toad Island bridge. In the course of the conversation Clapley mentioned he was headed to a friend's farm near Lake Okeechobee for some off-road bird shooting, and he'd be delighted if Stoat joined him.

"Oh, and I've got the rest of your money," Clapley added.

Stoat took the interstate to U.S. 27 and sped north toward Clewiston. An hour later he located Clapley, waiting in a field of bare dirt that not so long ago had been a tomato patch. The field had been baited heavily with seeds, and all that remained for the two hunters was to wait for the doves to show up. It wasn't much of a challenge but that was fine with Palmer Stoat, who hadn't yet shaken the bleary bone-ache from his hangover. Clapley set up a roomy canvas shooting blind and broke out a bottle of expensive scotch. With a matching flourish, Stoat produced two large cigars from a pocket of his hunting vest. The men drank and puffed and told pussy-related lies until the birds started arriving. The blind was spacious enough for both men to fire their shotguns simultaneously, and in only two hours they shot forty-one doves, very few of which were actually airborne at the time. The rest of the doves were on the ground, obliviously pecking up birdseed, when they got blasted. The men didn't even need a retriever, since the doves all succumbed within twenty yards of the portable blind, where the bulk of the food had been sprinkled.

At dusk the men quit shooting and removed their earmuffs. Clapley began picking up the small ruffled bodies and dropping them in a camo duffel. Behind him walked the wobbly Stoat, his shotgun propped butt-first across his shoulder.

"How many a these tasty little gumdrops you want?" Clapley asked.

"Not many, Bob. Just enough for me and the wife."

Later, when he got home and began to sober up, Stoat realized that Robert Clapley had forgotten to give him the $50,000 check.

When Desie arrived, Palmer was plucking the birds in the kitchen. He got up to hug her but she ducked out of reach.

He said, "Tell me what happened, sweetie. Are you all right?"

"Like you care."

And so it went for nearly an hour—Stoat apologizing for coming home so bombed the previous night that he'd failed to notice Desie was missing; apologizing for not being on the airplane to meet her in Gainesville; apologizing for not personally picking her up at the Fort Lauderdale airport (although he'd sent a chauffeured Town Car!); apologizing for failing to comment upon her odd attire—baggy sweatpants and an orange mesh University of Florida football jersey, purchased in haste at a campus bookstore; apologizing for not inquiring sooner if the deranged kidnapper had raped her or roughed her up; and, finally, apologizing for stacking dead doves on the kitchen table.

Then Desie said: "Aren't you even going to ask about Boodle?"

So Stoat apologized again, this time for not being properly concerned about the abducted family pet.

"Where is he, hon?"

"The kidnapper's still got him," Desie announced.

"Oh, this is crazy."

"You're not going to like it."

"How much does he want?" Stoat asked.

"He's not after money."

"Then what?"

Desie repeated what the strange young dognapper had instructed her to say. She omitted the fact that she was the one who'd tipped him off to the Shearwater project.

When Stoat heard the kidnapper's demand, he cackled.

"Palmer, the man is *serious.*"

"Really."

"You'd better do what he wants."

"Or what," said Stoat. "He's going to kill my dog? My *dog?*"

"He says he will."

Again Stoat chuckled, and resumed cleaning the birds. "Come on, Des. The sickest bastard in the whole world isn't going to hurt a Labrador retriever. Especially Boodle—everybody falls head over heels for Boodle."

Exhausted though she was, Desie couldn't help but watch as her husband meticulously tugged out the gray feathers one by one and placed them in a soft velvety pile. Naked, the doves looked too scrawny to eat. The breasts were gaunt and the flesh was pocked unattractively with purple-tinged holes from the shotgun pellets.

He said, "Oh, I almost forgot—the package from Panama City?"

"On the porch," Desie said. "What is it, anyway?"

"Stationery."

"In Tupperware?"

"Oh . . . well, yeah," her husband stammered. "Keeps out the humidity. It's good stuff. Embossed."

"Cut the crap, Palmer. It's powder."

"You opened it!"

"Yeah. My husband the smack dealer. No wonder you didn't want it sent by regular mail."

Stoat threw back his head and laughed. "Heroin? Now you think I'm moving heroin! Oh, that's priceless."

"Then what is it?" Desie demanded angrily. "What's in the Tupperware? Tell me, Palmer."

So he did, adding: "But I wanted it to be a surprise."

She stared at him. "Rhino sex powder."

"Hon, they don't always shoot the animals to get the horns. That's a common myth."

"You're unbelievable," Desie said.

"I just thought it might liven things up for you and me. Hey, can it hurt to try?"

Wordlessly she stood up and went to the bedroom.

"Aren't you hungry?" Stoat called hopefully after her. "Marisa's firing up the barbecue."

It took another forty-five minutes to finish with the heads and the skins of the birds. Not wishing to stink up his garbage can with the innards, he wrapped them in butcher paper and carried it across the backyard, through the hedge, to the well-manicured property of his neighbors, the Clarks, where he dumped the whole mess in the goldfish pond. Ned and Susan Clark, Stoat happened to know, were on a gambling cruise to Nassau.

After Stoat returned to the house, he sent the cook home, stored the doves in the refrigerator, stood for a long time under a hot shower and pondered what to do about Desirata. He didn't believe the kidnap story but took it as proof that something was seriously amiss, something was unraveling inside her mind. Maybe she'd run off with some guy on a whim, then changed her mind. Or maybe she'd simply freaked out and bolted. Manic depression, multiple-personality syndrome— Stoat had heard of these illnesses but was unclear about the symptoms. This much was true: Given the hinky events of the past twenty-four hours, he had come to suspect that his own unhappy spouse had conspired in the defacing of his prize taxidermy, the trashing of the red BMW, and even the infesting of his luxury sport-utility vehicle with shit-eating insects.

A cry for help, Palmer Stoat figured. Obviously the kid's got some loose shingles.

But whatever weird was happening within Desie, it was the part of her yarn about the dog that Stoat couldn't sort out. What had she done with poor Boodle, and why?

He toweled off and crawled into bed. He felt her go tense when he slipped an arm around her waist.

"You OK?" he asked.

"Never felt better."

"You smell good."

"Compared to a sack of dead pigeons, I hope so."

"I know you're upset, sweetie. I think we should talk."

"Well, I think we should be calling the police." Desie knew he wouldn't do it, but she was ticked off that he hadn't raised the prospect. What concerned husband wouldn't at least consider notifying the authorities after an intruder breaks into his home and takes off with his wife! So maybe it hadn't been a *real* kidnapping (since it was Desie's idea to go), but Palmer didn't know that.

He said, "Sweetie, we can't possibly get the police involved."

"Why not? You said he'll never hurt the dog, so what've we got to lose?"

"Because it'll be all over the TV and the newspapers, that's why. My clients rely on me to be low-profile and discreet," he explained. "This would be a disaster, Desie. I'd be a laughing stock. 'Dognapper Targets Prominent Lobbyist.' Jesus Hubbard Christ, can you imagine the headlines?"

She squirmed out of his embrace.

Stoat said, "Honestly, how could I show my face in Tallahassee or Washington? A story like that, I'm telling you, it might turn up in a Letterman monologue. Try to understand what that could do to my business."

"Fine," she said curtly.

"Don't worry. We'll get our puppy back."

"Then you'll do what this maniac wants. It's the only way," she said.

With an exaggerated sigh, Palmer rolled on his back. "It's *not* the only way. Trust me."

Desie turned to face him. "Please just do what he says."

"You can't be serious."

She said, "It's just a bridge, Palmer. One lousy bridge to one lousy little island. They'll get by fine without it."

"You don't know what you're talking about. Besides, it's already done. I couldn't stop it even if I wanted to, which I don't."

"Don't lie to me. Not about this."

Stoat sucked in his breath, wondering: What the hell does she mean by *that*?

Desie said what she'd been told to say by the dog-napper: "Your buddy Governor Dick—he hasn't signed the budget bill yet, has he? Tell him to veto the money for the bridge."

"OK, that's it." Stoat sat up and reached for the lamp. "Darling, you've obviously lost your goddamned mind."

She closed her eyes but kept her cheek to the pillow. "Otherwise we'll never see the dog again," she said. "The lunatic has already changed his name, Palmer. He calls him McGuinn."

"Yeah. Whatever." What a whacked-out imagination she has, Stoat thought. He'd had no idea.

Desie stiffened beside him. "So you think I'm out of my mind? Isn't that what you just said?"

Palmer bowed his head and gingerly massaged his tender temples. "Look, Des, let's please finish talking about this tomorrow. I'm having a tough day's night."

His wife groaned in exasperation and rolled over.

Robert Clapley celebrated in his own special style. He returned with his share of the dove kill to the oceanfront condominium his company owned in Palm Beach. There he cooked the birds in a light wine sauce and lovingly served them to Katya and Tish, whom Clapley half-whimsically referred to as Barbie One and Barbie Two.

Katya was from Russia; Tish was from the Czech Republic. They were both five ten and weighed approximately 130 pounds. Clapley didn't know their last names, or their true ages, and didn't ask. He had met them six months earlier on South Beach, at an all-night party thrown by a bisexual German real-estate tycoon. The women told Clapley they were models and had come to Miami for new career opportunities. Steady fashion work was hard to come by in Eastern Europe, and the pay was lousy compared with that in France or the States. Robert Clapley thought Katya and Tish looked a bit flashy for big-time modeling, but they were plenty attractive enough for him. The fellow who'd thrown the party had taken Clapley aside and confided that it was he who had purchased the transatlantic plane tickets for Katya and Tish, and half a dozen other women who were exceptionally eager to come to America. The man had chosen them from an array of more than one hundred who had appeared on an audition videotape mailed to him by a "talent agency" in Moscow.

"But don't get the wrong idea, Bob. These girls are *not* common prostitutes," the man had assured Clapley.

No, Katya and Tish were not common. Within a week Clapley had installed them in one of his part-time residences, the sixteenth-floor Palm Beach condo, which featured a seven-jet Jacuzzi, a Bose sound system and a million-dollar view of the Atlantic Ocean from every room. Katya and Tish were in heaven, and demonstrated their gratitude to Clapley with ferocious ardor. Occasionally they would go out to actual modeling try-outs, but for the most part they filled their days with swimming, sunning, shopping and watching American soap operas. When eventually it came time for their visas to expire, Katya and Tish were crestfallen. They appealed to their generous new boyfriend, Bob, who suggested he might be able to fix their immigration problems in exchange for a favor; not a small favor, though.

Robert Clapley had been the youngest of five children, and the only boy. At some point in an otherwise unremarkable childhood, young Bob had developed a somewhat unnatural interest in Barbie dolls, which his sisters collected like marbles. In fact there were so many Barbies and Barbie playhouses and Barbie wardrobes in the Clapley household that Robert's sisters never seemed to notice when one or two of the dolls went missing, and in any case wouldn't have thought to accuse their meek little brother. Robert's attraction to the Barbies was more than a fleeting puerile curiosity; three of the voluptuous eleven-and-a-half-inch icons—Wedding Day Barbie, Cinderella Barbie and Disco Barbie (plus assorted costumes)—covertly accompanied Clapley when he went off to college at age eighteen. Later, running dope twice monthly from Cartagena to South Bimini, Clapley was never without his favorite Live-Action Barbie, zipped snugly into the fur-lined pocket of his leather flight jacket.

What did he so adore about the plastic dolls? Their pneumatic and shapely flawlessness, to be sure. Each Barbie was dependably perfect to the eye and feel. That Clapley's obsession had an eccentric sexual component, there was no doubt, but he would have argued on the side of harmless fantasy over perversion. And indeed he treated the toy Barbies with the utmost veneration and civility, undressing them only long enough to change (or iron) their exquisite miniature outfits. Innocent or not, Robert Clapley knew enough to guard his secret; who would have understood? Clapley himself was vexed by the doll fixation, and as he got older began to doubt he would ever outgrow it—until he met Katya and Tish. Instantaneously the future appeared to Clapley in dual thunderbolts of lust. The statuesque immigrants represented a luminous opportunity for a therapeutic breakthrough; the transcendence of appetites from toy to flesh, from Barbie worship to Barbie carnality. In other words: from boy to man.

So strong was their desire to remain in the United States (and retain twenty-four-hour spa privileges at Robert Clapley's condominium tower), that Katya and Tish weren't completely unreceptive to his ambitiously twisted proposal. Matching the hair was a cinch; the blond hue of Clapley's choosing came in a brand-name bottle. The surgery, however—to begin with identically sized breast implants—was the cause of some trepidation for the two women.

There's absolutely nothing to worry about! Clapley insisted. America has the best doctors in the world!

Ultimately, Katya and Tish were persuaded to go along, cajoled and flattered and spoiled as they were by their enthusiastic young host. And Clapley was enthralled to observe the concurrent transformations, each cosmetic refinement bringing him closer to his dream of living live-in Barbies. No, it wouldn't be long now!

He sat at the head of the dinner table, sipping a chardonnay and beaming as Katya and Tish hungrily hacked at the scorched little bird carcasses. Palmer Stoat seems like a fellow who would appreciate this setup,

Clapley thought cheerily. I can't wait to see his face when I introduce him to the girls.

And Stoat, like every man who'd recently met Katya and Tish, undoubtedly would lean over to his host and whisper: Wow, Bob, are those really twins?

And Robert Clapley would smile and answer the way he always did.

No, but they will be soon.

Vecker Darby's house blew up and burned down while Twilly Spree was asleep. Twilly would notice the photograph in the newspaper two days later, and sleep just as soundly that night. "Justice," he'd mutter to McGuinn, whose chin rested on his knee. "Justice, boy. That's all it is." The dog would sleep fine, too.

They were parked in palmetto scrub off a dirt road near Zolfo Springs when Vecker Darby came into their lives. It was close to midnight. Presumably, Desirata Stoat was home in Fort Lauderdale with her worthless dickhead of a husband, and Twilly found himself thinking about her. He was sitting in the rental car with an empty pizza box on his lap. McGuinn already had downed supper, four heaping cups of premium dry dog food; Desie had strictly instructed Twilly on which brand to purchase. Vet's orders, she'd said. Typically, McGuinn wolfed the whole pile in about fourteen seconds. Afterward Twilly would sneak out the antibiotic pills, each concealed in a square-folded slice of rare roast beef, which McGuinn eagerly inhaled.

Twilly had the radio turned up loud for Derek and the Dominoes, so at first he didn't hear Vecker Darby's flatbed truck. Certainly he didn't see it, as Vecker Darby was driving without headlights. Twilly was drumming his fingertips on the pizza box and wondering if, in retrospect, he'd been too hasty in his decision to ditch Mrs. Stoat in Bronson. Not that she would run to the cops; he had a strong feeling she wouldn't. No, what bothered Twilly was how he sort of missed her. She was good company; plus, she had a lovely laugh. The dog was terrific, a real champ, but he didn't light up the car the way Desie Stoat did.

I wonder if I'll ever see her again, Twilly thought.

When the song ended, he turned off the radio. That's when he heard the truck nearby—specifically, the grinding hydraulics of the flatbed being tilted. McGuinn raised his huge black head and barked. Hush! Twilly whispered. He slipped from the car and circled back through the scrub until he gained a clear view of the truck and what the driver was doing. As the incline of the flatbed steepened, the truck's unbound cargo began sliding off the back—assorted barrels, drums, tanks and cylinders, tumbling one after another down a gentle mossy embankment toward the banks of the Peace River, where Twilly Spree had hoped to spend a soothing, restful night.

The driver, whose name Twilly wouldn't learn until he saw it in the paper, didn't bother to watch his own handiwork. He leaned one hip against the fender and smoked a cigarette and waited until the whole load went down the slope. Then he lowered the flatbed, climbed in the cab and drove the five miles home. Vecker Darby was still in the shower when Twilly hot-wired the truck and raced back to the river to retrieve the barrels, drums, tanks and cylinders. Two hours later, when Twilly returned, Vecker Darby was sleeping in his favorite Naugahyde recliner with six empty Coors cans at his feet and the Playboy Channel blaring on the television.

He failed to awaken when one of the bedroom windows was pried open and the screen was cut, and therefore didn't see the broken-off end of a plastic rain gutter being inserted into his house by a stranger clad in Vecker Darby's own canary yellow hazmat moon suit (which Vecker Darby almost never wore but stored faithfully under the seat of his truck, in case of encountering an EPA inspector).

Nor did Vecker Darby awaken during the following ninety minutes, during which approximately 197 gallons of virulent and combustible fluids were funneled from barrels, drums, tanks and cylinders directly into the house. The resulting toxic soup contained the ingredients of xylene, benzyl phythlate, methanol, toluene, ethyl benzene, ethylene oxide and common formaldehyde, any of which would have caused a grave and lasting damage to the Peace River. The risk to an occupied home dwelling was equally dire but would prove far more spectacular, visually.

What finally aroused Vecker Darby from sleep were the caustic fumes. He arose, coughing violently and keenly aware that something was amiss. He fully intended to exit the premises, after first emptying his bloated bladder of beer. Conceivably, he would have survived a brief detour to the bathroom had he not (out of dull, brainless habit) lighted up a Marlboro on the way.

From the stark photograph in the Fort Myers *News Press*, it appeared that Vecker Darby's house had burned all the way to the slab. He had lived alone in what was once a small orange grove, miles out of town, so that no one became aware of the inferno until it was spotted by the pilot of a commercial jetliner. By the time the fire engines arrived, even the victim's flatbed truck had melted to a skeletal husk. The newspaper article identified Vecker Darby as the owner of a private waste-disposal firm, servicing industrial clients from Sarasota to Naples. Farther down the story, it was noted that the late Mr. Darby had once paid a $275 fine for illegally dumping used hypodermics, surgical dressings and other contaminated waste in a public Dumpster behind a Cape Coral kindergarten.

Twilly Spree read the article about Vecker Darby while standing at a pay phone in the Seminole Indian service plaza on the cross-state expressway known as Alligator Alley. Twilly was waiting to call Desie Stoat at the prearranged hour. She picked up on the second ring.

"Twilly?"

It was the first time he'd heard her say his name, and it gave him an odd, though not uneasy, feeling.

"Yeah, it's me," Twilly said. "Can you talk?"

"Just for a minute."

"Did you inform your husband of the threat?"

"I did, yes."

"And?"

"He doesn't believe it," Desie said.

"Doesn't believe what—that I'll assassinate his dog?"

From Desie's end came a perturbed sigh. "Palmer doesn't believe you've got the dog, Twilly. He doesn't believe there was a kidnapping. He doesn't even believe there's a *you*. He thinks I flipped my wig and made up the whole story."

"Don't tell me this."

"We had a terrible fight. He wants me to see a shrink."

Twilly said, "But his dog's missing! What does he say about that?"

"He thinks I sent Boodle to my mother's."

"Jesus, what for?"

"All the way to Georgia."

Twilly said, "You're married to a jackass."

Desie said, "I gotta go."

"I'll call back in two days. Meanwhile, tell your husband to watch for a FedEx delivery."

"Oh no. What're you going to do now?"

"Make him a believer," Twilly said.

EIGHT

Desirata Brock was born in Memphis and raised in Atlanta. Her mother was a pediatrician and her father was a mechanic for Delta Air Lines. Desie attended Georgia State University with the plan of becoming a schoolteacher but was sidetracked in her senior year by her engagement to a professional basketball player named Gorbak Didovlic, who stood a shade over seven feet tall and spoke no English.

Dido, as he was known in the NBA, was a rookie backup center for the Atlanta Hawks. He had spotted Desie on a tennis court and sent one of the Hawks trainers to get her phone number. Dido was considerate enough to bring a Serbo-Croatian interpreter along on their first two dates, but the third time Dido arrived alone at Desie's apartment. They went to dinner and then to a club. Dido was surprisingly garrulous, and although Desie could understand nothing he said, she sensed in his impenetrably consonanted monologues a quaint sort of immigrant innocence. It wouldn't be the last time she misread a man.

Shortly after one in the morning, Desie tapped on the face of her wristwatch to show Dido it was time to leave. He took her home, walked her to the doorstep and kissed her tenderly on the crown of her head, the only part of her body that he could reach with his lips, without dropping to one knee. Then he placed his enormous slender hands on her shoulders and began speaking in a hushed, ardent tone. Desie, who was exhausted, nodded and smiled warmly and murmured all-purpose responses like "That's so sweet," or "I know what you mean." But in fact she hadn't a clue what Dido meant, for the next morning a large diamond engagement ring was delivered to her door. It arrived with a note; two notes actually—Dido's original, scribbled in pencil on notepaper bearing the Reebok logo, and the laborious translation, which said: "I am so very happy you are to be my wife. Our life together will be full of many funs and pleasures. Thank you plenty for saying yes. Your truest love, Gorbak."

Desie was stunned to learn that Dido had proposed marriage, and even more stunned to find out she had accepted. But that's what Dido insisted had happened, and Desie took the man at his word; it seemed romantic, in a quirky sitcom way. She dropped out of college with the idea of accompanying her new fiancé on the NBA tour. She imagined that traveling with Dido would be an exciting way to see the country's greatest cities; in particular, she was looking forward to New York, Boston and Chicago. But through his Serbian interpreter (whom the Hawks provided to Dido on a full-time basis), Dido explained to Desie that wives and girl-friends weren't allowed to accompany basketball players on the road. He would, however, be "plenty much happy" if she attended all the home games in Atlanta. "Is better that way," the interpreter added. "Also, you can stay in school and get smartened." Desie wasn't entirely sure it was Dido talking, but she told the interpreter she'd think about it.

The first basketball game she attended was a kick. January something, 1988. For a while Desie saved the ticket stub in her antique sewing box. The Hawks beat the Chicago Bulls 107–103. Dido played most of the third quarter and blocked four shots. Desie got to sit close to courtside, in a section with the other wives and girlfriends. Most of them, like her, were young and exceptionally attractive. At halftime the women laughed and gossiped. Desie didn't follow professional basketball, and so was unaware how huge the sport was becoming. One of the Hawks' wives pointed out a prematurely bald Chicago player, practicing jump shots, and said he was paid more than $5 million a year, not including endorsement fees. Desie was astounded. She wondered aloud how much Dido was making, and one of the Hawks' wives (who memorized all the team stats) was pleased to inform her. It was a truly boggling sum of money for a twenty-two-year-old man, or for anybody. Desie did the arithmetic in her head: Dido's salary worked out to $10,500 *per game.*

"See that ring on your finger?" the Hawk's wife said, lifting Desie's left hand. "One night's work. And that's if he got it retail."

Desie didn't return to college. Dido set her up in a bigger apartment in the Buckhead area, bought her a Firebird convertible (two nights' work, at least) and arranged for private tennis lessons at a nearby country club. Reebok supplied free shoes.

The engagement lasted a day shy of three months. It ended when Desie decided on a whim to fly to Detroit, of all places, to surprise Dido on the road for his birthday. When she knocked on his door at the Ritz-Carlton, she was met by a raven-haired woman wearing chrome-hoop earrings and latex bicycle pants, and no top. Tattooed on the woman's left breast was a grinning skull with a cowboy hat.

The topless visitor turned out to be a local exotic dancer who spoke fluent Serbo-Croatian, in addition to English. One of the Pistons players had introduced her to Dido at a bachelor party. Desie chatted politely with the woman until Dido returned from the basketball game. Unfortunately, he had sent his interpreter home early—reasoning there'd be no need, with a bilingual stripper—so Dido found himself mostly lost during Desie's agitated discourse. Certainly her mood needed no translation; Dido had picked up on the anger even before she'd flushed her diamond engagement ring down the toilet.

He tried to make up after the team returned to Atlanta, but Desie refused to see him. She moved out of the Buckhead apartment and went to stay with her parents. One day, when Dido showed up at the house, Desie turned the garden hose on him. Being rejected sent him into a glum frame of mind that deleteriously affected his already marginal performance on the basketball court. One wretched night, filling in for a flu-bound Moses Malone, Dido scored only three points, snagged precisely one rebound, turned the ball over five times and fouled out by the middle of the third quarter. The following morning he was traded to the Golden State Warriors, and Desie never saw him again, not even on television.

Oh, you'll find somebody new, her mother assured her. You just got off on the wrong foot.

But Desie couldn't seem to find the right one. In her twenties she was engaged three other times but never married. Twice she returned the rings without rancor, but one she kept. It had been given to her by a fiancé named Andrew Beck, with whom Desie was nearly in love. Andrew Beck produced and directed campaign commercials for political candidates, but his background was as an artist. For years he had seriously painted and sculpted and nearly starved. Then he got into television and became wealthy, as were all of Desie's fiancés. She told herself this was coincidence but knew better. In any case, she felt strongly about Andrew, who had a dreamily creative and distant side. Desie was captivated, as she'd never before been with a man who was even slightly enigmatic. Andrew couldn't stand politics and generally detested the senators and congressmen who paid so exorbitantly for his image-shaping skills. Desie came to admire Andrew for hating his own work—only a highly principled man would stand up and admit to wasting his God-given talent on something so shallow, manipulative and deceptive as a thirty-second campaign commercial.

The downside of Andrew Beck's commendable candor was that he often went around brooding and depressed. Desie blamed herself for what happened next. She had persuaded Andrew to see a psychologist, who urged him to seek an outlet for releasing his inner fountain of angst. Andrew chose body piercing and embarked on a zealous program of self-mutilation. He began with three small holes in each earlobe and advanced quickly to the eyebrows, one cheek and both nostrils. And he didn't stop there. He wore studs and pegs made only of the finest silver, and before long he bristled from so many man-made orifices that commercial air travel became impractical, due to delays caused by the metal detectors. With each new attachment Andrew's visage became more grotesque, although it didn't seem to bother his politician clients; Andrew's professional services were in greater demand than ever. Desie, on the other hand, could hardly bear to look at him. She held out hope that it was just a phase, even after Andrew got his tongue pierced to accommodate a size 4/0 tarpon hook. Desie appreciated the symbolism but not the tactile effect. In fact, sex with Andrew had already become too much of an obstacle course, body ornaments snagging and jabbing her at the most inopportune moments.

But she cared for him so she kept trying, until the evening he showed up with a tiny fourteen-karat Cupid's arrow pinned through the folds of his scrotum. It was then Desie realized there was no saving the relationship, and she moved home with her folks. She hung on to the engagement ring not for sentimental reasons, but because she feared Andrew Beck might otherwise put it to some perversely self-decorative use.

Less than a week later, Desie got a phone call from Palmer Stoat. She had met him only once, during an editing session at Andrew's studio. Andrew had been videotaping trial campaign spots for a man named Dick Artemus, who was planning to run for the governorship of Florida. Palmer Stoat had accompanied Artemus to Atlanta, and sat beside him while the "Vote for Dick" commercials were screened. Desie was there to prevent Andrew from offending Artemus (whom he abhorred) and thereby pissing away a $175,000 production contract.

In the studio Stoat began flirting with Desie, until she made it plain she was spoken for. Stoat apologized convincingly and didn't say another word, although he hardly took his eyes off her all afternoon. Desie never did figure out how he learned so quickly of her breakup with Andrew Beck, but Palmer wasted no time with phone calls, flowers and first-class plane tickets. Initially Desie put him off but in the end he wore her down with his slick enthusiasm—she had always been a sucker for pampering and flattery, and Palmer was a virtuoso. Desie's parents seemed to adore him (which should have been a warning signal) and urged her to give the nice young gentleman a fair chance. Only later, when she'd married Palmer and moved away to Fort Lauderdale, did it occur to Desie that her folks had been trying to nudge her out of the house. (Two days after the wedding, her father brought in a team of carpenters to convert her bedroom into a gym.)

She couldn't deny that Stoat treated her well: the Beemer, the canal-front house off Las Olas, all the shopping she could stand. And while the physical relationship between Desie and her husband wasn't acrobatic or fiery, it was mostly pleasurable. Morphologically, Palmer was a bit doughy for Desie's taste, but at least he didn't look like a damn Christmas tree when he took off his clothes. Not one of Palmer's pallid body parts was pierced, pinned or spangled, which was a treat for his new bride. It was nice, if not exactly rapturous, to make love without fear of puncture or abrasion.

Desie felt so liberated that on their honeymoon night in Tortola she was able to remain aroused—and not dissolve into giggles—when Palmer panted into her ear: "Come on, baby, light my candle."

"Fire," she whispered gently.

"What?"

"It's 'fire,' honey. The song goes, 'Come on, baby, light my fire.'"

"No way. I saw that fella do a show down at Dinner Key before he croaked—"

"Palmer," Desie said, changing the subject, "can I get on top now?"

It was three months before he brought the Polaroid camera into bed. Desie went along but she didn't approve—the flash was annoying, as were Palmer's stage directions. Moreover, the snapshots came out so blurry and shabbily composed that she couldn't understand how her husband found them titillating. Did that make him a weirdo? After being with Andrew Beck, nothing short of a medieval mace and chain-mail suit would have seemed kinky to Desie.

She did, however, draw the line at cigars. Palmer wanted her to try one in the bedroom, before and possibly during sex.

"No chance," Desie said.

"It's that goddamn Bill Clinton, isn't it? Him and his twisted bimbos, they've given the whole cigar scene a bad name. Honest, Des, all I want you to do is *smoke* one."

"The answer is no, and it's got nothing to do with the president."

"Then what?" Palmer Stoat rattled off the names of several cigar-puffing movie starlets. "Come on," he pleaded, "it's a very erotic look."

"It's a very stupid look. Not to mention the nausea that goes with it."

"Oh, Desie, *please*."

"They cause cancer, you know," she said. "Tumors in the soft palate. You find *that* erotic, Palmer?"

He never again mentioned cigar sex. But now: rhinoceros horns. Desie was appalled. Killing one was bad enough, but this!

Admittedly, she and Palmer hadn't been making love so often. Desie knew why she wasn't feeling amorous—she wasn't happy with herself or the marriage; wasn't even certain she still *liked* her husband all that much. And she was aware he seemed to have lost interest, as well. Maybe he kept girlfriends in Tallahassee and Washington, or maybe he didn't. Maybe he was being truthful when he said that the only reason he'd purchased the black-market rhino powder was to rekindle their romance.

Desie didn't know what to do. Materially she had secured a good comfortable life; she was scared to think of starting over. But the emptiness in her heart was scary, too; scarier by the day. She didn't view herself as one of those wives who could accept a marital chill as inevitable; pretend it wasn't there, distract themselves with spas and overseas travel and home-improvement projects.

Or perhaps she could. To Desie, being alone sounded less appealing than being in a not-so-torrid marriage. Some of her friends had it worse; they had husbands who didn't give a shit. At least Palmer was trying, or appearing to try. His hope for a two-day erection was either endearing or idiotic, depending on his true motives.

In any case, Desie was so infuriated by the way he ridiculed her kidnap story that she ordered him to sleep in one of the guest rooms.

"I'll find you a shrink. The best in town," Palmer Stoat told her. "Please, Des. You're just a little confused."

"I prefer to stay confused," she said, "for now." Firmly she closed the bedroom door in his face.

All of a sudden McGuinn quit eating and became lethargic. At first Twilly didn't know why. Then he found the lint-covered cluster of antibiotic pills on the car floor, beneath the backseat. All this time the dog had been pretending to swallow—scarfing down the roast-beef envelopes while somehow concealing the chalky tablets under his tongue. Then, when Twilly wasn't looking, he'd spit them out.

So the stubborn mutt probably has a post-op infection, Twilly thought. From the phone book he picked a nearby veterinarian's office. There the receptionist took out a clipboard and asked him some questions.

"Name of the pet?"

Twilly told her.

"Breed?"

"Labrador retriever."

"Age?"

"Five," Twilly guessed.

"Weight?"

"One twenty. Maybe heavier."

"Is he neutered?"

"Check for yourself."

"No thanks," the receptionist said.

"See? Balls."

"Why don't you have him lie down again, Mr. Spree."

"Down, boy," Twilly said obediently.

"Would you like us to go ahead and neuter him?"

"I'm not the one you should be asking," said Twilly.

"We've got a special this month on cats and dogs," the receptionist told him. "You get a twenty-five-dollar rebate from the Humane Society."

"Is that twenty-five per testicle?"

"No, Mr. Spree."

Twilly sensed the Lab gazing up at him. "Cats and dogs only?"

"That's right."

"Too bad."

The receptionist ignored his last remark. A tall frizzy-haired woman in a pink lab coat came out to collect McGuinn. Twilly followed her to an examination room and together they hoisted the dog onto a stainless-steel table. In came the veterinarian, a slightly built fellow in his sixties. He had a reddish gray mustache and wore thick-rimmed eyeglasses, and he didn't say much. He listened to McGuinn's heartbeat, palpated his abdomen and examined the sutures.

Without looking up, the doctor asked, "What was the reason for the surgery?"

Twilly said, "I don't know." Desie had promised to tell him, but never did.

"I don't understand. Isn't this your dog?"

"Actually, I just found him a few days ago."

"Then how do you know his name?"

"I had to call him something besides 'boy.'"

The veterinarian turned and eyed Twilly dubiously. Twilly made up a story about finding the Labrador wandering the shoulder of Interstate 75 near Sarasota. He assured the veterinarian he was taking an advertisement in the local newspaper, in the hope of locating the dog's owner.

"No rabies tags?" the veterinarian asked.

"No, sir."

"No collar?"

"Nope," Twilly said. The collar and the tag were in the car.

"A dog like this—it seems hard to believe. This animal has champion bloodlines."

"I sure wouldn't know about that."

The veterinarian stroked McGuinn's snout. "Somebody cared enough to take him in for surgery. Doesn't make any sense they'd abandon him afterward. Not to me, it doesn't."

Twilly shrugged. "Humans are hard to figure. The point is, I care about him, too. Otherwise I wouldn't be here."

"No, I suppose not."

"I got worried when he stopped eating."

"Yes, it's good you brought him in." The veterinarian lifted McGuinn's upper lip and peered at the pale gums. "Mr. Spree, do you mind waiting in the other room?"

Twilly returned to the reception area and took a seat across from two maternal-looking women, each with an obese cat on her lap. Next to Twilly sat a sharp-featured man clutching a brushed leather valise, from which a small shaggy head—no larger than an apple—would emerge intermittently. Its moist brown eyes would dart edgily about the room until the man whispered something, and then the tiny canine head would pop out of sight.

The sharp-featured man noticed Twilly staring, then pulled the valise protectively to his chest. Abruptly he got up and moved three chairs away.

"So," Twilly said affably, "what's your hamster's name?"

The young man snatched up a veterinary magazine and pretended to read. The other pet owners seemed equally disinclined to chat. Twilly assumed they disapproved of his attire—he was shirtless and barefoot, and wore only a pair of old chinos. The rest of his clothes were at a laundromat down the street.

"Ah well," he said, and folded his arms. Before long he fell asleep and, as always, did not dream. He awoke to see the face of the frizzy-haired woman in the pink lab coat.

"Mr. Spree? Mr. Spree?"

"Yes. Sorry."

"Dr. Whitcomb needs to see you right away."

Twilly rose so fast, it made him wobbly. "Is something wrong?" he asked the woman in pink.

"Please. Come right now."

The dog predated Desirata. It was a gift from Dag Magnusson, president of the Magnusson Phosphate Company, who knew that Palmer Stoat loved to hunt. Dag Magnusson had purchased the dog from a breeder of field-trial champion Labradors in Hibbing, Minnesota. The one selected by Dag Magnusson was the pick of the litter and cost fifteen hundred dollars. Stoat named him Boodle as an inside joke, although the dog technically wasn't a bribe but rather a reward for arranging one.

Dag Magnusson had sought out Stoat because a Magnusson mine in Polk County was about to be shut down by the EPA for polluting a community lake with chemical runoff. The chemical was so vile that it exterminated all life-forms larger than amoebas, and the government was contemplating a whopping six-figure fine against Magnusson Phosphate, in addition to padlocking the facility. The situation was so politically touchy—and the lake so odiferously befouled—that not even the sluttiest congressman could be induced to intervene.

So Palmer Stoat tried another approach. He put Dag Magnusson in touch with a regional EPA administrator who was known to have a weak spot for trout fishing. Dag Magnusson invited the EPA man to accompany him on a trip to a private stretch of blue-ribbon river in western Montana, and it was there the lucky fellow nailed his first twenty-inch rainbow. The fish had barely stopped flopping when the EPA quietly began settling its differences with Magnusson Phosphate, which ultimately agreed to pay a $3,900 fine and erect large warning signs on the shores of the poisoned lake in Polk County. Dag Magnusson was delighted with the outcome, and decided that Palmer Stoat deserved something more than his customarily exorbitant fee.

Hence the dog. Stoat's wife at the time (his second) protested, but to no avail. The wife's name was Abbie, and she had no patience for puppy piddle or puppy poop. Few humans are able to resist the spunky charms of a six-week-old Labrador retriever, but Abbie could and did. She was resolutely not, by her own admission, "an animal person." She felt that anything with fur belonged on a hanger, not under the dining-room table licking her pedicured toes. Abbie's attitude toward the puppy was so glacially resentful that it alarmed her husband, who was amused, if not smitten, by his rambunctious new pooch. Palmer Stoat had been mentally compiling reasons to divorce Abbie, and her aversion to Boodle immediately vaulted to the top of his list (replacing, temporarily, her aversion to oral-genital contact).

In the end, Stoat was able to turn his wife's dislike of the puppy to his own legal advantage. One evening he returned home from Tallahassee to find Abbie hysterically flogging the young dog with a rolled-up copy of *Women's Wear Daily*. Boodle was nearly a year old and already ninety-plus pounds, so he wasn't the least bit harmed or even unnerved by Abbie's outburst (and failed to make a connection between the spanking and the coral red Rossetti sling-back that had become his newest chew toy). The dog thought Abbie was playing, and throughout the attack he kept wagging his truncheon-like tail in appreciation of the rare display of attention. Palmer Stoat burst into the laundry room and wrested the rolled-up fashion magazine from his wife's fist. Within a week he presented her with divorce papers. Abbie signed without a fight, rather than face the lurid accusations of animal cruelty that her husband had vowed to publicize.

After she was gone, Stoat briefly set out to make a hunting dog of his blood-champion Lab. Boodle proved excellent at fetching but not so good at retrieving. He could find a downed mallard in the thickest cattails but invariably he kept swimming. By the time Stoat and his hunting companions chased down the dog, there was too little remaining of the bedraggled game bird to cook. Stoat went through half a dozen Labrador trainers before giving up on Boodle; the retrieval talents for which his canine lineage was famous obviously had skipped a generation. Stoat consigned the dog to household-protection duties, for which he seemed well suited, given his daunting size and midnight blackness.

So Boodle had settled in as lord of the manor. Stoat was undeniably fond of the animal, and enjoyed the company on those rare nights he wasn't away traveling, or drinking at Swain's. To his delight Stoat also discovered that, unlike the vanquished Abbie, most women adored large huggable dogs and were attracted to men who owned them. Boodle (Palmer Stoat would brag to his buddies) turned out to be a "big-time chick magnet." Certainly it had worked on Desie, who'd fallen instantly for the dog. Naïvely she had regarded Boodle's exuberantly sunny disposition as a positive reflection on his master. Such a happy pooch, she reasoned, could only have been raised by a patient, caring, unselfish man. Desie believed you could tell as much about a potential suitor from his pet as from his automobile, wardrobe and CD collection. Boodle being a riotously content and gentle dog, it seemed unthinkable that Palmer Stoat could be a conniving shitweasel.

Although Desie's view of her husband had grown darker after their marriage, her affection for the dog had deepened. Now Boodle/McGuinn was in the custody of a disturbed young man who might or might not prove to be a maniac, and Desie couldn't convince her husband that it was true. Several days passed before the envelope arrived via Federal Express late one afternoon. Desie wondered what Twilly Spree possibly could have sent that would "make a believer" of her doubting husband. A photograph of the dog, she guessed; the dog depicted in obvious jeopardy. But how—tethered to a railroad crossing? Tied up with a revolver pressed to his head? Desie cringed at the possibilities.

Palmer's flight from Tallahassee was late, so he didn't arrive home until half past eleven, after Desie was in bed. She heard him go into the den, where she'd left the package; heard him open the top drawer of his desk, where he kept the gold-plated scissors. For several moments she heard nothing else, and then came a quavering bleat that didn't sound anything like her husband, though it was.

Desie ran to the den and found him standing away from the desk, pointing spasmodically with the scissors.

"What is it, Palmer?"

"Eeeaaaaaahhh!" he cried.

Desie stepped forward to see what was in the FedEx envelope. At first she thought it was just a sock, a thin, shiny wrinkled black sock, but that wouldn't make any sense. Desie picked up the velvety thing and suddenly it looked familiar, and then she let out a cry of her own.

It was the severed ear of a dog, a large dog. A large black Labrador.

Desie dropped the thing, and it landed like a dead bat on the pale carpet. "Jesus!" she gasped.

Her flushed and trembling husband bolted for the bathroom. Desie pounded furiously on the door. "Now do you believe me?" she shouted over the roar of retching. "How about it, Palmer? Do you believe me now, you smart-assed sonofabitch?"

NINE

Twilly missed McGuinn. Missed the sound of his panting, the musky warmth of his fur.

It's only a dog, he thought. I got through my whole childhood without so much as a goldfish for a pet, so why all the guilt over a damn dog?

For two days Twilly Spree drove, scouting the likeliest locations. Okeechobee Road in west Dade. Sunrise Boulevard in Fort Lauderdale. Dixie Highway in North Miami. U.S.1 from Kendall Drive to Florida City. And all the time he was missing McGuinn.

I'm going soft, Twilly grumbled. I'm definitely slipping here.

On the third day, after finally finding what he needed, he returned to the veterinary clinic. The frizzy-haired lady in pink met him in the reception area and took him to Dr. Whitcomb's private office. The veterinarian, who was on the telephone, motioned Twilly to a chair. The lady in pink closed the door on her way out.

As soon as Dr. Whitcomb hung up, Twilly said: "Well?"

"Yes. You ought to have a look." The veterinarian took a small round object from the top drawer. He handed it to Twilly, who rolled it in the palm of his hand. Seeing the object on an X ray was one thing; holding it was something else, a handful of guilt.

It was a glass eye from the stuffed head of an animal.

"And you've got no idea," Dr. Whitcomb was saying, "how your dog came to ingest something like this?"

"Beats me," Twilly lied. "I told you, I just found him a few days ago."

"Labs'll eat just about anything," the doctor remarked.

"Evidently."

Now Twilly knew the truth: He was the one responsible for the dog's sickness. If he hadn't removed the eyeballs from Palmer Stoat's taxidermy, McGuinn wouldn't have found the damn things and swallowed them.

Twilly wondered why Desie hadn't told him. He might've returned the dog to Stoat if he'd known the truth about the surgery. Now he felt purely rotten.

"A glass eye," Dr. Whitcomb was saying, "imagine that."

"And it got stuck inside him?"

"Basically, yes. Pretty far down the chute, too."

Twilly said, "God. The poor guy needed another operation?"

"No, Mr. Spree. A laxative."

The door swung open and McGuinn clambered into the office, trailing his leash. Excitedly he whirled around twice before burrowing his snout in Twill's crotch, the customary Labrador greeting.

"A very potent laxative," Dr. Whitcomb added, "and plenty of it."

Twilly found himself hugging the dog fiercely. He

could feel McGuinn's tongue, as thick as a cow's, lathering his right ear.

"You sure he'll be OK?"

"Fine," said Dr. Whitcomb, "but pretty soon he'll need those staples taken out of his belly."

From a damp crumple of cash Twilly counted out a thousand dollars in fifties, which he handed to the veterinarian.

"No, Mr. Spree, this is way too much."

"It is not."

"But—"

"Don't argue, just take it. Maybe next time somebody can't afford to pay, then. . . ."

"That's a good idea," said Dr. Whitcomb. "Thank you."

He followed Twilly and McGuinn to the parking lot, where the dog methodically peed on the tires of five late-model cars, including the doctor's.

"Can I ask a favor?" the veterinarian said. "It's about that fake eyeball. Mr. Spree, would you mind if I kept it for my collection?"

"That depends," said Twilly, "on the collection."

"Weird Things Dogs Eat," Dr. Whitcomb said. "I've got doorstops, earrings, fountain pens, cigarette lighters, car keys. This one Lab—Rachel was her name—she swallowed a cellular phone! And here's the funny part: It kept ringing inside her stomach. That's how her owners figured out what'd happened."

Twilly reached into his shirt for Palmer Stoat's Cape buffalo eye. He tossed it underhand to the veterinarian. "It's all yours, Doc."

Dr. Whitcomb looked amused as he fingered the

glossy orb. "Crazy dog. How'd you suppose he got hold of something like this?"

Twilly shrugged. "Crazy damn dog," he said.

Why couldn't he stop thinking of Desie?

Her neck, in particular—the pale snowy slope between her pearl-spangled earlobe and her collarbone. Twilly had a grand weakness for the female neck. The last time he'd seen one as alluring as Desie's, it nearly got him killed.

The neck had been attached to a woman named Lucy, and Twilly didn't know about the pharmaceuticals and the booze and the bipolar disorder. All he knew was that Lucy had an indisputably fabulous neck, and that she freely let him nuzzle her there. She was also nice enough to have sex with him, which meant he quickly fell in love with her and moved in. They had known each other sixteen days.

Lucy, it turned out, was not well. She took lots of self-prescribed medicine and washed it down with Bombay gin. Some nights she was the happiest person on the planet, a joy to behold. And some nights she was a skank monster, violent and paranoid and gun-crazy. Twilly had never known a woman so fond of handguns. Lucy owned several, mostly semi-automatics. "My father was a policeman," she would say by way of explanation. Whenever Twilly came across one of Lucy's firearms, he would secretly take it from the house and throw it down a nearby manhole. But she always seemed to have another at the ready; where she hid all those guns was a mystery. Sometimes she shot at the telephone; sometimes it was the television. Once she shot the bagel toaster while Twilly was fixing breakfast. Another time she shot out her personal computer because one of her drug connections had E-mailed to say he was out of Percocet. That was the same afternoon she ran next door and shot her neighbor's scarlet macaw for squawking during her naptime (Lucy needed lots of naps). The police took Lucy downtown but no charges were filed, since she promptly reimbursed the grief-stricken bird owner and agreed to undergo counseling. There the therapists found Lucy to be a model of stability—engaging and self-aware and repentant. Happy, too. One of the happiest patients they'd ever seen. But of course they didn't have to live with her.

To Lucy's credit, she never purposely tried to shoot Twilly, although on several occasions she nearly hit him by accident. For all her vast gun-handling experience, she was a surprisingly lousy shot. Yet during fourteen hair-raising weeks under the same roof, Twilly's fear of taking a bullet was outweighed by his neck-nuzzling lust. It was, he realized later, another appalling example of his own deficient judgment.

Twilly never knew which Lucy was coming through the front door until he leaned down to kiss her neck, which was the first thing he always did. If it was Happy Lucy, she would sigh and press close against him. If it was Bipolar Lucy, she would shove him away and beeline for the medicine cabinet, and then the gin. Later a loaded handgun or two might appear. Most boyfriends would have wisely bolted after the first drunken shooting episode, but Twilly stayed. He was infatuated with the Happy Lucy. He truly believed he could mend her. Whenever Bipolar Lucy surfaced, Twilly declined to do the sensible thing, which was run like a scalded gerbil. Instead he hovered at the scene, endeavoring to soothe and coax and *communicate*. He was always trying to talk Lucy down; he dearly wanted to be the one to catch her when she fell. And that's how he nearly died.

Lucy worked at an acupuncture clinic, keeping the books. One day the doctor caught her in an error—a minor mathematical transposition that resulted in a $3.60 overstatement of the accounts receivable. The doctor made a remark that Lucy deemed unfairly harsh, and she arrived home in a moist-eyed fury that told Twilly she'd stopped for cocktails and toot along the way. For once he knew better than to attempt a neck nuzzle. Lucy disappeared into the bathroom and emerged five minutes later, naked, with an empty pharmacy bottle clenched in her teeth and a 9-mm Beretta in her right hand. Twilly, who remembered she was left-handed, prudently stepped back while she did her Elvis routine, shooting up the TV and the stereo and even the Mr. Coffee. Many rounds were required, due to Lucy's poor marksmanship, yet there was little risk of anyone calling the police. Lucy considerately used a muzzle suppressor to mute the gunshots.

Twilly made a practice of counting, so he'd know when the clip was empty. His near-fatal mistake that night was assuming Lucy was too fucked up to reload. After she'd exhausted herself and collapsed in bed, Twilly waited patiently for her ragged and fitful snoring. Then he slipped beneath the sheets, enfolded her in his arms and held her as still as a baby for a long time. Soon her breathing became soft and regular. Through his shirt Twilly could feel the steel coldness of the Beretta, which Lucy continued to clutch with both hands between her breasts. The snout of the silencer pressed ominously against Twilly's ribs, but he wasn't afraid. He thought the gun was empty; he clearly remembered Lucy pulling the trigger over and over until the only noise from the gun was a dull click. He didn't know about the spare clip that she'd stashed inside a tampon box under the bathroom sink.

So on Twilly's part it was carelessness, embracing an unconscious dope-addled psychotic without first confiscating her weapon. His second mistake was succumbing at the worst possible moment to raw desire. By chance Twilly had aligned his comforting hug of Lucy in such a way that his chin came to rest on one of her shoulders. He calculated that a slight turn of the head could put his lips in direct contact with her bare silken neck, and this proved blissfully true.

And perhaps if Twilly had stopped there—perhaps if he'd been content with a chaste and feathery peck— then he wouldn't have ended up on a stretcher in the emergency room. But Lucy's neck was a truly glorious sight and, gun or no gun, Twilly could not resist kissing it. The sensation (or possibly it was the sound of ardent smacking) jarred Lucy from her turbulent, gargoyle-filled stupor. She stiffened in Twilly's arms, opened one bloodshot eye and emitted a hollow startled cry. Then she pulled the trigger, and drifted back to sleep.

The bullet furrowed along Twilly's chest, rattling across his rib cage as if it were a washboard, then exiting above the collarbone. So copious and darkly hued was the seepage of blood that Twilly feared he might be mortally wounded. He snatched the top sheet off the bed (rearranging the zonked Lucy) and knotted it around his thorax; a full body tourniquet. Then he drove to the nearest hospital, informing the doctors that he'd accidentally shot himself while cleaning a pistol. X rays showed that Lucy's slug had missed puncturing a jugular vein—and likely killing Twilly Spree—by scarcely two inches.

She hadn't meant to shoot him; she was scared, that's all, and too ripped to recognize him.

Twilly never told Lucy what she'd done. He did not return to the house, and never saw her again. More than a year had passed since the shooting, and during that time Twilly had avoided all lip-to-neck contact, the experience being indelibly connected to the muffled thump of a Beretta. Even in the throes of lovemaking, he remained scrupulous about the location of his kisses, and banished all thoughts of delicious forays into the nape region.

Until he met Desie. Twilly wanted very much to see the intriguing Mrs. Stoat again, despite the imminent risk of arrest and imprisonment. He wanted not only to be near her but to apologize for leaving the glass eyeballs lying around for McGuinn to swallow; wanted her to know how remorseful he felt.

The dog was the connection, the link to Desie. Having the dog beside him buoyed Twilly's spirits and gave him something resembling hope. So what if Desie was married to an irredeemably soulless pig? Everybody makes mistakes, Twilly thought. Look at me.

McGuinn instantly knew something was wrong—he could smell it in the car. His nose twitched and the hair bristled on his withers.

"Chill out," Twilly said.

But the beast hurdled into the backseat and started digging frenetically at the upholstery.

"Oh stop," said Twilly.

McGuinn was trying to claw through the cushions and get into the trunk of the car.

"No!" Twilly commanded. "Bad boy!" Finally he was forced to pull off the road and park. He snatched the end of McGuinn's leash and gave a stiff yank.

"You wanna see? OK, fine." Twilly got out, pulling the dog behind him. "You're not gonna like it, sport. That, I can promise."

He popped open the trunk and McGuinn charged forward. Just as suddenly he drew back, his legs splaying crookedly, like a moose on thin ice. He let out a puppy noise, half bark and half whimper.

Twilly said, "I warned you, dummy."

Inside the car trunk was a dead Labrador retriever. Twilly had found it in south Miami-Dade County at the intersection of 152nd Street and U.S. 1, where it had been struck by a car. The dog couldn't have been dead more than two hours when Twilly spotted it in the median, bundled it in bubble wrap and placed it on a makeshift bed of dry ice in the rental car. The dog wasn't as hefty as McGuinn, but Twilly thought it would do fine; correct species, correct color phase.

Before spotting the black Lab, Twilly had searched 220 miles of highway and counted thirty-seven other dog carcasses—mostly mutts, but also a golden retriever, two Irish setters, a yellow Lab and a pair of purebred Jack Russell terriers with matching rhinestone collars. The Russells had perished side by side in a school zone on Coconut Grove's busy Bayshore Drive. Twilly speculated it might have been a double suicide, if dogs were capable of such plotting. Evidence of a cold and heartless master was the fact that the two stumpy bodies of the Russells lay uncollected in the roadway; they would have easily fit in a grocery bag. It took Twilly twenty minutes to bury the dogs between the roots of an ancient banyan tree. Before that, he had jotted down the numbers off the rabies tags, so that someday—when he had more time—he could track down the owner of the terriers and ruin his or her day.

The roadkill Lab wore no tags or identification collar. Twilly was saddened to think it might be a stray, but he would have been equally depressed to know it was somebody's beloved pet; a child's best buddy, or an old widow's faithful companion. A dead dog was just a sad thing, period. Twilly didn't feel good about what he had to do, but the animal was long past suffering and the cause seemed worthy.

McGuinn was pacing behind the rental car. He whined and kept his head low, and every few steps he would glance apprehensively toward the trunk, as if expecting the dead Lab to spring out and attack. Twilly calmed McGuinn and put him in the front seat. As an extra precaution, Twilly tethered the leash to the steering wheel. Then he walked back to the rear of the car and snapped open his pocketknife, a splendid three-inch Al Mar from Japan. The blade was wicked enough to shave tinsel.

Twilly was glad the dead dog's eyes were shut. He stroked its silky brow and said: "Better it's me than the damn buzzards." Afterward he tucked the severed ear in his back pocket and drove around Miami until he spotted a FedEx truck on the Don Shula Expressway. For a two-hundred-dollar tip the driver was pleased to pull over for an unscheduled pickup.

TEN

The king-sized hot tub was outdoors, on the scalloped balcony of Robert Clapley's beachfront condominium. All four of them peeled off their clothes and slipped into the water—Clapley, Katya, Tish and Palmer Stoat, who needed three cognacs to relax. Stoat was self-conscious about his pudginess, and slightly creeped out by the two Barbies; he wished Clapley hadn't told him the details.

"Twins!" Clapley had chortled.

"No kidding."

"Identical twins—in time for next Christmas!"

"They speak English, Bob?"

"Damn little," Clapley had replied, "and I intend to keep it that way."

Now one of the Barbies was attempting to straddle Stoat in a balmy swirl beneath tropical stars, and Stoat caught himself peeking under her immense high-floating breasts for tell-tale surgical scars. Gradually the cognac began to soothe him.

"In Moscow," Clapley was saying, "there's a school where they go to become world-class fellatrixes."

"A what?"

"Blow-job artists," Clapley explained. "An actual school—you hear what I'm saying!"

"Oh, I hear you." Stoat thinking: They can hear you all the way to St. Augustine, dipshit.

Robert Clapley got very loud when he was coked up and drunk. "I'd like to be there for final exams!" he said with a salacious grunt. "I'd like to personally grade *those* SATs—"

"Which one's from Russia?" Stoat inquired.

Clapley pointed at the Barbie now laboring to wrap her legs around Stoat's waist. "Yours!" he said. "You old horndog!"

"And she . . . went . . . to . . . this . . . 'school'?"

"She's the one who told me about it. Isn't that right, Katya? Show Mr. Stoat what you learned."

"Me, too!" exclaimed Tish. Her vast bosom pushed a wake like a shrimp trawler as she sloshed across the tub to join her future twin. They spread Palmer Stoat's legs and, with merry jostling, squeezed between them.

He said, "Really, Bob."

Robert Clapley laughed. "I should get the camcorder!"

"Not unless you want to see it in pieces." Normally Stoat was more of a sport, but not tonight. Desie was heavy on his mind; also, the severed dog ear that had been delivered by the FedEx man.

Clapley said, "You need to relax, kiddo."

"I just stopped by to talk some business, Bob. I didn't mean to make an evening of it."

"Hell, we can chat later. How often in a guy's lifetime does he have a chance to get sucked off by two semi-identical six-foot dolls? I'm guessing this isn't a weekly event for you, Palmer, so please shut the hell up and enjoy. I need to make a couple calls."

Clapley climbed agilely out of the tub. Stoat could

hear him talking on the phone but couldn't see over the tops of the two Barbies, each of whose head was stacked with at least one linear foot of shiny bleached hair. The women tugged and stroked and prodded at Palmer Stoat until finally, not wishing to seem the ungrateful guest, he closed his eyes and submitted. He enjoyed the moment, but not so much that he forgot his reason for being there.

By the time Clapley finished his calls, the Barbies were done, out of the tub and in the shower. Stoat floated back with his legs extended, frog-like. He pretended to gaze at the stars.

Clapley said, "How'd you like that twin sandwich?"

Stoat whistled appreciatively. "Blond sugar, like the song says."

"Yea, brother." Clapley was too trashed to dispute the lyric. "Listen, I know why you're here."

Stoat slowly righted himself, tucking his pink knees beneath him. How could Robert Clapley know! Was it possible, Stoat wondered, that the maniacal ear-mutilating dognapper had contacted his client?

Clapley said, "I believe I still owe you some money."

"Yeah, you do." Stoat was much relieved.

They moved to the den, both wearing long towels and matching terrycloth bath slippers. Clapley sat behind a glass-topped desk and opened his checkbook.

"It completely slipped my mind," he said, "last time you were here."

"That's quite all right, Bob."

"Now . . . how much was it?"

"Fifty thousand," Stoat replied, thinking: Asshole. He knows damn well how much.

"Fifty? Boy, that's a shitload of shotgun shells."

Clapley, alluding to the bird-hunting trip. That and the kinky Barbie action was aimed at hustling a discount, Stoat concluded. Well, Bobby boy, you can bite me.

Robert Clapley waited a couple beats, but Stoat retained his anticipatory demeanor.

"Right. Fifty it is." Clapley strained to sound gracious.

Palmer Stoat enjoyed watching the man write out the check. Clapley's discomfiture was manifest, and Stoat didn't mind prolonging it. An important principle was at stake; a matter of respect. Stoat considered himself a professional, and in the lobbyist trade a pro didn't tolerate being jerked around for his fee, particularly by baby-faced ex-smugglers with Barbie fetishes. Stoat had come to Clapley's condo intending to warn him of a temporary snag with the Toad Island bridge appropriation. Stoat had been prepared to let Clapley hold the balance of his fee until the situation with the extortionist dognapper got resolved. But Clapley had so annoyed Palmer Stoat with his coy cheapness—"*how much was it?*"—that Stoat changed his mind about the money. He'd pocket it and say nothing. Besides, if Desie left him—as she'd threatened to do if Stoat didn't meet the dognapper's demands—he would be needing the extra fifty grand (and more) for divorce lawyers.

"Here you go." Clapley capped his Mont Blanc and slid the check toward Stoat.

"Thanks, Bob." Stoat's smile could have passed for sincere. He didn't take the check immediately, but left it lying faceup on the glass desktop.

Clapley said, "Dick was right about you."

"Dick has his moments."

"So, when's he supposed to sign the budget?"

"Week or two, I expect," Stoat said.

"Fan-fucking-tastic. The sooner they can get started on the new bridge, the sooner I can slap together some model homes."

One of the Barbies walked in carrying a tray with two cognacs and two large cigars. She was wearing a blood-red catalog-style teddy with lacy bra cups. Clapley whistled when she leaned over to set down the drinks.

"Thank you, *darling*," he said in a leering tone. Then, to Palmer Stoat: "Hey, how'd you like that double-barreled hummer in the hot tub?"

"Great." Stoat thinking: Christ, how many times do I have to say it? "One of the great blow jobs of all time, Bob."

"And all because she buckled down and stayed in school. You know what they say, Palmer: A tongue is a terrible thing to waste." Clapley winked at the departing Barbie, who responded with a perky four-fingered wave. After she closed the door, he said, "That was Katya. I dream of the day when I can't tell 'em apart."

"Shouldn't be long now," Stoat said, encouragingly.

They spent a few ceremonial moments clipping and lighting the cigars. Then Robert Clapley raised his glass in a toast.

"To Shearwater Island," he said.

"Amen," said Palmer Stoat.

"And good company."

"The best, Bob."

They sipped cognac and blew smoke rings toward the ceiling. Clapley told a crude joke about a nearsighted rabbi. Stoat told one about a farsighted cheerleader. Again Clapley raised his drink.

"Here's to doing business again one day, you and me."

"Anytime," Stoat said, thinking: It'll be sooner than you think, dipshit.

As soon as Palmer had left for Palm Beach, Desie opened the freezer and removed the plastic Baggie containing the dog ear. She examined it with a mixture of revulsion and forensic curiosity. The ear didn't seem large enough to be one of Boodle's, but she couldn't be certain. That it belonged to a big black dog was indisputable. If that dog turned out to be hers, then Twilly Spree was a savage monster and Desie had horribly misjudged him.

Equally mortifying was her own culpability in the crime. After all, it was she who'd told Twilly about what was happening at Toad Island; it was she who'd given him the crazy idea of saving the place. Why? Because she'd wanted to see the smugness wiped off her husband's face, wanted to appraise Palmer's reaction when one of his slick fixes went awry. But how could she have known that young Twilly Spree would carry things so far?

Desie returned the dog ear to the freezer—placing it out of sight, behind a half-gallon of rum-raisin ice cream—and went to draw a hot bath. At noon the maid knocked on the door and said a "Mister Ezra Pound" was on the telephone. Desie asked the maid to hand her the portable.

It was Twilly's voice on the other end. "Well, does he believe it now?"

Desie said, "I'd say so, judging by the way he hurled his dinner. Where are you?"

"Not far."

"Please tell me it's not Boodle's ear."

"The name's McGuinn, remember?"

"But it's not his ear, is it? God, please don't say you sliced off that poor dog's ear. Not over a bunch of dead toads."

Twilly said, "I didn't. I would never."

"I *knew* it."

"But this isn't about toads, it's about pillage. We're dealing with an immoral, unforgivable crime." Twilly sighed in frustration. "Don't you read the papers, Mrs. Stoat? Can't you see who's running the show?"

Desie said, "Take it easy." The last thing she wanted to do was set him off.

"Now I've got a question for you," Twilly said. "Why didn't you tell me the truth about your dog?"

"Uh-oh," said Desie.

Twilly recounted the visit to the veterinarian, and the unsavory retrieval of the glass buffalo eye.

"It wasn't your fault. He'll eat anything," Desie said.

"It most certainly *was* my fault."

"How's he doing now? That's the important thing."

"He seems OK," Twilly said, "but he misses you."

"I miss him, too."

"How much?" asked Twilly. "What I mean is, do you want to see him?"

"Yes!"

"That way, you can count his ears. See for yourself that I'm no puppy slasher."

"Of course I want to see him." Desie climbed out of

the water and put on a robe, switching hands with the phone. "Where are you now?" she asked Twilly again.

"But you can't tell your dickhead husband, OK? He's got to believe it's McGuinn's ear, or the whole plan goes bust. Can you promise me? Because if Palmer finds out the truth, neither of you will ever see this animal again. I won't hurt him, Mrs. Stoat, I'm sure you already figured that out. But I swear to God you'll never lay eyes on him again."

Desie knew he wasn't bluffing. She knew he was angry enough to punish her husband, and that he wouldn't stop with snatching the family pet. She said, "Twilly, I won't tell him about the ear. Look, I've trusted you. Now it's your turn to trust me."

Still dripping from the bath, she padded to the kitchen and got a notepad. Twilly made her read back his directions after she'd jotted them down.

"Can I bring you anything?" she said.

There was a pause on the line. "Yes, I'd like a book."

"Poetry?" Desie, thinking of his Ezra Pound approach.

"I'm not in the mood. But anything by John D. Mac-Donald would be terrific. And also some Tic Tacs. Spearmint, if it's not too much trouble."

Desie caught herself smiling. "No trouble," she said. Something brushed her bare toes and she jumped—it was only the maid, diligently mopping the drops on the kitchen tile.

"How do you know McGuinn misses me?"

"Sometimes he gets mopey," Twilly said.

"Maybe it's Palmer he misses."

"Be serious. I'll see you later."

"Wait. About this ear—what do I do with it?"

"Whatever you want," said Twilly. "Hang it on the Christmas tree, for all I care. Or nail it to the wall, with the rest of your husband's dead animal parts."

Desie thought: Boy, he *is* in a shitty mood.

She said, "I'm just curious. If it's not Boodle's—"

"McGuinn!"

"Sorry. If it's not *McGuinn's* ear—"

"And it's not. Didn't I tell you?"

"Right, you did," Desie said. "And that's why I can't help being curious. Anybody would—a gross item like this arrives on your doorstep. But now I'm thinking: Do I really want to know where it came from?"

"You do not," said Twilly Spree. "Definitely not."

Dick Artemus had known Palmer Stoat three years. They'd first met on a quail-hunting plantation in Thomasville, Georgia, across the state line from Tallahassee. At the time, Dick Artemus was the mayor of Jacksonville, and also the multimillionaire owner of seven Toyota dealerships, all prosperous. For the usual reasons he decided he needed to be governor of Florida, and methodically began ingratiating himself with all the major players in state politics. One was Palmer Stoat, the well-known lobbyist, problem fixer and deal broker.

Stoat had been ambivalent about meeting Dick Artemus, as he'd recently purchased a Toyota Land Cruiser that had given him nothing but grief. One of the electric windows shorted out, the CD player got jammed on Cat Stevens, and the four-wheel drive functioned only in reverse. These annoyances were brought to Dick Artemus's attention by a mutual acquaintance of Palmer Stoat, and two days later a flatbed hauling a brand-new Land Cruiser pulled into Stoat's driveway. The next morning, Stoat chartered a plane for Thomasville.

The quails were so quick that he actually managed to hit a few. Another pleasant surprise was Dick Artemus, who turned out to be glib, sufficiently charming and presentable, with the obligatory flawless dentition and mane of silver-gray hair. The man could actually win this thing, Palmer Stoat thought—Artemus was three inches taller and ten times better-looking than any of the Democrats.

In Stoat's occupation it was unwise to take sides (because one never knew when the political tides might change), but he discreetly arranged introductions between Dick Artemus and Florida's heaviest campaign donors, most of whom happened to be Stoat's clients from industry, real estate and agriculture. They were favorably impressed by the handsome automobile tycoon. By midsummer, two months before the Republican primary, Dick Artemus had collected more than $4 million in contributions, much of it traceable and even legitimate. He went on to capture the general election by a breezy margin of 200,000 votes.

Dick Artemus never forgot the value of Palmer Stoat's early guidance, because Palmer Stoat wouldn't let him forget. Usually it was the lobbyist who needed a favor but occasionally the governor himself made the phone call. They cut back on the weekend hunting trips, as both men agreed it would be imprudent to be seen spending time together. Stoat couldn't afford to piss off the Democrats, while Dick Artemus couldn't afford to be branded the stooge of some oily wheeler-dealer lobbyist. The two remained friendly, if not close. When (after less than a year!) Palmer Stoat traded in the Toyota for a new Range Rover, Dick Artemus diplomatically hid his disappointment. He had re-election to worry about; he would need Stoat's connections.

So naturally the governor said yes when Palmer called to request a rare meeting alone. Lisa June Peterson, the aide who took the call, knew it was a serious matter because Stoat didn't try to flirt with her over the phone, or invite her out for drinks, or ask for her dress size so he could buy her a little something the next time he was in Milan. No, Palmer Stoat sounded more tense and distracted than Lisa June Peterson had ever heard him.

Dick Artemus set up one of his famous private lunches at the governor's mansion, and made sure Stoat arrived through the service entrance, out of view of visitors and journalists. The menu featured sautéed baby lobsters, quite illegal to possess, which had been confiscated from poachers by the marine patrol in Key Largo and then transported by state helicopter to Tallahassee. (Anyone who asked questions was told the undersized crustaceans were being donated to the kitchen of a local church orphanage, and on infrequent occasions—when the governor had a prior dinner commitment, for example—that act of charity would actually come to pass.)

The lobsters were so runty that Palmer Stoat immediately abandoned the fork and went to his fingers. Dick Artemus couldn't help but notice how Stoat delicately stacked the empty carapaces on his butter plate, a display of meticulousness that contrasted oddly with his wet sloppy chewing.

"The bridge," Stoat said, after his second glass of wine.

"Which bridge?"

"Toad Island. The Shearwater project." Stoat had a baby lobster plugged in each cheek. It made him appear mottled and goggle-eyed, like a grouper.

Dick Artemus said, "What's the problem, Palmer? The bridge money is in the budget—it's a done deal."

"Well, I need you to undo it."

"Is this a joke?"

"No," Stoat said, "it's a matter of life and death."

"That's not good enough," said the governor.

"Dick, you've got to veto the bridge."

"You're completely insane."

"No, you listen up." Palmer Stoat wiped his butter-slick hands on a linen napkin and slugged down the rest of his wine. Then he told Dick Artemus the whole story about the missing dog; about the deranged lunatic who broke into his house and stole Boodle and vowed to murder the animal if Robert Clapley got that new bridge; about how Desie was threatening to leave him if he didn't do what the dognapper demanded; about how he couldn't afford another costly divorce, couldn't afford to have a humiliating story like this splashed all over the newspapers and television; and, finally, about how much he loved his big dopey pooch and didn't want him to die.

The governor replied with a murmur of disappointment. "It's that fucking Willie Vasquez-Washington, isn't it? He wants something else from me."

Palmer Stoat rose off his chair. "You think I'd make up something like this—a *dog* abduction, for Chrissake!—to cover for a greedy two-bit cock sucker like Willie V? He's nothing to me, Dick, a jigaboo gnat on the fucking windshield of life!"

"OK, keep it down." Three hundred Brownie scouts were touring the governor's mansion, and Dick Artemus preferred that their tender ears be spared Stoat's profane braying.

"This is my reputation I'm talking about," Stoat continued. "My marriage, my financial situation, my whole future—"

"What kind of dog?" the governor asked.

"Black Lab."

Dick Artemus smiled fondly. "Aw, they're great. I've had three of 'em."

"Then you know," Stoat said.

"Yeah, yeah. I sure loved those hounds, Palmer, but I wouldn't have tanked a twenty-eight-million-dollar public works project for one. I mean, there's love and then there's love." The governor raised his palms.

Stoat said, "I'm not talking about *killing* the bridge project, my friend. You sign a line-item veto next week. Maybe Clapley screams and hollers for a little while. Same for Roothaus. My crazy dognapper reads in the papers how the Shearwater deal is suddenly DOA, and he lets Boodle go free and everything's hunky-dory."

"Boodle?" Dick Artemus said quizzically.

"That's his name—long story. Anyhow, soon as I get back my dog, here's what you should do, Dick. You call the legislature back to Tallahassee for a special session."

"All for a bridge? You can't be serious. I'll get slaughtered by the press."

In agitation Stoat lunged for a fresh bottle of wine. "Dick, in the immortal words of Jethro Tull, sometimes you're as thick as a stick."

The governor glanced at his wristwatch and said, "How about cutting to the chase."

"OK," said Stoat. "You're not calling a special session for one lousy bridge, you're calling it for *education*. You aren't happy with how your colleagues in the House and Senate hacked up your education package—"

"That's the truth."

"—and so you're bringing them back to Tallahassee to finish the job, on behalf of all the children of Florida. You say they deserve bigger classrooms, more teachers, newer books, and so on. You follow me?"

The governor grinned. "Let me guess. Robert Clapley intends to build a public school on Shearwater Island."

"I expect he'll be receptive to the idea, yes."

"But school buses are heavy vehicles, aren't they?"

"Especially when they're full, that's absolutely right." Palmer Stoat was pleased. There was hope yet for Dick Artemus. "You can't have a bus loaded with innocent little kids going back and forth across the bay on a rickety old bridge."

"Too dangerous," the governor agreed.

"Risky as hell. And how can you put a price tag on a child's safety?"

"You can't," said Dick Artemus.

Stoat's voice rose melodramatically to the occasion. "Try telling Mom and Dad that little Jimmy doesn't deserve a safe new bridge for his first school bus ride to Shearwater Elementary. See if they don't think twenty-eight million dollars is a small price to pay. . . ."

The governor's eyes twinkled. "You're a stone genius, Palmer."

"Not so fast. We've got lots of phone calls to make."

The governor canted one eyebrow. "We?"

"Hell, Dick, you *said* you liked dogs."

This is craziness, thought Dick Artemus, whacko world. That he was even considering such a scheme was a measure of how desperately he wanted to keep Palmer Stoat on his side.

Said the governor: "I assume Bob Clapley's on board for all this nonsense."

"Oh, I'll handle Clapley," Stoat said with the flick of a hand. "He doesn't give a damn how he gets the bridge, as long as he gets it. Don't you worry about Clapley."

"Fine, then."

"In fact, I'd keep my distance from him until we get this ironed out."

"You're the man, Palmer."

They talked about basketball and hunting and women until they were done with dessert, homemade pecan pie topped with vanilla ice cream. Stoat was putting on his coat when the governor said: "Your kooky dognapper—how do you know he's not fulla shit?"

"Because he sent me a goddamn ear, that's how," Stoat said. "An ear off a real dog."

The governor was dumbfounded. "Yours?"

"I don't know for sure. It's very possible," Stoat acknowledged, "but even if it isn't Boodle's ear, you see what I'm up against. He hacked the damn thing off a dog, *some* dog *somewhere*. That's the point. An actual ear, Dick, which he then sent to me via Federal fucking Express. Just so you appreciate what we're dealing with."

"Yes. I get the picture." The governor looked shaken. He was thinking: Again with the "we"?

ELEVEN

Palmer took Desie to a seafood restaurant on Las Olas
Boulevard, where she was so distracted by his table
manners that she hardly ate a bite. He'd ordered two
dozen oysters, slurping them with such sibilant exuber-
ance that customers at nearby tables had fallen silent in
disgust. Now Palmer was arranging the empty oyster
shells around the rim of his plate, six identical piles of
four. He was chattering away, seemingly unaware of his
deviant tidying. Desie was as perplexed as she was
embarrassed. Wasn't this the same slob who had, on
the drive to the restaurant, lobbed an empty coffee cup
and three handfuls of junk mail out of the Range Rover?
Desie didn't know the clinical name of her husband's
disorder, but the symptoms were not subtle; anything
he couldn't eat, drink or reorganize got chucked.

"You're not listening to me," said Palmer Stoat.

"Sorry."

"What're you staring at?"

"Nothing."

"Is there something wrong with your scrod?"

"It's fine, Palmer. Go on, now. Tell me what Dick
said."

"He said he'll do it."

"Are you serious?" Desie had assumed there was no chance.

"For me, he'll do it," said Stoat self-importantly. "He'll kill the bridge."

"That's fantastic."

"Yeah, well, it's gonna cost me big-time. Bob Clapley'll want my testicles on a key chain before this is over, and he won't be alone. Twenty-eight million bucks buys an army of enemies, Des."

She said, "What's more important—another stupid golf resort or saving your dog's life?"

"Fine. Fine. When do we get the big guy back?"

"When it makes the newspapers, about the bridge veto. That's when the kidnapper will let Boodle go. He said he'll be in touch in the meantime."

"Wonderful." Stoat signaled for the check. "Too bad you didn't get his name."

"Palmer, he's a criminal. They don't give out business cards." Desie didn't understand why she continued to protect Twilly Spree, but it was no time to change her story.

Stoat said, "I'm just curious is all. It's gotta be somebody who knows me. Somebody I pissed off somewhere up the line. *Seriously* pissed off, to break into my house and snatch my goddamn Labrador."

"What's the difference?" she said. "You said everything's set. Governor Dick's going to do what you asked, then we get Boodle back and all the fuss is over. Right?"

"That would be the plan," said her husband. Then, turning to the waiter: "Could you please see that my wife's entrée is taken off our bill? The scrod was so freezer-burned she couldn't eat it."

"For heaven's sake," Desie said.

Driving home, Palmer slid his free hand beneath her skirt. "You proud of me?" he asked.

"I am." Involuntarily she pressed her knees together.

"How proud?"

Desie felt her chest tighten. She locked her eyes straight ahead, as if watching the traffic.

"Proud enough for a little you-know-what?"

"Palmer." But she was leaden with guilt. Of course she'd have sex with him tonight—after what he'd done for the dog, how could she say no?

"It's been a couple of weeks," he noted.

"I know. A rough couple of weeks."

"For both of us, sweetheart. So how about it? Lilac candles. A bottle of French wine—"

"Sounds nice," said Desie.

"—and maybe a spoonful of rhino dust for some extra-special excitement."

"No!"

"Des, come on."

"No way, Palmer. *No way*!" She removed his hand from inside her panties and told him to mind the road. It took three traffic lights for Stoat to compose himself and rally for the salvage operation.

"You're right," he said to Desie. "Forget the rhino horn, forget I even mentioned it. I'm sorry."

"Promise me you'll throw it away."

"I promise," Stoat lied. Already he was thinking about the intriguing call girl he'd met the other night at Swain's, the one who fucked only Republicans. Certainly *she* would have no liberal qualms about aphrodisiacs harvested from endangered species. Nor would Roberta, the free-spirited, prodigiously implanted blonde who was Stoat's occasional travel companion. For the promise of a new and improved orgasm, Roberta would've killed the rhinoceros with her own bare hands.

But to his wife, Palmer Stoat declared: "I'll toss the stuff first thing in the morning."

"Thank you."

With a sly sideways glance, he said: "Does that mean we're still on for later?"

"I suppose." Desie turned her head, pretending to scout the bikinis in the display window of a beachwear shop. She felt the spiderish return of Palmer's fingers between her legs. He left them there after the light turned green.

"You look soooooo gorgeous tonight," he said. "I can't wait to see the pictures!"

Lord, Desie thought. The shutterbug routine again.

"Palmer, I'm not really in the mood."

"Since when? Come on, darling, learn to relax."

Stoat stopped at a convenience store, where he purchased three packs of Polaroid film. He compulsively tore them open inside the truck, throwing the empty boxes into the parking lot. Desie got out and retrieved each one, much to her husband's consternation.

"What's gotten into you?" he demanded.

"Just drive," she told him. "Just take me home."

So we can get it over with.

That night Twilly Spree was pulled over by a policeman on Route A1A in the snowbird community of Lauderdale-by-the-Sea. Twilly thought he knew why: There had been another incident of anger mismanagement, this one involving four college students, two personal watercrafts and a large volume of beer.

It had happened after Twilly returned the rented Chevrolet Corsica and transferred McGuinn to the black pickup truck. Twilly was minding his own affairs, waiting in traffic on the Commercial Boulevard drawbridge, when he noticed two Jet Skis racing at break-ass speed down the Intra-coastal Waterway. One Jet Ski was white with bright blue stripes; the other was white with red stripes. Each carried a matching pair of riders—a young stud at the helm with a young babe behind him, arms locked around his waist. They were jumping the wakes of yachts, buzzing the sailboats, spraying the bait netters and otherwise announcing their drunken idiocy to the world. Such brain-dead antics were so commonplace among water bikers that it was hardly noteworthy, and Twilly Spree would have paid no further attention except that the drawbridge was still up and he was stuck for entertainment. Besides, there was a better-than-average chance that the bozos would crash their noisy toys head-on into the seawall at fifty miles per hour—and Twilly was always eager to see Darwin vindicated in such cinematic style.

Back and forth the Jet Skis went, bitch-howling like runaway chain saws. A frightened pelican took off from a piling, and instantly both water bikes lit out in a deafening pursuit. Twilly jumped from his truck and ran to the bridge rail. McGuinn poked his snout out the window and whined.

It was over in less than a minute. At first the bird flew low to the water, struggling to gain speed. The Jet Ski riders came swiftly from behind, the afternoon rays glinting off their beer cans. All four kids let loose at the same time, just as the pelican began its ascent. Three of the cans missed the bird, but one struck the crook of a wing. The exploding cartwheel of gold mist told Twilly the beer can was full, as heavy as a rock. The pelican went down in an ungainly spin, landing backward with its beak agape. The water bikers circled the splash once and then sped off, up the Intracoastal in a frothy streak. They were too far away for Twilly to see if they were laughing, but he chose to assume they were. He watched a river taxi retrieve the injured pelican, which was flogging the water with its good wing, trying to lift off.

Twilly got in his truck and turned up the radio and scratched McGuinn under the chin and waited for the bridge to go down. Then he shot free of the traffic and drove north like a psychopath along the waterfront, searching for the marina where the water bikers had put in. At dusk he finally caught up with them, at a public wharf in Pompano Beach. They were winching the Jet Skis up on a tandem trailer that was hitched to a black Cadillac Seville coupe, new but dirty from a long road trip. The expensive car, which bore Maryland license tags, probably belonged to somebody's father. The kids obviously were on spring break from college, and even more obviously drunk. The two young studs had put in some serious gym time, and they wore mesh tank tops to advertise the results. Their girlfriends were both slender and brunette, possibly sisters, and too cadaverously pale for the neon thongs they wore. Their bare bike-wrinkled butt cheeks looked like pita loaves.

Twilly's initial impulse was to ram the Cadillac so hard that it would roll in reverse down the boat ramp. That way he could sink the car and the Jet Skis and all cash and valuables therein. Unfortunately, the Caddy substantially outweighed Twilly's pickup truck, making such an impact problematic. Twilly didn't give a hoot about himself, but there was McGuinn to consider—the last thing the poor dog needed was whiplash.

And besides, Twilly reasoned to himself, what would be accomplished by petty property destruction? The insurance company would replace the luxury coupe and the Jet Skis, and no important lessons would have been learned. The water bikers would fail to see any connection between the vandalism against their belongings and their cruel attack on the pelican. To Twilly, that was unacceptable. Vengeance, he believed, ought never to be ambiguous.

So he clipped McGuinn to the leash and got out of the truck. The two tipsy college girls spotted the huge dog and scampered over, their sandals flopping on the asphalt. They knelt beside McCuinn, cooing and giggling while he licked their salty sunburned faces. This, Twilly had counted on, as Labrador retrievers were magnets for children and women. The beefy college boyfriends wandered up with an air of sullen, incipient jealousy; as trashed as they were, they still resented not being the center of attention. While the girls fawned over the dog, Twilly struck up a conversation with the boyfriends about their nifty water bikes—how fast they went, how much they cost, what kind of mileage they got. The two guys loosened up quickly and started to brag about how their Jet Skis had been illegally modified to go much faster than the factory recommended. Twilly asked if he could have a close-up look. He told them he'd never ridden one before, but said it looked like a blast. And the boyfriends said sure, come on.

Twilly asked the girlfriends if they'd mind keeping an eye on the dog, and they said: Mind? We wanna take him home to Ocean City with us! What's his name, anyway?

Beowulf, said Twilly.

Aw, thassadorable, said one of the girlfriends.

As Twilly followed the boyfriends across the parking lot toward the Cadillac with the tandem trailer, he asked if there was an extra beer in the cooler. And that was the last thing the girlfriends remembered overhearing until Twilly returned a few minutes later and took the dog by the leash. The college girls hugged "Beowulf" and crooned their smoochy good-byes. Then they wobbled to their feet and glanced around for their boyfriends, at which point Twilly Spree lowered his voice and said: "I saw what you dipshits did to that pelican."

"Uh?" said one of the girlfriends.

The other grabbed her elbow and said, "Whadhesay?"

"Don't ever come back here," Twilly advised. "Not ever. Now go call the fire department. Hurry."

The trunk of the Cadillac was open. So was the cooler inside. The boyfriends were stretched out on the ground, faceup at a forty-five-degree angle to each other; like the hands of a broken clock. One had a fractured cheekbone, denoted by a rising purple bruise. The other had a severely dislocated jaw, also festooned with an angry raw contusion. Nearby lay two misshapen Budweiser cans, fizzing beer bubbles on the pavement. The drunken girlfriends began to wail, and from the cooler they frantically scooped bare handfuls of ice cubes, which they attempted to affix on the lumpy wounds of their drunken boyfriends. The college girls were so absorbed in first aid that they didn't notice the two water bikes smoldering ominously on the trailer, soon to burst into flames.

As much as he would've enjoyed it, Twilly Spree didn't wait around for the fire. Later, when the flashing blue police lights appeared in his rearview mirror, he concluded that the two girlfriends hadn't been quite as intoxicated as he thought. He figured they'd taken note of his pickup truck, perhaps even memorizing the license plate. It was a dispiriting turn of events, for Twilly couldn't afford to go back to jail. Not now anyway; not with the Toad Island mission unresolved. The timing of his outburst against the young pelican molesters couldn't have been worse, and he was mad at himself for losing control. Again.

The Lauderdale-by-the-Sea police officer was a polite young fellow not much older than Twilly. He stood back from the truck, peering into the cab and shining a powerful flashlight on McGuinn, who started barking theatrically. The officer seemed relieved that it was a dog and not a large dark-skinned person sharing the front seat with Twilly. He asked Twilly to step out and show his driver's license. Twilly did as he was told. He easily could have disarmed and outrun the young cop, but he couldn't abandon McGuinn. No, they were going down together, man and beast.

The policeman said: "Sir, I noticed you were driving erratically."

Twilly was elated—a routine traffic stop! "Yes. Yes, I *was* driving erratically!"

"Is there a reason?"

"Yes, sir. I accidentally dropped a Liv-A-Snap on my lap, and the dog went for it." This was the absolute truth. "At that moment," Twilly said, "I'm sure I began driving erratically."

"It's a big dog you got there," the officer allowed.

"And rambunctious," added Twilly. "I'm sorry if we alarmed you."

"Mind taking a Breathalyzer?"

"Not at all."

"Because I definitely smell beer."

"I didn't drink it. It got spilled on me," Twilly said, without elaboration.

He passed the breath test with flying colors. The young policeman got on the radio to check for outstanding warrants, but Twilly came up clean. The officer walked back to the truck and gave it a once-over with the flashlight, the beam of which settled upon an old steamer trunk in the cargo bed.

"Mind if I look inside?" the policeman asked.

"I'd rather you didn't," Twilly said.

"Whatcha got in there?"

"You'd never believe it."

"I can call in a K-9 unit, Mr. Spree. If you want to do this the hard way."

"K-9s in Lauderdale-by-the-Sea," Twilly marveled. "What are they sniffing for, bootleg Metamucil?"

A second squad car brought a trained German shepherd named Spike. Twilly and McGuinn were ordered to stand back and observe. Twilly spied the Labrador looking up at him querulously. "You're right," Twilly muttered to the dog. "I'm an asshole."

The young cop lowered the tailgate, and the trained German shepherd sprung into the bed of the pickup. One whiff at the steamer chest and Spike went white-eyed—yapping, snapping, scratching at the locks, turning circles.

"God Almighty," said the K-9 cop.

"I got the trunk at a yard sale," Twilly said. "They said it came over on the *Queen Mary*." True enough.

"The hell you got in there, son?"

Twilly sighed. He approached the pickup and said, "May I?"

"Do it," said the younger cop.

Twilly flipped the latches and opened the lid of the chest. When Spike the drug-sniffing shepherd saw what was inside, he vaulted off the tailgate and bounded, whimpering, into the cage of his master's squad car. Both policemen trained their lights on the contents of the steamer trunk.

The K-9 cop, trying not to sound shocked: "What's the story here?"

"It's dead," said Twilly.

"I'm listening."

"That's just ice, dry ice. It's not dope."

"What a helpful guy," said the K-9 cop.

"There's no law against possessing a dead dog," Twilly asserted, although he wasn't certain.

The officers stared at the roadkill Labrador. One of them said: "Happened to the ear?"

"Vulture," replied Twilly.

"So, why are you driving around with this . . . this item in your truck?" the younger cop asked.

"Because he's a deeply twisted fuckhead?" the K-9 officer suggested.

"I'm on my way to bury it," Twilly explained.

"Where?"

"The beach."

"Let me guess. Because Labs love the water?"

Twilly nodded. "Something like that."

The younger cop said nothing as he wrote Twilly a ticket for improper lane changing. Nor did he reply when Twilly asked if he'd ever lost a beloved pet himself.

"Look, this is *not* what you think," Twilly persisted. "He got hit by a car. He deserves a decent burial."

"Whatever." The young policeman handed him the ticket. "You can pay by mail."

"I don't blame you for being suspicious."

The K-9 officer said, "On the off chance you're telling the truth, don't try to bury this damn thing on the public beach."

"Why not? Is there a law against it?"

"I don't know and I don't care. Understand?"

The younger cop bent to stroke McGuinn's neck. "If I stop your truck again," he said to Twilly, "and there's *two* dead dogs inside, I'm going to shoot your ass. Law or no law."

"Your candor is appreciated," Twilly said.

After the policemen left, he drove south along A1A to Fort Lauderdale, where he parked across from Bahia Mar. He hoisted the steamer trunk out of his truck and, walking backward, dragged it along the sand. He stopped behind the Yankee Clipper Hotel and dug for more than an hour with his bare hands. No one stopped to ask what he was doing but around the steamer trunk a small crowd of curious tourists gathered, many of them Europeans. They acted as if they anticipated entertainment; a magic act, perhaps, or a busker! Twilly opened the lid to show them what was inside before he covered it up with sand. Afterward one of the tourists, a slight gray-bearded man, stepped up to the fresh grave and said a prayer in Danish. Soon he was joined by the others, each murmuring reverently in their native tongue. Twilly was deeply moved. He hugged the Dane, and then each of the other tourists one by one. Then he stripped off his clothes and dove into the ocean. When he got out of the water, he was alone on the beach.

He picked up Desie on Federal Highway, at the south end of the New River Tunnel.

"A really super idea," she remarked when she got in the truck. "They think I'm a hooker, standing out here on the corner. I had a dozen guys stop and ask how much for a blow job."

"What did you tell them?"

"Very funny."

"Well," said Twilly, "you don't look like a hooker."

"Aw, what a sweet thing to say."

"Aren't we the sarcastic one?"

"Sorry," Desie said, "but I had a shitty day. And a fairly shitty night, too, come to think of it. Where's my dog?"

"Someplace safe."

"No more games, Twilly. Please."

"I had to be sure you came alone."

"Another vote of confidence. What're you staring at?"

"Nothing."

"Blue jeans, sandals and a Donna Karan pullover—is that what street-walkers are wearing these days?"

Twilly said, "You look great. That's what I'm staring at."

"Well, don't." Self-consciously she pulled her hair back into a ponytail, tucking it into a blue elastic band. This gave Twilly quite a lovely angle on her neck.

"What's in the shopping bag, Mrs. Stoat?"

When she showed him, he broke into a grin. It was a paperback edition of *The Dreadful Lemon Sky*, a box of Tic Tacs, a jumbo bag of Liv-A-Snaps and a compact disc called *Back From Rio*, a solo album by Roger McGuinn, the dog's namesake.

Twilly slipped the CD into his dashboard stereo. "This is an extremely nice surprise. Thank you."

"Welcome."

"What's the matter?"

"Nothing." Desie sniffled. "Everything." She was biting her lower lip.

"I'll shut up now," said Twilly. But they weren't even halfway to Miami Beach when he noticed her left foot tapping in time to the music. Twilly thought: She'll be all right. And it was nice with her sitting beside him again.

He'd reserved two ocean-view rooms at the Delano. Desie was incredulous. "The dog gets his own?" she asked in the elevator.

"The dog snores," Twilly explained, "and also farts."

"How'd you sneak him past the front desk?"

"Kate Moss is staying here."

"Go on," Desie said.

"She and her actor boyfriend. What's his name— Johnny Damon?"

"Johnny Depp."

"Right," Twilly said. "This is Johnny's dog. Johnny

doesn't go anywhere without him. Johnny and the dog are inseparable."

"And they went for that?"

"Seemed to."

"Lord," said Desie.

The elevator was lit in red but the rooms were done entirely in white, top to bottom. McGuinn was so excited to see Desie that he dribbled pee on the alabaster tile. She took a white towel from the white bathroom and got on her knees to wipe up McGuinn's piddle. The dog thought she wanted to play—he flattened to a half crouch and began to bark uproariously.

"Hush!" Desie said, but she was soon laughing and rolling around on the floor with the dog. She noticed that the surgical staples had been removed from his belly.

"He's doing fine," said Twilly.

"Is he taking his pills?"

"*No problemo.*"

"Roast beef?"

"No, he got hip to that. Now we're doing pork chops."

Desie went to the minibar, which was also white. She was reaching for a Diet Coke when she noticed it—a plastic Baggie. She picked it up, recognized what was inside and hastily put it back, between the table wafers and the Toblerone chocolate bar. With a gasp she said, "My God, Twilly."

He plopped down helplessly on the corner of the bed. McGuinn trotted to the other side of the room and tentatively positioned himself by the door.

"Where did it come from?" Desie asked.

"Same place as the ear."

Desie closed the door of the minibar.

"Don't worry," Twilly said, "I didn't kill anything. He was dead when I found him."

"On the road?" Desie spoke so softly that Twilly could barely hear her. "Did you find him on the road?"

"Yep."

Her eyes cut back toward the minibar. "What a weird coincidence, huh? Another black Lab."

"No coincidence. I was looking for one. I drove all over creation."

Desie sighed. "That's what I was afraid of."

"Well, what the hell was I supposed to do?" Twilly rose from the bed and began to pace. "And it worked, didn't it? The Great White Hunter fell for it."

"Yes, he did."

"Right, so don't give me that what-a-poor-sick-soul-you-are look. The animal was already dead, OK? He didn't need the ear anymore!"

Desie motioned him to sit down. She joined him on the bed and said, "Calm down, for heaven's sake. I'm surprised is all. I'm not being judgmental."

"Good."

"It's just . . . I thought the ear was enough. I mean, I thought it worked like a charm. Governor Dick did what you wanted, didn't he? He vetoed the Shearwater bridge."

"Well, speaking from experience, it never hurts"— Twilly shooting to his feet again—"it never hurts to add an exclamation point."

"All right."

"So there's no ambiguity, no confusion whatsoever."

Desie said, "I understand."

"Excellent. Now, we'll need a cigar box."

"OK."

"A special cigar box," Twilly said. "Are you going to help me or not?"

"Would you please chill out? Of course I'll help. But first—"

"What?"

"First, I think I know somebody," Desie said, turning toward the door, "who needs a nice long w-a-l-k. . . ."

McGuinn's ebony ears shot up and his tail began flogging the tile.

TWELVE

"I spoke to the governor."

Jesus, that wasn't what Palmer Stoat wanted to hear from Robert Clapley; not while Stoat was tied to a bar stool, trussed up with an electrical cord in his own kitchen, the maid off for the day and a blond stranger with a stubby-barreled gun standing over him.

And Robert Clapley pacing back and forth, saying things such as: "Palmer, you are a fuckweasel of the lowest order. Is that not true?"

This, less than two hours after Stoat had phoned Clapley to break the news about the governor's intention to veto the Shearwater Island bridge appropriation. Stoat, laying it off on Willie Vasquez-Washington—that sneaky spade/spic/redskin!—Stoat claiming it was Willie backing out of the deal, busting the governor's balls to make him sign some bullshit budget rider guaranteeing minority contractors for the new Miami baseball stadium. Haitian plasterers, Cuban drywallers, Miccosukee plumbers—God only knows what all Willie was demanding! Stoat telling Clapley: It's race politics, Bob. Amateur hour. Has nothing to do with you or me.

And Clapley, going ballistic (as Stoat had anticipated), hollering into the phone about betrayal, low-life double cross, revenge. And Stoat meanwhile working to soothe his young client, saying he had a plan to save the bridge. Wouldn't be easy, Stoat had confided, but he was pretty sure he could pull it off. Then telling Clapley about the special session of the legislature that Dick Artemus had planned—for beefing up the education budget, Stoat had explained. There'd be tons of dough to go around, too, plenty for Clapley's bridge. All he had to do was build an elementary school on Shearwater Island.

"Name it after yourself!" Stoat had enthused.

On the other end of the line there was a long silence that should have given Stoat the jitters, but it didn't. Then Robert Clapley saying, in a tone that was far too level: "A school."

You bet, Stoat had said. Don't you see, Bob? A school needs school buses, and a school bus cannot possibly cross that creaky old wooden bridge to the island. So they'll just have to build you a new one. They can't possibly say no!

More silence on Clapley's end, then what sounded like a grunt—and Stoat still not picking up on the inclemency of the situation.

"I think this is perfectly doable, Bob. I believe I can set this up."

And Clapley, still in a monotone: "For how much?"

"Another fifty ought to do it."

"Another fifty."

"Plus expenses. There'll be some travel," Stoat had added. "And some dinners, I expect."

"Let me get back to you, Palmer."

Which were Robert Clapley's last words on the matter, until he showed up unannounced at Stoat's house. Him and the freak in the houndstooth checked suit. The man was short and broadly constructed, with incongruously moussed-up hair—dyed, too, because the ends were egg white and spiky, giving the effect of quills. Clapley's man looked like he had a blond porcupine stapled to his skull.

Stoat had opened the front door and in they came. Before greetings could be exchanged, the spiky blond man had whipped out a stubby pistol, bound Stoat to the bar stool and dragged the bar stool into the kitchen. There Robert Clapley paced in front of the bay window, his diamond ear stud glinting when he spun on his heels.

He began by addressing Stoat as follows: "Palmer, you are a world-class turd fondler."

And so on, ending with: "I spoke to the governor."

"Oh." Stoat experienced a liquid flutter far, far down in his colon. He went icy at the prospect of being shot point-blank, which now seemed likely. Bitterly he thought of the Glock in the Range Rover's glove compartment, and of the .38 in his bedroom, both useless in his singular moment of dire peril.

"Dick told me everything," Clapley was saying. "Told me this was entirely your idea, the veto, on account of your fucking dog got kidnapped by some mystery maniac. Can this possibly be true? Of course not. There's no earthly way."

Stoat said, "The guy sent me an ear."

"Do tell." Robert Clapley put his tan face close to Stoat's. He wore a mocking smile. Palmer Stoat was struck—no, overwhelmed—by Clapley's cologne, which smelled like a fruit salad gone bad.

"The dog's ear, Bob. The guy cut it off and sent it to me."

Clapley chuckled harshly and moved away. "Yeah,

Dick told me all about that, the FedEx delivery. I say it's bullshit. *Creative* bullshit, Palmer, but bullshit nonetheless. I say you're nothing but a world-class turd fondler who's making up stories in order to shake me down for an extra fifty large. Please give me one good reason not to trust my instincts."

Then, as if on impulse, Blond Porcupine Man seized a handful of Stoat's hair, jerked back his head, pried open his mouth, inserted something warm and soft, closed his mouth and then continued to hold his jaws shut. This was achieved, with viselike effect, by placing a thumb beneath Palmer Stoat's surgically resculpted chin, and a stiff finger inside each nostril.

Robert Clapley saying: "Before I became a real estate developer, I was engaged in another line of work—not exporting VCRs, either, as you've probably figured out. Mr. Gash here was on my payroll, Palmer. I'm sure even you can figure out what he did for me, job description-wise. Nod if you understand."

It wasn't easy, with Mr. Gash clamping his face, but Stoat managed to nod. He was also desperately trying not to throw up, as he would likely choke to death on his own trapped vomit. The gag reflex had been triggered when the small soft object Mr. Gash had dropped into Stoat's mouth began to squirm; when Stoat finally identified the odd tickling sensation as movement—ambulation, it felt like, something crawling across his tongue, moistly nosing into the pouch of his right cheek. Stoat's doll-sized blue eyes puckered into a squint, and with a violent moan he began shaking his head.

Robert Clapley said to Mr. Gash: "Aw, let him go."

And Mr. Gash released Stoat's face, allowing him to unhinge his jaws and expel (in addition to the tuna casserole he'd eaten for lunch) a live baby rat. The rat was dappled pink and nearly hairless, no bigger than a Vienna sausage. It landed unharmed on the kitchen counter, next to a bottle of Tabasco sauce, and began to creep away.

Later, after Stoat finished hacking and splurting, Clapley placed a hand on the back of his neck. "That's a little something from the old days, the rat-in-the-mouth number. Worked then, works now."

"Lets you know we're serious." The first utterance by Mr. Gash. He had a deceptive voice, as mild as a chaplain's, and it sent a frigid bolt up Stoat's spine.

Clapley said, "Palmer, I assume you've now got something to say. Help me fill in the missing pieces."

And Stoat, who had never before faced torture or death, willed himself to swallow. He grimaced at the taste of his own bile, spit copiously on the tile and croaked: "The freezer. Look in the goddamn freezer." Jerking his chin toward the huge custom Sub-Zero that Desie had picked out for the kitchen.

Mr. Gash opened the door, peeked inside, turned to Clapley and shrugged.

Stoat blurted: "Behind the ice cream!" Praying that Desie hadn't moved the damn thing, or thrown it in the trash.

Mr. Gash, reaching into the freezer compartment and moving things around, taking things out—a pair of steaks, a box of frozen peas, a do-it-yourself pizza, a carton of rum raisin—dropping them on the floor. Then giving a barely audible "Hmmmm," and withdrawing from the freezer the clear Baggie containing the dog ear.

"See!" cried Stoat.

Mr. Gash tapped the frosty ear into the palm of his

hand. He examined it closely, holding it to the light as if it were an autumn leaf, or a shred of rare parchment.

Then he turned and said: "Yeah, it's real. But so fucking what?"

But Robert Clapley knew what the severed ear in the freezer meant. It meant that Palmer Stoat (turd fondler though he was) was telling the truth about the dognapping. Stoat was capable of many tawdry things, Clapley knew, but hacking off a dog's ear wasn't one of them. A fellow like Mr. Gash, he might do it on a friendly bet. But not Stoat; not for fifty grand, or five hundred grand. He couldn't hurt a puppy dog, his or anybody else's.

So Robert Clapley told Mr. Gash to untie Stoat, then allowed the sweaty wretch a few moments to freshen up and get dressed. When Stoat finally emerged from the bathroom—his face puffy and damp—Clapley motioned him to take a seat. Mr. Gash was gone.

"Now, Palmer," Clapley said. "Why don't you start at chapter one."

So Stoat told him the whole story. Afterward, Clapley rocked back and folded his arms. "See, this is exactly why I'll never have kids. Never! Because the world's such a diseased and perverted place. This is one of the sickest goddamn things I ever heard of, this business with the ear."

"Yeah," said Stoat without much fervor. In his cheeks he could still feel the tickle of Clapley's rat.

And Clapley ranted on: "Stealing and mutilating a man's dog, Jesus Christ, this must be one diseased cocksucker. And you've got no idea who he is?"

"No, Bob."

"Or where he is?"

"Nope."

"What about your wife?"

"She's met him. He grabbed her, too," Stoat said, "but he let her go."

Robert Clapley frowned. "I wonder why he did that. Let her go, I mean."

"Beats me." Stoat was exhausted. He wanted this creep out of his house.

"Would you mind if I spoke to Mrs. Stoat?"

"She's not here now."

"Then whenever."

Stoat said, "Why?"

"To find out as much as possible about your sicko dognapper. So I'll know what I'm up against."

"Up against, *when*?"

"When I send Mr. Gash after him, Palmer. Don't be such a chowder-head." Clapley smiled matter-of-factly and tapped his knuckles on the kitchen table. "When I send Mr. Gash to go find this deranged bastard and kill him."

Stoat nodded as if the plan was not only logical but routine—anything to please Clapley and hasten his departure, leaving Stoat free to go get drunk. He was so shaken and wrung-out that he could barely restrain himself from fleeing the house at a dead run. And, Christ, now the man was talking about *murder*.

"One thing I've learned about the world," Clapley was saying, "is that shitheads like this won't go away. They say they will but they never do. Suppose Dick vetoes my bridge, and this pervo puppy-slasher actually frees your dog, or what's left of your dog. What d'you think happens as soon as he finds out we're getting the bridge anyway?"

Stoat said, "OK, I see your point."

"He'll pull some other crazy stunt."

"Probably."

"Not only inconvenient to me but very expensive."

"Not to mention vicious," said Stoat.

"So the only sensible thing to do, Palmer, is waste the fucker. As we used to say in the old days."

"Did you tell that to the governor?"

"Oh sure. He said he'd loan me his MAC-10." Robert Clapley drummed the table impatiently. "What the hell's the matter with you? *No,* I didn't tell the governor."

Clapley informed Stoat that he, too, was a dog lover at heart. He would go along with the veto scam so that Stoat's Labrador retriever might be saved, and also to buy Mr. Gash some time to get a bead on this lunatic kidnapper.

"But I'm not building any elementary schools on Shearwater Island, not with my hard-laundered money. I made this crystal clear to our friend Governor Dick, and he said not to worry. He said it's all for show, the school item, and nobody'll remember to check on it later, after the bridge is up."

Stoat said, "The governor's right. They'll forget about it."

"So we'll get this little problem straightened out. I'm not concerned about that," said Clapley, "but I am disappointed in you, Palmer. After all I've done for you, the dove hunt and the free pussy and so forth. . . ."

"You're right, Bob. I should've told you as soon as it happened."

"Oh, not telling me was disappointing enough. But on top of it all you try to rip me off . . . that takes kryptonite balls! Not just blaming Rainbow Willie for the veto but exploiting the dog situation for your own gain—I mean, that's about the lowest thing imaginable."

Stoat said, miserably, "I'm sorry." He should have had a backup plan; should have guessed that the hot-headed Clapley might contact the governor directly; should have known that Dick Artemus would've ignored Stoat's instructions and taken Clapley's phone call, Clapley being a platinum-plated campaign donor and Dick being an obsequious glad-handing maggot.

"I thought it was all bullshit, until I saw the ear." Clapley pointed solemnly toward the freezer. "I thought, Hell, Palmer's gotta be making it up, that weirdness about the dog ear. A fifty-thousand-dollar line of bullshit is what I figured. But you weren't making it up."

"I'm afraid not."

"Which makes it worse. Which makes *you* worse," Clapley said. "Worse than the worst of turd fondlers, is this not true?"

Stoat, dull-eyed and slump-shouldered: "What do you want from me, Bob?"

"Fifty thousand bucks' worth of fun," Clapley replied without hesitation. "Let's start with a cheetah for the wall. I remember you told me about a place where I could shoot one. A place right here in Florida, so I wouldn't have to fly to Bumfuck, Africa, or wherever."

"Yes. It's called the Wilderness Veldt Plantation."

"Where you got your black rhino!"

"Right," Stoat said.

"So how about let's go there on a cheetah hunt. All expenses paid by you."

"No problem, Bob." Stoat thinking: Easy enough. One phone call to Durgess. "It'll take a little time to set up," he told Clapley, "in case they don't have a cat on the property. Then they'll have to order one."

"All the way from Africa? That could be months."

"No, no. They get 'em from zoos, circuses, private collectors. Two-day air freight. Three tops."

Robert Clapley said, "I want a goody."

"Of course."

"A prime pelt."

"Guaranteed." Stoat was dying for a drink and a cigar at Swain's. Something to kill the reek of fear, and also the aftertaste of rodent. Maybe Estelle the Republican prostitute would be there to listen to his tale of terror.

"A cheetah would be fantastic, really fantastic," Robert Clapley was saying.

"I'll call you soon with the details."

"Terrific. Now, what else?"

Stoat shook his head helplessly. "What else do you want?"

"Something for the Barbies. Something special."

Stoat sagged in relief. "I've got just the thing." Opening a cupboard and removing the opaque Tupperware container; popping the lid and showing Clapley what was inside.

"Is that what I think it is?" Clapley wasn't pleased. "I hauled all kinds a shit in my day, but I never used the stuff. As a matter of policy, Palmer."

"It's not dope, Bob. It's rhinoceros horn. Powdered rhinoceros horn."

"Wow." Clapley, leaned closer, using a pinkie finger to touch the fine grains. "I heard about this," he said.

"The Barbies will love you for it. And love you and love you and love you." Stoat winked.

"No shit?"

"Magical erections, amigo. I want a full report."

Stoat inwardly congratulated himself for remembering about the rhino powder. Now he and Clapley were back to being buddies, almost. Clapley closed the Tupperware and tucked it like a football under one arm. Palmer Stoat felt a wave of liberation as he escorted him to the door.

"What exactly do I do with this stuff?" Clapley was saying. "Snort it or smoke it, or what?"

"Put some in your wine," Stoat advised. "You drink wine? Sprinkle some in there." That's what the Chinese man in Panama City had instructed.

"But how much? How much should I use?" asked Clapley.

Palmer Stoat didn't know the answer; he'd forgotten to question Mr. Yee about dosages. So Stoat told Clapley: "Normally I'd say a tablespoon, but for you, two. One for each Barbie."

Clapley laughed. "Well, I *do* try not to play favorites."

"Exactly!" Now Stoat was laughing, too.

"Good night, Palmer. Sorry if Mr. Gash gave you a fright, but it's important to get these things out in the open."

"Speaking of which"—Stoat, giving a worried backward glance over his shoulder—"I almost forgot, Bob. What about that damn rat?"

"Oh, you keep it," said Clapley amiably. "It's yours."

Contrary to popular assumption, Lisa June Peterson was not sleeping with her boss. To be sure, she had been hired by Dick Artemus with that in mind. The three names, the long straw-blond hair, the impeccable Tri Delt credentials from Florida State—she was everything the new governor desired in a junior staff assistant. But his lubricious plans for Lisa June had been derailed by her unexpected and dazzling competency, which made her too valuable to be a mistress. Dick Artemus was not a brilliant man but he appreciated talent, especially talent that made him look good. Lisa June was meticulous, quick-thinking and intuitive, and she advanced quickly to the important position of executive assistant—gatekeeper to the governor's office. Nobody got a personal audience with Dick Artemus unless Lisa June Peterson checked off on it. No phone call reached the governor's desk without ringing first at Lisa June's. And, consequently, it was largely because of her that Dick Artemus's office appeared to run smoothly.

He would have been disappointed to know that Lisa June Peterson's fierce and protective efficiency had nothing to do with loyalty. She was assiduous and responsible by nature. It was not the rare honor of working for a governor that had drawn her to the job but rather a keen and calculating curiosity. Lisa June wanted to learn how government really worked, wanted to know who held the true power, and how they'd gotten it. She was looking down the road—long after Dick Artemus had returned to his Toyota tent jamborees in Jacksonville—to a day when she herself could be a serious player, putting to good use all the tricks she'd learned, all the contacts she'd made while baby-sitting Governor Dick. . . .

"Where do you see yourself, hon?" he'd ask her now and then.

And she would answer: "Someday I'd like to be a lobbyist."

Dick Artemus would crinkle his face as if he'd just stepped in dog shit, as if lobbying was the most loathsome job in the universe. Lisa June Peterson was always tempted to say something sarcastic about the lustrous ethical standards of your average car salesman....

But she held her tongue, and took the calls. For someone who professed to despise lobbyists, the new governor counted plenty of them as friends. And they were (Lisa June was the first to admit) a mostly purulent lot. Neggy Keele, the NRA's seedy point man in Tallahassee, sprung instantly to mind. So did Carl Bandsaw, the pinstriped hustler who represented sugarcane growers and phosphate miners. And then there was sweaty-faced Palmer Stoat, the boss hog of them all. No cause was too abhorrent for Stoat—he'd work for anybody and anything, if the price was right. In addition to the requisite lack of a conscience, Stoat had been blessed with a monumental ego; he was openly proud of what he did. He considered it prestigious, the fixing of deals.

Other lobbyists didn't try to sleep with Lisa June Peterson because they assumed she was sleeping with the governor. Dick Artemus did nothing to discourage the rumor, nor did Lisa June herself. It made life easier, not having to fend off so many drooling scumbags. Palmer Stoat was the only one who didn't seem to care. In fact, he often hinted to Lisa June that he and the governor had "shared" other women, as if inviting her to join some exclusive club. She declined firmly but without reproach. In two years Dick Artemus himself had made only one drunken pass at Lisa June Peterson, late one evening when she was alone at her desk. He had come at her from behind, reaching around and cupping both hands on her breasts. Lisa June hadn't protested or squirmed or yelled—she had simply put down the telephone and said: "You've got sixty seconds, Governor."

"To do what?" Dick Artemus had asked, his breath sour and boozy.

"Touch 'em," Lisa June had said, "and you'd better make the most of it, because this is all you'll ever get from me. No blow jobs, no hand jobs, no intercourse, nothing. This is it, Governor, your one minute of glory. Fondle away."

He had recoiled as if he'd stuck his hands in a nest of yellow jackets, then shakily retreated to the executive toilet until Lisa June Peterson went home. To the governor's vast relief, she never mentioned the incident again. Nor did she interfere with, or comment upon, his many liaisons with other staff members. Dick Artemus mistook Lisa June's silence for discretion, when in truth it was plain disinterest. She was no more surprised or appalled by the governor's oafish behavior than she was by that of legislators, cabinet members or (yes) lobbyists. Far from being dispirited by their aggregate sliminess, Lisa June Peterson found in it a cause for hope. She could run circles around these lecherous, easily distracted clowns, and in time she would.

Until then, she would continue to watch, listen and learn. Every morning she arrived at work at eight sharp, poised and cordial and always prepared—as she was on this day, one of the rare days when Dick Artemus had beaten her to the office. He was waiting at his desk when she brought him a cup of coffee. He asked her to close the door and sit down.

"I've got a little problem, Lisa June."

He always used both names.

"Yes, sir?"

"I need to find a man that's been missing awhile."

Lisa June said, "I'll call FDLE right away."

That was the Florida Department of Law Enforcement, the state equivalent of the FBI.

The governor shook his head. "Naw, there's a better way to handle this. If I give you a name, can you get me some information?"

"Certainly."

"Take as much time as you need. The whole day," Dick Artemus said. "It's real important, Lisa June."

He told her the man's name, and what he'd done. She looked surprised.

"I've never heard of him," she said.

"It was before your time, hon."

"But, still. . . ."

"Ancient history," said the governor. "When were you born?"

"Nineteen seventy-five."

Dick Artemus smiled. "Sweet Jesus, you weren't even out of diapers when it happened."

Lisa June Peterson spent the morning at the state archives, her lunch break on the telephone, and the afternoon in the morgue of the Tallahassee *Democrat*. That evening she returned to the governor's office with two cardboard boxes of files and newspaper clippings.

"It's all old stuff," she reported. "Too old. He could be dead by now."

"Oh, I seriously doubt it. Who could find out for us?" asked Dick Artemus. "Who would know where he might be?"

Lisa June passed the governor a sheet of paper. It was the copy of a letter from a Highway Patrolman to his troop commander, a seemingly routine request for transfer. In red ink Lisa June had circled the name at the bottom of the letter.

"*He* could probably find out," she said, "and he's still with the department."

"Good," said the governor. "Anything else I oughta know?"

"Yes, there is." Lisa June Peterson handed him a copy of another letter. This one was signed by the man himself.

Dick Artemus read it and said: "Excellent. This is excellent. Thank you, Lisa June."

"You're welcome."

She went home, showered, skipped dinner, got into bed and lay there all night with her eyes wide open. She couldn't stop thinking about the missing man, wondering why Dick Artemus wanted to find him after so many years.

Car salesman turned governor.

How it fried Dick Artemus to hear himself described that way, the snotty implication being that all car salesmen were cagey and duplicitous, unworthy of holding public office. At first Dick Artemus had fought back, pridefully pointing out that his dealerships sold only Toyotas, the most popular and reliable automobile on the face of the planet. A quality vehicle, he'd said. Top-rated by all the important consumer magazines!

But the governor's media advisers told him he sounded not only petty but self-promotional, and that folks who loved their new Camry did not necessarily love the guy who'd sold it to them. The media advisers told Dick Artemus that the best thing he could do for his future political career was make voters *forget* he'd ever been a car salesman (not that the Democrats would ever let them forget). Take the high road, the media advisers told Dick Artemus. Act gubernatorial.

So Dick Artemus dutifully had programmed himself not to respond to the jokes and jabs about his past life, though it wasn't easy. He was a proud fellow. Moreover, he believed he wouldn't have made it to the governor's mansion had it not been for all those hard sweaty Florida summers on automobile lots. That's where you learned your people skills, Dick Artemus would tell his staff. That's where you learned your sincerity and your flattery and your graciousness. That's where you learned to smile until your cheeks cramped and your gums dried out.

Running for public office was a cakewalk, Dick Artemus liked to say, compared to moving 107 light pickups in one year (which he had done, single-handedly, in 1988). Even after winning the election, the new governor frequently found himself falling back on his proven Toyota-selling techniques when dealing with balky lobbyists, legislators and constituents. Wasn't politics all about persuasion? And wasn't that what Dick Artemus had been doing his entire adult life, persuading reluctant and suspicious people to overextend themselves?

While Dick Artemus felt unprepared for some facets of his job, he remained confident in his ability to sell anybody anything. (In interviews he insisted on describing himself as "a people person's people person," though the phrase induced muted groans from his staff.) The governor's abiding faith in his own charms led to many private meetings at the mansion. One-on-one, he liked to say, that's how I do business. And even his most cynical aides admitted that Dick Artemus was the best they'd ever seen, one-on-one. He could talk the fleas off a dog, they'd say. He could talk the buzzards off a shit wagon.

And talking was what Dick Artemus was doing now. Loosening his necktie, rolling up his cuffs, relaxing in a leather chair in his private study, the tall hardwood shelves lined with books he'd never cracked. Talking one-on-one to a black man wearing the stiff gray uniform of the state Highway Patrol. Sewn on one shoulder of the uniform was a patch depicting a ripe Florida orange, a pleasing sunburst of color to take a tourist's mind off the $180 speeding ticket he was being written.

The black trooper sitting in the governor's study had a strong handsome face and broad shoulders. He looked to be in his late forties or early fifties, wisps of silver visible in his short-cropped hair.

Dick Artemus said, "Well? Has it changed much since you worked here?" He was referring to the governor's mansion.

"Not much," the trooper said, with a polite smile.

"You're a lieutenant now?"

"Yes, sir."

"That's impressive," said the governor. Both of them

knew why: The Highway Patrol was not famous for promoting minorities.

"Your wife?"

"She's fine, sir."

"She was a trooper, too?"

"That's right."

"Never went back?"

"No, sir."

Dick Artemus nodded to show his approval. "One in the family's enough. It's dangerous as hell out there on the road."

As if the lieutenant needed reminding.

"Which is why I asked you to stop by, Jim"—as if the trooper had a choice—"for this private chat," said the governor. "I've got a problem that needs to be handled quickly and quietly. A delicate situation involving a highly unstable individual—a nutcase, if I can be blunt—who's on the loose out there . . . *somewhere.*" Dick Artemus motioned somberly toward the window.

The trooper's expression never changed, but the governor sensed an onset of discomfort, a newfound wariness in the man's gaze. Artemus picked up on it immediately; he'd encountered the same vibe a thousand times before, with customers at Dick's Toyota Land, USA.

"What I'm about to tell you," the governor said, leaning forward, "must remain in the strictest confidence."

The trooper, whose name was Jim Tile, said, "Of course."

And Dick Artemus told him the story, almost the whole story, about the young man who'd kidnapped

Palmer Stoat's dog and FedExed him one of the ears, in order to stop a new bridge from being built to a place called Toad Island.

"Or Shearwater, which is the developer's Yuppie-ass name for it," the governor added. "Point is, I didn't call you here to talk about rescuing some jerkoff lobbyist's dog—that's been taken care of. The problem is this young man, who has the potential—and I'm no shrink—but I'd say he's got the potential to hurt or even kill someone if we don't find him fast."

"And then what?" asked the black trooper.

"Get him some help, of course. Professional help, Lieutenant Tile. That's what the young man needs."

"Do you know his name?"

"Nope," said the governor.

"What he looks like?"

"We can find out. He was seen in a bar called Swain's, down in Lauderdale."

"Where is he now? What's the best guess?"

"No earthly idea, my friend." Dick Artemus was amused by the trooper's straight-faced questions, entertained by the charade.

Jim Tile said, "Then there's not much I can do."

"Is that so." The governor smiled now. Not the carlot smile, either, or the campaign smile. This was the OK-let's-cut-the-bullshit smile. "Look here, Jim, you know damn well what I need you to do."

The trooper momentarily glanced away. Dick Artemus could see the cable-thick cords of his neck go tight.

"So, tell me. How is our former governor these days? And don't say, 'Which one?' You *know* which one. The crazy one. Clinton Tyree."

"I don't know, sir. I haven't spoken to him in at least a year, probably longer."

"But you do know where to find him?"

"No, sir," said Jim Tile. Technically it was the truth. He knew *how* to find the ex-governor, but not *where*.

Dick Artemus got up, stretched his arms and ambled to the window. "The old-timers still talk about him around here. He wasn't even in office, what, two years, before he disappeared. And still he's the one they always talk about. 'Where is he?' 'What's he done now?' 'Did they catch him yet?' 'You think he's still alive?' Man, it's the crazy fuckers that always capture the public imagination, huh? What is old Clint calling himself these days?"

The black trooper said, "I don't know. I call him Governor."

He said it so deadpan that Dick Artemus whipped around. And what Dick Artemus saw in Jim Tile's expression was worse than distrust, or even disliking. It was a bloodless and humiliating indifference.

"Look here, Jim, you were here when it happened. You were his bodyguard, for God's sake."

"And his friend."

"You bet," said the governor, "his friend, of course. When I say 'crazy,' you know what I mean. There's good crazy and bad crazy. And this kid who's hacking up Labrador retrievers to make a political statement, that's the bad kind of crazy."

"I'm sure you'll find him, sir." Jim Tile rose from the chair. He was several inches taller than Dick Artemus, big hair and all.

But the governor, selling hard, pressed on. "Skunk," he said, "I believe that's what he calls himself. Or is it

Skink? See, Lieutenant, I've done my homework. Because I was as curious as anybody, hearing all this talk, all the rumors. You know he never even sat for a portrait? In the whole mansion there's nothing, not a picture or a plaque—nothing—to show he ever lived here. So hell, yes, I was curious."

Jim Tile said, "Sir, I'm sorry but I ought to be going. I teach a DUI school downtown that starts in twenty minutes."

"This'll take only five." Dick Artemus casually sidled in front of the door. "This Toad Island bridge, it's a twenty-eight-million-dollar item. The folks who want those contracts gave quite a bit of money to my campaign. So it's gonna get done, this damn bridge, one way or another. You can bet the farm on that. Now—about this crazy boy, he's got the potential to make some ugly headlines, and that I don't need. Neither do my loyal friends at the future Shearwater Island resort.

"But even worse, I get the distinct feeling this boy's whacko behavior has put his own welfare in jeopardy. This information goes no further than you and me, Lieutenant. All I'll say is this: Some of the characters involved in this project aren't so nice. Am I proud to be their choice for governor?" Dick Artemus snorted. "That's a whole 'nother issue. But for now, I need to make sure nothing awful happens to this crazy dognapper, because, a, no young man deserves to die over something stupid like this and, b, that would be one ugly headline. A goddamn nightmare of a headline, can we all agree on that?"

The trooper said, "You really think they'd murder him?"

"Fucking A. And if he's half as crazy as I think, he

won't go quietly. He'll make a big splash, like all these nutty ecoterrorists. And then Shearwater gets on the front pages, and before long some prick reporter follows the trail of slime directly to yours truly. Who, by the way, is hoping to be re-elected in a couple years."

"Sir, I see your problem," Jim Tile said.

"Good."

"But he won't do it. Assuming I can even find him—in a million years I don't think he'd ever agree to help."

"And *I* think you're wrong." Dick Artemus walked to a maple credenza and picked up a brown office envelope. Both ends were taped shut. "Give this to the former governor, please. That's all I'm asking, Jim. Just make sure it reaches him, and then you're free of the whole mess. Whatever he decides, he decides. It's all laid out for him in black and white."

The governor handed the envelope to the trooper. "This is not a request, Lieutenant."

"Yes, sir, I know. I'll do what I can." Jim Tile spoke with such a blazing lack of enthusiasm that Dick Artemus abandoned his plans for an inducement: A job offer is what he'd been prepared to offer. An opportunity for the trooper to get off the highway and rest his tired middle-aged butt. Step out of the hot polyester uniform and into a nice suit. Return to the governor's mansion and ride security.

But Dick Artemus didn't waste his time trolling the idea by Jim Tile. He knew a cold customer when he saw one. The lieutenant would do what he was asked, but he would act strictly out of duty. Nothing more. The man had no interest in hitching his future to the governor's star, one-on-one.

"The truth is," Dick Artemus said, "after all I've

heard, I'd like to meet your legendary friend someday myself. Under different circumstances, of course."

"I'll be sure to pass that along."

After the trooper was gone, the governor poured himself some fine bourbon and sat back to reflect on simpler times, when the worst thing he had to do was sell cherry-red pinstriping to helpless widows in two-door Corollas.

THIRTEEN

Estella was the name.

"Would you care for a drink?" asked Palmer Stoat. Then, to the bartender: "A vodka martini for my gorgeous guest."

The prostitute smiled tolerantly. "I remember you, too."

"I'm glad, Estella."

"You were quite the chatty one." She wore a violet cocktail dress and matching stockings. "You told me about a fishing trip with George Bush."

"Yes, that's right," Stoat said. "And you said he was the most underrated president since Hoover."

"He got a bum rap in the media, Bush did. Because he wasn't a smoothy, some TV glamour boy with big teeth." Estella's lipstick was a shade or two darker than her cocktail dress. She had nice skin and wore little makeup. Her hair, however, was myriad shades of blond. "I would've done him for free," she confided, "just to say thanks, Mr. Commander in Chief, for the Gulf War. He did a helluva number on those shitbird Iraqis."

Stoat said, "Plus he's a very nice guy. Very down-to-earth." Estella slid closer to the bar. "I saw him lose a hundred-pound tarpon at the boat," said Stoat. "The line snagged on the propeller and that's all she wrote. And he was such a damn good sport about it."

"Doesn't surprise me one bit." The prostitute plucked the cigar from Stoat's mouth and took a couple of dainty puffs. "How about President Reagan?" she asked. "Ever meet him?"

Man oh man, thought Stoat. This is just what the doctor ordered. "Several times," he said matter-of-factly to Estella. "Talk about impressive. Talk about charisma."

She returned the cigar, slipping it between his lips. "Tell me some stories, Palmer."

He felt a small hand settle confidently between his legs. To hell with Robert Clapley and Porcupine Head, Stoat thought. To hell with the dognapper and the Shearwater bridge. Even Desie—where the hell had *she* gone today? Well, to hell with her, too.

Because Stoat was at Swain's now, buzzing sweetly in a familiar cloud of blue haze, alcohol and perfume. He leaned close to the call girl and said: "Ronnie once told me a dirty joke."

Another self-aggrandizing lie. Reagan had never spoken so much as a word to him. "Wanna hear it?"

Estella was practically straddling Palmer Stoat now, the bar stool listing precariously. "Tell me!" She nudged him purposefully with a breast. "Come on, you, tell me!"

But as Stoat struggled to remember the punch line to the joke about the horny one-eyed parrot, the bartender (who'd told Stoat the joke in the first place) touched his sleeve and said: "Sorry to bother you, but this just came by courier."

Which highly annoyed Stoat, as Estella's hand was

now tugging on a part of him that craved tugging. Stoat was ready to wave off the bartender when he noticed what the man was holding: a cigar box. Even through the smoke Stoat recognized the distinctively ornate label, the official seal of the Republic of Cuba, and of course could not suppress his excitement.

Pulling away from the call girl, even as her fingers worked on his zipper. Reaching across the bar for the cigar box, assuming it to be a gift from a grateful client. Thinking of how many years he'd been trying to get a line on this particular blend. Already imagining the best place to display the box in his bookcase, among his other treasures.

Stoat taking the box with both hands and noticing first that the seal had been broken, and, second, that the box seemed too light.

Setting it on the polished oak bar and opening the lid—Estella watching, her chin on his shoulder—to find no cigars inside the box, not a single one.

Only the paw of an animal; a black shorthaired dog paw, severed neatly at the bone.

"What's that?" The prostitute craned to see.

Stoat was dumbstruck with disgust, the lunatic once again violating his sanctum.

"Lemme look," Estella said, releasing the tab on Stoat's zipper and extending the same inquisitive hand—she was a nimble one, Stoat had to admit—for the cigar box.

"Don't," he warned, too late.

Now she had the ghastly curio out of the box, turning it first one way and then another; tracing her painted fingernails around the velvety paw pads, playfully flicking at the sharp dewclaw.

"Palmer, is this some sorta joke? This can't be real."

Stoat clutched lugubriously at his drink. "I gotta go."

"Wow." Now Estella the prostitute was stroking the severed paw gently, as if it were alive. "Sure *feels* real," she remarked.

"Put it back, please. Back in the box."

"Holy Christ, Palmer!" In newfound revulsion she dropped the furry thing. It fell with a sploosh, stump-first into his brandy; lifeless doggy toenails hooking on the rim of the glass. Palmer Stoat snatched up the Cuban cigar box and made for the door.

Desie asked to see where he had buried the dead Labrador.

Twilly said, "You don't believe me."

"I believe you."

"No, you don't."

So they drove all the way back to Lauderdale. McGuinn rode in the bed of the pickup. The rush of seventy-mile-per-hour wind on the interstate made his ears stand out like bat wings. Desie said she wished she had a camera. Every time she spun around to look at the dog, Twilly got an amber glimpse of her neckline in the sodium streetlights. He liked the fact she wanted to see for herself about the other dog. Of course she would—after all, she was married to a compulsive bullshit artist. Why would she believe anything said to her by any man?

The beach behind the Yankee Clipper was nearly deserted, cast in a pinkish all-night dusk by the lights of the old hotel. The breeze had stiffened, and with it the splash and hiss of the surf. Twilly led Desie to the grave.

He said, "I suppose you want me to dig it up."

"That won't be necessary."

McGuinn sniffed intently at the fresh-turned sand.

"Ten bucks says he pees on it," Twilly said.

McGuinn cocked his head, as if he understood, and began circling a target zone.

"No!" Desie snatched up the leash and tugged the dog away from the grave. "This is so sad," she said.

"Yes."

"Didn't it creep you out? Cutting off the ear and the paw—"

"It's getting late, Mrs. Stoat. Time for you to go home."

"I left my purse at the Delano."

"We'll mail it to you," Twilly said.

"With my car keys and my house keys."

"Anything else?"

"Yes. My birth-control pills."

And I had to ask, Twilly thought. He nearly dozed off on the drive back to Miami Beach. Up in the hotel room he decided on a scalding shower, to rouse himself for more driving. From the bathroom he called to Desie: "Phone your husband and tell him you're on the way."

When Twilly came out, he found her in the white bed with the white covers pulled up to her throat. She said, "I'm afraid I got sand in your sheets. What time is it?"

"One-fifteen."

"I think I want to stay."

"I think I want you to stay."

"You're in no shape to drive."

"That's the only reason?"

"That's what I'm telling myself, yes."

"All right, stay. Because I'm in no shape to drive."

"Thank you," Desie said. "But no sex."

"Furthest thing from my mind."

Then McGuinn jumped on the bed and began licking her chin. Twilly said, "I could demand equal time."

"He's just a dog," said Desie. "You're a crazed felon."

"Move over."

That's how they spent the night, the three of them under a blanket at the Delano; Desie sandwiched in the middle. She awoke at dawn to husky dog breath, McGuinn's bullish head on the pillow beside her. Desie tried to turn over but she couldn't—Twilly's face was buried in the crook of her neck, his lips pressed softly against her skin. She didn't know it but he was dreaming.

For the first time ever.

Mr. Gash had spent the day listening to 911 tapes. He couldn't get enough of them. Off late-night television he had mail-ordered *The World's Most Bloodcurdling Emergency Calls*, Volumes 1–3. The recordings had been tape-recorded by police departments all over the country, and somebody had gotten the slick idea to compile them into a Best of 911 series and sell them on cassettes and CDs. Only the *F* word was edited out, to protect children who might be listening.

CALLER: 911? 911?

DISPATCHER: This is the police department. Do you have an emergency?

CALLER: Yeah, my one brother, he's stabbing the shit out of my other brother.

DISPATCHER: A stabbing, did you say?

CALLER: Yeah, you better send somebody out here fast. There's [bleeping] blood all over the drapes. He's gone crazy, you got to send somebody fast, fore he goes and kills us all.

DISPATCHER: Could you describe the weapon, ma'am?

CALLER: It's a knife, for Christ's sake. A huge [bleeping] butcher knife. It's got a wood handle and at the other end it's real pointy. Get the picture?

DISPATCHER: OK, OK, settle down. Where's your brother at now?

CALLER: On the floor. Where the hell do you think he's at? He's on the floor bleeding to death. He looks like a piece of [bleeping] Swiss cheese, except with catsup.

DISPATCHER: No, the brother with the butcher knife. Where's he at?

CALLER: In the kitchen. Probably getting another goddamn beer. Are you guys coming? 'Cause if you're not, just let me know so I can go ahead and slit my throat. To save my drunken crazy-ass brother the trouble.

DISPATCHER: Easy now, we've got units on the way. Can you stay on the phone? Are you in a safe place?

CALLER: Safe? Oh Christ, yeah. I'm locked in the [bleeping] bathroom of a double-wide house trailer, it's like Fort [bleeping] Knox in here. I'm snug as a bug in a goddamned rug—what's the matter with you people! Hell no, I'm not safe. A cat fart could knock down this whole damn place. . . .

DISPATCHER: Ma'am, try to stay calm.

CALLER: Oh Jesus, that's him! I hear him outside!! Clete, you back off from here! You leave me be, else I'm tellin' Mama what you did to Lippy, I swear to God! Don't you . . . now don't you dare open this door! Clete . . . goddammit, I got the cops on the phone—no! I told you no—

DISPATCHER: Ma'am, is that him? Is that your brother you're talking to?

CALLER: No, it's Garth [bleeping] Brooks. What's the matter with you morons—hey, Clete, stop that shit right now! No, no . . . put that thing down, you hear? Put it away!!!!

DISPATCHER: Ma'am? Hello? Are you all right?

Mr. Gash was exhilarated by the sound of fear in human voices. Fury, panic, despair—it was all there on the 911 calls, the full cycle of primal desperation.

Daddy's on a rampage.

Baby's in the swimming pool.

Momma took some pills.

There's a stranger at the bedroom window.

And yet, somehow, somebody makes it to a telephone and phones for help.

To Mr. Gash, this was better than theater, better than literature, better than music. True life is what it was; true life unspooling. He never tired of the 911 tapes. He even redubbed his favorites and set them to classical music—Mahler for domestic disputes, Tchaikovsky for cardiac arrests, and so on.

The emergency tapes kept his mind off the grinding traffic, and he listened to them all the way to Toad Island, the morning after he'd roughed up Palmer Stoat. For the long drive north, Mr. Gash had selected the *Best-of-House-Fire Calls*, with background accompaniment by Shostakovich.

DISPATCHER: Is there an emergency?

CALLER: Hurry! My house is on fire! It's on fire!

DISPATCHER: Where are you, sir?

CALLER: Inside! Inside the house!

DISPATCHER: Where inside the house?

CALLER: The bedroom, I'm pretty sure! Hurry, man, it's all on fire! Everything!

DISPATCHER: The trucks are on the way—

CALLER: I was basing under the Christmas tree, see—

DISPATCHER: Sir, you need to exit the dwelling immediately.

CALLER: Freebasing, see? And somehow, man, I don't know what happened but all of a sudden there's a flash and the tree's lit up, I mean bigtime. Next thing, all the Christmas presents, they're on fire, too, and before long the whole scene is smoke. . . .

DISPATCHER: Sir, you need to get out of the house immediately. Right now.

CALLER: You hurry, that's the main thing. Hurry! 'Cause I don't have a goddamn clue where "out" is. You understand what I'm saying. I am one lost mother[bleeper], OK?

The tapes were aural tapestry to Mr. Gash. From a

lone scream he could fully visualize the interior of a house, its bare halls and cluttered bedrooms; the faded carpets and the functional furniture, the oversized paintings and tense-looking family photographs. And of course he could see the orange flames licking at the walls.

"Ouch," he said aloud as he drove.

Toad Island was the logical place to start hunting for the man he was supposed to murder. Possibly the fellow lived there, or at least must have visited the place. Why else would he give two shits about Robert Clapley's bridge?

Mr. Gash's first stop was the home of Nils Fishback, the island's self-crowned "mayor" and Clapley's onetime political adversary. Clapley had told Mr. Gash it was Fishback who'd know the inside dope on any malcontents among the residents.

"Get off my damn property!" was Nils Fishback's intemperate greeting to Mr. Gash.

"Mr. Clapley sent me."

"What for?" Fishback demanded. "What's with the hair, jocko—you from England or somethin'?"

The old man was stationed on the front lawn. He was shoeless and shirtless, a bandanna knotted around his neck. The bandanna was milky yellow, as was Fishback's long beard and also his toenails. He appeared not to have bathed for some time.

"Can't you tell I'm busy?" Fishback pointed at a moving van in the driveway. Two beefy men were lugging a long plaid sofa up the ramp to the truck.

Mr. Gash said: "This'll only take a minute."

"I don't have a minute."

"What you don't have," said Mr. Gash, "is manners."

He intercepted the two movers and advised them to take a thirty-minute break. Then he grabbed Nils Fishback by one of his bony elbows and dragged him into the house and tied his ankles and wrists with a Dacron curtain sash and pushed him into a bathtub. After a short search Mr. Gash found a bar of Dial antiperspirant soap, untouched, which he forcefully inserted into Fishback's mouth.

"You probably feel like puking," Mr. Gash said, "but of course you can't."

From the tub Fishback stared up with wild, horsey eyes.

"Here's what I need from you," said Mr. Gash. He was hovering, a gun held loosely in one hand.

"There's a man causing Mr. Clapley lots of grief over the new bridge. What I need to know, 'Mr. Mayor,' is who would do something like this? Somebody out here on the island is my guess. Some creep trying to squeeze more money from my good friend Mr. Clapley."

Nils Fishback shook his head frantically. Mr. Gash laughed. He had been made aware of Fishback's lucrative real estate sellout. "Oh, I know it's not you," he told the old man. "From what I hear, you got no complaints. You made out like a bandit on this deal."

Now Fishback was nodding. Mr. Gash set the handgun on the toilet seat and took out a penknife, which he used to pry the cake of Dial from Fishback's mouth. The soap came out embedded with expensive porcelain bridgework. Immediately the mayor wriggled upright and began vomiting in his own lap. Mr. Gash turned on the shower, picked up his gun and left the bathroom.

When Nils Fishback emerged, he was the consummate host, all southern graciousness and hospitality. He fixed fresh coffee and powdered doughnuts for Mr. Gash, and told him of a rumor going around the island.

"About a guy who works for Roothaus, Clapley's engineering firm. This guy's all—what is it they say these days?—*conflicted* about his job. He's been getting drunked up at night, roamin' around saying it's a damn crime, what Clapley's set to do to this island."

"Crime?" Mr. Gash was amused.

"Crime against nature, the young man said. I believe he's some kind a biologist." Nils Fishback paused to readjust his dental bridge. Slivers of orange soap were visible between his front teeth.

He said, "Tree-hugger type, that's the rumor."

"But he works for Roothaus," said Mr. Gash, "who works for Clapley. Ha!" Mr. Gash knit his brow. "What ever happened to good old-fashioned loyalty? This is excellent coffee, by the way."

Fishback said: "Thanks. The young fella's name is Brinkman or Brickman. Somethin' like that. They say he's a doctor of biology."

"I appreciate the information."

Fishback fingered his sodden beard apprehensively. "Keep in mind, it's only a rumor. I don't wanna see nobody get hurt, because there might be nothin' to it. People say all kinds a crazy shit when they drink."

Mr. Gash rose and handed his empty cup to Fishback. "Well, these sorts of stories need to be checked out. Where you moving to, Mayor?"

"Vegas."

"Whoa. Land of opportunity."

"No, it's just I got sinus problems."

Mr. Gash smiled encouragingly. "You'll love it there."

Krimmler had warned Dr. Steven Brinkman to curtail his drinking, but it wasn't easy. Brinkman was depressed so much of the time. He had nearly completed the biological survey of Toad Island without documenting one endangered species. That was splendid tidings for Roger Roothaus and Robert Clapley, but not for the remaining wildlife; not for the ospreys or the raccoons, not for the gray squirrels or the brown tree snails, not for the whip-tailed lizards or the western sandpipers. Because now, Brinkman knew, there was no way to block the Shearwater resort. The creeps who'd bulldozed the tiny oak toads would do the same to all other creatures in their path, and no law or authority could stop them. So Dr. Brinkman's exhaustively detailed catalog of Toad Island's birds, mammals, reptiles, amphibians, insects and flora was for all practical purposes a death list, or that's how the young biologist had come to think of it.

Sometimes, at night, he would sneak into the construction trailer to brood over the impressive Shearwater mock-up—how verdant and woody the layout looked in miniature! But Brinkman knew it was an illusion created by those two immense golf courses—a wild, rolling splash of green rimmed by houses and condos, a chemical hue of emerald found nowhere in nature. And the suckers were lining up to buy! Occasionally Brinkman would crouch by the scale model in mordant contemplation of Clapley's "nature trail"—a linear quarter-mile trek through a scraggle of pines at the north hook of the island. And there was the scenic little salt-water creek, for kayaks and canoes. In the mock-up the creek was painted sky blue, but in real life (Brinkman knew) the water would be tea-colored and silted. A school of mullet would be cause for great excitement. Meanwhile Clapley's people would be leveling hundreds of acres for homesites, parking lots, the airstrip, the heliport and that frigging shooting range; they'd be dredging pristine estuary for the yacht harbor and water-sports complex and desalinization plants. Along the beach rose the dreaded high-rises; on the model, each sixteen-story tower was the size of a pack of Marlboro mediums.

Steven Brinkman felt awful about his complicity in the Shearwater juggernaut, and about his career calling in general. Go with the private sector—that's what his old man had advised him. His old man, who'd spent twenty-six years with the U.S. Forest Service and had nothing positive to say about government work. If I had it to do all over again, he'd grumble, I'd jump on that job with the timber company. Private sector, son, all the way!

And though it was the handsome salary that had induced Steven Brinkman to sign on with Roger Roothaus, he also honestly thought he could make a difference. Fresh out of school, he naïvely believed it was possible to find middle ground between the granola-head bunny lovers and the ruthless corporate despoilers. He believed science and common sense could bring both sides together, believed wholeheartedly in the future of "environmental engineering."

Then they put him to work counting butterflies and toads and field mice. And before long, Brinkman was also counting the days until he could go home. He didn't want to be on Toad Island when the clearing started. And he would never return afterward, to see if it ended up looking like the scale model.

For living quarters, Roothaus had provided a second-hand Winnebago but Steven Brinkman rarely used it, choosing instead to sleep under the stars in the doomed woods. Here he could drink recklessly without drawing Krimmler's ire. Most evenings he'd build a campfire and play R.E.M. on the small boom box that his sister had given him. The locals had long ago pegged Brinkman as a flake, and let him be.

Rarely was his outdoor solitude interrupted by anything noisier than a hoot owl, so he was therefore surprised to see a stocky stranger clomping into his camp. The man's blond hair was eccentrically spiked, but it was the houndstooth suit that put Brinkman on edge, even after half a quart of Stoli.

"I'm looking for a dog," the man announced, in a voice that was almost soothing.

Brinkman tottered to his feet. "Who're you?"

"A black Labrador retriever is what I'm looking for."

Brinkman shrugged. "No dog here."

"Possibly with one ear cut off. I don't suppose you'd know anything about that."

"No—"

In a flash the man pinned him against the trunk of a pine tree. "I work for Mr. Robert Clapley," he said.

"Me, too," said Brinkman. "What's the matter with you?"

"Are you Steven Brinkman?"

"Dr. Brinkman. Yeah, now—"

"The troublemaker?"

Brinkman struggled to break free. "What? I'm a field biologist."

The spiky-haired man grabbed him by the throat. "Where's the god damn dog, *Doctor*?"

Brinkman spluttered a protest but Clapley's man knocked him down with a punch to the gut. "Jesus, you don't know what I'm talking about," the man said disgustedly. He kicked through the campsite, swearing. "You don't have the goddamn dog. You're not the one."

"No." Brinkman was on his knees, gasping.

"But you're still a troublemaker. Mr. Clapley doesn't like troublemakers." The man took out a pistol. "And you're trashed on top of it. Not good."

Brinkman fearfully threw up his dirt-smeared palms. "There was a guy here, a couple days ago. He had a black Lab."

"Go on." The man brushed a moth off his lapel.

"On the beach. Guy my age. Very tan. He had a big black Lab."

"How many ears?"

"Two, I think." Brinkman was pretty sure he would've remembered otherwise.

"What else, doctor?"

The man placed the gun to Brinkman's temple. Brinkman had been drinking so heavily that he couldn't even pee in his pants, couldn't make neurotransmitter contact with his own bladder.

He said, "The guy drove a black pickup truck. And there was a woman."

"What'd she look like?"

"Beautiful," Brinkman said. "Outstanding." The Stoli was kicking in magnificently.

The spiky-haired man whacked him with the butt of the pistol. "'Beautiful' covers a lot of territory, doesn't it?"

Brinkman tried to collect himself. He felt a warm bubble of blood between his eyebrows. "She was a brunette, in her early thirties. Hair so long"—Brinkman, using both hands to indicate the length—"and the dog seemed to be hers. The Lab."

"So they weren't, like, a couple."

"Is it Mr. Clapley's dog? Those people—did they steal it?"

The man in the checked suit smirked. "Do I look like a person who wastes his time chasing lost pets? Seriously? Would I need a gun for that? Here, whistle dick, have another drink."

He shoved the Stoli bottle at Steven Brinkman, who took a swig and pondered what the blond man had said. He was a professional killer, of course. Clapley had sent him to the island to murder somebody, over something to do with a dog. Brinkman was too drunk to find it anything but hilarious, and he began to giggle.

The man said, "Shut up and tell me the guy's name."

"He never said." Again Brinkman felt the cold poke of the gun barrel against his temple. "They never gave their names. Neither one," he told the spiky-haired man. "Why would I lie?"

"I intend to find out."

Then, as sometimes happened with vodka, Steven Brinkman experienced a precipitous mood plunge. He remembered that he'd sort of liked the tan young man and the outstandingly beautiful woman with the friendly black dog. They had seemed entirely sympathetic and properly appalled about what was happening out here; the burying of the toads, for instance. Not everyone cared about toads.

And now here I am, Brinkman thought morosely, ratting them out to some punk-headed hit man. Just like I ratted out *Bufo quercicus* to Krimmler. Ratted out the whole blessed island. What a cowardly dork I am! Brinkman grieved.

"The name," said the killer. "I'm counting to six."

"Six?" Brinkman blurted.

"It's a lucky number for me. Three is another good one," the killer said. "Want me to count to three instead? One . . . two . . ."

Brinkman wrapped one hand around the gun barrel. "Look, I don't know the guy's name, but I know where he's camping tonight."

"That would be progress." Clapley's man holstered the gun and motioned for Brinkman to lead the way.

The biologist picked up a gas lantern and set off through the woods, though not stealthily. He was exceedingly tipsy and barely able to hoist his feet, much less direct them on a course. As he plowed ahead, pin-balling off tree trunks and stumbling through scrub, Brinkman heard the blond stranger cursing bitterly from behind. Undoubtedly the pine boughs and thorny vines were taking a nappy toll on the houndstooth suit.

Brinkman's idea—it would hardly qualify as a plan—was to tromp along until he found a clearing in which he could wheel around and clobber Clapley's man with the lantern. Only fine vodka could have imbued Brinkman with such grandiose estimations of his own strength and agility, but the anger in his heart was true and untainted. The spiky-headed intruder had become an ideally crude and lethal symbol for Shearwater and its attendant evils. Wouldn't it be cool to knock out the bastard and turn him over to the cops? And then? Sit back and watch Robert Clapley squirm, trying to explain such shenanigans to the media—a hired thug with a gun, turned loose to hunt down "troublemakers" on the island! Brinkman grinned, somewhat prematurely, at the headline.

Suddenly he found himself stepping out of the pines and into a broad opening, which filled with the lantern's pale yellow light. Brinkman saw squat machines, furrows and mounds of dry dirt—and, beneath his boots, a corrugated track. He knew where he was; a good place to do it, too. He gulped for the cool salty air and quickened his pace.

"Hey, shithead." It was Clapley's man.

Dr. Brinkman didn't turn all the way around, but from the corner of an eye he spotted the shadow—a flickery figure projected by lantern light on the blade of a bulldozer, like a puppet on a wall.

"Hey, you think this is funny?"

Clapley's man, striding faster now, coming up behind him. Dr. Brinkman deliberately slowed his pace, laboring to clear the buzz from his head, straining to gauge the proximity of the killer's footsteps, knowing the timing of this grand move had to be absolutely flawless . . . flawless timing, unfortunately, not being a typical side effect of massive vodka consumption.

So that when Steven Brinkman spun and swung the hefty lantern, Clapley's man was still five yards from reaching him, and safely out of range. Centrifugal physics whirled Brinkman almost 360 degrees, an involuntary rotation halted only by the force of the lantern striking the tire of a four-ton backhoe. Brinkman saw a white-pink flash and then a bright blue flash, heard one sharp pop and then another louder one—the lantern exploding, followed by something else. Brinkman went down in darkness, finding it fascinating (in a way that only a drunk man could) to feel the onrushing dampness of his own blood yet no pain from the bullet. He tried to run without getting up, his legs cycling haplessly in the dirt until he was breathless.

The clearing had become shockingly silent, and Brinkman momentarily rejoiced in the possibility that Clapley's man had taken him for dead and run off. But then Brinkman heard the bulldozer start, backfiring once before lurching into gear. Then he knew. Even with his brain awash in Stoli, he knew what was coming next; knew he should have been terrified to the marrow. But Steven Brinkman mainly felt tired, so tired and chilly and wet that all he wanted now was to sleep. Anyplace would do, anyplace where he could lie down would be dandy. Even someplace deep in the ground, among tiny man-mulched toads.

FOURTEEN

Twilly dreamed about Marco Island. He dreamed he was a boy, jogging the bone white beach and calling out for his father. The long strand of shore was stacked as far as he could see with ghastly high-rise apartments and condominiums. The structures rose supernaturally into the clouds, blocking the sunshine and casting immense chilly shadows over the beach where young Twilly ran, a shoe box full of seashells tucked under his arm.

In the dream, the first he could ever remember, Twilly heard Little Phil from somewhere on the far side of the high-rises; a voice echoing gaily along the concrete canyon. Twilly kept running, searching for a way between the buildings. But there was no path, no alley, no beckoning sliver of light: Each tower abutted the next, forming a steep unbroken wall—infinitely high, infinitely long—that served to blockade the island's entire shore.

Twilly Spree ran and ran, shouting his father's name. Above the boy's head flew laughing gulls and ring-billed gulls and sandwich terns, and around his bare legs skittered sanderlings and dowitchers and plovers. He noticed the tide was rising uncommonly fast, so he ran harder, kicking up soft splashes. In the dream Twilly couldn't make out his father's words, but the tone suggested that Little Phil was not addressing his lost son but closing a real-estate deal; Twilly recognized the counterfeit buoyancy and contrived friendliness.

Still the boy ran hard, for the beach was disappearing beneath him. The salt water had reached his ankles—shockingly cold, too cold for swimming—and Twilly dropped the shoe box so he could pump with both arms to make himself run faster. The sting of the salt caused his eyes to well up, and the shoreline ahead grew blurry. In the dream Twilly wondered how the tide could be racing in so swiftly, because there was no storm pushing behind it, not the smallest breath of wind. Beyond, the water lay as flat and featureless as polished glass!

Yet now it was rising to Twilly's kneecaps, and running had become impossible. The boy was seized by a paralyzing chill, as if a spike of ice had been hammered into his spine. Through the blur he could make out the W-shaped silhouettes of seabirds wheeling and slanting and skimming insanely above the roiled foam. He wondered why the birds didn't simply fly upward and away, far out to the Gulf, but instead they went crashing blindly into the monolith of buildings; dull concussions of feather and bone. In wild whirling torrents the birds smashed themselves into windowpanes and balconies and awnings and sliding doors, and before long the façades of the hulking high rises were freckled top to bottom with bloody smudges. Twilly Spree no longer heard his father's voice.

In the dream he squeezed his eyes closed so that he would no longer see the birds dying. He stopped trying to move his legs because the water had reached his waist, water so frigid that it would surely kill him in minutes. Twilly wondered how the sea could be so

unbearably chilly—in southern Florida! Latitude
twenty-six degrees!—but then the answer came to him,
and so simple. The water was cold because there was
no sun to warm it; because the goddamned skyscrapers
on the beach had blotted out every ray of sunlight,
leaving the Gulf in a perpetual unholy shade. So it got
plenty cold. Sure it did.

Twilly decided to float. In the dream the water was
up to his armpits and he was fighting so frantically to
catch his breath that he was making weird peeping
noises, like a tree frog. Not acceptable, nossir!
Floating—now there's a nifty idea. Float on my back,
let the tide carry me up to one of these buildings, where
I'll just climb outta this freezing soup. And keep
climbing as high and as long as it takes to get dry,
climbing like the clever little froggy I am. Water's gotta
lay down sometime, right?

In the dream Twilly opened his stinging eyelids and
began to float, yipping for breath. He drifted up to a
condo, maybe a thousand stories tall, and hooked his
arms over a balcony rail. He hung there hoping to
regain some strength. Bobbing all around him in the
foam were the bodies of seabirds, tawny clumps with
rent beaks, clenched yellow claws, disheveled red-
smeared plumage. . . .

The boy struggled to hoist himself out of the frigid
water and onto the dry terrace. He raised his chin to
the rail but that was as high as he got, because standing
there in baggy wet Jockey shorts on the balcony was
his father, Little Phil. Cupped in his outstretched palms
were hundreds of tiny striped toads, bug-eyed and
bubble-cheeked, peeping with such ungodly shrillness
that it hurt Twilly Spree's ears.

And in the dream he cried out. He shut his eyes and let go of the rail and fell back into the flow, the current spinning him like a sodden chunk of timber. Something soft touched his cheek and he swiped at it, thinking it was a dead sandpiper or a gull.

But it wasn't. It was Desie's hand. Twilly opened his eyes and could not believe where he was: lying warm in her arms. He could hear her heart.

"Everything's all right now," she told him.

"Yes." He felt a light kiss on his forehead.

"You're shaking."

He said, "So that's what they call dreaming."

"Let me get you another blanket."

"No, don't move."

"All right," Desie said.

"I don't want you to go."

"All right."

"I mean *ever*," Twilly said.

"Oh."

"Consider it. Please."

The house was dark and silent. No one had set the alarm. Palmer Stoat opened the door. He called out Desie's name and started flipping on light switches. He checked the master bedroom, the guest bedrooms, the porch, the whole house. His wife wasn't home, and Stoat was miffed. He was eager to show her the latest atrocity—the dog paw in the Cuban cigar box. He wanted to sit her down and make her recall every detail about the crazy man who'd snatched Boodle. And he wanted her to tell it all to that sadistic porcupine-haired goon of Robert Clapley's, so then the dognapper could be hunted down.

And killed.

"I want him dead."

Palmer Stoat, hollow-eyed in front of the bathroom mirror. He looked like hell. His face was splotchy, his hair mussed into damp wisps. In the bright vanity lights he could even see the shiny crease on his chin where the surgeon had inserted the rubber implant.

"I want him dead." Stoat said the words aloud, to hear how severe it sounded. Truly he *did* want the man killed . . . whacked, snuffed, offed, done, whatever guys like Mr. Gash called it. The man deserved to die, this young smart-ass, for interfering with the $28 million bridge deal that Palmer Stoat had so skillfully orchestrated; for abducting good-natured Boodle; for using severed dog parts as a lever of extortion; for mucking up Palmer Stoat's marriage . . . how, Stoat wasn't sure. But ever since she'd encountered the dognapper, Desie had been acting oddly. Case in point: Here it was ten-thirty at night and she wasn't home. Mrs. Palmer Stoat, not home!

He stalked to the den and took his throne among the glass-eyed game fish and gaping animal heads. He dialed the governor's mansion and demanded to speak to Dick Artemus. A valet named Sean—Oh perfect! It had to be a Sean!—informed Stoat that the governor had gone to bed early and could not be disturbed, which meant Dick Artemus was off screwing Lisa June Peterson or one of his other triple-named ex-sorority sister aides. Palmer Stoat, who eyed the cigar box on the desk in front of him, believed the arrival of the paw merited a personal conversation with Florida's governor. Stoat felt it was vital for Dick Artemus to know that the dognapper was keeping on the pressure. Stoat felt Governor Dick needed reminding to veto the Shearwater bridge as soon as possible, and to make damn sure it hit the newspapers so the dognapper would see it.

But no—protective, diligent young Sean wouldn't put the call through to the fornicating ex-Toyota salesman!

"What's your full given name, son!" Palmer Stoat thundered over the phone.

"Sean David Gallagher."

"And do you enjoy working at the governor's mansion? Because one word from me about your obstinate attitude and you'll be back at the fucking Pizza Hut, Windexing the sneeze hood over the salad bar. You follow, son?"

"I'll give Governor Artemus your message, Mr. Stoat."

"Do that, sport."

"And I'll also say hi to my father for you."

"Your father?" Stoat sniffed. "Who the hell's your father?"

"Johnny Gallagher. He's Speaker Pro Tem of the House."

"Oh. Right." Palmer Stoat mumbled something conciliatory and hung up. Goddamn kids these days, he fumed, can't even get a job without the old man's juice.

Stoat opened the cigar box and peeked again at the dog paw. "Jesus, what next," he said, slapping the lid shut.

He tried to remember what the guy had looked like that night at Swain's, passing him that snarky note. The suntan, the flowered shirt. . . . Stoat had figured the guy for a boat bum, a mate on a yacht. But the face? He was young, Stoat remembered. But the bar had been smoky, Stoat had been half-trashed, and the kid had been wearing dark shades, so . . . no luck with the face. Desie was the one nasty Mr. Gash should consult. She's the one who'd spent time with the dognapper.

But the thought of Mr. Gash alone with Desirata made Palmer Stoat cringe. What a scary little prick he was! Stoat wondered if the disgusting baby rat was still alive—mewling and crawling half-blind through his cereal cupboard, no doubt! It was unbelievable. Shocking, really. One of the most powerful human beings in the state of Florida, and here his lofty shining universe had been reduced to a tabloid freak show— dog dismemberers and Barbie-doll fetishists and armed punk-haired sadists who crammed rodents down his gullet!

Thank God they didn't know about it, all those people who feared and needed and sucked up to Palmer Stoat, big-time lobbyist. All those important men and women clogging up his voice mail in Tallahassee . . . the mayor of Orlando, seeking Stoat's deft hand in obtaining $45 million in federal highway funds—Disney World, demanding yet another exit off Interstate 4; the president of a slot-machine company, imploring Stoat to arrange a private dinner with the chief of the Seminole Indian tribe; a United States congresswoman from West Palm Beach, begging for box seats to the Marlins home opener (not for her personally, but for five sugar-company executives who'd persuaded their Jamaican and Haitian cane pickers to donate generously—well beyond their means, in fact—to the congresswoman's reelection account).

That was Palmer Stoat's world. Those were his

people. This other sicko shit, it had to stop. It *would* stop, too, once Porcupine Head tracked down the creep who was holding poor Boodle.

Stoat opened the top drawer of his desk and found a favorite stack of sex Polaroids. He had taken them in Paris, while he and Desie were on a weeklong junket paid for by a multinational rock-mining conglomerate. There wasn't much of Desie to be seen in the photographs—here a thigh, there a shoulder—but it was enough to give her husband a pang in his heart and a tingle in his groin. Where the hell was she?

Palmer Stoat noticed the message light blinking on his answering machine. He punched the PLAY button and leaned back. The first message was from Robert Clapley, sounding uncharacteristically edgy and out of breath.

"It's about that rhino powder," he said on the tape. "Call me right away, Palmer. Soon as you get this message!"

The second call, thirty minutes later, also from Clapley: "Palmer, you there? I gotta talk to you. It's the Barbies, they're. . . . Call me, OK? No matter how late."

The third message on Stoat's machine was from Desie. When he heard her voice, he quickly rocked forward and turned up the volume.

"Palmer, I'm all right. I'm going to be gone for a few days. I just need some time away. Please don't worry, uh . . . we'll talk when I get home, OK?"

She didn't sound upset or frightened. She sounded perfectly calm. But there was something quite alarming on the tape—a noise in the background. It happened the moment before Desie said good-bye.

Palmer Stoat listened to the message three times, to

be sure. The noise was familiar and unmistakable: a dog barking.

Not just any dog, either. It was Boodle.

Stoat moaned and pressed his fleshy knuckles to his forehead. Now the sick bastard had gone and snatched his wife!

Again.

On a warm breezy morning in late April, twelve Japanese men and women stepped from an air-conditioned charter bus that had parked on the shoulder of a two-lane road in North Key Largo. The travelers paired off and climbed into half a dozen candy-colored canoes. Under a creamy porcelain sky they began paddling down a winding creek called Steamboat toward Barnes Sound, where they planned to eat box lunches and turn around. The entire trip was supposed to take four hours, but the canoeists went missing for almost three days. Eventually they were found trudging along County Road 905 in the dead of night and, except for a few scrapes and insect bites, were all found to be in excellent health. Oddly, though, they refused to tell police what had happened to them, and fled from reporters seeking interviews.

The men and women were employed by Matsibu-Com, one of Tokyo's most prolific construction companies. Timber being scarce and exorbitant in Japan, MatsibuCom imported millions of board feet annually from the United States; specifically, Montana and Idaho, where entire mountains had been clear-cut, essentially razed down to dusty bald domes, for the purpose of enhancing Tokyo's skyline and, not incidentally,

MatsibuCom's profit margin. Having weathered Asia's financial upheaval in relatively robust shape, the company rewarded a dozen of its top executives with a group vacation to Florida. They would begin the week at unavoidable Walt Disney World and finish down in the Keys, at the upscale (and safely Republican) Ocean Reef Club. Ironically, the MatsibuCom executives expressed an interest in ecotourism activities, and so the Steamboat Creek canoe trip was arranged. The men and women were told they might come across manatees, indigo snakes, bald eagles and perhaps even the elusive North American crocodile (which lived in the mangrove lakes and grew to a length of fourteen feet). Many rolls of film were purchased in anticipation.

When the Japanese failed to return on time from the expedition, an intense search was launched using ultralight planes, airboats, skiffs and swamp buggies. Governor Dick Artemus even dispatched a pair of state helicopters to assist (a modest favor, in his view, compared to the free membership he'd been given at Ocean Reef on the day of his inauguration). Meanwhile, Florida tourism officials gloomily pondered how many millennia it would take for the industry to recover if it came to pass that twelve foreign business executives had been devoured by crocodiles—or perished under some equally horrific circumstances—while vacationing in the Sunshine State.

Publicly, authorities stuck to the theory that the Japanese visitors were "lost" in the mangrove creek system, although reporters found no shortage of locals who were both skeptical and happy to be quoted. Steamboat Creek was about as complicated to navigate as Interstate 95, and a thousand times safer. Fear of foul play rose with the ominous discovery of the missing canoes, shot full of holes and strung together with blue ski rope. The canoes had been hung off the Card Sound Bridge to dangle and spin high over the Intracoastal Waterway, like the baubled tail of an oversized kite. Boaters stopped to snap pictures until police showed up and hastily cut down the rope. The spectacle of the bullet-riddled boats all but vanquished hopes that the MatsibuCom executives would be found safe. It now appeared that they'd been abducted by either psychopaths or terrorists—a far more devastating scenario, publicity-wise, than a simple crocodile attack. A dour-faced contingent from the Japanese consulate in Miami arrived by private jet at Ocean Reef, where they were given a suite of waterfront rooms and unlimited long-distance privileges. Meanwhile, in Washington, a team of FBI forensic experts already had packed for the trip to Florida—they awaited only the somber phone call, reporting that the decomposing bodies had been located.

Then the dozen Japanese canoeists surprised everybody by turning up alive, unharmed and closemouthed. By daybreak on April 30, the MatsibuCom men and women were on a chartered Gulfstream 5, speeding back to Tokyo. The local press milked what it could from the ecotour-gone-awry angle, but in the absence of first-person quotes (and corpses), the story faded quickly from the headlines.

Lt. Jim Tile had heard about it before it made the TV news; the state Highway Patrol sent five road troopers and its top K-9 unit to join the search for the important visitors. The discovery of the canoes—and the emphatic manner in which they'd been sabotaged and strung up for display—confirmed Jim Tile's suspicions about the incident on Steamboat Creek. He was hopeful the Japanese would remain silent, so that no other authorities would make the connection. Obviously Dick Artemus had not. Jim Tile purposely hadn't shared his theory about the ecotour abduction with the governor during their brief meeting in Tallahassee.

That afternoon, though, the trooper dialed the voice-mail number they customarily used to trade messages—he and his friend, the long-ago governor—and was annoyed to find the line disconnected. So he packed an overnight bag, kissed Brenda good-bye and drove south nonstop, virtually the full length of the state. The sun had been up an hour by the time he arrived at the gatehouse of the Ocean Reef Club in North Key Largo. The trooper was admitted to the premises by a surly young security guard who apparently had failed the rudimentary knuckle-dragging literacy quiz required to join regular police departments. The guard reluctantly escorted Jim Tile to the club's executive offices, where—after producing a letter of introduction from the attorney general—the trooper was permitted to examine a roll of film that had been found in a camera bag left behind by one of the Japanese canoeists.

The film had been developed into a black-and-white contact sheet by the local sheriff's lab technician, who had understandably failed to recognize its evidentiary value: Thirty-five of the thirty-six frames were dominated by a blurred finger in the foreground—not an uncommon phenomenon, when a 35-mm camera was placed in the excitable hands of a tourist. But, to Jim Tile, the finger in the snapshots from Steamboat Creek did not appear to be the wayward pinkie of a slightly built Japanese business executive, but rather the fleshy, hairy, crooked, scarred-up middle digit of a six-foot-six Anglo-American hermit with a furious sense of humor.

The last photograph on the roll, the only photograph without the finger, was of equal interest to the trooper. He turned to the slug-like security guard and said: "Does the club have a boat I can borrow? A skiff would do fine."

"We keep a twelve-footer tied up at the marina. But I can't letcha take it out by yourself. That'd be 'gainst policy."

Jim Tile folded the contact sheet and slipped it into a brown office envelope, the same envelope Dick Artemus had handed to him at the governor's mansion.

"So, where's the marina?" the trooper asked the security guard.

"You ain't authorized."

"I know. That's why you're coming with me."

It was a shallow-draft johnboat, powered by a fifteen-horse outboard. The guard, whose name was Gale, cranked the engine on the third pull. Over his ill-fitting uniform he buckled a bright orange life vest, and told Jim Tile to do the same.

"Policy," Gale explained.

"Fair enough."

"Kin you swim?"

"Yep," said the trooper.

"No shit? I thought black guys couldn't swim."

"Where you from, Gale?"

"Lake City."

"Lake City, Florida?"

"Is they another one?"

"And you never met a black person that could swim?"

"Sure, in the catfish ponds and so forth. But I'm talking about the ocean, man. *Salt* water."

"And that's a different deal?"

"Way different," the guard said matter-of-factly. "That's how come the life jackets."

They crossed Card Sound behind a northerly breeze, the johnboat's squared-off hull slapping on the brows of the waves. Gale entered the mouth of Steamboat Creek at full throttle but slowed beneath the low bridge.

He said to the trooper, up in the bow: "How far you need to go?"

"I'll tell you when we get there, Gale."

"Is that a .357 you got?"

"It is."

"I don't got my carry permit yet. But at home I keep a Smith .38 by the bed."

"Good choice," said Jim Tile.

"I b'lieve I'll get somethin' heavier for the streets."

"See the eagle? Up there in the top of that tree." The trooper pointed.

"Cool!" exclaimed Gale the security guard. "Now for that, you need a pump gun, twenty-gauge minimum. . . . Hey, I gotta stop'n take a leak."

"Then stop," said Jim Tile.

"I drank about a gallon of Sanka this morning and I'm fit to 'splode."

"Anywhere's fine, Gale."

The guard cut the engine and the boat coasted silently in the milky green water. Gale removed the life vest and modestly turned around to urinate off the stern. The featherweight boat swung sidelong in the current, and at that moment an ill-timed gust of wind disrupted Gale's golden outflow, blowing it back on the front of his uniform. He let out a yowl and clumsily zipped himself up.

"Goddammit. *That* won't work." He started the engine and idled the nose of the boat into the trees, up against the bank. Stepping out, he snagged one foot on a barnacled root and nearly went down. "Be right back," he told the state trooper.

"Take your time, Gale."

To escape the messy effect of the breeze, the security guard clomped twenty yards into the woods before choosing a spot to unzip. He was midstream—and pissing gloriously, like a stallion—when he heard the *chuk-a-chuk* of the outboard motor. Gale strained to halt his mighty cascade, tucked in his pecker and charged back toward the water's edge. When he got there, the johnboat was gone.

Jim Tile headed down Steamboat Creek at half throttle. A school of finger mullet scattered in silvery streaks ahead of the bow. From behind he heard Gale the security guard bellowing hoarsely in the mangroves. He hoped the young man wouldn't do something completely idiotic, such as attempt to *walk* out.

As he followed the creek, the trooper closely scanned the shoreline along both sides. He wasn't expecting an obvious sign; a flotilla of searchers had been up and down the waterway and found nothing. Jim Tile knew his friend would be careful not to leave tracks. The trooper shed the life vest and reached inside his shirt, where he'd hidden the brown envelope. He took out the contact sheet and glanced once more at frame 36.

The photo had been snapped with the camera

pointed aimlessly downward, as if the shutter had been triggered by mistake. And even though the picture was underlit and out of focus, Jim Tile could make out a patch of water, a three-pronged mangrove sprout and—wedged in the trident-like root—a soda-pop can. Schweppes, it looked like.

A Schweppes ginger ale, of all the unlikely brands.

At least it was *something*. Jim Tile started scouring the waterline for cans, and he found plenty: Coke, Diet Coke, Pepsi, Diet Pepsi, Mountain Dew, Dr Pepper, Orange Crush, Budweiser, Busch, Colt .45, Michelob—it was sickening. People are such slobs, the trooper thought, trashing such a fine and unspoiled place. Who could be so inexcusably disrespectful of God's creation? Jim Tile had grown up in neighborhoods where there was more broken glass than grass on the ground, but his mother would've knocked him on his scrawny black butt if she'd caught him throwing a soda can anywhere but in a trash bin. . . .

The trooper had twisted the throttle down so that the johnboat was barely cutting a wake. Back and forth across the creek he tacked, scooping up floating cans where he saw them; easy to spot, glinting in the bright sun. But no Schweppes. Jim Tile felt foolish for chasing such a weak clue—he knew that weather skidded flotsam all over these creeks. And if the tide rose too high, the trident-shaped mangrove bud would be submerged anyway; invisible. The trooper crumpled the photographic contact sheet and shoved it into his pocket.

Still he kept searching the banks, mechanically collecting other cans and bottles and paper cups. Soon the inside of the johnboat began to look like a Dumpster.

He was turning a wide bend in the creek when something caught his attention—not a ginger-ale can or a three-pronged mangrove sprout, but a slash of canary yellow paint. It appeared as a subtle vector across a cluster of tubular stalks, a yard above the waterline, where somebody had dragged something heavy and brightly painted into the trees. Something like a canoe.

Jim Tile tied off the bow and rolled up his trousers and pulled off his shoes. He bird-stepped from the johnboat and gingerly made his way into the snarl of trees. His left foot poked something smooth and metallic: The Schweppes can from the photograph, trapped beneath the surface by its mangrove talon. The trooper moved ahead, excruciatingly, the soles of his feet rasped by roots and shards of broken mollusks. He slipped repeatedly, and twice nearly pitched onto his face. Jim Tile was aware that he sounded like a herd of drunken buffalo, and not for a moment did he entertain the fantasy that he could sneak up on the governor. It would have been impossible, even on dry land.

The trees thinned and the trooper found a bleached rocky ridge that led him to the edge of a shallow tannic-looking lake. He realized he had stumbled into the federal crocodile refuge, a fact that impelled him to sit down, slap the spiders off his ankles and reconsider the practical boundaries of friendship.

Jim Tile was parched, exhausted, well lacerated—and no great fan of carnivorous reptiles. He rose with rictus-grim determination. Rocking on tender feet, he cupped both hands to his mouth.

"HEY!" he yelled out across the lake. "IT'S ME!"

High overhead, a lone osprey piped.

"I'M TOO OLD FOR THIS SHIT!" Jim Tile shouted.

Nothing.

"YOU HEAR ME? GODDAMN CROCODILES—
YOU THINK THAT'S FUNNY? I GOT A WIFE, GOV-
ERNOR! I GOT PERSONAL RESPONSIBILITIES!"

The trooper was shouting nearly at the top of his
lungs.

"COME ON OUT, MAN, I'M SERIOUS! SERIOUS
AS A FUCKING HEART ATTACK! YOU COME
OUT!"

Jim Tile sucked in his breath and sat down again.
He folded both arms across his knees and rested his
head. He would've strangled a nun for a drop of warm
ginger ale.

Then came the gunshot, followed by two, three, four
more. The trooper raised up and smiled.

"Melodramatic sonofabitch," he said.

The man whom Jim Tile had been sent to find was
almost sixty now, but he stood formidably erect and
broad-shouldered. Beneath a thin plastic shower cap his
pate gleamed egg pink and freshly shorn. He had taken
to wearing a kilt and little else; a kilt fashioned from a
checkered racing flag. Jiffy Lube 300, the man said, I
sort of stole it. He offered no explanation whatsoever
for the origin of his weapon, an AK-47.

The man had grown out his silver beard in two
extravagant tendrils, one blossoming from each cheek.
The coils hung like vines down his broad leathery chest,
and were so intricately braided that Jim Tile wondered
if a woman had done it. Fastened by a ribbon to the
end of each braid was the hooked beak of a large bird.
Vultures, the man acknowledged. Big fuckers, too. His

tangled eyebrows were canted at a familiar angle of disapproval, and somewhere he had gotten himself a new glass eye. This one had a crimson iris, as stunning as a fresh-bloomed hibiscus. Jim Tile found the effect disarming, and somewhat creepy.

The one-eyed kilted man had once been a popular and nationally famous figure, a war hero turned political crusader; brash, incorruptible and of course doomed to fail. It was Jim Tile who had driven the limousine that finally carried the man away from the governor's mansion, away from Tallahassee and a creeping volcanic insanity. It was Jim Tile who had delivered him—his ranting friend—into a private and sometimes violent wilderness, and who had endeavored for more than two decades to keep track of him, watch over him, stop him when he needed to be stopped.

The trooper had done the best he could, but there had been the occasional, unpreventable eruption. Gunplay. Arson. Wanton destruction of property. Even homicide—yes, his friend had killed a few men since leaving Tallahassee. Jim Tile was sure of it. He was equally sure the men must have behaved very badly, and that in any case the Lord, above all, was best qualified to judge Clinton Tyree. That day would come soon enough. In the meantime, Jim Tile would remain recklessly loyal to the man now known as "Skink."

"How's your lovely bride?"

"Just fine," the trooper replied.

"Still like your steaks scorched?" The ex-governor was bending over a crude fire pit, flames flicking perilously at the ringlets of his beard.

Jim Tile said, "What's on the menu tonight?" It was

a most necessary question; his friend's dining habits were eclectic in the extreme.

"Prime filet of llama!"

"Llama," said the trooper, pensively. "Should I even ask?"

"A circus came to town. I swear to God, up in Naranja, a genuine carny."

"Uh-oh."

"Not what you think," Skink said. "Poor thing fell off a truck ramp and fractured both front legs. The girl who owned the critter, she didn't have the heart to put it down herself."

"I get the picture."

"So I did it as a favor. Plus you know how I feel about wasting meat."

Jim Tile said, "What in the world were you doing at a circus?"

Skink grinned; the same charming matinee-idol grin that had gotten him elected. "Romance, Lieutenant. It didn't last long, but it was fairly wonderful for a while."

"She do the beard?"

"Yessir. You like it?" Skink stroked his lush silvery braids. "The beaks were my touch. They're fresh."

"So I noticed."

"Had a little run-in with these two birds. They took an unhealthy interest in my llama."

Jim Tile shook his head. "But you know the law on buzzards. They're protected."

"Not too effectively, in my experience." Skink flipped the steaks in the pan and stepped back from the sizzle. He used a corner of the kilt to wipe a spatter of hot grease off his glass eye. "You're here about the Japanese, right?"

"No," said the trooper, "but I am curious."

"You know who they worked for? MatsibuCom, those greedy, forest-nuking, river-wrecking bastards. But they're strong little buggers, one-on-one, even the ladies. Fiberglass canoes are heavier than you think, Jim. Two miles they hauled 'em on their shoulders, through some pretty thick cover."

"What exactly did you do to those folks, Governor?"

"Nothing. We talked. We hiked. Went for a ride. Nibbled on some llama cutlets. I showed them a few sights, too. Immature bald eagle. Butterfly hatch. Baby crocs." Skink shrugged. "I believe I broadened their horizons."

"They didn't have much to say when they got back."

"I should hope not. I explained to them how seriously I value my privacy. Hey, all we got for refreshments is good old H-two-oh. That OK?"

"Perfect," said Jim Tile. It had been a long time since he had seen the man so talkative. "It's nice to find you in a civilized mood."

"Afterglow, brother." Skink spoke wistfully. "The Human Slinky—that was her circus name. Said she was limber in places other women don't even have places. She made me laugh, Jim. I've gotten to where that counts more than . . . well, that other stuff. Which means I'm either getting real old or real smart. Brenda make you laugh?"

"All the time."

"Fantastic. How about we shut up now and eat?"

Cooked well done, the llama tasted fine. After lunch Skink snatched up his assault rifle and led the trooper at a brisk pace down a sparse trail, past an abandoned cockfighting ring and across County 905 to his new base camp. He had set it up in the buggy shade of an ancient mangrove canopy, within earshot of the ocean. There was no tent but there was a genuine NASCAR Dodge, number 77, blue and gold and plastered bumper-to-bumper with colorful decals: Purolator, Delco, Firestone, Rain-X, Autolite, Bose, BellSouth, Outback Steak House, Sudafed and more. The governor caught Jim Tile staring and said: "From that obscene racetrack up in Homestead. Fifty million dollars of tax money they spent. The car came from there."

"You swiped it."

"Correct."

"Because . . ."

"The godawful noise, Jim. You could hear it all the way across Card Sound. Gave me the worst migraine— you know how I get."

Dumbstruck, the trooper walked a circle around the stolen stock car.

"It's just the body," Skink said. "No engine block or tranny."

"Then how'd you manage?"

"It was on an eighteen-wheeler. The crew parked it behind the Mutineer after the race—the dopes, though I guess they were bright enough to win. They hung the checkered flag off the CB antenna, bless their little hillbilly hearts." Skink paused to admire his new kilt. "Anyhow, the car is where I sleep these days."

The auto theft was one more thing Jim Tile wished he didn't know about. "Where's the truck rig?" he asked uneasily.

"Farther down the shore, toward the abandoned marina. That's where I keep all my books, except for the Graham Greene. Those, I'm traveling with." Skink slid his butt up on the shiny hood of the NASCAR Dodge. Idly he twirled the buzzard beaks on the ends of his beard. "So let's hear the bad news, Jim."

The trooper eyed him squarely. "They want you to hunt down a man. Some wild young kid who's hiding out in the boonies. Seems he reminds them of a junior Clinton Tyree."

"They being . . ."

"Our current governor, the Honorable Dick Artemus."

Skink snorted. "Never heard of him."

"Well, he's heard of you. Wants to meet you someday."

At this, Skink hooted. The trooper went on: "This boy they want you to find, he's been trying to stop a new bridge from getting built."

"I expect he's got a name."

"Unknown."

"Where are they putting this bridge?"

"Place called Toad Island, up on the Gulf. The boy's kidnapped the pet dog of some important guy, some asshole buddy of the governor. And now the governor's pal is receiving pooch parts via Federal Express."

Skink's eyebrows arched. "FedEx? That could run into some money, depending on the size of the animal."

"It's a Labrador, I'm told." Jim Tile reached for his friend's canteen and took a swig of water. "The point is, Governor Artemus is keen on getting this bridge built—"

"Like I care—"

"—and he wants this disturbed young fellow tracked down and apprehended at your earliest convenience. Please don't look at me that way."

Skink said, "I'm no damn bounty hunter."

"I'm aware of that."

"And, furthermore, I wouldn't know Dick Artemus from an elephant hemorrhoid. I don't give two shits about him and I don't give two shits about his bridge, though I do feel badly about the dismembered canine. Now"—Skink, boosting himself off the hood of the race car—"you may return to Tallahassee, my large Negro friend, and advise the governor to go fuck himself, repeatedly and without lubricants, at my behest."

"Not so fast." The trooper reached under his shirt for the brown envelope, damp with sweat. "He told me to give this to you. He thought it might change your mind. I'm afraid he's right."

"What the hell is it?"

"See for yourself."

"You peeked?"

"Certainly," said Jim Tile.

Inside the envelope was a single piece of paper, to which The Honorable Richard Artemus had been wise enough not to affix his name. The man known as Skink read the paper twice, silently. He looked up and said, "The bastard might be bluffing."

"He might be."

"On the other hand. . . ." Skink turned, and for several moments he gazed off through the mangroves, toward the sounds of the waves on the coral. "God-dammit, Jim."

"Yeah."

"I don't see another way but to do this thing."

"Not one you could live with, I agree."

"So now what?"

"Take me back to wherever the hell I parked that

little boat. I'll go up to Ocean Reef and make some calls. Then we'll meet up tonight outside the Last Chance, say ten o'clock."

"All right." For once Skink sounded old and worn-out. He slung the AK-47 over his shoulder and adjusted his shower cap.

Jim Tile said, "I got a feeling you'll get another uninvited guest today. A fat-assed Cracker rent-a-badge—Gale would be his name. He'll be lost and thirsty and chewed up, and he'll be screaming bloody murder about some crazy nigger cop ditching him on Steamboat Creek. Otherwise he's mostly harmless."

"I'll show him the way to the road."

"I'd appreciate that, Governor."

On the trek out, the two men came across a full-grown crocodile with a blue heron clamped in its jaws. The beast lay in the reeds on the edge of a brackish pond, its massive corrugated tail blocking Skink's footpath. He stopped to watch, motioning for the trooper to do the same. The idea of using their guns would not have occurred to either man. Respectfully they waited while the reptile, spraying feathers, gulped down the magnificent stilt-legged bird.

"A sad sight," whispered Skink, "but also a beautiful one. Because you and I and the six billion other selfish members of our species didn't interfere."

"Honestly, I wouldn't dream of it."

Jim Tile was relieved when the crocodile skidded off the muddy bank and into the lake. Twenty minutes later the two men reached the johnboat. Skink held it steady while the trooper climbed in. The motor was cold and didn't crank until the fifth pull. Skink eased the bow away from the mangroves and gave a light push.

"See you tonight," he said.

"Wait, there's one more thing," said Jim Tile. The engine coughed and stopped. The boat began to drift, slowly.

Skink said, "Tell me later, Jim."

"No, I need to tell you now. Artemus says somebody else is out hunting for this boy. Somebody bad."

"Imagine that."

"Well, you need to know." The trooper waved. "Ten o'clock sharp?"

Skink nodded heavily. "With bells on." He bent over and plucked the Schweppes can out of the roots. He tossed it into the johnboat, where it clattered against the others.

The trooper chuckled. "Nice shot." He jerked the starter cord and the outboard motor hiccuped to life.

Skink stood on the shore, twirling his twin buzzard beaks. "Jim, I'm sorry. I truly am."

"For what, Governor?"

"For whatever's coming," he said. "I'm sorry in advance." Then he turned and splashed into the trees.

FIFTEEN

As agreed, Governor Dick Artemus vetoed from the state budget all $27.7 million set aside for "the Toad Island–Shearwater bridge and highway-improvement project." Other funds blocked by the governor included $17.5 million for the construction and promotion of a Southern Bowler's Hall of Fame in Zolfo Springs; $14.2 million for the "agronomic testing" of a technique to genetically remove the navel-like aperture from navel oranges; $2.6 million to rebuild Aqua Quake, a simulated tidal-wave attraction owned by the uncle of a state senator, and destroyed in a fire of dubious origin; and $375,000 to commence a captive breeding program for the endangered rose-bellied salamander, of which only seven specimens (all males) were known to survive.

In all, Dick Artemus used a line-item veto to eliminate more than $75 million in boondoggles. Except for the Toad Island bridge, all had been proposed by Democrats. Among the items *not* vetoed by the governor were numerous frivolities initiated by his fellow Republicans, including: $24.2 million to redesign a private golf course in Sarasota, ostensibly to attract a PGA tournament but in truth to spruce up the back nine for the chairman of the House Appropriations Committee, who owned three prime lots along the fourteenth fairway; $8.4 million for the purchase of an abandoned South Dade tomato farm liberally appraised at $561,000, purportedly to expand the crucial buffer around Everglades National Park, but actually to enrich the absentee owners of the property, who had contributed magnanimously to the state Republican Committee; $19.1 million to pave and widen to six lanes a gravel road leading to a 312-acre cow pasture in Collier County, said pasture being the as-yet-unannounced future site of a mammoth outlet mall, its silent developer partners including the wife, sister-in-law and niece of the Republican Speaker of the House.

None of the pet projects overlooked by Governor Dick Artemus made the newspapers, but the vetos did. Desie found the list in the Fort Lauderdale *Sun-Sentinel*, beneath the following headline:

GOVERNOR AXES $75 MILLION FROM BUDGET
DECLARES WAR ON POLITICAL "PORK"

Desie read the story aloud to Twilly Spree in the truck.

"Be happy," she told him. "You did it. The bridge is history."

Twilly said, "We'll see." He held one hand on the steering wheel and one hand out the window of the pickup, cupping air. He nodded when Desie asked if he was still thinking about the dream.

She said, "You know what a psychologist would say? A psychologist would say you had a breakthrough."

"Anything's possible." Twilly didn't seem unhappy or upset; only absorbed.

Desie said, "Do you remember asking me to stay?"

"Yes."

"Why did you?"

"Because I was scared."

"Of what—more dreams?"

Twilly smiled. "No, not dreams." He adjusted the rearview to check on McGuinn, riding in the bed of the truck. "You think he's OK back there?"

"Oh, he's loving life," Desie said.

"I think he ought to be riding with us."

"Twilly, he's in heaven."

"But what if it starts to rain—"

"He's a Labrador!"

"But he's been sick. He shouldn't be out in the weather."

Twilly parked on the shoulder and brought McGuinn into the cab, between him and Desie. It proved to be a cramped arrangement, made worse by an onset of canine flatulence.

"From the dog food," Desie explained. "Liver-flavored is the worst."

Twilly grimaced. He got off at the next exit and stopped at a Buick dealership, where he traded in the pickup truck on a 1992 Roadmaster station wagon. The entire transaction took twenty-one minutes, Twilly making up the difference in cash that he peeled from a wad in his denim jacket. Desie watched, intrigued.

"This is the largest domestic passenger vehicle ever manufactured in the United States," Twilly announced, loading McGuinn into the cavernous rear compartment. "Now you can fart all you want."

And off they went again.

Desie almost asked where Twilly had gotten the money, but it didn't matter. He could've robbed a church and still she wouldn't have wanted to go home. She understood him no better than she understood herself, but she felt unaccountably comfortable at his side. Sometimes she caught him glancing sideways at her—it was a look no other man had ever given her, a combination of naked desire, penetrating curiosity and also sadness. Finally she said: "What in the world is going through your head?"

"How beautiful you are."

"Please."

"OK. How much I want to sleep with you?"

"No, Twilly. There's more."

"You're right. I keep forgetting how complicated I am." He took a slow breath and interlocked both hands at the top of the steering wheel. "What I'm thinking," he said, "is how much I *want* to need you."

"That's a better answer," Desie said. "Not as flattering as the others, but a little more original."

"What if it's the truth?"

"And what if I feel the same way?"

Twilly let out a soft whistle.

"Exactly," she said.

"So we're both off the rails."

"A case could be made, yes."

He was silent for several miles. Then he said: "Just for the record, I *do* want to sleep with you."

"Oh, I know." Desie tried not to look pleased.

"What are your views on that?"

"We'll discuss it later," she said, "when you-know-who is asleep." She cut her eyes toward the rear of the station wagon.

"The dog?" Twilly said.

"My *husband's* dog. I'd feel weird doing it in front of him—cheating on his master."

"He licks his butt in front of *us*."

"This isn't about modesty, it's about guilt. And let's talk about something else," Desie said, "such as: Where the heck are we going?"

"I don't know. I'm just following this car."

"Why?" Desie said. It was a cobalt four-door Lexus with a Michigan license plate. "May I ask why?"

"Because I can't help myself," said Twilly. "About twenty miles back she tossed a cigarette, a lit cigarette. With piney woods on both sides of the road!"

"So she's an idiot. So what?"

"Luckily it landed in a puddle. Otherwise there could've been a fire."

Swell, Desie thought, I'm riding with Smokey the Bear.

"All right, Twilly, she threw a cigarette," Desie said, "and the point of following her is. . . ."

Inside the blue Lexus was only one person, the driver, a woman with an alarming electric mane of curly hair. She appeared to be yakking on a cellular phone.

Desie said: "You do this often—stalk total strangers?"

"The woods look dry."

"Twilly, there's lots of dumb people in this world and you can't be mad at all of 'em."

"Thanks, Mom."

"Please don't tailgate."

Twilly pointed. "Did you see that?"

Desie had seen it: the woman in the Lexus, tossing another smoldering butt. Twilly's fists were clamped on the steering wheel, and the cords of his neck stood out like cables, yet no trace of anger was visible in his face. What frightened Desie was the gelid calm in his eyes.

She heard him say, "I bet that car's got a huge gas tank."

"Twilly, you can't possibly go through life like this."

She was digging her fingernails into the armrest. They were inches from the bumper of the Lexus. If the idiot woman touched the brakes, they'd all be dead.

Desie said, "You think you can *fix* these people? You think you can actually teach 'em something?"

"Call me an optimist."

"Look at her, for God's sake. She's in a whole different world. Another universe."

Gradually Twilly slid back a couple of car lengths.

Desie said, "I'm an expert, remember? I'm married to one of them."

"And it never makes you mad?"

"Twilly, it made me nuts. That's why I'm here with you," she said. "But now you've got me so scared I'm about to wet my pants, so please back off. Forget about her."

Twilly shifted restlessly. The driver of the Lexus had no clue; her tangly head, wreathed in smoke, bobbed and twitched as she chattered into the phone.

"Please." Desie touched his wrist.

"OK."

He eased off the gas. The cobalt Lexus began to pull away, and as it did a can of Sprite flew out the window and bounced into the scrub. Desie sighed defeatedly. Twilly stomped the accelerator and the station wagon shot forward. He got tight on the bumper again, this time punching the horn.

"Jesus," Desie gasped. "I can practically see her dandruff."

"Well, I believe she finally knows we're here."

The woman in the Lexus anxiously fumbled with the rearview mirror, which had been angled downward for makeup application instead of traffic visibility.

"Moment of truth," Twilly announced.

"I'm begging you," Desie said. Ahead of them, the idiot driver was now frantically jerking the Lexus all over the road.

Twilly wore a wistful expression. "Admit it," he said to Desie. "It would be a glorious sight, that car going up in flames—and her hopping around like a cricket in the firelight, screeching into that damn phone. . . ."

"Don't do this," Desie said.

"But you can see it, can't you? How such an idea might take hold—after what she's done?"

"Yes, I understand. I'm angry, too." Which was true. And the scene Twilly described would not have been completely unsatisfying, Desie had to admit. But, God, it was nuts. . . .

The Lexus began to slow down, and so did Twilly. The curly-haired woman clumsily veered onto the shoulder, gravel flying. Desie's pulse pounded at her temples, and her mouth felt like dry clay. She could feel the car shudder when Twilly pumped the brakes. Groggily, McGuinn sat up, anticipating a walk.

The Roadmaster eased up alongside the Lexus. The driver cowered behind the wheel. She wore enormous rectangular sunglasses, which spared Desie from seeing the dread in her eyes.

Twilly glowered at the woman but abruptly turned

away. Desie watched him draw a deep breath. She was holding hers.

Then, to her surprise, the station wagon began to roll. "Maybe some other time," Twilly said quietly.

Desie leaned across and kissed him. "It's all right."

"Honey, where's the Tom Petty CD?"

"Right here."

She felt a rush as Twilly gunned the big car toward the interstate. He cranked up the music.

"'One foot in the grave,'" he sang.

"'And one foot on the pedal,'" sang Desirata Stoat. She was glad to be with a man who got the words right.

"This is all your fault," said Robert Clapley.

"I beg your pardon."

"You're the one who gave me that shit."

"In the first place," said Palmer Stoat, "it was for *you* to use, not the girls. That's my understanding of powdered rhinoceros horn, Bob. It's a male stimulant. In the second place, only a certifiable moron would smoke the stuff—you mix it in your drink. You know, like NutraSweet?"

They were in the doorway of the master bedroom at Clapley's Palm Beach condominium, which reeked of garlic and hashish and stale sweat. The place was a wreck. The mirror hung crooked and cracked, and the king-sized mattress lay half on the floor; the silk bed-sheets were knotted in a sticky-looking heap. Above the headboard, the walls were marked with greasy partial imprints of hands and feet and buttocks.

"Fucking olive oil," Robert Clapley growled. "And I mean *fucking* olive oil."

"What else they were taking," Stoat asked, "besides the rhino powder?"

"Hash, ecstasy, God knows what—trust me, you'd need a moon suit to go in their bathroom." Clapley laughed mirthlessly. "Some asshole they met at the spa sent up some Quaaludes. When's the last time you ever *saw* an actual Quaalude, Palmer? You can't find that shit in a pharmaceutical museum."

The men moved to the bay window that overlooked the sundeck, where Katya and Tish floated toe-to-toe in the Jacuzzi, with their eyes closed. Today they did not look much like Barbie dolls. They looked like whored-up junkies. In fact they were so blotched and bloated and unappetizing that Palmer Stoat almost felt sorry for Robert Clapley—almost, but not quite. This was, after all, the same prick who'd called him a turd fondler; the same prick who'd threatened him and brought that psycho Porcupine Head into his home. Therefore it was impossible for Stoat to be wholly sympathetic to Clapley's predicament.

"Where does it stand now, Bob? Between you and the twins."

"Limp is how it stands," Clapley said. Nervously he tightened the sash on his bathrobe. Stoat noticed a fresh scab on one earlobe, where once there had been a diamond stud.

"Here's the thing. The last couple days were wild, real carny stuff," said Clapley. "Truth is, the rhino horn didn't do a damn thing for me except ruin a perfectly good bourbon. But the girls, Palmer, they think it's some kind of supercharged jingle crack. . . ."

"But they were stoned, anyway."

"The point is," Clapley said, raising a hand, "the

point is, they think it was the rhinoceros powder that gave 'em the big wet high. They *believe*, Palmer, and that's ninety percent of what dope is about: believing in it. And these are not—let me remind you, pardner—these are not the most sophisticated ladies you'll ever meet. They escape from a dull, cold, miserable place and end up in beautiful sunny South Florida, a.k.a. paradise. Everything's supposed to be new and exciting here. Everything's supposed to be better. Not just the weather but the drugs and the cock and the parties. The whole nine yards."

Through the tinted glass Stoat studied the two nude women in the tub, their impossibly round implants poking out of the water like shiny harbor buoys. The bright sun was brutally harsh on their facial features; puffy eyelids, puffy lips. Their sodden, matted hair looked like clumps of blond sargassum—Stoat could see by the dark roots it was time for refresher dye jobs. He heard Clapley say: "They want more."

"They used it all up?"

Clapley nodded grimly. "And now they want more."

"Bob, that shit is extremely hard to come by."

"I can imagine."

"No, you can't. You have no idea."

"Problem is, they're supposed to get their chins done next week," Robert Clapley said. "I've got the top chin guy in the whole goddamn world flying in first-class from São Paulo. But the girls—get this—first thing this morning they announce: No more sex and no more surgery and no more Barbie wardrobe until we get rhino dust. That's what they call it, rhino dust."

"How adorable." Palmer Stoat, stroking his own artificially sculpted chin. "My advice, Bob? Deport these ingrates straight back to the motherland, then get on with your life."

Clapley looked pained. "You don't understand. I had plans for these two. I had a timetable."

"Bob, you can always find new Barbies to climb your little staircase to heaven. Florida's crawling with 'em."

"Not like these. Not twins."

"But they're *not* really twins, for Christ's sake—"

Robert Clapley seized Stoat's arm. "I have too much invested here. And not just time and money, Palmer. This is an important project to me. *They*"—jerking his head toward the hot tub—"are important to me."

A project, Stoat mused. Like customizing Chevys.

"Christmas," Clapley was saying. "We're right on schedule to be finished by the Christmas holidays—everything, head to toe. That's how close we are."

"They're hookers, Bob. They'll do whatever you tell them."

"Not anymore." Clapley wheeled away from the window. "Not without the rhino dust."

Palmer Stoat followed him into the living room. "I'll make some calls. I can't promise anything."

"Thank you." Clapley sagged into an overstuffed chair.

"But I'm not responsible for what might happen. They could croak smoking that stuff. They could fall down dead right before your eyes. Where'd they get such a damn fool idea?"

"TV probably. For some reason they decided to put the shit in a pipe. They were sucking it out of a glass pipe. Then they were sucking on me—"

"Enough. I get the picture," Stoat said.

"Then Spa Boy showed up and they were sucking on

him, and he was sucking on them. . . ." Robert Clapley clicked his teeth. "Oh, it was a regular tropical suckfest, Palmer. You should've been here."

"No thanks. I had my own excitement."

"Yeah?" Clapley gave a halfhearted leer.

"That's what I need to talk to you about. The dog-napper."

"What now?"

"He sent me a paw," Stoat said, "in a Cuban cigar box."

Clapley grunted. "To go with the ear? Man, that's cold."

"Here's what else, Bob. He's got my wife."

"Still? I thought—didn't you tell me he let her go?"

"He did," said Stoat. "But he got her again."

"How, for God's sake?"

"Who knows. Point is, he's most definitely got her."

"Plus the dog?" Clapley asked.

"That's right."

"Damn." Clapley looked exasperated. "What a sick fucking world. Sick, sick, sick."

"Speaking of which," said Palmer Stoat, "your charming Mr. Gash—where might he be, Bob?"

"Shearwater Island, last I heard. Hunting for the sicko dognapper."

Palmer Stoat said, "Call him off, please."

"What for?"

"I don't want him anywhere near my wife. Call him off until this puppy-slicing freak lets her go."

"What if he doesn't let her go?"

"He will," Stoat said. "Governor Dick vetoed your twenty-eight-million-dollar bridge. It was in the papers this morning."

The veto was a very sore subject with Clapley. "You're damn lucky to be alive," he reminded Palmer Stoat.

"I know, I know. The point is, Bob, that's all the dognapper guy asked for—the veto. So now he'll think he won."

Clapley fidgeted impatiently. "And you're saying this twerp is as good as his word. Some demented fruitcake who's mailing you chunks of your pet dog—him you trust. Is that about the size of it?"

"Look, I want him out of the picture as much as you do. Once Desie's free, then Mr. Gash can go do his thing and you can get on with Shearwater. Just give it a couple days, that's all I'm asking. Until she's home safe and sound."

"The dog, too?" Robert Clapley said. "Or should I say, what's left of the dog."

Stoat ignored the snideness. "When does Mr. Gash usually check in?"

"When there's a result to report."

"Next time he calls—"

"I'll be sure to relay your concerns," Clapley said, "and in the meantime, you'll make inquiries about purchasing another rhinoceros horn."

Stoat nodded. "If I find one, it won't be cheap."

"When did perfection ever come cheap?" Clapley smiled wearily. "Do your best, Palmer."

A commotion arose from outside, on the deck. Clapley hurried to the door, Stoat at his heels. The two Barbies were fighting in the Jacuzzi, throwing punches and shrieking in two thickly dissonant tongues. As Clapley waded haplessly into the hot tub, Palmer Stoat could not help but reflect once more on the seedy, disturbing downturn his own life had taken. Here he was, standing in the scorching sun like a eunuch servant, obediently holding a silk robe for a man—his own client!—who had filled both pockets with dolls. Not only dolls but a tiny hand mirror and makeup kits and a hairbrush, too!

Stoat held the miniature brush, no larger than a stick of Dentyne, in the palm of one hand. The bristles were exquisitely fine and the handle—my God, could it possibly be? Stoat squinted in amazement. Pearl!

Slowly he looked up, beyond the sordid tumble of yowling flesh in the Jacuzzi, toward the tranquil gem blue of the Atlantic. What's happening to this country of ours? Stoat wondered ruefully. What's happening to me?

SIXTEEN

No, Mr. Gash was not a patient man.

And Toad Island was a drag; no trace of the dick-faced boy he was supposed to murder.

After much searching, Mr. Gash located a tolerable motel on the mainland. He chose not to call Robert Clapley, as there was nothing to report except for the drunken biologist whom Mr. Gash had shot and buried with the backhoe. No bonus points there.

So Mr. Gash got in his car and returned to Toad Island. All morning he drove back and forth across the old bridge, with a favorite 911 compilation in the tape deck: *Snipers in the Workplace*, accompanied by an overdub of Tchaikovsky's Symphony no. 3 in D Major.

CALLER: It's Tim! Tim from the ramp! He's gone totally batshit! He's shooting all the god-damned supervisors!

DISPATCHER: What's your last name, Tim?

CALLER: I AM NOT TIM! Tim's the shooter!!!

DISPATCHER: You say he's got a gun?

CALLER: Hell yes. He's got, like, FIVE guns! You better send some cops fast!

DISPATCHER: Sir? Sir?

CALLER: You hear that? Holy Christ.

DISPATCHER: Was that gunfire?

CALLER: Well, it ain't the [bleeping] Fourth a July. Is somebody on the way yet?

DISPATCHER: Yes, sir, we've got units en route. Could you give me a description of the suspect?

CALLER: He's about six two, two hundred forty pounds, dark curly hair.

DISPATCHER: What's his full name?

CALLER: Hell, I got no idea. He doesn't even work for me, OK? Tim is all I know—Tim, the day-shift loading-ramp guy.

DISPATCHER: Does he have any—sir, you there? Sir?

CALLER: Yeah, I'm still here. Can't you hear all those shots? Don't you understand what's going on here? All [bleeping] hell is breaking loose. The man is runnin' from office to office, poppin' the supervisors—

DISPATCHER: Does this Tim have any distinguishing features, any scars or tattoos?

CALLER: No, lady, but he won't be hard to pick out. He'll be the only one with five smoking handguns. In fact, he'll be the only one here with a pulse, if the cops don't show up real soon. . . . Oh Jesus!

DISPATCHER: Sir?

CALLER: Hey there, Timmy boy! . . . Howzit goin', bro? . . . Yeah, it's me. . . . Oh, just catchin' a few z's here in the old broom closet. . . . So how's it going? Man, you look really stressed—

DISPATCHER: Sir, please don't hang up. Sir?

Mr. Gash was buoyed by the panic that infused the tape recording; it connected him to a more familiar realm, and temporarily relieved his sense of dreary isolation on Toad Island. Back and forth across the bridge he went, reasoning that it was the best way to monitor who was coming and going. No cars or trucks could slip past, while small boats approaching from the mainland would be visible from the low span.

But even with his 911 emergency tapes in the car, Mr. Gash found himself battling boredom and impatience. Part of him wanted to bag the Clapley job and rush home to his comfortable apartment on South Beach, where he could change to a clean houndstooth suit and get some sushi on Lincoln Road and then head to the clubs, scouting for girls. One was never enough for Mr. Gash. Oh, he was way past one-on-one. Two was all right but three was even better. In his apartment Mr. Gash had a custom-made bed, double the width of a standard king. Bolted into the overhead ceiling beams was a pulley rig, to which was attached a harness made of the choicest green iguana hides. A furniture upholsterer on Washington Avenue had tailored the lizard-skin harness to fit Mr. Gash's block-like torso; first-rate work, too, and reasonably priced.

That's what Mr. Gash was daydreaming about doing—dangling from his ceiling above three writhing long-legged women, one of them wielding platinum ice tongs—when a station wagon carrying a large dog sped past going the other direction, across the bridge toward the island. Mr. Gash was sniggering as he wheeled around to follow. He could see the dog's pitch-black head jutting from a window; Mr. Gash was almost certain it was a Labrador. And, from a quarter of a mile away, Mr. Gash counted only one black ear flapping in the wind.

Bingo! he thought, and eagerly stepped on the gas.

The dog, it turned out, was a black Labrador retriever. Both ears, however, were intact—the one invisible to Mr. Gash had merely been turned inside out. The dog's name was Howard and he belonged to Ann and Larry Dooling of Reston, Virginia. They did not resemble the young couple described to Mr. Gash by the fatally dweebish Dr. Brinkman. The Doolings were in their mid-sixties; she was retired from the Smithsonian, he from the U.S. Commerce Department. They had come to Florida for the sunshine, and to Toad Island in particular for the beach, where Mr. Gash had approached them on the pretense of seeking directions. Once he determined they were tourist goobs, not ecoterrorists or dognapping extortionists, he endeavored to terminate the conversation and clear out.

But Larry Dooling slapped a cold sweaty Budweiser in his hand and said: "We been all over this damn state, looking for a decent beach. By 'decent,' I mean peaceful and quiet."

"The brochures," chimed Ann Dooling, "are *very* misleading."

Howard the dog sniffed the tops of Mr. Gash's shoes while Larry Dooling recounted the many beaches in Florida that had disappointed them on their travels. "Fort Lauderdale, of course—just try to find a parking space there, I dare ya'. Miami we steered clear of. Vero was OK but they had a shark warning posted, so we couldn't swim. Palm Beach, it was poison jellyfish. And what possessed us to take a chance on Daytona, I'll never know."

"Don't forget Clearwater," interjected Ann Dooling. "What a zoo—all those college kids!"

The couple's voices bore like titanium augers into Mr. Gash's skull. When the woman remarked for the third time upon his "modern hairstyle," Mr. Gash enthusiastically immersed himself in another daydream. He imagined the Doolings writhing from toxic jellyfish stings; imagined he was listening to them not on a sunny beach but in the cool dark privacy of his own apartment, in 5.1 Dolby Surround sound.

He imagined the Doolings on a 911 emergency tape.

"Aren't you warm in that suit?" Ann Dooling asked.

Oh, part of him wanted to peel off the houndstooth coat and let the Doolings eyeball his gun; wanted to watch their jaws drop as he snatched it from the holster and leveled it to their shiny cocoa-buttered foreheads—the yappy goobs rendered speechless at last. . . .

But it was broad daylight and nearby on the sand were children playing Frisbee. So Mr. Gash tossed his beer can, turned away and tromped disgustedly to the car.

He made it halfway across the old bridge when he spotted another station wagon coming fast the other way; a Buick Roadmaster woody, the mother of all wagons, carrying another couple, another black dog with its head out the window.

Mr. Gash reflexively braked. Then he thought: Fuck *that*. I'm all tapped out on tourists today. What he needed now was a stack of porny magazines and a bottle of Meyer's. So he kept driving, away from Toad Island.

Tomorrow, Mr. Gash told himself. Tomorrow I'll come back to check out the Roadmaster.

In the spring of 1966, two brothers went to Vietnam. One came back a hero, the other came back a casualty. Doyle Tyree was riding in an army Jeep when it turned over, ten miles outside of Nha Trang. The driver, a sergeant, died instantly. Doyle Tyree suffered a broken leg and grave head injuries, and he was airlifted stateside to spend six weeks in a VA hospital. To his everlasting torment, the Jeep accident had not been caused by hostile fire but by recklessness. He and his sergeant had polished off a case of Hong Kong ale and decided to go carp fishing in a flooded rice paddy—carp fishing after dark in a combat zone! All because Doyle Tyree was homesick for Florida and worried out of his mind about his little brother, Clint, who was playing sniper somewhere out in the steamy highland fog, among the Cong and the leeches and the cobras.

They had grown up on a fine little bass lake, all the Tyree boys, but it was Doyle and Clint who could never get enough of the place—after school and Saturday mornings, and Sundays, too, when church let out. And it wasn't the fishing so much as the good hours together and the unbroken peace—the breeze bending the cattails, the sunlight shimmering the slick-flat water, the turtles on the logs and the gators in the lilies and the querulous calls of the meadowlarks drifting down from the pastures. Doyle Tyree was wretched with longing and loneliness when he suggested to his sergeant that they go carp fishing that evening, not even knowing if there *were* carp or any other damn fish in the flooded-out rice paddy; knowing only that in the twilight it reminded him of the lake back home. So they'd cut down bamboo shoots for poles and bowed sewing needles into hooks and for bait swiped a bread loaf from the mess, then grabbed up their remaining bottles of ale—bitter and piss-warm, but who cared?—and set off to catch some major motherfucking carps. The dirt road was unlit and potholed but ultimately it was the damn goat that did the job, some sleepy peasant's runaway goat. When the sergeant swerved to avoid it, the Jeep flipped (as those army Jeeps would do) and kept on flipping until an ox-drawn wagon stopped it as conclusively as a concrete wall.

And Doyle Tyree awoke in a chilly white room in Atlanta, Georgia, with steel pins in his femur and a plate in his head and more guilt and shame on his twenty-five-year-old soul than seemed bearable. He asked to return to duty in Vietnam, which was not unusual for soldiers injured under such circumstances, but the request was turned down and he was handed an honorable discharge. So back to Florida he went, to wait for his heroic little brother. Only after Clint returned safely from the jungle, only after they'd hugged and laughed and spent a misty morning on the family lake, only then did Doyle Tyree allow the breakdown to begin. Within a week he was gone, and nobody knew where.

It was many years before his brother found him. By then Clinton Tyree was governor and had at his disposal the entire state law-enforcement infrastructure, which on occasion displayed bursts of efficiency. The governor's brother, who had been using the name of his dead sergeant from Vietnam, was unmasked by a sharp-eyed clerk during a routine fingerprint screen. The fingerprint data located Doyle Tyree in an Orlando jail cell, where he was doing thirty days for trespassing. He had been arrested after pitching his sleeping bag and firing up a Sterno camp stove inside the tower of Cinderella's Castle at Walt Disney World—the thirty-sixth time it had happened during a two-year stretch. Disney police figured Doyle Tyree for a wino, but in fact he had not swallowed a drop of alcohol since that night outside of Nha Trang. He was bailed out of the Orlando jail, bathed, shaved, dressed up and brought to Tallahassee on a government plane.

For Clinton Tyree, the reunion was agony. Doyle grasped his hand and for a moment the dead-looking eyes seemed to spark, but he uttered not one word for the full hour they were together at the governor's mansion; sat ramrod-straight on the edge of the leather sofa and stared blankly at the sprig of mint floating in his iced tea. Eventually Clinton Tyree said, "Doyle, for God's sake, what can I do to help?"

Doyle Tyree took from his brother's breast pocket a ballpoint pen—a cheap give-away souvenir, imprinted with the state seal—and wrote something in tiny block letters on the skin of his own bare arm. Doyle Tyree pressed so forcefully that each new letter drew from his flesh a drop of dark blood. What he wrote was: PUT ME SOMEWHERE SAFE.

A week later, he began work as the keeper of a small lighthouse at Peregrine Bay, not far from Hobe Sound. The red-striped tower, a feature tourist attraction of the Peregrine Bay State Park, had not been functional for almost four decades, and it had no more need of a live-in keeper than would a mausoleum. But it was indeed a safe place for the governor's unraveled brother, whose hiring at a modest $17,300 a year was the one and only act of nepotism committed by Clinton Tyree.

Who scrupulously made note of it in his personal files, to which he attached a copy of Doyle Tyree's military and medical records. Also attached was the letter Clinton himself had written to the division of parks, politely requesting a position for his brother.

The letter was one of the documents that Lisa June Peterson had dutifully shown to her boss, Dick Artemus, the current governor of Florida, upon delivering the boxes of background material about Clinton Tyree. Lisa June Peterson had also reported that the name Doyle Tyree continued to appear on the state payroll—at his original salary—suggesting that he was still encamped at the top of the Peregrine Bay lighthouse.

Which Dick Artemus was now threatening to condemn and demolish if Clinton Tyree turned him down and refused to go after the deranged young extortionist who was cutting up dogs in protest of the Shearwater project.

That was the ball-grabbing gist of the unsigned demand delivered by Lt. Jim Tile to the man now known as Skink: "Your poor, derelict, mentally unhinged brother will be tossed out on the street unless you do as I say. Sorry, Governor Tyree, but these are lean times in government," the letter had said. "What with cutbacks in the Park Service—there's simply no slack in the budget, no extra money to pay for a seldom-seen keeper of a defunct lighthouse.

"Unless you agree to help."

So he did.

Lisa June Peterson had become uncharacteristically

intrigued by the subject of her research, the only man ever to quit the governorship of Florida. She'd devoured the old newspaper clippings that charted Clinton Tyree's rise and fall—from charismatic star athlete and decorated-veteran candidate to baleful subversive and party outcast. If half the quotes attributed to the man were accurate, Lisa June mused, then quitting had probably saved his life. Somebody surely would've assassinated him otherwise. It was one thing to recite the standard gospel of environmentalism—for heaven's sake, even the Republicans had learned to rhapsodize about the Everglades!—but to rail so vituperatively against growth in a state owned and operated by banks, builders and real-estate developers. . . .

Political suicide, marveled Lisa June Peterson. The man would've had more success trying to legalize LSD.

To an avid student of government, Clinton Tyree's stay in Tallahassee was as fascinating as it was brief. He was probably right about almost everything, thought Lisa June Peterson, yet he did almost everything wrong. He cursed at press conferences. He gave radical speeches, quoting from Dylan, John Lennon and Lenny Bruce. He let himself go, shambling barefoot and unshaven around the capitol. As popular as Clinton Tyree had been with the common folk of Florida, he'd stood no chance—none whatsoever—of disabling the machinery of greed and converting the legislature to a body of foresight and honest ethics. It was boggling to think a sane person would even try.

But perhaps Tyree was not sane. Look at his brother, thought Lisa June Peterson; maybe it runs in the family. Look at the way the governor had blown town, fleeing the capitol after his Cabinet had betrayed him by closing a wildlife preserve and selling the seaside property to well-connected developers. So swift and complete was Tyree's disappearance that people initially thought he'd been kidnapped or murdered, or even had done himself in—until the letter of resignation arrived, the angry slash of a signature verified by FBI experts. Lisa June Peterson had made two photocopies of the historic missive; one for Dick Artemus and one for her scrapbook.

For a short while after Clinton Tyree vanished, the newspapers had been full of gossip and speculation. Then nothing. Not a single journalist had been able to find him for an interview or a photograph. Over the years his name had popped up intermittently in the files of the state Department of Law Enforcement—purported sightings in connection with certain crimes, some quite bizarre. But Lisa June Peterson had found no record of an arrest, and in fact no solid proof of the ex-governor's involvement. Yet the mere idea he was still alive, brooding in some gnarly wilderness hermitage, was beguiling.

I'd give anything to meet him, Lisa June thought. I'd love to find out if he really snapped.

Never would she have guessed what her boss wanted with her research. She didn't know Dick Artemus had stayed up until 4:00 a.m. one night, grubbing through the documents and clippings until he seized with excitement upon the tragic story of Doyle Tyree, the ex-governor's brother. Nor did Lisa June Peterson know about the unsigned communiqué given by her boss to the black state trooper, or the icy nature of her boss's threat.

And so she was unaware of the event she had set in

motion: a man coming wounded and bitter out of deep swamp; a man such as she had never known, or imagined.

"Money is no object," Palmer Stoat said into the phone.

On the other end was Durgess. "This ain't only about money. It's about major jail time."

"The Chinaman hung up on me."

"Yessir. He don't like telephones."

"One lousy horn is all I need," Stoat said. "Can't you reach out to him? Tell him the money's no object."

Durgess said, "You gotta understand, it's not been a good year for the rhino trade. Some of the boys we normally use, they got busted and went to jail."

"Does he know who I am? The Chinaman," said Stoat, "does he know how well connected I am?"

"Sir, you shot the last rhino we had on-site. Used to be Mr. Yee could do business direct with Africa, but Africa's shut down for a couple months. Africa got too hot."

Palmer Stoat paused to light up an H. Upmann, only to find the taste metallic and sugary. It was then he remembered, with revulsion, the cherry cough drop in his cheek. Violently he spit the lozenge onto his desk.

"You mean to tell me," he said to Durgess, "that for the obscene price of fifty thousand dollars, your intrepid Mr. Yee cannot locate one single solitary rhinoceros horn anywhere on planet Earth?"

"I didn't say that," said Durgess. "There's a private zoo in Argentina wants to sell us an old male that's all broke down with arthritis."

"And he's still got his horns?"

"Damn well better," Durgess said.

"Perfect. How soon can you get him?"

"We're workin' on it. They tell me a month or so."

"Not good enough," Stoat said.

"Lemme see what I can do."

"Hey, while I got you on the line"—Stoat, giving the Upmann another try—"how's my head mount coming? Did you get with your fiberglass guy?"

"He's on the case," Durgess said. "Says it'll look better'n the real thing, time he gets done. Nobody'll know it's fake except you and me."

"I can't wait," Palmer Stoat said. "I can't wait to see that magnificent beast on the wall."

"You bet."

Stoat failed to detect the mockery in Durgess's tone, and he hung up, satisfied that he'd lit a blaze under the guide's slothful butt. Stoat fastidiously nubbed the ash of his cigar and went to shower. He carried a portable phone into the bathroom, in case Desie called from Hostage World, wherever. . . .

The lights went out while Stoat had a head covered with shampoo lather. He groped in the dark, cursing and spitting flecks of soapy foam, until he found the shower knobs. When he tried to open the door, it wouldn't budge. He leaned a shoulder to the glass, with no better result.

Through stinging eyes Stoat saw a hulking shadow on the other side of the shower door. A cry died in his throat as he thought: Mr. Gash again. Who else could it be?

Then the glass disintegrated, an earsplitting echo off the imported Italian marble. The door fell in pieces around Stoat's bare feet. Afterward the only sound in the bathroom was his own stark, rapid breathing. He felt a stinging sensation on his right leg, and a warm trickling toward his ankle.

The shadow no longer loomed face-to-face; now it was seated on the toilet, evidently evacuating its bowels.

"Mr. Gash?" The words came out of Palmer Stoat in a choke.

"Wrong," the shadow said.

"Then who are you?"

"Your friend Dick sent me," the shadow man said. "Dick the governor. Something about a missing pooch."

"Yes!"

"Suppose you tell me."

"Now? Here?"

The lights came on. Palmer Stoat squinted, raising one hand to his brow. With the other hand he covered his shrunken genitals. Broken glass lay everywhere; it was a miracle he'd only been nicked.

"Start talking," said the shadow man. "Hurry, soldier, life is passing us by."

As Stoat's eyes adjusted, the broad-shouldered figure on the toilet came into focus. He had sun-beaten features and a silvery beard, exotically platted into two long strands. Tied to each of the strands was a beak, yellow and stained like old parchment. The man wore ancient mud-caked boots and a dirty orange rain jacket. Bunched at his ankles was a legless checkered garment that might have been a kilt. On his head the man wore a cheap plastic shower cap, through which shone a shiny bald scalp. Something was odd about his eyes, but Stoat couldn't decide what it was.

"Do you have a name?" he asked.

"Call me captain." The visitor spoke in a low rumble, like oncoming thunder.

"All right, *captain*." Stoat didn't feel quite so terrified, with the guy sitting where he was. "Why didn't you just ring the doorbell?" Stoat said. "Why break into the house? And why'd you bust the shower door?"

"To put you in the proper frame of mind," the man replied. "Also, I was in the mood for some serious goddamn noise."

"Dick Artemus sent you?"

"Sort of."

"Why—to get my dog back?"

"That's right. I'm from Animal Control." The man barked sarcastically.

Palmer Stoat fought to stay calm. Considering the political stakes, it almost made sense that Governor Dick would recruit his own tracker to take care of the dognapper—maybe not to kill him but certainly to stop him before he caused more trouble. But where had the governor found such a crazed and reckless brute? Stoat wondered. He was like Grizzly Adams on PCP.

Stoat asked: "Are you a manhunter?"

"More like a shit scraper," the visitor replied, "and I'm starting with you."

"Look, I'll tell you the whole story, everything, but first let me towel off and put on some clothes. Please."

"Nope. You stay right there." The man rose and reached for the toilet paper. "In my experience," he said, hoisting his checkered kilt, "men who are buck naked and scared nutless tend to be more forthcoming. They tend to have better memories. So let's hear your sad doggy story."

Stoat realized what was bothering him about the manhunter's eyes: They didn't match. The left eyeball was artificial and featured a brilliant crimson iris. Stoat wondered where one would procure such a spooky item, and why.

"Are you going to start talking," the man said, "or just stand there looking ridiculous."

Palmer Stoat talked and talked, nude and dripping in the shower stall amid the broken glass. He talked until the dripping stopped and he had completely dried. He told the one-eyed stranger everything he thought might help in the manhunt—about the tailgater in the black pickup truck; about the cruel trashing of Desie's Beemer convertible; about the break-in at his house and the perverse defacing of his trophy taxidermy; about the swarm of dung beetles set loose inside his sports-utility vehicle; about Boodle's abduction and the ensuing eco-extortion demand; about the resort project turning Toad Island into Shearwater Island, and the ingenious wheeling and dealing required to get a new bridge funded; about the mocking note from the stranger in sunglasses at Swain's, probably the damn dognapper himself; about the severed ear arriving soon after, by FedEx, followed by the paw in the cigar box; about the governor agreeing to veto the bridge; about how Stoat was expecting the lunatic to free his beloved Labrador any day now, and also his wife—

Here he was interrupted by the man with the crimson eye.

"Hold on, sport. Nobody said anything about a woman hostage."

"Well, he's got her," Stoat said. "I'm ninety-nine percent sure. That's why the situation is so dicey, why it would be better for you to wait until after he lets Desie go."

The man said, "What makes you so sure she'll want to come home?"

Palmer Stoat frowned. "Why wouldn't she?" Then, as an afterthought: "You don't know my wife."

"No, but I know these situations." The man handed a towel to Stoat and said: "Show me this room where you keep your dead animals."

Stoat wrapped the towel around his waist and tiptoed through the shattered glass. He led the bearded man down the hall to the den. Stoat began giving a stalk-by-stalk history of each mount, but he was barely into the Canadian lynx saga when "the captain" ordered him to shut up.

"All I want to know," the man said to Stoat, "is what exactly he did in here."

"Pried out the eyes and left them on my desk."

"Just the mammals, or the fish, too?"

"All of them." Stoat shook his head somberly. "Every single eyeball. He arranged them in a pattern. A pentagram, according to Desie."

"No shit?" The captain grinned.

"You don't find that sick?"

"Actually, I admire the boy's style."

Palmer Stoat thought: He *would* think it's cute. Him with his moldy rain suit and funky fifty-cent shower cap and weird fake eye. But then again, Stoat mused, who better to track down a perverted sicko than another perverted sicko?

"You shot all these critters for what reason, exactly?" The man was at the long wall, appraising the stuffed

Cape buffalo head. Being so tall, he stood nearly nose-to-nose with the great horned ungulate.

"You shot them, why—for fun or food or what, exactly?" he asked again, twirling the bird beaks on the platted ends of his beard.

"Sport," Stoat answered warily. "For the sport of it."

"Ah."

"You look like you do some hunting yourself."

"On occasion, yes," the man said.

"Whereabouts?"

"The road, usually. Any busy road. Most of what I'm after is already dead. You understand."

Dear God, thought Palmer Stoat: *Another* professional hit man. This one shoots his victims on the highway, while they're stuck in traffic!

"But certain times of the year," the visitor added, "I'll take a buck deer or a turkey."

Stoat felt a wavelet of relief, perceived a sliver of common ground. "I got my first whitetail when I was seventeen," he volunteered. "An eight-pointer."

The one-eyed man said, "That's a good animal."

"It was. It really was. From then on I was hooked on hunting." Stoat thickly laid on the good-ole-boy routine, and with it the southern accent. "And now, hell, lookit me. I'm runnin' outta wall space! The other day I got a black rhino—"

"A rhino! Well, congratulations."

"Thank you, cap'n. My first ever. It was quite a thrill."

"Oh, I'll bet. You cook him?"

Stoat wasn't sure he'd heard right. "I'm gettin' the head mounted," he went on, "but I jest don't know where to hang the dang thing—"

"On account a ya'll runnin' outta gawdamn wall space!"

"Right." Stoat gave a brittle chuckle. The big sonofabitch was making fun of him.

"Sit your ass down," the man said, pointing toward the desk. The leather chair felt cool against Palmer Stoat's bare back; he tried to cross his flabby thighs but the bath towel was wrapped too snugly. The bearded one-eyed man walked around the desk and stood directly behind the leather chair. The only way Stoat could see the man was to cock his head straight back. From that upside-down vantage, the captain's visage appeared amiable enough.

"So you're a lobbyist," he said to Stoat.

"That's right." Stoat began to explain his unsung role in the machinations of representative government, but the one-eyed man slammed a fist so hard on the polished wood that Stoat's picture frames toppled.

"I know what you do," the man said mildly. "I know all about the likes of you."

Palmer Stoat made a mental note to call a Realtor first thing tomorrow and put his house on the market; it had become a chamber of torture, practically every room violated by demented intruders—first the dognapper, then the sadistic Mr. Gash and now this nutty bald cyclops. . . .

"I've only got one question," the man said to Stoat. "Where is this Toad Island?"

"Up the Gulf Coast. I'm not exactly sure where."

"You're not sure?"

"No . . . captain . . . I've never been there," Stoat said.

"That's beautiful. You sold the place out. Single-handedly greased the skids so it could be 'transformed' into a golfer's paradise—isn't that what you told me?"

Stoat nodded wanly. Those had been his exact words.

"Another fabulous golfer's paradise. Just what the world needs," the one-eyed man said, "and you did all this having never set foot on the island, having never laid eyes on the place. Correct?"

In a voice so timorous that he scarcely recognized it, Palmer Stoat said: "That's how it goes down. I work the political side of the street, that's all. I've got nothing to do with the thing itself."

The man laughed barrenly. "'The thing itself'! You mean the monstrosity?"

Stoat swallowed hard. His neck muscles hurt from looking upward at such a steep angle.

"A client calls me about some piece of legislation he's got an interest in," he said. "So I make a phone call or two. Maybe take some senator and his secretary out for a nice dinner. That's all I do. That's how it goes down."

"And for that you get paid how much?"

"Depends," Stoat replied.

"For the Shearwater bridge?"

"A hundred thousand dollars was the agreement." Palmer Stoat could not help himself, he was such a peacock. Even when faced with a life-threatening situation, he couldn't resist broadcasting his obscenely exorbitant fees.

The captain said, "And you have no trouble looking at yourself in the mirror every morning?"

Stoat reddened.

"Incredible," the man said. He came purposefully around the leather chair and with one hand easily overturned the heavy desk. Then he kicked the chair out from under Stoat, dumping him on his butt. The towel came untied and Stoat lunged for it, but the one-eyed man snatched it away and, with a theatrical flair, flung it cape-like across the horns of the stuffed buffalo.

Then he wheeled to stand over Stoat, a bloated harp seal wriggling across the carpet. "I'm going to do this job for your buddy Dick," the man growled, "only because I don't see how *not* to."

"Thank you," cheeped the cowering lobbyist.

"As for your dog, if he's really missing an ear or a paw or even a toenail, I'll deal appropriately with the young fellow who did it." The captain paused in contemplation.

"As for your wife—is that her?"—pointing at the upended picture frame on the floor, and not waiting for Stoat's answer. "If I find her alive," the man said, pacing now, "I'll set her loose. What she does then, that's up to her. But I do intend to advise her to consider all options. I intend to tell her she can surely do better, much better, than the sorry likes of you."

Palmer Stoat had crawled into a corner, beneath a stacked glass display of antique cigar boxes. The bearded man approached, his legs bare and grime-streaked below the hem of the kilt. Stoat shielded his head with his arms. He heard the big man humming. It was a tune Stoat recognized from an old Beach Boys album—"Wouldn't It Be Great," or something like that.

He peeked out to see, inches from his face, the intruder's muddy boots.

"What I ought to do," Palmer Stoat heard the man say, "I ought to kick the living shit out of you. That's what would lift my spirits. That's what would put a spring in my step, ha! But I suppose I won't." The man dropped to one knee, his good eye settling piercingly on Stoat while the crimson orb wandered.

"Don't hurt me," said Stoat, lowering his arms.

"It's so tempting."

"Please don't."

The bearded man dangled the two bird beaks for Stoat to examine. "Vultures," he said. "They caught me in a bad mood."

Stoat closed his eyes and held them shut until he was alone. He didn't move from the floor for two hours, long after the intruder had departed. He remained bunched in the corner, his chin propped on his pallid knees, and tried to gather himself. Every time he thought about the last thing the captain had said, Palmer Stoat shuddered.

"Your wife is a very attractive woman."

SEVENTEEN

The dog was having a grand time.

That's the thing about being a Labrador retriever—you were born for fun. Seldom was your loopy, freewheeling mind cluttered by contemplation, and never at all by somber worry; every day was a romp. What else could there possibly be to life? Eating was a thrill. Pissing was a treat. Shitting was a joy. And licking your own balls? Bliss. And everywhere you went were gullible humans who patted and hugged and fussed over you.

So the dog was having a blast, cruising in the station wagon with Twilly Spree and Desirata Stoat. The new name? Fine. McGuinn was just fine. Boodle had been OK, too. Truthfully, the dog didn't care *what* they called him; he would've answered to anything. "Come on, Buttface, it's dinnertime!"—and he would've come galloping just as rapturously, his truncheon of a tail wagging just as fast. He couldn't help it. Labradors operated by the philosophy that life was too brief for anything but fun and mischief and spontaneous carnality.

Did he miss Palmer Stoat? It was impossible to know, the canine memory being more sensually absorbent than sentimental; more stocked with sounds and smells than emotions. McGuinn's brain was forever imprinted with the smell of Stoat's cigars, for example, and the jangle of his drunken late-night fumbling at the front door. And just as surely he could recall those brisk dawns in the duck blind, when Stoat was still trying to make a legitimate retriever out of him—the frenzied flutter of bird wings, the *pop-pop-pop* of shotguns, the ring of men's voices. Lodged in McGuinn's memory bank was every path he'd ever run, every tomcat he'd ever treed, every leg he'd tried to hump. But whether he truly missed his master's companionship, who could say. Labradors tended to live exclusively, gleefully, obliviously in the moment.

And at the moment McGuinn was happy. He had always liked Desie, who was warm and adoring and smelled absolutely glorious. And the strong young man, the one who had carried him from Palmer Stoat's house, he was friendly and caring and tolerable, aroma-wise. As for that morbid bit with the dog in the steamer trunk—well, McGuinn already had put the incident behind him. Out of sight, out of mind. That was the Lab credo.

For now he was glad to be back at Toad Island, where he could run the long beach and gnaw on driftwood and go bounding at will into the cool salty surf. He loped effortlessly, scattering the seabirds, with scarcely a twinge of pain from the place on his tummy where the stitches had been removed. So energetic were his shoreline frolics that McGuinn exhausted himself by day's end, and fell asleep as soon as they got back to the room. Someone stroked his flank and he knew, without looking, that the sweetly perfumed hand belonged to Desie. In gratitude the dog thumped his tail but elected not to rise—he wasn't in the mood for another pill, and it was usually Desie who administered the pills.

But what was this? Something being draped across his face—a piece of cloth smelling vaguely of soap. The dog blinked open one eye: blackness. What had she done? McGuinn was too pooped to investigate. Like all Labradors, he frequently was puzzled by human behavior, and spent almost no time trying to figure it out. Soon there were unfamiliar noises from the bed, murmurs between Desie and the young man, but this was of no immediate concern to McGuinn, who was fast asleep and chasing seagulls by the surf.

Twilly Spree said: "I can't believe you blindfolded him."

Desie tugged the sheet to her chin. "He's Palmer's dog. I'm sorry, but I feel funny about this."

She moved closer, and Twilly slipped an arm around her. He said, "I guess this means we have to be extra quiet, too."

"We have to be quiet, anyway. Mrs. Stinson is in the next room," Desie said.

Mrs. Stinson was the proprietress of Toad Island's only bed-and-breakfast. She stiffly had declared a no-dogs policy, and was in the process of turning them away when Twilly had produced a one-hundred-dollar bill and offered it as a "pet surcharge." Not only did Mrs. Stinson rent them the nicest room in the house but she brought McGuinn his own platter of beef Stroganoff.

Twilly said, "Mrs. Stinson is downstairs watching wrestling on Pay-Per-View."

"We should be quiet, just the same," said Desie. "Now I think you ought to kiss me."

"Look at the dog."

"I don't want to look at the dog."

"A purple bandanna."

"It's mauve," Desie said.

Twilly was trying not to laugh.

"You're making fun of me," said Desie.

"No, I'm not. I think you're fantastic. I think I could search a thousand years and not find another woman who felt guilty about fooling around in front of her husband's dog."

"They're very intuitive, animals are. So would you please stop?"

"I'm not laughing. But just look at him," Twilly said. "If only we had a camera."

"That's it." Desie reached over and turned off the lamp. Then she climbed on top of Twilly, lifted his hands and placed them on her breasts. "Now, you listen," she said, keeping her voice low. "You told me you wanted to make love."

"I do." McGuinn looked outrageous. It was all Twilly could do not to crack up.

Desie said, "Did you notice I'm in my birthday suit?"

"Yup."

"And what am I doing?"

"Straddling me?"

"That's correct And are those your hands on my boobs?"

"They are."

"And did you happen to notice," Desie said, "where *my* hand is?"

"I most certainly did."

"So can we please get on with this," she said, "because it's one of the big unanswered questions about this whole deal, about me running off with you, Twilly—this subject."

"The sex?"

Desie sighed. "Right. The sex. Thank God I don't have to spell everything out." She squeezed him playfully under the covers.

He smiled up at her. "Nothing like a little pressure the first time out."

"Oh, you can handle it." Desie, squeezing him harder. "You can *definitely* handle it."

"Hey! Watch those fingernails."

"Hush," she said, and kissed him on the mouth.

They were not so quiet, and not so still. Afterward, Desie rolled off and put her head next to Twilly's on Mrs. Stinson's handmade linen pillowcases. Desie could tell by the frequent rise and fall of his chest that he wasn't drowsy; he was wired. She switched on the lamp and he burst out laughing.

"Now what?" She snapped upright and saw McGuinn sitting wide awake at the foot of the bed. His tail was bebopping and his ears were cocked and he looked like the happiest creature in the whole world, even with a ludicrous mauve blindfold.

Twilly whispered: "Dear God, we've traumatized him for life."

Desie broke into a giggle. Twilly removed the bandanna from the dog and put out the light. In the darkness he was soothed by the soft syncopations of their breathing, Desie's and McGuinn's, but he didn't fall asleep. At dawn he rose and pulled on a pair of jeans and a sweatshirt. Desie stirred when she heard him murmur: "Time for a walk."

She propped herself on one elbow. "Come back to bed. He doesn't need a walk."

"Not him. Me."

She sat up, the sheet falling away from her breasts. "Where you going?"

"The bridge," said Twilly.

"Why?"

"You coming?"

"It's nippy out, Twilly. And I'm beat."

He turned to McGuinn. "Well, how about you?"

The dog was up in an instant, spinning euphorically at Twilly's feet. A walk—was he kidding? Did he even *have* to ask?

Krimmler had worked nineteen years for Roger Roothaus. He had been hired because of his reputation as a relentless prick. When Krimmler was on-site, construction moved along swiftly because Krimmler whipped it along. The faster a project got completed, the less money it cost the developer, and the more profit and glory accrued to the engineering firm of Roothaus and Son. Krimmler abhorred sloth and delay, and would let nothing—including, on occasion, the law—stand in the path of his bulldozers. Unless otherwise instructed by Roger Roothaus personally, Krimmler began each day with the mission of flattening, burying or excavating something substantial. Nothing gladdened his soul so much as the sharp crack of an oak tree toppling under a steel blade. Nothing fogged him in gloom so much as the sight of earth-moving machinery sitting idle.

Krimmler's antipathy toward nature was traceable to one seminal event: At age six, while attending a Lutheran church picnic, he'd been bitten on the scrotum by a wild chipmunk. The incident was not unprovoked—Krimmler's mischievous older brother had snatched the frightened animal from a log and dropped it down Krimmler's corduroy trousers—and the bite itself had barely drawn blood. Nevertheless, Krimmler was traumatized to such a degree that he became phobic about the outdoors and all creatures dwelling there. In his imagination every uncut tree loomed as a musky, mysterious hideout for savage scrotum-nipping chipmunks, not to mention snakes and raccoons and spiders and bobcats . . . even bats!

Young Krimmler felt truly safe only in the city, shielded by concrete and steel and glass. It was the comfort drawn there—in the cool sterile shadows of skyscrapers—that propelled him toward a career in engineering. Krimmler proved ideally suited to work for land developers, each new mall and subdivision and high-rise and warehouse park bringing him that much closer to his secret fantasy of a world without trees, without wilderness; a world of bricks and pavement and perfect order; a world, in short, without chipmunks. It was inevitable Krimmler would end up in Florida, where developers and bankers bought the politicians who ran the government. The state was urbanizing itself faster than any other place on the planet, faster than any other place in the history of man. Each day 450 acres of wild forest disappeared beneath bulldozers across Florida, and Krimmler was pleased to be on the forefront, proud to be doing his part.

Early on, Roger Roothaus had recognized the value

of placing such a zealot on-site as a project supervisor. So long as a single sapling remained upright, Krimmler was impatient, irascible and darkly obsessed. The construction foremen hated him because he never let up, and would accept none of the standard excuses for delay. To Krimmler, a lightning storm was no reason to shut down and run for shelter, but rather a splendid opportunity to perform unauthorized land clearing, later to be blamed on the violent weather. He would permit nothing to waylay the machines, which he regarded with the same paternal fondness that George Patton had felt for his tanks.

Krimmler regarded each new construction project as a battle, one step in a martial conquest. And so it was with the Shearwater Island resort. Krimmler lost no sleep over the fate of the oak toads, nor did he derive particular joy from it; burying the little critters was simply the most practical way to deal with the situation. As for the sudden disappearance of Brinkman, the pain-in-the-ass biologist, Krimmler couldn't be bothered to organize a search.

What'm I now, a goddamn baby-sitter? he'd griped to Roothaus. The guy's a lush. Probably got all tanked up on vodka and fell off that old bridge—speaking of which, what's all this shit I see in the newspaper. . . .

"Not to worry," Roger Roothaus had assured him.

"But is it true? The governor vetoed the bridge money!"

"A technicality," Roger Roothaus had said. "We get it back in a month or two. All twenty-eight mil."

"But what about the meantime?"

"Just chill for a while."

"But I got a survey crew coming over from Gainesville this week—"

"Calm down. It's a political thing," Roger Roothaus had said. "A long story, and nothing you've got to worry about. We just need to chill out for a spell. Take some time off. Go up to Cedar Key and do some fishing."

"Like hell," Krimmler had said. "Forget the bridge, I've still got serious acreage to clear. I've got the drivers ready to—"

"No. Not now." The words of Roger Roothaus had hit Krimmler like a punch in the gut. "Mr. Clapley says to lay low for now, OK? No activity onsite, he says. There's a small problem, he's handling it. Says it shouldn't take long."

"What kind a problem?" Krimmler had protested. "What in the hell kind a problem could shut down the whole job?"

"Mr. Clapley didn't say. But he's the boss chief, OK? He's paying the bills. So I don't want no trouble."

Krimmler had hung up, fuming. He was fuming when he went to bed, alone in the luxury camper that he drove from site to site. And he was still fuming the next morning when he woke up and heard the goddamned mockingbirds singing in the tops of the goddamned pines, heard the footsteps of a goddamned squirrel scampering across the camper's aluminum roof—a *squirrel*, which was a second goddamned cousin to a chipmunk, only bolder and bigger and filthier!

Wretched was the only way to describe Krimmler's state after the Roothaus phone call; wretched in the milky tranquillity of the island morning, wretched without the growling, grinding gears of his beloved front-end loaders and backhoes and bulldozers. And when the surveyors showed up at the construction trailer at 7:00 a.m. sharp (a minor miracle in itself!), Krimmler could not bring himself to send them away, just because some shithead politicians were monkeying around with the bridge deal. Because the bridge was absolutely crucial to the project; without it, Shearwater Island would forever remain Toad Island. It had been hairy enough (and plenty expensive!) hauling the earth-moving equipment, one piece at a time, across the old wooden span. A fully loaded cement truck would never make it, and without cement you've got no goddamned seaside resort. Without cement you've got jack.

So why not get the bridge surveying out of the way? Krimmler reasoned. What harm could come of *that*? It would be one less chore for later, one less delay after the money finally shook loose in Tallahassee. To hell with "laying low," Krimmler thought. Roger'll thank me for this later.

So he led the surveyors to the old bridge and sat on the hood of the truck and watched them work—moving their tripod back and forth, calling coordinates to one another, spray-painting orange X's on the ground to mark critical locations. It was tedious and boring, but Krimmler hung around because the alternative was to sulk by himself in the trailer, listening to the goddamned birds and hydrophobic squirrels. The bridge survey was the closest thing to progress that was happening on Toad Island at the moment, and Krimmler felt a powerful need to be there. Once the surveyors were gone, that would be all for . . . well, who knew for *how* long. Krimmler willed himself not to fret about that. For now, perched on the hood of a Roothaus and Son

F-150 pickup, he would be sustained by the click of the tripod and the sibilant *fffttt* of the aerosol spray-paint cans. Briefly he closed his eyes to envision the gleaming new bridge, fastened to the bottom muck of the Gulf with stupendous concrete pillars, each as big around as a goddamn sequoia. . . .

"Hello there."

Krimmler stiffened, his eyes opening to a leery squint. "Who're *you?*"

It was a young man with a deep weathered tan and sun-bleached hair. He wore a navy sweatshirt and jeans, but no shoes. His feet were caramel brown.

"Just a tourist," he said.

"You don't look like a tourist."

"Really. Then what do I look like?" The young man gave a grin that put Krimmler on edge.

"All I meant," said the engineer, "was, you know, the suntan. Any darker and you'd be speaking Jamaican. Whereas most of the tourists we see around here are white as a fish belly."

"Well, I'm what you call a professional tourist," the young man said, "so I'm out in the sunshine all the time. What're you guys doing?" He jerked his chin in the direction of the surveyors. "Is this for that big golfing resort everybody's talking about?"

Krimmler said, "You play golf?"

"Where do you think I got this tan."

From the young man's air of casual confidence, Krimmler sensed that he might be living off a trust fund, or possibly socked-away dope earnings. Krimmler began to address him not as a scruffy pest but as a potential customer and future member of the Shearwater Island Country Club.

"We're building two championship courses," Krimmler said, "one designed by Nicklaus, the other by Raymond Floyd."

The young man whistled, turning to gaze at the island. "Two golf courses," he marveled. "Where you gonna put 'em?"

"Oh, there's plenty of space," Krimmler said, "once you rearrange a few trees."

"Ah." The young man looked back, again with the odd weightless grin.

"We'll have condos, town houses and custom estate homes," Krimmler went on. "The fairway lots are selling like Beanie Babies. You're interested, they've got some color handouts at the sales trailer."

"Raymond Floyd, you say?"

"That's right. He's doing the south course."

"Well, I'm impressed," the young man said. "And all this?"

"For the new bridge," said Krimmler. "Four lanes. Sixty-foot clearance."

"But isn't this the one I read about in the paper?"

"Naw."

"The one the governor just vetoed?"

"Forget what you see in the news," Krimmler told the young man. "The bridge is a done deal. The resort's a done deal. We're good to go."

"Is that right."

"Soon," Krimmler said, with a wink. "Real soon."

He heard a cry and, wheeling, saw one of the surveyors huffing after a big black dog. The dog somehow had gotten its leash caught up with the instrument tripod and was dragging the thing across the pavement like a crippled mantis.

"Hey, stop!" Krimmler yelled. "Stop, goddammit!"

The tan young man stepped away from Krimmler's side and broke into a run. He chased down the dopey dog and untangled the tripod, which he returned with its broken Sokkia transit to the slow-footed surveyor. Krimmler got there in time to hear the young man apologizing, and to watch him press a crisp wad of cash into the surveyor's palm. Then off they went, the black dog at the young man's heels, crossing the old wooden bridge toward the island.

"Hey!" Krimmler called brightly after them. "Don't forget to swing by the sales office and pick up a brochure!"

EIGHTEEN

When Krimmler returned to the travel trailer, he was alarmed to see lights in the windows. Approaching the front door, he heard a throb of excited voices.

She's stabbing me! The crazy . . . ugh! . . . bitch is . . . agh! . . . stabbing me!!!

Calm down. Please try to calm down.

Stay calm? There's a fondue . . . ugh! . . . fork in my ass! HELP!

Sir, we've got units on the way.

No, Debbie, not there! You promised, NOT THERE! Yaaaggghh—Jesus, look whatchu done now! You crazy damn bitch!!

Krimmler was turning to flee when the trailer door flew open. In a blur he was tackled, dragged inside and heaved like a sack of fertilizer onto the sour carpet. He expected to behold chaos, a deranged harpy with a bloody cheese fork poised over a dying boyfriend. . . .

But the only person in Krimmler's Winnebago was a powerfully built man with blond hair, which had been moussed into peculiar white-tipped spikes. The man wore a houndstooth suit and brown leather shoes with zippers down the ankles, like Gerry and the Pacemakers might have worn in 1964.

The interior of the trailer showed no evidence of a

savage stabbing. The cries and shrieks of crazed Debbie's victim had come from Krimmler's stereo speakers. The spiky-haired stranger twisted down the volume knob and positioned himself in a captain's chair, which he spun to face Krimmler.

"I work for Mr. Clapley," the man said. He had a deceptively gentle voice.

"I work for Mr. Clapley, too." Krimmler began to rise from the floor, but the spiky-haired man produced a handgun and motioned him to be still.

"You were talking to a guy this morning. Barefoot guy with a dog," said the stranger. "Over by the bridge, remember?"

"Sure."

"I was watching. Who was he?"

Krimmler shrugged. "Just some tourist. He wanted to know about the new golf courses. I sent him to the sales office."

"What else?"

"That's it. Why'd you bust into my place? Can't I get up now?"

"Nope," said the man in the houndstooth suit. "Did he ask about the new bridge?"

Krimmler nodded.

"Well?"

"I told him it was a done deal."

"Why'd you tell him that?"

"Because he acted like he had money," Krimmler said. "Mr. Clapley *is* still in the business of selling property, isn't he?"

The stranger popped a cassette out of Krimmler's stereo console. He placed it in an inside pocket of his suit jacket, all the time keeping the gun on display in his other hand. Krimmler wondered why Robert Clapley would employ such a thug. Possibly the stranger was lying about that, though it didn't really matter at the moment. Krimmler was unfailingly respectful of firearms.

"I never saw this goddamned guy before," he told the spiky-haired stranger. "He didn't say his name, and I didn't think to ask."

"Is he with a woman?"

"I got no idea."

"Yesterday I saw a couple in a Buick station wagon crossing to the island," the stranger said. "They had a dog in the car."

"Anything's possible," Krimmler said restlessly. "Look, I told you everything I know."

"Well, he acts like a troublemaker. Didn't he strike you as a troublemaker?" The man went into Krimmler's refrigerator for a beer. "Was he pissed when you told him about the new bridge?"

"Not that I could tell," Krimmler said. "Why the hell would he care about a bridge?"

The man with the gun was silent for a few moments. Then he said: "It's a helluva sound system you got in this cozy little tin can."

"Yeah. Thanks."

"You can actually hear the people *out of breath* on those tapes. You can hear them wheezing and gasping and shit. It's just amazing what's possible on a first-rate sound system."

"The speakers are brand-new," Krimmler said. "From Germany."

The spiky-haired man opened the beer and took a

swallow. "So. This troublemaker with the black dog—where would he be staying on the island?"

"If he's not camping out, then he's probably at Mrs. Stinson's bed-and-breakfast."

"And where's that?"

Krimmler gave directions. The man holstered his gun. He told Krimmler it was all right to get up off the floor.

"Can I ask your name?"

"Gash."

"You really work for Clapley?"

"I do. Ask him yourself." The stranger turned for the door.

"That tape you were listening to," said Krimmler, "was that for real? Was that you on there, calling for help?"

The man laughed—a creepy and unsettling gurgle that made Krimmler sorry he'd asked.

"That's good," Mr. Gash said. "That's really rich."

"Look, I didn't mean anything."

"Hey, it's OK. I'm laughing because the man on that tape, he's dead. Dead as a fucking doornail. Those were his last mortal words you heard: 'You crazy damn bitch!!' The last living breath out of his mouth."

Mr. Gash chuckled again, then stepped into the night.

It was nine-thirty, and Lisa June Peterson was alone in her office, which adjoined the governor's own. When the phone rang, she assumed it was Douglas, the probate attorney she'd been dating. Every time Douglas called, the first question was: "What're you wearing, Lisa June?"

So tonight, being in a frisky mood, she picked up the phone and said: "No panties!"

And a male voice, deeper and older-sounding than Douglas's, responded: "Me neither, hon."

The governor's executive assistant gasped.

"Ah, sweet youth," the voice said.

Lisa June Peterson stammered an apology. "I'm so— I thought you were somebody else."

"Some days I think the same thing."

"What can I do for you?" Lisa June asked.

"Get me an appointment with the governor."

"I'm afraid he's out of town." Lisa June, trying to recover, hoping to sound cool and professional.

The caller said: "Then I'll catch up with him later."

She was troubled by something in the man's tone— not menace, exactly, but a blunt certainty of purpose. "Maybe I can help," she said.

"I seriously doubt it."

"I can try to reach him. Does Governor Artemus know you?"

"Apparently so," the man said.

"May I have your name?"

"Tyree. You need me to spell it?"

"No." Lisa June Peterson was floored. "Is this some kind of a joke?"

"Anything but."

"You're *Governor* Tyree—no bullshit?"

"Since when do fine young ladies use that word in formal conversation? I am shocked to the marrow."

Lisa June Peterson already was on her feet, collecting her purse and car keys. "Where are you now?" she asked the caller.

"Pay phone down on Monroe."

"Meet me in front of the capitol. Ten minutes."

"Why?"

She said, "I drive a Taurus wagon. I'm wearing a blue dress and glasses."

"And no panties, 'member?"

Nothing in Lisa June Peterson's experience prepared her for the sight of Clinton Tyree. First his size—he looked as big as a refrigerator. Then the wardrobe—he was dressed like a squeegee man: boots, homemade kilt and shower cap. As he got in her car, the dome light offered an egg-white glimpse of shaved scalp, a ruby glint from a prosthetic eye. But it wasn't until they were seated side by side on upturned cinder blocks in front of a campfire that Lisa June Peterson got a good look at the lush cheek braids and the bleached bird beaks adorning them.

"Buzzards," the former governor said. "Bad day."

His face was saddle-brown and creased, but it opened to the same killer smile Lisa June remembered from her research; from those early newspaper photographs, before things went weird. The inaugural smile.

She said, "It's really you."

"Just the chassis, hon."

They were in a wooded lot outside of town, near the municipal airport. The ex-governor was skinning out a dead fox he'd scavenged on the Apalachee Parkway. He said it had been struck by a motorcycle; said he could tell by the nature of the dent in the animal's skull.

"What should I call you?" Lisa June Peterson asked.

"Let me think on that. You hungry?"

"I was." She turned away while he worked at the haunches of the dead fox with a small knife.

He said, "This is my first time back to Tallahassee."

"Where do you live now?"

"You know what's tasty? Possum done right."

Lisa June said, "I'll keep my eyes peeled."

"Tell me again what it is you do for Mr. Richard Artemus."

She told him.

Clinton Tyree said: "I had an 'executive assistant,' too. She tried, she honestly did. But I was pretty much an impossible case."

"I know all about it."

"How? You were just a baby."

Lisa June Peterson told him about the research that Governor Artemus has asked her to do. She did not tell him the scheme that had been kicking around her head, keeping her up nights; her idea to do a book about Clinton Tyree, Florida's lost governor.

"Did your boss say what he wanted with my files?" The grin again. "No, I didn't think so."

"Tell me," said Lisa June.

"You poor thing."

"What is it?"

"Your Governor Dickie has an errand for me, darling, and not a pleasant one. If I don't oblige, he's going to throw my poor helpless brother out on the street, where he will surely succumb to confusion. So here I am."

Lisa June felt a stab of guilt. "Doyle?"

Clinton Tyree raised a furry eyebrow. "Yes. My brother Doyle. I suppose *that* was in your damn research, too."

"I'm so sorry." But she was thinking: Dick Artemus isn't capable of such a cold-blooded extortion.

The ex-governor speared the sliced pieces of fox on

the point of a whittled oak branch, balancing it over the flames. "The reason I came to see him—your boss—is to let him know the dire ramifications of a double cross. He needs to be aware of how seriously I regard the terms of this deal."

Lisa June Peterson said: "Isn't it possible you misunderstood?"

Clinton Tyree gazed down at her with a ragged weariness. Then he dug into a dusty backpack and brought out a brown envelope crookedly folded and dappled with stains. Lisa June opened it and read the typed letter that had been delivered to Clinton Tyree by his best friend, Lt. Jim Tile. It didn't matter that there was no signature at the bottom—Lisa June recognized the bloated phrasing, the comical misspellings, the plodding run-on sentences. The author of the threat could only be the Honorable Richard Artemus, governor of Florida.

"My God." Despondently she folded the letter. "I can hardly believe it."

Clinton Tyree snatched her under the arms, drawing her face close to his. "What *I* can't believe," he rumbled, "is that your boss had the piss-poor, shit-for-brains judgment to come fuck with *me*. Me of all people."

His crimson eye jittered up toward the stars, but the good eye was fixed steady and lucid with wrath. "Anything bad happens to my brother from all this nonsense, someone's going to die a slow, wretched death involving multiple orifices. You get the picture, don't you?"

Lisa June Peterson nodded. The ex-governor eased her to the ground. "Try some fox leg," he said.

"No, thanks."

"I advise you to eat."

"Maybe just a bite."

"People speak of me as Skink. You call me captain."

"OK," said Lisa June.

"Any reason you need to be home tonight?"

"No. Not really."

"Dandy," said Clinton Tyree, stoking the campfire. "That'll give us time to get to know each other."

The flight from Fort Lauderdale to Gainesville took ninety minutes, plenty of time for Palmer Stoat to reflect on a productive half day of work. With a two-minute phone call he'd made forty grand. The woman on the other end was the chairperson of the Miami-Dade County Commission, who had obligingly moved to the bottom of the night's agenda an item of large importance to Palmer Stoat. It was a motion to award the exclusive fried-banana concession at Miami International Airport to a person named Lester "Large Louie" Buccione, who for the purpose of subverting minority set-aside requirements was now representing himself as Lestorino Luis Banderas, Hispanic-American.

To avoid the unappetizing prospect of competitive bidding, Lester/Lestorino had procured the lobbying services of Palmer Stoat, whose sway with Miami-Dade commissioners was well known. Once he had identified the necessary loophole and lined up the requisite voting majority, all that remained for Stoat was to make sure the fried-banana contract was placed far down on the agenda, so that the "debate" would be held no sooner than midnight. The strategy was to minimize public input by minimizing public attendance. A sparse crowd meant sparse opposition, reducing the likelihood that some skittish commissioner might get cold feet and screw up the whole thing.

It was a cardinal rule of political deal fixing: The later the vote, the better. So stultifying was the average government meeting that not even the hardiest of civic gadflies could endure from gavel to gavel. Generally, the only souls who remained to the wee hours were being paid to sit there—lawyers, lobbyists, stenographers and a few drowsy reporters. And since the shadiest deals were saved for the end, when the chamber was emptiest, competition was fierce for space at the tail of the agenda.

Lester Buccione had been elated to learn that the fried-banana contract would be taken up last, in tomb-like tranquillity, and that for this favor the chairperson of the Miami-Dade Commission had demanded only that one of her deadbeat cousins be hired as a part-time cashier at one of Lester's new fried-banana kiosks. So pleased was "Lestorino" that he had promptly messengered to Palmer Stoat's home a cashier's check for the $40,000 fee, which divinely had mended Stoat's tattered confidence—five-digit reassurance that the planet had not skittered off its axis, that the rightful order of the urban food chain had not been perverted, despite the harrowing madness that had ruptured Stoat's personal universe.

He had been fingering the check from Lester Buccione, savoring its crisp affirmation, when out of the blue his missing wife had telephoned and asked him to charter another plane to Gainesville. Right away! And Palmer Stoat had thought: Thank God she's finally come to her senses. He would fly up to get her and then they would go away for a while, somewhere secluded and safe from the demented dog dismemberer, the lascivious bald cyclops, the sadistic Blond Porcupine Man, the doll-stroking Clapley. . . .

The plane landed at half-past two. Stoat searched for Desie inside the terminal but she wasn't there. One of his cell phones rang—Stoat carried three—and he snatched it from a pocket. Durgess was on the line: No luck so far with the rhino, but good news about Robert Clapley's cheetah! They'd found one in Hamburg, of all places, at a children's zoo. The cat would arrive within days at the Wilderness Veldt Plantation, where it would be caged, washed and fattened up in advance of the big hunt. Anytime you're ready! said Durgess, more perky than Stoat had ever heard him. I'll inform Mr. Clapley, Stoat said, and get back to you.

He walked to the airport parking lot and squinted into the sunlight, not knowing exactly what to look for. A horn honked twice. Stoat turned and saw a white Buick station wagon approaching slowly. A man was driving; no sign of Desie. The car stopped beside Palmer Stoat and the passenger door swung open. Stoat got in. In the backseat lay Boodle, an orange-and-blue sponge football pinned beneath his two front paws. His tail thwapped playfully when he saw Stoat, but he clung to the toy. Stoat reached back and stroked the dog's head.

"That's the best you can do?" the driver said.

"He stinks," said Stoat.

"Damn right he stinks. He spent the morning running cows. Now give him a hug."

Not in a two-thousand-dollar suit I won't, thought Stoat. "You're the one from Swain's," he said to the driver. "Where the hell's my wife?"

The station wagon started moving.

"You hear me?"

"Patience," said the driver, who looked about twenty years old. He wore a dark blue sweatshirt and loose faded jeans and sunglasses. He had shaggy bleached-out hair, and his skin was as brown as a surfer's. He drove barefoot.

Palmer Stoat said, "You tried to scare me into thinking you cut up my dog. What kind of sick bastard would do that?"

"The determined kind."

"Where'd you get the ear and the paw?"

"Not important," the young man said.

"Where's Desie?"

"Whew, that cologne you're wearing. . . ."

"WHERE IS MY WIFE?"

The Roadmaster was heading north, toward Starke, at seventy-five miles an hour. Stoat angrily clenched his hands; moist, soft fists that looked about as menacing as biscuits.

"Where the hell are you taking me? What's your name?" Stoat was emboldened by the fact that the dog-napper appeared to be unarmed. "You're going to jail, you know that, junior? And the longer you keep my wife and dog, the longer your sorry ass is gonna be locked up."

The driver said: "That blonde you sometimes travel with, the one with the Gucci bag—does Desie know about her?"

"What!" Stoat, straining to sound indignant but thinking: How in the world does he know about Roberta?

"The one I saw you with at the Lauderdale airport, the one who tickled your tonsils with her tongue."

Stoat wilted. He felt a thousand years old. "All right. You made your damn point."

"You hungry?" the driver asked.

He turned into a McDonald's and ordered chocolate shakes, fries and double cheeseburgers. As he pulled back on the highway, he handed the bag to Palmer Stoat and said, "Help yourself."

The food smelled glorious. Stoat came to life, and he quickly went to work on the cheeseburgers. Boodle dropped the foam football and sat up to mooch handouts. The driver warned Stoat not to feed the dog anything from the McDonald's bag.

"Doctor's orders," the young man said.

"It's all your fault he got sick in the first place." Stoat spoke through bulging, blue-veined, burger-filled cheeks. "You're the one who yanked all the glass eyeballs out of my trophy heads. That's what he ate, the big dope—those taxidermy eyes."

"From the trophy heads. Yes, I know."

"And did Desie tell you what his surgery cost?"

The driver fiddled with the knobs on the stereo system. Stoat recognized the music; a rock song he'd heard a few times on the radio.

"I tell you what," the young man said, "these speakers aren't half-bad."

"Why'd you steal my dog?" Stoat swiped at his lips with a paper napkin. "Let's hear it. This ought to be good." He finished engulfing one double cheeseburger, then wadded the greasy wax wrapper.

The young man's eyebrows arched, but he didn't look away from the highway. He said to Stoat: "Don't tell me you haven't figured it out."

"Figured *what* out?"

"How I chose you. How all this rough stuff got started—you honestly don't know?"

"All I know," Stoat said with a snort, "is that you're some kinda goddamn psycho and I did what you wanted and now I'm here to collect my wife and my dog." He fumbled on the door panel for the window switch.

"Oh brother," said the driver.

Stoat looked annoyed. "What now?"

The driver groaned. "I don't believe this."

"Believe what?" said Palmer Stoat, clueless. Casually he tossed the balled-up cheeseburger wrapper out of the speeding car.

"Believe what?" he asked again, a split second before his brainpain detonated and the world went black as pitch.

NINETEEN

In Twilly Spree's next dream he was down in the Everglades and it was raining hawks. He was running again, running the shoreline of Cape Sable, and the birds were falling everywhere, shot from the sky. In the dream Desie was running barefoot beside him. They were snatching up the bloodied hawks from the sugar-white sand, hoping to find one still alive; one they could save. McGuinn was in Twilly's dream, too, being chased in circles by a scrawny three-legged bobcat—it might have been hilarious, except for all the birds hitting the beach like russet feather bombs. In the dream Twilly saw a speck on the horizon, and as he drew closer the speck became the figure of a man on the crest of a dune; a man with a long gun pointed at the sky. Heedlessly Twilly ran on, shouting for the hawk killer to stop. The man lowered his weapon and spun around to see who was coming. He went rigid and raised the barrel again, this time taking aim at Twilly. In the dream Twilly lowered his shoulders and ran as fast as he could toward the hawk killer. He was astonished when he heard Desie coming up the dune behind him, running even faster. Twilly saw the muzzle flash at the instant Desie's hand touched his shoulder.

Except it wasn't Desie's hand, it was his mother's.

Amy Spree gently shook her son awake, saying, "My Lord, Twilly, were you dreaming? When did *this* start?"

Twilly sat up, chilled with sweat. "About a week ago."

"And what do you dream about?"

"Running on beaches."

"After all these years! How wonderful."

"And dead birds," Twilly said.

"Oh my. You want a drink?"

"No thanks, Mom."

"Your friend is relaxing out on the deck," said Amy Spree.

"I'm coming."

"The man with the pillowcase over his head?"

"Yes, Mom."

"She says it's her husband."

"Correct."

"Oh, Twilly. What next?"

Amy Spree was a stunning woman of fifty-five. She had flawless white skin and shy sea-green eyes and elegant silver-streaked hair. Twilly found it ironic that in divorcehood his mother had chosen Flagler Beach, given both her aversion to tropical sunlight and her previous attachment to a philandering swine who hawked oceanfront property for a living. But Amy Spree said she was soothed by the Atlantic sunrises (which were too brief to inflict facial wrinkles), and harbored no lingering bitterness toward Little Phil (whom she dismissed as "confused and insecure"). Furthermore, Amy Spree said, the shore was a perfect place to practice her dance and clarinet and yoga, all of which required solitude.

Which her son interrupted once a year, on her birthday.

"I never know what to get you," Twilly said.

"Nonsense," his mother clucked. "I got the best present in the world when you knocked on the door."

They were in the kitchen. Amy Spree was preparing a pitcher of unsweetened iced tea for Twilly, his new lady friend and her husband, who was trussed to a white wicker rocking chair once favored by Twilly's father.

"How about a dog?" Twilly asked his mother. "Wouldn't you like a dog?"

"*That* dog?" Amy Spree eyed McGuinn, who had hungrily positioned himself at the refrigerator door. "I don't think so," said Amy Spree. "I'm happy with my bonsai trees. But thank you just the same."

She put on a straw hat as broad as a garbage-can lid. Then she carried a glass of tea outside to Desirata Stoat, on the deck overlooking the ocean. Twilly came out later, dragging Palmer Stoat in the rocking chair. Twilly placed him on the deck, next to Desie. Twilly sat down on a cedar bench with his mother.

Amy Spree said, "I am not by nature a nosy person."

"It's all right," said Desie, "you deserve to know." She looked questioningly at Twilly, as if to say: Where do we start?

He shrugged. "Mrs. Stoat's husband is a congenital litterbug, mother. An irredeemable slob and defiler. I can't seem to teach him any manners."

Desie cut in: "There's an island over on the Gulf Coast. My husband's clients intend to bulldoze it into a golf retirement resort. A pretty little island."

Twilly's mother nodded. "I was married to such a

man," she said with a frown. "I was young. I went along."

An unhappy noise came from Palmer Stoat. The pillowcase puckered in and out at his mouth. Desie put one foot on the chair and began to rock him slowly.

"What's the matter?" she asked her husband. "You getting thirsty?"

Twilly said, "His gourd hurts. I whacked him pretty hard."

"For tossing garbage out of the car," Desie explained to Twilly's mother.

"Oh dear," said Amy Spree. "He's always had trouble controlling his anger. Ever since he was a boy."

"He's still a boy," Desie said fondly.

Amy Spree smiled.

"That's enough of *that*," said Twilly. He jerked the pillowcase from Palmer Stoat's head and peeled the hurricane tape off his mouth. "Say hello to my mom," Twilly told him.

"Hello," Stoat mumbled, squinting into the sunlight.

"How are you?" said Amy Spree.

"Shitty." Stoat's cheeks were flushed and his lips were gnawed. His left temple featured a knot the size of a plum.

"Mr. Stoat," said Twilly, "please tell my mother about the bridge."

Palmer Stoat blinked slowly, like a bullfrog waking out of hibernation. Desie continued to rock him with her foot.

"Tell her how you lied to me about the bridge," Twilly said, "lied about the governor killing the bridge so the island would be saved. Mother, Mr. Stoat is a close personal friend of Governor Richard Artemus."

"Really?" said Amy Spree.

Stoat worked up a glower for Twilly. "You don't know what you're talking about."

Twilly raised his hands in disgust. "You said the bridge was dead but, lo and behold, what do I encounter this very morning on Toad Island? A survey team, Mother. Measuring for—surprise, surprise!—a new bridge."

"Uh-oh," said Amy Spree.

"Without it, Mr. Stoat's clients can't build their fancy resort, because they can't get their cement trucks across the water."

"Yes, son, I understand."

McGuinn ambled onto the deck. He sniffed the knots at Palmer Stoat's wrists, then leisurely poked his nose in his master's groin.

"Boodle, no!" Stoat bucked in the rocking chair. "Stop, goddammit!"

Amy Spree turned her head, stifling a giggle. On the beach behind the deck were half a dozen young surfers, shirtless, with their boards under their arms. They were staring out morosely at the flat water. Amy Spree thought the scene would make a good picture, photography being her newest hobby. McGuinn trotted down the steps to make friends.

"So what now?" Twilly slapped his palms loudly against his thighs. "That's the question of the day, Desie. What do I do with this lying, littering shithead of a husband you've got?"

Desie looked at Twilly's mother, who looked at Palmer Stoat. Stoat cleared his throat and said: "Give me another chance."

"Are you talking to me," said Twilly, "or your wife?"

"Both."

"Palmer," Desie said, "I'm not sure I want to come home."

"Oh, for God's sake." Stoat huffed impatiently. "What is it you want, Desie?"

"Honestly I don't know."

"You want to be Bonnie Parker, is that it? Or maybe Patty Hearst? You want to end up a newspaper headline."

"I just want—"

"Fine. Then don't come home," said Palmer Stoat. "Don't even bother."

Amy Spree rose. "Son, I need some help downstairs in the garage."

"Relax, Mom," Twilly said. "It's all right."

Amy Spree sat down. Desie Stoat took her foot off the chair, and her husband rocked to a stop.

"Do whatever you want," he snarled at his wife. "Fuck you. Fuck that stupid Labrador retriever. To hell with the both of you."

Twilly's mother said: "There's no need for profanity."

"Lady, I'm tied to a goddamn chair!"

Desie said, "Oh please. It's not like you've been a model husband the last two years."

Stoat made a noise like a football going flat. "You'll be hearing from my lawyers, Desirata. Now: One of you fruitcakes better untie me." He twisted his neck to get a fix on Twilly Spree. "And with regard to the Toad Island bridge, junior, there's not a damn thing you or anyone else on God's green earth can do to stop it. You can have my wife and you can have my dog, but that new bridge is going up whether you like it or not. It's what we call a foregone conclusion, junior—no matter how many paws and ears and dog balls you send out. So take off these ropes this minute, before I start raising holy hell."

Never had Desie seen her husband so infuriated. His face was swollen up like an eggplant.

She said, "Palmer, why did you have to lie?"

Before Stoat could tee off on her again, Twilly slapped a fresh strip of hurricane tape across his lips. The pillowcase came down over wide hate-filled eyes.

Amy Spree said, "Son, don't be too rough with the man."

Twilly hauled the rocking chair indoors while Desie whistled for McGuinn. Later Amy Spree served dinner, broiled shrimp over rice under a homemade tomato-basil sauce. They brought Palmer Stoat to the table but he made clear, with a series of snide-sounding grunts, that he wasn't particularly hungry.

"There's plenty more," said Twilly's mother, "if you change your mind. And I apologize, kids, for not having wine."

"Mom gave up drinking," Twilly explained to Desie.

"But if I'd known you were coming, I would have picked up a bottle of nice Merlot," said Amy Spree.

"We're just fine. The food is fantastic," Desie said.

"What about your puppy?"

"He'll eat later, Mrs. Spree. There's a bag of chow in the car."

Dessert was a chocolate cheesecake. Twilly was cutting a second slice when his mother said, "Your father was asking about you."

"You still talk to him?"

"He calls now and again. Between flings."

"So how's waterfront moving out on the West Coast?" Twilly said.

"That's what I wanted to tell you. He quit the business!"

"I don't believe that. Quit, or retired?"

"Actually, they took away his real-estate license."

"In California?"

"He didn't go into all the gory details."

Twilly was incredulous. "Don't you have to disembowel somebody to lose your real-estate license in California?"

"Son, I couldn't believe it, either. Know what he's selling now? Digital home-entertainment systems. He mailed me a color brochure but I can't make sense of it."

Twilly said, "You know what gets me, Mom? He could've quit the business after Big Phil died. All that money—Dad didn't need to hawk one more lousy foot of beach. He could've moved to the Bahamas and gone fishing."

"No, he could not," said Amy Spree. "Because it's in his blood, Twilly. Selling oceanfront is in his blood."

"Please don't say that."

"Excuse me," Desie interjected, "but Palmer acts like he needs to use the little boy's room."

"Again?" Twilly rose irritably. "Jesus, his bladder's smaller than his conscience."

Later Amy Spree walked them downstairs, where her son hoisted the rocking chair (with Palmer Stoat, squirming against the ropes) into the station wagon.

She said, "Twilly, what're you going to do with him? For heaven's sake, think about this. You're twenty-six years old."

"You want to take his picture, Mother? He likes to get his picture made. Isn't that right, Palmer?"

From under the puckering pillowcase came a snort.

"Polaroids especially," said Twilly.

Desie blushed. From the rocker came a dejected moan.

Amy Spree said: "Twilly, please don't do something you'll come to regret." Then, turning to Desie: "You stay on his case, all right? He's got to buckle down and work on that anger."

Twilly slid behind the wheel, with Desie on the other side and McGuinn hunkered between them, drooling on the dashboard.

"I love you, son," said Amy Spree. "Here, I wrapped the rest of the cheesecake."

"I love you, too, Mom. Happy birthday."

"Thanks for remembering."

"And I'll bring back the rocking chair."

"No hurry."

"Might be next year," said Twilly, "maybe sooner."

"Whenever," said his mother. "I know you're busy."

Word of the governor's veto somehow reached Switzerland. Robert Clapley was floored when one of the bankers financing Shearwater Island called him up in the middle of the night. "Vot hippen to ze bridge?" All the way from Geneva at two-thirty in the morning—like he'd never heard of international time zones, the icy-blooded bastard.

Yet Clapley was wide-awake, skull abuzz, when the phone rang. All night long he'd been trying to contact Palmer Stoat, as the Barbies were on a bimbo rampage for more rhinoceros powder. Clapley had returned from Tampa and found them locked in the bathroom, a boom box blasting fusion dance music from behind the door. An hour later the two women emerged arm in arm, giggling. Katya's hair was tinted electric-pink to match her tube top, and from the sun-bronzed cleft between her breasts arose an ornate henna fer-de-lance, fangs bared and dripping venom. By contrast, Tish had dressed up as a man, complete with a costume mustache, in Clapley's favorite charcoal gray Armani.

He was struck helpless with horror. The women looked vulgar and deviant—anti-Barbies! They announced they were going to a strip club near the airport for amateur night. First prize: a thousand bucks.

"I'll give you two thousand," Clapley pleaded, "to stay home with me."

"You got horn?" Katya, with a cruel wink. "No? Then we go score some." And merrily they had breezed out the door.

On the telephone, the banker from Geneva was saying: "Ze bridge, Mr. Clapley, vot hippen?"

And over and over Robert Clapley tried to make the stubborn blockhead understand there was no cause for alarm. Honest. Trust me. The governor's a close personal friend. The veto was nothing but a sly deception. The new bridge is good to go. Shearwater Island is a done fucking deal.

"So relax, Rolf, for God's sake." Clapley was fuming. He'd answered the phone only because he thought it might be that fuckweasel Stoat, finally returning his calls, or possibly the Palm Beach County vice squad, with precious Katya and Tish in custody. . . .

"But ze newspaper said—"

"I told you, Rolf, it's just politics. Jerkwater Florida politics, that's all."

"Yes, but you see, Mr. Clapley, with a line of credit as large as vot ve extended to you—"

"Yeah, I know what you ex-shtended—"

"Von hundred ten million, U.S."

"I'm keenly aware of the amount, Rolf."

"News such as this vood naturally cause some concern. It is understandable, no? Given our exposure."

"Sure. So let me say it *one more time*. And feel free to pass this along to all your associates at the bank: There's nothing to worry about, OK? Now you say it."

From the other end: "Vot?"

"Your turn," said Robert Clapley. "Repeat after me: THERE IS NOTHING TO WORRY ABOUT. Come on, Rolf, let me hear you."

The problem was: Clapley was unaccustomed to dealing with bankers. He was used to dealing with dopers—criminals, to be sure, but far more flexible and pragmatic when something went wrong. The average drug smuggler lived in a world crawling with fuckoffs, deadbeats and screwups; not a day of his life unfolded exactly as planned. He transacted narcotics, guns and cash, routinely taking insane risks that young Rolf in Geneva could not possibly fathom. Exposure? thought Robert Clapley. This cheesebrain doesn't know the meaning of the word.

"Oh, Rolf?"

"Dere is nutting to vorry bout."

"Thattaboy," said Clapley.

He had resorted to Swiss bankers only because the Shearwater project had become too big for dope money —or at least Robert Clapley's kind of dope money. Oh,

Toad Island he'd bought up all by himself, no sweat. However, more serious dough was needed to clear the place and remake it into a world-class golf and leisure community. Clapley's only other project, a seventeen-story apartment tower off Brickell Avenue in Miami, had been financed entirely with marijuana and cocaine profits, which Clapley had washed and loaned to himself through a phony Dutch holding company. He would have loved to work the same scam with Shearwater Island but he didn't have $100-odd million in loose cash lying around, and the only people who did were people who didn't need Robert Clapley to invest it for them: seasoned Colombian money launderers who favored commercial real estate over residential.

So Clapley had gone looking for his first-ever legitimate partners and wound up with the Swiss bankers, who had been so impressed by the balance sheet on the Brickell Avenue tower that they'd offered him a generous line of credit for developing and marketing his scenic island getaway on Florida's Gulf Coast. Afterward, the bankers mostly had left Clapley alone—so much so that he'd been lulled into complacency.

Because, obviously, they'd been keeping a cold blue Aryan eye on his ass. How else would they have found out that Dick Artemus had vetoed the damn Shearwater bridge?

Still, Clapley sensed that young Rolf was uncomfortable in the role of edgy inquisitor, that he wanted very much to be stoic and unflappable in the Swiss banker tradition. . . .

"Surely this sort of minor snafu has come up before."

Rolf said, "Yah, shore. Snafus all ze time."

"So there's no cause to get all hot and bothered," said Clapley. "And Rolf?"

"Yah."

"Next time, don't call at such a wicked hour. I've got ladies here."

"Oh."

"That's ladies, plural," said Clapley, with a suggestive chuckle.

"Again, sir, my apologies. But ve can hope for no more surprises? That vood be good."

"Oh, that vood be vunderful," chided Robert Clapley, perceiving starch in the young banker's tone, and not liking it. "Now it's time to say goodbye. Somebody's knocking at the door."

"Ah. Perhaps one of your ladies plural."

"Good night, again, Rolf."

Clapley put on a silk robe that almost matched his pajamas. He hurried to the peephole and let out a burble of glee. Palmer Stoat!

Clapley snatched open the door. "You got my rhino dust!"

"No, Bob. Something better."

As Stoat walked past him, Clapley inhaled a foul wave of heat, halitosis and perspiration. The lobbyist looked awful; blotchy and damp-skinned, a nasty purple bruise shining on his head.

"It's about Toad Island," he said, trudging uninvited toward the kitchen. "Where are the future twins?"

"Mass," said Clapley.

"What for—to show off their kneeling?" Stoat was wheezing as if he'd walked all sixteen flights. "By the way, I lined up your cheetah hunt."

"Swell. But what I need right now, more than oxygen, is the horn off a dead rhinoceros."

Palmer Stoat waved a sticky-looking palm. "It's in the works, Bob. On my mother's grave. But that's not what I came here to tell you." He removed a carton of orange juice from the refrigerator and a bottle of Absolut from the liquor cabinet. He fixed himself an extremely tall screwdriver and told Robert Clapley all that had happened to him in the clutches of the maniac dognapper.

"Plus, now he's brainwashed my wife. So here's what I did, Bob. Here's your big news. I advised this fucker—whose name is Twilly, by the way—I told him to keep Desie, keep the damn dog and quit wasting our time. The bridge is going up, I told him. Toad Island's history. So fuck off!" Palmer Stoat smacked his liver-colored lips and smiled.

Clapley shrugged. "That's it?"

Stoat's piggy wet eyes narrowed. "Yes, Bob, and that's plenty. No more extortion. The guy's got nothing I care about. He can't stop us and he can't hurt us."

"You're only half-right," said Clapley, "as usual."

"No, Bob. He's pathetic."

"Really."

"He doesn't matter anymore." Palmer Stoat made this a pronouncement. "He's a gnat. He's a no-place man."

"That's 'nowhere man.'"

"What can he do to us now? What's he got left?" Stoat gave a sickly grin. "He shot his wad, Bob."

Robert Clapley was thinking how unwell Stoat looked. He was reminded of the day Stoat almost swallowed the baby rat.

"So what're you saying, Palmer?"

"Onward and upward is what I'm saying." Stoat tipped another shot of vodka into his drink. "From now on, it's full speed ahead. You build your bridge and dig those pretty golf courses—me, I'm getting a divorce and a new dog."

"You say this diseased cocksucker's name is Twilly."

"Forget about him, Bob. He's Desie's headache now."

Clapley frowned. "No, Palmer, I can't forget about him. He went to a lot of trouble to make his point with you. I expect he's not done screwing with Shearwater yet."

"For God's sake, what's he gonna do—throw himself in front of the bulldozers? Let him be," Stoat said. "It's over, Bob. Call off Mr. Gash and send him back to Liquid, or whatever-the-hell club you found him at."

"I'm afraid that's not possible."

Stoat gingerly pressed the chilled tumbler of vodka to the knot on his head. "Meaning you don't want to, right?"

"Meaning it's not possible, Palmer. Even if I *did* want to," Clapley said. "Mr. Gash isn't communicating with me at the moment. He gets these moods."

Palmer Stoat shut his eyes. Down one pallid cheek rolled a single clear droplet from the vodka glass. "Would he hurt Desie?"

"Under certain conditions, sure," Clapley said. "Hell, you met the man. He's a primitive. Take a hot shower, Palmer, you'll feel better. Later we'll go look for the twins."

*

All night he waited in vain for the Buick station wagon. He was parked in a grove of pines not far from Mrs. Stinson's bed-and-breakfast. Playing over and over in the tape deck was one of his most prized 911s—a private bootleg not for sale anywhere at any price, not even on the Internet. Mr. Gash had learned of the recording one afternoon while hanging in his custom iguana-skin sex harness from the rafters of his air-conditioned South Beach apartment. One of the three women in bed below him fortuitously turned out to be a police dispatcher trainee from Winnipeg, Canada, who had a friend who had a friend who worked fire rescue in Duluth, Minnesota, where the bizarre incident was rumored to have occurred.

For three hundred dollars Mr. Gash had procured the tape recording, raw and unedited. He set the conversation to Mozart's Offertory in D Minor, "Misericordias Domini."

CALLER: I've got an emergency!
DISPATCHER: Go ahead.
CALLER: My wife thinks I'm in Eau Claire!
DISPATCHER: Sir?
CALLER: But I'm eighteen thousand feet over Duluth and dropping like a fucking stone!
DISPATCHER: Sir, this is Duluth fire rescue. Please state your emergency.
CALLER: OK, here's my emergency. I'm on an airplane that's about to fucking crash. We lost an engine, maybe both engines—whoaaaaa, Jesus!—and we're coming down, and my wife thinks I'm in Eau Claire, Wisconsin.
DISPATCHER: You're on a plane?

CALLER: Yes! Yes! I'm calling from a cellular.

DISPATCHER: And you're in Duluth?

CALLER: No, but I'm getting closer every second. Oh God! Oh God, we're ro—ro—rolling!

DISPATCHER: Hold on, sir, hold on. . . .

CALLER: Please, you gotta call my wife. Tell her the company sent me upstate at the last minute. Tell her . . . I dunno, make something up, I don't give a shit . . . anything!

DISPATCHER: Sir, I'm . . . sir, did your pilot have a heart attack?

CALLER: No! I'd let you talk to him but he's kinda busy right now, trying to pull us outta this nosedive . . . whooaaaaa . . . Mother Mary . . . whooaaaaaaa!!!

DISPATCHER: What type of aircraft? Can you give me a flight number?

CALLER: I don't know. . . . Oh God, it's so dizzy, so dizzy, oh Jesus . . . I think I see, uh, cornfields. . . . My wife's name is Miriam, OK? Phone number is area . . . uh, area code—

DISPATCHER: Cornfields? Anything else? Can you see Duluth yet?

CALLER: Oooooeeeeeeeehhhhh. . . .

DISPATCHER: Sir, I need a location or I can't assign units.

CALLER: It's way too late for units, mister. . . . Whoaaaaaaa . . . you just . . . whoaaaaaa, Jesus, you just tell 'em to look for the giant smoking hole in the ground. That'll be us. . . . Oh fuck me, FUCK MEEEEEEEEEE! . . .

DISPATCHER: Sir, I have to put you on hold but don't hang up. Sir? You there?

Mr. Gash was tantalized by the call—the idea that a cheating husband aboard a crashing airplane would find the composure to dial 911 just to cover his doomed ass. What admirable futility! What charming desperation!

A dozen times he replayed the tape. Everything was on there, eighteen thousand feet of gut-heaving panic. Everything was there but the fatal impact and explosion.

Too late for units.

Man, thought Mr. Gash, was that poor bastard ever right.

Mr. Gash's Duluth connection had enclosed a newspaper clipping with the cassette. The flight was a twin-engine commuter out of St. Paul. It went down in a farm field; twenty-one dead, no survivors. Local authorities didn't release the name of the passenger who had placed the telephone call from the cabin; they said it would upset the relatives. The original 911 tape was turned over to the National Transportation Safety Board and sealed as evidence in the accident investigation. The version sent to Mr. Gash was a second-generation copy of high quality.

Suddenly he thought of something to make the recording even more dramatic: Redub it with a symphonic piece, one that ended with a crashlike crescendo of cymbals—a musical simulation of an aircraft breaking up as it smashes into the ground.

Sir? You there?

Boom, booooooom, KA-BOOOOOOOM!

"Oh, yeah," Mr. Gash murmured. He got out of the car to stretch. It was nearly daylight on Toad Island, and still there was no sign of the troublemaker, the woman, the black dog or the Buick Roadmaster.

Mr. Gash went down the street to the bed-and-breakfast. He ambled up the porch steps and knocked. Mrs. Stinson called him around to the kitchen, where she was making muffins. At the screen door she greeted him warily, studying his oily spiked hair with unmasked disapproval.

Mr. Gash said, "I'm looking for a guy with a black dog."

"Who're you?"

"He's driving a big station wagon. Might have a woman along."

"I said, who are you?"

"The guy owes me some money," said Mr. Gash. "He owes everybody money, so if I were you I'd be careful."

Mrs. Stinson offered a chilly smile through the screen. "Well, he paid me cash. In advance."

"I'll be damned."

"So get on outta here before I call the law. You two settle this some other time, 'cause I don't allow no trouble."

Mr. Gash put one hand against the door. He made it appear casual, as if he was only leaning. "Is he here now? That dog is dangerous, by the way. Killed some little girl down in Clewiston. Ripped her throat out. That's another reason this guy's on the run. Was he here last night?"

"I don't know where they went, mister. All I know is, the room's paid for and I'm doing my muffins, because breakfast is part of the package." Mrs. Stinson took a step back, positioning herself (Mr. Gash noticed) within reach of a wall phone.

"As for that dog of his," she said, "he's about as scary as a goldfish, and not much smarter. So you get on outta here. I mean it."

"You don't know this guy, ma'am. He's bad news."

"I don't know *you*," Mrs. Stinson barked. "Now go! You and your fairy hairdo."

Mr. Gash was about to punch through the screen when he heard a car turn the corner. He spun around, his heartbeat quickening because he thought it was the young troublemaker, returning in the Buick woody.

It wasn't. It was a black-and-tan Highway Patrol cruiser.

"How about that!" said Mrs. Stinson.

Mr. Gash edged away from her door. He watched the state police car go by the house, a black uniformed trooper at the wheel. In the backseat cage of the car was the form of a man, a prisoner slumped sideways against a door as if he had passed out. Mr. Gash wasn't sure, but it seemed like the trooper slowed down a little when he passed the bed-and-breakfast.

From behind him, Mr. Gash heard Mrs. Stinson chortle: "Ha! You still wanna chat, smart-mouth?"

As soon as the police cruiser was out of sight, Mr. Gash stepped off the porch and began to walk. He had a story ready, just in case: The car wouldn't start. He went to the bed-and-breakfast to use the phone. Next thing he knows, the old hag starts raving at him like some nut. . . .

On the road Mr. Gash saw no sign of the Highway Patrolman. He got to his car and kept walking; circled the block at an easygoing pace and returned. Better safe than sorry, he thought. It was probably nothing at all. Probably just some DUI that the state trooper was carting off to jail. That's about all they were good for, Mr. Gash mused, busting drunks.

He pulled off his houndstooth jacket and laid it on

the front seat. Then he stepped behind a pine tree to take a leak. He was zipping up when he heard movement—something on the edge of the trees, near the car. Mr. Gash took out his gun and peered around the trunk of the pine. He saw a bum crouched by the side of the road.

Mr. Gash stole out from behind the tree. The bum had his back to him; a big sonofabitch, too. When he stood up, he was nearly a foot taller than Mr. Gash. He appeared to be wearing a white-and-black checkered skirt over bare legs and hiking boots.

With confidence Mr. Gash returned the gun to his shoulder holster. He smiled to himself, thinking: This dolly would be a hit on Ocean Drive.

When the bum turned around, Mr. Gash reconsidered his assessment.

"Take it easy, pops." Hoping the man took notice of the gun under his arm.

The bum said nothing. He wore a cheap shower cap on his head, and he had a jittery red eyeball that looked like a party gag. A silvery beard hung off his cheeks in two ropy braids, each decorated with a hooked beak. In one of his huge hands the bum held by its tail an opossum, its jaw slack and its fur crusty with blood. In the other hand was a paperback book.

Mr. Gash said, "Where'd you come from?"

The man smiled broadly, startling Mr. Gash. He had never seen a bum with such perfect teeth, much whiter than his own.

"Nice dress," said Mr. Gash, testing the guy.

"Actually it's a kilt. Made it myself."

"You got a name?"

"Not today," said the bum.

"I hope you weren't planning to steal my car."

The bum grinned again. He shook his head no, in a manner suggesting that Mr. Gash's car wasn't worth stealing.

Mr. Gash pointed at the opossum and said, "Your little pal got a name?"

"Yeah: Lunch. He got hit by a dirt bike."

Mr. Gash thought the bum seemed oddly at ease, being interrogated by a stranger with a handgun.

"You didn't answer my question, pops. Where'd you come from?"

The bum held up the book. "You should read this."

"What is it?" Mr. Gash said.

"*The Comedians*. By Graham Greene."

"Never heard of him."

"He would have enjoyed meeting you."

"The hell's *that* supposed to mean?" Mr. Gash took two steps toward the car. He was creeped out by the guy's attitude, the nonchalant way he handled the dead opossum.

The bum said, "I'll loan you my copy."

Mr. Gash got in his car and started the engine. The bum came closer.

"Stop right there, pops," said Mr. Gash, whipping out the semi-automatic. The guy stopped. His weird red iris was aimed up toward the treetops, while his normal eye regarded Mr. Gash with a blank and unnerving indifference.

Mr. Gash waggled the gun barrel and said, "You never saw me, understand?"

"Sure."

"Or the car."

"Fine."

"The fuck are you staring at?"

There it was again—that toothpaste-commercial smile.

"Nice hair," the bum said to Mr. Gash.

"I ought to kill you, pops. Just for that I ought to shoot your sorry homeless ass. . . ."

But the bum in the homemade checkered skirt turned away. Toting his paperback book and his roadkill opossum, he slowly made his way into the pines, as if Mr. Gash wasn't there; wasn't pointing a loaded gun at his back, threatening to blow him away on the count of six.

Mr. Gash sped off, burning rubber. What a mother-freaking nutcase! he thought. I hate this place and I hate this job.

A whole goddamn island full of troublemakers!

Mr. Gash turned on the tape and punched the REWIND button.

Very soon, he reminded himself. Then I get to go home.

TWENTY

The first few times Twilly and Desie made love, McGuinn paid no attention; just curled up on the floor and snoozed. Then one night—the night they freed Palmer—the dog suddenly displayed a rambunctious interest in what was happening up on the mattress. Desie was on the verge of what promised to be a memorable moment when the bed frame heaved violently, and Twilly let out a groan that was notably devoid of rapture. All movement ceased, and the springs fell dolefully silent. Desie felt hot liver-biscuit breath on her cheeks and a crushing weight upon her chest. By the quavering glow of the motel-room television, she saw that the Labrador had leapt upon Twilly's bare back and planted himself there, all 128 pounds. That alone would have distracted Twilly (who was nothing if not focused while in Desie's embrace), but the dog had made himself impossible to ignore by clamping his jaws to the base of Twilly's neck, as if snatching an unsuspecting jackrabbit.

"Bad boy," Twilly scolded through clenched teeth.

McGuinn was not biting hard, and he didn't seem angry or even agitated. He was, however, intent.

"Bad dog," Twilly tried again.

Desie whispered, "I think he's feeling left out."

"What do you suggest?"

"Are you hurt?"

"Only my concentration," Twilly said.

Desie released the headboard and slipped her arms around Twilly's shoulders. She hooked her fingertips inside the Labrador's cheeks and tugged gently. McGuinn compliantly let go. Ears pricked in curiosity, the huge dog stared down at Desie. She could hear his tail thwumping cheerfully against Twilly's thighs.

"Good boy," Twilly said, the words muffled by Desie's right breast. "Wanna go for a w-a-l-k?"

McGuinn scrambled off the bed and bounded to the door. Desie used a corner of the top sheet to sop the dog slobber from Twilly's neck, which also featured a detailed imprint of canine dentition.

"No bleeding," Desie reported.

"How about hickeys?"

"Maybe he was having a bad dream."

"Or a really good one."

They tried again later, after McGuinn's walk. They waited until they heard him snoring on the carpet near the television. This time it was Twilly whose promising climax got thwarted—the dog flew in out of nowhere, knocking the wind out of Twilly, and knocking Twilly out of Desie.

"Bad boy," Twilly rasped. He was highly annoyed. "You're a bad, bad boy. A rotten, miserable, worthless boy."

"He's biting your neck again!"

"He certainly is."

"Maybe I'm making too much noise when we do it," Desie said. "Maybe he thinks you're hurting me."

"No excuses. He's not a puppy anymore."

But the more strenuously Desie tried to prize open

the dog's jaws, the more intractable his grip became. To McGuinn it was a new game, and Labradors loved to play games.

"Well, I intend to get some rest," Twilly said. "If the dumb bastard doesn't let go of me by morning, I'm killing him."

And to sleep Twilly went, a jumbo-sized Labrador retriever attached to his neck. Soon the dog was sleeping, too, as placidly as if he'd dozed off with his favorite rubber ball in his mouth. Desie lay rigid in the bed, listening to both of them enjoy a deep, restful slumber. She thought: So this is my status at age thirty-two and a half—alone with a kinky dog and my kidnapper-lover in a twenty-nine-dollar motel room in Fort Pierce, Florida. What interesting choices I've made! Roll the highlights, please, starting with untrustworthy Gorbak Didovlic, the not-so-gifted NBA rookie; brilliant Andrew Beck, the self-perforating producer of deceptive political commercials; slick-talking Palmer Stoat, the tiresomely devious husband whom we dumped only two hours earlier at a Cracker Barrel restaurant off Interstate 95.

And finally young Twilly Spree, who would probably love me faithfully and forever in his own charming adolescent way, but who has no ambition beyond wreaking havoc, and no imaginable future that doesn't include felony prison time. The man of my dreams!

Fun? Big fun. Major adrenaline rush. Mysteriously wealthy, and other surprises galore. Then what? Desie wondered. Then he'll be gone, of course.

Well, there was still Palmer. Deceitful asshole though he was, Desie nonetheless had felt a twinge of pity at the sight of him tied up and hooded in the rocking chair.

And the expression on his pie-shaped face when Twilly removed the sweat-stained pillowcase and cut the ropes—a look of malignant contempt, manufactured for Desie's benefit. See how serious I am!

But he'd take her back in a heartbeat, her husband would. Palmer required a sharp-looking wife, one who would put up with his conveniently ambiguous travel plans and his unsportsmanlike hunting trips and all that Polaroid weirdness in the bedroom. Palmer knew he had a good thing in Desie, and he also knew what divorces cost. So, sure, he'd take her back.

That would be the easiest road for Desie, too, but she couldn't take it. She would not be able to look at her husband without thinking of tiny orange-striped toads, bulldozed into goop.

Her folks in Atlanta—they'd be glad to have her home for a while. Mom was busy with her medical practice, but Dad would be retiring soon from Delta. Maybe I could start back at GSU, Desie thought, finish up on my teaching degree.

Yeah, right. And afterward I'll move to Appalachia and live in a tin shanty and do volunteer work with the learning disabled. Who the hell am I kidding?

Twilly stirred when Desie stroked his brow.

"You awake?"

"Am now," he said.

"Dreaming?"

"I dunno. Is there a giant black dog on my back?"

"I'm afraid so."

"Then I wasn't dreaming," Twilly said.

"I've been lying here wondering . . . what happens now?"

"The itinerary, you mean."

"The agenda," she said.

"Well, first, I intend to seriously fuck things up so Shearwater never gets built."

Desie cupped his chin in her hands. "You can't stop it."

"I can try."

"They'll fix it so you can't. Palmer and the governor. I'm sorry but that's a fact," said Desie. "If they say the bridge is a done deal, it's done."

"Just watch."

"There's nothing you can do, Twilly, short of killing somebody."

"I agree."

"My God."

"What?"

"Don't even joke about that," Desie said. "Nothing like this is worth taking a human life."

"No? What's the life of an island worth? I'd be curious to know." Twilly reached behind his head and flicked McGuinn smartly on the tip of the nose. The dog awoke with a startled yelp, releasing his hold on Twilly's neck. He jumped to the floor and began to paw, optimistically, at the doorjamb.

Twilly rose on one arm to face Desie. "Ever been to Marco Island? You can't imagine how they mauled that place."

"I know, honey, but—"

"If you'd seen it when you were a kid and then now, you'd say it was a crime. You'd say somebody ought to have their nuts shot off for what they did. And you'd be right."

Desie said, "If you're trying to scare me off, you're doing a fine job."

"You asked me a question."

Desie pulled him into her arms. "I'm sorry. We can talk about this in the morning."

As if it could end differently.

"The whole damn island," she heard him murmur. "I can't let that happen again."

Dick Artemus offered Lisa June Peterson a drink. He was on his third. She said no thanks.

"Still drivin' that Taurus?" he asked her.

"Yes, sir."

"You break my heart, Lisa June. I can put you in a brand-new Camry coupe, at cost."

"I'm fine, Governor. Thanks, just the same."

The phone on his desk rang and rang. Dick Artemus made no move to pick it up. "Is Dorothy gone home already? Jesus Christ."

"It's six-thirty. She's got kids," Lisa June Peterson said. She reached across the desk and punched a button on the telephone console. Instantly the ringer went mute.

The governor savored his bourbon. He winked and said: "Whaddya got for me?"

Lisa June thought: Great, he's half-trashed. "Two things. About this special session—before we send out the press release, you should know that Willie Vasquez-Washington is pitching a conniption. He says he doesn't want to fly back to Tallahassee next week, doesn't want his vacation interrupted. He says he's going to make himself a royal pain in the ass if you drag the House and Senate back into session—"

"Those his words?" Dick Artemus grimaced. "'Royal pain in the ass.' But you told him this was for schools, right? For the education budget."

Lisa June Peterson patiently explained to the bleary governor that Willie Vasquez-Washington was no fool; that he'd quickly figured out the true purpose for the special legislative session, namely to revive the Toad Island bridge project on behalf of the governor's buddies—

"Hell, they aren't my buddies!" Dick Artemus spluttered. "They aren't my pals, they aren't my partners. They're just some solid business folks who contributed to the campaign. Goddamn that Willie, he ain't no saint himself. . . ."

Lisa June Peterson informed her boss that Willie Vasquez-Washington didn't know (or care) why the governor had vetoed the bridge appropriation in the first place, but he promised to make the governor suffer dearly for screwing up his travel plans.

"He's going skiing in Banff," Lisa June reported. "Taking the whole family."

Dick Artemus sniffed. "Who's payin' for *that*?"

"I can find out."

"Naw. Hell." The governor puffed his cheeks in disgust. "Y'know, I never had to deal with shit like this in Toyota Land. What else, Lisa June? Let's have it."

"Clinton Tyree came to see you the other night, when you were in Orlando."

Dick Artemus straightened in the chair. "Damn. What'd he want? What'd he say?"

"He said he'll do what you asked him to—"

"Fannnnn-tastic!"

"—but he'll come back to Tallahassee and murder you if anything happens to his brother Doyle. Murder you slowly, he asked me to emphasize."

"Oh, for God's sake." The governor forced out a chuckle.

Lisa June said, "He mentioned the following items: a pitchfork, handcuffs, a fifty-five-gallon drum of lye and a coral snake."

"He's a nut," the governor said.

"He's also serious."

"Well, don't worry, 'cause nuthin's gonna happen to brother Doyle. For God's sake." Dick Artemus groped distractedly for the bourbon bottle. "Poor Lisa June, you're probably wonderin' what the hell you got yourself into with this crazy job. You can't figger out what the heck's goin' on."

Lisa June Peterson said, "I know what's going on. He showed me the letter you wrote."

"What letter!" Dick Artemus protested. Then, sheepishly: "OK, scratch that. Yeah, I wrote it. See, sometimes. . . ."

He gazed with a drowsy bemusement into his glass.

Lisa June said, "Sometimes what?"

"Sometimes in this world you gotta do things that aren't so nice."

"For the sake of a golf course."

"Don't get me started, darling. It's a lot more complicated than that." The governor raised his face to offer a paternal smile. "There's a natural order to consider. A certain way things work. You know that, Lisa June. That's how it's always been. You can't change it and I can't change it and some crazy old homicidal hermit—

Skink, isn't that what he calls himself?—well, he damn sure can't change it, neither."

Lisa June Peterson stood up, smoothing her skirt. "Thanks for the pep talk, Governor."

"Aw, don't get sulky on me. Sit down, now. Tell me what he looked like. Tell me what happened, I'm dyin' to hear."

But even if Dick Artemus had been sober, Lisa June couldn't have brought herself to share what had happened at the campfire—that the ex-governor had kept her up all night with a fevered monologue; that he had told her true stories of old Florida, that he had ranted and incanted and bellowed at the stars, stomping back and forth, weeping from one eye while the other smoldered as red as a coal; that he had painted teardrops on his bare scalp with fox blood; that he had torn his queer checkered kilt while scrambling up a tree, and that she'd put it back together with three safety pins that she'd found in a corner of her purse; that he'd kissed her, and she'd kissed him back.

Lisa June Peterson couldn't have brought herself to tell her boss that she'd left Clinton Tyree snoring naked and sweaty in the woods a mere ten miles from the capitol, or that she'd rushed home with the intention of putting it all down on paper—everything he'd said and done, and *said* he'd done—saving it for the book she planned to write. Because when she got home to her apartment, showered, fixed a cup of hot tea and sat down with a legal pad, she could not put down a word. Not one.

"Nothing much happened," Lisa June Peterson told the governor.

Dick Artemus rocked forward and planted his elbows on his desk. "Well, what does he look like? He's a big fucker, according to the files."

"He's big," Lisa June confirmed.

"Taller'n me?"

"He looks old," Lisa June said.

"He *is* old. What else?"

"And sad."

"But he's still freaky, I bet."

"I've seen freakier," said Lisa June.

"Aw, you're pissed at me. Don't be like this." Dick Artemus held out his arms imploringly. "I wasn't really gonna evict the man's brother from that lighthouse, Lisa June. You honestly think I'd do something as shitty as that?"

"The letter was enough."

"Oh, for God's sake." The governor grabbed his bourbon and leaned back, balancing the glass on his lap. "All I want him to do is find that crazy kid with the dog. That's all."

"Oh, he'll find him," Lisa June Peterson said. "Now, how do you want to deal with the Honorable Representative Vasquez-Washington?"

"That fucking Willie." Dick Artemus hacked out a bitter laugh. "You know what to do, Lisa June. Call Palmer Stoat. Get him to make things right."

"Yes, sir."

"Hey. What happened to your knee?" The governor, craning his neck for a better angle.

"Just a scrape," said Lisa June thinking: I knew I should've worn hose today, Dick Artemus being an incorrigible ogler of legs.

"Ooooch," he said. "How'd that happen?"

"Climbing a tree," said Lisa June Peterson.

"This I gotta hear."

"No, you don't."

The name of the strip club was Pube's.

Upon bribing the bouncer, Robert Clapley was dismayed to be informed that the Barbies had easily won first place in the amateur contest, snatched up the thousand-dollar cash prize and departed the premises with an individual named Avalon Brown, who claimed to be an independent film producer from Jamaica.

"I feel sick," Clapley said to Palmer Stoat.

"Don't. It's the best thing that could happen to you," Stoat said, "getting rid of those two junkie sluts."

"Knock it off, Palmer. I need those girls."

"Yeah, like you need rectal polyps."

Stoat was in a sour and restless mood. All around him were frisky nude women, dancing on tabletops, yet he couldn't stop thinking about Desie and the Polaroid.

But those nights were over, as was his marriage.

"Let's go," Clapley said. "Maybe they went back to the apartment."

Palmer Stoat raised a hand. "Hang on." The stage announcer was introducing the entrants for the final event, a Pamela Anderson Lee look-alike contest.

"Whoa, momma!" Stoat piped.

"If I had a grapefruit knife," said Robert Clapley, "I'd gouge out my eyeballs."

"Bob, are you kidding? They're gorgeous."

"They're grotesque. Cheap trash."

"As opposed to your classy twins," Stoat said archly, "Princess Grace and Princess Di, who are presently double-fellating some Rastafarian pornographer in exchange for a whole half a gram of Bolivian talc."

Clapley seized Stoat by the collar. "Palmer, you're a goddamn pig."

"We're both pigs, Bob, so relax. Chill out. I'll get you a rhino horn and then you'll win your precious Barbies back." Stoat pulled free of Clapley's clutch. "Anyway, there's nothing you can do to me that hasn't already been done—starting with that fucking rodent your charming Mr. Gash gagged me with."

"That was after you tried to rip me off," Clapley reminded him, "double-billing me for the bridge fix. Or was it triple-billing?"

"So maybe I got a little greedy. But still. . . ."

Onstage, thirteen Pamela Anderson Lees were dancing, or at least bobbling, to the theme music from the *Baywatch* television series. Palmer Stoat sighed in glassy wonderment. "Man, we live in incredible times. Look at all that!"

"I'm outta here."

"Go ahead. I'll grab a taxi." Stoat's gaze was riveted to the pneumatic spectacle onstage. It was just what he needed to take his mind off Desie.

"Don't call me again until Governor Dickhead signs over the bridge money and you've got your hands on some rhinoceros dust. Those are the only two goddamn news bulletins I want from you. Understand?"

Stoat grunted a vague assent. "Bob, before you take off. . . ."

"What now, Palmer?"

"How about another Cuban?"

Robert Clapley slapped a cigar on the table. "Turd fondler," he said.

"Sweet dreams, Bob."

TWENTY-ONE

On a cool May night, an unmarked panel truck delivered a plywood crate to the Wilderness Veldt Plantation. The crate had been shipped directly to a private airstrip in Ocala, Florida, thereby avoiding port-of-entry inspections by the U.S. Customs Service, Fish and Wildlife and other agencies that would have claimed a jurisdictional interest.

At the Wilderness Veldt Plantation, the scuffed box was loaded onto a flatbed and transported to a low-slung, windowless barn known as Quarantine One. Less than an hour later, Durgess was summoned from home. He was met outside the facility by a man named Asa Lando, whose job title at the hunting ranch was Supervisor of Game.

"How bad?" Durgess asked.

Asa Lando spat in the dirt.

Durgess frowned. "All right, lemme take a look."

The barn was divided into eight gated stalls, fenced with heavy-gauge mesh from the ground to the beams. Each stall had an overhead fan, a heater and a galvanized steel trough for food and water. The Hamburg delivery was in stall number three.

Durgess said: "You gotta be kiddin'."

"I wish." Asa Lando knew he was in trouble. It was his responsibility to procure animals for the hunts.

"First off," Durgess began, "this ain't no cheetah."

"I know—"

"It's a ocelot or a margay. Hell, it can't weigh no more'n thirty-five pounds."

Asa Lando said, "No shit, Durge. I got eyes. I can see it ain't no cheetah. That's why I woke you outta bed."

"Second of all," said Durgess, "it's only got two goddamn legs."

"I can *count*, too." Asa sullenly poked the toe of his boot into the sawdust. "Could be worse."

Durgess glared. "How? If he came in a jar?"

"Look, this ain't the first time we run into this sorta situation," Asa reminded him. "We got plenty clients happy to shoot gimped-out game."

"Not this client," Durgess said. One time they'd gotten away with a three-legged wildebeest, but two legs was out of the question, especially for a big cat.

Morosely the men stared through the fencing. With plucky agility, the ocelot hopped over and began rubbing its butt against the links.

"I wonder what the hell happened to him," Durgess said.

"Doc Terrell says he was likely a-born that way— one front leg, one back leg. All things considered, he's got an awful decent disposition."

Durgess cheerlessly agreed. "Tell me again where you got him."

"Uncle Wilhelm's Petting Zoo," Asa said. "They got rid of him on account he was eatin' all their parrots.

Don't ask me how he caught the damn things, but I guess he taught hisself to jump like a motherfucker."

"And how much did we pay?" Durgess braced himself.

"Five grand, minus freight."

"Sweet Jesus."

"C.O.D."

"Asa, buddy, we got a serious problem." Durgess explained that one of their best customers, Palmer Stoat, was bringing a bigshot business associate to Wilderness Veldt to shoot a cheetah, a full-grown African cheetah.

"It's a big kill," Durgess said gravely. "Big money."

Asa eyed the wiry cat. "Maybe we can fatten him up 'tween now and then."

"Sure," Durgess said. "Staple on a couple fake legs while we're at it. Lord, Asa, sometimes I wonder 'bout you."

But the Supervisor of Game wasn't ready to admit failure. "Three hundred yards, Durge, one cat looks like another to these bozos. Remember Gummy the Lion?"

Durgess flicked his hand in disgust. Formerly known as Maximilian III, Gummy the Lion had been the star of a trained-animal act at a roadside casino outside Reno, Nevada. Old age and a lifelong affinity for chocolate-chip ice cream claimed first the big cat's canines and eventually all its teeth, so Max had been retired and sold to a wildlife wholesaler, who had in turn peddled the animal to the Wilderness Veldt Plantation. Even Asa Lando had been aghast when they'd uncrated it. Durgess had figured they were stuck with a new pet—who'd pay good money to shoot a senile, toothless lion?

A moron named Nick Teeble, it turned out. Eighteen

thousand dollars he'd paid. That was how badly the retired tobacco executive had wanted a lion skin for the stone fireplace in his Costa Rican vacation chalet. It had been Asa who had sized up Nick Teeble for the phony he was; Asa who had persuaded Durgess to use the enfeebled Gummy in the canned hunt. And Asa had been right: Nick Teeble was both oblivious and incompetent, an ideal combination for Wilderness Veldt. It had taken Nick Teeble seven shots to hit the lion, whose disinclination to run or even stir from its nap was attributable to a complete and irreversible deafness (brought about by twenty-one years of performing in front of a very loud, very bad casino brass combo).

Durgess said to Asa Lando: "That was different. Teeble was a chump."

"*All* our customers are chumps," Asa Lando pointed out. "They damn sure ain't hunters. They just want somethin' large and dead for the wall. Talk about chumps, you can start with your Mr. Stoat."

"The man he's bringing here has done real big-game trips. He won't go for no Gummy routine," Durgess asserted. "He ain't gonna buy it if we tell him he *shot* two legs off that cat."

Asa Lando said, unflaggingly: "Don't be so sure."

"Hey, the man wants a cheetah, which is the fastest land mammal in the whole entire world. This poor critter here"—Durgess gestured at the lopsided ocelot—"couldn't outrun my granny's wheelchair."

As if on cue, the cat hip-hopped itself in a clockwise motion, hoisted its tail and sprayed through the mesh of the cage, dappling both men's pants.

"Damn!" cried Asa Lando, jumping back from the stall.

Durgess turned and trudged out of the building.

Riding in silence, they crossed the old bridge in late afternoon. Twilly Spree headed for the beach instead of the bed-and-breakfast, even though they were hungry. He hoped a sunset would improve Desie's spirits.

But a front was pushing through, and the horizon disappeared behind rolling purple-tinged clouds. A grayness fell suddenly over the shore and a cool, wet-smelling breeze sprung off the Gulf. Twilly and Desie held hands loosely as they walked. McGuinn loped ahead to harass the terns and gulls.

"Rain's coming," Twilly said.

"It feels great." Desie took a long deep breath.

"At each end of this beach is where they want to put those condos," said Twilly, "like sixteen-story bookends. 'Luxury units starting in the low two hundreds!'" This was straight off a new billboard that Robert Clapley had erected on U.S. 19. Twilly had noticed it that morning while driving back to the island.

Desie said, "I've got a question. You don't have to answer if you don't want."

"OK."

"Two questions, actually. Have you ever killed a person?"

Twilly thought of Vecker Darby's house exploding in a chemical cloud with Vecker Darby, slow-footed toxic dumper, still inside.

"Have you?" Desie asked.

"Indirectly."

"What kind of answer is that?"

"A careful one," Twilly said.

"Would you do it again? Over toads? Honey, you *arrest* somebody for mushing toads. You don't murder them."

Twilly let her hand slip from his fingers. "Desie, it's not just the toads, and you know it."

"Then what—over condos? Two lousy high-rises? You act like they're paving the whole coast."

"And you're beginning to sound like your husband."

Desie stopped in her tracks, the tail of a wave washing over the tops of her feet. A gust of wind blew the hair away from her neck, her astonishingly lovely neck, and Twilly fought the impulse to kiss her there.

She said, "This is all my fault."

"What is?"

"I should never have told you about this island, about what they're planning to do."

"Why not? It's horrible what they're planning."

"Yes, but now you're talking about killing people, which is also wrong," said Desie, "not to mention a crime, and I don't particularly want to see you go to jail. Jail would not be good for this relationship, Twilly."

He said, "If it wasn't Shearwater, it'd be something else. If it wasn't this island, it would be another. That's what you need to understand."

"And if it wasn't me with you here on this beach, it would be someone else. Right?"

"Please don't." Twilly reached for her waist but she spun away, heading back (he assumed) toward the car.

"Desie!"

"Not now," she called over her shoulder.

From the other direction came an outburst of

barking. At first Twilly thought it was another big dog, because he'd never heard McGuinn make such a racket.

But it was him. Twilly could see the familiar black hulk far down the beach, alternately crouching and dashing circles around somebody on the sand. The behavior looked anything but playful.

Twilly broke into a run. A nasty dog-bite episode was the last thing he needed to deal with—the ambulance, the cops, the wailing victim. Just my luck, Twilly thought glumly. How can you possibly piss off a Labrador retriever? Short of hammering them with a baseball bat, they'd put up with just about anything. Yet someone had managed to piss off ultra-mellow McGuinn. Probably some idiot tourist, Twilly fumed, or his idiot kids.

He jogged faster, kicking up water whenever a wave slid across his path. The run reminded him of his two dreams, without all the dead birds and the panic. Ahead on the beach, McGuinn continued to carry on. Twilly now could see what was upsetting the dog—a stocky, sawed-off guy in a suit. The man was lunging with both arms at the Labrador, which kept darting out of reach.

What now? Twilly wondered.

As he drew closer, he shouted for the dog to come. But McGuinn was in manic mode and scarcely turned his head to acknowledge Twilly's voice. The stranger reacted, though. He stopped grabbing for the dog and arranged himself into a pose of calm and casual waitfulness.

Twilly prepared for trouble. He pulled up and walked the last twenty yards, to catch his breath and assess the situation. Immediately, McGuinn positioned himself between Twilly and the stranger, who clearly was no tourist. The man wore a rumpled houndstooth suit and ankle-high leather shoes with zippers. He had a blond dye job and a chopped haircut that belonged on somebody with pimples and a runny nose.

"Down!" Twilly said to McGuinn.

But the Lab kept snapping and snarling, his lush coat bristling like a boar's. Twilly was impressed. Like Desie, he believed animals possessed an innate sense of danger—and he believed McGuinn's intuition was correct about the out-of-place stranger.

"Obedience school," the man said. "Or try one of those electrified collars. That'll do the trick."

"He bite you?" Twilly's tone made it clear he was not stricken with concern for the stranger's health.

"Naw. We're just playing. What's his name?"

"You might be playing," Twilly said to the man, "but he's not."

McGuinn lowered himself on all fours. He rumbled a low growl and panted unblinkingly. His haunches remained bunched and taut, as if readying to launch at the stranger.

"What's his name?" the man asked again.

Twilly told him.

"Sounds Irish," the man remarked. His eyes cut back and forth between Twilly and the dog. "You Irish?" he said to Twilly.

"You'll have to do better than this."

The stranger acted innocent. "What do you mean? I'm just trying to be friendly."

Twilly said, "Cut the shit."

The weather was coming up on them fast. A cold raindrop hit the side of Twilly's neck. The man with the spiky hair took a fat one on the nose. He wiped it dry with the sleeve of his jacket.

"Rain'll ruin those shoes of yours," Twilly said, "in about two minutes flat."

"Let me worry about the footwear," the stranger said, but he glanced down anyway at his feet. Twilly knew he was thinking about how much the brown leather shoes had cost.

"McGuinn! Let's go." Twilly clapped his hands loudly.

The dog wouldn't move, wouldn't shift his stare from the man in the musty-smelling suit. The Labrador had retained little from his short-lived time as a hunting dog in training, but one thing that had stayed with him was an alertness to guns. A human with a gun carried himself in a distinctly different manner. The Palmer Stoat who clomped through the marsh with a 20-gauge propped on his shoulder practically was a separate species from the Palmer Stoat who each night clipped McGuinn to a leash and covertly led him next door to crap on the neighbor's garden. To Stoat and his human hunter friends, the transformation in themselves—bearing, gait, demeanor and voice—was so subtle they didn't notice, yet it was glaringly obvious to McGuinn. A visual sighting of the gun itself was superfluous; humans who carried them had an unmistakable presence. Even their perspiration smelled different—not worse, for in the ever-ripe world of dogs there was hardly such a thing as a bad odor. Just different ones.

For a moment the stranger acted as if he wanted to make friends. He reached a hand beneath his moldy-smelling coat and said, "Here, boy. I've got something you'll like. . . ."

McGuinn, cocking his head, licking his chops, never taking his hopeful brown eyes off the stranger's hand, which emerged from under the coat with . . .

The gun. Had to be.

Now, from behind, the Labrador heard the young man say:

"Stay, boy. Don't move!"

Never had McGuinn detected such urgency in a command. He decided, on a whim, to obey.

There was another gun-toting human on Toad Island: Krimmler, who had taken to carrying a loaded .357 after Robert Clapley's hired freak accosted him in the Winnebago.

The pistol added to Krimmler's nervousness, and he had plenty of time to be nervous. Construction on the Shearwater resort project remained suspended, and the lush new quiet on the island made Krimmler restless and edgy—it was the very sound of Nature, gradually reclaiming the ground plowed up by his beloved bulldozers. One morning he was appalled to find a green shoot sprouting in the old dirt tracks of a frontend loader. A baby tree! Krimmler thought, ripping it from the soil. A baby tree that would otherwise grow to be a tall chipmunk-harboring tree!

The tranquillity that had once merely annoyed Krimmler now turned him into a paranoid basket case. At night he slept with the .357 under his pillow, half-certain he accidentally would shoot off his own ear while groping for the gun in a moment of dire need. By day he tucked it in the front of his pants, half-certain he accidentally would shoot off his genitals if danger surfaced.

Krimmler did not, as it turned out, shoot off any of his own body parts. He went for the .357 exactly once, dislodging it from his waistband and knocking it all the way down his baggy right pants leg. It landed with a clunk on the flimsy floor of the construction trailer, where it was retrieved by the smiling bald-headed bum with the racing flag around his waist.

"You rascal," the bum said to Krimmler.

"Gimme that!" Krimmler exclaimed.

The bum tapped the bullets out of the cylinder, then handed the empty gun to the engineer.

"Good way to shoot off your pecker," the bum remarked.

"What do you want!"

"I'm looking for a young man, a woman and a dog. A black Labrador retriever."

Krimmler said, "What is this! Don't tell me you work for Mr. Clapley, too?"

The bald bum began twirling the long, grungy-looking braids of his beard. Some sort of shrunken-looking artifact was attached to each end.

He said, "The Lab might be missing an ear. Other parts, too."

"I'll tell you the same thing I told that other guy," Krimmler said. This bounty hunter was even bigger and worse-dressed than Mr. Gash. He also had a bad eye, which made him appear even more unstable.

"I don't know where your boy is," Krimmler said, "or his goddamned dog, either. If he's not camping at the beach, he's probably at the b-and-b. Or maybe he left the island. Tourists sometimes do, you know."

The bum said, "I don't work for Clapley."

"I knew it, you asshole!"

"I work for Governor Richard Artemus."

"Right," said Krimmler, "and I'm Tipper Gore."

"One question, sir."

"Go fuck yourself," Krimmler said, "but first go take a bath."

That's when the bum slapped Krimmler. He slapped him with an open hand—Krimmler saw it coming. Slapped him with an open hand so hard it knocked Krimmler unconscious for forty-five minutes. When he awoke, he was naked and halfway up a tall pine tree, wedged loosely in the crotch of three branches. The scratchy bark was murder on his armpits and balls. His jaw throbbed from the blow.

The sky had clouded and the wind had kicked up cold from the west. Krimmler felt himself swaying with the tree. On a nearby limb sat the bum in the racing-flag skirt. He was sipping a cream soda and reading (with his normal eye) a paperback book.

He glanced up at Krimmler and said: "One question, sir."

"Anything," Krimmler said weakly. He had never been more terrified. The treetops undoubtedly were full of goddamned squirrels, mean as timber wolves!

The bum said, "What 'other guy'?"

"The one with the snuff tape."

"Tell me more." The bum closed his book and put it in the pocket of his rain jacket, along with his empty cream-soda can.

"He had a tape of some poor slob dying. Getting stabbed to death by his girlfriend. Live, as it happened." Krimmler was scared to look down, as he was afraid of heights. He was also scared to look up, for fear of seeing one of those squirrels or possibly even a band of mutant chipmunks. So he squeezed his eyes shut.

The bum said: "What'd this other guy look like?"

"Short. Muscle-bound. Bad suit, and hair to match."

"Blondish?" the bum inquired. "Spiked out like a hedgehog?"

"That's him!" Krimmler felt relieved. Now the bum knew he was being truthful, and therefore had no compelling reason (other than Krimmler's general obnoxiousness) to push him out of the tree. The bum rose to stretch his arms, the pine bough creaking under his considerable weight. At the sound, Krimmler opened his eyes.

The bum asked, "What's the guy's name?"

"Gash," Krimmler replied. A chilly raindrop landed on his bare thigh, causing him to shiver. Another drop fell on his back.

"Last name or first?"

"Mr. Gash is what he called himself."

"What did he want with the young man and the dog?"

"He said Mr. Clapley had sent him. He said the kid was a troublemaker. I didn't ask him what he meant." The rising wind made the pine needles thrum. Krimmler clawed his fingernails into the bark. "Can you please get me down from here?"

"I can," said the bum, hopping to a lower branch, "but I don't believe I will."

"Why the hell not! What're you doing!"

"Gotta go," the bum informed the quaking Krimmler. "Bath time."

TWENTY-TWO

The man in the zippered shoes said, "I've killed my share of dogs."

"I don't doubt it," said Twilly.

"Kitty cats, too."

"Oh, I believe you."

"And one time, some jerkwad's pet monkey. Bernardo was his name. Bernardo the baboon. Came right out of his halter and went for my scalp," the man said. "They say monkeys are so smart? Bullshit. Dogs're smarter."

"Yeah," said Twilly.

"But I'll shoot this one, you try and get cute."

"Well, he's not mine."

"What're you saying?" The rain was flattening the spikes in the man's hair. He held his right arm straight, the gun trained on the Labrador's brow. "You don't care if I pop this mutt?"

Twilly said, "I didn't say that. I said he doesn't belong to me. He belongs to the guy who sent you here."

"Wrong!" The man made a noise like the buzzer on a TV game show. "He belongs to a major asshole named Palmer Stoat."

"Didn't he hire you?"

The man cackled and made the sarcastic buzzer noise again. "Would I work for a fuckhead like that? Ha!"

"What was I thinking," Twilly said.

"Mr. Clapley's the one that hired me."

"Ah."

"To clean out the troublemakers. Now, how about you get a move on. Call the damn dog and let's go," the man said, "before we get soaked. Where's your car?"

"That way." Twilly nodded down the beach.

"Your lady friend?"

"Gone." Twilly thinking: God, I hope so. "We had a fight. She split."

"Too bad. I had some plans."

Twilly changed the subject. "Can I ask you something?"

"My name is Mr. Gash."

That's when Twilly became aware that the man in the brown zippered shoes intended to kill him. The man would not have offered his name unless he knew Twilly wouldn't be alive to repeat it.

"Can I ask you something?"

"Long as your feet keep moving," said the man.

They were walking along the windswept shoreline, Twilly with McGuinn at his heels. Mr. Gash followed a few feet behind. He was taking care not to get his shoes wet in the surf.

"Why are you pointing the gun at the dog," Twilly said, "and not at me?"

"Because I saw how you hauled ass up here when you thought Fido was in trouble. You care more about that dumb hound than you do about yourself," Mr. Gash said. "So I figure you won't try any crazy shit long as I keep the piece aimed at Fido's brain, which I'm sure is no bigger than a stick of Dentyne."

Twilly reached down and scratched the crown of McGuinn's head. The Lab wagged his tail appreciatively. He seemed to have lost interest in the strange-smelling human with the gun.

"Also," said Mr. Gash, "it'll be cool to watch you watch the dog die. Because that's what has to happen. I gotta do Fido first."

"How come?"

"Think about it, man. I shoot you first, the dog goes batshit. I shoot the dog first, what the hell're *you* going to do—bite me in the balls? I seriously doubt it."

Twilly said, "Good point."

His legs felt leaden and his arms were cold; the temperature was dropping rapidly ahead of the weather front. The salt spray stung, so Twilly kept his eyes lowered as he walked. He could see Desie's footprints in the sand, pointing in the same direction.

Mr. Gash was saying: "I got tape of a hellacious dog attack. Chow named Brutus. The owner's on the phone yelling for help and Brutus gets him by the nuts and will not let go. The 911 operator tells the guy to, quick, try and distract the dog. So the poor fucker, he dumps a pot of Folger's decaf on Brutus and the last thing on the tape is this scream that goes on forever. Damn dog took everything! I mean the whole package."

"Ouch," said Twilly.

"You should hear it."

"How'd you get a tape of something like that?" said Twilly thinking: The more pertinent question is: Why?

Mr. Gash said, "I got my sources. Where's your god-damned car, anyway? I'm getting drenched."

"Not far."

Twilly was crestfallen to spy the Roadmaster behind a scrub-covered sand dune, where he had parked it. He had hoped Desie would see the keys in the ignition and drive back to the bed-and-breakfast, to sulk or pack her bag or whatever.

Maybe she decided to walk, thought Twilly. The important thing was that she was somewhere else, somewhere safe. . . .

But she wasn't. She was lying down in the backseat. Mr. Gash tapped the gun barrel against the rain-streaked window. Desie sat up quizzically and put her face near the glass. Mr. Gash showed her the semi-automatic and told her to unlock the door. When she hesitated, he grabbed McGuinn's collar, jerked the dog off the ground and jammed the gun to its neck.

The door flew open.

Mr. Gash beamed. "Lookie there, Fido. She loves you, too."

The trooper got to the old bridge before he changed his mind. He whipped the cruiser around and drove back to look for his friend. Thirty minutes later he found him, naked on a dune. The governor stood with his face upturned, his arms outstretched—letting the rain and wind beat him clean.

Jim Tile honked and flashed his headlights. The man who called himself Skink peered indignantly through the slashing downpour. When he saw the Highway

Patrol car, he stalked across the sand and heaved himself, dripping luxuriantly, into the front seat.

"I thought we said our good-byes," he growled, wringing out his beard.

"I forgot to give you something."

The man nodded absently. "FYI: Governor Dickhead was right. They sent someone after this boy. The boy with the dog."

Jim Tile said, "He's twenty-six years old."

"Still a boy," Skink said. "And he's here on the island, like we figured. I believe I met the man they sent to kill him."

"Then I'm glad I came back."

"You can't stay."

"I know," said the trooper.

"You've got Brenda to consider. Pensions and medical benefits and such. You can't be mixed up in shit like this."

"Nothing says I can't take off the uniform, Governor, at least for a few minutes."

"Nothing except for common sense."

"Where's your damn clothes?"

"Hung in a tree," said Skink. "What'd you bring me, Jim?"

The trooper jerked a thumb toward the trunk of the cruiser.

"Pop it open for me, would you?" Skink got out in the rain and went to the rear of the car. He returned with the package, which Jim Tile had wrapped in butcher's paper.

Skink smiled, hefting the item up and down in one hand. "You old rascal! I'm guessing Smith & Wesson."

The trooper told him the gun was clean; no serial

numbers. "One of my men took it off a coke mule in Okaloosa County. Very slick operation, too—eighteen-year-old Cuban kid driving a yellow Land Rover thirty-seven miles per hour at three in the morning on Interstate 10. It's a wonder we noticed him."

Skink borrowed a handkerchief to swipe the condensation off his glass eye. "I don't get it. You're the one told me not to bring the AK-47."

"Guess I'm getting nervous in my old age," the trooper said. "There's something else in the glove compartment. You go ahead and take it."

Skink opened the latch and scowled. "No, Jim, I hate these damn things." It was a cellular phone.

"Please. As a favor," the trooper said. "It will significantly improve my response time."

Skink closed his palm around the phone. "You better hit the road," he said grumpily. "This damn car stands out like the proverbial turd in the punch bowl."

"And you don't?"

"I'll be getting dressed momentarily."

"Oh, then you'll *really* blend in," Jim Tile said.

Skink got out of the police cruiser and tucked the heavy brown package under one arm. Before closing the door, he leaned in and said, "My love to your bride."

"Governor, I don't hear from you in twenty-four hours," the trooper said, "I'm coming back to this damn island."

"You don't hear from me in eight, don't even bother."

Skink gave a thumbs-up. Then he turned and began to run across the windblown dunes. It was a meandering, waggle-stepped, butt-wiggling run, and Jim Tile couldn't help but laugh.

He watched his friend disappear into the hazy

yellow-gray of the storm. Then he wheeled the car around and headed for the mainland.

CALLER: Help me! Help me, God, please, oh God, help. . . .

DISPATCHER: What's the problem, sir?

CALLER: She set fire to my hair! I'm burning up, oh God, please!

DISPATCHER: Hang on, sir, we've got a truck on the way. We've got help coming. Can you make it to the bathroom? Try to get to the bathroom and turn on the shower.

CALLER: I can't, I can't move. . . . She tied me to the damn bed. She . . . I'm tied to the bed with, like—oh Jesus, my hair!—clothesline. Aaagggggghhhoooooohhhh. . . .

DISPATCHER: Can you roll over? Sir, can you turn over?

CALLER: Cindy, no! Cindy, don't! CINDY!

DISPATCHER: Sir, if you're tied to the bed, then how—

CALLER: She held the phone to my ear, the sick bitch. She dialed 911 and put the phone to my ear and now . . . ooohhhhhhh. . . . Stop! . . . Now she's doing marshmallows. My hair's on fire and she's cooking. . . . Stop, God, stop, I'm burning up, Cindy! . . . Marsh—oh Jesus!—mallows. . . . Cindy, you crazy psycho bitch. . . .

Mr. Gash turned down the volume and said, "See? That's what love gets you. Man's wife ties him to the bedposts, pretending like she's gonna screw his brains out. Instead she puts a lighter to his hair and roasts marshmallows in the flames."

Desie said, "That was real?"

"Oh yes, Virginia." Mr. Gash popped the tape out of the console, and read from the stick-on label. "Tacoma, Washington. March tenth, 1994. Victim's name was Appleman. Junior Appleman."

"Did he die?"

"Eventually," Mr. Gash reported. "Took about six weeks. According to the newspaper, the Applemans had been having serious domestic problems. The best part: He lied to the dispatcher. It wasn't clothesline she tied him up with, it was pantyhose. He was too embarrassed to say so. Even on fire! But my point is, romance is fucking deadly. Look at you two!"

Twilly and Desie traded glances.

"You wouldn't be here right now, about to die," Mr. Gash added, "if you guys hadn't gotten romantically involved. I'd bet the farm on it."

They were all in the station wagon, parked among the bulldozers in the woods. Desie recognized the place from Dr. Brinkman's tour of the island. Night had fallen, and the rain had ebbed to a drizzle. The only light inside the car came from the dome lamp, which Mr. Gash had illuminated while playing the 911 cassette for his captives. He was next to Twilly Spree in the front seat. Desie sat behind them with McGuinn, who noisily had buried his snout in a sack of dry dog food and was therefore heedless of the semi-automatic pointed at his head.

Mr. Gash said to Desie, "What's your name, babe?"

"Never mind."

Mr. Gash held the gun in his right hand, propped

against the headrest. With his other hand he pawed through Desie's purse until he found her driver's license. When he saw the name on it, he said, "Shit."

Desie shrunk in her seat.

"Nobody told me. I wonder why," Mr. Gash mused. "They told me about the dog but not the wife!"

Twilly said, "Her husband didn't know."

"Didn't care is more like it."

"You're making a mistake," said Twilly. Of course the man in the brown zippered shoes ignored him.

"Well, 'Mrs. Stoat,' I had big plans for tonight. I was going to drive you back to the mainland and hook up with a couple party girls. Introduce you to the wonderful world of multiple sex partners." Mr. Gash was studying Desie's photograph on the license. "I like the highlighting job on these bangs. It's a good look for you."

Desie resisted the impulse to comment upon the killer's platinum-tinted eyebrows.

"How exactly do you pronounce your name?" Mr. Gash asked. "Dez-eye-rotta? Is that close?"

"'Desie' is fine."

"Like the Cuban guy on the old Lucy show."

"Close enough."

"Take off your earrings," Mr. Gash told her. "I've got a friend in Miami, an Italian girl, she'll look wicked hot in those. Almost as hot as you."

Desie removed the pearl studs and handed them over.

Mr. Gash said, "You're way too pretty for that crybaby porker of a husband. And since I haven't been laid in six days, I say what the hell. I say go for it."

Twilly tensed. "Don't be an idiot. Clapley isn't paying you to molest the wives of his friends."

"Friend? According to Mr. Clapley, Stoat's nothing—

and I quote—but a 'turd fondler.' Besides," said Mr. Gash, "my job is cleaning out the troublemakers. And, Mrs. Stoat, sleeping with a troublemaker makes you a troublemaker, too."

Desie pretended to stare out the fogged-up windows. A tear crawled down one cheek.

"The way I see it," Mr. Gash went on, "is a murder-suicide. The young hothead boyfriend. The married woman who refuses to leave her rich husband. The lovers argue. Boyfriend goes postal. Whacks the broad, whacks the puppy dog, and then finally he whacks himself. Of course, they find the weapon"—Mr. Gash, nodding at his own—"at the scene."

Twilly said, "Not very original."

"The murdered dog makes it different. That's what the cops'll be talking about," said Mr. Gash. "'What kind of creep would hurt an innocent dog?' Speaking of which, before I shoot you I've gotta ask: Where'd you get that damn ear, the one you sent to Stoat? Jesus, was he freaked!"

Twilly shifted slightly in the driver's seat. He braced his back against the door and casually took his right arm off the steering wheel.

"You really collect those horrible tapes?" Desie's voice was like acid.

"By the trunkload." Mr. Gash flashed a savage smile.

For a few moments, a chorus of ragged breathing was the only sound in the car; all three humans, including Mr. Gash, were on edge. Twilly glanced over the seat to check on McGuinn, who had finished off the dog food and was now mouthing the paper sack. The Lab wore an all-too-familiar expression of postprandial contentment.

God, Twilly thought, please don't let him fart. This psycho punk would shoot him in a heartbeat.

Mr. Gash was saying, "Whoever finds your bodies, the first thing they'll do is call 911. You could be nothing but skeletons and still they'll call emergency." Mr. Gash paused to relish the irony. "Know what I'm going to do, Mrs. Stoat? I'm going to get the tape of that phone call, as a remembrance of our one and only night together. What do you think of that?"

"I think you're a monster."

"'Possible human remains.' That's what the cops call those cases."

Desie Stoat said, "Please don't shoot my dog."

"You crack me up," said Mr. Gash.

"I'll do anything you want. Anything."

Desie sat forward and pinched the damp sleeve of Mr. Gash's houndstooth coat.

"*Anything*, Mrs. Stoat? Because I've got a very active imagination."

"Yes, we can tell by your wardrobe," said Twilly. He drew his right hand into a fist, mentally calibrating the distance to Mr. Gash's chin.

Desie was saying, "Please. There's no need to do that."

Mr. Gash shrugged. "Sorry, babe. The mutt dies first."

"Then I hope you're into necrophilia," she told him, trembling, "because if you shoot McGuinn, you're in for the worst sex of your whole life. That's a promise."

Mr. Gash pursed his waxy-looking lips and grew pensive. Twilly could tell that Desie's threat had hit home; the killer's kinky fantasies were in ruins.

Finally he said, "OK, I'll let him go."

Desie frowned. "Here? You can't just let him go."
"Why the hell not."
Twilly said, "He's been sick. He's on medicine."
"Better sick than dead."
"He's a dog, not a turtle. You don't just let him go," Desie protested. "He doesn't know how to hunt for himself—what's he going to eat out here?"
"You guys, for starters," said Mr. Gash. "Dogs go for fresh meat, is my understanding."
Desie blanched. Mr. Gash was paying close attention to her reaction, savoring it. Twilly saw an opportunity. He coiled his shoulder muscles, drew a deep breath and—
Then it hit him, rank and unmistakable. McGuinn!
Mr. Gash's nose twitched. His face contorted into a gargoyle scowl. "Aw, who cut the cheese? Did *he* do that!"
"What are you talking about?" Twilly, laboring to breathe through his mouth.
"I don't smell anything," insisted Desie, though her eyes had begun to well.
"Your damn dog passed gas!"
Mr. Gash was up on his knees, cursing furiously and waving the semi-automatic. McGuinn wore that liquid expression of pure lovable innocence well known to all owners of Labrador retrievers. The Look had evolved over hundreds of years as an essential survival trait, to charm exasperated humans into forgiveness.
Unfortunately, Mr. Gash was immune. "Roll down the goddamn windows!" he gasped at Twilly.
"I can't. They're electric and you took the car keys."
Mr. Gash dug the ignition key out of his pocket and twisted it into the switch on the steering column. Then

he threw himself across Twilly's lap and feverishly began mashing all the window buttons on the door panel. Mr. Gash remained in that position long enough to gag Twilly with a miasmal body funk that, by comparison, made dog flatulence smell like orange blossoms.

Had Twilly been able to draw an untainted breath, he likely could have reached around and broken Mr. Gash's neck, or at least his firing arm. But the stench off the gamy houndstooth suit had a paralyzing effect, and by the time Twilly recovered, Mr. Gash had thrust the upper half of his torso across the front seat and placed the gun barrel squarely between McGuinn's calm, still-guileless eyes.

"You were home free, Fido. Then you had to go and fart."

Desie cried out and threw both arms around the Lab's trunk-like neck.

For several moments, nobody moved. A piney breeze rushed through the open windows of the Roadmaster. Twilly hoped it might refresh Mr. Gash and cool his fury.

It did not. He cocked the hammer.

"Back to Plan A," he said.

Twilly dove across the seat and slammed his right fist into Mr. Gash's rib cage, the nearest availing target. The punch didn't land right—Twilly had expected the sting of bone against bone but the impact was softer, as if he'd slugged a sofa. He could not have foreseen that Mr. Gash would be wearing, beneath the jacket, holster and long-sleeved shirt, a padded corset of cured rattlesnake hides.

The device had been fashioned by the same Washington Avenue upholstery wizard who'd customized Mr.

Gash's iguana-skin sex harness. Why Mr. Gash would don a corset undergarment was a question Twilly never would get to ask. The answer: The killer had a vain streak when it came to his physique. He was driven to take measures that artificially streamlined his midsection, which in recent years had shown signs of incipient tubbiness—an unnerving development that Mr. Gash bitterly blamed on the dull sedentary lifestyle of a hit man. It was an occupation that neither required nor allowed much physical exercise; plane trips, car rides, endless stakeouts in motel rooms and bars. For Mr. Gash, already self-conscious about his short stature, the sight of a marbled, thickening belly was intolerable. A discreetly tailored corset seemed a good temporary solution, at least until he found time to join a spa. And because he lived on South Beach, not just any corset would do. Yet that's all Mr. Gash could find when he went shopping: starchy medical corsets, white or beige; no colors, no patterns. Mr. Gash wanted something with élan, something that didn't look like a flab-binding swathe, something he wouldn't be ashamed to display when stripping off his clothes for the women he took home, something intriguing enough to divert their eyes away from his gelatinous tummy.

Snakeskin was the obvious choice. With snakeskin you couldn't go wrong anywhere on Ocean Drive. Mr. Gash had chosen Eastern diamond-back because the women who consented to go home with him typically were danger freaks and would therefore (Mr. Gash reasoned) be more aroused by the remains of a venomous serpent than those of a common boa or python. And over time the rattlesnake-hide corset had served Mr. Gash very well, both socially and cosmetically.

When he wasn't wearing it, he felt shy and bloated—and, oddly, shorter! Without the corset, Mr. Gash would not have fit comfortably (or even attempted to fit) into his trademark houndstooth ensemble.

None of this was known to Twilly Spree. All he knew was that he hit the man with an exceptionally good punch and that the man sagged but did not keel, gulped but did not cry out, grimaced but did not roll his eyes in the manner of the soon-to-be unconscious. So Twilly clutched Mr. Gash desperately around the waist, struggling to flip him backward and get at the gun. That's when a bomb went off in Twilly's right eardrum, and white-hot starbursts exploded in his eye sockets. He hoped it was the beginning of another dream, but it wasn't.

TWENTY-THREE

The breeze felt good. More important to McGuinn, it *tasted* good; a tantalizing smorgasbord for doggy senses. There was the tangy trace of boar raccoon, the musky whiff of mother opossum, the familiar fumes of randy tomcat—and a host of intriguing new woodland scents that required immediate investigation. The night beckoned McGuinn and, once the dog food was gone, he saw no reason not to answer the call.

Except for Desie.

Desie kept hugging him, and nothing in the world was more pleasurable to a Labrador retriever than the cooing affection of a female human. They smelled fantastic! So McGuinn was torn between the primal urge to prowl and mark territory and the not-so-primal urge to be coddled and stroked.

The gunshot clinched it—so loud it made him jump, yet nevertheless triggering one of the few learned responses to have lodged for more than a day or two in his quicksand memory. A gunshot meant McGuinn was supposed to run! This he explicitly recalled from all those frosty dawns in the marsh with Palmer Stoat. A gunshot meant ducks falling from the sky! Warm, wet, tasty ducks! Ducks to be scented out and snapped floating from the pond, carried off at a gallop to be eagerly gnawed upon until hollering male humans up and snatched them away. That's what gunfire meant to McGuinn.

So he vaulted from the station wagon—out of Desie's loving arms, through an open window (yipping as his surgical wound grazed the lock button), into the misting darkness in quest of . . . ducks? But where?

Mr. Gash watched him run away and said, "That solves the dog problem."

He pushed Twilly Spree's lifeless form out of the car, pulled the door shut, and climbed into the backseat with Desie. He considered moving her to the rear cargo bed, but it was cluttered with mangled chew toys and carpeted with Labrador sheddings. Mr. Gash preferred sex that did not require a head-to-toe vacuuming afterward.

"Take off your clothes." He placed the gun to Desie's temple. Mechanically she removed her sweatshirt, bra and jeans. Mr. Gash shook himself out of the hounds-tooth coat and with his free hand folded it neatly into a square.

"Stick this under your head," he told Desie.

"What about your pants?" She was so frightened, so strung out with terror that her own voice seemed to be echoing from a cavern; some remote, untouchable part of her consciousness that urged her to stall, drag it out, keep the monster occupied as long as you can.

As awful as it might get.

"My pants?" said Mr. Gash.

"They're wet."

"Yeah, they are. From the *rain*."

"I know," Desie said, "but it's cold on my skin. Could you please take them off? The shirt, too." She was lying on her back, covering her nipples with her hands. Now it was purely about survival; nothing could be done for Twilly, who was either dead or dying. Desie would cry for him later, if she made it.

Mr. Gash sat poised on the edge of the seat. "Don't you move," he told her. "Don't you even blink."

He unzipped his brown shoes and placed them under the seat. Then he tugged off his damp trousers and laid them across one of the headrests. Next came the shoulder holster, then the shirt.

"What's that?" Desie asked. Even in the dark she could tell it was a most unusual garment.

"Bulletproof vest," Mr. Gash lied.

"Is that from a snake?"

"Sure is. Wanna touch?"

"No."

"It's dead. Go on and touch it."

Desie did what she was told, tracing her fingertips across the corrugated scales of the hide. She shivered not at the sensation but at the thought of where it had come from.

"Please take that off, too," she said.

As Mr. Gash fumbled to unlace the corset, he said, "Mrs. Stoat, I don't think you get it. This isn't a goddamn honeymoon, it's what the cops would call an aggravated sexual battery. And you're making me more damn aggravated by the minute."

When he climbed on top of her, she robotically positioned a hand on each of his shoulders, which felt greased and lumpy. Something hard poked her neck, and she correctly assumed it was the handgun.

Mr. Gash said, "Oh shit."

"What?"

"There's a leak in this damned car."

Desie looked up and noticed a dime-sized hole in the Roadmaster's roof. The hole was from the bullet that accidentally fired from the killer's gun when he smacked it against Twilly Spree's head. Now water was dripping from the hole onto Mr. Gash's bare torso.

"Right down the crack of my ass," he reported sourly.

He sat up and hastily plugged the leak with a wadded-up discount coupon for chicken-flavored Purina. Then he again lowered himself on Desie, saying, "Now. *Finally.*"

She resolved not to fight; Mr. Gash was too muscular. But she had another plan: to will herself paralyzed from the neck down, so she wouldn't feel him. It was a technique Desie had developed while engaged to the multi-baubled Andrew Beck. Later, the self-numbing hypnosis had proved useful with Palmer Stoat, during the nights when his Polaroid antics became tedious.

Her trick was to imagine she was living in a borrowed body, through which she could see and speak but not feel. And at first she didn't feel anything of Mr. Gash.

"Gimme second." His breathing came in a heavy rhythm, as if he was practicing a meditation. "Just hang on," he said.

Elatedly, Desie thought: The creep can't get it up!

But relief gave way to gloom, for she realized he would kill her anyway—probably even sooner now, in a violent rage of frustration.

"Help me out here, babe."

He was grinding against her with somber determination. His hipbones banged into her hipbones, his chest slapped against her breasts, his chin dug into her forehead. . . .

Desie fought off waves of nausea—the man stank of rancid perspiration, syrupy cologne and unlaundered clothes.

"I'm not . . . used to . . . this." Mr. Gash, panting gaseously.

The rank heat of his breath made Desie shudder.

"Used to what—women?" she said. "You bi?"

"No! What I'm not . . . used to . . . is *one* woman. I'm used to . . . more."

"How many more?"

"Two . . . three. Sometimes four." He told her what he liked to do (and have done to him) while hanging in his lizard-skin sling from the ceiling.

"Whew," Desie said. "Can't help you there, chief."

Mr. Gash stopped grinding and pushed himself up on his arms. "Sure you can. There's lots of things you can do, Mrs. Stoat."

Twilly awoke facedown in mud. He blew clods out both nostrils when he lifted his head.

His head! He'd never known such pain. He tried to spit and again nearly blacked out. His left ear clanged like a fire alarm. The whole side of his skull felt flaming hot; liquid and distended.

Twilly thought: I guess I've finally been shot. He was incensed but not especially afraid, which was a chronic problem in his life—anger supplanting normal, well-founded fears. Twilly had an unhealthy lack of concern for his own safety.

He rolled over and saw stars. They vanished behind a wispy curtain of fast-moving clouds. It was night-time and a hard rain was ending. Twilly didn't know where he was, or what he was doing there, but he had a hunch somebody would bring him up to speed. He raised an exploratory hand to his head and located a large raw knot, but no bullet wound. His fingers came back sticky so he held them in front of his face to check the color of the blood; the brighter the better. That's when he knew he'd lost the vision in his left eye.

"Hell," he muttered.

With a forefinger Twilly gingerly probed the socket and was relieved to find the eyeball externally intact. Slowly he raised on his forearms, teetering in the sloppy mud. Overhead the stars and clouds spun madly around the treetops. Twilly waited patiently for the world to slow down. With his good eye he discerned bulky motionless shapes on either side of him—to his left, a bulldozer; to his right, a boat-sized station wagon.

Progress, he told himself.

Gradually the locomotive ringing subsided and Twilly could make out distinct noises—the wind in the pines, an incongruous jingling in the understory, almost like sleigh bells. . . .

And, from inside the car, a muffled struggle.

Twilly tried to stand, bracing himself on the fender. He noticed it was shimmying. Once on his feet, he felt dizzy and sick to his stomach. Meanwhile the jingling sounded closer, causing him to speculate it was all inside his head; something loose or broken.

But the station wagon *was* rocking—not much, but enough to keep Twilly's shaky equilibrium in flux. Miserably he sunk to his knees and listed against the car, his cheek mashed against the cool steel. He groped for purchase and found a door handle.

There he hung like a drunken rock climber until the latch clicked and the heavy door swung open. Twilly lost his grip and slid limply to the mud. He lay blinking at the heavens as his eardrums pealed with the jingle bells of the oncoming sleigh. Where's the snow? he wondered sleepily.

Moments later, Twilly saw the sleigh shoot over him, a hulking black shadow that momentarily blotted out the stars and the clouds. He smelled it, too, though it didn't smell like Christmas. It smelled like a big wet dog. From inside the car came a startled cry, and suddenly Twilly remembered where he was, and what was happening. He remembered everything.

"He thinks it's a game," Desie explained.

"Make him let go!"

"He won't hurt you."

"Get him off me, goddammit, so I can kill him."

The mutt was riding Mr. Gash as if he were a pony. The wet, filthy mutt! Its yellow fangs were planted on his neck—not hard enough to break the skin, but firmly enough to bring severe distress to Mr. Gash, who was not an animal lover. (He regarded the 911 tape of the testicle-chomping chow as one of the most harrowing in his extensive collection.)

"I've shot dogs," he hissed at Desie, "for a lot less than this."

"He thinks we're playing."

"You mean he's pulled this shit before? While you were screwing?"

"To him it's wrestling. He hates to be left out." The combined weight and aromas of the two animals, the Lab and Mr. Gash, made it difficult for Desie to speak up.

"Who taught him how to open a car door?" Mr. Gash said snidely.

"I dunno. That's a new one."

"Make him get off! He weighs a fucking ton."

Weakly, Desie said, "McGuinn, down!"

The dog held its position. They heard a tail flopping mirthfully against the upholstery.

"Jesus, he's drooling all over me!" Mr. Gash cried.

Desie saw a strand of slobber glistening from one of his earlobes. He swung the gun away from her neck and reached it behind his own head, so the barrel was jammed to the Labrador's jaw.

"Big mistake," said Desie.

"What?" The dumb mutt *had* to die—first, because he had interrupted Mr. Gash's strenuous efforts to achieve an erection; second, because he had fouled Mr. Gash's hair with spit.

"You have any idea," Desie said, "how hard that dog's head is?"

"What're you saying, Mrs. Stoat? This is a forty-five-caliber handgun."

"I'm saying his noggin is like a cinder block. The bullet could bounce off him and wind up in you or me. It's something to think about, that's all."

Mr. Gash did think about it. She had a point. The beast was glommed to his very spine, after all. Plus, it would be a blind shot, backhanded over the shoulder. Very risky.

"Shit," said Mr. Gash. The evening was not playing

out as he had hoped. "How long does he usually hang on?"

"Till he gets bored. Or hungry." Desie felt suffocated and claustrophobic.

"He farts again, I'm definitely pulling the trigger."

"Tell that to *him*," she muttered at Mr. Gash, "not me."

Twilly Spree was on all fours in the slop, peering up into the backseat through the open door. In the greenish glow of the dome light he saw Desirata Stoat and her dog, with Mr. Gash sandwiched obscenely between them. None of them could see Twilly, who listened only briefly to the taut conversation before scooting like a water bug underneath the Roadmaster.

He thought: Crazy damn dog, he'll get her killed.

It wouldn't take much for Mr. Gash to blow a gasket and start shooting. The challenge was to get McGuinn off the killer, then somehow get the killer off Desie.

"Let go a me, you dumb bastard! Let go a me!" The rising fury of Mr. Gash.

Twilly licked his lips and tried to whistle. Nothing came out—he was trembling too much from the damp cold.

He heard Desie cry out: "What're you doing!"

Then Mr. Gash: "Making do."

The car began rocking again. Twilly vigorously rubbed the clamminess from his cheeks. He was striving for a specific two-note whistle; the whistle used to summon McGuinn for supper. Twilly puckered and blew. This time it worked.

The station wagon stopped shaking. There was a

shout, a splash, an inquisitive bark. The dog had let go of the killer and was out of the car, hunting for the source of the dinner call. Twilly could track McGuinn's pacing by the tinkling of his collar. It was only a matter of moments before the ever-hungry Lab sniffed out Twilly's hiding place.

"Who made that noise!" Mr. Gash bellowed from the backseat.

"What noise?" came Desie's voice. "That bird, you mean."

"It was no goddamned bird."

Twilly whistled again, this time with a whimsical lilt. He saw McGuinn's legs stiffen—all senses on full alert. The dog was zeroing in.

Not yet, Twilly thought, please. He heard more movement above him: Mr. Gash, scrambling from the station wagon.

"That's it," the killer was saying, "somebody's out there. Some asshole troublemaker."

Twilly sucked in his breath as McGuinn's twitching snout appeared below the rear bumper. The dog began to whine and scratch at the ground. No! Twilly thought. *Stay!*

Finally, the two pale feet Twilly was awaiting emerged from the car and descended into view. They disappeared into the mud as the killer stood up.

"Damn," Mr. Gash rasped. "That's cold."

From Twilly's vantage, the bony white ankles looked like aspen saplings. He clasped a hand around each one and jerked. The killer went down hard and unquietly. McGuinn retreated, moon-howling in confusion.

Twilly wriggled from under the car and hurled himself upon the thrashing Mr. Gash. The resulting splatter of muck glooped uncannily into Twilly's good eye, completing his decline to full sightlessness. Wild punches landed harmlessly upon the brawny arms and shoulders of Mr. Gash, who simply bucked Twilly aside, raised his gun and fired.

This time Twilly knew it for a fact: He was shot. The slug slammed into the right side of his chest and knocked him goony. He didn't fall so much as fold.

He heard the wind blowing. Desie sobbing. That weird sleigh-bell jingling in the trees. His own heart pounding.

Twilly believed he could even hear the blood squirting from the hole in his ribs.

And a strange new voice, possibly imaginary.

"I'll take it from here," it said, very deeply.

"What? Like hell you will." That was Mr. Gash, the killer.

"The boy comes with me."

"Ha! Pops, I should've shot your ass, back up the road. Now get the fuck outta here."

"Mister, run! Go get help! Please." That would be Desie.

"Shut up, Mrs. Stoat"—the killer again—"while I blow this sorry old fart's head off."

"I said, the boy's mine." The deep voice, astoundingly calm.

"You mental or what? I guess maybe so," Mr. Gash said. "Whatever. It's just one more dead troublemaker to me."

Twilly felt himself sliding away, as if he were on a raft spinning languidly downriver. If this was dying, it wasn't half-bad. And if it was only a dream, he had no desire to awaken. Twenty-six years of unspent dreams is what they owed him.

On impulse he decided to summon McGuinn—a dog was always good company on a river.

"*I said, the boy is mine.*"

Who's he talking about? Twilly wondered. What boy?

He also wondered why he could no longer hear himself whistling, why suddenly he couldn't hear anything at all.

TWENTY-FOUR

"What is it you want, Willie?"

The age-old question. Palmer Stoat tinkled the ice cubes in his glass and awaited a reply from the vice chairman of the House Appropriations Committee.

"You and your rude-ass manners," Willie Vasquez-Washington said. "Man, I'll tell you what I want. I want the Honorable Richard Artemus to not fuck with my spring snow skiing, Palmer. I want to be in Canada next week. I do *not* want to be in Tallahassee for some bullshit 'special session.'"

"Now, Willie, it's too late—"

"Don't 'now Willie' me. This isn't about the schools budget, amigo, it's about that dumb-ass bridge to that dumb-ass Cracker island, which I thought—no, which you *told* me!—was all ironed out a few weeks ago. And then. . . ." Willie Vasquez-Washington paused to sip his Long Island iced tea. "Then your Governor Dick goes and vetoes the item. His own baby! Why?"

Palmer Stoat responded with his standard you-don't-really-want-to-know roll of the eyes. They were sitting at the bar in Swain's, the last place on the planet where Stoat wanted to retell the squalid dognapping saga. After all, it was here the lunatic had sent the infamous phantom paw. The bartender was even rumored to have named a new drink after it, to Stoat's mortification.

"Fine. Don't tell me," said Willie Vasquez-Washington. "But guess what? It ain't my problem, Palmer."

"Hey, you got your inner-city community center."

"Don't start with that."

"Excuse me. Community *Outreach* Center," said Stoat. "Nine million bucks, wasn't it?"

"Back off!"

"Look, all I'm saying. . . ." The lobbyist dropped his voice, for he did not wish to appear to be insulting an Afro-Haitian-Hispanic-Asian-Native American, or any combination thereof (assuming Willie Vasquez-Washington was telling the truth about at least one of the many minorities he professed to be). In any case, the upscale cigar-savoring clientele at Swain's was relentlessly Anglo-Saxon, so the presence of a person of color (especially one as impeccably attired as Representative Vasquez-Washington) raised almost as many eyebrows as had the sight of the severed Labrador paw.

"Willie, all I'm saying," Palmer Stoat continued, "is that the governor kept his end of the deal. He did right by you. Can't you help him out of this one lousy jam? These were circumstances beyond his control."

"Sorry, man."

"We can't pull this off without you."

"I'm aware of that," said Willie Vasquez-Washington, drumming his fingernails on the oak. "Any other time, Palmer, but not now. I've been planning this vacation for years."

Which was a complete crock, Stoat knew. The junket was being paid for secretly by a big HMO as a show of gratitude to Willie Vasquez-Washington, whose timely intervention had aborted a potentially embarrassing investigation of certain questionable medical practices; to wit, the HMO encouraging its minimum-wage switchboard operators to make over-the-phone surgical decisions for critically ill patients. What a stroke of good fortune (Stoat reflected wryly) that Willie Vasquez-Washington played golf every Saturday with the State Insurance Commissioner.

"Willie, how's this? We fly you in for the Toad Island vote, then fly you straight back to Banff. We'll get a Lear."

Willie Vasquez-Washington eyed Stoat as if he were a worm on a Triscuit. "And you're supposed to be so damn sharp? Lemme spell it out for you, my brother: I cannot skip the special session and go skiing, like I want. Why? Because they would crucify my ass in the newspapers, on account of the newspapers have bought into the governor's bullshit. They think we're all headed back to the capital to vote more money for poor little schoolkids. Because, see, the papers don't know jack about your bridge scam. So I am one stuck-ass motherfucker, you follow?"

Now it was Willie Vasquez-Washington's turn to lower his voice. "I'm stuck, man. I gotta go to this session, which means no skiing, which means the wife and kids will be supremely hacked off, which means—sorry!—no new bridge for Honorable Dick and his friends."

Palmer Stoat calmly waved for another round. He handed a genuine Montecristo Especial No. 2 to Willie Vasquez-Washington, and lighted it for him. Stoat was mildly annoyed by this impasse, but not greatly worried. He was adept at smoothing over problems among self-important shitheads. Stoat hoped someday to be doing it full-time in Washington, D.C., where self-importance was the prevailing culture, but for now he was content to hone his skills in the swamp of teeming greed known as Florida. Access, influence, introductions—that's what all lobbyists peddled. But the best of them also were fast-thinking, resourceful and creative; crisis solvers. And Palmer Stoat regarded himself as one of the very best in the business. A virtuoso.

Shearwater! Jesus H. Christ, what a cluster fuck. It had cost him his wife and his dog and nearly his life, but he would not let it cost him his reputation as a fixer. No, this cursed deal *would* get done. The bridge would get funded. The cement trucks would roll and the high rises would rise and the golf courses would get sodded. The governor would be happy, Robert Clapley would be happy, everybody would be happy—even Willie Vasquez-Washington, the maggot. And afterward they would all say it never would have come together except for the wizardly lobbying of Palmer Stoat.

Who now whispered through a tingling blue haze to the vice chairman of the House Appropriations Committee: "He wants to talk to you, Willie."

"I thought that was your job."

"Face-to-face."

"What the hell for?"

"Dick's a people person," Stoat said.

"He's a damn Toyota salesman."

"He wants to make this up to you, Willie. He wants to know what he can do to make things right."

"Before the session starts, I bet."

Stoat nodded conspiratorially. "They'll be some

money floating around next week. How's your district fixed for schools? You need another school?"

"Man. You serious?" Willie Vasquez-Washington laughed harshly. "Suburbs get all the new schools."

"Not necessarily," said Palmer Stoat. "There's state pie, federal matching, lottery spill. Listen, you think about it."

"I am not believin' this shit."

Stoat took out a fountain pen and wrote something in neat block letters on a paper cocktail napkin. He slid it down the bar to Willie Vasquez-Washington, who chuckled and rolled the cigar from one corner of his mouth to the other.

Then he said: "OK, OK, I'll meet with him. Where?"

"I've got an idea. You ever been on a real big-game safari?"

"Not since I took the bone out of my nose, you asshole."

"No, Willie, this you'll dig. Trust me." Stoat winked and signaled for the check.

Willie Vasquez-Washington's gaze once more fell upon the cocktail napkin, which he discreetly palmed and deposited in an ashtray. On the drive back to Miami, he thought about the words Palmer Stoat had written down, and envisioned them five feet high, chiseled into a marble façade.

WILLIE VASQUEZ-WASHINGTON SENIOR HIGH SCHOOL

Asa Lando urged Durgess to check out the horn; the horn was first-rate. Durgess could not disagree. However. . . .

"This rhino is how old?" he asked.

"I don't honestly know," said Asa Lando. "They said nineteen."

"Yeah? Then I'm still in diapers."

It was the most ancient rhinoceros Durgess had ever seen; even older and more feeble than the one procured for Palmer Stoat. This one was heavier by at least five hundred pounds, which was but a small consolation to Durgess. The animal had come to the Wilderness Veldt Plantation from a wildlife theme park outside Buenos Aires. The park had "retired" the rhino because it was now sleeping, on average, twenty-one hours a day. Tourists assumed it was made from plaster of paris.

"You said money was no object."

Durgess raised a hand. "You're right. I won't even ask."

"His name's El Jefe." Asa Lando pronounced it "Jeffy," with a hard *J*.

"Why'd you tell me that?" Durgess snapped. "I don't wanna know his name." The guide slept better by pretending that the animals at Wilderness Veldt actually were wild, making the hunts less of a charade. But named quarry usually meant tamed quarry, and even Durgess could not delude himself into believing there was a shred of sport to the chase. It was no more suspenseful, or dangerous, than stalking a pet hamster.

"El Jeffy means 'the boss,'" Asa Lando elaborated, "in Spanish. They also had a name for him in American but I forgot what."

"Knock it off. Just knock it off."

Durgess leaned glumly against the gate of the rhino's stall in Quarantine One. The giant creature was on its knees, in a bed of straw, wheezing in a deep and potentially unwakable slumber. Its hide was splotched floridly with some exotic seeping strain of eczema. Bottleflies buzzed around its parchment-like ears, and its crusted eyelids were scrunched into slits.

Asa Lando said: "What'd ya expect, Durge? He's been locked in a box for five damn days."

With a mop handle Durgess gingerly prodded the narcoleptic pachyderm. Its crinkled gray skin twitched, but no cognitive response was evident.

"Besides," said Asa Lando, "you said it didn't matter, long as the horns was OK. Any rhinoceros I could find, is what you said."

Durgess cracked his knuckles. "I know, Asa. It ain't your fault."

"On short notice, you can't hope for much. Not with endangereds such as rhinos and elephants. You pretty much gotta take what's out there, Durge."

"It's awright." Durgess could see that El Jefe once had been a strapping specimen, well fed and well cared for. Now it was just old, impossibly old, and physically wasted from the long sweltering flight.

"Can he run," Durgess asked, "even a little bit?"

Asa Lando shook his head solemnly.

"Well, can he *walk*?"

"Now and again," said Asa Lando. "He walked outta the travel crate."

"Hooray."

"Course, that was downhill."

"Well, hell," Durgess said impatiently. "He must move around enough to eat. Lookit the size of the bastard."

Asa Lando cleared his throat. "See, they, uh, brought all his food to him—branches and shrubs and such. He pretty much just stood in the same spot all day long, eatin' whatever they dumped in front of his face. Give him a big shady tree, they told me, and he won't go nowheres."

Durgess said, "I'm sure."

"Which is how I figure we'll set up the kill shot. Under one a them giant live oaks."

"Oaks we got," Durgess sighed.

He thought: Maybe we can get us two birds with one stone. Maybe Mr. Stoat's big-shot hunter would go for a jenna-wine African rhinoceros over a cheetah; even a sleepy rhino was an impressive sight. And El Jefe's front horn *was* primo—fifty grand is what Stoat said he could get for a decent one. Durgess idly wondered if the mysterious Mr. Yee might be enticed into a bidding war. . . .

"I gotta make a phone call," Durgess said to Asa Lando.

"One more thing. It might could help."

"What?"

"He stomped a man to death, Durge."

"No shit!"

"Six, seven years ago. Some superdumb tourist," Asa Lando said, "hopped on his back so the wife could take a picture. Like he was ridin' a bronco. Old El Jeffy went nuts is what them Argentinos told me. Threw the tourist fellow to the ground and mushed his head like a tangelo. Made all the papers in South America."

Durgess smiled crookedly. "So it ain't just any rhino we got here, Asa. It's a *killer* rhino. A world-famous killer rhino."

"Exactly right. That help?"

"You bet your ass," Durgess said. "Call me when he wakes up."

Mr. Gash couldn't believe that the bum with the crimson eye and the weird checkered skirt had showed up in the dead of night, in the middle of the woods. And packing a pistol!

"I said, the boy is mine."

Mr. Gash leered. "You're into *that*, huh, pops? A rump ranger."

"I'll take the woman, too." The bum motioned with the gun toward the station wagon containing Desirata Stoat.

"Pops, you can have the 'boy.' He's dying anyway. But the lady," said Mr. Gash, waving with his own gun, "she stays with me. Now get the fuck outta here. I'm counting to six."

The bum flashed his teeth. The braids of his beard were dripping after his jog through the rain; tiny perfect globes, rolling off the bleached buzzard beaks. Mr. Gash was unnerved by the sight, as he was by the man's eerie calm. Being cold and unclothed had put Mr. Gash at a psychological disadvantage in the standoff. By rights he should have felt cocksure, a single-action Smith being no match for his trusty semi-automatic. Yet all it would take would be one lucky shot in the dark—and even a bum could get lucky.

Mr. Gash elected to proceed carefully, lest his pecker be blown off.

He said to the bum: "You can have the dog, too."

"I was hungry enough, Mr. Gash, I just might."

"What kinda sick kink you into, pops?" Mr. Gash

levered himself to one knee. His foot made a sucking sound when he tugged it out of the mud. He was somewhat flattered that the bum knew his name.

"The governor sent me, Mr. Gash. I'll take over from here."

"Hooo! The governor!"

"Yessir. To fetch that young man."

"Well, Mr. Robert Clapley sent *me*," said Mr. Gash, "to do the exact same thing. And my guess is Mr. Clapley pays a whole lot handsomer than the governor. So we got a conflict, don't we?"

A jingling came from the pines, and McGuinn's shadow appeared at the edge of the clearing. The second gunshot had launched the dog on another fruitless search for falling ducks, and he had returned only to encounter yet another human with a gun; an uncommonly large human who smelled of fried opossum and wood smoke. McGuinn's mouth began to water. Unspooling his tongue, he trotted forward to greet the stranger in the customary Labrador manner.

Mr. Gash saw what was coming and steadied his arm, preparing to fire. Here was the opportunity he'd been awaiting: The bum wouldn't be able to ignore the dog. *Nobody* could ignore that loony pain-in-the-ass mutt. And the moment the bum got distracted, Mr. Gash would shoot him in the heart.

From the car, Desie called out: "McGuinn! Come, boy!"

Naturally the dog paid no attention. On his way to meet the stranger, he stepped blithely over Twilly Spree, sprawled bleeding on the ground.

"Bad boy! Come!" Desie shouted, to no avail.

McGuinn sensed that the extra-large human with the

gun presented no menace, but rather the promise of an opossum snack. It was imperative to make friends. . . .

As the dog's nose disappeared beneath the hem of the bum's checkered kilt, Mr. Gash's forefinger tightened on the trigger. He was waiting for the bum to react— to recoil in surprise, yell in protest, shove the dog away. Something. Anything.

But the bum didn't even flinch; wouldn't take his good eye (or the .357) off Mr. Gash. He merely stood there smiling, a smile so luminous as to be visible on a moonless night.

Smiling, while a filthy 128-pound hairball sniffed at his privates! Mr. Gash was disgusted.

"You're one sick bastard," he spat at the bum.

A voice from behind Mr. Gash: "Look who's talking."

He turned to see Desie at the car door, modeling his snakeskin corset. Assuming that the perverted bum would be transfixed by Mrs. Stoat, Mr. Gash decided to seize his chance.

"You're all sick!" he snarled.

In the moment between uttering those words and pulling the trigger, something unexpected happened to Mr. Gash. The bum shot him twice. The first slug clipped off his right kneecap, toppling him sideways. The second slug, striking him on the way down, went through one cheek and out the other.

Flopping about, Mr. Gash felt a large boot descend firmly on his throat, and the semi-automatic being pried from his fingers. He began to choke violently on a gob of mud, and he was slipping into blackness when a huge fist snatched him by the hair and jerked him upright to a sitting position. There he coughed volcanically until he was able to expel the gob.

But it wasn't mud. It was an important segment of Mr. Gash's tongue, raggedly severed by the bum's second bullet. Only when he endeavored to speak did Mr. Gash comprehend the debilitating nature of his wound.

"Zhhooo zhhaa off mah fugghy ung!"

The bum tweaked Mr. Gash's chin. "Not bad, sport. You could've been a rap star."

"Zhoooo zhhuuhh of a bizhhh!"

The bum hoisted Mr. Gash by the armpits and heaved him headfirst into the leering grille of the Buick. Mr. Gash crumpled into a grimy naked heap on the ground, and he would have preferred to remain there indefinitely until his multitude of fiery pains abated. The bum, however, had other plans.

Twilly was no longer floating down a river. He was lying flat on a tailgate. The good news was, his vision had returned, more or less. Two silhouettes hovered over him: Mrs. Desirata Stoat and a tall hoary stranger with silvery twines growing from each side of his face. The stranger was using a finger to probe the gurgling hole in Twilly's thorax.

"Hold still, son," the man advised.

"Who are you?"

"You call me captain, but for now shut up."

Desie said, "Honey, you lost some blood."

Twilly nodded dully. It wouldn't have surprised him to learn he'd lost every drop. He could barely hoist his eyelids. "You OK?" he asked Desie. "He hurt you?"

"Nothing that three or four months in a scalding bath won't cure. But no, he didn't get what he was after," she said, "thanks to you and McGuinn and this gentleman."

Twilly swallowed a deep breath. "Somebody's been shooting a gun. I smell it."

"Son, I told you to hush," the captain said. Then to Desie: "You got something clean I can use on him?"

She retrieved her bra from inside the car. With a pocketknife, the captain cut a swatch of padding from one of the cups. He folded the foam into a makeshift plug, which he gently worked into Twilly's wound.

"Somewhere in my raincoat," the captain said to Desie, "there's a phone. Can you get it for me?"

Twilly shut his eyes. Moments later Desie took his hands, her touch supernaturally hot. He was losing it; slipping under. He heard the beeps of a keypad, followed by half a conversation. The captain's voice trailed Twilly into a dream, his third ever. He believed it might be his last.

"Jim, you awake?"

In the dream Twilly was on a beach that looked very much like Toad Island. It was straight-up noon.

"Listen, how many helicopters they got waiting around on the governor these days? . . . Because I need to borrow one. The fastest they got."

In the dream Twilly was chasing after a black dog, and the dog was chasing after a man. They all were running hard.

"It's the kid, Jim. . . . Gunshot to the chest. Be nice if they could round up a doctor for the ride."

In Twilly's dream he somehow caught up with the dog, passing it with a terrific kick of speed. Rapidly he gained ground on the man who was running away. Drawing closer, Twilly saw that the man was wearing baggy Jockey shorts and a sleeveless undershirt. He looked scrawny and old, too old to be moving so fast.

"*We're still on the island. He can set the chopper down on the beach.*"

Twilly tackled the man from behind. He rolled him over in the sand and was about to uncork a punch when he saw it was his father. In the dream, Little Phil Spree blinked up at his son and chirped, "The coast is clear! The coast is clear!"

"*I've got the man who shot the boy. . . . I haven't decided yet, Jim, but don't you worry your pretty head.*"

In the dream the dog began to bark madly and spin; a frantic feral spell. Twilly Spree pulled away from his father and sprung to his feet. All along the shore, as far as he could see in both directions, were shiny mustard-yellow bulldozers. Poised on every dune! Blades glinting in the sun, the dozers were aligned in ready position at identical angles, like a division of panzers. "The coast is clear!" crooned Twilly's father.

"*The woman's doing all right. I expect she'll want to ride along in the whirlybird. . . . She's nodding yes. Also, there's a station wagon here that oughta be disposed of pretty quick.*"

Twilly ran headlong for the water. The black dog followed him in, baying insanely. The Gulf was chilly and mirror-calm. When the dog finally quit barking, Twilly could hear his father chanting mindlessly on the beach—and also the fearsome rumble of the bulldozers, chewing up the island. In the dream Twilly waited for the dog to catch up, and together they struck out for the horizon. The sky over the water darkened with birds that were spooked from the island by the din of the earth-moving machines. As he swam farther and farther out to sea, Twilly grew afraid that the gulls and terns and skimmers would start tumbling down like before, blood-spattered and broken. If that happened, he wouldn't be able to bear it—he was too weak and too lost. If the birds came down again, it would be over, Twilly knew. In such a morbid rain, he would drown. He would not survive his own dream.

"Good news. I'm coming in on that chopper, too. . . . I got a little errand to run and you're gonna help me, Lieutenant. . . . Because you wouldn't want to miss it for the world, that's why."

TWENTY-FIVE

Oh, Mr. Gash put up a fight.

Not a great fight, but then again, he was minus a kneecap and most of his tongue. So pain was a factor. Plus he was stark naked, which seriously compromised his freewheeling style of personal combat. Nonetheless, he managed to get off a couple of right hooks that would have knocked most men to their knees.

The punches had no discernible effect upon the bum in the checkered skirt, who at the time was lugging Mr. Gash down the slope of a hill. The hill was not a natural formation, for Toad Island was as flat as a skillet. The hill had been created by earth-moving machines. It was a steep mound of scraped-up soil, scrub and tree stumps; the debris of a road-grading incursion through the pine woods. The bum had slung Mr. Gash over one shoulder, like a sack of lime, and charged down the soft-packed bank. He seemed to be in a hurry. Mr. Gash slugged at him frenetically, landing at least two monster blows—one to the ribs, one to the kidneys. Nothing; not even a grunt of acknowledgment. The bum kept to his mission. Mr. Gash flailed and spluttered incoherently. He knew something bad was coming. He just didn't know what.

At the bottom of the hill, the bum dumped him and turned to go back up.

Now what? thought Mr. Gash. He made one last ferocious swipe at the man but came away with only the pinned-together checkered skirt, which turned out to be a flag of the sort waved at the finish line of automobile races. Mr. Gash used it to sop the blood from the holes in his cheeks. The stump of his tongue stung like a mother. He lay in the mulch and pondered his options, which were limited. Because his mangled right leg was useless, escape by running, walking or crawling was impossible. He would have to wriggle, and wriggle swiftly, assuming the bum was not finished with him.

With a mournful effort, Mr. Gash rolled himself over. He reached out both arms, dug his fingers into the sodden grit and pulled himself forward until his chin touched his knuckles. Total linear progress: Two feet, max.

Mr. Gash thought: This sucks. He felt the tickle of an insect on his buttocks and flogged at it awkwardly. From the other side of the man-made hill came the *chug-chugging* of an engine, too rackety to be a car. Steadily it got louder. Mr. Gash craned his neck, squinting into the gloom. Of course he knew what he was hearing. He'd driven one of the damn things himself, the night he took care of that troublemaker Brinkman. Now the rig loomed directly above him, on the crest of the slope. Mr. Gash recognized the blocky square-edged outline. He could smell the acrid exhaust. A tall figure emerged from the cab, then reached back inside—undoubtedly to release the brake.

"Fuugghh me," Mr. Gash groaned.

The bulldozer jolted clangorously downhill. Rapidly, Mr. Gash tried to drag himself out of its path, and he almost made it. Only half of him got pinned under the track; the lower half.

So his lungs still worked, which was encouraging. Another positive sign was the surprising lack of pain below his waist. Mr. Gash concluded that the bulldozer had not crushed his torso so much as embedded it in the spongy turf. His immediate concern were the diesel fumes being belched into his face. His eyes burned and his stomach roiled—obviously the dozer's exhaust pipes had been damaged in the descent. Eventually the machine would run out of fuel and its engine would cut off, but Mr. Gash wondered if he could stay conscious until then, inhaling from a noxious cloud. He felt simultaneously sleepy and convulsive.

A pair of dirt-caked hiking boots appeared before him. Then the bulldozer hiccuped once and went silent. As the smoke dissipated, Mr. Gash raised up on his forearms and drank in the fresh breeze. Crouched beside him was the bum, his glass eye gleaming like a polished ruby in the starlight.

"You're gonna die out here," he said to Mr. Gash.

"Ungh-ungh."

"Yeah, you are, Iggy. It's all over."

"Iggy"? Now the fucker's making fun of my hair! Mr. Gash boiled.

"You're dying even as we speak," the bum said. "Trust me. I know a thing or two about roadkill. You qualify."

"Ungh-ungh!"

"In case you haven't noticed, your ass is lying under a Cat D6. That's twenty tons of serious steel," said the bum. "I don't know about making peace with God, but it might be a good time to tell the young lady you're sorry for trying to hurt her. Want me to go get her?"

Mr. Gash said, "Fuugghh oooh, popff."

The bum stood up. "That's a mighty poor attitude," he said, "for a man who's bleeding out of both ears. Now, if you'll excuse me, Iggy, I've gotta go track down some fool dog."

"FUUGGHH OOOOH!"

Mr. Gash's head sagged. Soon he heard the crunch of the bum's heavy footsteps fading into the woods.

What an idiot, thought Mr. Gash. He should've shot me! I'll be out of here by dawn!

Hastily he began trying to dig himself out from beneath the track of the bulldozer. The task was arduous. Being pinned on his tummy, Mr. Gash was forced to reach behind himself and work his arms like turtle flippers. After twenty grueling minutes Mr. Gash quit in exhaustion. He fell asleep with a centipede skittling across his shoulder blade. He was too weary to slap it away.

Hours later a helicopter awakened him. It was daylight; a high rose-tinged sky. Mr. Gash couldn't see the chopper but he could hear the egg-beater percussion of the rotors as it landed nearby. He lifted his head and gave an unholy wail; pain had found him. Horrible, nerve-shearing, bone-snapping pain. He observed, despairingly, that all his frantic digging had accomplished little. A pitiable few handfuls of dirt had been scalloped around each leg, upon which the Caterpillar D6 remained steadfastly parked. Mr. Gash could not drag himself a single millimeter out from under it. After a third attempt, he gave up.

Instead of escape, he now focused on survival. The helicopter, of course. It would be lifting off soon—Mr. Gash could tell by the accelerating whine of the engines. Anxiously he scanned the ground within his reach, searching for something, anything, to draw the pilot's attention. His eyes fixed upon a silky-looking wad in the muck. It was the crazy bum's skirt—the checkered racing flag, now lavishly spotted with Mr. Gash's dried blood. He snatched it up and shook off the loose dirt.

With a head-splitting roar, a black-and-gray jet helicopter appeared over the spires of the pines. With both hands Mr. Gash raised the checkered flag. He began a wildly exaggerated wave, flopping his upper body back and forth like a rubber windshield wiper. It was a completely new experience for Mr. Gash: desperation. He swung the flag with the fervor of a drunken soccer hooligan, for he feared the pilot couldn't see him, grime-smeared and half-interred beneath a bulldozer.

He was right. The chopper circled the clearing once but didn't hover. It banked sharply to the north and hummed off.

The flag dropped from Mr. Gash's hands. He was in the purest mortal agony. From the waist down: dead. From the waist up: every cell a burning cinder. His head thundered. His arms were cement. His throat was broken glass on the scabby nub of his tongue. Sickening trickles ran down the fuzz of both jawlines, all the way to Mr. Gash's chin—warm blood from his ears.

That fucking troublemaker of a bum had been right. It was over.

Or maybe not.

Mr. Gash noticed a small object on the ground, something he couldn't have spotted in the dark. It lay a few precious feet out of reach, partially hidden by a palmetto frond. It was black and rectangular and plastic-looking, like the remote control of a VCR, or the clip to a Glock.

Or a cellular telephone.

Mr. Gash used a broken branch to retrieve it. Woozily, he mashed at the POWER button with his forefinger. The phone emitted a perky bleep and lit up with a peachy glow. Mr. Gash stared at the numbers on the keypad. A desolate smirk came to his whitening lips.

Palmer Stoat said, "Good news, Bob."

"Better be."

They met at noon in Pube's; this time in a champagne booth reserved for private friction dancing.

Stoat said, "Remember the other night we were here? Well, I got a date afterward with one of the Pamela Anderson Lees."

"You're a pig," Robert Clapley remarked mirthlessly.

"Back to the bachelor life for me. I'm moving on!"

"That's your news?"

"No," said Palmer Stoat. "The news is big."

Clapley looked as if he hadn't slept in a year. Sullenly he fingered the gold link chain on his neck. A dancer approached the table and introduced herself as Cindi with an *i*. Clapley gave her a ten and sent her away.

Stoat said, "I take it you haven't found your Barbies."

"They called me."

"Hey! It's a start."

"From the residence of Mr. Avalon Brown." Robert Clapley took a slug of bourbon. "Mr. Brown is recruiting investors for his newest feature-film project.

Katya and Tish thought it would be nice of me to help out. They, of course, would get starring roles in the movie."

"Which is titled . . ."

"*Double Your Pleasure.*"

"Ah. An art film." Palmer Stoat smiled commiseratingly. "And how much have you agreed to invest?"

"For a hundred thousand dollars, Mr. Avalon Brown promises to make me a full partner," Clapley said. "For a tenth of that, I could have him killed."

Inwardly, Stoat shuddered. A messy homicide scandal could wreck everything: the Shearwater deal, Dick Artemus's re-election chances and (last but not least) Stoat's own career.

He lay a consoling hand on Clapley's shoulder. "Bob, for the last time, forget about those two tramps. You've got to move on, the way I'm moving on."

"I can't."

"Sure you can. Join me on the Palmer pussy patrol." Clapley said, "Know what I've got in my pants?"

"Dolls?"

"Righto."

"How many?" Stoat asked dispiritedly.

"Two in each pocket."

"These would be the Vibrator Barbies?"

"Screw you, Palmer. I miss the twins. I want them back," Robert Clapley said, waving off another dancer. "They say I don't help with the movie, they're cutting off all their hair and moving to Kingston."

"Sunny Jamaica."

"World headquarters of Avalon Brown Productions."

"Let 'em go," Stoat said. "I'm begging you."

"Are you deaf? It's *not* going to happen." Clapley

gave a brittle laugh. "That's why men like Mr. Gash exist—and prosper. Because of situations like this."

Stoat said, "Speaking of which, here's some of that good news I promised. That pesky problem we've been having up at Toad Island is all taken care of. The kid who grabbed my dog is in the hospital with a forty-five-caliber hole in his chest."

"Fantastic! That means Mr. Gash is available for a new job."

"I don't know about Mr. Gash. My information comes directly from the governor," Stoat said, "and he wasn't too clear on the details. The important thing is, that nutty kid is finally out of the picture. And, oh yeah, Desie and Boodle are OK, too. Not that I give a shit."

Robert Clapley found himself gazing past Stoat, at a dancer performing in a nearby booth. She had long golden hair, high conical breasts and pouty lacquered lips.

"Close." Clapley was talking strictly to himself. "If only she was taller."

"Jesus Hubbard Christ. You want to hear the rest, or you want to go diddle with your dollies?" Palmer Stoat unsheathed a Cohiba and fired it up with a flourish. He took his sweet time.

Without looking away from the woman, Clapley said, "Tell me about the bridge money. Tell me it's all set."

"We're almost there, Bob. It's ninety-nine percent a done deal."

"Who's the one percent?"

"Willie Vasquez-Washington."

"Again!"

"Don't worry. He's almost there."

Robert Clapley sneered. "I've heard that one before. How tall you think that girl is? The blonde."

"Gee, Bob, it's awful hard to tell while she's got her feet hooked behind her ears."

"I assume you've got another plan."

"Oh, a good one."

"Do tell."

"We're taking Rainbow Willie on a hunting trip. You, me and Governor Dick. At that private game reserve I told you about up in Marion County," Stoat said. "We're gonna hunt, drink, smoke and tell stories. And we're gonna make friends with Willie, whatever it takes."

Clapley scowled. "Whoa. That little prick is *not* getting my trophy cat."

"That's the other thing I came to tell you. Durgess, my guide, he says they sent the ranch a bum cheetah. A stone gimp."

"That's good news?"

"No, Bob, the good news is, he's got a rhinoceros instead. A genuine killer rhino." Stoat paused suspensefully. "Stomped a man to death a few years back."

Robert Clapley's head snapped around. Tremulously he sat forward. "And the horn?"

"Huge," Stoat whispered. "Major stud dust."

"God. That's fantastic."

Clapley's hands dove under the table, into his pockets. Stoat pretended not to notice.

"When's the hunt?" Clapley was breathless.

"This weekend. Durgess said the sooner the better."

"Yes! They'll come back to me now, for sure. Katya and Tish, I know they will." Clapley was radiant. "They'll come running home for the good stuff—especially when they find out I'm going to shoot the big bastard myself. A killer rhino. Can you imagine? They'll dump that ganja turd in a heartbeat."

"In which case, you wouldn't have to kill him, right?" Stoat cringed whenever he thought of Porcupine Head amok.

Clapley shrugged. "Frankly, I'd rather spend my money on something else. Mr. Gash isn't cheap." Clapley snatched a cigar out of Stoat's pocket. "And neither are you, Palmer. How much is all this extra fun going to cost me? Remember, you owed me the cheetah and then some. So . . . how much?"

"Not a dime, Bob. The hunt is on me."

"That's mighty kind."

"But the horn you've got to buy separately," Stoat said, "at the price we discussed. Rules of the house."

"Glad to do it," said Clapley. "Oh, by the way, these Cohibas of yours are counterfeit."

"What! No way."

"You can tell by the labels, Palmer. See these tiny black dots? They're supposed to be raised up, so you can feel 'em with your fingertips. That's how they come from the factory in La Habana. But these you got"—Clapley, wagging one in front of Stoat's nose—"see, the dots are smooth to the touch. That means they're el fake-o."

"No way," Stoat huffed. "Three hundred dollars a box at the Marina Hemingway. No way they're knock-offs." He removed the cigar from his lips and set it, unaffectionately, on the table's edge. He hunched close to examine the label.

Robert Clapley stood to leave. He patted Stoat on the back and said, "Don't worry, buddy. I'll get us some real McCoys, for the big rhinoceros hunt."

At that moment, a Florida Highway Patrol car entered the black wrought-iron gate of the governor's mansion in Tallahassee. At the door, a plain-clothes FDLE agent waved Lt. Jim Tile inside, but not before giving his two companions a hard skeptical look. One was a black dog. The other was a man who was not properly attired for lunch with the chief executive.

Lisa June Peterson was waiting for them.

"Nice to see you again," Skink said, kissing her cheek. "You look ever-lovely."

Lisa June's cheeks flushed. Jim Tile shot a laser glare at his friend, who beamed innocently.

"I got him to shower," the trooper said, "but that's all."

"He looks fine," said Lisa June Peterson.

Former Governor Clinton Tyree wore hiking boots, his blaze orange rain jacket with matching trousers, a new shower cap (with a daisy pattern) and a vest made from Chihuahua pelts.

"For special occasions," he explained.

"Dear Lord," Jim Tile said.

"It's truly one of a kind."

Lisa June said nothing; surely there was a story behind the vest, and just as surely she didn't want to hear it. She knelt to scratch McGuinn's chin. "Aw, what a handsome boy."

"An OK dog," Skink conceded, "but definitely not the brightest bulb in the chandelier."

Lisa June took the former governor's arm. "Come on. He's waiting for you."

"Oh, I'm tingling with excitement."

"Don't start," Jim Tile said. "You promised."

Skink told Lisa June: "Hon, don't mind Jim. He's just pissed because I lost his cell phone."

She led them to the dining room. Lunch was hearts-of-palm salad, conch chowder, medallions of venison and Key lime pie.

"An all-Florida menu," Lisa June announced with a whimsical curtsy, "in yore onna, suh!"

Skink parked himself at the head of the long table. The trooper said, without irony, "That's the governor's place, Governor."

"Yes, Jim, I remember."

"Don't do this."

"Do what?"

Lisa June said, "It's fine, Lieutenant. Governor Artemus has been fully briefed."

"With all due respect, I seriously doubt that."

Through a side door burst Dick Artemus; dapper, energized and primed to charm. His face was fresh-scrubbed and ruddy, his hair lustrous and ardently brushed, his green eyes clear and twinkling. When Clinton Tyree stood up, the governor bear-hugged him as if he were a long-lost twin.

"The one and only! I can't believe you're here!" Dick Artemus looked positively misty.

Dropping to one knee, he fondly grabbed McGuinn by the ruff and made *coo-cheee-coo* sounds. "Hey, boy,

I'm glad to see you still got both ears. That bad man didn't hurt you after all!"

Skink glanced skeptically at Jim Tile.

"This is quite an honor," Dick Artemus said, rising.

"Why?" Skink asked.

"Because you're a legend, Governor."

"I'm a goddamned footnote in a history book. That's all."

"How about a glass of orange juice?" Lisa June Peterson suggested.

"Thanks. Heavy on the pulp," Skink said.

Dick Artemus exclaimed: "Me, too! The best OJ is the kind you gotta chew. What're those little beauties tied to the ends of your beard—may I ask?"

"Buzzard beaks."

"Ah! I was gonna guess eagles." Dick Artemus signaled to one of the stewards. "Sean, an orange juice for the governor and how about a screwdriver for me. And you folks?"

In unison, Jim Tile and Lisa June Peterson declined a beverage.

"So, tell me," Dick Artemus burbled to Skink, "how's the old place look? Seven hundred North Adams Street."

"About the same."

"Bring back memories?"

"More like hives."

The governor was undaunted. "Was the gym built when you were here? Would you like a tour?"

Skink looked at Lisa June. "Is he for real?" He threw back his head and cackled. "A tour!"

Lunch was more small talk; Dick Artemus was the world champion of small talkers. Lt. Jim Tile was strung drum-tight, and he finished his meal as rapidly as decent manners allowed. He had argued vigorously against such a meeting, as there was no telling how Clinton Tyree would react upon returning to the mansion after so many years. The trooper also held no expectation that the ex-governor would take a liking to the present governor, or for that matter show him even a trace of respect. Nothing good could come of the visit, Jim Tile had warned Lisa June Peterson, who had promised to warn the governor.

But Dick Artemus wasn't worried, for he believed he was the most irresistible sonofabitch in the whole world. He believed he could make *anyone* like him. And he had been flattered to learn that the legendary Clinton Tyree wanted to meet him.

"Tell me about your eye," he chirped.

"If you tell me about your hair."

Lisa June, helpfully: "Governor Tyree lost the eye many years ago, during a violent robbery."

"Actually, it was more of an old-fashioned assault," Skink said, inhaling a frothy sliver of pie. "I go through glass eyeballs like underwear. A friend of mine found this one in Belgrade." He tapped the crimson iris with a tine of his silver dessert fork. "Said she got it off a Gypsy king, and I choose to believe her. She had quite a circus background."

The governor nodded as if this were conversation he heard every day. His attention was broken by something poking him between his legs—the Labrador, lobbying for a handout. Dick Artemus genially slipped the dog a chunk of corn bread.

"Let's talk turkey," he said. "First, I want to thank you, Governor, for finding this troubled young man."

"Unfortunately, someone else found him first."

"Yes. Lieutenant Tile notified me as soon as he heard. He also told me how you risked your life to get the kid out alive."

"A promise is a promise." Skink put down the fork with a sharp clink. "I kept mine."

"Yes. You sure did." The governor shifted uneasily, then pretended it was because of the dog nosing him beneath the table. Lisa June Peterson knew better. So did Jim Tile.

Skink said, "You said you're going to get the boy some counseling."

"That's right."

"Where?"

"Uh . . . well, wherever he wants," Dick Artemus fumbled. "How's he doing, by the way? How bad was he hit?"

"He'll make it. He's tough," Skink said. "Why're all those cops outside his hospital room?"

"For his own protection," the governor replied matter-of-factly. "Somebody tried to kill him, remember?"

"So he's not under arrest?"

"Not to my knowledge. Mr. Stoat isn't interested in prosecuting. He says the publicity of a trial would be unwelcome, and I couldn't agree more."

"All right," said Skink, planting his elbows on the table. "Now, what about my brother?"

"Yes?" The governor snuck an anxious glance at Lisa June Peterson.

"Doyle," she said.

"Right. Doyle Tyree!" said Dick Artemus, awash

with relief. "The lighthouse keeper. Certainly he can stay there as long as he wants. Hillsborough Inlet, right?"

"Peregrine Bay." Again Skink turned to Lisa June Peterson. "Would you and Jim mind if I spoke to the governor in private?"

Lisa June tried to object and Jim Tile weighed in with a grave sigh, but Dick Artemus brushed them off. "Of course they don't mind. Lisa June, why don't you take this puppy out back and introduce him to some of our magnificent old Leon County pine trees." Dick Artemus had a speech to give in thirty minutes, and he didn't wish to be seen with dog snot on his inseam.

Once they were alone, the former governor said to the present governor: "What about that island?"

"It'll be real nice when they're done."

"It's real nice now," Skink said. "Ever been there?"

Dick Artemus said he hadn't. "Look, you remember how this stuff works." He drained his glass down to the ice cubes, chasing the last of the vodka. "The guy wrote some major checks to my campaign. In return, he expects a little consideration. Slack, if you want to call it that. And I've gotta say, he's done most everything by the book with this Shearwater thing. The zoning, the permits, the wildlife surveys—it all looks kosher. That's what my people say."

"You oughta at least see the place before you let 'em wreck it."

"Governor, I appreciate how you feel."

"You don't appreciate shit."

"What're you doing? Hey, let go!"

*

The bulldozer dream kept rerunning itself, the snarling chorus of machines chasing Twilly Spree farther and farther from shore. The way it finally ended was: The gulls began falling from the sky, just as Twilly had dreaded. The birds were stiff before they hit the water and they hurtled down like rocks, splashing around his head. He dove to escape, but whenever he surfaced for a breath he got struck; a sickening *thwock* against his skull. Twilly soon lost the strength to swim, and he found himself sinking into an icy whorl of cobalt and foam. It felt like talons pulling him down, death clawing at his bare legs. Then something powerful took hold of him and tugged him upward, out of the swirling cold and free of the grasping claws.

The black dog! It was like a damn Disney flick, a plucky hound swimming to the rescue, dragging him to the top for air. . . .

Except it wasn't a dog bringing him up. It was Desie, one arm behind his head, holding him upright while she adjusted the pillows. The first thing Twilly saw when he opened his eyes was the pale cleft at the base of her neck. He leaned forward to kiss it, a deed that (judging by the pain) split open his chest.

Desie was smiling. "Somebody's feeling better."

"Lots," Twilly gasped.

"Don't try to talk," she said, "or smooch."

She pecked him on the forehead; not a good sign. They always pecked him on the forehead right before they said good-bye.

"I'm sorry about everything," he told her.

"Why? I was there because I wanted to be."

"You leaving?"

She nodded. "Hot-lanta. Spend some catch-up time with the folks."

"I love you," Twilly said blearily, though it was absolutely true. It was also true he would fall in love with the next woman who slept with him, as always.

Desie Stoat said, "I know you do."

"You look incredible."

"It's the Demerol, darling. I look like hell. Get some rest now."

"What about that man. . . ."

"Oh!" Desie tweaked his ankle through the blanket. "You'll never guess who he is!"

When she told him, Twilly acted as if he'd been mainlined with pure adrenaline. His head rocked off the bed and he blurted: "I know that name! From my mother."

"Clinton Tyree?"

"The whole story! She thought he was a hero. My father said he was a nut."

Desie said, "Well, he hit on me in the helicopter."

"See? That proves he's sane." Twilly flashed a weak smile before sinking back on the pillows.

"He also expressed an extremely low opinion of my husband. He said a school-yard flasher would be a step up."

Twilly chuckled. A nurse bustled in to fiddle with the drip on his IV bag. She told him to get some sleep, and on her way out favored Desie with a scalding glare.

"I spoke to Palmer this morning. Just to let him know I'm OK," Desie said. "He sounded happy as a clam. He's going hunting this weekend with Governor Dick and—guess who else—Robert Clapley. I suppose they're celebrating Shearwater."

Twilly grunted curiously. "Hunting for what? Where?"

"Honey, even if I knew, I'd never tell." Desie wore a sad smile. She traced a finger lightly down his cheek. "All that crazy talk about killing somebody—you keep it up, hotshot, you're headed for an early grave. Call me selfish but I don't want to be around when it happens."

Twilly Spree spoke out of a fog. "Have faith," he said.

Desie laughed ruefully. "Faith I've got. It's good sense I'm dangerously short of."

When she stood up to go, Twilly saw she was wearing a new sundress: sea green with spaghetti straps. It put a knot in his heart.

"I need a favor. It's McGuinn," Desie said. "Could you keep him until I get squared away? My mom's deathly allergic to dogs."

"What about Palmer?"

"Nossir. I might not get much out of this divorce, Twilly, but my husband is *not* keeping McGuinn. Please, can you take care of him?"

"Sure." Twilly liked the dog and he liked the idea of seeing Desie again, when she came to collect him. "Where is he now?"

"With Lieutenant Tile and you-know-who. The motel where I'm staying won't take pets." Desie picked up her purse. "I've got a flight to catch. Promise me one more thing."

"Shoot."

She put one knee on the edge of the bed and leaned forward to kiss him; a proper kiss this time. Then she whispered, "Don't make love to anyone else in front of the dog. He'll be so confused."

"Promise." Playfully, Twilly tried to grab her straps, but she slipped away.

"Be good. There're four humongous cops outside your door with nobody to pound on."

Twilly tried a feeble salute. He could barely lift his arm.

"Good-bye, hon," Desie said.

"Wait. That other guy, Gash. . . ."

Her eyes hardened. "Freak accident," she said.

"It happens." Suddenly Twilly was very sleepy. "Love you, Desie."

"So long, tiger."

CALLER: Hep meh! Peezh!

DISPATCHER: Do you have an emergency?

CALLER: Yeah, I gah a emoozhezhee! I gah a fugghy boo-gozer oh meh azzhhh!

DISPATCHER: "Boo-gozer"? Sir, I'm sorry, but you'll have to speak more clearly. This is Levy County Fire Rescue, do you have an emergency to report?

CALLER: Yeah! Hep! Mah baggh is boge! Ah bing zzhaa eng mah fay! I ngee hep!

DISPATCHER: Sir, do you speak English?

CALLER: Eh izzh Engizh! Mah ung gaw zzha off! Whif ah gung!

DISPATCHER: Hang on, Mr. Boogozer, I'm transferring you to someone who can take the information. . . .

CALLER: Ngooohh! Hep! Peezh!

DISPATCHER TWO: Diga. ¿Dónde estás?

CALLER: Aaaaaagghh!!!

DISPATCHER TWO: ¿Tienes un emergencia?

CALLER: Oh fugghh. I gaw die.
DISPATCHER TWO: Señor, por favor, no entiendo nada que estás diciendo.
CALLER: Hep! . . . Hep!

TWENTY-SIX

As a car salesman Dick Artemus encountered plenty of pissed-off folks—furious, frothing, beet-faced customers who believed they'd been gypped, deceived, baited, switched or otherwise butt-fucked. They were brought to Dick Artemus because of his silky demeanor, his indefatigable geniality, his astounding knack for making the most distraught saps feel good about themselves— indeed, about the whole human race! Regardless of how egregiously they'd been screwed over, no customers walked out of Dick Artemus's office angry; they emerged placid, if not radiantly serene. It was a gift, the other car salesmen would marvel. A guy like Dick came along maybe once every fifty years.

As governor of Florida, this preternatural talent for bullshitting had served Dick Artemus exquisitely. Even his most virulent political enemies conceded he was impossible not to like, one-on-one. So how could it be, Dick Artemus wondered abjectly, that Clinton Tyree alone was immune to his personal magnetism? The man did *not* like him; detested him, in fact. Dick Artemus could draw no other conclusion, given that the ex-governor now held him by the throat, pinned to the wood-paneled wall of the gubernatorial dining room. It had happened so fast—dragged like a rag doll across the table, through the remaining tangy crescent of Key lime pie—that Dick Artemus had not had time to ring for Sean or the bodyguards.

Clinton Tyree's brows twitched and his glass eyeball fluttered, and his grip was so hateful that the governor could not gulp out a word. That's the problem, Dick Artemus lamented. If only this crazy bastard would ease up, maybe I could talk my way out of this mess.

In the tumult Clinton Tyree had lost his shower cap, and his refulgent bullet-headed baldness further enhanced the aura of menace. Looming inches from the governor's meringue-smudged nose, he said: "I oughta open you up like a mackerel."

It hurt Dick Artemus to blink, his face was so pinched.

"Nothing must happen to disturb my brother. *Ever*," the ex-governor whispered hoarsely.

Dick Artemus managed a nod, the hinges of his jaw painfully obstructed by the brute's thumb and forefinger.

"What exactly do you believe in, sir?"

"Uh?" peeped Dick Artemus.

"The vision thing. What's yours—tract homes and shopping malls and trailer parks as far as the eye can see? More, more, more? More people, more cars, more roads, more houses." Clinton Tyree's breath was hot on the governor's cheeks. "More, more, more," he said. "More, more, more, more, more, more, more...."

Dick Artemus felt his feet dangling—the madman was hoisting him one-handed by the neck. A terrified squeak escaped from the governor.

"I didn't fit here, Dick," Clinton Tyree was saying. "But you! This is your place and your time. Selling is what you do best, and every blessed inch of this state is for sale. Same as when I had your job, Dickie, only the stakes are higher now because there's less of the good stuff to divvy up. How many islands are left untouched?"

Clinton Tyree laughed mordantly and let Dick Artemus slide down the wall. He hunched over him like a grave digger. "I know what I *ought* to do to you," he said. "But that might get my friends in hot water, so instead. . . ."

And the next thing the governor knew, he had been stripped of his coat, shirt and necktie. He lay bare-chested on the floor, with 240 pounds of one-eyed psychopath kneeling on his spine.

"What the hell're you doing?" he cried, then his head was roughly jerked backward until he could see the pitiless vermilion glow of Clinton Tyree's dead eye.

"Hush now, Governor Dick."

So Dick Artemus shut up and concentrated on bladder control, to preserve his dignity as well as the gubernatorial carpet. If Clinton Tyree did not intend to kill him, then what was he up to? Dick Artemus shivered when he felt his trousers being loosened and yanked down.

He thought: Aw Jesus, it's just like *Deliverance*.

Involuntarily his anus puckered, and he found himself suddenly ambivalent about the possibility of being rescued mid-sodomy—the headlines might be more excruciating than the crime. The only governor of Florida to be boned by a former governor on the floor of the governor's mansion! There's one for the history books, Dick Artemus thought disconsolately, and more than just a damn footnote.

Even worse than the threat of public humiliation was

the potential political fallout. Was Florida ready to re-elect a defiled chief executive? Dick Artemus had his doubts. He remembered how the audience felt about the Ned Beatty character at the end of the movie—you were sorry for the guy, but no one was standing in line for his next canoe trip.

A calloused paw grabbed one of the governor's buttocks and he girded for the worst. Then: an unexpected sensation, like a dry twig scratching up and down his flesh, or the lusty play of a woman's fingernails—sharp, yet pleasing. Dick Artemus remained motionless and oddly becalmed. He wondered what the big freak was doing, straddling his cheeks and humming so quietly to himself.

The bizarre proceeding was disrupted when a door opened and a woman shouted Clinton Tyree's name. Dick Artemus twisted his neck and saw Lisa June Peterson and Lt. Jim Tile each fastening themselves to one of the ex-governor's arms, pulling him away—the madman grinning yet submissive—out of the dining room.

Dick Artemus lurched to his feet and tugged up his pants and smoothed his tousled hair. Not a word would be said about this—Lisa June and the trooper could be counted upon for that. No one would ever know! He hurried to the bedroom for a freshly pressed shirt and notified his driver he was ready. And in the car on the way to the Planters Club, Dick Artemus breezily reviewed the notes for his speech, as if nothing out of the ordinary had happened. It was only later, after leaving the dais to a round of polite applause, that Dick Artemus discovered what Clinton Tyree had done to him. The FDLE agent standing outside the men's room heard a sob and flung open the door to see the governor of Florida with blood-flecked boxer shorts bunched at his ankles, his milk-white bum thrust toward the mirror. He was appraising himself woefully over one shoulder.

"Sir?" the agent said.

"Go away!" croaked Dick Artemus. "Out!"

But the agent already had seen it. And he could read it, too, even backward in the mirror:

The word SHAME in scabbing pink letters across the governor's bare ass, where it had been meticulously etched with a buzzard beak.

Jim Tile said, "This time you've outdone yourself."

"Jail?" Skink asked.

"Or the nuthouse."

Lisa June Peterson said, "Are you kidding? Nobody's going to jail. This never happened."

They were heading to the hospital in Jim Tile's patrol car. The trooper and Lisa June sat up front. McGuinn and the ex-governor were curled in two aromatic heaps—one black and one fluorescent orange—on the backseat, in the prisoner cage.

"Imagine if Governor Artemus orders Governor Tyree prosecuted," Lisa June was saying. "Once the story leaks out, Lord, it's front-page news all over the country—and not the kind you clip out for the family scrapbook, if you're Dick Artemus."

From the backseat: "What's the big deal? He won't scar."

Jim Tile said, "I believe you're missing the point."

"Two weeks, his scrawny butt'll be as good as new. What?" Skink perked up. "Lisa June, are you giggling?"

"No."

"Yes, you are!"

"Well, it was . . ."

"Funny?" Skink prompted.

"Not what I expected to see, that's all." Lisa June Peterson tried to compose herself. "You on top of him. Him with his fanny showing. . . ."

Thinking about the scene, Jim Tile had to chuckle, as well. "When can I go home?" he said.

From the backseat: "Soon as we spring the boy."

Lisa June addressed both of them. "If anyone asks, here's what happened today: Governor Richard Artemus held a cordial, uneventful private lunch with former Governor Clinton Tyree. They discussed—let's see—bass fishing, Florida history, the restructuring of the state Cabinet—and the strenuous job demands of the office of chief executive. The meeting lasted less than an hour, after which former Governor Tyree declined a tour of the refurbished residence, due to a previous commitment to visit a friend in a local hospital. All agreed?"

"Sounds good to me," Jim Tile said.

"It will sound even better to Governor Artemus. Trust me."

Skink sat up in the cage. "But what about that bridge?"

Jim Tile said, "Don't even think about it."

"Hell, I'm just curious."

"Your work is done here, Governor."

"Oh, relax, Lieutenant."

Lisa June Peterson said, "They'll reappropriate the bridge funding next week, during the special session. Once that happens, Shearwater is a go."

Skink sagged forward, hooking sun-bronzed fingers in the steel mesh. "So the veto was bullshit. They lied to the boy."

"Of course they did. They thought he was going to kill your buddy." Lisa June nodded toward the dozing dog. "It was extortion, captain. They couldn't cave in."

"Plus the bridge is a twenty-eight-million-dollar item."

"There's that, yes."

"And let's not forget that Governor Pencil Dick is dearly beholden to Shearwater's developer."

"Agreed," Lisa June Peterson said, "but the point is, everything worked out. Mr. Stoat's dog is safe. Mr. Stoat's wife is safe. And the young man, Mr. Spree, will get the professional help he needs. . . ."

Skink snorted. "The island, however, is fucked."

A cheerless silence settled over the occupants of the patrol car. Jim Tile thought: This is precisely what I was afraid of. This was the danger they risked, bringing him out of the swamp on such heartless terms.

The trooper said, "Governor, where will you take the kid?"

"A safe place. Don't you worry."

"Until he's feeling better?"

"Sure."

"Then what?" Lisa June asked.

"Then he's free to burn down the goddamn capitol building if he wants. I'm not his father," Skink groused, "and I'm not his rabbi." Once again he drew himself caterpillar-like into a ball, resting his shaved dome on the car seat. The Labrador awoke briefly and licked him on the brow.

As Jim Tile wheeled up to the hospital entrance, Lisa

June Peterson asked: "You sure about this? He's OK to travel?"

The trooper explained that Twilly Spree's gunshot wound was a through-and-through; minor damage to the right lung, two fractured ribs, no major veins or arteries nicked.

"Lucky fella," Jim Tile said. "In any case, he's safer with him"—cutting his eyes toward the backseat—"than anyplace else. Somebody wanted the young man dead. Maybe still does."

"What if those officers upstairs won't let him out?"

"Miss Peterson, three of those troopers are being evaluated next month for promotions. Guess who's one of the evaluators?" Jim Tile removed his mirrored sunglasses and folded them into a breast pocket. "I don't think they'll raise a fuss if Mr. Spree decides to check himself out."

From the backseat: "You ever been there?"

"Excuse me, Governor?"

"Jim, I'm talking to Lisa June. Darling, you ever been down to Toad Island?"

"No."

"You just might like it."

"I'm sure I would," she said.

"No, I meant you might like it *the way it is*. Without the fairways and yacht basins and all the touristy crap."

Lisa June Peterson turned to face him. "I know exactly what you meant, captain."

Jim Tile parked in the shade and left the back windows cracked, so the dog could get some fresh air. While a nurse changed Twilly Spree's dressing, the three of them—Skink, Lisa June and Jim Tile—waited outside the hospital room. Jim Tile spoke quietly to the four young troopers posted at the door, then led them down the hall for coffee. Skink flopped cross-legged on the bare floor. Lisa June borrowed a spring-backed chair from the nursing station and sat next to him.

He eyed her with an avuncular amusement. "So, you're going to stay put here in Tallahassee. Learn the ropes. Be a star." The ex-governor winked.

"Maybe I'll write a book about you instead."

"I enjoy Graham Greene. I'd like to think he would have found me interesting," Skink mused, "or at least moral."

"I do," Lisa June said.

"No, you write a book about Governor Dickless instead—and publish it before the next election. Wouldn't that be a kick in the kumquats!" Skink's mandrill howl startled a middle-aged patient wearing a neck brace and rolling an IV rig down the hallway. The man made a wobbly U-turn and steamed back toward the safety of his room.

Lisa June Peterson lowered her voice. "Look, I was thinking. . . ."

"Me, too." The captain, playfully pinching one of her ankles.

"Not about *that*."

"Well, you should. It'll do you good."

"The new bridge," Lisa June whispered. "Shearwater."

"Yeah?"

"The deal's not sewn up yet. There's one more meeting." She told him who would be there. "And Palmer Stoat, too, of course. He set the whole thing up. It's a hunting trip."

Skink's thatched eyebrows hopped. "Where?"

"That's the problem. They're going to a private game ranch outside Ocala. You need an invitation to get in."

"Darling, please."

"But let's say you did get in," Lisa June continued. "I was thinking you could talk to them about Toad Island. Talk to them the way you talked to me about Florida that night by the campfire. Who knows, maybe they'd agree to scale down the project. Leave some free beach and a few trees at least. If you can just get Dick on your side—"

"Oh, Lisa June—"

"Listen! If you can get Dick on your side, the others might go along. He can be incredibly persuasive, believe me. You haven't seen him at his best."

"I should hope not," said Skink, toying with his buzzard beaks. "Lisa June, I just whittled a serious insult into the man's rear end. He ain't never *ever* gonna be on my side. And you know that." The captain leaned sideways and smooched one of her kneecaps. "But I sincerely appreciate the information."

The door to Twilly Spree's room opened and they both got up. A pleasant freckle-faced nurse reported that Mr. Spree was improving by the hour.

Lisa June Peterson tugged Skink's sleeve. "I'd better be getting back to the capitol. The boss has a busy afternoon."

"Don't you want to meet the notorious psycho dog-napper?"

"Better not. I just might like him."

Skink nodded. "That would be confusing, wouldn't it?"

"Heartbreaking is more like it," she said, "if something bad were to happen."

When he wrapped his great arms around her, Lisa June felt bundled and hidden; safe. He told her: "Between you and Jim, I've never seen such worriers."

From somewhere in the deep crinkly folds of his embrace he heard her ask: "But it wouldn't hurt to try, would it? Talking sense to them, I mean. What could it hurt?"

"It's a hunting trip, darling. Can't be talking out loud during a hunt. You gotta stay real quiet, in order to sneak up on the varmints." Skink pressed his lips to her forehead. "Sorry for making a mess of lunch. How about a rain check?"

"Anytime."

"Bye now, Lisa June."

"Good-bye, Governor."

They had sex on the lion-skin rug in the den, under the dull glassy gaze of the fish and wild animals Palmer Stoat had killed: the Cape buffalo, the timber wolf, the tuft-eared lynx, the bull elk, the striped marlin, the tarpon. . . .

Afterward, Estella, the right-wing prostitute from Swain's, asked: "You miss her?"

"Miss her? I booted her!" Stoat proclaimed. "The dog's a different story. Boodle was good company."

"You're fulla shit."

"How about another drink?"

"Why not," she said.

They were both nude, and smoking Havana's finest. Romeo y Julieta was the brand. Palmer Stoat was delighted to have found a partner who would keep a lit cigar in her mouth during athletic intercourse. Later, if he could get it up again, he would snap some pictures—the two of them going at it, stogie-to-stogie, like dueling smokestacks!

Her scotch freshened, Estella rolled on one side and stroked the frizzy auburn mane of the lion skin. "You shot this stud muffin yourself?"

"I told you, sweetheart. I shot all of 'em." Stoat fondly patted the tawny hide, as if it were the flank of a favorite saddle horse. "This sumbitch was tough, too. Took me three slugs at point-blank."

It would have taken only one had Stoat not been bowled off his feet by the pack of fourteen half-starved hounds that Durgess had deployed to tree the exhausted cat. While falling, Stoat had squeezed off two wild rounds that struck a hapless grackle and a cabbage palm, respectively. These colorful details were not shared with rapt Estella.

"Tell me about Africa," she said, pursing her painted lips to launch a halo of blue smoke.

"Africa. Yes." Most everything he knew about Africa came from National Geographic TV specials.

"Where did you go to 'bag' this lion—Kenya?"

"That's right. Kenya." Stoat ran a dry tongue across his lips, dawbing at the honeyed sheen of Johnnie Walker. "Africa is . . . amazing," he ventured. "Incredible."

"Oh, I'd give anything to go there someday." Estella said it dreamily, with a shake of her hair.

Balancing a drink in one hand, Stoat carefully pivoted on his side and fitted himself to the slope of her bottom, spoon-style. "It's so big," he said quietly. "Africa is."

"Big. Yes." Estella arched seductively and Stoat deftly

drew back, so as not to ignite her multi-hued locks with his cigar.

"Sweetheart, it would take years to see it all."

"We should go together, Palmer. You could hunt and I could go antiquing," she said. "No charge for the sex, either. You pay for my plane tickets, the nookie is free."

Stoat was tempted to say yes. God knows he needed to get away. And as soon as the legislature finished its final bit of nonsense next week . . . well, why not a safari vacation to Africa? By the time he returned, the movers would have cleaned out Desie's stuff and the house would feel like his own again. Stoat could begin remodeling for bachelorhood. (He had changed his mind about moving; it would take years to find a place with such an ideal trophy room.)

"Let me see what I can do with my schedule," he told Estella, meaning he first wanted to float the Africa idea past his preferred choice of an overseas companion, the Pamela Anderson look-alike from Pube's. At the moment Stoat could not recall her Christian name, though he was sure he'd copied it on a cocktail napkin and saved it in his billfold.

"What's that empty spot?" said Estella, pointing at a conspicuous space on the animal wall.

"That's for my black rhino. I bagged it a couple weeks ago."

"A rhinoceros!"

"Magnificent beast," Palmer Stoat said, taking a prodigious drag. "You'll see for yourself, when the mount is finished."

"You went *back* to Africa? When was this?" Estella asked. "How come you never told me?"

"That's because we're always talking politics,

babe. Anyway, it was a quickie trip, just for a couple days," he added dismissively. "I believe it was the same weekend you went to that Quayle-for-President brunch."

She wriggled around to face him on the lion skin. "Let me get this straight. You went all the way to Kenya for a weekend? God, you must really love to hunt."

"Oh, I do. And I'm going back Saturday." Instantly, Stoat was sorry he'd said it.

Estella sat up excitedly, sloshing scotch on both of them. "Can I go, too, Palmer? Please?"

"No, honey, it's business this time. I'm taking along an important client. I promised him a rhino like mine."

"Aw, come on. I'll stay out of your way."

"Sorry, sweetheart."

"Then bring me back a nice present, all right? And not just cheapo beads or a grass skirt. A cool wood carving, or maybe—I know!—a Masai spear."

"Consider it done." Stoat, thinking dismally: Where am I going to find something like *that* in Ocala, Florida?

"Wow. All the way to Africa." Estella raised her violet-rimmed lashes to the long wall of stuffed animal heads and laminated fish—Stoat's prize trophies. She said: "I've never even fired a cap pistol, Palmer, but every year I give a little money to the NRA. I am totally behind the Second Amendment."

"Me, too. As you can tell." Stoat airily swept his arm toward the blank-eyed taxidermy. "Like the song says, happiness is a hot gun."

Estella smiled inquisitively. "I don't think I ever heard that one."

TWENTY-SEVEN

Krimmler couldn't sleep.

I might never sleep again, he thought.

And Roger Roothaus had not believed the "bum in the tree" story!

Asked Krimmler if he'd been drinking. Suggested he take a vacation, drive the Winnebago up to Cedar Key or Destin.

"Nothing's happening on the island anyway," Roger Roothaus had said. "Not until we hear otherwise from Mr. Clapley. So go enjoy yourself. It's on me."

Krimmler protested. Insisted he felt fine. A bum really *did* break into my camper and beat me up and drag me up a goddamn tree. And left me stranded there, Roger! I had to crawl down in a blinding rainstorm. Nearly broke my ass.

Man, I'm worried about you, Roothaus had said.

You should be!

Don't say a word about this to Mr. Clapley, OK?

But Clapley sent a guy, too, another freak who busted into my place and roughed me up. He had snuff tapes—

I gotta take another call, Roothaus had said curtly. You get off the rock for a while, Karl. I'm serious.

But Krimmler had no intention of leaving Toad Island, because a general never abandoned the battleground, even for an all-expenses-paid beach vacation. So Krimmler loaded his .357 and hunkered down in the Winnebago to await the next intruder.

Hours passed and nobody came, but the pulse of the island murmured ominously at his door. The breeze. The seabirds. The rustle and sigh of the leaves. Krimmler was a haunted man. Besieged by Nature, he possessed the will and armaments to fight back—but no troops. Truly he was alone.

Oh, to hear the familiar backfire of an overloaded dump truck, the plangent buzz of chain saws, the metallic spine-jolting *ploink* of a pile driver . . . how Krimmler's soul would have cartwheeled with joy!

But the earth-moving machines he so loved sat mute and untended, and with each passing moment the cursed island resurged; stirred, blossomed, flexed to life. Locked inside the dank-smelling travel camper, Krimmler began to worry for his own sanity. He was teased and tormented by every cry of a sandpiper, every trill of a raccoon, every emboldened bark of a squirrel (which he had come to dread nearly as much as he dreaded chipmunks). The onset of a blustery dusk only seemed to amplify the primeval racket at Krimmler's door, and to drown the din he slammed a Tom Jones CD into the stereo. He turned on all the lights, wedged a deck chair under the doorknob, crawled under the covers—and waited for a slumber that would not come.

Outside the window, Toad Island mocked him.

Krimmler plugged his ears and thought: I might never sleep again.

He squeezed his eyelids together and spun a plot. At dawn he would commandeer one of the bulldozers and start mowing down trees, purely for therapy. Jump into a D6 and plow a wide dusty trench through some quiet, piney thicket. Fuck you, squirrels. Welcome to your future.

Krimmler smirked at the idea.

After a while he sat up and listened. The Winnebago had fallen silent except for a steady dripping on the roof from wet branches overhead. Hurriedly Krimmler snatched up the .357 and went to put in another CD.

That's when he heard the cry, unlike anything he'd heard before. It began as a low guttural moan and built to a winding, slow-waning scream. The hair rose on Krimmler's forearms and his tongue turned to chalk. The scream was mighty enough to be that of a large cat, such as a panther, but nerdy Dr. Brinkman had said all panthers had long ago been shot or driven out of northwest Florida. In fact (Krimmler recalled), Roger Roothaus had explicitly inquired about the possibility of panthers on Toad Island, because the animals were listed as a protected species. One measly lump of scat and Uncle Sam could padlock the whole Shearwater operation, possibly forever.

Again the unearthly cry arose. Krimmler shuddered. What else could it possibly be but a panther? That goddamn Brinkman! He lied to us, Krimmler thought— a closet bunny-hugger, as I always suspected! That would explain why he disappeared all of a sudden; probably ran off to squeal to the feds.

Krimmler jerked open the door of the Winnebago and glared into the blue fog and drizzle. The cat scream seemed to be coming from the same upland grove where he had ordered the oak toads buried. The quavering yowl sounded almost human, like a man slowly dying.

Hepppppppppppppppppmeeeeeeeeeeeeeeeeeeeeeee!!!

Well, sort of human, Krimmler mused. If you let your imagination run wild.

He stepped into a pair of canvas work trousers and pulled on a wind-breaker. Grabbing the pistol and a flashlight, he stalked into the mist. To hell with that drunken snitch Brinkman, wherever he is, Krimmler seethed. This bugshit island *will* be tamed; cleared, dredged, drained, graded, platted, paved, stuccoed, painted and reborn as something of tangible, enduring human value—a world-class golf and leisure resort.

To Krimmler, the screaming in the night was a call to arms. He would not cower and he would not retreat, and he would not allow Shearwater to be thwarted by some smelly, spavined, tick-infested feline. Not after so much work and so much money and so much bullshit politics.

I'll kill the damn thing myself, Krimmler vowed.

Again the night was cleaved by wailing, and Krimmler struck out toward it in a defiant rage. This panther is beyond endangered, he thought. This fucker is doomed.

His charge was halted momentarily when he slipped on a log, the fall shattering his flashlight. Quickly he gathered himself and marched on, slashing with his gun arm to clear a path through the silhouetted trees. The feral cry drew him to the clearing where the toad-mulching bulldozers were parked, and in a frenzy Krimmler started firing the moment he burst from the woods.

"Here, kitty, kitty!" he exulted with a mad leer.

Hepppppppppppppppppmeeeeeeeeeeeeeeeeeeeeeee!!!

*

Besides the money, what Robert Clapley missed most about the drug business was the respect. If you were known to be a smuggler of serious weight, the average low-life schmuck wouldn't dream of screwing with you.

A schmuck such as Avalon Brown, for instance—making Clapley stew for forty-five minutes in the lobby of the Marlin Hotel while he attended to "important business" upstairs with the two Barbies.

Although Avalon Brown obviously found it amusing to be rude to a wealthy American real-estate developer, he would never (Clapley was certain) treat a major importer of cocaine with such reckless disrespect. The longer Clapley had to wait, the more his thoughts turned to Mr. Gash—now, there was a fellow who could teach Avalon Brown some manners, and would be pleased to do so.

Clapley wondered why Mr. Gash had not phoned from Toad Island. Shootings, even if not fatal to the target, customarily resulted in a first-person report from the field. Maybe Mr. Gash was sulking, Clapley speculated, because the dognapper had survived. Mr. Gash took a great deal of pride in his work.

Still, he ought to call soon, Clapley thought. Wait'll I tell him about Avalon Brown—a turd fondler like that would be just the thing to brighten Mr. Gash's spirits; the sort of assignment he'd been known to do for free.

"Bobby?"

In the lobby stood Katya and Tish, aloof but not outwardly sullen. There was no sign of Jamaica's answer to Stanley Kubrick.

"Bobby, Mr. Brown vonts to know vere is movie money."

"My lawyers are drawing up the partnership papers. Let's go eat lunch," Robert Clapley said.

As they strolled to the News Café, Clapley was nearly overcome by distress. The Barbies looked ghoulish. They had frizzed their hair and dyed it as black as onyx, shading lips and eyelids to match. They wore musty lace shawls over loose diaphanous halters, tight leather pants and buckled, open-toed shoes as clunky as tugboats. It was criminal, Clapley lamented silently. The women were *made* for short skirts and high heels; hell, he ought to know. He was the design engineer! At no small expense, he had re-formed Katya and Tish into perfect twin images of *the* American beauty icon. And here was the thanks he got: rebellion. Toenails painted black!

Over cappuccinos and bagels, he asked: "You girls miss me?"

"Shore, Bobby," Tish said.

"Score any rhino dust yet?"

Tish shook her head tightly. Katya dropped her eyes.

"No luck, huh?" Clapley clucked in mock sympathy.

"Just cocaine. Cocaine is bo-rink," said Katya, crunching into a toasted raisin bagel.

"Very boring," Robert Clapley agreed. "What's with the new look? Is that for your movie?"

"Is casual Goth, Bobby." By way of explanation, Tish pointed to a silver crucifix hanging from her neck. Katya was wearing one, too, Clapley noticed.

"Goth? You mean bats and vampires and shit like that."

"Ya," Katya said, "and blude vership."

"Also, good dance clubs," Tish added.

Clapley chuckled caustically. "Blood worship and rave. You're definitely in the right town."

His whole body twitched and perspired with wanton anxiety. Every ounce of concentration was required to steady the coffee cup in his hands. Meanwhile, the Barbies were giddily diverted by a shirtless young man racing backward on Rollerblades; the requisite ponytail, Oakley shades and a white cockatoo on one shoulder.

"Girls." Robert Clapley felt like a teacher who hears giggling in the back of the classroom. "Katya! Tish!"

Their naughty smiles evaporated.

"Do you still want some rhino dust?"

Tish glanced at Katya, who cocked an unplucked eyebrow.

"Vere?" she asked suspiciously.

"The condo in Palm Beach."

"Ven? You have now?"

"Not today," Clapley said. "Day after tomorrow."

Tish said, "No boolshit, Bobby? You got horn?"

"I will."

"How you find? Vere it is?" Katya demanded.

Clapley could hardly bear to look at them, their hair and makeup were so appalling. Plus, they were noshing like a pair of starved heifers!

"Vere you get dis horn?" Katya persisted.

"From a real rhinoceros. I'll be shooting it myself."

Tish froze, her waxy cheeks bulging with bagel. Katya sat forward, the pink tip of tongue showing between her front teeth, like a kitten's.

"Black rhino. A monster," Robert Clapley said. "The hunt is all set for Saturday morning."

"You shoot rhino? No boolshit?"

"That's right."

"What if you don't hit?"

"Then it will probably kill me. Just like it killed another man a few years ago." Clapley affected a rueful sigh. "A truly awful thing, it was. The guide says this is an extremely dangerous animal. A rogue."

The Barbies sat big-eyed and transfixed. Another teenaged Rollerblader skated past, swinging his spandex-covered buns, but the women remained riveted upon the great white hunter.

"Don't you worry. I *won't* miss," Clapley told them. "I never miss."

Katya said, "Big gun, ya?"

"The biggest."

"Then, after, you bring home horn!"

"Only if you'll be there waiting."

The women nodded in syncopated enthusiasm.

"Fantastic. But you can't tell anyone, especially not Mr. Brown," Clapley warned. "This is very risky, what I'm doing for you. I could get in lots of trouble."

"OK, Bobby."

"Not to mention trampled to death."

Katya tenderly put a hand on top of Clapley's. "We love, Bobby, that you would do such risky things for us. To shoot so dangerous rhino."

"Haven't I always given you whatever you wanted? Haven't I? You and Tish asked for more horn, and this is the only way I can get it for you. Putting my life on the line."

"Thank you, Bobby."

"So, I'll see you both Saturday night? With *blond* hair. Please?"

Tish tittered. "Tall shoes, too."

"That would be fantastic." So much for the Goth shit, Robert Clapley thought. He was rapturous with triumph and longing; soon his twins would be home.

In the lobby of the Marlin, he hugged both of them and said: "I trust Mr. Avalon Brown got you a nice oceanfront suite."

Tish looked questioningly at Katya, who seemed embarrassed.

"No? Well, maybe after the movie's a big hit." Clapley leaned in for good-bye kisses, wincing at the fumes of a sickly, unfamiliar perfume.

"What is that?" he wheezed politely.

"Name is called Undead," Katya replied. "I think by Calvin."

"Lovely. Tell Mr. Brown I'll be in touch."

"Be careful to shoot rhino, Bobby."

"Don't worry about me," Clapley said. "Oh, I almost forgot. Dr. Mujera will be flying in from South America next week. Just a reminder." He tapped an index finger on his chin. "Assuming you girls are still interested."

"Maybe," Katya said, guardedly.

"Ya, maybe," Tish said.

"Only the best for you two. Right? He's the top guy in the whole world."

"But Mr. Brown says he loves our chins, like is now."

"Is that so," Clapley said thinly.

"Good chins for movie light-ink," Tish elaborated.

"Soft," Katya added. "He says soft angles look better. Not sharp, like on American models."

"Dr. Mujera has operated on many, many international movie stars."

"For real, Bobby? Chins of movie stars?"

"I'll speak to Mr. Brown myself. I believe he'll be

very pleased with the doctor's qualifications." Robert Clapley looked at his wristwatch. "As a matter of fact, I've got some time now. Why don't you girls phone the room and ask Mr. Brown to join us for a drink?"

"No," Katya said. "Massage lady is there."

"Two o'clock every day," said Tish.

"The massage lady?"

"He says is for stress," Katya explained.

Clapley offered an understanding smile. "Mr. Brown must be under a lot of pressure."

"See you Saturday, Bobby. We party like before, OK?"

"Baby, I can't wait."

"And good lucks with black rhino!"

"Don't worry about me," Robert Clapley told his future Barbie twins. "You just get busy fixing that beautiful hair of yours."

When they put him in the Highway Patrol car, Twilly Spree was loaded on painkillers, which worked out fine because McGuinn immediately pounced on his chest to say hello. It still hurt like hell, but not enough to make Twilly pass out.

The first stop was a Barnett bank, where he made a cash withdrawal that by chance equaled, almost to the dollar, three whole years of Lt. Jim Tile's Highway Patrol salary. Even the former governor was taken aback.

"Inheritance," Twilly said thickly. "My grandfather's spinning in his grave."

The next stop was a GM dealership on the way out of Tallahassee.

"What for?" the captain demanded.

"We need a car."

"I walk most everywhere."

"Well, I don't," Twilly said, "not with a hole in my lung."

Jim Tile appeared highly entertained. Twilly sensed that Clinton Tyree was accustomed to running the show.

"Can I call you Governor?"

"Rather you didn't."

"Mr. Tyree? Or how about Skink?"

"Neither."

"All right, *captain*," Twilly said, "I just wanted to thank you for what you did on the island."

"You're most welcome."

"But I was wondering how you happened to be there."

"Spring break," Skink said. "Now, let's get you some wheels."

With McGuinn in mind, Twilly picked out another used Roadmaster wagon, this one navy blue. While he filled out the paperwork in the salesman's cubicle, the trooper, the captain and the big dog ambled around the showroom. None of the other salesmen dared to go near them. Afterward, in the parking lot, Jim Tile admired the big Buick. McGuinn was sprawled in the back, Twilly was in the front passenger seat and Skink was behind the wheel.

"I don't really want to know where you three are headed," the trooper said, "but, Governor, I do want to know what you did with that gun I gave you."

"Gulf of Mexico, Jim."

"You wouldn't lie to me?"

"I threw it out of the chopper. Ask the boy."

Twilly nodded. It was true. The pilot wisely had asked no questions.

"But the cell phone is a sad story, Jim. I must've dropped it in the woods," Skink said. "The great state of Florida should buy you a new one. Tell Governor Dick I said so."

Jim Tile circled to Twilly's side of the car and leaned down at the window. "I assume you know whom you're traveling with."

"I do," Twilly said.

"He is a dear friend of mine, son, but he's not necessarily a role model."

Skink cut in: "Another public service announcement from the Highway Patrol!"

Twilly shrugged. "I'm just looking for peace and quiet, Lieutenant. My whole mortal being aches."

"Then you should take it easy. Real easy." The trooper returned to the driver's side. Clearly something was bothering him.

Skink said, "Jim, you believe the size of this thing!"

"How long since you drove a car?"

"Been awhile."

"Yeah, and how long since you had a license?"

"Twenty-two years. Maybe twenty-three. Why?" The captain idly walked his fingers along the steering wheel. Twilly had to grin.

"Tell you what I'm going to do," Jim Tile said. "I'm going to leave right now, so that I don't see you actually steer this boat off the lot. Because then I'd have to pull you over and write you a damn ticket."

Skink's eye danced mischievously. "I would frame it, Jim."

"Do me a favor, Governor. This young man's already

been through one shitstorm and nearly didn't make it. Don't give him any crazy new ideas."

"There's no room in his head for more. Am I right, boy?"

Twilly, deadpan: "I've turned over a new leaf."

The trooper put on his wire-rimmed sunglasses. "Might as well be talking to the damn dog," he muttered.

Clinton Tyree reached up and chucked him on the shoulder. Jim Tile gravely appraised his road Stetson, the brim of which had been nibbled ragged by McGuinn.

"Governor, I'll say it again: I'm too old for this shit."

"You are, Jim. Now, go home to your bride."

"I don't want to read about you two in the paper. Please."

Skink plucked off the trooper's shades and bent them to fit his face.

"Elusive and reclusive! That's us."

"Just take care. Please," Jim Tile said.

As soon as he was gone, they drove straight for the interstate. Twilly drifted in and out of codeine heaven, never dreaming. Near Lake City the captain excitedly awakened him to point out a dead hog on the shoulder of the highway.

"We could live off that for two weeks!"

Twilly sat up, rubbing his eyes. "Why are you stopping?"

"Waste not, want not."

"You love bacon that much, let me buy you a Denny's franchise," Twilly said. "But I'll be damned if you're stashing a four-hundred-pound pig corpse in my new station wagon. No offense, captain."

In the back of the car, McGuinn whined and fidgeted.

"Probably gotta pee," Skink concluded.

"Makes two of us," Twilly said.

"No, makes three."

They all got out and walked toward the fringe of the woods. The ex-governor glanced longingly over his shoulder, toward the roadkill hog. McGuinn sniffed at it briefly before loping off to explore a rabbit trail. Twilly decided to let him roam for a few minutes.

When they got back to the car, the captain asked Twilly how he felt.

"Stoned. Sore." With a grunt, Twilly boosted himself onto the hood. "And lucky," he added.

Skink rested one boot on the bumper. He peeled off the shower cap and rubbed a bronze knuckle back and forth across the stubble of his scalp. He said, "We've got some decisions to make, Master Spree."

"My mother saved all the clippings from when you disappeared. Every time there was a new story, she'd read it to us over breakfast," Twilly recalled. "Drove my father up a wall. My father sold beachfront."

Skink whistled sarcastically. "The big leagues. More, more, more."

"He said you must be some kind of Communist. He said anybody who was anti-development was anti-American."

"So your daddy's a patriot, huh? Life, liberty and the pursuit of real-estate commissions."

"My mother said you were just a man trying to save a place he loved."

"And failing spectacularly."

"A folk hero, she said."

Skink seemed amused. "Your mother sounds like a

romantic." He refitted the shower cap snugly on his skull. "You were in, what, kindergarten? First grade? You can't possibly remember back that far."

"For years afterward she talked about you," Twilly said, "maybe just to give my dad the needle. Or maybe because she was secretly on your side. She voted for you, that I know."

"Jesus, stop right there—"

"I think you'd like her. My mother."

Skink pried off the sunglasses and studied his own reflection in the shine off the car's fender. With two fingers he repositioned the crimson eye, more or less aligning it with his real one. Then he set his gaze on Twilly Spree and said, "Son, I can't tell you what to do with your life—hell, you've seen what I've done with mine. But I will tell you there's probably no peace for people like you and me in this world. Somebody's got to be angry or nothing gets fixed. That's what we were put here for, to stay pissed off."

Twilly said, "They made me take a class for it, captain. I was not cured."

"A class?"

"Anger management. I'm perfectly serious."

Skink hooted. "For Christ's sake, what about *greed* management? Everybody in this state should get a course in *that*. You fail, they haul your sorry ass to the border and throw you out of Florida."

"I blew up my uncle's bank," Twilly said.

"So what!" Skink exclaimed. "Nothing shameful about anger, boy. Sometimes it's the only sane and logical and moral reaction. Jesus, you don't take a class to make it go away! You take a drink or a goddamn bullet. Or you stand and fight the bastards."

The ex-governor canted his chin to the sky and boomed:

> *"Know ye the land where the cypress and myrtle*
> *Are emblems of deeds that are done in their clime;*
> *Where the rage of the vultures, the love of the turtle,*
> *Now melt into sorrow, now madden to crime?"*

Quietly, Twilly said, "But I'm already there, captain."

"I know you are, son." Slowly he lowered his head, the braids of his beard trailing down like strands of silver moss. The two bird beaks touched hooks as they dangled at his chest.

"Lord Byron?" Twilly asked.

Skink nodded, looking pleased. "The Bride of Abydos."

With a thumb Twilly tested his bandaged wound. The pain was bearable, even though the dope was wearing off. He said, "I suppose you heard about this big-game trip."

"Yes, sir."

"You wouldn't happen to know where it is."

Here was Skink's chance to end it. He could not.

"I do know where," he said, and repeated what Lisa June Peterson had told him.

"So, what do you think?" Twilly asked.

"I think a canned hunt is as low as it gets."

"That's not what I mean."

"Ah. You mean as the potential scene of an ambush?"

"Well, I keep thinking about Toad Island," Twilly said, "and how to stop that damn bridge."

Skink's blazing eye was fixed on the highway, the cars and trucks streaking past. "Look at these fuckers," he said softly, as if to himself. "Where could they all be going?"

Twilly slid off the hood of the station wagon. "I'll tell you where *I'm* going, Governor, I'm going to Ocala. And on the way I intend to stop at a friendly firearms retailer and purchase a high-powered rifle. Want one?"

"The recoil will do wonders for your shoulder."

"Yeah, it'll hurt like a sonofabitch, I imagine." Twilly plucked the car keys from Skink's fingers. "You don't want to come, I can drop you in Lake City."

"That's how you treat a folk hero? Lake City?"

"It's hot out here. Let's get back on the road."

Skink said, "Did I miss something? Is there a plan?"

"Not just yet." Twilly Spree licked his lips and whistled for the dog.

TWENTY-EIGHT

Durgess warmed his hands on a cup of coffee while Asa Lando gassed up the big forklift. It was three hours until sunrise.

"You sure about this?" Durgess asked.

"He ain't moved since yesterday noon."

"You mean he ain't woke up."

"No, Durge. He ain't *moved*."

"But he's still breathin', right?"

Asa Lando said, "For sure. They said he even took a dump."

"Glory be."

"Point is, it's perfectly safe. Jeffy isn't going anywheres."

Durgess poured his coffee in the dirt and entered the building marked Quarantine One. Asa Lando drove the forklift around from the rear. The rhinoceros was on its chest and knees, a position the veterinarian had described as "sternal recumbency." The vet had also estimated the animal's age at thirty-plus and used the word *dottering*, which Asa Lando took to mean "at death's door." Time was of the essence.

Durgess opened the stall and Asa Lando rolled in atop the forklift. They couldn't tell if the rhino was awake or asleep, but Durgess kept a rifle ready. El

Jefe exhibited no awareness of the advancing machine. Durgess thought he saw one of the ears twitch as Asa Lando cautiously slid the steel tines beneath the rhino's massive underbelly. Slowly the fork began to rise, and a tired gassy sigh escaped the animal's bristly nostrils. Hoisted off the matted straw, the great armored head sagged and the stringy tail swatted listlessly at a swarm of horseflies. The stumpy legs hung motionless, like four scuffed gray drums.

"Easy now," Durgess called, as Asa Lando backed out the forklift and headed for the flatbed truck. Durgess was astounded: Suspended eight feet in the air, the rhinoceros was as docile as a dime-store turtle. A tranquilizer dart would have put the damn thing into a coma.

In preparation for the fragile cargo, Asa Lando had padded the truck bed with two layers of king-sized mattresses. Upon being deposited there, the pachyderm blinked twice (which Durgess optimistically interpreted as a sign of curiosity). Asa tossed up an armful of fresh-cut branches and said, "Here go, Mr. El Jeffy. Breakfast time!"

Durgess himself had selected the location for the kill: an ancient moss-covered live oak that stood alone at the blue-green cleft of two vast grassy slopes, about a mile from the Wilderness Veldt lodge. A hundred years ago the land had produced citrus and cotton, but back-to-back winter freezes had prompted a switch to more durable crops—watermelon, cabbage and crookneck squash. It was the sons and grandsons of those early vegetable growers who eventually abandoned the farm fields and sold out to the Wilderness Veldt Plantation Corporation, which turned out to be co-owned by a

Tokyo-based shellfish cartel and a Miami Beach swim-suit designer named Minton Tweeze.

In the dark it took Durgess a half hour to find the designated oak tree—he was driving the flatbed slowly so as not to lose Asa Lando, who was following with the forklift. Durgess parked the truck so that its headlights illuminated the clearing around the craggy trunk of the old tree. Before unloading the rhino, Durgess looped one end of a heavy cattle rope around its neck. The other end he secured to the trailer hitch of the flatbed.

"Why bother?" Asa Lando said.

"I got fifty thousand excellent reasons."

But the rhino never made a move to break free; in fact, it made no movement at all. When Asa lowered the animal to the ground, it settled immediately to its knees, its drowsy demeanor unchanged. If it was happy to be outdoors again, neither Durgess nor Asa Lando could tell. They might as well have been rearranging statuary.

Uneasily, Durgess studied Robert Clapley's high-priced quarry in the twin beams of the truck lights. "Asa, he don't look so good."

"Old age. That's what he's dyin' from."

"Long as he makes it till morning." Durgess cocked his head and put a tobacco-stained finger to his lips. "You hear a dog bark?"

"No, but I heard a wheeze." Asa Lando jerked a thumb toward the rhino. "Chest cold. Doc Terrell says he probably picked it up on the aeroplane."

Durgess hastily stubbed out his cigarette. "Christ. A rhinoceros with fucking asthma."

"Comes and goes, Durge. Same with the arthritis."

"To hell with that. I heard a dog out there, I swear I did."

He cupped a hand to his ear and listened: Nothing. Asa Lando shrugged. "I'm tellin' you, it's Jeffy got a chest wheeze. That's all."

Durgess edged toward the somnolent load and unslipped the rope. It seemed unnecessarily harsh to keep the aged creature tied down, as some prey had to be (due to the incompetent riflery of Wilderness Veldt clients, most of whom had no reasonable chance of hitting anything that wasn't tethered to a stake).

Asa Lando took out a camera and snapped a picture of the rhinoceros, for posting on the Wilderness Veldt's Web site. Then he heaved a bale of wheat in front of the animal, which acknowledged the gesture with a gravelly sniff.

"Well, Durge, that's it. All we can do now is go back to the lodge until dawn."

"And say our prayers," Durgess said. "What if he up and dies, Asa? You think he'll fall over on one side, or will he stay . . . you know. . . ."

"Upright? That's a good question."

"Because if he don't fall, I mean, if he just sorta keeps on his knees. . . ."

Asa Lando brightened. "They won't even know!"

"There's a strong possibility," Durgess agreed. "The damn thing could be stone-dead and. . . ."

"From fifty yards away, how could they tell?"

"That's what I'm sayin', Asa. These clowns'll never figger it out. Long as Jeffy here don't keel over before they actually squeeze off a shot."

Durgess took a step closer, into the spear of white

light and swirling insects. He peered skeptically at the motionless rhino. "You still with us, old-timer?"

"He is," Asa Lando said. "Unless that's a puddle of *your* piss on the grass."

The hunting party had come in the night before and, against Durgess's advice, celebrated into the late hours with rich desserts, cognac and Cuban cigars. It was rare that the governor was able to cut loose and relax without fear of ending up in a snarky newspaper column—ordinarily he was careful not to be seen socializing so intimately with insider lobbyists such as Palmer Stoat or shady campaign donors such as Robert Clapley. And upon first arriving at the Wilderness Veldt, Dick Artemus had been subdued and remote, his wariness heightened by a recent unsettling event inside the governor's mansion.

Gradually, however, the chief executive began to feel at ease within the gated privacy of the Wilderness Veldt Plantation, drinking fine whiskey and trading bawdy stories in cracked leather chairs by a cozy stone fireplace. This was what it must have been like in the good old days, the governor thought wistfully, when the state's most important business was conducted far from the stuffy, sterile confines of the capitol—hammered into law by sporting men, over smoky poker games at saloons and fish camps and hunting lodges; convivial settings that encouraged frank language and unabashed horse trading, free from the scrutiny of overzealous journalists and an uninformed public.

Willie Vasquez-Washington, however, wasn't so comfortable among the walnut gun cabinets and the stuffed animal heads, which unblinkingly stared down at him from their stations high on the log walls. Like the governor, Willie Vasquez-Washington also felt as if he'd taken a step backward to another time—a time when a person of his color would not have been welcome at the Wilderness Veldt Plantation unless he wore burgundy doublets and waistcoats, and carried trays of Apalachicola oysters (as efficient young Ramon was doing now). Nor was Willie Vasquez-Washington especially enthralled by the company at the lodge. He had yet to succumb to the famous charms of Dick Artemus, while Palmer Stoat was, well, Palmer Stoat— solicitous, amiably transparent and as interesting as cold grits. Willie Vasquez-Washington was no more favorably impressed by Robert Clapley, the cocky young developer of Shearwater, who had greeted him with a conspicuously firm handshake and a growl: "So you're the guy who's trying to fuck me out of a new bridge."

It was Willie Vasquez-Washington's fervent wish that the political deal could be settled that night, over dinner and drinks, so he would be spared the next day's rhinoceros hunt. Half-drunk white men with high-powered firearms made him extremely nervous. And while Willie Vasquez-Washington was not, in any sense of the term, a nature freak, he had no particular desire to watch some poor animal get shot by the likes of Clapley.

So Willie Vasquez-Washington attempted on several occasions to draw the governor aside, in order to state his simple proposal: A new high school in exchange for a yea vote on the Toad Island bridge appropriation. But Dick Artemus was caught up in the frothy mood of the pre-hunt festivities, and he was unwilling to tear himself away from the hearth. Nor was Palmer Stoat a helpful intermediary; whenever Willie Vasquez-Washington approached him, the man's face was so crammed with food that his response was indecipherable. In the soft cast of the firelight, Stoat's damp bloated countenance resembled that of an immense albino blowfish. What meager table manners he had maintained while sober deteriorated vividly under the double-barreled effects of Rémy Martin and babyback ribs. The ripe spray erupting from Stoat's churning mouth presented not only an unsavory visual spectacle but also (Willie Vasquez-Washington suspected) a health hazard. The prudent move was to back off, safely out of range.

At 1:00 a.m., Willie Vasquez-Washington gave up. He headed upstairs to bed just as Stoat and Clapley broke into besotted song:

> *"You can't always do who you want,*
> *No, you can't always do who you want. . . ."*

They stopped at a shop with a Confederate flag nailed to the door, on U.S. 301 between Starke and Waldo. Twilly Spree purchased a Remington 30.06 with a scope and a box of bullets. Clinton Tyree got Zeiss nightscope binoculars and a secondhand army Colt .45, for use at close range. A five-hundred-dollar cash "donation" toward the new Moose Lodge served to expedite the paperwork and inspire a suddenly genial clerk to overlook the brief waiting period normally required for handgun purchases in Florida.

Skink and Twilly stopped for dog food, camo garb and other supplies in the town of McIntosh, seventeen miles outside Ocala. At a diner there, a shy ponderous waitress named Beverly blossomed before their very eyes into a svelte southern version of Rosie O'Donnell—a transformation hastened by a hundred-dollar tip and the gift of a one-of-a-kind Chihuahua hide vest, which Skink good-naturedly took off and presented to her on the spot. Beverly pulled up a chair and offered numerous scandalous anecdotes about what went on at the Wilderness Veldt Plantation and, more importantly, flawless directions to it. By nightfall Twilly and Skink were comfortably encamped on the north end of the spread, having conquered the barbed ten-foot fence with a bolt cutter. The ex-governor built a small fire ring in a concealed palmetto thicket, while Twilly took McGuinn to scout the area. The dog was like a dervish on the leash, pulling so hard in so many different directions that it nearly dislocated Twilly's acutely tender right shoulder. By the time they returned to the campsite, Skink had dinner cooking over the flames—for Twilly, a rib-eye steak and two baked potatoes; for himself, braised rabbit, alligator tail and fried-water moccasin, all plucked, freshly smote, off a bountiful two-mile stretch of pavement south of Micanopy.

Skink said, "Any sign of the warriors?"

"No, but I could see the lights of the main lodge at the top of a hill. I'm guessing it's three-quarters of a mile from here." Twilly looped McGuinn's leash over one ankle and sat down with a jug of water by the fire. The dog rested its chin on its paws, gazing up longingly at the sizzling meat.

"Still no brainstorm?" Skink inquired.

"Truth is, we ought to just shoot the fuckers."

"It's your call, son."

"How about some input?" Twilly wanted the captain

to assure him there was another way to save Toad Island, besides committing murder.

Instead Skink said, "I've tried everything else and look where it's got me."

"You're just tired is all."

"You don't know the half of it."

They ate in restive silence, the night settling upon them like a dewy gray shroud. Even McGuinn inched closer to the fire. Twilly thought of Desie—he missed her, but he was glad she wasn't with him now.

"I propose we sleep on it," said Skink, crunching on the last curl of snake.

Twilly shook his head. "I won't be sleeping tonight."

"We could always just snatch 'em, I suppose."

"Yeah."

"Make a political statement."

"Oh yeah. Just what the world needs," Twilly said.

"Plus, hostages are a lot of work. You've gotta feed 'em and take 'em to the john and wash their dirty underwear so they don't stink up the car. And listen to all their goddamn whining, sweet Jesus!" Skink laughed contemptuously.

"On the other hand," Twilly said, "if we kill them, then the entire Federal Bureau of Investigation will be chasing us. That's not a happy prospect."

The ex-governor pried loose his glass eye and tossed it to Twilly, who held it up before the fire. The thing appeared surreal and distant, a glowering red sun.

"Beats a plain old patch," Skink said, swabbing the empty socket.

Twilly handed the prosthetic eye back to him. "What do you think they'll be hunting tomorrow?"

"Something big and slow."

"And when it's over, they'll gather around the fireplace, drink a toast to the dead animal and then get down to business. Make their greedy deal and shake hands. And that gorgeous little island on the Gulf will be permanently fucked."

"That's how it usually goes."

"I can't sit still for that, captain."

Skink tugged off his boots and placed them next to the binoculars case. In a pocket of his rain suit he found a joint, which he wedged into his mouth. He lowered his face to the edge of the flames until the end of the doobie began to glow.

"Son, I can't sit still for it, either," he said. "Never could. Want a hit?"

Twilly said no thanks.

"You ever licked toads to get high?" Skink asked.

"Nope."

"Don't."

Twilly said, "I should warn you, I'm not much of a shot."

"Maybe you won't have to be." Skink dragged heavily on the joint. "All kinds of bad shit can happen to foolish men in the woods."

"Still, a plan would be helpful."

"It would, son."

Twilly stretched out, using McGuinn as a pillow. The rhythmic rise and fall of the dog's chest was soothing. Skink dumped water on the fire, and the aroma of wood smoke mingled sweetly with the marijuana.

"What time is it, Governor?"

"Late. You get some rest, we'll figure something out."

"They've got more guns than we do."

"That's undoubtedly true."

453

The Labrador stirred slightly beneath Twilly's head, and he reached up to scratch the dog's chin. One of McGuinn's hind legs started to kick spasmodically.

Twilly said, "There's him to consider, too."

"No need to bring him along. We can tie him to a tree, where he'll be safe."

"And what happens to him if we don't make it back?"

The captain exhaled heavily. "Good point."

Twilly Spree fell asleep and had another dream. This time he dreamed he was falling. There was a bullet hole in his chest, and as he fell he leaked a curlicued contrail of blood. Far below him were a break of green waves and a long white beach, and in the sky all around him were the seabirds, falling at the same velocity; lifeless clumps of bent feathers and twisted beaks. Somewhere above was the faint, fading sound of a helicopter. In the dream Twilly snatched wildly at the falling gulls until he got one. Clutching the broken bird to his breast, he plummeted in a clockwise spin toward the beach. He landed hard on his back, and was knocked momentarily senseless. When he awoke, Twilly glanced down and saw that the gull had come to life and flown away, out of his hands. It was dark.

And Clinton Tyree was looming over him. Around his neck was a pair of binoculars. Hefted in his arms like an overstuffed duffel was McGuinn, looking chastened.

Twilly raised his head. "What?"

"A flatbed and a forklift. You won't believe it."

Skink rekindled the fire and made coffee. Wordlessly they changed into camouflage jumpsuits and broke out the guns and ammunition. Twilly removed the dog's collar, so it wouldn't jingle.

"Hey, captain, I got one for you. Not a plan but a poem."

"Good man."

"'I should have been a pair of ragged claws,'" Twilly said, "'Scuttling across the floors of silent seas.'"

The former governor of Florida clapped his hands in delight. "More!" he exhorted. "More, more, more!" His laughter crashed like a hailstorm through the tall trees and scrub.

Durgess awoke everybody an hour before dawn. No one in the hunting party had the stomach for a hearty breakfast, so the four men gathered quietly around the table for coffee, aspirins, Imodium and, in Robert Clapley's case, two Bloody Marys. Willie Vasquez-Washington had correctly guessed that khaki would be the fashion order of the day. He wondered if Clapley, Stoat and Governor Dick had purchased their nearly identical big-game wardrobes at a sale (although Stoat's absurd cowboy hat somewhat set him apart).

The mood at the table was subdued; a few lame hangover jokes, and halfhearted inquiries about the weather. Durgess sat down to explain how the hunt would be organized. Because the rhinoceros was Clapley's kill, he and Durgess would go first into the bush. Asa Lando would follow twenty or so yards behind, accompanied by the governor, Palmer Stoat and Willie Vasquez-Washington. Ten yards behind them would be the governor's two regular bodyguards.

Weaponry was the next subject, Robert Clapley announcing he had come armed with a .460 Weatherby, "the Testarrosa of hunting rifles."

Durgess said, "That's all we'll need." Thinking: A slingshot and a pebble would probably do the job.

Not to be outdone, Stoat declared he was bringing his .458 Winchester Magnum.

"My choice, too," interjected Dick Artemus, who had never shot at anything larger, or more menacing, than a grouse. The governor had yet to fire the powerful Winchester, which he had received as a bribe six years earlier while serving on the Jacksonville City Council.

It was hopeless to object, but Durgess felt obliged. "Mr. Clapley's gun is plenty. I'll be armed and so will Asa, in case the animal gives us any trouble. And so will the governor's men." The FDLE bodyguards had lightweight Ruger assault rifles, semi-automatics.

"He's right," Clapley chimed in. He didn't want anybody else sneaking a shot at his trophy rhino.

"Just hold on," Palmer Stoat said to Durgess. "You said this was a killer, right? A rogue."

"Yessir."

"Then—no disrespect meant to you, Bob, or to Dick's security people—but I intend to protect myself out there. I'm bringing my own rifle."

"Me, too," the governor said. "The more the merrier."

Durgess relented without comment. It was always the same story with these big-city shitheads, always a dick-measuring contest. One guy gets a gun, they *all* gotta have one.

The guide turned to Willie Vasquez-Washington. "You a Winchester man, too?"

"Nikkormat. Pictures is all I'm shooting."

"That's cool." Once Durgess had turned down an offer to guide big-game photo safaris in South Africa because he'd heard that hunters tipped better than photographers. Sometimes, on mornings such as this, Durgess wished he'd taken the gig anyway.

Robert Clapley said, "One thing we've got to get straight right now. It's about the horn—I'm taking that sucker home with me. *Today*."

Durgess thought: Sure, tough guy. Soon as we see the dough. Otherwise Mr. Yee awaits, cash in hand.

"The horn? What in the world you gonna do with that?" Willie Vasquez-Washington asked.

Palmer Stoat explained how rhinoceros horn was ground into an illicit powder that was sold as an aphrodisiac. "It didn't put any extra lead in Bob's pencil, but his two blond babeniks went animal for the stuff."

Willie Vasquez-Washington chortled in astonishment.

"They got so wet, Bob needed a spatula to scrape 'em off the sheets." Stoat winked archly at Clapley, who turned as red as his tomato cocktail.

Still hollow-eyed from the night before, Dick Artemus gamely looked up from his coffee cup. "I heard about that stuff from a buddy works for Toyota HQ. These horns are very pricey, he says, plus you've got to go all the way to Hong Kong or Bangkok to find one. Supposedly you sprinkle it in your *sake* and get a hard-on that lasts longer than a hockey season."

"Some men do, but not Bob," Palmer Stoat chirped.

Willie Vasquez-Washington couldn't believe what he was hearing—Clapley clearly was more excited about scoring the sex powder than stalking the formidable African rhinoceros. White guys were truly pathetic, the worst, when it came to fretting about their dicks.

Addressing the table, Robert Clapley said, "Palmer

disapproves of my two ladies, though I suspect he's just jealous. They have exotic tastes, it's true—and talents to match."

There was a ripple of appreciative laughter.

"So bring a hacksaw for the horn," Clapley instructed Durgess firmly.

"Yessir."

"You know what's also supposed to be good for boners? Bull testicles," the governor volunteered informatively. "Rocky Mountain oysters is what they call 'em out West. Can you imagine eating barbecued bull's balls?"

Durgess rose sluggishly, as if cloaked in cast iron. "We best be movin' out now," he told the men. "I'll go fetch Asa. You fellas meet us in front."

"With our guns," Palmer Stoat added.

"Yessir. With your guns," Durgess said, with dull resignation.

TWENTY-NINE

They found a knoll with a clear downhill view of the towering moss-draped oak, which stood alone at the confluence of two slopes. The men laid down in the tallest grass to wait, Twilly sighting with the Remington while Skink scanned with the field glasses. McGuinn sat restlessly between them, nosing the foggy dawn air. The end of his leash was looped once around Skink's axhandle wrist.

"Is it alive?" said Twilly, squinting through the rifle scope.

"Hard to say," Skink said.

They were talking about the black rhinoceros.

"Lookie there!"

"What?"

Skink, who needed only half of the binoculars, said: "It's eating. See for yourself."

Twilly positioned the crosshairs and saw twin puffs of mist rising from the beast's horned snout. Its prehensile upper lip browsed feebly at a bale of hay.

"Looks about a thousand years old," Twilly said.

Skink sounded somber. "If we're going to do this thing, whatever it is, it's gotta happen before they plug that poor sonofabitch. That I won't watch, you understand?"

McGuinn edged cagily toward the slope, but Skink yanked him on his butt. Twilly pointed on a line with his rifle: "Here they come, captain."

The hunting party arrived in a zebra-striped Chevy Suburban, parking no more than two hundred yards from the solitary oak. Eight men in all, the group made no effort at stealth. The great El Jefe, masticating serenely beneath the tree, seemed oblivious to the slamming doors, clicking gun bolts and unmuffled male voices.

At the front of the truck they held a brief huddle— Skink spotted the orange flare of a match—before the stalk began in earnest. Two men headed out first, both armed. Twilly didn't recognize either of them but he knew one had to be Robert Clapley.

Four men followed in a second group. Twilly didn't need a scope to pick out Desie's husband. He remembered Palmer Stoat's oversized cowboy hat from that first day, when he had pursued the obnoxious litterbug down the Florida Turnpike. Another giveaway was the bobbing cigar; downwind or upwind, only a stooge such as Stoat would smoke while tracking big game.

Skink said, "There's your boy." He recognized Stoat's dough-ball physique from the night he'd broken into the lobbyist's house and usurped his bathroom. Seeing him again now, in such an inexcusable circumstance, Skink was even less inclined toward mercy. Twilly Spree had related how all the madness had started—Stoat blithely chucking hamburger cartons out the window of his Range Rover. The ex-governor had understood perfectly Twilly's infuriated reaction, for such atrocious misbehavior could not be overlooked. In Skink's view, which he kept to himself, Twilly had shown uncommon restraint.

In the same contingent of hunters as Palmer Stoat marched the governor, looking theatrically chipper in an Aussie bush hat. Dick Artemus carried his gun in a way that suggested he practiced everything except shooting. A third man, leaner and darker, held a long-lensed camera but no weapon. The fourth man in the group walked out front with a rifle at the ready; he was older and wiry-looking, dressed more like a mechanic than a hunter.

The last two members of the motley safari stayed many paces behind and shouldered shorter rifles—semi-automatics, Skink somberly informed Twilly. The men wore jeans, running shoes and navy blue windbreakers with the letters FDLE visible on the back.

"Governor Dick's bodyguards," Skink said, "with Mini-14s, if I'm not mistaken."

Twilly didn't like the odds. The sun was rising behind the knoll, which meant he and the captain would get some cover from the glare. But still. . . .

Skink nudged him. "Make the call, son. I'm not getting any younger."

Like a disjointed centipede, the hunting party advanced tentatively along the cleft at the base of the grassy slopes. Drawing closer to their prey, the two men out front altered their walk to a furtive stoop, pausing every few steps to rest on their haunches and strategize. The one doing all the pointing would be the guide, Twilly figured, while Robert Clapley would be the one bedecked like an Eddie Bauer model.

Viewed from a distant perch, the stalk unfolded as comic mime of a true wild hunt. Whenever the lead duo halted and crouched, the men trailing behind would do the same. The bare grass offered the trackers neither protection nor concealment, but none was necessary. The killer rhinoceros continued chewing, unperturbed.

"If you had to take out one of them," Twilly said to Skink, "who would it be—Governor Dickless?"

"Waste of ammo. They got assembly lines that crank out assholes like him. He wouldn't even be missed."

"Stoat, then?"

"Maybe, but purely for the entertainment. Tallahassee has more lobbyists than termites," Skink said.

"That leaves only Mr. Clapley." Twilly closed one eye and framed the developer square in the crosshairs. Clapley's face appeared intent with predatory concentration. Twilly carefully rested a forefinger on the Remington's trigger.

Skink said: "It's his project. His goddamned bridge. His hired goon who tried to kill you."

Twilly exhaled slowly, to relax his shooting arm. The hunting guide and Clapley had approached to within forty yards of the rhinoceros.

"On the other hand," Skink was saying, "it might be more productive just to snatch the bastard and haul him down to the Glades for three or four months. Just you and me, re-educating his ass on the Shark River."

Twilly turned his head. "Captain?"

"Could be fun. Like a high-school field trip for young Bob Clapley, or holiday camp!" Skink mused. "We'll send him home a new man—after the banks have called in his construction loans, of course. . . ."

"Captain!"

"It's your call, son."

"I *know* it's my call. Where's the damn dog?"

"The dog?" Skink sprung up and looked around anxiously. "Oh Jesus."

So many enthralling smells!

McGuinn reveled in the country morning: Sunrise, on the crest of a green hill, where seemingly everything—leaves, rocks, blades of grass, the dew itself—was laced with strange intoxicating scents. Large animals, McGuinn concluded from their potent musks; jumbos. What could they be? And what sort of place was this?

Although most of the smells that reached the hill were too faint to merit more than a cursory sniff or a territorial spritz of pee, one scent in particular hung fresh and warm, cutting pungently through the light fog. McGuinn was itching to bolt loose and track it.

The scent was not that of a domestic cat or another dog. Definitely not duck or seagull. Negative also for deer, rabbit, raccoon, skunk, muskrat, mouse, toad, turtle or snake. This earthy new animal odor was unlike any the dog had previously encountered. It made his hair bristle and his nose quiver, and it was so heavy in the air that it must have been exuded by a creature of massive proportion. McGuinn yearned to chase down this primordial behemoth and thrash it mercilessly . . . or at least pester it for a while, until he found something better to do.

In the distance a vehicle stopped and emptied out a new bunch of humans, and soon McGuinn detected other aromas—gasoline exhaust, sunblock, aftershave, coffee, cigar smoke and gun oil. But it was the smell of the mystery beast that beckoned irresistibly. The dog glanced around and saw that nobody was paying attention to him. The young man, Desie's friend, was preoccupied with pointing a gun down the hill. Similarly distracted was his travel companion, the hairy-faced man who was perfumed indelibly with burnt wood and dead opossum, and on whose wrist was limply fastened the cursed leash.

McGuinn levered his butt imperceptibly off the grass, scooted backward a couple of inches, then sat down again. Neither of the men looked up. So McGuinn did it again, and still again, until the slack in the leash was gone and all that remained was to coil his muscles and execute The Lunge—a heedless, headlong escape maneuver familiar to all owners of Labrador retrievers. During many an evening walk, McGuinn had employed The Lunge to excellent effect, leaving Palmer Stoat or Desie standing empty-handed, snatching at thin air, while he dashed off to deal with an insolent Siamese, or to take a dip in the New River. The dog was well aware he was exceptionally fast, and virtually impossible for humans to overtake on foot.

Once he made his break.

This time it happened so smoothly that it was anticlimactic. McGuinn surged forward and the leash simply came free, slipping so cleanly off the hand of the hairy-faced man that he didn't feel it. The next thing the dog knew, he was barreling away, unnoticed and unpursued. Down the long slope he ran—ears unfurled, tongue streaming, velvet nose to the grass—faster and faster until he was but a black streak, hurtling past the dumbstruck hunters. He heard a flurry of agitated voices, then a familiar angry command—"Boodle, no!"—which he gleefully disregarded. Onward he sped, the leash flopping at his heels, the powerful alien fragrance reeling him in as if he were a barracuda hooked on a wire. Directly ahead loomed a gnarled mossy tree, and beneath it stood a great horned creature so immense and unflinching, McGuinn thought at first that it was made of stone.

But, no, smell it! A piquant blend of mulchy digestive vapors, sour body mold and steaming shit. With a self-congratulatory howl, the dog bore in. He circled first one way and then the other before dropping to a snarling crouch behind the animal's gargantuan armor-plated flanks. McGuinn expected the beast to wheel in self-defense, yet the stately rump remained motionless. McGuinn inched around cautiously to confront the snouted end, where he initiated a sequence of spirited head fakes, left and right, to feign a charge. Yet the creature did not shirk, bridle or jump at its tormentor's well-choreographed hysterics. The creature did not move; merely stared at the dog through crinkled, gnat-covered slits.

McGuinn was flabbergasted. Even the laziest, stupidest dairy cow would have spooked by now! The dog backed off to catch his breath and sort through his options (which, given a Lab's cognitive limitations, were modest and few). He affected a baleful pearly drool, only to stare in bewilderment as the monster placidly resumed nibbling from its bale of forage. Incredible!

Then came the approach of measured footsteps, followed by urgent human whispers. McGuinn knew what that meant: No more fun here. Soon someone would be snatching up his leash and jerking the choke chain. Time was running out. One last try: The dog growled, flattened his ears and insinuated himself into a wolf-like slink. Once more he began circling the torpid brute, which (McGuinn noticed) had ceased chewing, its jaws bewhiskered with sodden sprouts. But now the dog directed his focus at the stern of his prey: a sparse cord of a tail, dangling invitingly.

A leap, a flash of fangs and McGuinn had it!

Instantly the beast erupted, whirling with such hellish might that the dog was flung off, landing hard against the trunk of the sturdy old oak. He scrambled upright and shook himself vigorously from head to tail. With a mixture of surprise and elation, he observed that the monster was running away—and pretty darn fast, too!

McGuinn broke into lusty pursuit, driven by ancient instincts but also by sheer joy. Was there a better way to spend a spring morning, racing free through cool green meadows, snapping at a pair of fleeing hindquarters while slow-footed humans yammered helplessly in protest?

Every dog dreamed of such adventure.

No one was more rattled than Palmer Stoat to see a black Labrador charging into the line of fire, because it looked like his dog—Jesus H. Christ, it *was* his dog!—gone for all these days, only to surface at the worst possible time in the worst possible place. Stoat felt an upswell of despair, knowing the dog wasn't running downhill to greet him, but rather to flush Robert Clapley's prize rhinoceros, thereby disrupting the hunt and possibly mucking up (yet again!) the Shearwater deal.

It was no less than a curse.

"Boodle, no!" Stoat yelled, cigar waggling. "Bad boy!"

A few yards ahead stood Clapley, his aggrieved expression revealing all: He wanted to shoot the dog, but Durgess wouldn't permit it. In fact, the guide was signaling all of them to remain still.

"Hold up here," Asa Lando dutifully instructed Stoat's group.

Dick Artemus leaned in and whispered, "Palmer, is that your damn fool dog?" Willie Vasquez-Washington chuckled and began shooting pictures. In mute wonderment the guides and hunters watched the Labrador circle and taunt the rhinoceros; even Asa Lando found it difficult not to be entertained. The dog really was a piece of work!

Palmer Stoat shaded a nervous eye toward Clapley, huddled in a heated discussion with Durgess. Of all those present, Stoat alone knew of Clapley's peculiar obsession. Stoat alone knew without asking that the man had brought dolls, and probably a miniature pearl-handled hairbrush, concealed inside his ammo vest. Stoat alone knew the wanton seed of Clapley's motivation (which had nothing to do with sport), and understood the true base nature of his panic. No rhino, no horn; no horn, no live Barbies! In such a fraught equation, one frolicsome Labrador carried zero weight.

Only too late did it dawn on Stoat that he should have taken Bob aside the night before and explained that the "killer" rhinoceros would not and could not escape, due to the insurmountable barbed fence that enclosed the Wilderness Veldt Plantation. And though the news might have taken a bit of luster off the hunt, it might also have lowered Robert Clapley's buggy anxiety to a saner level, at which he might not have attempted to sight his Weatherby on something so inconsequential as a pesky hound. From the spot where Stoat knelt, he could see Clapley trying again and again to raise the gun barrel, only to have it slapped down by Durgess.

In desperation Stoat bellowed: "Boodle! Come!"

Dick Artemus stuck two fingers in his cheeks and gave a whistle that sounded like the screak of a tubercular macaw. The Labrador failed to respond. Peering at the confrontation through a 500-mm lens, Willie Vasquez-Washington could make out amazing details— the electric green bottleflies buzzing about the rhino's rear end, the shining strands of spittle on the dog's chin. ... .

And when the Lab suddenly leapt forward and seized the rhino's tail, it was Willie Vasquez-Washington who loudly piped: "Look at that crazy sonofabitch!"

Palmer Stoat saw the rhinoceros spin. He saw Boodle windmilling through the air. He saw Robert Clapley shake free of Durgess and jump to his feet. And then he saw the rhino take off, his idiot dog biting at its heels. The beast vectored first one direction and then another, ascending halfway up the northernmost slope before deferring to gravity. With a resolute snort, the rhino arced back downhill toward the three groups of men, whom it might easily have mistaken for shrubbery or grazing antelopes (given the rhinoceros's notoriously poor vision). Arbitrarily it picked for an escape route the twenty-yard gap between the first two groups. The dog bayed merrily in pursuit.

Because of the rhino's barge-like girth and laconic-looking trot, the swiftness of its advance was misjudged by both Stoat and Clapley—though not by the two guides, whose awe at the decrepit pachyderm's resurgence was outweighed by their aversion to violent death. Durgess, who anticipated the next phase of the fiasco, grimly flattened himself to the ground. Asa Lando spun on one heel and ran for the live oak. Governor Dick Artemus took the cue; dropped his gun and hit the grass ass-first. His two bodyguards dashed forward, seizing him roughly under the armpits and dragging him toward the zebra-striped truck. Meanwhile, Willie Vasquez-Washington backpedaled, snapping pictures in hasty retreat.

And Palmer Stoat, faced with a charging African rhinoceros, raised his rifle and took aim. Exactly sixty-six feet away, Robert Clapley did the same. Both men were too adrenalized to recognize their respective vulnerabilities in the lethal geometry of a cross fire. Both were too caught up in the heart-pounding maleness of the moment to sidestep manifest disaster.

It had been years since Stoat had shot an animal that was more or less ambulatory, and he trembled excitedly as he drew a bead on the grizzled brow of the lumbering rhino. As for Clapley, killing it would be more than a display of *machismo*—it would fulfill a fantasy that consumed him night and day. Through his rifle scope (laughably unnecessary at such close range), Clapley breathlessly admired the rhino's immense horn. He imagined presenting the hair-encrusted totem—upright and daunting—on a satin pillow to the twin Barbies, who would be curled up nude and perfumed and (he fervidly hoped) blond. He envisioned a grateful glow in their nearly completed faces. Next week: the chins. By Christmas: perfection.

As the rhinoceros thundered on a straight line between them, Clapley and Stoat swung their gun barrels to lead the beast, as they would a dove on the wing. Except, of course, they were not aiming upward, but level.

"Hold your fire!" Durgess shouted, strictly for the record.

That night, drinking heavily at a bar in McIntosh, neither he nor Asa Lando would be able to say which of the fools had fired first. Judging by the stereophonic roar of gunfire—and the instantaneous results—Robert Clapley and Palmer Stoat could have pulled their triggers simultaneously. Both of them completely missed the rhinoceros, naturally, and both went down very hard—Clapley, from the Weatherby's bone-jarring recoil; Stoat, from a combination of recoil and shrapnel.

Reconstructing the split-second mishap wasn't easy but, with some help from Master Jack Daniel, Durgess and Asa Lando would conclude that Stoat's slug must have struck the trunk of the oak at the instant Clapley's slug struck Stoat's Winchester, which more or less exploded in Stoat's arms. At that point the lobbyist was not dead, although his right shoulder had been seriously pulped by splintered gun stock.

Asa Lando would recall looking down from the tree and seeing Stoat, hatless and dazed, struggling to his knees. Likewise, Durgess would remember helping Robert Clapley to an identical position, so that the two hunters were facing each other like rival prairie dogs. But the guides well knew that Stoat wasn't staring at Clapley, and Clapley wasn't staring at Stoat—both men were scanning intently for a fresh rhinoceros corpse.

"You missed," Durgess informed Clapley.

"What?" Clapley's ears ringing from the gunshot.

"Mr. Stoat missed, too," Durgess added, by way of consolation.

"What?"

As Durgess stood up to scout for the runaway rhino, he heard frantic shouting from high in the live oak: Asa Lando, trying to warn him. The ground under Durgess's boots began to shake—that's what he would talk about later.

Like a damn earthquake, Asa. Could you feel it, too?

The rhinoceros had cut back unexpectedly and now was rumbling up from behind the scattered hunting party; prey turned predator. There was no time to flee. Asa squawked from the tree. Palmer Stoat spit his broken cigar and gaped. Durgess dove for Robert Clapley but Clapley wasn't there; he was down on all fours, scrambling after his rifle. Helplessly Durgess rolled himself into a ball and waited to be crushed. Beneath him the earth was coming unsprung, a demonic trampoline.

Durgess felt the rhinoceros blow past like a steam locomotive, wheezing and huffing. He peeked up in time to see an outstretched black shape silhouetted briefly against the creamy pink sky, and to feel Labrador toenails scuff his forehead. Durgess decided he was in no hurry to get up, a decision reinforced by the sound of Clapley shrieking.

The guide would remember remaining motionless until hearing a man's heavy footsteps, and feeling a shadow settle over him. He would remember rocking up slowly, expecting to see Asa, but facing instead a bearded apparition with a gleaming grin and a molten red eye that might have been plucked from the skull of the devil himself.

"We've come for the dog," the apparition said.

While being dragged to safety, the governor lost the tender scabs on his buttocks. By the time the bodyguards got him to the Suburban, he had bled through his khaki trousers—the word SHAME appearing chimerically across his ass, like stigmata. If Willie Vasquez-Washington noticed, he didn't say so. He and Dick Artemus were hustled into the backseat. The FDLE agents hopped up front, locked the doors and radioed for a helicopter and ambulances.

Riding back to the lodge, the governor looked drained and shaken, his great cliff of silver hair now a tornadic nest. He sank low in the seat. Willie Vasquez-Washington rode ramrod-straight, a fervent amazement on his face.

"Sweet Jesus," he said. "Did you see that!"

"Willie?"

"Those poor fuckers."

"Willie!"

"Yeah?"

"I was never here. You were never here." The governor placed a clammy hand on Willie Vasquez-Washington's knee. "Can we agree on that?"

The vice chairman of the House Appropriations Committee rubbed his jaw thoughtfully. With his other hand he touched a button on the Nikkormat, still hanging from his neck, and set off the automatic rewind. The hum from a swarm of wasps would not have been more unsettling to Dick Artemus.

Ruefully his eyes fell on the camera. "You got some pictures, huh?"

Willie Vasquez-Washington nodded. "A whole roll."

"Color or black-and-white?"

"Oh, color."

Dick Artemus turned and stared straight ahead. Just then, a white-tailed buck crashed out of the cabbage palms and entered the path in front of the truck. The agent who was driving stomped the accelerator and swerved expertly around the deer.

"Nice move!" Willie Vasquez-Washington cheered, bouncing in the seat.

The governor never flinched, never blinked.

"Willie," he said, wearily.

"Yeah?"

"What is it you want?"

Twilly Spree tried to go after McGuinn but he was chased down and tackled by Clinton Tyree, who whispered in his ear: "Let it happen, son."

Said it with such a startling serenity that Twilly understood, finally, what sustained the man—an indefatigable faith that Nature eventually settles all scores, sets all things straight.

So they let the dog go, then watched as the rhinoceros snorted to action. It ran halfway up the slope before turning back toward the hunting party, which dissolved in bedlam. Viewed from the bank of the knoll, the debacle unfolded with eerie, slow-motion inevitability— the two idiots swinging their rifles as the beleaguered rhino attempted to cut between them, a triangulated aim turning linear and deadly. And when the shots rang out, it indeed appeared that Palmer Stoat and Robert Clapley had managed to blast one another in a brainless cross fire.

Skink and Twilly were quite surprised to see both men lever to their knees. They were somewhat less surprised to see the rhino swing around once more, this time charging blind from behind the shooters.

Skink sucked in his breath. "Say good night, Gracie."

Clapley was groping inanely in the grass when the rhinoceros scooped him up at a full trot. His screams carried up the slope, echoing among the caws of grumpy crows. Like a frog on a gig, Clapley frantically tried to push himself off the rhino's horn (which at forty-nine centimeters would have been considered truly a splendid prize). Furiously the animal bucked its head, tossing and goring Clapley as it ran.

Ran directly at the injured Palmer Stoat, whose Winchester was in pieces and whose reflexes were in disarray. Stoat spastically waved one pudgy arm in an attempt to intimidate the beast (which, Skink later noted, couldn't possibly have seen him anyway; not with Robert Clapley's body impaled so obtrusively on its nose). With McGuinn nipping at its hocks, the rhinoceros—all two and one-quarter tons of it—flattened Stoat as effortlessly as a beer truck.

Twilly and Skink waited to come down off the hill until the animal had run out of steam, and the zebra-striped Suburban carrying the governor and his bodyguards had sped away. One of the guides remained on the ground, balled up like an armadillo. Skink checked on him first, while Twilly went through the messy formality of examining Palmer Stoat. The lobbyist's eyes were open, fixed somewhere infinite and unreachable. They reminded Twilly of the glassy orbs he'd removed from Stoat's animal heads.

The exhausted rhinoceros had returned to the shade of the live oak and collapsed to its knees. From thirty yards away, Skink and Twilly could hear the animal wheezing and see the heat rippling off its thick hide. Across the prow-like snout hung Robert Clapley, limp and contorted.

Skink asked Twilly: "What's with the dog?"

Once the armor-plated behemoth had quit playing runaway, McGuinn had grown bored and sniffed elsewhere for mischief: The tree. A human was up in the tree! The dog decisively stationed himself beneath the tall oak and commenced a barking fit, punctuated by the occasional lunge.

To the man in the branches, Twilly said: "You OK up there?"

"Pretty much. Anyway, who the hell are you?" It was the other hunting guide, the one dressed like a mechanic.

"Nobody. We just came for the dog."

"That's yours? You see what all he did?" The man in the tree was highly upset. "You see the holy shitstorm he caused, your damn dog!"

"I know, I know. He's been a very bad boy."

Twilly whistled the dinner whistle. McGuinn, having already lost track of the time of day, fell for it. Sheepishly he lowered his head, tucked his tail and sidled toward Twilly in a well-practiced pose of contrition. Twilly grabbed the leash and held on tight. He didn't want the dog to see what had happened to his former master.

Skink ambled up and seized McGuinn in a jovial

bear hug. The Labrador chomped one of Skink's cheek braids and began to tug, Skink giggling like a schoolboy.

Twilly said, "We'd better go."

"No, son. Not just yet."

He got up, took out the .45 and strode purposefully toward the rhinoceros.

"What are you doing?" Twilly called out. In the tumult he'd left his Remington up on the knoll. "Don't!"

As Skink approached the rhinoceros, a voice from the tree inquired: "Are you fuckin' nuts?"

"Hush up," said the former governor of Florida.

The rhino sensed him coming and struggled to rise.

"Easy there. Easy." Skink stepped gingerly, edging closer. His arm gradually reached out, the blue barrel of the Colt pointing squarely at the animal's brainpan— or so it appeared to Twilly, who had kept back. Morosely he wondered why Skink would kill the old rhino now; perhaps to spare it from being shot by somebody else, a cop or a game warden. Meanwhile, McGuinn bucked at the leash, thinking the opossum-smelling man had cooked up a fun new game.

"Hey, what're you doing?" Twilly shouted again at Skink.

The rhino's view remained obstructed by the lumpy object snagged on its horn. El Jefe could not clearly see either the silver-bearded man or the gun at its face, which was just as well, though the man had no intention of harm.

Watching Skink's arm stiffen, Twilly braced for the clap of a gunshot. None came, for Skink didn't place the weapon to the ancient animal's brow. Instead he touched it firmly to Robert Clapley's unblinking right eye, to make absolutely sure the fucker was dead. Satisfied, he stepped back and lowered the gun. The man in the tree hopped down and scampered away. McGuinn barked indignantly, which made the rhinoceros stir once more. With a volcanic grunt and a violent head shake, it launched Robert Clapley's beanbag body, which landed in a khaki heap.

Skink went over and poked it with a boot. Twilly saw him bend over and pick something up off the ground. Later, striding up the slope, he removed the article from his pocket and showed it to Twilly. "What do you make of *this?*" he asked.

It was a voluptuous blond doll, dressed in a skimpy deerhide outfit of the style Maureen O'Sullivan wore in the old Johnny Weismuller movies. Barbie as Jane.

"Came off Clapley," Skink reported, with a troubled frown. "A girl's doll."

Twilly Spree nodded. "Sick world."

THIRTY

It was seventy-seven steps to the top of the lighthouse. He counted each one as he went up the circular stairwell. Where the steps ended stood a warped door with flaking barn-red paint and no outside knob. The former governor of Florida gave three hard raps, waited a few moments, then knocked again. Eventually he heard movement on the other side; more a shuffling than a footfall.

"Doyle?"

Nothing.

"Doyle, it's me. Clint."

He could hear his brother breathing.

"Are you all right?"

The only light slanting into the stone column came from a row of narrow salt-caked windows. Littering the floor from wall to wall were envelopes—hundreds of identical envelopes, yellowed and unopened. Payroll checks from the State of Florida. It had been a very long time since Clinton Tyree had seen one.

In the shadows he noticed a crate of fresh oranges, three one-gallon water jugs and, stacked nearby like library books, two dozen boxes of Minute rice. It was rice he smelled now, cooking on the other side of the door.

"Doyle?"

He so wanted to lay eyes on his brother.

"I'm not going to stay. I just need to know you're all right."

Clinton Tyree leaned his shoulder to the wood. The door held fast. He heard more shuffling; the scrape of metal chair legs across a pine floor, the sibilant protest of a cheap cushion being sat upon, emphatically. His brother had taken a position.

"The park rangers said there are people bringing you food. Doyle, is that true?"

Nothing.

"Because if there's anything you need, I'll get it for you. Groceries, medicine, whatever. Anything at all."

Books, magazines, paintings, a VCR, a grand piano . . . how about a whole new life? Jesus, Clinton Tyree thought, who am I kidding here?

He heard the chair scoot closer to the door. Then came a metallic click, like a Zippo lighter or a pocket-knife being opened. Then he thought he heard a murmur.

"Doyle?"

Still not a word.

"The reason I came—look, I just wanted to tell you that you never have to leave this place if you don't want. It's all been taken care of. Don't be frightened ever again, because you're safe here, OK? For as long as you want. I give you my word."

There was another click behind the door, and then two solid footsteps. Clinton Tyree pressed a cheek to the briny wood and sensed more than heard his brother on the other side, doing the same.

"Doyle, please," he whispered. "Please."

He heard a bolt slide, and he stepped back. The door cracked and an arm came out slowly; an old man's arm, pallid and spidered with violet veins. On the underside, between the wrist and the elbow, were faded striations of an old scar. The hand was large, but bony and raw-looking. Clinton Tyree grabbed it and squeezed with all his heart, and found his brother still strong. The pale wrist twisted back and forth against his grip, and that's when he noticed the new wound on the meat of the forearm, letters etched into flesh—*i love you*—blooming in droplets as bright as rose petals.

Then Doyle Tyree snatched his hand away and closed the door in his brother's face.

As he descended the lighthouse, the former governor of Florida counted all seventy-seven steps again. When he reached the bottom he got on his belly and wedged through a gap in the plywood that had been nailed over the entrance to keep out vandals and curious tourists.

From the darkness of the beaconage, Clinton Tyree emerged, squinting like a newborn, into a stunning spring morning. He stood and turned his tear-streaked face to the cool breeze blowing in off the Atlantic. He could see tarpon crashing a school of mullet beyond the break.

The plywood barricade to the tower was papered with official notices, faded and salt-curled:

NO TRESPASSING
CLOSED TO THE PUBLIC UNTIL FURTHER NOTICE
STATE PROPERTY—KEEP OUT

But someone recently had tacked a business card to the plywood. The tack was shiny, not rusted, and the card stood out white and crisp. Clinton Tyree put his good eye to it and smiled. The inaugural smile.

LISA JUNE PETERSON
Executive Assistant
Office of the Governor

He took the card off the board and slipped it under the elastic band of his shower cap. Then he trudged down the beach, over the dunes and through the sea oats, across the street to the Peregrine Bay Visitor Center and Scenic Boardwalk, where the navy blue Roadmaster was parked.

Palmer Stoat was buried with his favorite Ping putter, a Polaroid camera and a box of Cuban Montecristo #2s, a cause for authentic mourning among the cigar buffs at the ceremony. The funeral service was held at a Presbyterian church in Tallahassee, the minister eulogizing Stoat as a civic pillar, champion of the democratic process, dedicated family man, lover of animals, and devoted friend to the powerful and common folk alike. Those attending the service included a prostitute, the night bartender from Swain's, a taxidermist, three United States congressmen, one retired senator, six sitting circuit judges, three dozen past and present municipal commissioners from throughout Florida, the lieutenant governor and forty-one current members of the state Legislature (most of whom had been elected with campaign funds raised by Stoat, and not because he admired their politics). Those sending lavish sprays of flowers included the Philip Morris Company, Shell

Oil, Roothaus and Son Engineering, Magnusson Phosphate Company, the Lake County Citrus Cooperative, U.S. Sugar, MatsibuCom Construction of Tokyo, Port Marco Properties, the Southern Timber Alliance, the National Rifle Association, University of Florida Blue Key, the Republican Executive Committee and the Democratic Executive Committee. Messages of regret arrived from Representative Willie Vasquez-Washington and Governor Richard Artemus, neither of whom could make it to the service.

"Our grief today should be assuaged," the minister said, in closing, "by the knowledge that Palmer's last day among us was spent happily at sport, with his close friend Bob Clapley—just the two of them, walking the great outdoors they loved so much."

Burial was at a nearby cemetery, which, fittingly, served as the final resting place for no less than twenty-one of Florida's all-time crookedest politicians. The joke around town was that the grave digger needed an auger instead of a shovel. The Stoats had attended the funerals of several of the dead thieves, including some convicted ones, so Desie was familiar with the layout. For Palmer she selected an unshaded plot on a bald mound overlooking Interstate 10. Since he had so often (and enthusiastically) predicted Florida would someday be as bustling as New York or California, she figured he would appreciate a roadside view of it coming to pass.

At the grave, more kind words were spoken. Desie, who sat in front with her parents and Palmer's only cousin, a defrocked podiatrist from Jacksonville, found herself weeping tears of true aching sadness—not over the eulogies (which were largely fiction), but over the unraveling of her own feelings about her husband, and how that had contributed to his untimely death. While she could take no blame for the freakish hunting mishap, it was also indisputable that the doomed rhino expedition had been precipitated by the dognapping crisis—and that the dognapping had been complicated by Desie's attraction to, and abetment of, Twilly Spree.

True, Palmer would still have been alive had he, early on, done the honorable thing and bailed out of the Shearwater fix. But there had been no chance of that, no reasonable expectation that her husband would suddenly discover an inner moral compass—and Desie should have known it.

So she was feeling guilt. And grief, too, because even as she kept no romantic love for Palmer, she also kept no hate. He was what he was, and it wasn't all rotten or she wouldn't have married him. There was a companionable, eager-to-please side of the man that, while it couldn't have been called warm, was lively enough to be missed and even grieved for. Putting the Polaroid in his coffin had been Desie's idea, an inside joke. Palmer would have laughed, she thought, although he undoubtedly would have preferred the bedroom snapshots. Those, she had destroyed.

As the casket was lowered, a murmuring rippled lightly through the mourners. Desie heard panting and felt something wet and velvety brush her fingers. She looked down to see McGuinn, nuzzling her clasped hands. The big dog had a black satin bow on his neck, and a chew toy clamped in his teeth. The toy was a rubber bullfrog with an orange stripe down its back. The frog croaked whenever McGuinn bit down on it, which was every ten or twelve seconds. A few people chuckled gently, grateful for the distraction, but the minister (who was busy walking through the valley of the shadow of death) raised his glacial eyes with no hint of amusement.

Not a dog person, Desie decided, and extracted the chew toy from McGuinn's jaws. The Labrador curled up at her feet and watched, curiously, as another big wooden box disappeared into the ground. He assumed it contained a one-eared dog, like the one in the box that had been buried on the beach. But if there was death in the air, McGuinn couldn't smell it for all the flowers.

Meanwhile, the widow Stoat glanced expectantly first over one shoulder and then the other, scanning the faces of the mourners. He wasn't there. She opened her hand and looked at the rubber toy, which actually resembled a toad more than a bullfrog. She turned it over in her palm and saw that someone had written in ballpoint ink across its pale yellow belly: *I dreamt of you!*

And then a postal box number in Everglades City, not far from Marco Island.

The sneeze set his lungs afire.

Twilly Spree grimaced. "You sure didn't have to jump on me like that."

"Oh, I damn sure did," Skink said. "I'd never catch you on a dead run downhill. You're way too fast for an old fart like me."

"Yeah, right. How much did you say you weigh?"

"I just figured you might not want to get shot again, so soon after the first time. And that's likely what would have happened out there with those two peckerheads blasting away with their cannons. Either that or the damn rhino would have stomped you into a tortilla."

"All right, all right—thank you," Twilly said sarcastically. "Thank you very much for jumping on my broken ribs. I'd forgotten how good that feels."

He sneezed again, the pain causing his eyes to well.

Skink said, "I've got an idea. Pull off at the next exit."

At a gas station they vacuumed the dog hair out of the station wagon—enough of it, Skink observed, for a whole new Labrador. Twilly's sneezing was cured. They headed southbound on the Florida Turnpike, which recently had been renamed (for reasons no one could adequately explain) after Ronald Reagan.

"Name a rest stop after him. *That* would make sense," Skink groused. "But the whole turnpike? Christ, he was still making cowboy movies when the damn thing was built."

Twilly said he didn't care if they dedicated the road to Kathie Lee Gifford, as long as they raised the toll to one hundred dollars per car.

"Not nearly high enough. Make it half a grand," Skink decreed. "Twice as much for Winnebagos."

Traffic was, as usual, rotten. Twilly felt a familiar downward skid in his mood.

"Where you headed now?" he asked the captain.

"Back to Crocodile Lakes, I suppose. My current residence is a cozy but well-ventilated NASCAR Dodge. You?"

"Everglades City."

Skink canted an eyebrow. "What for?"

"Strategic positioning," Twilly said. "Or maybe just to catch some red-fish. Who knows."

"Oh man."

"Hey, there's something I've been meaning to ask: All these years, you never thought about leaving?"

"Every single day, son."

"Where to?" Twilly said.

"Bahamas. Turks and Caicos. Find some flyspeck island too small for a Club Med. Once I bought a ticket to the Grenadines and got all the way to Miami International—"

"But you couldn't get on the plane."

"No, I could not. It felt like I was sneaking out the back door on a dying friend."

Twilly said, "I know."

Skink hung his head out the car and roared like a gut-shot bear. "Damn Florida," he said.

For ten miles they rode in silence. Then Twilly felt the heat of that gaze—and from the corner of an eye he saw the buzzard beaks, twirling counterclockwise on the tails of the burnished braids.

Skink said, "Son, I can't tell you how to handle the pain, or where to find a season of peace—or even one night's worth. I just hope you have better luck at it than I did."

"Governor, I hope I do half as well."

With a tired smile, Skink said, "Then I've got only one piece of advice: If she's crazy enough to write you, be sure to write back."

"Gee. I'll try to force myself. By the way, how'd it go with your brother?"

"You've been so good not to ask."

"Yeah, well, it's been a hundred miles," Twilly said, "so I'm asking now."

"It went fine. We had a good talk." And, in a way,

they had. Skink dug out Jim Tile's mirrored sunglasses and pinched them to the bridge of his nose. "You taking the Trail across?"

Twilly nodded. "I thought I would. Nice straight shot."

"And an awful pretty drive. Drop me at Krome Avenue, I'll hitch to the Keys."

"Like hell. I want to see this alleged race car." Twilly reached for the stereo. "Is Neil Young OK with you?"

"Neil Young would be superb."

So they flew past the exit for the Tamiami Trail and remained on the Ronald Reagan Turnpike. It was the tail of rush hour and the traffic was still clotted; frenzied. The unspoken question bubbling like nitroglycerin inside the Buick Roadmaster was whether they could make it through Miami, whether they could actually get out of the godforsaken city before somebody did *something* that simply couldn't be overlooked. . . .

And somehow they did get out, navigating onward through the turgid hellhole of west Kendall toward Snapper Creek, Cutler Ridge, Homestead—until finally the highway delivered them, more or less sane, to Florida City. They glowered at the blighted dreck of mini-marts and fast-food pits until escaping on Card Sound Road, bounded only by scrub and wetlands, and aiming the prow of the Buick toward North Key Largo; both men breathing easier, Twilly humming and Skink even tapping his boots to the music, when—

"You see that?" Twilly stiffened at the wheel.

"See what?"

"That black Firebird ahead."

"What about it," Skink said.

But of course he had seen what Twilly had seen: a

beer bottle fly out the front passenger's window, spooking a great blue heron off the canal bank.

"Asshole," Twilly muttered, knuckles tightening on the wheel.

Another airborne beer bottle, this time from the driver's side. Skink counted four bobbing heads inside the Firebird—two couples, launching a festive vacation. They looked young. The car was a rental.

"Unbelievable," Twilly said.

No, it's not, Skink thought dismally. More, more, more. . . .

The next item of litter from the Firebird was a plastic go-cup, followed by a lighted cigarette butt, which skittered into the crackling dry grass along the shoulder of the road.

Skink swore. Twilly hit the brakes, threw the station wagon into reverse and backed up to the spot where the cigarette had landed. He jumped from the car and stomped out the small flame, and kept on stomping in tight circles for a full minute. It looked like excellent therapy. Skink felt like joining him.

When Twilly got back in the driver's seat, he calmly put the pedal to the floor. Skink watched the speedometer tick all the way up to 110. The Firebird was no longer a distant speck on the blacktop; it was getting bigger rapidly.

"I was wondering," Twilly said, perfectly composed. "You in a rush to get home?"

Skink thought about it; thought about everything. Palmer Stoat. Dick Artemus. Doyle. Twilly. The hardworking heron whose supper was so rudely interrupted by a beer bottle.

And he thought of the two couples in the Firebird,

laughing and drinking but plainly oblivious to the two unkempt, deeply disturbed men riding their bumper. How else to explain what happened next—an Altoids tin casually ejected through the Firebird's sunroof. It glanced off the windshield of the pursuing station wagon and landed, as trash, in the water.

Twilly clicked his tongue impatiently. "Well, Governor? Shall we?"

He thought: Oh, what the hell.

"Anytime you're ready, son."

EPILOGUE

With the death of **Robert Clapley**, the Zurich-based SwissOne Banc Group withdrew all lines of credit for the Shearwater Island Development Corporation, which immediately folded. At a bankruptcy auction arranged by Clapley's estate, his extensive waterfront holdings on Toad Island were sold to an anonymous buyer, who eventually renamed it Amy Island and deeded every parcel for preservation. No new bridge was built.

Norva Stinson, the only remaining private landowner on Toad Island, staunchly refused to sell her tiny bed-and-breakfast to the Nature Conservancy for any sum less than $575,000—six times its appraised value. Her demand was politely rejected, and Mrs. Stinson still lives in the house today, subsisting mainly on canned donations from a local church group.

Three months after the collapse of the Shearwater project, bird-watchers hiking on Toad Island discovered a man's skeleton. The legs had been crushed by an enormous weight, and a Nokia cellular telephone was clutched in the bones of one hand. FBI pathologists later identified the remains as **Darian Lee Gash**, a convicted felon, registered sex offender and well-known player on the South Beach club scene. The cause of death was determined to be bullet wounds from two different .357-caliber handguns, only one of which was ever recovered.

The 911 tape recording of Mr. Gash's frantic, though largely unintelligible, plea for help has been included in Volume Four of *The World's Most Blood-curdling Emergency Calls*, and widely marketed on television and the Internet. The cassette is priced at $9.95 and the compact disc is $13.95, not including shipping and handling.

The body of **Karl Krimmler** was found in the shallows of a brackish marsh in the pine uplands of Toad Island. He was pinned inside the cab of a Caterpillar D-6 bulldozer that he inexplicably had driven at full throttle into the water. An autopsy determined he had drowned, the pathologist noting "a large number of viable tadpoles in the victim's upper trachea." In the same marsh, police divers discovered a Smith & Wesson model .357 pistol that was later linked to the shooting of Darian Lee Gash. Because of Mr. Gash's checkered past, detectives theorized that the deaths of the two men were a sordid murder-suicide. The remains of **Dr. Steven Brinkman** were never recovered.

Following the botched rhinoceros "hunt," the **Wilderness Veldt Plantation** was raided by federal wildlife agents, who broke into the compounds and discovered twelve impalas, eight Thompson's gazelles, a defanged Malaysian cobra, a juvenile Cape buffalo, three missing circus chimpanzees, a troop of heavily sedated baboons, a mule painted to resemble a zebra, and a feisty two-legged ocelot. The facility was swiftly shut down by the U.S. Attorney's Office, which alleged multiple violations of the Endangered Species Act and other statutes. The rhinoceros known as **El Jefe** was safely recaptured, tranquilized and transported to a protected game reserve in Kenya, not far from where it had been born thirty-one years earlier. Its massive front horn was painlessly removed, so that the animal would have no value to poachers or hunters.

John Randolph Durgess relocated to West Texas, where he took a job as a guide on a private 22,000-acre hunting reserve called Serengeti Pines. There he was killed and partially devoured by a wild cougar, which had jumped the fence to feast on imported dik-diks.

Asa Lando was hired as an animal handler at Walt Disney World's Animal Kingdom theme park, near Orlando. Two months later he was quietly dismissed, following the unexplained disappearance of the attraction's only male cheetah.

Double Your Pleasure, Double Your Pain, featuring **Katya Gudonov** and **Tish Karpinski**, was released by Avalon Brown Productions and went instantly to home video. Within weeks, the Mattel Corporation obtained an emergency injunction prohibiting the two stars of the film from "performing, portraying, attiring, advertising or in any way representing themselves as Barbie dolls, a trademarked symbol; this order to include but not expressly be limited to such oral and visual depictions as 'Goth Barbies,' 'Undead Barbies,' and 'Double-

Jointed Vampire Barbies.'" Both women received unfriendly visits from agents of the U.S. Immigration and Naturalization Service, and soon thereafter left the United States on an extended working vacation to the Caribbean.

Estella Hyde, also known to Fort Lauderdale vice officers as Crystal Barr, Raven McCollum and Raven Bush, became volunteer treasurer of the Broward County Chapter of Citizens for Quayle. During a fund-raising brunch for the former vice president at Pier 66, she met and befriended Governor Dick Artemus, who soon afterward invited her to Tallahassee to serve on the Public Service Commission.

After surrendering his California real-estate license to avoid prosecution, **Phillip Spree, Jr.**, moved to Beaufort, South Carolina, where he specialized in peddling oceanfront property on low-lying barrier islands. Before long, Little Phil came to believe his own bubbly sales pitch, and built himself a getaway house on pilings at the edge of the Atlantic. He, his fourth wife and their architect perished there one summer, when Hurricane Barbara smashed the beach bungalow to matchsticks.

Amy Spree married her yoga instructor and moved to Cassadaga, Florida, where she is faithfully visited by her son every year on her birthday.

Lt. Jim Tile retired from the Florida Highway Patrol and opened a fish camp and diner near Apalachicola. The following Christmas, he received in the mail a gaily wrapped package. Inside was a new Nokia cellular phone, the speed dial programmed to an unlisted number in North Key Largo. Callers are treated to a voice-mail greeting that consists entirely of the solo guitar lead-in to "Fortunate Son," by Creedence Clearwater Revival.

Lisa June Peterson resigned her job as executive assistant to Governor Dick Artemus and went to work as a lobbyist for the Clean Water Action Group. The following spring, she was instrumental in pushing for a new anti-pollution law that resulted in a $5,000-a-day fine against a notoriously virulent Magnusson Phosphate plant in Polk County. As a result, mine owner Dag Magnusson angrily switched political parties and spent the rest of his days bitterly funneling thousands of dollars in illicit campaign contributions to Democratic candidates.

Ten months after the hunting fiasco at Wilderness Veldt, a groundbreaking ceremony was held in Miami on the future site of the **Willie Vasquez-Washington Senior High School**. Governor Dick Artemus attended the event and posed graciously with the honoree, both men wielding gold-painted shovels while photographers took their picture.

The **Peregrine Bay Lighthouse** remains closed to the public, though on occasion mariners along Florida's southeast coast claim to see a bright light flashing at the dome of the barber-striped tower. The Coast Guard routinely discounts these sightings as an illusion caused by foul weather, since the lighthouse is known to be empty and out of service.

Carl Hiaasen

SKIN TIGHT

Acknowledgement

For his advice, expertise, and good humour, I am grateful to Dr Gerard Grau, and also to his former surgical nurse Connie, who is my wife.

ONE

On the third of January, a leaden, blustery day, two tourists from Covington, Tennessee, removed their sensible shoes to go strolling on the beach at Key Biscayne.

When they got to the old Cape Florida lighthouse, the young man and his fiancée sat down on the damp sand to watch the ocean crash hard across the brown boulders at the point of the island. There was a salt haze in the air, and it stung the young man's eyes so that when he spotted the thing floating, it took several moments to focus on what it was.

'It's a big dead fish,' his fiancée said. 'Maybe a porpoise.'

'I don't believe so,' said the young man. He stood up, dusted off the seat of his trousers, and walked to the edge of the surf. As the thing floated closer, the young man began to wonder about his legal responsibilities, providing it turned out to be what he thought it was. Oh yes, he had heard about Miami; this sort of stuff happened every day.

'Let's go back now,' he said abruptly to his fiancée.

'No, I want to see what it is. It doesn't look like a fish any more.'

The young man scanned the beach and saw they were all alone, thanks to the lousy weather. He also knew from a brochure back at the hotel that the lighthouse was long ago abandoned, so there would be no one watching from above.

'It's a dead body,' he said grimly to his fiancée.

'Come off it.'

At that instant a big, lisping breaker took the thing on its crest and carried it all the way to the beach, where it stuck – the nose of the dead man grounding as a keel in the sand.

The young man's fiancée stared down at the corpse and said, 'Geez, you're right.'

The young man sucked in his breath and took a step back.

'Should we turn it over?' his fiancée asked. 'Maybe he's still alive.'

'Don't touch it. He's dead.'

'How do you know?'

The young man pointed with a bare toe. 'See that hole?'

'That's a hole?'

She bent over and studied a stain on the shirt. The stain was the colour of rust and the size of a sand dollar.

'Well, he didn't just drown,' the young man announced.

His fiancée shivered a little and buttoned her sweater. 'So what do we do now?'

'Now we get out of here.'

'Shouldn't we call the police?'

'It's our vacation, Cheryl. Besides, we're a half-hour's walk to the nearest phone.'

The young man was getting nervous; he thought he heard a boat's engine somewhere around the point of the island, on the bay side.

The woman tourist said, 'Just a second.' She unsnapped the black leather case that held her trusty Canon Sure-Shot.

'What are you doing?'

'I want a picture, Thomas.' She already had the camera up to her eye.

'Are you crazy?'

'Otherwise no one back home will believe us. I mean, we come all the way down to Miami and what happens? Remember how your brother was making murder jokes before we left? It's unreal. Stand to the right a little, Thomas, and pretend to look down at it.'

'Pretend, hell.'

'Come on, one picture.'

'No,' the man said, eyeing the corpse.

'Please? You used up a whole roll on Flipper.'

The woman snapped the picture and said, 'That's good. Now you take one of me.'

'Well, hurry it up,' the young man grumped. The wind was blowing harder from the north-east, moaning through the whippy Australian pines behind them. The sound of the boat engine, wherever it was, had faded away.

The young man's fiancée struck a pose next to the dead body: she pointed at it and made a sour face, crinkling her zinc-coated nose.

'I can't believe this,' the young man said, lining up the photograph.

'Me neither, Thomas. A real live dead body – just like on the TV show. Yuk!'

'Yeah, yuk,' said the young man. 'Fucking yuk is right.'

*

The day had begun with only a light, cool breeze and a rim of broken raspberry clouds out toward the Bahamas. Stranahan was up early, frying eggs and chasing the gulls off the roof. He lived in an old stilt house on the shallow tidal flats of Biscayne Bay, a mile from the tip of Cape Florida. The house had a small generator powered by a four-bladed windmill, but no air-conditioning. Except for a few days in August and September, there was always a decent breeze. That was one nice thing about living on the water.

There were maybe a dozen other houses in the stretch of Biscayne Bay known as Stiltsville, but none were inhabited; rich owners used them for weekend parties, and their kids got drunk on them in the summer. The rest of the time they served as fancy split-level toilets for seagulls and cormorants.

Stranahan had purchased his house dirt-cheap at a government auction. The previous owner was a Venezuelan cocaine courier who had been shot thirteen times in a serious business dispute, then indicted posthumously. No sooner had the corpse been air-freighted back to Caracas than Customs agents seized the stilt house, along with three condos, two Porsches, a one-eyed scarlet macaw, and a yacht with a hot tub. The hot tub was where the Venezuelan had met his spectacular death, so bidding was feverish. Likewise the macaw – a material witness to its owner's murder – fetched top dollar; before the auction, mischievous Customs agents had taught the bird to say, 'Duck, you shithead!'

By the time the stilt house had come up on the block, nobody was interested. Stranahan had picked it up for forty thousand and change.

He coveted the solitude of the flats, and was delighted

to be the only human soul living in Stiltsville. His house, barn-red with brown shutters, sat three hundred yards off the main channel, so most of the weekend boat traffic travelled clear of him. Occasionally a drunk or a total moron would try to clear the banks with a big cabin cruiser, but they did not get far, and they got no sympathy or assistance from the big man in the barn-red house.

January third was a weekday and, with the weather blackening out east, there wouldn't be many boaters out. Stranahan savoured this fact as he sat on the sun deck, eating his eggs and Canadian bacon right out of the frying pan. When a pair of fat, dirty gulls swooped in to nag him for the leftovers, he picked up a BB pistol and opened fire. The birds screeched off in the direction of the Miami skyline, and Stranahan hoped they would not stop until they got there.

After breakfast he pulled on a pair of stringy denim cutoffs and started doing push-ups. He stopped at one hundred and five, and went inside to get some orange juice. From the kitchen he heard a boat coming and checked out the window. It was a yellow bonefish skiff, racing heedlessly across the shallows. Stranahan smiled; he knew all the local guides. Sometimes he'd let them use his house for a bathroom stop, if they had a particularly shy female customer who didn't want to hang it over the side of the boat.

Stranahan poured two cups of hot coffee and went back out on the deck. The yellow skiff was idling up to the dock, which was below the house itself and served as a boat garage. The guide waved up at Stranahan and tied off from the bow. The man's client, an inordinately pale fellow, was preoccupied trying to decide which of four different grades of sunscreen to slather on his milky arms. The guide hopped out of the skiff and climbed up to the sun deck.

'Morning, Captain.' Stranahan handed a mug of coffee to the guide, who accepted it with a friendly grunt. The two men had known each other many years, but this was only the second or third occasion that the captain had gotten out of his boat and come up to the stilt house. Stranahan waited to hear the reason.

When he put down the empty cup, the guide said: 'Mick, you expecting company?'

'No.'

'There was a man this morning.'

'At the marina?'

'No, out here. Asking which house was yours.' The guide glanced over the railing at his client, who now was practising with a fly rod, snapping the line like a horsewhip.

Stranahan laughed and said, 'Looks like a winner.'

'Looks like a long goddamn day,' the captain muttered.

'Tell me about this guy.'

'He flagged me down over by the radio towers. He was in a white Seacraft, a twenty-footer. I thought he was having engine trouble but all he wanted was to know which house was yours. I sent him down toward Elliott Key, so I hope he wasn't a friend. Said he was.'

'Did he give you a name?'

'Tim is what he said.'

Stranahan said the only Tim he knew was an ex-homicide cop named Gavigan.

'That's it,' the fishing guide said. 'Tim Gavigan is what he said.'

'Skinny redhead?'

'Nope.'

'Shit,' said Stranahan. Of course it wasn't Timmy Gavigan. Gavigan was busy dying of lung cancer in the VA.

The captain said, 'You want me to hang close today?'

'Hell, no, you got your sport down there, he's raring to go.'

'Fuck it, Mick, he wouldn't know a bonefish from a sperm whale. Anyway, I've got a few choice spots right around here – maybe we'll luck out.'

'Not with this breeze, buddy; the flats are already pea soup. You go on down south, I'll be all right. He's probably just some process-server.'

'Somebody's sure to tell him which house.'

'Yeah, I figure so,' Stranahan said. 'A white Seacraft, you said?'

'Twenty-footer,' the guide repeated. Before he started down the stairs, he said, 'The guy's got some size to him, too.'

'Thanks for the info.'

Stranahan watched the yellow skiff shoot south, across the flats, until all he could see was the long zipper of foam in its wake. The guide would be heading to Sand Key, Stranahan thought, or maybe all the way to Caesar Creek – well out of radio range. As if the damn radio still worked.

By three o'clock in the afternoon, the wind had stiffened, and the sky and the water had acquired the same purple shade of grey. Stranahan slipped into long jeans and a light jacket. He put on his sneakers, too; at the time he didn't think about why he did this, but much later it came to him: splinters. From running on the wooden deck. The raw two-by-fours were hell on bare feet, so Stranahan had put on his sneakers. In case he had to run.

The Seacraft was noisy. Stranahan heard it coming two miles away. He found the white speck through his field glasses and watched it plough through the hard chop. The boat was heading straight for Stranahan's stilt house and staying clean in the channels, too.

Figures, Stranahan thought sourly. Probably one of the park rangers down at Elliott Key told the guy which house; just trying to be helpful.

He got up and closed the brown shutters from the outside. Through the field glasses he took one more long look at the man in the Seacraft, who was still a half mile away. Stranahan did not recognize the man, but could tell he was from up North – the guy made a point of shirt-sleeves, on this kind of a day, and the dumbest-looking sunglasses ever made.

Stranahan slipped inside the house and closed the door behind him. There was no way to lock it from the inside; there was no reason, usually. With the shutters down the inside of the house was pitch-black, but Stranahan knew every corner of each room. In this house he had ridden out two hurricanes – baby ones, but nasty just the same. He had spent both storms in total darkness, because the wind knifed through the walls and played hell with the lanterns, and the last thing you wanted was an indoor fire.

So Stranahan knew the house in the dark.

He selected his place and waited.

After a few minutes the pitch of the Seacraft's engines

dropped an octave, and Stranahan figured the boat was slowing down. The guy would be eyeing the place closely, trying to figure out the best way up on the flat. There was a narrow cut in the marl, maybe four feet deep at high tide and wide enough for one boat. If the guy saw it and made this his entry, he would certainly spot Stranahan's aluminium skiff tied up under the water tanks. And then he would know.

Stranahan heard the Seacraft's engines chewing up the marly bottom. The guy had missed the deep cut.

Stranahan heard the big boat thud into the pilings at the west end of the house. He could hear the guy clunking around in the bow, grunting as he tried to tie it off against the tide, which was filling fast. Stranahan heard – and felt – the man hoist himself out of the boat and climb to the main deck of the house. He heard the man say: 'Anybody home?'

The man did not have a light step; the captain was right – he was a big one. By the vibrations of the plank-boards, Stranahan charted the intruder's movements.

Finally the guy knocked on the door and said: 'Hey! Hello there!'

When no one answered, the guy just opened the door.

He stood framed in the afternoon light, such as it was, and Stranahan got a pretty good look. The man had removed his sunglasses. As he peered into the dark house, his right hand went to the waist of his trousers.

'State your business,' Stranahan said from the shadows.

'Oh, hey!' The man stepped backward onto the deck, forfeiting his silhouette for detail. Stranahan did not recognize the face – an odd and lumpy one, skin stretched tightly over squared cheekbones. Also, the nose didn't match the eyes and chin. Stranahan wondered if the guy had ever been in a bad car wreck.

The man said: 'I ran out of gas, and I was wondering if you had a couple gallons to get me back to the marina. I'll be happy to pay.'

'Sorry,' Stranahan said.

The guy looked for the source of the voice, but he couldn't see a damn thing in the shuttered-up house.

'Hey, pal, you OK?'

'Just fine,' Stranahan said.

'Well, then, would you mind stepping out where I can see you?'

With his left hand Stranahan grabbed the leg of a barstool and sent it skidding along the bare floor to no place in particular. He just wanted to see what the asshole would do, and he was not disappointed. The guy took a short-barrelled pistol out of his pants and held it behind his back. Then he took two steps forward until he was completely inside the house. He took another slow step toward the spot where the broken barstool lay, only now he was holding the pistol in front of him.

Stranahan, who had squeezed himself into a spot between the freezer and the pantry, had seen enough of the damn gun.

'Over here,' he said to the stranger.

And when the guy spun around to get a bead on where the voice was coming from, Mick Stranahan lunged out of the shadows and stabbed him straight through with a stuffed marlin head he had gotten off the wall.

It was a fine blue marlin, maybe four hundred pounds, and whoever caught it had decided to mount only the head and shoulders, down to the spike of the dorsal. The trophy fish had come with the Venezuelan's house and hung in the living room, where Stranahan had grown accustomed to its indigo stripes, its raging glass eye and its fearsome black sword. In a way it was a shame to mess it up, but Stranahan knew the BB gun would be useless against a real revolver.

The taxidermied fish was not as heavy as Stranahan anticipated, but it was cumbersome; Stranahan concentrated on his aim as he charged the intruder. It paid off.

The marlin's bill split the man's breastbone, tore his aorta, and severed his spine. He died before Stranahan got a chance to ask him any questions. The final puzzled look on the man's face suggested that he was not expecting to be gored by a giant stuffed fish head.

The intruder carried no identification, no wallet, no wedding ring; just the keys to a rented Thunderbird. Aboard the Seacraft, which was also rented, Stranahan found an Igloo cooler with two six-packs of Corona and a couple of cheap spinning rods that the killer had brought along just for looks.

Stranahan heaved the body into the Seacraft and took the boat out into the Biscayne Channel. There he pushed the dead guy overboard, tossed the pistol into deep water, rinsed down the decks, dove off the stern, and swam back toward the stilt house. In fifteen minutes his knees hit the mud bank, and he waded the last seventy-five yards to the dock.

That night there was no sunset to speak of, because of the dreary skies, but Stranahan sat on the deck anyway. As he stared out to the west, he tried to figure out who wanted him dead, and why. He considered this a priority.

TWO

On the fourth day of January, the sun came out, and Dr Rudy Graveline smiled. The sun was very good for business. It baked and fried and pitted the facial flesh, and seeded the pores with vile microscopic cancers that would eventually sprout and require excision. Dr Rudy Graveline was a plastic surgeon, and he dearly loved to see the sun.

He was in a fine mood, anyway, because it was January. In Florida, January is the heart of the winter tourist season and a bonanza time for cosmetic surgeons. Thousands of older men and women who flock down for the warm weather also use the occasion to improve their features. Tummy tucks, nose jobs, boob jobs, butt jobs, fat suctions, face lifts, you name it. And they always beg for an appointment in January, so that the scars will be healed by the time they go back North in the spring.

Dr Rudy Graveline could not accommodate all the snowbirds, but he did his damnedest. All four surgical theatres at the Whispering Palms Spa were booked from dawn to dusk in January, February, and half-way into March. Most of the patients asked especially for Dr Graveline, whose reputation greatly exceeded his talents. While Rudy usually farmed the cases out to the eight other plastic surgeons on staff, many patients got the impression that Dr Graveline himself had performed their surgery. This is because Rudy would often come in and pat their wrinkled hands until they nodded off, blissfully, under the nitrous or IV Valium. At that point Rudy would turn them over to one of his younger and more competent protégés.

Dr Graveline saved himself for the richest patients. The regulars got cut on every winter, and Rudy counted on their business. He reassured his surgical hypochondriacs that there was nothing abnormal about having a fifth, sixth, or seventh blepharoplasty in as many years. *Does it make you feel better about yourself?* Rudy would ask them. *Then it's worth it, isn't it? Of course it is.*

Such a patient was Madeleine Margaret Wilhoit, age sixty-nine, of North Palm Beach. In the course of their acquaintance, there was scarcely a square inch of Madeleine's substantial physique that Dr Rudy Graveline had not altered. Whatever he did and whatever he charged, Madeleine was always delighted. And she always came back the next year for more. Though Madeleine's face reminded Dr Graveline in many ways of a camel, he was fond of her. She was the kind of steady patient that offshore trust funds are made of.

On January fourth, buoyed by the warm sunny drive to Whispering Palms, Rudy Graveline set about the task of repairing for the fifth, sixth, or seventh time (he couldn't remember exactly) the upper eyelids of Madeleine Margaret Wilhoit. Given the dromedarain texture of the woman's skin, the mission was doomed and Rudy knew it. Any cosmetic improvement would have to take place exclusively in Madeleine's imagination, but Rudy (knowing she would be ecstatic) pressed on.

Midway through the operation, the telephone on the wall let out two beeps. With a gowned elbow the operating-room nurse deftly punched the intercom box and told the caller that Dr Graveline was in the middle of surgery and not available.

'It's fucking important, tell him,' said a sullen male voice, which Rudy instantly recognized.

He asked the nurse and the anaesthetist to leave the operating room for a few minutes. When they were gone, he said to the phone box: 'Go ahead. This is me.'

The phone call was made from a pay booth in Atlantic City, New Jersey, not that it would have mattered to Rudy. Jersey was all he knew, all he needed to know.

'You want the report?' the man asked.

'Of course.'

'It went lousy.'

Rudy sighed and stared down at the violet vectors he had inked around Madeleine's eyes. 'How lousy?' the surgeon said to the phone box.

'The ultimate fucking lousy.'

Rudy tried to imagine the face on the other end of the line, in New Jersey. In the old days he could guess a face by the voice on the phone. This particular voice sounded fat and lardy, with black curly eyebrows and mean dark eyes.

'So what now?' the doctor asked.

'Keep the other half of your money.'

What a prince, Rudy thought.

'What if I want you to try again?'

'Fine by me.'

'So what'll *that* cost?'

'Same,' said Curly Eyebrows. 'Deal's a deal.'

'Can I think on it?'

'Sure. I'll call back tomorrow.'

Rudy said, 'It's just that I didn't count on any problems.'

'The problem's not yours. Anyway, this shit happens.'

'I understand,' Dr Graveline said.

The man in New Jersey hung up, and Madeleine Margaret Wilhoit started to squirm. It occurred to Rudy that maybe the old bag wasn't asleep after all, and that maybe she'd heard the whole conversation.

'Madeleine?' he whispered in her ear.

'Unnggggh.'

'Are you OK?'

'Fine, Papa,' Madeleine drooled. 'When do I get to ride in the sailboat?'

Rudy Graveline smiled, then buzzed for the nurse and anaesthetist to come back and help him finish the job.

During his time at the State Attorney's Office, Mick Stranahan had helped put many people in jail. Most of them were out now, even the murderers, due to a federal court order requiring the state of Florida to seasonally purge its overcrowded prisons. Stranahan accepted the fact that some of these ex-cons harboured bitterness against him, and that more than a few would be delighted to see him dead. For this reason, Stranahan was exceedingly cautious about visitors. He was not a paranoid person, but took a practical view of risk: when someone pulls a gun at your front door, there's really no point to asking what he wants. The answer is obvious, and so is the solution.

The gunman who came to the stilt house was the fifth person that Mick Stranahan had killed in his lifetime.

The first two were North Vietnamese Army regulars who were laying trip wire for land mines near the town of Dak Mat Lop in the Central Highlands. Stranahan surprised the young soldiers by using his sidearm instead of his M-16, and by not missing. It happened during the second week of May 1969, when Stranahan was barely twenty years old.

The third person he killed was a Miami holdup man named Thomas Henry Thomas, who made the mistake of sticking up a fried-chicken joint while Stranahan was standing in line for a nine-piece box of Extra Double Crispy. To supplement the paltry seventy-eight dollars he had grabbed from the cash register, Thomas Henry Thomas decided to confiscate the wallets and purses of each customer. It went rather smoothly until he came down the line to Mick Stranahan, who calmly took away Thomas Henry Thomas's .38-calibre Charter Arms revolver and shot him twice in the right temporal lobe. In appreciation, the fried-chicken franchise presented Stranahan with three months' worth of discount coupons and offered to put his likeness on every carton of Chicken Chunkettes sold during the month of December 1977. Being broke and savagely divorced, Stranahan took the coupons but declined the celebrity photo.

The shooting of Thomas Henry Thomas (his obvious character flaws aside) was deemed serious enough to dissuade both the Miami and metropolitan Dade County police from hiring Mick Stranahan as an officer.

His virulent refusal to take any routine psychological tests also militated against him. However, the State Attorney's Office was in dire need of a streetwise investigator, and was delighted to hire a highly decorated war veteran, even at the relatively tender age of twenty-nine.

The fourth and most important person that Mick Stranahan killed was a crooked Dade County judge named Raleigh Goomer. Judge Goomer's speciality was shaking down defence lawyers in exchange for ridiculous bond reductions, which allowed dangerous felons to get out of jail and skip town. It was Stranahan who caught Judge Goomer at this game and arrested him taking a payoff at a strip joint near the Miami airport. On the trip to the jail, Judge Goomer apparently panicked, pulled a .22 somewhere out of his black nylon socks, and fired three shots at Mick Stranahan. Hit twice in the right thigh, Stranahan still managed to seize the gun, twist the barrel up the judge's right nostril, and fire.

A special prosecutor sent down from Tampa presented the case to the grand jury, and the grand jury agreed that the killing of Judge Raleigh Goomer was probably self-defence, though a point-blank nostril shot did seem extreme. Even though Stranahan was cleared, he obviously could no longer be employed by the State Attorney's Office. Pressure for his dismissal came most intensely from other crooked judges, several of whom stated that they were afraid to have Mr Stranahan testifying in their court-rooms.

On June 7, 1988, Mick Stranahan resigned from the prosecutor's staff. The press release called it early retirement, and disclosed that Stranahan would be receiving full disability compensation as a result of injuries suffered in the Goomer shooting. Stranahan wasn't disabled at all, but his family connection with a notorious personal-injury lawyer was sufficient to terrify the county into paying him off. When Stranahan said he didn't want the money, the county promptly doubled its offer and threw in a motorized wheelchair. Stranahan gave up.

Not long afterwards, he moved out to Stiltsville and made friends with the fish.

A marine patrol boat pulled up to Mick Stranahan's place at half past noon. Stranahan was on the top deck, dropping a line for mangrove snappers down below.

'Got a second?' asked the marine patrol officer, a sharp young Cuban named Luis Córdova. Stranahan liked him all right.

'Come on up,' he said.

Stranahan reeled in his bait and put the fishing rod down. He dumped four dead snappers out of the bucket and gutted them one at a time, tossing their creamy innards in the water.

Córdova was talking about the body that had washed up on Cape Florida.

'Rangers found it yesterday evening,' he said. 'Lemon shark got the left foot.'

'That happens,' Stranahan said, skinning one of the fish fillets.

'The ME says it was one hell of a stab wound.'

'I'm gonna fry these up for sandwiches,' Stranahan said. 'You interested in lunch?'

Córdova shook his head. 'No, Mick, there's some jerks poaching lobster down at Boca Chita so I gotta be on my way. Metro asked me to poke around out here, see if somebody saw anything. And since you're the only one out here . . .'

Stranahan glanced up from the fish-cleaning. 'I don't remember much going on yesterday,' he said. 'Weather was piss-poor, that I know.'

He tossed the fish skeletons, heads still attached, over the rail.

'Well, Metro's not all that excited,' Córdova said.

'How come? Who's the stiff?'

'Name of Tony Traviola, wise guy. Jersey state police got a fat jacket on him. Tony the Eel, loan-collector type. Not a very nice man, from what I understand.'

Stranahan said, 'They think it's a mob hit?'

'I don't know what they think.'

Stranahan carried the fillets into the house and ran them under the tap. He was careful with the water, since the tanks were low. Córdova accepted a glass of iced tea and stood next to Stranahan in the kitchen, watching him roll the fillets in egg yolk and bread crumbs. Normally Stranahan preferred to be left alone when he cooked, but he didn't want Luis Córdova to go just yet.

'They found the guy's boat, too,' the marine patrolman went on. 'It was a rental out of Haulover. White Seacraft.'

Stranahan said he hadn't seen one of those lately.

'Few specks of blood was all they found,' Córdova said. 'Somebody cleaned it pretty good.'

Stranahan laid the snapper fillets in a half-inch of oil in a frying pan. The stove didn't seem to be working, so he got on his knees and checked the pilot light – dead, as usual. He put a match to it and, before long, the fish started to sizzle.

Córdova sat down on one of the wicker barstools.

'So why don't they think it was the mob?' Stranahan asked.

'I didn't say they didn't, Mick.'

Stranahan smiled and opened a bottle of beer.

Córdova shrugged. 'They don't tell me every little thing.'

'First of all, they wouldn't bring him all the way down to Florida to do it, would they, Luis? They got the exact same ocean up in Jersey. So Tony the Eel was already here on business.'

'Makes sense,' Córdova nodded.

'Second, why didn't they just shoot him? Knives are for kids, not pros.'

Córdova took the bait. 'Wasn't a knife,' he said. 'It was too big, the ME said. More like a javelin.'

'That's not like the guineas.'

'No,' Córdova agreed.

Stranahan made three fish sandwiches and gave one to the marine patrolman, who had forgotten about going after the lobster poachers, if there ever were any.

'The other weird thing,' he said through a mouthful of bread, 'is the guy's face.'

'What about it?'

'It didn't match the mug shot, not even close. They made him through fingerprints and dentals, but when they got the mugs back from the FBI it looked like a different guy altogether. So Metro calls the Bureau and says you made a mistake, and they say the hell we did, that's Tony Traviola. They go back and forth for about two hours until somebody has the brains to call the ME.' Córdova stopped to gulp some iced tea; the fish was steaming in his cheeks.

Stranahan said, 'And?'

'Plastic surgery.'

'No shit?'

'At least five different operations, from his eyes to his chin. Tony the Eel, he was a regular Michael Jackson. His own mother wouldn't have known him.'

Stranahan opened another beer and sat down. 'Why would a bum like Traviola get his face remade?'

Córdova said, 'Traviola did a nickel for extortion, got out of Rahway about two years ago. Not long afterwards a Purolator truck gets hit, but the robbers turn up dead three days later – without the loot. Classic mob rip. The feds put a warrant out for Traviola, hung his snapshot in every post office along the Eastern seaboard.'

'Good reason to get the old schnoz bobbed,' Stranahan said.

'That's what they figure.' Córdova got up and rinsed his plate in the sink.

Stranahan was impressed. 'You didn't get all this out of Metro, did you?'

Córdova laughed. 'Hey, even the grouper troopers got a computer.'

This was a good kid, Stranahan thought, a good cop. Maybe there was hope for the world after all.

'I see you went out and got the newspaper,' the marine patrolman remarked. 'What's the occasion, you got a pony running at Gulfstream?'

Hell, Stranahan thought, that was a stupid move. On the counter was the *Herald*, open to the page with the story about the dead floater. Miami being what it is, the floater story was only two paragraphs long, wedged under a tiny headline between a one-ton coke bust and a double homicide on the river. Maybe Luis Córdova wouldn't notice.

'You must've got up early to get to the marina and back,' he said.

'Grocery run,' Stranahan lied. 'Besides, it was a nice morning for a boat ride. How was the fish?'

'Delicious, Mick.' Córdova slapped him on the shoulder and said so long.

Stranahan walked out on the deck and watched Córdova untie his patrol boat, a grey Mako outboard with a blue police light mounted on the centre console.

'If anything comes up, I'll give you a call, Luis.'

'No sweat, it's Metro's party,' the marine patrolman said. 'Guy sounds like a dirtbag, anyway.'

'Yeah,' Stranahan said, 'I feel sorry for that shark, the one that ate his foot.'

Córdova chuckled. 'Yeah, he'll be puking for a week.'

Stranahan waved as the police boat pulled away. He was pleased to see Luis Córdova heading south toward Boca Chita, as Luis had said he would. He was also pleased that the young officer had not asked him about the blue marlin head on the living room wall, about why the sword was mended together with fresh hurricane tape.

Timmy Gavigan had looked like death for most of his adult life. Now he had an excuse.

His coppery hair had fallen out in thickets, revealing patches of pale freckled scalp. His face, once round and florid, looked like somebody had let the air out.

From his hospital bed Timmy Gavigan said, 'Mick, can you believe this fucking food?' He picked up a chunk of grey meat off the tray and held it up with two fingers, like an important piece of evidence. 'This is your government in action, Mick. Same fuckers that want to put lasers in outer space can't fry a Salisbury steak.'

Stranahan said, 'I'll go get us some take-out.'

'Forget it.'

'You're not hungry?'

'I got about five gallons of poison in my bloodstream, Mick. Some new formula, experimental super juice. I told 'em to go ahead, why the hell not? If it kills just one of those goddamn cells, then I'm for it.'

Stranahan smiled and sat down.

'A man came out to see me the other day. He was using your name, Tim.'

Gavigan's laugh rattled. 'Not too bright. Didn't he know we was friends?'

'Yeah, that's what I mean. He was telling people he was you, trying to find out where my house was.'

'But he didn't tell *you* he was me?'

'No,' Stranahan said.

Gavigan's blue eyes seemed to light up. 'Did he find your place?'

'Unfortunately.'

'And?'

Stranahan thought about how to handle it.

'Hey, Mick, I haven't got loads of time, OK? I mean, I could check out of this life any second now, so don't make me choke the goddamn story out of you.'

Stranahan said, 'It turns out he was a bad guy from back East. Killer for the mob.'

'*Was?*' Gavigan grinned. 'So that's it. And here I thought you'd come by just to see how your old pal was hanging in.'

'That, too,' Stranahan said.

'But first you want me to help you figure it out, how this pasta-breath tied us together.'

'I don't like the fact he was using your name.'

'How d'you think I feel?' Gavigan handed Stranahan the dinner tray and told him to set it on the floor. He folded his papery hands on his lap, over the thin woollen blanket. 'How would he know we was friends, Mick? You never call, never send candy. Missed my birthday three years in a row.'

'That's not true, Timmy. Two years ago I sent a strippergram.'

'You sent that broad? I thought she just showed up lonely at the station and picked out the handsomest cop. Hell, Mick, I took her to Grand Bahama for a week, damn near married her.'

Stranahan was feeling better; Timmy knew something. Stranahan could tell from the eyes. It had come back to him.

Gavigan said, 'Mick, that girl had the finest nipples I ever saw. I meant to thank you.'

'Any time.'

'Like Susan B. Anthony dollars, that's how big they were. Same shape, too. Octagonal.' Gavigan winked. 'You remember the Barletta thing?'

'Sure.' A missing-person's case that had turned into a possible kidnap. The victim was a twenty-two-year-old University of Miami student. Victoria Barletta: brown eyes, black hair, five eight, one hundred and thirty pounds. Disappeared on a rainy March afternoon.

Still unsolved.

'We had our names in the paper,' Gavigan said. 'I still got the clipping.'

Stranahan remembered. There was a press conference. Victoria's parents offered a $10,000 reward. Timmy was there from Homicide, Stranahan from the State Attorney's Office. Both of them were quoted in the story, which ran on the front pages of the *Herald* and the *Miami News*.

Gavigan coughed in a way that startled Mick Stranahan. It sounded like Timmy's lungs had turned to custard.

'Hand me that cup,' Gavigan said. 'Know what? That was the only time we made the papers together.'

'Timmy, we got in the papers all the time.'

'Yeah, but not together.' He slurped down some ginger ale and pointed a bony finger at Stranahan. 'Not together, bucko, trust me. I save all the clippings for my scrapbook. Don't you?'

Stranahan said no.

'You *wouldn't*.' Gavigan hacked out a laugh.

'So you think this Mafia guy got it out of the papers?'

'Not the Mafia guy,' Gavigan said, 'but the guy who hired him. It's a good possibility.'

'The Barletta thing was four years ago, Timmy.'

'Hey, I ain't the only one who keeps scrapbooks.' He yawned. 'Think hard on this, Mick, it's probably important.'

Stranahan stood up and said, 'You get some rest, buddy.'

'I'm glad you took care of that prick who was using my name.'

'Hey, I don't know what you're talking about.'

'Yeah, you do.' Gavigan smiled. 'Anyway, I'm glad you took care of him. He had no business lying like that, using my name.'

Stranahan pulled the blanket up to his friend's neck.

'Good night, Timmy.'

'Be careful, Mick,' the old cop said. 'Hey, and when I croak, you save the newspaper clipping, OK? Glue it on the last page of my scrapbook.'

'It's a promise.'

'Unless it don't make the papers.'

'It'll make the damn papers,' Stranahan said. 'Buried back in the truss ads, where you belong.'

Timmy Gavigan laughed so hard, he had to ring the nurse for oxygen.

THREE

Four days after the Mafia man came to murder him, Mick Stranahan got up early and took the skiff to the marina. There he jump-started his old Chrysler Imperial and drove down to Gables-by-the-Sea, a ritzy but misnomered neighbourhood where his sister Kate lived with her degenerate lawyer husband and three teenaged daughters from two previous marriages (his, not hers). The subdivision was nowhere near the ocean but fronted a series of man-made canals that emptied into Biscayne Bay. No one complained about this marketing deception, as it was understood by buyers and sellers alike that Gables-by-the-Sea sounded much more toney than Gables-on-the-Canal. The price of the real estate duly reflected this exaggeration.

Stranahan's sister lived in a big split-level house with five bedrooms, a swimming pool, a sauna, and a putting green in the yard. Her lawyer husband even bought a thirty-foot sailboat to go with the dock out back, although he couldn't tell his fore from his aft. The sight of the sparkling white mast poking over the top of the big house made Stranahan shake his head as he pulled into the driveway – Kate's husband was positively born for South Florida.

When Stranahan's sister came to the door, she said, 'Well, look who's here.'

Stranahan kissed her and said, 'Is Jocko home?'

'His name's not Jocko.'

'He's a circus ape, Katie, that's a fact.'

'His name's not Jocko, so lay off.'

'Where's the blue Beemer?'

'We traded it.'

Stranahan followed his sister into the living room, where one of the girls was watching MTV and never looked up.

'Traded for what?'

'A Maserati,' Kate said, adding: 'The sedan, not the sporty one.'

'Perfect,' Stranahan said.

Kate made a sad face, and Stranahan gave her a little hug; it killed him to think his little sister had married a sleazeball ambulance chaser. Kipper Garth's face was on highway billboards up and down the Gold Coast – 'If you've had an accident, somebody somewhere owes you money!!! Dial 555-TORT.' Kipper Garth's firm was called The Friendly Solicitors, and it proved to be a marvellously lucrative racket. Kipper Garth culled through thousands of greedy complainants, dumping the losers and farming out the good cases to legitimate personal-injury lawyers, with whom he would split the fees fifty-fifty. In this way Kipper Garth made hundreds of thousands of dollars without ever setting his Bally loafers on a courtroom floor, which (given his general ignorance of the law) was a blessing for his clients.

'He's playing tennis,' Kate said.

'I'm sorry for what I said,' Stranahan told her. 'You know how I feel.'

'I wish you'd give him a chance, Mick. He's got some fine qualities.'

If you like tapeworms, Stranahan thought. He could scarcely hear Kate over the Def Leppard video on the television, so he motioned her to the kitchen.

'I came by to pick up my shotgun,' he said.

His sister's eyes went from green to grey, like when they were kids and she was onto him.

'I got a seagull problem out at the house,' Stranahan said.

Kate said, 'Oh? What happened to those plastic owls?'

'Didn't work,' Stranahan said. 'Gulls just crapped all over 'em.'

They went into Kipper Garth's study, the square footage of which exceeded that of Stranahan's entire house. His shotgun, a Remington pump, was locked up with some fancy filigreed bird guns in a maplewood rack. Kate got the key from a drawer in her husband's desk. Stranahan took the Remington down and looked it over.

Kate noticed his expression and said, 'Kip used it once or twice up North. For pheasant.'

'He could've cleaned off the mud, at least.'

'Sorry, Mick.'

'The man is hopeless.'

Kate touched his arm and said, 'He'll be home in an hour. Would you stay?'

'I can't.'

'As a favour, please? I'd like you to straighten out this lawsuit nonsense once and for all.'

'Nothing to straighten out, Katie. The little monkey wants to sue me, fine. I understand.'

The dispute stemmed from a pending disbarment proceeding against Kipper Garth, who stood accused of defrauding an insurance company. One of Kipper Garth's clients had claimed eighty per cent disability after tripping over a rake on the seventeenth hole of a golf course. Three days after the suit had been filed, the man was dumb enough to enter the 26-kilometre Orange Bowl Marathon, dumb enough to finish third, and dumb enough to give interviews to several TV sportscasters.

It was such an egregious scam that even the Florida Bar couldn't ignore it, and with no encouragement Mick Stranahan had stepped forward to testify against his own brother-in-law. Some of what Stranahan had said was fact, and some was opinion; Kipper Garth liked none of it and had threatened to sue for defamation.

'It's getting ridiculous,' Kate said. 'It really is.'

'Don't worry, he won't file,' Stranahan said. 'He couldn't find the goddamn courthouse with a map.'

'Will you ever let up? This is my husband you're talking about.'

Stranahan shrugged. 'He's treating you well?'

'Like a princess. Now will you let up?'

'Sure, Katie.'

At the door, she gave him a worried look and said, 'Be careful with the gun, Mick.'

'No problem,' he said. 'Tell Jocko I was here.'

'Not hello? Or maybe Happy New Year?'

'No, just tell him I was here. That's all.'

Stranahan got back to the marina and wrapped the shotgun in an oilcloth and slipped it lengthwise under the seats of the skiff. He headed south in a biting wind, taking spray over the port side and bouncing hard in the troughs. It took twenty-five minutes to reach the stilt house; Stranahan idled in on a low tide. As soon as he tied off, he heard voices up above and bare feet on the planks.

He unwrapped the shotgun and crept up the stairs.

Three naked women were stretched out sunning on the deck. One of them, a slender brunette, looked up and screamed. The others reflexively scrambled for their towels.

Stranahan said, 'What are you doing on my house?'

'Are you going to shoot us?' the brunette asked.

'I doubt it.'

'We didn't know this place was yours,' said another woman, a bleached blonde with substantial breasts.

Stranahan muttered and opened the door, which was padlocked from the outside. This happened occasionally – sunbathers or drunken kids climbing up on the place when he wasn't home. He put the gun away, got a cold beer, and came back out. The women had wrapped themselves up and were gathering their lotions and Sony Walkmans.

'Where's your boat?' Stranahan asked.

'Way out there,' the brunette said, pointing.

Stranahan squinted into the glare. It looked like a big red Formula, towing two skiers. 'Boyfriends?' he said.

The bleached blonde nodded. 'They said this place was deserted. Honest, we didn't know. They'll be back at four.'

'It's all right, you can stay,' he said. 'It's a nice day for the water.' Then he went back inside to clean the shotgun. Before long the third woman, a true blonde, came in and asked for a glass of water.

'Take a beer,' Stranahan said. 'I'm saving the water.'

She was back to her naked state. Stranahan tried to concentrate on the Remington.

'I'm a model,' she announced, and started talking. Name's Tina, nineteen years old, born in Detroit but moved down here when she was still a baby, likes to model but hates some of the creeps who take the pictures.

'My career is really taking off,' she declared. She sat down on a bar stool, crossed her legs, folded her arms under her breasts.

'So what do you do?' she asked.

'I'm retired.'

'You look awful young to be retired. You must be rich.'

'A billionaire,' Stranahan said, peering through the shiny blue barrel of the shotgun. 'Maybe even a trillionaire. I'm not sure.'

Tina smiled. 'Right,' she said. 'You ever watch *Miami Vice*? I've been on there twice. Both times I played prostitutes, but at least I had some good lines.'

'I don't have a television,' Stranahan said. 'Sorry I missed it.'

'Know what else? I dated Don Johnson.'

'I bet that looks good on the resumé.'

'He's a really nice guy,' Tina remarked, 'not like they say.'

Stranahan glanced up and said, 'I think your tan's fading.'

Tina the model looked down at herself, seemed to get tangled up in a thought. 'Can I ask you a favour?'

A headache was taking seed in Mick Stranahan's brain. He actually felt it sprouting, like ragweed, out of the base of his skull.

Tina stood up and said: 'I want you to look at my boobs.'

'I have. They're lovely.'

'Please, look again. Closer.'

Stranahan screwed the Remington shut and laid it across his lap. He sat up straight and looked directly at Tina's breasts. They seemed exquisite in all respects.

She said, 'Are they lined up OK?'

'Appear to be.'

'Reason I ask, I had one of those operations. You know, a boob job. For the kind of modelling I do, it was necessary. I mean, I was about a thirty-two A, if you can imagine.'

Stranahan just shook his head. He felt unable to contribute to the conversation.

'Anyway, I paid three grand for this boob job and it's really helped, workwise. Except the other day I did a *Penthouse* tryout and the photog makes some remark about my tits. Says I got a gravity problem on the left side.'

Stranahan studied the two breasts and said, 'Would that be your left or my left?'

'Mine.'

'Well, he's nuts,' Stranahan said. 'They're both perfect.'

'You're not just saying that?'

'I'll prove it,' he said, thinking: I can't believe I'm doing this. He went to the pantry and rummaged noisily until he found what he was searching for, a carpenter's level.

Tina eyed it and said, 'I've seen one of those.'

'Hold still,' Stranahan said.

'What are you going to do?'

'Just watch the bubble.'

The level was a galvanized steel ruler with a clear cylinder of amber liquid fixed in the middle. Inside the cylinder was a bubble of air, which moved in the liquid according to the angle being measured. If the surface was dead level, the bubble sat at the midway point of the cylinder.

Stranahan placed the tool across Tina's chest, so that each end rested lightly on a nipple.

'Now look down slowly, Tina.'

''Kay.'

'Where's the bubble?' he said.

'Smack dab in the centre.'

'Right,' Stranahan said. 'See – they're lined up perfectly.'

He lifted the ruler off her chest and set it on the bar. Tina beamed and gave herself a little squeeze, which caused her to bounce in a truly wonderful way. Stranahan decided to clean the shotgun one more time.

'Well, back to the sunshine,' Tina laughed, sprinting bare-assed out the door.

'Back to the sunshine,' Mick Stranahan said, thinking that there was no sight in the world like a young lady completely at ease with herself, even if it cost three grand to get that way.

At four-thirty, the red Formula full of husky boyfriends roared up. Stranahan was reading on the sun deck, paying little attention to the naked women. The water was way too shallow for the ski boat, so the boyfriends idled it about fifty yards from the stilt house. After a manly huddle, one of them hopped to the bow and shouted at Mick Stranahan.

'Hey, what the hell are you doing?'

Stranahan glanced up from the newspaper and said nothing. Tina called out to the boat, 'It's OK. He lives here.'

'Put your clothes on!' hollered one of the guys in the boat, probably Tina's boyfriend.

Tina wiggled into a T-shirt. All the boyfriends appeared to be fairly agitated by Stranahan's presence among the nude women. Stranahan stood up and told the girls the water was too low for the ski boat.

'I'll run you out there in the skiff,' he said.

'You better not, Richie's real upset,' Tina said.

'Richie should have more faith in his fellow man.'

The three young women gathered their towels and suntan oils and clambered awkwardly into Stranahan's skiff. He jacked the outboard up a couple notches, so the prop wouldn't hit bottom, and steered out toward the red Formula in the channel. Once alongside the ski boat, he helped the girls climb up one at a time. Tina even gave him a peck on the cheek as she left.

The boyfriends were every bit as dumb and full of themselves as Stranahan figured. Each one wore a gold chain on his chest, which said it all.

'What was that about?' snarled the boyfriend called Richie, after witnessing Tina's goodbye peck.

'Nothing,' Tina said. 'He's an all-right guy.'

Stranahan had already let go, and the skiff had drifted a few yards beyond the ski boat, when Richie slapped Tina for being such a slut. Then he pointed out at Stranahan and yelled something extremely rude.

The boyfriends were quite surprised to see the aluminium skiff coming back at them, fast. They were equally amazed at the nimbleness with which the big stranger hopped onto the bow of their boat.

Richie took an impressive roundhouse swing at the guy, but the next thing the other boyfriends knew, Richie was flat on his back with the ski rope tied around both feet. Suddenly he was in the water, and the boat was moving, and Richie was dragging in the salt spray and yowling at the top of his lungs. The other boyfriends tried to seize the throttle, but the stranger knocked them down quickly and with a minimum of effort.

After about three-quarters of a mile, Tina and the other women asked Stranahan to please stop the speedboat, and he did. He grabbed the ski rope and hauled Richie back in, and they all watched him vomit up sea water for ten minutes straight.

'You're a stupid young man,' Stranahan counselled. 'Don't ever come out here again.'

Then Stranahan got in the skiff and went back to the stilt house, and the Formula sped away. Stranahan fixed himself a drink and stretched out on the sun deck. He was troubled by what was happening to the bay, when boatloads of idiots could spoil the whole afternoon. It was becoming a regular annoyance, and Stranahan could foresee a time when he might have to move away.

By late afternoon most of the other boats had cleared out of Stiltsville, except for a cabin cruiser that anchored on the south side of the radio towers in about four feet of water. A very odd location, Stranahan thought. On this boat he counted three people; one seemed to be pointing something big and black in the direction of Stranahan's house.

Stranahan went inside and came back with the shotgun, utterly useless at five hundred yards, and the binoculars, which were not. Quickly he got the cabin cruiser into focus and determined that what was being aimed at him was not a big gun, but a portable television camera.

The people in the cabin cruiser were taking his picture.

This was the capper. First the Mafia hit man, then the nude sunbathers and their troglodyte boyfriends, now a bloody TV crew. Stranahan turned his back to the cabin cruiser and kicked off his trousers. This would give them something to think about: moon over Miami. He was in such sour spirits that he didn't even peek over his shoulder to see their reaction when he bent over.

Watching the sun slide low, Mick Stranahan perceived the syncopation of these events as providential; things had changed on the water, all was no longer calm. The emotion that accompanied this realization was not fear, or even anxiety, but disappointment. All these days the tranquillity of the bay, its bright and relentless beauty, had lulled him into thinking the world was not so rotten after all.

The minicam on the cabin cruiser reminded him otherwise. Mick Stranahan had no idea what the bastards wanted, but he was sorely tempted to hop in the skiff and go find out. In the end, he simply finished his gin and tonic and went back inside the stilt house. At dusk, when the light was gone, the boat pulled anchor and motored away.

FOUR

After quitting the State Attorney's Office, Stranahan had kept his gold investigator's badge to remind people that he used to work there, in case he needed to get back inside. Like now.

A young assistant state attorney, whose name was Dreeson, took Stranahan to an interview room and handed him the Barletta file, which must have weighed four pounds. In an officious voice, the young prosecutor said: 'You can sit here and make notes, Mr Stranahan. But it's still an open case, so don't take anything out.'

'You mean I can't blow my nose on the affidavits?'

Dreeson made a face and shut the door, hard.

Stranahan opened the jacket, and the first thing to fall out was a photograph of Victoria Barletta. Class picture, clipped from the 1985 University of Miami student yearbook. Long dark hair, brushed to a shine; big dark eyes; a long, sharp nose, probably her old man's; gorgeous Italian smile, warm and laughing and honest.

Stranahan set the picture aside. He had never met the girl, never would.

He skimmed the statements taken so long ago by himself and Timmy Gavigan: the parents, the boyfriend, the sorority sisters. The details of the case came back to him quickly in a cold flood.

On March 12, 1986, Victoria Barletta had gotten up early, jogged three miles around the campus, showered, attended a 9 a.m. class in advanced public relations, met her boyfriend at a breakfast shop near Mark Light Field, then bicycled to an 11 a.m. seminar on the history of television news. Afterwards, Vicky went back to the Alpha Chi Omega house, changed into jeans, sneakers, and a sweatshirt, and asked a sorority sister to give her a lift to a doctor's appointment in South Miami, only three miles from the university.

The appointment was scheduled for 1:30 p.m. at a medical building called the Durkos Center. As Vicky got out of the car, she instructed her friend to come back at about 5 p.m. and pick her up. Then she went inside and got a nose job and was never seen again.

According to a doctor and a nurse at the clinic, Vicky Barletta left the office at about 4:50 p.m. to wait on the bus bench out front for her ride back to campus. Her face was splotched, her eyes swollen to slits, and her nose heavily bandaged – not exactly a tempting sight for your average trolling rapist, Timmy Gavigan had pointed out.

Still, they both knew better than to rule it out. One minute the girl was on the bench, the next she was gone.

Three county buses had stopped there between 4:50 and 5:14 p.m., when Vicky's friend finally arrived at the clinic. None of the bus drivers remembered seeing a woman with a busted-up face get on board.

So the cops were left to assume that somebody snatched Victoria Barletta off the bus bench moments after she emerged from the Durkos Center.

The case was treated like a kidnapping, though Gavigan and Stranahan suspected otherwise. The Barlettas had no money and no access to any; Vicky's father was half-owner of a car wash in Evanston, Illinois. Aside from a couple of cranks, there were no ransom calls made to the family, or to the police. The girl was just plain gone, and undoubtedly dead.

Rereading the file four years later, Mick Stranahan began to feel frustrated all over again. It was the damnedest thing: Vicky had told no one – not her parents, her boyfriend, nobody – about the cosmetic surgery; apparently it was meant to be a surprise.

Stranahan and Timmy Gavigan had spent a total of fifteen hours interviewing Vicky's boyfriend and wound up believing him. The kid had cried pathetically; he used to tease Vicky about her shnoz. 'My little anteater,' he used to call her. The boyfriend had been shattered by what happened, and blamed himself: his birthday was March twentieth. Obviously, he sobbed, the new nose was Vicky's present to him.

From a homicide investigator's point of view, the secrecy with which Victoria Barletta planned her doctor's visit meant something else: it limited the suspects to somebody who just happened to be passing by, a random psychopath.

A killer who was never caught.

A victim who was never found.

That was how Mick Stranahan remembered it. He scribbled a few names and numbers on a pad, stuffed everything into the file, then carried it back to a pock-faced clerk.

'Tell me something,' Stranahan said. 'How'd you happen to have this one downtown?'

The clerk said, 'What do you mean?'

'I mean, this place didn't used to be so efficient. Used to take two weeks to dig out an old case like this.'

'You just got lucky,' the clerk said. 'We pulled the file from the warehouse a week ago.'

'This file here?' Stranahan tapped the green folder. 'Same one?'

'Mr Eckert wanted to see it.'

Gerry Eckert was the State Attorney. He hadn't personally gone to court in at least sixteen years, so Stranahan doubted if he even remembered how to read a file.

'So how's old Gerry doing?'

'Just dandy,' said the clerk, as if Eckert were his closest, dearest pal in the world. 'He's doing real good.'

'Don't tell me he's finally gonna pop somebody in this case.'

'I don't think so, Mr Stranahan. He just wanted to refresh his memory before he went on TV. The Reynaldo Flemm show.'

Stranahan whistled. Reynaldo Flemm was a television journalist who specialized in sensational crime cases. He was nationally famous for getting beaten up on camera, usually by the very hoodlums he was trying to interview. No matter what kind of elaborate disguise Reynaldo Flemm would devise, he was always too vain to cover his face. Naturally the crooks would recognize him instantly and bash the living shit out of him. For pure action footage, it was hard to beat; Reynaldo Flemm's specials were among the highest-rated programmes on television.

'So Gerry's hit the big time,' Stranahan said.

'Yep,' the clerk said.

'What did he say about this case?'

'Mr Eckert?'

'Yeah, what did he tell this TV guy?'

The clerk said, 'Well, I wasn't there for the taping. But from what I heard, Mr Eckert said the whole thing is still a mystery.'

'Well, that's true enough.'

'And Mr Eckert told Mr Flemm that he wouldn't be one bit surprised if someday it turns out that Victoria Barletta ran away. Just took one look at her face and ran away. Otherwise, why haven't they found a body?'

Stranahan thought: Eckert hasn't changed a bit, still dumb as a bull gator.

'I can't wait to see the show,' Stranahan remarked.

'It's scheduled to be on March twelfth at 9 p.m.' The clerk held up a piece of paper. 'We got a memo from Mr Eckert today.'

The man from New Jersey did not call Dr Rudy Graveline again for four days. Then, on the afternoon of January eighth, Rudy got a message on his beeper. The beeper went off at a bad moment, when Rudy happened to be screwing the young wife of a Miami Dolphins wide receiver. The woman had come to Whispering Palms for a simple consult – a tiny pink scar along her jawline, could it be fixed? – and the next thing she knew, the doctor had her talking about all kinds of personal things, including how lonely it got at home during the football season when Jake's mind was on the game and nothing else. Well, the next thing she knew, the doctor was taking her to lunch in his black Jaguar sedan with the great Dolby sound system, and the football player's wife found herself thinking how the rich smell of leather upholstery made her hot, really hot, and then – as if he could read her mind – the doctor suddenly pulled off the Julia Tuttle Causeway, parked the Jag in some pepper trees, and started to gnaw her panties off. He even made cute little squirrel noises as he nuzzled between her legs.

Before long the doctor was merrily pounding away while the football player's wife gazed up at him through the spokes of the walnut steering wheel, under which her head had become uncomfortably wedged.

When the beeper went off on Dr Graveline's belt, he scarcely missed a beat. He glanced down at the phone number (glowing in bright green numerals) and snatched the car phone from its cradle in the glove box. With one hand he managed to dial the long-distance number even as he finished with the football player's wife, who by this time was silently counting down, hoping he'd hurry it up. She'd had about all she could take of the smell of new leather.

Dr Graveline pulled away just as the phone started ringing somewhere in New Jersey.

The man answered on the fourth ring. 'Yeah, what?'

'It's me. Rudy.'

'You been jogging or what?'

'Something like that.'

'Sounds like you're gonna have a fuckin' heart attack.'

Dr Graveline said: 'Give me a second to catch my breath.'

The football player's wife was squirming back into her slacks. The look on her face suggested disappointment at her partner's performance, but Rudy Graveline did not notice.

'About the deal,' he said. 'I don't think so.'

Curly Eyebrows in New Jersey said: 'Your problem musta gone away.'

'Not really.'

'Then what?'

'I'm going to get somebody local.'

The man in New Jersey started to laugh. He laughed and laughed until he began to wheeze.

'Doc, this is a big mistake. Local is no good.'

'I've got a guy in mind,' Dr Graveline said.

'A Cuban, right? Crazy fuckin' Cuban, I knew it.'

'No, he's not a Cuban.'

'One of my people?'

'No,' Rudy said. 'He's by himself.'

Again Curly Eyebrows laughed. 'Nobody is by himself, Doc. Nobody in this business.'

'This one is different,' Rudy said. Different wasn't the word for it. 'Anyway, I just wanted to let you know, so you wouldn't send anybody else.'

'Suit yourself.'

'And I'm sorry about the other fellow.'

'Don't bring up that shit, hear? You're on one of those cellular phones, I can tell. I hate them things, Doc, they ain't safe. They give off all kinds of fucked-up microwaves, anybody can listen in.'

Dr Graveline said, 'I don't think so.'

'Yeah, well, I read where people can listen on their blenders and hair dryers and shit. Pick up everything you say.'

The football player's wife was brushing on fresh make-up, using the vanity mirror on the back of the sun visor.

The man in Jersey said: 'Your luck, some broad's pickin' us up on her electric dildo. Every word.'

'Talk to you later,' Rudy said.

'One piece of advice,' said Curly Eyebrows. 'This guy you lined up for the job, don't tell him your life story. I mean it, Doc. Give him the name, the address, the dough, and that's it.'

'Oh, I can trust him,' Dr Graveline said.

'Like hell,' laughed the man in New Jersey, and hung up.

The football player's wife flipped the sun visor up, closed her compact, and said, 'Business?'

'Yes, I dabble in real estate.' Rudy zipped up his pants. 'I've decided to go with a Miami broker.'

The woman shrugged. She noticed her pink bikini panties on the floor-mat, and quickly put them in her purse. They were ruined; the doctor had chewed a hole in them.

'Can I drive your car back to the office?' she asked.

'No,' said Rudy Graveline. He got out and walked around to the driver's side. The football player's wife slid across the seat, and Rudy got in.

'I almost forgot,' the woman said, fingering the place on her jaw, 'about my scar.'

'A cinch,' the doctor said. 'We can do it under local anaesthetic, make it smooth as silk.'

The football player's wife smiled. 'Really?'

'Oh sure, it's easy,' Rudy said, steering the Jaguar back on the highway. 'But I was wondering about something else . . .'

'Yes?'

'You won't mind some friendly professional advice?'

'Of course not.' The woman's voice held an edge of concern.

'Well, I couldn't help but notice,' Dr Graveline said, 'when we were making love . . .'

'Yes?'

Without taking his eyes off the road, he reached down and patted her hip. 'You could use a little suction around the saddlebags.'

The football player's wife turned away and blinked.

'Please don't be embarrassed,' the doctor said. 'This is my speciality, after all. Believe me, darling, I've got an eye for perfection, and you're only an inch or two away.'

She took a little breath and said, 'Around the thighs?'

'That's all.'

'How much would it cost?' she asked with a trace of a sniffle.

Rudy Graveline smiled warmly and passed her a monogrammed handkerchief. 'Less than you think,' he said.

The cabin cruiser with the camera crew came back again, anchored in the same place. Stranahan sighed and spat hard into the tide. He was in no mood for this.

He was standing on the dock with a spinning rod in his hands, catching pinfish from around the pilings of the stilt house. Suspended motionless in the gin-clear water below was a dark blue log, or so it would have appeared to the average tourist. The log measured about five feet long and, when properly motivated, could streak through the water at about sixty knots to make a kill. Teeth were the trademark of the Great Barracuda, and the monster specimen that Mick Stranahan called

Liza had once left thirteen needle-sharp incisors in a large plastic mullet that some moron had trolled through the Biscayne Channel. Since that episode the barracuda had more or less camped beneath Stranahan's place. Every afternoon he went out and caught for its supper a few dollar-sized pinfish, which he tossed off the dock, and which the barracuda devoured in lightning flashes that churned the water and sent the mangrove snappers diving for cover. Liza's teeth had long since grown back.

Because of his preoccupation with the camera boat, Mick Stranahan allowed the last pinfish to stay on the line longer than he should have. It tugged back and forth, sparkling just below the surface until the barracuda ran out of patience. Before Stranahan could react, the big fish rocketed from under the stilt house and severed the majority of the pinfish as cleanly as a scalpel; a quivering pair of fish lips was all that remained on Stranahan's hook.

'Nice shot,' he mumbled and stored the rod away.

He climbed into the skiff and motored off the flat, toward the cabin cruiser. The photographer immediately put down the video camera; Stranahan could see him conferring with the rest of the crew. There was a brief and clumsy attempt to raise the anchor, followed by the sound of the boat's engine whining impotently in the way that cold outboards do. Finally the crew gave up and just waited for the big man in the skiff, who by now was within hailing distance.

A stocky man with a lacquered helmet of black hair and a stiff bottle-brush moustache stood on the transom of the boat and shouted, 'Ahoy there!'

Stranahan cut the motor and let the skiff coast up to

the cabin cruiser. He tied off on a deck cleat, stood up, and said, 'Did I hear you right? Did you actually say *ahoy?*'

The man with the moustache nodded uneasily.

'Where did you learn that, watching pirate movies? Jesus Christ, I can't believe you said that. *Ahoy there!* Give me a break.' Stranahan was really aggravated. He jumped into the bigger boat and said, 'Which one of you assholes is Reynaldo Flemm? Let me guess; it's Captain Blood here.'

The stocky man with the moustache puffed out his chest and said, 'Watch it, pal!' – which took a certain amount of courage, since Mick Stranahan was holding a stainless-steel tarpon gaff in his right hand. Flemm's crew – an overweight cameraman and an athletic young woman in blue jeans – kept one eye on their precious equipment and the other on the stranger with the steel hook.

Stranahan said, 'Why have you been taking my picture?'

'For a story,' Flemm said. 'For television.'

'What's the story?'

'I'm not at liberty to say.'

Stranahan frowned. 'What's it got to do with Vicky Barletta?'

Reynaldo Flemm shook his head. 'In due time, Mr Stranahan. When we're ready to do the interview.'

Stranahan said, 'I'm ready to do the interview now.'

Flemm smiled in a superior way. 'Sorry.'

Stranahan slipped the tarpon gaff between Reynaldo Flemm's legs and gave a little jerk. The tip of the blade not only poked through Reynaldo Flemm's Banana Republic trousers, but also through his thirty-dollar bikini underpants (flamenco red), which he had purchased at a boutique in Coconut Grove. The cold point of the gaff came to rest on Reynaldo Flemm's scrotum, and at this frightful instant the air rushed from his intestinal tract with a sharp noise that seemed to punctuate Mick Stranahan's request.

'The interview,' he said again to Flemm, who nodded energetically.

But words escaped the television celebrity. Try as he might, Flemm could only burble in clipped phrases. Fear, and the absence of cue cards, had robbed him of cogent conversation.

The young woman in blue jeans stepped forward from the cabin of the boat and said, 'Please, Mr Stranahan, we didn't mean to intrude.'

'Of course you did.'

'My name is Christina Marks. I'm the producer of this segment.'

'Segment of what?' Stranahan asked.

'Of the Reynaldo Flemm show. *In Your Face*. You must have seen it.'

'Never.'

For Reynaldo, Stranahan knew, this was worse than a gaff in the balls.

'Come on,' Christina Marks said.

'Honest,' Stranahan said. 'You see a TV dish over on my house?'

'Well, no.'

'There you go. Now, what's this all about? And hurry it up, your man here looks like his legs are cramping.'

Indeed, Reynaldo Flemm was shaking on his tiptoes. Stranahan eased the gaff down just a notch or two.

Christina Marks said: 'Do you know a nurse named Maggie Gonzalez?'

'Nope,' Stranahan said.

'Are you sure?'

'Give me a hint.'

'She worked at the Durkos Medical Center.'

'OK, now I remember.' He had taken her statement the day after Victoria Barletta had vanished. Timmy Gavigan had done the doctor, while Stranahan had taken the nurse. He had scanned the affidavits in the State Attorney's file that morning.

'You sure about the last name?' Stranahan asked.

'Sorry – Gonzalez is her married name. Back then it was Orestes.'

'So let's have the rest.'

'About a month ago, in New York, she came to us.'

'To me,' croaked Reynaldo Flemm.

'Shut up,' said Stranahan.

Christina Marks went on: 'She said she had some important information about the Barletta case. She indicated she was willing to talk on camera.'

'To me,' Flemm said, before Stranahan tweaked him once more with the tarpon gaff.

'But first,' Christina Marks said, 'she said she had to speak to you, Mr Stranahan.'

'About what?'

'All she said was that she needed to talk to you first, because you could do something about it. And don't ask me about what, because I don't know. We gave her six hundred bucks, put her on a plane to Florida, and never saw her again. She was supposed to be back two weeks ago last Monday.' Christina Marks put her hands in her pockets. 'That's all there is. We came down here to look for Maggie Gonzalez, and you're the best lead we had.'

Stranahan removed the gaff from Reynaldo Flemm's crotch and tossed it into the bow of his skiff. Almost instantly, Flemm leapt from the stern and bolted for the cabin. 'Get tape of that fucker,' he cried at the cameraman, 'so we can prosecute his fat ass!'

'Ray, knock it off,' said Christina Marks.

Stranahan liked the way she talked down to the big star. 'Tell him,' he said, 'that if he points that goddamn camera at me again, he'll be auditioning for the Elephant Man on Broadway. That's how seriously I'll mess up his face.'

'Ray,' she said, 'did you hear that?'

'Roll tape! Roll tape!' Flemm was all over the cameraman.

Wearily, Stranahan got back into his skiff and said, 'Miss Marks, the interview is over.'

Now it was her turn to be angry. She hopped up on the transom, tennis shoes squeaking on the teak. 'Wait a minute, that's it?'

Stranahan looked up from his little boat. 'I haven't seen Maggie Gonzalez since the day after the Barletta girl disappeared. That's the truth. I don't know whether she took your money and went south or what, but I haven't heard from her.'

'He's lying,' sneered Reynaldo Flemm, and he stormed into the cabin to sulk. A gust of wind had made a comical nest of his hair.

Stranahan hand-cranked the outboard and slipped it into gear.

'I'm at the Sonesta,' Christina Marks said to him, 'if Maggie Gonzalez should call.'

Not likely, Stranahan thought. Not very likely at all.

'How the hell did you find me, anyway?' he called out to the young TV producer.

'Your ex-wife,' Christina Marks called back from the cabin cruiser.

'Which one?'

'Number four.'

That would be Chloe, Stranahan thought. Naturally.

'How much did it cost you?' he shouted.

Sheepishly, Christina Marks held up five fingers.

'You got off light,' Mick Stranahan said, and turned the skiff homeward.

FIVE

Christina Marks was in bed, reading an old *New Yorker*, when somebody rapped on the door of the hotel room. She was hoping it might be Mick Stranahan, but it wasn't.

'Hello, Ray.'

As Reynaldo Flemm breezed in, he patted her on the rump.

'Cute,' Christina said, closing the door. 'I was getting ready to turn in.'

'I brought some wine.'

'No, thanks.'

Reynaldo Flemm turned on the television and made himself at home. He was wearing another pair of khaki Banana Republic trousers and a baggy denim shirt. He smelled like a bucket of Brut. In a single motion he scissored his legs and propped his white high-top Air Jordans on the coffee table.

Christina Marks tightened the sash on her bathrobe and sat down at the other end of the sofa. 'I'm tired, Ray,' she said.

He acted like he didn't hear it. 'This Stranahan guy, he's the key to it,' Flemm said. 'I think we should follow him tomorrow.'

'Oh, please.'

'Rent a van. A van with smoked window panels. We set the camera on a tripod in back. I'll be driving, so Willie gets the angle over my . . . let's see, it'd be my right shoulder. Great shot, through the windshield as we follow this big prick—'

'Willie gets carsick,' Christina Marks said.

Reynaldo Flemm cackled scornfully.

'It's a lousy idea,' Christina said. She wanted him to go away, now.

'What, you trust that Stranahan?'

'No,' she said, but in a way she did trust him. At least more than she trusted Maggie Gonzalez; there was something squirrelly about the woman's sudden need to fly to Miami. Why had she said she wanted to see Stranahan? Where had she really gone?

Reynaldo Flemm wasn't remotely concerned about Maggie's motives – good video was good video – but Christina Marks wanted to know more about the woman. She had better things to do than sit in a steaming van, tailing a guy who, if he caught them, would probably destroy every piece of electronics in their possession.

'So, what other leads we got?' Reynaldo Flemm demanded. 'Tell me that.'

'Maggie's probably got family here,' Christina said, 'and friends.'

'Dull, dull, dull.'

'Hard work is dull sometimes,' Christina said sharply, 'but how would you know?'

Flemm sat up straight and flared his upper lip like a chihuahua. 'You can't talk to me like that! You just remember who's the star.'

'And you just remember who writes all your lines.

And who does all your dull, dull research. Remember who tells you what questions to ask. And who edits these pieces so you don't come off looking like a pompous airhead.' Except that's exactly how Reynaldo came off, most of the time. There was no way around it, no postproduction wizardry that could disguise the man's true personality on tape.

Reynaldo Flemm shrugged. His attention had been stolen by something on the television: Mike Wallace of CBS was a guest on the Letterman show. Flemm punched up the volume and inched to the edge of the sofa.

'You know how old that geezer is?' he said, pointing at Wallace. 'I'm half his age.'

Christina Marks held her tongue.

Reynaldo said, 'I bet *his* producer sleeps with him any time he wants.' He glanced sideways at Christina.

She got up, went to the door, and held it open. 'Go back to your room, Ray.'

'Aw, come on, I was kidding.'

'No, you weren't.'

'All right, I wasn't. Come on, Chris, close the door. Let's open the wine.'

'Good night, Ray.'

He got up and turned off the TV. He was sulking.

'I'm sorry,' he said.

'You sure are.'

Christina Marks held all the cards. Reynaldo Flemm needed her far worse than she needed him. Not only was she very talented, but she knew things about Reynaldo Flemm that he did not wish the whole world of television to know. About the time she caught him beating himself up, for example. It happened at a Hyatt House in Atlanta. Flemm was supposed to be out interviewing street-gang members, but Christina found him in the bathroom of his hotel room, thwacking himself in the cheek with a sock full of parking tokens. Reynaldo's idea was to give himself a nasty shiner, then go on camera and breathlessly report that an infamous gang leader named Rapper Otis had assaulted him.

Reynaldo Flemm had begged Christina Marks not to tell the executive producers about the sock incident, and she hadn't; the weeping is what got to her. She couldn't bear it.

For keeping this and other weird secrets, Christina felt secure in her job, certainly secure enough to tell Reynaldo Flemm to go pound salt every time he put the make on her.

On the way out the door, he said, 'I still say we get up early and follow this Stranahan guy.'

'And I still say no.'

'But, Chris, he *knows* something.'

'Yeah, Ray, he knows how to hurt people.'

Christina couldn't be sure, but she thought she saw a hungry spark in the eyes of Reynaldo Flemm.

The next morning Stranahan left the skiff at the marina, got the Chrysler and drove back across the Rickenbacker Causeway to the mainland. Next to him on the front seat was his yellow notepad, open to the page where he had jotted the names and numbers from the Barletta file. The first place he went was the Durkos Medical Center, except it wasn't there any more. The building was now occupied entirely by dentists: nine of them, according to Stranahan's count from the office directory. He went looking for the building manager.

Every door and hallway reverberated with the nerve-stabbing whine of high-speed dental drills; soon Stranahan's molars started to throb, and he began to feel claustrophobic. He enlisted a friendly janitor to lead him to the superintendent, a mammoth olive-coloured woman who introduced herself as Marlee Jones.

Stranahan handed Marlee Jones a card and told her what he wanted. She glanced at the card and shrugged. 'I don't have to tell you nothing,' she said, displaying the kind of public-spirited co-operation that Stranahan had come to appreciate among the Miami citizenry.

'No, you don't have to tell me nothing,' he said to Marlee, 'but I can make it possible for a county code inspector to brighten your morning tomorrow, and the day after that, and every single day until you die of old age.' Stranahan picked up a broom and stabbed the wooden handle into the foam-tile ceiling. 'Looks like pure asbestos to me,' he said. 'Sure hate for the feds to find out.'

Marlee Jones scowled, exhibiting an impressive array of gold teeth: bribes, no doubt, from her tenants. She shuffled to a metal desk and opened a bottom drawer and got out a black ledger. 'All right, smartass, what was that name?'

'Durkos.' Stranahan spelled it. 'A medical group. They were here as of March twelfth, four years ago.'

'Well, as of April first, four years ago, they was gone.' Marlee started to close the ledger, but Stranahan put his hand on the page.

'May I look?'

'It's just numbers, mister.'

'Aw, let me give it a whirl.' Stranahan took the ledger from Marlee Jones and ran down the columns with his forefinger. The Durkos Medical Trust, Inc., had been sole tenant of the building for two years, but had vacated within weeks after Victoria Barletta's disappearance. The ledger showed that the company had paid its lease and security deposits through May. Stranahan thought it was peculiar that, after moving out, the medical group never got a refund.

'Maybe they didn't ask,' Marlee Jones said.

'Doctors are the cheapest human beings alive,' Stranahan said. 'For fifteen grand they don't just ask, they hire lawyers.'

Again Marlee Jones shrugged. 'Some people be in a big damn hurry.'

'What do you remember about it?'

'Who says I was here?'

'This handwriting in the ledger book – it's the same as on these receipts.' Stranahan tapped a finger on a pile of rental coupons. Marlee Jones appeared to be having a spell of high blood pressure.

Stranahan asked again: 'So what do you remember?'

With a groan Marlee Jones heaved her bottom into the chair behind the desk. She said, 'One night they cleared out. Must've backed up a trailer truck, who knows. I came in, the place was empty, except for a bunch of cheapo paintings on the walls. Cats with big eyes, that sorta shit.'

'Were they all surgeons?'

'Seemed like it. But they wasn't partners.'

'Durkos the main man?'

'Was no Durkos that I heard of. Big man was a Dr Graveyard, something like that. The other four guys worked for him. How come I know this is, the day after all the stuff is gone, a couple of the other doctors showed up dressed for work. They couldn't believe their office was emptied.'

Graveline was the name of the surgeon who had operated on Vicky Barletta. There was no point to correcting Marlee Jones on the name. Stranahan said, 'This Dr Graveyard, he didn't even tell the other doctors about the move?'

'This is Miami, lots of people in a big-time hurry.'

'Yeah, but not many pay in advance.'

Marlee Jones finally laughed. 'You right about that.'

'Did anybody leave a forwarding address?'

'Nope.'

Stranahan handed Marlee Jones the ledger book.

'You be through with me?' she asked.

'Yes, ma'am.'

'For good?'

'Most likely.'

'Then can I ask who is it you're workin' for?'

'Myself,' said Mick Stranahan.

Since the day that the Durkos Medical Center had ceased to exist, the life of Nurse Maggie Orestes had gotten complicated. She had gone to work in the emergency room at Jackson Hospital, where one night she had met a man named Ricky Gonzalez. The reason for Ricky Gonzalez's visit to the emergency room was that he had accidentally been run over by a turbocharged Ferrari during the annual running of the Miami Grand Prix. Ricky was a race-car promoter, and he had been posing for pictures with Lorenzo Lamas in pit row, not paying close attention when the Ferrari had roared in and run over both his feet. Ricky broke a total of fourteen bones, while Lorenzo Lamas escaped without a scratch.

Nurse Maggie Orestes attended to Ricky Gonzalez in the emergency room before they put him under for surgery. He was young, dashing, full of promises – and so cheerful, considering what had happened.

A month later they were married at a Catholic church in Hialeah. Ricky persuaded Maggie to quit nursing and be a full-time hostess for the many important social functions that race-car promoters must necessarily conduct. Maggie had hoped she would come to enjoy car racing and the people involved in it, but she didn't. It was noisy and stupid and boring, and the people were worse. Maggie and Ricky had some fierce arguments, and she was on the verge of walking out of the marriage when the second pit-row accident happened.

This time it was a Porsche, and Ricky wasn't so lucky. After the service they cremated him in his complimentary silver Purolator racing jacket, which turned out to be fireproof, so they had to cremate that portion twice. Lorenzo Lamas sent a wreath all the way from Malibu, California. At the wake Ricky's lawyer came up to Maggie Gonzalez and told her the bad news: first, her husband had no life insurance; second, he had emptied their joint bank accounts to pay for his cocaine habit. Maggie had known nothing about the drug problem, but in retrospect it explained her late husband's irrepressible high spirits and also his lack of caution around the race track.

A widowhood of destitution did not appeal to Maggie Gonzalez. She went back to being a nurse with a plan to nail herself a rich doctor or at least his money. In eighteen months she had been through three of them, all disasters – a married pediatrician, a divorced radiologist, and a urologist who wore women's underwear and who wound up giving Maggie a stubborn venereal disease. When she dumped the urologist, he got her fired from the hospital and filed a phoney complaint with the state nursing board.

All this left Maggie Gonzalez with a molten hatred of men and a mind for vengeance.

Money is what pushed her to the brink. With the mortgage payment on her duplex coming due, and only eighty-eight bucks in the checking account, Maggie decided to go ahead and do it. Part of the motive was financial desperation, true, but there was also a delicious hint of excitement – payback, to the sonofabitch who'd started it all.

First Maggie used her Visa card to buy a plane ticket to New York, where she caught a cab to the midtown offices of Reynaldo Flemm, the famous television journalist. There she told producer Christina Marks the story of Victoria Barletta, and cut a deal.

Five thousand dollars to repeat it on camera – that's as high as Reynaldo's people would go. Maggie Gonzalez was disappointed; it was, after all, one hell of a story.

That night Christina Marks got Maggie a room at the Goreham Hotel, and she lay there watching Robin Leach on TV and worrying about the risks she was taking. She remembered the State Attorney's investigator who had questioned her nearly four years ago, and how she had lied to him. God, what was she thinking of now? Flemm's people would fly straight to Miami and interview the investigator – Stranahan was his name – and he'd tell them she'd never said a word about all this when it happened. Her credibility would be shot, and so would the five grand. Out the window.

Maggie realized she had to do something about Stranahan.

And also about Dr Rudy Graveline.

Graveline was a dangerous creep. To rat on Rudy – well, he had warned her. And rewarded her, in a sense. A decent severance, glowing references for a new job. That was after he closed down the Durkos Center.

Lying there, Maggie got another idea. It was wild, but it just might work. The next morning she went back to Christina Marks and made up a vague story about how she had to go see Investigator Stranahan right away, otherwise no TV show. Reluctantly the producer gave her a plane ticket and six hundred in expenses.

Of course, Maggie had no intention of visiting Mick Stranahan. When she got back to Florida, she drove directly to the Whispering Palms Spa and Surgery Center in beautiful Bal Harbour. Dr Rudy Graveline was very surprised to see her. He led her into a private office and closed the door.

'You look frightened,' the surgeon said.

'I am.'

'And a little bouncy in the bottom.'

'I eat when I'm frightened,' Maggie said, keeping her cool.

'So what is it?' Rudy asked.

'Vicky Barletta,' she said. 'Somebody's making a fuss.'

'Oh.' Rudy Graveline appeared calm. 'Who?'

'One of the investigators. A man named Stranahan.'

'I don't remember him,' Rudy said.

'I do. He's scary.'

'Did he speak to you?'

Maggie shook her head. 'Worse than that,' she said. 'Some TV people came to my place. They're doing a special on missing persons.'

'Christ, don't tell me.'

'Stranahan's going to talk.'

Rudy said, 'But what does he know?'

Maggie blinked. 'I'm worried, Dr Graveline. It's going to break open all over again.'

'No way.'

Maggie's notion was to get Stranahan out of the way. Whether Dr Graveline bribed him, terrorized him, or worse was immaterial; Rudy could get to anybody. Those who stood in his way either got with the programme or got run over. One time another surgeon had done a corrective rhinoplasty on one of Rudy's botched-up patients, then badmouthed Rudy at a medical society cocktail party. Rudy got so furious that he paid two goons to trash the other doctor's office, but not before stealing his medical files. Soon, the other doctor's surgical patients received personal letters thanking them for being so understanding while he battled that terrible heroin addiction, which now seemed to be under control. Well, almost . . . By the end of the month, the other doctor had closed what was left of his practice and moved to British Columbia.

Maggie Gonzalez was counting on Rudy Graveline to overreact again; she wanted him worried about Stranahan to the exclusion of all others. By the time the doctor turned on the tube and discovered who was the real threat, Maggie would be long gone. And out of reach.

She went on: 'They won't leave me alone, these TV people. They said the case is going to a grand jury. They said Stranahan's going to testify.' She fished in her purse for a tissue. 'I thought you ought to know.'

Rudy Graveline thanked her for coming. He told her not to worry, everything was going to be fine. He suggested she get out of town for a few weeks, and she said that was probably a good idea. He asked if there was anywhere in particular she wanted to go, and she said New York. The doctor said New York is a swell place to visit around Christmas time, and he wrote out a personal cheque for twenty-five hundred dollars. He recommended that Maggie stay gone for at least a month, and said to call if she needed more money. *When*, Maggie said. Not *if* she needed more money, but when.

Later that same afternoon, Dr Rudy Graveline had locked his office door and made a telephone call to a seafood restaurant in New Jersey. He talked to a man who probably had curly eyebrows, a man who promised to send somebody down around the first of the year.

On the day that Tony Traviola, the first hit man, arrived to kill Mick Stranahan, Maggie Gonzalez was in a tenth-floor room at the Essex House hotel. The room had a view of Central Park, where Maggie was taking skating lessons at Donald Trump's ice rink. She planned to lay low for a few more weeks, maybe stop in for a chat at *20/20*. A little competition never hurt. Maybe Reynaldo Flemm would get worried enough to jack up his offer. Five grand sucked, it really did.

*

Dr Rudy Graveline made an appointment with the second killer for January tenth at three in the afternoon. The man arrived at Whispering Palms a half hour early and sat quietly in the waiting room, scaring the hell out of the other patients.

Rudy knew him only as Chemo, a cruel but descriptive nickname, for he truly did appear to be in the final grim stages of chemotherapy. Black hair sprouted in random wisps from a blue-veined scalp. His lips were thin and papery, the colour of wet cement. Red-rimmed eyes peered back at gawkers with a dull and chilling indifference; the hooded lids blinked slowly, pellucid as a salamander's. And the skin – the skin is what made people gasp, what emptied the waiting room at Whispering Palms. Chemo's skin looked like breakfast cereal, like somebody had glued Rice Krispies to every square centimetre of his face.

This, and the fact that he stood six foot nine, made Chemo a memorable sight.

Dr Graveline was not alarmed, because he knew how Chemo had come to look this way: it was not melanoma, but a freak electrolysis accident in Scranton, many years before. While burning two ingrown hair follicles off the tip of Chemo's nose, an elderly dermatologist had suffered a crippling stroke and lost all hand-eye co-ordination. Valiantly the old doctor had tried to complete the procedure, but in so doing managed to incinerate every normal pore within range of the electrified needle. Since Chemo had eaten five Valiums for breakfast, he was fast asleep on the table when the tragedy occurred. When he awoke to find his whole face blistered up like a lobster, he immediately garrotted the dermatologist and fled the State of Pennsylvania for ever.

Chemo had spent the better part of five years on the lam, seeking medical relief; ointments proved futile, and in fact a faulty prescription had caused the startling Rice Krispie effect. Eventually Chemo came to believe that the only hope was cosmetic surgery, and his quest for a miracle brought him naturally to Florida and naturally into the care of Dr Rudy Graveline.

At three sharp, Rudy motioned Chemo into the consultation room. Chemo ducked as he entered and shut the door behind him. He sat in an overstuffed chair and blinked moistly at Dr Graveline.

Rudy said: 'And how are we doing today?'

Chemo grunted. 'How do you think?'

'When you were here a few weeks ago, we discussed a treatment plan. You remember?'

'Yep,' Chemo said.

'And a payment plan, too.'

'How could I forget?' Chemo said.

Dr Graveline ignored the sarcasm; the man had every right to be bitter.

'Dermabrasion is expensive,' Rudy said.

'I don't know why,' Chemo said. 'You just stick my face in a belt sander, right?'

The doctor smiled patiently. 'It's a bit more sophisticated than that—'

'But the principle's the same.'

Rudy nodded. 'Roughly speaking.'

'So how can it be two hundred bucks a pop?'

'Two hundred and ten,' Rudy corrected. 'Because it requires uncommonly steady hands. You can appreciate that, I'm sure.'

Chemo smiled at the remark. Rudy wished he hadn't; the smile was harrowing, a deadly weapon all by itself. Chemo looked like he'd been teething on cinderblocks.

'I *did* get a job,' he said.

Dr Graveline agreed that was a start.

'At the Gay Bidet,' Chemo said. 'It's a punk club down on South Beach. I'm a greeter.' Again with the smile.

'A greeter,' said Rudy. 'Well, well.'

'I keep out the scum,' Chemo explained.

Rudy asked about the pay. Chemo said he got six bucks an hour, not including tips.

'Not bad,' Rudy said, 'but still . . .' He scribbled some figures on a pad, then took a calculator out of his desk and punched on it for a while. All very dramatic.

Chemo stretched his neck to look. 'What's the damage?'

'I figure twenty-four visits, that's a minimum,' Rudy said. 'Say we do one square inch every session.'

'Shit, just do it all at once.'

'Can't,' Rudy lied, 'not with dermabrasion. Say twenty-four visits at two ten each, that's—'

'Five thousand and forty dollars,' Chemo muttered. 'Jesus H. Christ.'

Dr Graveline said: 'I don't need it all at once. Give me half to start.'

'Jesus H. Christ.'

Rudy put the calculator away.

'I just started at the club a week ago,' Chemo said. 'I gotta buy groceries.'

Rudy came around the desk and sat down on the edge. In a fatherly tone he asked: 'You have Blue Cross?'

'The fuck, I'm a fugitive, remember?'

'Of course.'

Rudy shook his head and mused. It was all so sad, that a great country like ours couldn't provide minimal health care to all its citizens.

'So I'm screwed,' Chemo said.

'Not necessarily.' Dr Graveline rubbed his chin. 'I've got an idea.'

'Yeah?'

'It's a job I need done.'

If Chemo had had eyebrows, they would have arched.

'If you could do this job,' Rudy went on, 'I think we could work a deal.'

'A discount?'

'I don't see why not.'

Idly, Chemo fingered the scales on his cheeks. 'What's the job?'

'I need you to kill somebody,' Rudy said.

'Who?'

'A man that could cause me some trouble.'

'What kind of trouble?'

'Could shut down Whispering Palms. Take away my medical licence. And that's for starters.'

Chemo ran a bloodless tongue across his lips. 'Who is this man?'

'His name is Mick Stranahan.'

'Where do I find him?'

'I'm not sure,' Rudy said. 'He's here in Miami somewhere.'

Chemo said that wasn't much of a lead. 'I figure a murder is worth at least five grand,' he said.

'Come on, he's not a cop or anything. He's just a

regular guy. Three thousand, tops.' Rudy was a bear
when it got down to money.

Chemo folded his huge bony hands. 'Twenty treatments, that's my final offer.'

Rudy worked it out in his head. 'That's forty-two
hundred dollars!'

'Right.'

'You sure drive a hard bargain,' Rudy said.

Chemo grinned triumphantly. 'So when can you start
on my face?'

'Soon as this chore is done.'

Chemo stood up. 'I suppose you'll want proof.'

Rudy Graveline hadn't really thought about it. He
said, 'A newspaper clipping would do.'

'Sure you don't want me to bring you something?'

'Like what?'

'A finger,' Chemo said, 'maybe one of his nuts.'

'That won't be necessary,' said Dr Graveline, 'really
it won't.'

SIX

Stranahan got Maggie Orestes Gonzalez's home address from a friend of his who worked for the state nursing board in Jacksonville. Although Maggie's licence was paid up to date, no current place of employment was listed on the file.

The address was a duplex apartment in a quiet old neighbourhood off Coral Way, in the Little Havana section of Miami. There was a chain-link fence around a sparse brown yard, a ceramic statue of Santa Barbara in the flower bed, and the customary burglar bars on every window. Stranahan propped open the screen door and knocked three times on the heavy pine frame. He wasn't surprised that no one was home.

To break into Maggie Gonzalez's apartment, Stranahan used a three-inch stainless-steel lockpick that he had confiscated from the mouth of an infamous condominium burglar named Wet Willie Jeeter. Wet Willie got his nickname because he only worked on rainy days; on sunny days he was a golf caddy at the Doral Country Club. When they went through Wet Willie's place after the arrest, the cops found seventeen personally autographed photos of Jack Nicklaus, going back to the 1967 Masters. What the cops did not find was any of

Wet Willie's burglar tools, due to the fact that Wet Willie kept them well hidden beneath his tongue.

Stranahan found them when he visited Wet Willie in the Dade County Jail, two weeks before the trial. The purpose of the visit was to make Wet Willie realize the wisdom of pleading guilty and saving the taxpayers the expense of trial. Unspoken was the fact that the State Attorney's Office had a miserably weak case and was desperate for a deal. Wet Willie told Stranahan thanks anyway, but he'd just as soon take his chances with a jury. Stranahan said fine and offered Wet Willie a stick of Dentyne, which the burglar popped into his mouth without thinking. The chewing dislodged the steel lock-picks, which immediately stuck fast in the Dentyne; the whole mess eventually lodged itself in Wet Willie's throat. For a few hectic minutes Stranahan thought he might have to perform an amateur tracheotomy, but miraculously the burglar coughed up the tiny tools and also a complete confession. Stranahan kept one of Wet Willie's lockpicks as a souvenir.

The lock on Maggie's door was a breeze.

Stranahan slipped inside and noticed how neat the place looked. Someone, probably a neighbour or a relative, had carefully stacked the unopened mail on a table near the front door. On the kitchen counter was a Princess-model telephone attached to an answering machine. Stranahan pressed the Rewind button, then Play, and listened to Maggie's voice say: 'Hi, I'm not home right now so you're listening to another one of those dumb answering machines. Please leave a brief message and I'll get back to you as soon as possible. Bye now!'

Stranahan played the rest of the tape, which was

blank. Either Maggie Gonzalez wasn't getting any calls, or someone was taking them for her, or she was phoning in for her own messages with one of those remote pocket beepers. Whatever the circumstances, it was a sign that she probably wasn't all that dead.

Other clues in the apartment pointed to travel. There was no luggage in the closets, no bras or underwear in the bedroom drawers, no make-up on the bathroom sink. The most interesting thing Stranahan found was crumpled in a waste basket in a corner of the living room: a bank deposit slip for twenty-five hundred dollars, dated the twenty-seventh of December.

Have a nice trip, Stranahan thought.

He let himself out, carefully locking the door behind him. Then he drove three blocks to a pay phone at a 7-Eleven, where he dialled Maggie's phone number and left a very important message on her machine.

At the end of the day, Christina Marks dropped her rented Ford Escort with the hotel valet, bought a copy of the *New York Times* at the shop in the lobby, and took the elevator up to her room. Before she could get the key out of the door, Mick Stranahan opened it from the other side.

'Come on in,' he said.

'Nice of you,' Christina said, 'considering it's my room.'

Stranahan noticed she had one of those trendy leather briefcase satchels that you wear over your shoulder. A couple of legal pads stuck out the top.

'You've been busy.'

'You want a drink?'

'Gin and tonic, thanks,' Stranahan said. After a pause: 'I was afraid the great Reynaldo might see me if I waited in the lobby.'

'So you got a key to my room?'

'Not exactly.'

Christina Marks handed him the drink. Then she poured herself a beer, and sat down in a rattan chair with garish floral pillows that were supposed to look tropical.

'I went to see Maggie's family today,' she said.

'Any luck?'

'No. Unfortunately, they don't speak English.'

Stranahan smiled and shook his head.

'What's so funny?' Christina said. 'Just because I don't speak Spanish?'

Stranahan said, 'Except for probably her grand-mother, all Maggie's family speaks perfect English. Perfect.'

'What?'

'Her father teaches physics at Palmetto High School. Her mother is an operator for Southern Bell. Her sister Consuela is a legal secretary, and her brother, what's-his-name . . .'

'Tomàs.'

'Tommy, yeah,' Stranahan said. 'He's a senior account executive at Merrill Lynch.'

Christina Marks put down her beer so decisively that it nearly broke the glass coffee table. 'I sat in the living room, talking to these people, and they just stared at me and said—'

'*No habla* English, *señora.*'

'Exactly.'

'Oldest trick in Miami,' Stranahan said. 'They just

didn't want to talk. Don't feel bad, they tried the same thing with me.'

'And I suppose you know Spanish.'

'Enough to make them think I knew more. They're worried about Maggie, actually. Been worried for some time. She's had some personal problems, Maggie has. Money problems, too – that much I found out before her old lady started having chest pains.'

'You're kidding.'

'Second oldest trick,' Stranahan said, smiling, 'but I was done anyway. I honestly don't think they know where she is.'

Christina Marks finished her beer and got another from the small hotel refrigerator. When she sat down again, she kicked off her shoes.

'So,' she said, 'you're ahead of us.'

'You and Reynaldo?'

'The crew,' Christina said, looking stung.

'No, I'm not ahead of you,' Stranahan said. 'Tell me what Maggie Gonzalez knows about Vicky Barletta.'

Christina said, 'I can't do that.'

'How much did you promise to pay?'

Again Christina shook her head.

'Know what I think?' Stranahan said. 'I think you and Ray are getting the hum job of your lives.'

'Pardon?'

'I think Maggie is sucking you off, big-time.'

Christina heard herself saying, 'You might be right.'

Stranahan softened his tone. 'Let me give you a hypothetical,' he said. 'This Maggie Gonzalez, whom you've never seen before, shows up in New York one day and offers to tell you a sensational story about a missing college coed. The way she tells it, the girl came to a terrible and ghastly end. And, conveniently, the way she tells it can't ever be proven or disproven. Why? Because it happened a long time ago. And the odds are, Christina, that Victoria Barletta is dead. And the odds are, whoever did it isn't about to come forward to say that Reynaldo Flemm got it all wrong when he told the story on national TV.'

Christina Marks leaned forward. 'Fine. All fine, except for one thing. She names names.'

'Maggie does?'

'Yes. She describes exactly how it happened and who did it.'

'And these people—'

'Person, singular.'

'He? She?'

'He,' Christina said.

'He's still alive?'

'Sure is.'

'Here in town?'

'That's right.'

'Jesus,' Stranahan said. He got up and fixed himself another gin. He dropped a couple of ice cubes, his hands were shaking so much. This was not good, he told himself, getting so excited was definitely not good.

He carried his drink back to the living room and said, 'Is it the doctor?'

'I can't say.' It would violate a confidence, Christina Marks explained. Journalists have to protect their sources. Stranahan finished half his drink before he spoke again. 'Are you any good?'

Christina looked at him curiously.

'At what you do,' he said irritably, 'are you any damn good?'

'Yes, I think so.'

'Can you keep the great Reynaldo out of my hair?'

'I'll try. Why?'

'Because,' Stranahan said, 'it would be to our mutual benefit to meet once in a while, just you and me.'

'Compare notes?'

'Something like that. I don't know why, but I think I can trust you.'

'Thanks.'

'I'm not saying I do, just that it's possible.'

He put down the glass and stood up.

'What's your stake in this?' Christina Marks asked.

'Truth, justice, whatever.'

'No, it's bigger than that.'

She was pretty sharp, he had to admit. But he wasn't ready to tell her about Tony the Eel and the marlin head.

As she walked Stranahan to the door, Christina said, 'I spent some time at the newspaper today.'

'Reading up, I suppose.'

'You've got quite a clip file,' she said. 'I suppose I ought to be scared of you.'

'You don't believe everything you read?'

'Of course not.' Christina Marks opened the door. 'Just tell me, how much of it was true?'

'All of it,' Mick Stranahan said, 'unfortunately.'

Of Stranahan's five ex-wives, only one had chosen to keep his last name: ex-wife number four, Chloe Simpkins Stranahan. Even after she remarried, Chloe hung on to his name as an act of unalloyed spite. Naturally she was listed in the Miami phone book; Stranahan had begged her to please get a nonpublished number, but Chloe had said that would defeat the whole purpose. 'This way, any girl who wants to call up and check on you, I can tell them the truth. That you're a dangerous lunatic. That's what I'll tell them when they call up, Mick – *honey, he was one dangerous lunatic.*'

Christina Marks had gotten all the Stranahan numbers from directory assistance. When she had called Chloe from New York, Chloe assumed it was just one of Mick's girlfriends, and had given a vitriolic and highly embellished account of their eight-month marriage and nine-month divorce. Finally Christina Marks had cut in and explained who she was and what she wanted, and Chloe Simpkins Stranahan had said: 'That'll cost you a grand.'

'Five hundred,' Christina countered.

'Bitch,' Chloe hissed. But when the cashier's cheque arrived the next afternoon by Federal Express, Chloe faithfully picked up the phone and called Christina Marks (collect) in New York and told her where to locate her dangerous lunatic of an ex-husband.

'Give him a disease for me, will you?' Chloe had said and then had hung up.

The hit man known as Chemo was not nearly as resourceful as Christina Marks, but he did know enough to check the telephone book for Stranahans. There were five, and Chemo wrote them all down.

The day after his meeting with Dr Rudy Graveline, Chemo went for a drive. His car was a royal blue 1980 Bonneville, with tinted windows. The tinted windows were essential to conceal Chemo's face, the mere glimpse of which could cause a high-speed pileup at any intersection.

Louis K. Stranahan was the first on Chemo's list. A

Miamian would have recognized the address as being in the middle of Liberty City, but Chemo did not. It occurred to him upon entering the neighbourhood that he should have asked Dr Graveline whether the man he was supposed to kill was black or white, because it might have saved some time.

The address was in the James Scott housing project, a bleak and tragic warren where few outsiders of any colour dared to go. Even on a bright winter day, the project gave off a dark and ominous heat. Chemo was oblivious; he saw no danger here, just work. He parked the Bonneville next to a fenced-in basketball court and got out. Almost instantly the kids on the court stopped playing. The basketball hit the rim and bounced lazily out of bounds, but no one ran to pick it up. They were all staring at Chemo. The only sound was the dental-drill rap of Run-DMC from a distant quadrophonic blaster.

'Hello, there,' Chemo said.

The kids from the project glanced at one another, trying to guess how they should play it; this was one of the tallest white motherfuckers they'd ever seen this side of the Interstate. Also, one of the ugliest.

'Game's full,' the biggest kid declared with a forced authority.

'Oh, I don't want to play,' Chemo said.

A look of relief spread among the players, and one of them jogged after the basketball.

'I'm looking for a man named Louis Stranahan.'

'He ain't here.'

'Where is he?'

'Gone.'

Chemo said, 'Does he have a brother named Mick?'

'He's got six brothers,' one of the basketball players volunteered. 'But no Mick.'

'There's a Dick,' said another teenager.

'And a Lawrence.'

Chemo took the list out of his pocket and frowned. Sure enough, Lawrence Stranahan was the second name from the phone book. The address was close by, too.

As Chemo stood there, cranelike, squinting at the piece of paper, the black kids loosened up a little. They started shooting a few hoops, horsing around. The white guy wasn't so scary after all; shit, there were eight of them and one of him.

'Where could I find Louis?' Chemo tried again.

'Raiford,' said two of the kids, simultaneously.

'Raiford,' Chemo repeated. 'That's a prison, isn't it?'

With this, all the teenagers doubled up, slapping fives, howling hysterically at this gangly freak with the fuzzballs on his head.

'Fuck, yeah, it's a prison,' one of them said finally.

Chemo scratched the top two Stranahans off his list. As he opened the door of the Bonneville, the black kid who was dribbling the basketball hollered, 'Hey, big man, you a movie star?'

'No,' Chemo said.

'I swear you are.'

'I swear I'm not.'

'Then how come I saw you in *Halloween III*?'

The kid bent over in a deep wheeze; he thought this was so damn funny. Chemo reached under the car seat and got a .22-calibre pistol, which was fitted with a cheap mail-order suppressor. Without saying a word, he took aim across the roof of the Bonneville and shot the basketball clean out of the kid's hands. The explosion sounded like the world's biggest fart, but the kids from the project didn't think it was funny. They ran like hell.

As Chemo drove away, he decided he had taught the youngsters a valuable lesson: never make fun of a man's complexion.

It was half past noon when Chemo found the third address, a two-storey Mediterranean-style house in Coral Gables. An ill-tempered Rottweiler was chained to the trunk of an olive tree in the front yard, but Chemo ambled past the big dog without incident; the animal merely cocked its head and watched, perhaps not sure if this odd extenuated creature was the same species he'd been trained to attack.

Chloe Simpkins Stranahan was on the phone to her husband's secretary when the doorbell rang.

'Tell him if he's not home by eight, I sell the Dali. Tell him that right now.' Chloe slammed down the phone and stalked to the door. She looked up at Chemo and said, 'How'd you get past the pooch?'

Chemo shrugged. He was wearing black Raybans, which he hoped would lessen the effect of his facial condition. If necessary, he was prepared to explain what had happened; it wouldn't be the first time.

Yet Chloe Simpkins Stranahan didn't mention it. She said, 'You selling something?'

'I'm looking for a man named Mick Stranahan.'

'He's a dangerous lunatic,' Chloe said. 'Come right in.'

Chemo removed the sunglasses and folded them into the top pocket of his shirt. He sat down in the living room, and put a hand on each of his bony kneecaps. At the wet bar Chloe fixed him a cold ginger ale. She acted like she didn't even notice what was wrong with his appearance.

'Who are you?' she asked.

'Collection agent,' Chemo said. Watching Chloe move around the house, he saw that she was a very beautiful woman: auburn hair, long legs, and a good figure. Listening to her, he could tell she was also hard as nails.

'Mick is my ex,' Chloe said. 'I have nothing good to say about him. Nothing.'

'He owe you money, too?'

She chuckled harshly. 'No, I took him for every goddamn dime. Cleaned his clock.' She drummed her ruby fingernails on the side of the ginger ale glass. 'I'm now married to a CPA,' she said. 'Has his own firm.'

'Nice to hear it,' Chemo said.

'Dull as a dog turd, but at least he's no lunatic.'

Chemo shifted in the chair. 'Lunatic, you keep saying that word. What do you mean? Is Mr Stranahan violent? Did he hit you?'

'Mick? Never. Not me,' Chloe said. 'But he did attack a friend of mine. A male-type friend.'

Chemo figured he ought to learn as much as possible about the man he was supposed to kill. He said to Chloe, 'What exactly did Mick do to this male-type friend?'

'It's hard for me to talk about it.' Chloe got up and dumped a jigger of vodka into her ginger ale. 'He was always on the road, Mick was. Never home. No doubt he was screwing around.'

'You know for a fact?'

'I'm sure of it.'

'So you got a . . . boyfriend.'

'You're a smart one,' Chloe said mordantly. 'A goddamn rocket scientist, you are. Yes, I got a *boyfriend*. And he loved me, this guy. He treated me like a queen.'

Chemo said, 'So one night Mr Stranahan gets home early from a trip and catches the two of you—'

'In action,' Chloe said. 'Don't get me wrong, I didn't plan it that way. God knows I didn't want him to walk in on us – you gotta know Mick, it's just not a safe situation.'

'Short fuse?'

'No fuse.'

'So then what?'

Chloe sighed. 'I can't believe I'm telling this to some stranger, a bill collector! Unbelievable.' She polished off her drink and got another. This time when she came back from the bar, she sat down on the divan next to Chemo; close enough that he could smell her perfume.

'I'm a talker,' she said with a soft smile. The smile certainly didn't go with the voice.

'And I'm a listener,' Chemo said.

'And I like you.'

'You do?' This broad is creepy, he thought, a real head case.

'I like you,' Chloe went on, 'and I'd like to help you with your problem.'

'Then just tell me,' Chemo said, 'where I can find your ex-husband.'

'How much are you willing to pay?'

'Ah, so that's it.'

'Everything's got a price,' Chloe said, 'especially good information.'

'Unfortunately, Mrs Stranahan, I don't have any money. Money is the reason I'm looking for Mick.'

Chloe crossed her legs, and Chemo noticed a very fine run in one of her nylon stockings; it seemed to go on for ever, all the way up her thigh. Who knew where it ended? Internally he cautioned himself against such distractions. Any moment now, she was going to say something about his Rice Krispie face – Chemo knew it.

'You're not a bill collector,' Chloe said sharply, 'so cut the shit.'

'All right,' Chemo said. Feverishly he set his limited imagination to work, trying to come up with another story.

'I don't care what you are.'

'You don't?'

'Nope. Long as you're not a friend of Mick's.'

Chemo said, 'I'm not a friend.'

'Then I'll help,' Chloe said, 'maybe.'

'What about the money?' Chemo said. 'The most I can do is a hundred dollars, maybe one-fifty.'

'Fine.'

'Fine?' Christ, he couldn't believe this woman. A hundred bucks.

She said, 'But before I agree to help, you ought to know everything. It would be irresponsible for me not to warn you what you're up against.'

'I can handle myself,' Chemo said with a cold smile. Even that – his fractured, cadaverous leer – didn't seem to bother Chloe Simpkins Stranahan.

She said, 'So you really don't want to know?'

'Go ahead, then, shoot. What did Stranahan do to your precious boyfriend?'

'He put Krazy Glue on his balls.'

'What?'

'A whole tube,' Chloe said. 'He glued the man to the hood of his car. By the balls. Stark naked, glued to the hood of an Eldorado convertible.'

'Jesus H. Christ,' Chemo said.

'Ever seen the hood ornament on a Cadillac?'

Chemo nodded.

'Think about it,' Chloe said grimly.

'And glue burns like hell,' Chemo remarked.

'Indeed it does.'

'So Mick came home, caught you two in the sack—'

'Right here on the divan.'

'Wherever,' Chemo said. 'Anyway, he hauls Mr Stud-hunk outside and glues him buck naked to the hood of his Caddy.'

'By the testicles.'

'Then what?'

'That's it,' Chloe said. 'Mick packed his suitcase and left. The paramedics came. What more is there?'

'Your male friend – is this the same guy you're married to?'

'No, it isn't,' Chloe said. 'My male-type friend never recovered from his encounter with Mick Stranahan. I mean *never recovered*. You understand what I'm saying?'

'I think so.'

'The doctors insisted there was nothing wrong, medically speaking. I mean, the glue peeled off with acetone, and in a few days the skin healed just like new. But, still, the man was never the same.'

Chemo said, 'It's a major trauma, Mrs Stranahan. It probably takes some time—'

He flinched as Chloe threw her cocktail glass against

the wall. 'Time?' she said. 'I gave him plenty of time, mister. And I tried every trick I knew, but he was a dead man after that night with Mick. It was like trying to screw linguini.'

Chemo could imagine the hellish bedroom scene. He felt himself shrivel, just thinking about it.

'I loved that man,' Chloe went on. 'At least, I was getting there. And Mick ruined everything. He couldn't just beat the shit out of him, like other jealous husbands. No, he had to torture the guy.'

In a way, Chemo admired Stranahan's style. Murder is the way Chemo himself would have handled the situation: a bullet in the base of the skull. For both of them.

Chloe Simpkins Stranahan was up and pacing now, arms folded across her chest, heels clicking on the Spanish tiles. 'So you see,' she said, 'this is why I hate my ex-husband so much.'

There had to be more, but who cared? Chemo said, 'You want to get even?'

'Boy, are you a swifty. Yes, I want to get even.'

'Then why should I pay you anything? You should pay *me*.'

Chloe had to smile. 'Good point.' She bent over and picked a chunk of broken glass out of the deep-pile carpet. She looked up at Chemo and asked, 'Who are you, anyway?'

'Doesn't matter, Mrs Stranahan. The question is, how bad do you want revenge on your ex-husband?'

'I guess that is the question,' Chloe said thoughtfully. 'How about another ginger ale?'

SEVEN

Of the four plastic surgeons who had worked with Dr Rudy Graveline at the Durkos Center, only one had remained in Miami after the clinic closed. His name was George Ginger, and Stranahan found him on a tennis court at Turnberry Isle in the middle of a weekday afternoon. Mixed doubles, naturally.

Stranahan watched the pudgy little man wheeze back and forth behind the baseline, and marvelled at the atrociousness of his hairpiece. It was one of those synthetic jobs, the kind you're supposed to be able to wear in the shower. In Dr George Ginger's case, the thing on his head looked a lot like a fresh road kill.

Each point in the tennis game became its own little comedy, and Stranahan wondered if this stop was a waste of time, an unconscious stall on his part. By now he knew exactly where to locate Rudy Graveline; the problem was, he didn't know what to ask him that would produce the truth. It was a long way from Vicky Barletta to Tony the Eel, and Stranahan still hadn't found the thread, if there was one. One way or another, Dr Graveline was central to the mystery, and Stranahan didn't want to spook him. For now, he wanted him safe and contented at Whispering Palms.

Stranahan strolled into the dead lane of the tennis court and said, 'Dr Ginger?'

'Yo!' said the doctor, huffing.

Stranahan knew about guys who said yo.

'We need to talk.'

'Do we now?' said Dr Ginger, missing an easy backhand. His doubles partner, a lanky, overtanned woman, shot Stranahan a dirty look.

'Just take a minute,' Stranahan said.

Dr Ginger picked up two of the tennis balls. 'Sorry, but I'm on serve.'

'No, you're not,' Stranahan said. 'And besides, that was the set.' He'd been following the match from a gazebo two courts over.

As Dr Ginger intently bounced one of the balls between his feet, the other players picked up their monogrammed club towels and calfskin racket covers and ambled off the court.

Solemnly George Ginger said, 'The tall fellow was my lawyer.'

'Every doctor should have a lawyer,' said Mick Stranahan. 'Especially surgeons.'

Ginger jammed the tennis balls into the pockets of his damp white shorts. 'What's this all about?'

'Rudy Graveline.'

'I've heard of him.'

This was going to be fun, Stranahan thought. He loved it when they played cool.

'You worked for him at the Durkos Center,' Stranahan said to George Ginger. 'Why don't you be a nice fellow and tell me about it?'

George Ginger motioned Stranahan to follow. He

picked a quiet patio table with an umbrella, not far from the pro shop.

'Who are you with?' the doctor enquired in a low voice.

'The board,' Stranahan said. Any board would do; Dr Ginger wouldn't press it.

After wiping his forehead for the umpteenth time, the doctor said, 'There were four of us – Kelly, Greer, Shulman, and me. Graveline was the managing partner.'

'Business was good?'

'It was getting there.'

'Then why did he close the place?'

'I'm still not certain,' George Ginger said.

'But you heard rumours.'

'Yes, we heard there was a problem with a patient. The sort of problem that might bring in the state.'

'One of Rudy's patients?'

George Ginger nodded. 'A young woman is what we heard.'

'Her name?'

'I don't know.' The doctor was quite a lousy liar.

'How bad a problem?' Stranahan went on.

'I don't know that, either. We assumed it was a major fuck-up, or else why would Graveline pull out so fast?'

'Didn't any of you guys bother to ask?'

'Hell, no. I've been to court before, buddy, and it's no damn fun. None of us wanted to get dragged down that road. Anyway, we show up for work one day and the place is empty. Later we get a certified cheque from Rudy with a note saying he's sorry for the incon-venience, but good luck with our careers. Before you know it, he's back in business at Bal Harbour – of all places – with a frigging assembly-line operation. A dozen boob jobs a day.'

Stranahan said, 'Why didn't you call him?'

'What for? Old times' sake?'

'That certified cheque, it must've been a good one.'

'It was,' Dr Ginger conceded, 'very generous.'

Stranahan picked up the doctor's graphite tennis racket and plucked idly at the strings. George Ginger eyed him worriedly. 'Do you remember the day the police came?' Stranahan asked. 'The day a young female patient disappeared from a bus bench in front of the clinic?'

'I was off that day.'

'That's not what I asked.' Stranahan studied him through the grid of the racket strings.

'I remember hearing about it,' George Ginger said lamely.

'That happened right before Dr Graveline split, didn't it?'

'I think so, yes.'

Stranahan said, 'You consider yourself a bright man, Dr Ginger? Don't look so insulted, it's a serious question.' He put the tennis racket down on the patio table.

'I consider myself to be intelligent, yes.'

'Well, then, didn't you wonder about the timing? A girl gets snatched from in front of your office, and a few weeks later the boss closes up shop. Could that be the fuck-up you guys heard about? What do you think?'

Sourly, George Ginger said, 'I can't imagine a connection.' He picked up his tennis racket and, with a touch of pique, zipped it into its carry case.

Stranahan stood up. 'Well, the important thing is,

you still got your medical licence. Now, where can I find the rest of the stooges?'

Dr Ginger wrapped the towel around his neck, a real jock gesture. 'Kelly moved to Michigan. Shulman's up in Atlanta, working for some HMO. Dr Greer is deceased, unfortunately.'

'Do tell.'

'Don't you guys have it in your files? I mean, when a doctor dies?'

'Not in every case,' Stranahan bluffed.

George Ginger said, 'It happened maybe six months after Durkos closed. A hunting accident up around Ocala.'

'Who else was there?'

'I really don't know,' the doctor said with an insipid shrug. 'I'm afraid I'm not clear about all the details.'

'Why,' said Mick Stranahan, 'am I not surprised?'

The Rudy Graveline system was brilliant in its simplicity: sting, persuade, operate, then flatter.

On the wall of each waiting room at Whispering Palms hung a creed: VANITY IS BEAUTIFUL. Similar maxims were posted in the hallways and examining rooms. WHAT'S WRONG WITH PERFECTION? was one of Rudy's favourites. Another: TO IMPROVE ONE'S SELF, IMPROVE ONE'S FACE. This one was framed in the spa, where post-op patients relaxed in the crucial days following their plastic surgery, when they didn't want to go out in public. Rudy had shrewdly recognized that an after-surgery spa would not only be a tremendous money-maker, it would also provide important positive feedback during recovery. Everyone there had fresh scars and bruises, so no patient was in a position to criticize another's results.

As best as he could, Reynaldo Flemm made mental notes of Whispering Palms during his tour. He was posing as a male exotic dancer who needed a blemish removed from his right buttock. For the purpose of disguise, Flemm had dyed his hair brown and greased it straight back; that was all he could bear to do to alter his appearance. Secretly, he loved it when people stared because they recognized him from television.

As it happened, the nurse who greeted him at Whispering Palms apparently never watched *In Your Face*. She treated Flemm as any other prospective patient. After a quick tour of the facilities, she led him to a consultation room, turned off the lights and showed him a videotape about the wonders of cosmetic surgery. Afterwards she turned the lights back on and asked if he had any questions.

'How much will it cost?' Reynaldo Flemm said.

'That depends on the size of the mole.'

'Oh, it's a big mole,' Reynaldo said. 'Like an olive.' He held up his thumb and forefinger to show her the size of his fictional growth.

The nurse said, 'May I see it?'

'No!'

'Surely you're not shy,' she said. 'Not in your line of work.'

'I'll show it to the doctor,' Flemm said. 'No one else.'

'Very well, I'll arrange for an appointment.'

'With Dr Graveline, please.'

The nurse smiled. 'Really, Mr LeTigre.'

Flemm had come up with the name Johnny LeTigre all by himself. It seemed perfect for a male go-go dancer.

'Dr Graveline doesn't do moles,' the nurse said in a chilly tone. 'One of our other excellent surgeons can take care of it quite easily.'

'It's Dr Graveline or nobody,' Flemm said firmly. 'This is my dancing career, my life we're talking about.'

'I'm sorry, but Dr Graveline is not available.'

'For ten grand I bet he is.'

The nurse tried not to seem surprised. 'I'll be right back,' she said lightly.

When he was alone, Reynaldo Flemm checked himself in the mirror to see how the disguise was holding up. All he needed was a date and time to see the doctor, then he'd come back with Willie and a camera for the showdown – not out on the street, but inside the clinic. And if Graveline ordered them out, Reynaldo and Willie would be sure to leave through the spa exit, tape rolling. It would be dynamite stuff; even Christina would have to admit it.

The nurse returned and said, 'Come with me, Mr LeTigre.'

'Where to?'

'Dr Graveline has agreed to see you.'

'Now?' Flemm squeaked.

'He only has a few minutes.'

A cold prickle of panic accompanied Reynaldo Flemm as he followed the nurse down a long pale-blue hallway. About to meet the target of his investigation and here he was, defenceless – no camera, no tape, no notebooks. He could blow the whole story if he wasn't careful. The only thing in Flemm's favour was the fact that he also had no script. He wouldn't know what to ask even if the opportunity presented itself.

The nurse abandoned him in a spacious office with a

grand view of north Biscayne Bay, foamy with white-caps. Reynaldo Flemm barely had time to snoop the joint over before Dr Rudy Graveline came in and introduced himself. Reynaldo took a good close look, in case he might later have to point him out to Willie from the TV van: lean build, medium height, sandy brown hair. Had a golfer's tan but not much muscle. Overall, not a bad-looking guy.

Rudy Graveline didn't waste any time. 'Let's see your little problem, Mr LeTigre.'

'Hold on a minute.'

'It's only a mole.'

'To you, maybe,' Reynaldo Flemm said. 'Before we go any further, I'd like to ask you some questions.' He paused, then: 'Questions about your background.'

Dr Graveline settled in behind a gleaming onyx desk and folded his hands. 'Fire away,' he said amiably.

'What medical school did you go to?'

'Harvard,' Rudy replied.

Reynaldo nodded approvingly. He asked, 'How long have you been in practice?'

'Sixteen years,' Dr Graveline said.

'Ah,' said Reynaldo Flemm. He couldn't think of much else to ask, which was fine with Rudy. Sometimes patients wanted to know how high the doctor had placed in his med school class (dead last), or whether he was certified by a national board of plastic and recon-structive surgeons (he was not). In truth, Rudy had barely squeaked through a residency in radiology and had never been trained in plastic surgery. Still, no law prevented him from declaring it to be his speciality; that was the beauty of the medical profession – once you got a degree, you could try whatever you damn well pleased, from brain surgery to gynaecology. Hospitals might do some checking, but never the patients. And failing at one or more specialties (as Rudy had), you could always leave town and try something else.

Still stalling, Reynaldo Flemm said, 'What's involved in an operation like this?'

'First we numb the area with a mild anaesthetic, then we use a small knife to remove the mole. If you need a couple sutures afterward, we do that, too.'

'What about a scar?'

'No scar, I guarantee it,' said Dr Graveline.

'For ten grand, you're damn right.'

The doctor said, 'I didn't realize male strippers made that much money.'

'They don't. It's inheritance.'

If Flemm had been paying attention, he would have noticed a hungry flicker in Dr Graveline's expression.

'Mr LeTigre, you won't mind some friendly professional advice?'

'Of course not.'

'Your nose,' Rudy ventured. 'I mean, as long as you're going to all the trouble of surgery.'

'What the hell is wrong with my nose?'

'It's about two sizes too large for your face. And, to be honest, your tummy could probably come down an inch or three. I can do a liposuction after we excise the mole.'

Reynaldo Flemm said, 'Are you kidding? There's nothing wrong with me.'

'Please don't be embarrassed,' Rudy said. 'This is my speciality. I just thought someone in a job like yours would want to look their very best.'

Flemm was getting furious. 'I *do* look my very best!'

Dr Graveline put his elbows on the desk and leaned forward. Gently he said, 'With all respect, Mr LeTigre, we seldom choose to see ourselves the way others do. It's human nature.'

'I've heard enough,' Reynaldo Flemm snapped.

'If it's the money, look, I'll do the mole and the fat suction as a package. Toss in the rhinoplasty for nothing, OK?'

Flemm said, 'I don't need a goddamn rhinoplasty.'

'Please,' said Dr Graveline, 'go home and think about it. Take a good critical look at yourself in the mirror.'

'Fuck you,' said Reynaldo Flemm, and stormed out of the office.

'It's no sin to have a big honker,' Rudy Graveline called after him. 'Nobody's *born* perfect!'

One hour later, as Rudy was fitting a Mentor Model 7000 Gel-Filled Mammary Prosthesis into the left breast of the future Miss Ecuador, he was summoned from the operating suite to take an urgent phone call from New York.

The semi-hysterical voice on the other end belonged to Maggie Gonzalez.

'Take some deep breaths,' Rudy advised.

'No, you listen. I got a message on my machine,' Maggie said. 'The phone machine at my house.'

'Who was it from?'

'Stranahan. That investigator.'

'Really?' Dr Graveline worked hard at staying calm; he took pride in his composure. He asked, 'What was the message, Maggie?'

'Three words: "*It won't work*." '

Dr Graveline repeated the message out loud. Maggie sounded like she was bouncing off the walls.

'Don't come back here for a while,' Rudy said. 'I'll wire you some more money.' He couldn't think clearly with Maggie hyperventilating into the phone, and he did need to think. *It won't work.* Damn, he didn't like the sound of that. How much did Stranahan know? Was it a bluff? Rudy Graveline wondered if he should call Chemo and tell him to speed things up.

'What are we going to do?' Maggie demanded.

'It's being done,' the doctor said.

'Good.' Maggie didn't ask specifically what was being done. Specifically, she didn't want to know.

After lunch, Mick Stranahan stopped by the VA hospital, but for the second day in a row the nurses told him that Timmy Gavigan was asleep. They said it had been another poor night, that the new medicine was still giving him fevers.

Stranahan was eager to hear what his friend remembered about Dr Rudy Graveline. Like most good cops, Timmy never forgot an interview; and like most cops, Timmy was the only one who could read his own handwriting. The Barletta file was full of Gavigan-type scribbles.

After leaving the VA, Stranahan drove back to the marina at Key Biscayne. On the skiff out to Stiltsville, he mentally catalogued everything he knew so far.

Vicky Barletta had disappeared, and was probably dead.

Her doctor had closed up shop a few weeks later and

bought out his four partners for fifty thousand dollars apiece.

One of those partners, Dr Kenneth Greer, had never cashed his cheque – this according to microfiche records at the bank.

Approximately seven months after Rudy Graveline closed the Durkos Center, Dr Kenneth Greer was shot to death while hunting deer in the Ocala National Forest. The sheriff's office had ruled it an accident.

The hunter who had somehow mistaken Kenneth Greer for a white-tail buck had given his name as T. B. Luckner of 1333 Carter Boulevard in Decatur, Georgia. If the sheriff in Ocala had troubled himself to check, he would have found that there was no such person and no such address.

The nurse who participated in Victoria Barletta's surgery had recently gone to New York to sell her story to a TV producer.

Shortly afterwards, a paid killer named Tony the Eel showed up to murder Mick Stranahan. Tony, with a brand-new face.

Then the TV producer arrived in Miami to take Stranahan's picture for a prime-time special.

All traced to a four-year-old kidnapping that Mick Stranahan had never solved.

As he steered the boat into the Biscayne Channel, angling out of the messy following chop, he gunned the outboard and made a beeline for his stilt house. The tide was up, making it safe to cross the flats.

On the way, he thought about Rudy Graveline.

Suppose the doctor had killed Vicky. Stranahan checked himself – make that Victoria, not Vicky. Better yet, just plain Barletta. No sense personalizing.

But suppose the doctor had killed her, and suppose Greer knew, or found out. Greer was the only one who didn't cash the buyout cheque – maybe he was holding out for more money, or maybe he was ready to blab to the authorities.

Either way, Dr Graveline would have had plenty of motive to silence him.

And if, for some reason, Dr Graveline had been led to believe that Mick Stranahan posed a similar threat, what would stop him from killing again?

Stranahan couldn't help but marvel at the possibility. Considering all the cons and ex-cons who'd love to see him dead – hoods, dopers, scammers, bikers, and stickup artists – it was ironic that the most likely suspect was some rich quack he'd never even met.

The more Stranahan learned about the case, and the more he thought about what he'd learned, the lousier he felt.

His spirits improved somewhat when he spotted his model friend Tina stretched out on the sun deck of the stilt house. He was especially pleased to notice that she was alone.

EIGHT

Stranahan caught four small snappers and fried them up for supper.

'Richie left me,' Tina was explaining. 'I mean, he put me out on your house and left. Can you believe that?'

Stranahan pretended to be listening as he foraged in the refrigerator. 'You want lemon or garlic salt?'

'Both,' Tina said. 'We had a fight and he ordered me to get off the boat. Then he drove away.'

She wore a baggy Jimmy Buffett T-shirt over a cranberry bikini bottom. Her wheat-coloured hair was pulled back in a ponytail, and a charm glinted at her throat; a tiny gold porpoise, it looked like.

'Richie deals a little coke,' Tina went on. 'That's what we were fighting about. Well, part of it.'

Stranahan said, 'Keep an eye on the biscuits so they don't burn.'

'Sure. Anyway, know what else we were fighting about? This is so dumb you won't believe it.'

Stranahan was dicing a pepper on the kitchen countertop. He was barefoot, wearing cutoff jeans and a khaki short-sleeved shirt, open to the chest. His hair was still damp from the shower. Overall, he felt much better about his situation.

Tina said, 'I got this modelling job and Richie, he

went crazy. All because I had to do some, you know, nudes. Just beach stuff, nobody out there but me and the photog. Richie says no way, you can't do it. And I said, you can't tell me what to do. Then – then! – he calls me a slut, and I say that's pretty rich coming from a two-bit doper. So then he slugs me in the stomach and tells me to get my butt out of the boat.' Tina paused for a sigh. 'Your house was closest.'

'You can stay for the night,' Stranahan said, sounding downright fatherly.

'What if Richie comes back?'

'Then we teach him some manners.'

Tina said, 'He's still pissed about the last time, when you dragged him through the water.'

'The biscuits,' Stranahan reminded her.

'Oh, yeah, sorry.' Tina pulled the hot tray out of the oven.

For at least thirteen minutes she didn't say anything, because the snapper was excellent and she was hungry. Stranahan found a bottle of white wine and poured two glasses. It was then Tina smiled and said, 'Got any candles?'

Stranahan played along, even though darkness still was an hour away. He lighted two stubby hurricane candles and set them on the oilskin tablecloth.

'This is really nice,' Tina said.

'Yes, it is.'

'I haven't found a single bone,' she said, chewing intently.

'Good.'

'Are you married, Mick?'

'Divorced,' he replied. 'Five times.'

'Wow.'

'My fault, every one,' he added. To some degree, he believed it. Each time the same thing had happened: he'd awakened one morning and felt nothing; not guilt or jealousy or anger, but an implacable numbness, which was worse. Like his blood had turned to novocaine overnight. He'd stared at the woman in his bed and become incredulous at the notion that this was a spouse, that he had married this person. He'd felt trapped and done a poor job of concealing it. By the fifth go-round, divorce had become an eerie out-of-body experience, except for the part with the lawyers.

'Were you fooling around a lot, or what?' Tina asked.

'It wasn't that,' Stranahan said.

'Then what? You're a nice-looking guy, I don't know why a girl would cut and run.'

Stranahan poured more wine for both of them.

'I wasn't much fun to be around.'

'Oh, I disagree,' Tina said with a perkiness that startled him.

Her eyes wandered up to the big mount on the living room wall. 'What happened to Mr Swordfish?'

'That's a marlin,' Stranahan said. 'He fell off the wall and broke his beak.'

'The tape looks pretty tacky, Mick.'

'Yeah, I know.'

After dinner they went out on the deck to watch the sun go down behind Coconut Grove. Stranahan tied a size 12 hook on his fishing line and baited it with a lint-sized shred of frozen shrimp. In fifteen minutes he caught five lively pinfish, which he dropped in a plastic bait bucket. Entranced, Tina sat cross-legged on the deck and watched the little fish swim frenetic circles inside the container.

Stranahan stowed the rod in the stilt house, came out, and picked up the bucket. 'I'll be right back.'

'Where you off to?'

'Downstairs, by the boat.'

'Can I come?'

He shrugged. 'You might not like it.'

'Like what?' Tina asked and followed him tentatively down the wooden stairs toward the water.

Liza hovered formidably in the usual place. Stranahan pointed at the huge barracuda and said, 'See there?'

'Wow, is that a shark?'

'No.'

He reached into the bucket and grabbed one of the pinfish, carefully folding the dorsal so it wouldn't prick his fingers.

Tina said, 'Now I get it.'

'She's like a pet,' Stranahan said. He tossed the pinfish into the water, and the barracuda devoured it in a silent mercury flash, all fangs. When the turbulence subsided, they saw that the big fish had returned to its station; it hung there as if it had never moved.

Impassively Stranahan tossed another pinfish and the barracuda repeated the kill.

Tina stood so close that Stranahan could feel her warm breath on his bare arm. 'Do they eat people?' she asked.

He could have hugged her right then.

'No,' he said, 'they don't eat people.'

'Good!'

'They do strike at shiny objects,' he said, 'so don't wear a bracelet if you're diving.'

'Seriously?'

'It's been known to happen.'

This time he scooped up two pinfish and lobbed them into the water simultaneously; the barracuda got them both in one fierce swipe.

'I call her Liza,' Stranahan said. 'Liza with a *z*.'

Tina nodded as if she thought it was a perfectly cute name. She asked if she could try a toss.

'You bet.' Stranahan got the last pinfish from the bucket and placed it carefully in the palm of her hand. 'Just throw it anywhere,' he said.

Tina leaned forward and called out, 'Here, Liza! Here you go!'

The little fish landed with a soft splash and spun a dizzy figure eight under the dock. The barracuda didn't move.

Stranahan smiled. In slow motion the addled pinfish corkscrewed its way to the bottom, taking refuge inside an old horse conch.

'What'd I do wrong?' Tina wondered.

'Not a thing,' Stranahan said. 'She wasn't hungry any more, that's all.'

'Maybe it's just me.'

'Maybe it is,' Stranahan said.

He took her by the hand and led her upstairs. He turned on the lights in the house and vented the shutters on both sides to catch the cool night breeze. On the roof, the windmill creaked as it picked up speed.

Tina made a place for herself on a faded lumpy sofa. She said, 'I always wondered what it's like out here in the dark.'

'Not much to do, I'm afraid.'

'No TV?'

'No TV,' Stranahan said.

'You want to make love?'

'There's an idea.'

'You already saw me naked.'

'I haven't forgotten,' Stranahan said. 'The thing is—'

'Don't worry about Richie. Anyway, this is just for fun. We'll keep it casual, OK?'

'I don't do anything casually,' Stranahan said. 'This is my problem.' He was constantly falling in love; how else would you explain five marriages, all to cocktail waitresses?

Tina peeled off the tropical T-shirt and draped it across a barstool. Rockette-style, she kicked her way out of her bikini bottoms and left them in a rumple on the floor.

'How about these tan lines, huh?'

'What tan lines?' he asked.

'Exactly.' Tina pulled the rubber band out of her ponytail and shook her hair free. Then she got back on the sofa and said, 'Watch this.' She stretched out and struck a smoky-eyed modelling pose – a half-turn up on one elbow, legs scissored, one arm shading her nipples.

'That looks great,' Stranahan said, amused but also uneasy.

'It's tough work on a beach,' Tina remarked. 'Sand sticks to places you wouldn't believe. I did a professional job, though.'

'I'm sure.'

'Thanks to you, I got my confidence back. About my boobs, I mean.' She glanced down at herself appraisingly.

'Confidence is everything in the modelling business,' she said. 'Somebody tells you that your ass is sagging or your tits don't match up, it's like emotional disaster. I was worried sick until you measured them with that carpenter's thing.'

'Glad I could help,' Stranahan said, trying to think of something, anything, more romantic.

She said, 'Anyone ever tell you that you've got Nick Nolte's nose?'

'That's all?' Stranahan said. Nick Nolte was a new one.

'Now, the eyes,' Tina said, 'your eyes are more like Sting's. I met him one time at the Strand.'

'Thank you,' Stranahan said. He didn't know who the hell she was talking about. Maybe one of those pro wrestlers from cable television.

Holding her pose, Tina motioned him to join her on the old sofa. When he did, she took his hands, placed them on her staunch new breasts, and held them there. Stranahan assumed a compliment was in order.

'They're perfect,' he said, squeezing politely.

Urgently Tina arched her back and rolled over, Stranahan hanging on like a rock climber.

While we're on the subject,' he said, 'could I get the name of your surgeon?'

Even before the electrolysis accident, Chemo had led a difficult life. His parents had belonged to a religious sect that believed in bigamy, vegetarianism, UFOs, and not paying federal income taxes; his mother, father, and three of their respective spouses were killed by the FBI during a bloody ten-day siege at a post office outside Grand Forks, North Dakota. Chemo, who was only six at the time, went to live with an aunt and uncle in the Amish country of western Pennsylvania. It was a rigorous and demanding period, especially since Chemo's aunt and uncle were not actually Amish themselves, but fair-weather Presbyterians fleeing a mail-fraud indictment out of Bergen County, New Jersey.

Using their hard-won embezzlements, the couple had purchased a modest farm and somehow managed to infiltrate the hermetic social structure of an Amish township. At first it was just another scam, a temporary cover until the heat was off. As the years passed, though, Chemo's aunt and uncle got authentically converted. They grew to love the simple pastoral ways and hearty fellowship of the farm folk; Chemo was devastated by their transformation. Growing up, he had come to resent the family's ruse, and consequently the Amish in general. The plain baggy clothes and strict table manners were bad enough, but it was the facial hair that drove him to fury. Amish men do not shave their chins, and Chemo's uncle insisted that, once attaining puberty, he adhere to custom. Since religious arguments held no sway with Chemo, it was the practical view that his uncle propounded: all fugitives need a disguise, and a good beard was hard to beat.

Chemo sullenly acceded, until the day of his twenty-first birthday when he got in his uncle's pick-up truck, drove down to the local branch of the Chemical Bank, threatened a teller with a pitchfork (the Amish own no pistols), and strolled off with seven thousand dollars and change. The first thing he bought was a Bic disposable safety razor.

The *Philadelphia Inquirer* reported that it was the only bank robbery by an Amish in the entire history of the commonwealth. Chemo himself was never arrested for the crime, but his aunt and uncle were unmasked, extradited back to New Jersey, tried and convicted of mail fraud, then shipped off to a country-club prison in north Florida. Their wheat farm was seized by the US government and sold at auction.

Once Chemo was free of the Amish, the foremost challenge of adulthood was avoiding manual labour, to which he had a chronic aversion. Crime seemed to be the most efficient way of making money without working up a sweat, so Chemo gave it a try. Unfortunately, nature had dealt him a cruel disadvantage: while six foot nine was the perfect height for an NBA forward, for a burglar it was disastrous. Chemo got stuck in the very first window he ever jimmied; he could break, but he could not enter.

Four months in a county jail passed too slowly. He thought often of his aunt and uncle, and upbraided himself for not taking advantage of their vast expertise. They could have taught him many secrets about white-collar crime, yet in his rebellious insolence he had never bothered to ask. Now it was too late – their most recent postcard from the Eglin prison camp had concluded with a religious limerick and the drawing of a happy face. Chemo knew they were lost for ever.

After finishing his stretch for the aborted burglary, he moved to a small town outside of Scranton and went to work for the city parks and recreation department. Before long, he parlayed a phoney but impressive resumé into the post of assistant city manager, a job that entitled him to a secretary and a municipal car. While the salary was only twenty thousand dollars a year, the secondary income derived from bribes and kickbacks was substantial. Chemo prospered as a shakedown artist, and the town prospered, too. He was delighted to discover how often the mutual interests of private enterprise and government seemed to intersect.

The high point of Chemo's municipal career was his savvy trashing of local zoning laws to allow a Mafia-owned-and-operated dog food plant to be built in the suburbs. Three hundred new jobs were created, and there was talk of running Chemo for mayor.

He greatly liked the idea and immediately began gouging illegal political contributions out of city contractors. Soon a campaign poster was designed, but Chemo recoiled when he saw the finished product: the four-foot photographic blowup of his face magnified the two ingrown hair follicles on the tip of his otherwise normal nose; the blemishes looked, in Chemo's own distraught simile, 'like two ticks fucking'. He ordered the campaign posters shredded, scheduled a second photo session, and drove straight to Scranton for the ill-fated electrolysis treatment.

The grisly mishap and subsequent murder of the offending doctor put an end to Chemo's political career. He swore off public service for ever.

They rented an Aquasport and docked it at Sunday's-on-the-Bay. They chose a table under the awning, near the water. Chemo ordered a ginger ale and Chloe Simpkins Stranahan got a vodka tonic, double.

'We'll wait till dusk,' Chemo said.

'Fine by me.' Chloe slurped her drink like a parched coyote. She was wearing a ridiculous white sailor's suit from Lord and Taylor's; she even had the cap. It was not ideal boatwear.

'I used to work in this joint,' Chloe said, as if to illustrate how far she'd come.

Chemo said, 'This is where you met Mick?'

'Unfortunately.'

The bar was packed for ladies' night. In addition to the standard assembly of slick Latin studs in lizard shoes, there were a dozen blond, husky mates off the charter boats. In contrast to the disco Dannies, the mates wore T-shirts and sandals and deep Gulf Stream tans, and they drank mostly beer. The competition for feminine attention was fierce, but Chemo planned to be long gone before any fights broke out. Besides, he didn't like sitting out in the open, where people could stare.

'Have you got your plan?' Chloe asked.

'The less you know, the better.'

'Oh, pardon me,' she said caustically. 'Pardon me, Mister James Fucking Bond.'

He blinked neutrally. A young pelican was preening itself on a nearby dock piling, and Chemo found this infinitely more fascinating than watching Chloe Simpkins Stranahan in a Shirley Temple sailor cap, sucking down vodkas. It offended him that someone so beautiful could be so repellent and obnoxious; it seemed damned unfair.

On the other hand, she had yet to make the first wisecrack about his face, so maybe she had one redeeming quality.

'This isn't going to get too heavy?' she said.

'Define heavy.'

Chloe stirred her drink pensively. 'Maybe you could just put a good scare in him.'

'Bet on it,' Chemo said.

'But you won't get too tough, right?'

'What is this, all of a sudden you're worried about him?'

'You can hate someone's guts and still worry about him.'

'Jesus H. Christ.'

Chloe said, 'Chill out, OK? I'm not backing down.'

Chemo toyed with one of the infrequent black wisps attached to his scalp. He said: 'Where does your husband think you are?'

'Shopping,' Chloe replied.

'Alone?'

'Sure.'

Chemo licked his lips and scanned the room. 'You see anybody you know?'

Chloe looked around and said, 'No. Why do you ask?'

'Just making sure. I don't want any surprises; neither do you.'

Chemo paid the tab, helped Chloe into the bow of the Aquasport and cast off the ropes. He checked his wristwatch: 5:15. Give it maybe an hour before nightfall. He handed Chloe a plastic map of Biscayne Bay with the pertinent channel markers circled in red ink. 'Keep that handy,' he shouted over the engine, 'case I get lost.'

She tapped the map with one of her stiletto fingernails. 'You can't miss the goddamn things, they're sticking three storeys out of the water.'

Fifteen minutes later, they were drifting through a Stiltsville channel with the boat's engine off. Chloe Simpkins Stranahan was complaining about her hair getting salty, while Chemo untangled the anchor ropes. The anchor was a big rusty clunker with a bent tongue.

He hauled it out of the Aquasport's forward hatch and laid it on the deck.

Then he took some binoculars from a canvas duffel and began scouting the stilt houses. 'Which one is it?' he asked.

'I told you, it's got a windmill.'

'I'm looking at three houses with windmills, so which is it? I'd like to get the anchor out before we float to frigging Nassau.'

Chloe huffed and took the binoculars. After a few moments she said, 'Well, they all look alike.'

'No shit.'

She admitted she had never been on her ex-husband's house before. 'But I've been by there in a boat.'

Chemo said, 'How do you know it was his?'

'Because I saw him. He was outside, fishing.'

'How long ago was this?'

'Three, maybe four months. What's the difference?'

Chemo said, 'Did Mick know it was you in the boat?'

'Sure he did, he dropped his damn pants.' Chloe handed Chemo the binoculars and pointed. 'That's the one, over there.'

'You sure?'

'Yes, Captain Ahab, I am.'

Chemo studied the stilt house through the field glasses. The windmill was turning and a skiff was tied up under the water tanks, but no one was outside.

'So now what?' Chloe asked.

'I'm thinking.'

'Know what I wish you'd do? I wish you'd do to him what he did to my male friend. Krazy Glue the bastard.'

'That would settle things, huh?'

Chloe's tone became grave. 'Mick Stranahan

destroyed a man without killing him. Can you think of anything worse?'

'Well,' Chemo said, reaching for the duffel, 'I didn't bring any glue. All I brought was this.' He took out the .22 pistol and screwed on the silencer.

Chloe made a gulping noise and grabbed the bow rail for support. So much for poise, Chemo thought.

'Don't worry, Mrs Stranahan, this is my just-in-case.' He laid the pistol on top of the boat's console. 'All I really need is a little friction.' Smiling, he held up a book of matches from Sunday's bar.

'You're going to burn the house down? That's great!' Chloe's eyes shone with relief. 'Burning the house, that'll freak him out.'

'Big-time,' Chemo agreed.

'Just what that dangerous lunatic deserves.'

'Right.'

Chloe looked at him mischievously. 'You promised to tell me who you really are.'

'No, I didn't.'

'At least tell me why you're doing this.'

'I'm being paid,' Chemo said.

'By who?'

'Nobody you know.'

'Another ex-wife, I'll bet.'

'What did I say?'

'Oh, all right.' Chloe stood up and peered over the gunwale at the slick green water. Chemo figured she was checking out her own reflection.

'Did you bring anything to drink?'

'No,' Chemo replied. 'No drinks.'

She folded her arms to show how peeved she was.

'You mean, I've got to stay out here till dark with nothing to drink.'

'Longer than that,' Chemo said. 'Midnight.'

'But Mick'll be asleep by then.'

'That's the idea, Mrs Stranahan.'

'But how will he know to get out of the house?'

Chemo laughed gruffly. 'Now who's the rocket scientist?'

Chloe's expression darkened. She pursed her lips and said, 'Wait a minute. I don't want you to kill him.'

'Who asked you?'

A change was taking place in Chloe's attitude, the way she regarded Chemo. It was as if she was seeing the man for the first time, and she was staring, which Chemo did not appreciate. Her and her tweezered eyebrows.

'You're a killer,' she said, reproachfully.

Chemo blinked amphibiously and plucked at one of the skin tags on his cheek. His eyes were round and wet and distant.

'You're a killer,' Chloe repeated, 'and you tricked me.'

Chemo said, 'You hate him so much, what do you care if he's dead or not?'

Her eyes flashed. 'I care because I still get a cheque from that son of a bitch as long as he's alive. He's dead, I get zip.'

Chemo was dumbstruck. 'You get alimony? But you're remarried! To a frigging CPA!'

'Let's just say Mick Stranahan didn't have the world's sharpest lawyer.'

'You are one greedy twat,' Chemo said acidly.

'Hey, it's one-fifty a month,' Chloe said. 'Barely covers the lawn service.'

She did not notice the hostility growing in Chemo's expression. 'Killing Mick Stranahan is out of the question,' she declared. 'Burn up the house, fine, but I don't want him dead.'

'Tough titties,' Chemo said.

'Look, I don't know who you are—'

'Sit,' Chemo said. 'And keep your damn voice down.'

The wind was kicking up, and he was afraid the argument might carry across the flats to the house.

Chloe sat down but was not about to shut up. 'You listen to me—'

'I said, keep your damn voice down!'

'Screw you, Velcro-face.'

Chemo's brow crinkled, his cheeks fluttered. He probably even flushed, though this was impossible to discern.

Velcro-face – there it was, finally. The insult. The witch just couldn't resist after all.

'Now what's the matter?' Chloe Simpkins Stranahan said. 'You look seasick.'

'I'm fine,' Chemo said. 'But you shouldn't call people names.'

Then he heaved the thirty-pound anchor into her lap, and watched her pitch over backwards in her silky sailor suit. The staccato trail of bubbles suggested that she was cursing him all the way to the bottom of the bay.

NINE

Tina woke up alone in bed. She wrapped herself in a sheet and padded groggily around the dark house, looking for Mick Stranahan. She found him outside, balanced on the deck rail with his hands on his hips. He was watching Old Man Chitworth's stilt house light up the sky; a crackling orange torch, visible for miles. The house seemed to sway on its wooden legs, an illusion caused by blasts of raw heat above the water.

Tina thought it was the most breathtaking thing she had ever seen, even better than Old Faithful. In the glow from the blaze she looked up at Stranahan's face and saw concern.

'Somebody living there?' she said.

'No.' Stranahan watched Old Man Chitworth's windmill fall, the flaming blades spinning faster in descent. It hit the water with a sizzle and hiss.

'What started the fire?' Tina asked.

'Arson,' Stranahan said matter-of-factly. 'I heard a boat.'

'Maybe it was an accident,' she suggested. 'Maybe somebody tossed a cigarette.'

'Gasoline,' Stranahan said. 'I smelled it.'

'Wow. Whoever owns that place has some serious enemies, I guess.'

'The man who owns that place just turned eighty-three,' Stranahan said. 'He's on tubes in a nursing home, all flaked out. Thinks he's Eddie Rickenbacker.'

A gust of wind prompted Tina to rearrange her sheet. She got a shiver and edged closer to Mick. She said, 'Some harmless old geezer. Then I don't get it.'

Stranahan said, 'Wrong house, that's all.' He hopped off the rail. 'Somebody fucked up.' So much for paradise, he thought; so much for peace and tranquillity.

Across the bay, from Dinner Key, came the whine of toy-like sirens. Stranahan didn't need binoculars to see the flashing blue dots from the advancing police boats.

Tina clutched his hand. She couldn't take her eyes off the fire. 'Mick, have you got enemies like that?'

'Hell, I've got *friends* like that.'

By midmorning the Chitworth house had burned to the waterline, and the flames died. All that remained sticking out were charred tips of the wood pilings, some still smouldering.

Tina was reading on a deck chair and Stranahan was doing push-ups when the marine patrol boat drove up and stopped. It was Luis Córdova and another man whom Stranahan did not expect.

'Now, there's something you don't see every day,' Stranahan announced, plenty loud. 'Two Cubans in a boat, and no beer.'

Luis Córdova grinned. The other man climbed noisily up on the dock and said, 'And here's something else you don't see every day: an Irishman up before noon, and still sober.'

The man's name was Al García, a homicide detective

for the Metro-Dade police. His J. C. Penney coat jacket was slung over one arm, and his shiny necktie was loosened halfway down his chest. García was not wild about boat rides, so he was in a gruff and unsettled mood. Also, there was the matter of the dead body.

'What dead body?' Mick Stranahan said.

Badger-like, García shuffled up the stairs to the house, with Stranahan and Luis Córdova following single file. García gave the place the once-over and waved courteously to Tina on her lounge chair. The detective half-turned to Stranahan and in a low voice said, 'What, you opened a half-way house for bimbos? Mick, you're a freaking saint, I swear.'

They went inside the stilt house and closed the door. 'Tell me about the dead body,' Stranahan said.

'Sit down. Hey, Luis, I could use some coffee.'

'A minute ago you were seasick,' Luis Córdova said.

'I'm feeling much better, OK?' García scowled theatrically as the young marine patrol officer went to the kitchen. 'Interdepartmental co-operation, that's the buzzword these days. Coffee's a damn good place to start.'

'Easy, man, Luis is a sharp kid.'

'He sure is. I wish he was ours.'

Stranahan said, 'Now about the body . . .'

García waved a meaty brown hand in the air, as if shooing an invisible horsefly. 'Mick, what are you doing way the fuck out here? Somehow I don't see you as Robinson Crusoe, sucking the milk out of raw coconuts.'

'It's real quiet out here.'

Luis Córdova brought three cups of hot coffee.

Al García smacked his lips as he drank. 'Quiet – is

that what you said? Jeez, you got dead gangsters floating around, not to mention burning houses—'

'Is this about Tony the Eel?'

'No,' Luis said seriously.

García put down his coffee cup and looked straight at Stranahan. 'When's the last time you saw Chloe?'

Suddenly Mick Stranahan did not feel so well.

'A couple months back,' he said. 'She was on a boat with some guy. I assumed it was her new husband. Why?'

'You mooned her.'

'Can you blame me?'

'We heard about it from the mister this morning.'

Stranahan braced to hear the whole story. Luis Códova opened a spiral notebook but didn't write much. Stranahan listened sombrely and occasionally looked out the window toward the channel where Al García said it had happened.

'A rusty anchor?' Stranahan said in disbelief.

'It got tangled in this silky thing she was wearing,' the detective explained. 'She went down like a sack of cement.' Sensitivity was not García's strong suit.

'The rope is what gave it away,' added Luis Córdova. 'One of the guys coming out to the fire saw the rope drifting up out of the current.'

'Hauled her right in,' García said, 'like a lobster pot.'

'Lord.'

García said, 'Fact is, we really shouldn't be telling you all this.'

'Why not?'

'Because you're the prime suspect.'

'That's very funny.' Stranahan looked at Luis Córdova. 'Is he kidding?'

The young marine patrolman shook his head.

García said, 'Mick, your track record is not so hot. I mean, you already got a few notches on your belt.'

'Not murder.'

'Chloe hated your guts,' Al García said, in the tone of a reminder.

'That's my motive? She hated my guts?'

'Then there's the dough.'

'You think I'd kill her over a crummy one hundred fifty dollars a month?'

'The principle,' Al García said, unwrapping a cigar. 'I think you just might do it over the principle of the thing.'

Stranahan leaned back with a tired sigh. He felt bad about Chloe's death, but mostly he felt curious. What the hell was she doing out here at night?

'I always heard good things about you,' Al García said, 'mainly from Timmy Gavigan.'

'Yeah, he said the same for you.'

'And the way Eckert dumped you from the State Attorney's, that was low.'

Stranahan shrugged. 'They don't forget it when you shoot a judge. It's bound to make people nervous.'

García made a great ceremony of lighting the cigar. Afterwards, he blew two rings of smoke and said, 'For what it's worth, Luis here doesn't think you did it.'

'It's the anchor business,' Luis Córdova explained, 'very strange.' He was trying to sound all business, as if the friendship meant nothing.

Stranahan said, 'The murder's got to be connected to the fire.'

'The fire was an arson,' Luis said. 'Boat gas and a match. These houses are nothing but tinder.' To make his point, he tapped the rubber heel of his shoe on the pine floor.

Stranahan said, 'I think you both ought to know: somebody wants to kill me.'

García's eyebrows shot up and he rolled the cigar from one side of his mouth to the other. 'Who is it, *chico*? Please, make my job easier.'

'I think it's a doctor. His name is Rudy Graveline. Write this down, Luis, please.'

'And why would this doctor want you dead?'

'I'm not sure, Al.'

'But you want me to roust him on a hunch.'

'No, I just want his name in a file somewhere. I want you to know who he is, just in case.'

García turned to Luis Córdova. 'Don't you love the fucking sound of that? *Just in case.* Luis, I think this is where we're supposed to give Mr Stranahan a lecture about taking the law into his own hands.'

Luis said, 'Don't take the law into your own hands, Mick.'

'Thank you, Luis.'

Al García flicked a stubby thumb through his black moustache. 'Just for the record, you didn't invite the lovely Chloe Simpkins Stranahan out here for a romantic reconciliation over fresh fish and wine?'

'No,' Stranahan said. Fish and wine – that fucking García must have scoped out the dirty dinner dishes.

'And the two of you didn't go for a boat ride?'

'No, Al.'

'And you didn't get in a sloppy drunken fight?'

'No.'

'And you didn't hook her to the anchor and drop her overboard?'

'Nope.'

'Luis, you get all that?'

Luis Córdova nodded as he jotted in the notebook. Shorthand, too; Stranahan was impressed.

García got up and went knocking around the house, making Stranahan very nervous. When the detective finally stopped prowling, he stood directly under the stuffed blue marlin. 'Mick, I don't have to tell you there's some guys in Homicide think you aced old Judge Goomer without provocation.'

'I know that, Al. There's some guys in Homicide used to be in business with Judge Goomer.'

'And I know *that*. Point is, they'll be looking at this Chloe thing real hard. Harder than normal.'

Stranahan said, 'There's no chance it was an accident?'

'No,' Luis Córdova interjected. 'No chance.'

'So,' said Al García, 'you see the position I'm in. Until we get another suspect, you're it. The good news is, we've got no physical evidence connecting you. The bad news is, we've got Chloe's manicurist.'

Stranahan groaned. 'Jesus, let's hear it.'

García ambled to a window, stuck his arm out and tapped cigar ash into the water.

'Chloe had her toenails done yesterday morning,' the detective said. 'Told the girl she was coming out here to clean your clock.'

'Lovely,' said Mick Stranahan.

There was a small rap on the door and Tina came in, fiddling with the strap on the top piece of her swimsuit. Al García beamed like he'd just won the lottery; a dreary day suddenly had been brightened.

Stranahan stood up. 'Tina, I want you to meet

Sergeant García and Officer Córdova. They're here on police business. Al, Luis, I'd like you to meet my alibi.'

'How do you do,' said Luis Córdova, shaking Tina's hand in a commendably official way.

García gave Stranahan another sideways look. 'I love it,' said the detective. 'I absolutely love this job.'

Christina Marks heard about the death of Chloe Simpkins Stranahan on the six o'clock news. The only thing she could think was that Mick had done it to pay Chloe back for siccing the TV crew on him. It was painful to believe, but the only other possibility was too far-fetched – that Chloe's murder was a coincidence of timing and had nothing to do with Mick or Victoria Barletta. This Christina Marks could not accept; she had to plan for the worst.

If Mick was the killer, that would be a problem.

If Chloe had blabbed about getting five hundred in tipster money from the Reynaldo Flemm show, that would be a problem too. The police would want to know everything, then the papers would get hold of it and the Barletta story would blow up prematurely.

Then there was the substantial problem of Reynaldo himself; Christina could just hear him hyping the hell out of Chloe's murder in the intro: 'The story you are about to see is so explosive that a confidential informant who provided us with key information was brutally murdered only days later . . .' *Brutally murdered* was one of Reynaldo's favourite on-camera redundancies. Once Christina had drolly asked Reynaldo if he'd ever heard of anyone being *gently* murdered, but he missed the point.

Sometimes, when he got particularly excited about a story, Reynaldo Flemm would actually try to write out the script himself, with comic results. The murder of Stranahan's ex-wife was just the sort of bombshell to inspire Reynaldo's muse, so Christina decided on a preemptive attack. She was reaching across the bed for the telephone when it rang.

It was Maggie Gonzalez, calling collect from somewhere in Manhattan.

'Miss Marks, I got a little problem.'

Christina said: 'We've been looking all over for you. What happened to your trip to Miami?'

'I went, I came back,' Maggie said. 'I told you, there's a problem down there.'

'So what've you been doing the last few weeks,' Christina said, 'besides spending our money?' Christina had just about had it with this ditz; she was beginning to think Mick was right, the girl was ripping them off.

Maggie said, 'Hey, I'm sorry I didn't call sooner. I was scared. Scared out of my mind.'

'We thought you might be dead.'

'No,' said Maggie, barely audible. A long pause suggested that she was fretting over the grim possibility.

'Don't you even want to know how the story is going?' Christina asked warily.

'That's the problem,' Maggie replied. 'That's what I want to talk to you about.'

'Oh?'

Then, almost as an afterthought, Maggie asked, 'Who've you interviewed so far?'

'Nobody,' Christina said. 'We've got a lot of legwork to do first.'

'I can't believe you haven't interviewed anybody!'

Maggie was trolling for something, Christina could tell. 'We're taking it slow,' Christina said. 'This is a sensitive piece.'

'No joke,' Maggie said. 'Real sensitive.'

Christina held the phone in the crook of her shoulder and dug a legal pad and felt-tip pen from her shoulder bag on the bed table.

Maggie went on: 'This whole thing could get me killed, and I think that's worth more than five thousand dollars.'

'But that was our agreement,' Christina said, scribbling along with the conversation.

'That was before I started getting threatening calls on my machine,' said Maggie Gonzalez.

'From who?'

'I don't know who,' Maggie lied. 'It sounded like Dr Graveline.'

'What kind of threats? What did they say?'

'*Threat* threats,' Maggie said impatiently. 'Enough to scare me shitless, OK? You guys tricked me into believing this was safe.'

'We did nothing of the sort.'

'Yeah, well, five thousand dollars isn't going to cut it any more. By the time this is finished, I'll probably have to pack up and move out of Miami. You got any idea what that'll cost?'

Christina Marks said, 'What's the bottom line here, Maggie?'

'The bottom line is, I talked to *20/20*.'

Perfect, Christina thought. The perfect ending to a perfect day.

'I met with an executive producer,' Maggie said.

'Lucky you,' said Christina Marks. 'How much did they offer?'

'Ten.'

'Ten thousand?'

'Right,' Maggie said. 'Plus a month in Mexico after the programme airs . . . you know, to let things cool off.'

'You thought of this all by yourself, or did you get an agent?'

'A what?'

'An agent. Every eyewitness to a murder ought to have his own booking agent, don't you think?'

Maggie sounded confused. 'Ten seemed like a good number,' she said. 'Could be better, of course.'

Christina Marks was dying to find out how much Maggie Gonzalez had told the producer at *20/20*, but instead of asking she said: 'Ten sounds like a winner, Maggie. Besides, I don't think we're interested in the story any more.'

During the long silence that followed, Christina tried to imagine the look on Maggie's face.

Finally: 'What do you mean, "not interested"?'

'It's just too old, too messy, too hard to prove,' Christina said. 'The fact that you waited four years to speak up really kills us in the credibility department . . .'

'Hold on—'

'By the way, are they still polygraphing all their sources over at *20/20*?'

But Maggie was too sharp. 'Getting back to the money,' she said, 'are you saying you won't even consider a counter-offer?'

'Exactly.'

'Have you talked this over with Mr Flemm?'

'Of course,' Christina Marks bluffed, forging blindly ahead.

'That's very weird,' remarked Maggie Gonzalez, 'because I just talked to Mr Flemm myself about ten minutes ago.'

Christina sagged back on the bed and closed her eyes. 'And?'

'And he offered me fifteen grand, plus six weeks in Hawaii.'

'I see,' Christina said thinly.

'Anyway, he said I should call you right away and smooth out the details.'

'Such as?'

'Reservations,' said Maggie Gonzalez. 'Maui would be my first choice.'

TEN

One of the wondrous things about Florida, Rudy Grave-line thought as he chewed on a jumbo shrimp, was the climate of unabashed corruption: there was absolutely no trouble from which money could not extricate you.

Rudy had learned this lesson years earlier when the state medical board had first tried to take away his licence. For the board it had been a long sticky process, reviewing the complaints of disfigured patients, comparing the 'before' and 'after' photographs, sifting through the minutiae of thirteen separate malpractice suits. Since the medical board was made up mostly of other doctors, Rudy Graveline had fully expected exoneration – physicians stick together like shit on a shoe.

But the grossness of Rudy's surgical mistakes was so astounding that even his peers could not ignore it; they recommended that he be suspended from the practice of medicine for ever. Rudy hired a Tallahassee lawyer and pushed the case to a state administrative hearing. The hearing officer acting as judge was not a doctor himself, but some schlump civil servant knocking down twenty-eight thousand a year, tops. At the end of the third day of testimony – some of it so ghastly that Rudy's own attorney became nauseated – Rudy noticed the hearing officer getting into a decrepit old Ford Fairmont to go home to his wife and four kids. This gave Rudy an idea. On the fourth day, he made a phone call. On the fifth day, a brand new Volvo station wagon with cruise control was delivered to the home of the hearing officer. On the sixth day, Dr Rudy Graveline was cleared of all charges against him.

The board immediately reinstated Rudy's licence and sealed all the records from the public and the press – thus honouring the long-held philosophy of Florida's medical establishment that the last persons who need to know about a doctor's incompetence are the patients.

Safe from the sanctions and scrutiny of his own profession, Dr Rudy Graveline viewed all outside threats as problems that could be handled politically; that is, with bribery. Which is why he was having a long lunch with Dade County Commissioner Roberto Pepsical, who was chatting about the next election.

'Shrimp good, no?' said Roberto, who pocketed one in each cheek.

'Excellent,' Rudy agreed. He pushed the cocktail platter aside and dabbed the corners of his mouth with a napkin. 'Bobby, I'd like to give each of you twenty-five.'

'Grand?' Roberto Pepsical flashed a mouthful of pink-flecked teeth. 'Twenty-five grand, are you serious?'

The man was a hog: a florid, jowly, pug-nosed, rheumy-eyed hog. A cosmetic surgeon's nightmare. Rudy Graveline couldn't bear to watch him eat. 'Not so loud,' he said to the commissioner. 'I know what the campaign law says, but there are ways to duck it.'

'Great!' said Roberto. He had an account in the Caymans; all the commissioners did, except for Lillian Atwater, who was trying out a phoney blind trust in the Dominican Republic.

Rudy said, 'First I've got to ask a favour.'

'Shoot.'

The doctor leaned forward, trying to ignore Roberto's hot gumbo breath. 'The vote on Old Cypress Towers,' Rudy said. 'The rezoning thing.'

Roberto Pepsical lunged for a crab leg and cracked it open with his front teeth. 'Nooooo problem,' he said.

Old Cypress Towers was one of Dr Rudy Graveline's many real estate projects and tax shelters: a thirty-three storey luxury apartment building with a nightclub and health spa planned for the top floor. Only trouble was, the land currently was zoned for low-density public use – parks, schools, ball fields, shit like that. Rudy needed five votes on the county commission to turn it around.

'No sweat,' Roberto reiterated. 'I'll talk to the others.'

The 'others' were the four commissioners who always got pieced out in Roberto Pepsical's crooked deals. The way the system was set up, each of the nine commissioners had his own crooked deals and his own set of locked votes. That way the tally always came out 5–4, but with different players on each side. The idea was to confuse the hell out of the newspaper reporters, who were always trying to figure out who on the commission was honest and who wasn't.

'One more thing,' Dr Rudy Graveline said.

'How about another beer?' asked Roberto Pepsical, eyeing his empty sweaty glass. 'You don't mind if I get one?'

'Go ahead,' Rudy said, biting back his disgust.

'Crab?' The commissioner brandished another buttery leg.

'No, thanks.' Rudy waited for him to wedge it in his

mouth, then said: 'Bobby, I also need you to keep your ears open.'

'For what?'

'Somebody who used to work for me is threatening to go to the cops, trying to bust my balls. They're making up stuff about some old surgical case.'

Roberto nodded and chewed in synchronization, like a mechanical dashboard ornament. Rudy found it very distracting.

He said, 'The whole thing's bullshit, honestly. A disgruntled employee.'

Roberto said, 'Boy, I know how it is.'

'But for a doctor, Bobby, it could be a disaster. My reputation, my livelihood, surely you can understand? That's why I need to know if the cops ever go for it.'

Roberto Pepsical said, 'I'll talk to the chief myself.'

'Only if you hear something.'

Roberto winked. 'I'll poke around.'

'I'd sure appreciate it,' Dr Graveline said. 'I can't afford a scandal, Bobby. Something like that, I'd probably have to leave town.'

The commissioner's brow furrowed as he contemplated his twenty-five large on the wing. 'Don't sweat it,' he said confidently to the doctor. 'Here, have a conch fritter.'

Chemo was in the waiting room when Rudy Graveline got back to Whispering Palms.

'I did it,' he announced.

Rudy quickly led him into the office.

'You got Stranahan?'

'Last night,' Chemo said matter-of-factly. 'So when can we get started on my face?'

Unbelievable, Rudy thought. Very scary, this guy.

'You mean the dermabrasion treatments.'

'Fucking A,' Chemo said. 'We had a deal.'

Rudy buzzed his secretary and asked her to bring him the morning *Herald*. After she went out again, Chemo said, 'It happened so late, probably didn't make the paper.'

'Hmmmm,' said Rudy Graveline, scanning the local news page. 'Maybe that's it – must have happened too late. Tell me about it, please.'

Chemo wet his dead-looking lips. 'I torched his house.' No expression at all. 'He was asleep.'

'You know this for a fact?'

'I watched it go up,' Chemo said. 'Nobody got out.' He crossed his long legs and stared dully at the doctor. The droopy lids made him look like he was about to doze off.

Rudy folded up the newspaper. 'I believe you,' he said to Chemo, 'but I'd like to be sure. By tomorrow it ought to be in the papers.'

Chemo rubbed the palm of one hand along his cheeks, making sandpaper sounds. Rudy Graveline wished he would knock it off.

'What about the TV?' Chemo asked. 'Does that count, if it makes the TV?'

'Of course.'

'Radio, too?'

'Certainly,' Rudy said. 'I told you before, no big deal. I don't need to see the actual corpse, OK, but we do need to be sure. It's very important, because this is a dangerous man.'

'*Was*,' Chemo said pointedly.

'Right. This was a dangerous man.' Rudy didn't mention Stranahan's ominous phone call on Maggie Gonzalez's answering machine. Better to limit the cast of characters, for Chemo's sake. Keep him focused.

'Maybe it's already on the radio,' Chemo said hopefully.

Rudy didn't want to put the guy in a mood. 'Tell you what,' he said in a generous tone, 'we'll go ahead and do the first treatment this afternoon.'

Chemo straightened up excitedly. 'No shit?'

'Why not?' the doctor said, standing. 'We'll try a little patch on your chin.'

'How about the nose?' Chemo said, touching himself there.

Rudy slipped on his glasses and came around the desk to where Chemo was sitting. Because of Chemo's height, even in the chair, the surgeon didn't have to lean over far to get a close-up look at the corrugated, cheesy mass that passed for Chemo's nose.

'Pretty rough terrain,' Rudy Graveline said, peering intently. 'Better to start slow and easy.'

'Fast and rough is fine with me.'

Rudy took off his glasses and struck an avuncular pose, a regular Marcus Welby. 'I want to be very careful,' he told Chemo. 'Yours is an extreme case.'

'You noticed.'

'The machine we use is a Stryker dermabrader—'

'I don't care if it's a fucking Black and Decker, let's just do it.'

'Scar tissue is tricky,' Rudy persisted. 'Some skin reacts better to sanding than others.' He couldn't help remembering what had happened to the last doctor who had screwed up Chemo's face. Getting murdered was even worse than getting sued for malpractice.

'One little step at a time,' Rudy cautioned. 'Trust me.'

'Fine, then start on the chin, whatever,' Chemo said with a wave of a pale hand. 'You're the doctor.'

Those magic words.

How Rudy Graveline loved to hear them.

Compared to other law firms, Kipper Garth's had the overhead problem dicked. He had one central office, no partners, no associates, no 'of counsels'. His major expenses were billboard advertising, cable, telephones (he had twenty lines), and, of course, secretaries (he called them legal aides, and employed fifteen). Kipper Garth's law practice was, in essence, a high-class boiler room.

The phones never stopped ringing. This was because Kipper Garth had shrewdly put up his billboards at the most dangerous traffic intersections in South Florida, so that the second thing every noncomatose accident victim saw (after the Jaws of Life) was Kipper Garth's phone number in nine-foot red letters: 555-TORT.

Winnowing the incoming cases took most of the time, so Kipper Garth delegated this task to his secretaries, who were undoubtedly more qualified anyway. Kipper Garth saved his own energy for selecting the referrals; some PI lawyers specialized in spinal cord injuries, others in orthopedics, still others in death-and-dismemberment. Though Kipper Garth was not one to judge a colleague's skill in the courtroom (not having *been* in a courtroom in at least a decade), he knew a fifty-fifty fee split when he saw it, and made his referrals accordingly.

The phone bank at Kipper Garth's firm looked and sounded like the catalogue-order department at Montgomery Ward. By contrast, the interior of Kipper Garth's private office was rich and staid, lit like an old library and just as quiet. This is where Mick Stranahan found his brother-in-law, practising his putting.

'You don't knock any more?' said Kipper Garth, eyeing a ten-footer into a Michelob stein.

'I came to make a little deal,' Stranahan said.

'This I gotta hear.' Kipper Garth wore grey European-cut slacks, a silk paisley necktie and a bone-coloured shirt, the French cuffs rolled up to his elbows. His salt-and-pepper hair had been dyed silver to make him look more trustworthy on billboards.

'Let's forget this disbarment thing,' Stranahan said.

Kipper Garth chuckled. 'It's a little late, Mick. You already testified, remember?'

'How about if I agree not to testify next time?'

Kipper Garth backed away from the next putt and looked up. 'Next time?'

'There's other cases kicking around the grievance committee, am I right?'

'But how do you—'

'Lawyers talk, Jocko.' Stranahan emptied the golf balls out of the beer stein and rolled them back across the carpet toward his brother-in-law. 'I've still got a few friends in town,' he said. 'I'm still plugged in.'

Kipper Garth leaned his putter in the corner behind his desk. 'I'm suing *you*, remember? Defamation, it's called.'

'Don't make me laugh.'

The lawyer's eyes narrowed. 'Mick, I know why you're here. Chloe's been killed and you're afraid you'll take the fall. You need a lawyer, so here you are, looking for a goddamn freebie.'

'I said don't make me laugh.'

'Then what is it?'

'Who's getting your malpractice stuff these days?'

Kipper Garth started flicking through his Rolodex; it was the biggest Rolodex that Stranahan had ever seen, the size of a pot roast. Kipper Garth said, 'I've got a couple main guys, why?'

'These guys you've got, can they get state records?'

'What kind of records?'

Christ, the man was lame. 'Discipline records,' Stranahan explained, 'from the medical board.'

'Gee, I don't know.'

'There's a shocker.'

'What's going on, Mick?'

'This: you help me out, I'll lay off of you. Permanently.'

Kipper Garth snorted. 'I'm supposed to be grateful? Pardon me if I don't give a shit.'

Naturally, thought Stranahan, it would come to this. The pertinent papers were wadded in his back pocket. He got them out, smoothed them with the heel of one hand and laid them out carefully, like solitaire cards, on Kipper Garth's desk.

The lawyer muttered, 'What the hell?'

'Pay attention,' Stranahan said. 'This one here is the bill of sale for your spiffy new Maserati. That's a Xerox of the cheque – fifty-seven thousand, eight something, what a joke. Anyway, the account that cheque was written on is your clients' trust account, Jocko. We're talking deep shit. Forget disbarment, we're talking felony.'

Kipper Garth's upper lip developed an odd tic.

'I'm paying it back,' he said hoarsely.

'Doesn't matter,' Mick Stranahan said. 'Now, some of this other crap – that's a hotel bill from the Grand Bay in Coconut Grove. Same weekend you told Katie you were in Boston with the ABA. Anyway, it's none of my business but you don't look like a man that could drink three bottles of Dom all by your lonesome. See, it's right there on the bill.' Stranahan pointed, but Kipper Garth's eyes were focused someplace else, some place far away. By now his lip was twitching like a porch lizard.

'You,' he said to Stranahan. 'You jerk.'

'Now what's this dinner for two, Jocko? My sister was at grandma's with the kids that night, if memory serves. Dinner for two at Max's Place, what exactly was that? Probably just a client, no?'

Kipper Garth collected himself and said, 'All right, Mick.'

'You understand the situation.'

'Yes.'

'It was easier than you think,' Stranahan said. 'See, once you're plugged in, it's hard to get unplugged. I mean, once you know this stuff is out there, it's real easy to find.' A half dozen phone calls was all it took.

Kipper Garth began folding the papers, creasing each one with a great deal of force.

Stranahan said, 'What scares you more, Jocko: the Florida Bar, the county jail, or an expensive divorce?'

Wearily, Kipper Garth said, 'Did you mean what you said before, about the disbarment and all that?'

'You're asking because you know I don't have to

deal, isn't that right? Maybe that's true – maybe you'd do me this favour for nothing. But fair is fair, and you ought to get something in return. So, yeah, I'll lay off. Just like I promised.'

Kipper Garth said, 'Then I'll talk to my guys about getting the damn state files. Give me a name, please.'

'Graveline,' said Stranahan. 'Dr Rudy Graveline.'

Kipper Garth winced. 'Jeez, I've heard that name. I think he's in my yacht club.'

Mick Stranahan clapped his hands. 'Yo ho ho,' he said.

Later, on the way to see her plastic surgeon, Tina asked Mick: 'Why didn't you make love to me last night?'

'I thought you enjoyed yourself.'

'It was sweet, but why'd you stop?'

Stranahan said: 'Because I've got this terrible habit of falling in love.'

Tina rolled her eyes. 'After one night?'

'True story,' Stranahan said. 'All five of the women I married, I proposed to them the first night we went to bed.'

'Before or after?' Tina asked.

'After,' he said. 'It's like a disease. The scary part is, they tend to say yes.'

'Not me.'

'I couldn't take that chance.'

'You're nuts,' Tina said. 'Does this mean we're never gonna do it?'

Stranahan sighed, feeling old and out of it. His ex-wife just gets murdered, some asshole doctor's trying to kill him, a TV crew is lurking around his house – all this, and Tina wants to know about getting laid, wants a time and date. Why didn't she believe him about the others?

He stopped at a self-service Shell station and filled three plastic Farm Stores jugs with regular unleaded. When he went up to pay, nobody said a word. He put the gallon jugs in the trunk of the Imperial and covered them with a bunch of boat rags.

Back in the car, Tina gave him a look. 'You didn't answer my question.'

'You've got a boyfriend,' Stranahan said, wishing he could've come up with something better, more original.

'Richie? Richie's history,' said Tina. '*No problema.*'

It always amazed Stranahan how they could make boyfriends disappear, snap, just like that.

'So,' Tina said, 'how about tonight?'

'How about I call you,' he said, 'when things cool off?'

'Yeah,' Tina muttered. 'Sure.'

Stranahan was glad when they got to the doctor's office. It was a two-storey peach stucco building in Coral Gables, a refurbished old house. The plastic surgeon's name was Dicer. Craig E. Dicer; a nice young fellow, too nice to say anything nasty about Rudy Graveline at first. Stranahan badged him and tried again. Dr Dicer took a good hard look at the gold State Attorney's investigator shield before he said: 'Is this off the record?'

'Sure,' said Stranahan, wondering: Where do these guys learn to talk like this?

'Graveline's a butcher,' Dr Dicer said. 'A hacker. Everybody in town's mopped up after him, one time or another. Fortunately, he doesn't do much surgery himself any more. He got wise, hired a bunch of young sharpies, all board certified. It's like a damn factory up there.'

'Whispering Palms?'

'You've seen it?' Dr Dicer asked.

Stranahan said no, but it was his next stop. 'If everybody in Miami knows that Graveline's a butcher, how does he get any patients?'

Dr Dicer laughed caustically. 'Hell, man, the patients don't know. You think some housewife wants her tits poofed goes downtown to the courthouse and looks up the lawsuits? No way. Rudy Graveline's got a big rep because he's socially connected. He did the mayor's niece's chin, this I know for a fact. And old Congressman Carberry? Graveline did his girlfriend's eyelids. Or somebody at Whispering Palms did; Rudy always takes the credit.'

Tina, who hadn't been saying much since the car, finally cut in. 'Talk to models and actresses,' she said. 'Whispering Palms is in. Like tofu.'

'Jesus,' said Stranahan.

Dr Dicer said, 'Can I ask why you're interested?'

'Really, you don't want to know,' Stranahan said.

'I guess not.'

'*I* want to know,' Tina said.

Stranahan pretended not to hear her. He said to Dr Dicer: 'One more question, then we'll let you get back to work. This is hypothetical.'

Dr Dicer nodded, folded his hands, got very studious looking.

Stranahan said: 'Is it possible to kill somebody during a nose job?'

By way of an answer, Dr Dicer took out a pink neoprene replica of a bisected human head, a bronze Crane mallet, and a small Cottle chisel. Then he demonstrated precisely how you could kill somebody during a nose job.

When Chemo got to the Gay Bidet, a punk band called the Chicken Chokers had just finished wringing their sweaty jock straps into a cocktail glass and guzzling it down on stage.

'You're late,' said Chemo's boss, a man named Freddie. 'We already had three fights.'

'Car trouble,' said Chemo. 'Radiator hose.' Not an apology, an explanation.

Freddie pointed at the small bandage and said, 'What happened to your chin?'

'A zit,' Chemo said.

'A zit, that's a good one.'

'What's that supposed to mean?'

'Nothing,' Freddie said. 'Don't mean nothing.' He had to watch the wisecracks around Chemo. The man made him nervous as a gerbil. Freaking seven-foot cadaver, other clubs would kill for a bouncer like that.

Freddie said, 'Here, you got a message.'

Chemo said thank you, went outside to a pay phone on Collins and called Dr Rudy Graveline's beeper. At the tone, Chemo punched in the number of the pay phone, hung up, and waited. All the way out here, he could hear the next band cranking up. The Crotch Rockets, it sounded like. Their big hit was *Lube-Job Lover*. Chemo found it somewhat derivative.

The telephone rang. Chemo waited for the third time before picking up.

'We have got a problem,' said Rudy Graveline, raspy, borderline terrified.

Chemo said, 'Aren't you going to ask about my chin?'

'No!'

'Well, it stings like hell.'

Dr Graveline said, 'I told you it would.'

Chemo said, 'How long've I gotta wear the Band-Aid?'

'Till it starts to heal, for Chrissakes. Look, I've got a major situation here and if you don't fix it, the only person's going to care about your complexion is the goddamn undertaker. One square inch of perfect chin, maybe you're thinking how gorgeous you look. Well, think open casket. How's that for gorgeous?'

Chemo absently touched his new bandage. 'Why're you so upset?'

'Mick Stranahan's alive.'

Chemo thought: The bitch in the sailor suit, she got the wrong house.

'By the way,' Rudy Graveline said angrily, 'I'd like to thank you for not telling me how you drowned the man's wife in the middle of Biscayne Bay. From what was on TV, I'm just assuming it was you. Had your subtle touch.' When Chemo didn't respond for several moments, the doctor said: 'Well?'

Chemo asked, 'Is that a siren at your end?'

'Yes,' Rudy said archly, 'yes, that would be a siren. Now, aren't you going to ask how I know that Stranahan's still alive?'

'All right,' Chemo said, 'how do you know?'

'Because,' the doctor said, 'the bastard just blew up my Jag.'

ELEVEN

Christina Marks knocked twice, and when no one answered she walked in. The man in the hospital bed had a plastic oxygen mask over his mouth. Lying there he looked as small as a child. The covers were pulled up to the folds of his neck. His face was mottled and drawn. When Christina approached the bed, the man's blue eyes opened slowly and he waved. When he lifted the oxygen mask away from his mouth, she saw that he was smiling.

'Detective Gavigan?'

'The one and only.'

'I'm Christina Marks.' She told him why she had come, what she wanted. When she mentioned Vicky Barletta, Timmy Gavigan made a zipper motion across his lips.

'What's the matter?' Christina asked.

'That's an open case, lady. I can't talk about it.' Timmy Gavigan's voice was hollow, like it was coming up a pipe from his dead lungs. 'We got regulations about talking to the media,' he said.

'Do you know Mick Stranahan?' Christina said.

'Sure I know Mick,' Timmy Gavigan said. 'Mick came to see me a while back.'

'About this case?'

'Mick's in my scrapbook,' Timmy Gavigan said, looking away.

Christina said, 'He's in some trouble.'

'He didn't get married again, the dumb bastard?'

'Not that kind of trouble,' Christina said. 'This time it was the Barletta case.'

'Mick's a big boy,' said Timmy Gavigan. 'My guess is, he can handle it.' He was smiling again. 'Honey, you sure are pretty.'

'Thank you,' said Christina.

'Can you believe, six months ago I'd be trying to charm you right into the sack. Now I can't even get up to take a whizz. Here a gorgeous woman comes to my room and I can't raise my goddamn head, much less anything else.'

She said, 'I'm sorry.'

'I know what you're thinking – a dying man, he's likely to say anything. But I mean it, you're something special. I got high standards, always did. I mean, hell, I might be dead, but I ain't blind.'

Christina laughed softly. Timmy Gavigan reached for the oxygen mask, took a couple of deep breaths, put it down again. 'Give me your hand,' he said to Christina Marks. 'Please, it's all right. What I got, you can't catch.'

Timmy Gavigan's skin was cold and papery. Christina gave a little squeeze and tried to pull away, but he held on. She noticed his eyes had a sparkle.

'You've been to the file?'

She nodded.

'I took a statement from that doctor, Rudy Something.'

Christina said, 'Yes, I read it.'

'Help me out,' said Timmy Gavigan, squinting in concentration. 'What the hell did he say again?'

'He said it was a routine procedure, nothing out of the ordinary.'

'Yeah, I remember now,' Timmy Gavigan said. 'He was a precious thing, too, all business. Said he'd done five thousand nose jobs and this was no different from the others. And I said maybe not, but this time your patient vanished from the face of the earth. And he said she was fine last time he saw her. Walked out of the office all by herself. And I said yeah, walked straight into the fucking twilight zone. Pardon my French.'

Christina Marks said, 'You've got a good memory.'

'Too bad I can't breathe with it.' Timmy Gavigan took another hit of oxygen. 'Fact is, we had no reason to think the doctor was involved. Besides, the nurse backed him up. What the hell was his name again?'

'Graveline.'

Timmy Gavigan nodded. 'Struck me as a little snot. If only you could arrest people for that.' He coughed, or maybe it was a chuckle. 'Did I mention I was dying?'

Christina said yes, she knew.

'Did you say you were on TV?'

'No, I'm just a producer.'

'Well, you're pretty enough to be on TV.'

'Thank you.'

'I'm not being very much help, I know,' said Timmy Gavigan. 'They got me loaded up on morphine. But I'm trying to think if there was something I left out.'

'It's all right, you've been helpful.'

She could tell that each breath was torture.

He said, 'Your idea is that the doctor did it, is that right? See, that's a new angle – let me think here.'

Christina said, 'It's just a theory.'

Timmy Gavigan shifted under the covers and turned slightly to face her. 'He had a brother, was that in the file?'

No, Christina said. Nothing about a brother.

'Probably not,' Timmy Gavigan said. 'It didn't seem important at the time. I mean, the doc wasn't even a suspect.'

'I understand.'

'But he did have a brother, I talked to him maybe ten minutes. Wasn't worth typing it up.' Timmy Gavigan motioned for a cup of water and Christina held it to his lips.

'Jesus, I must be a sight,' he said. 'Anyway, the reason I mention it – let's say the doctor croaked Vicky. Don't know why, but let's say he did. What to do about the body? That's a big problem. Bodies are damn tough to get rid of, Jimmy Hoffa being the exception.'

'What does the doctor's brother do?'

Timmy Gavigan grinned, and colour flashed to his cheeks. 'That's my point, honey. The brother was a tree trimmer.'

Christina tried to look pleased at this new information, but mostly she looked puzzled.

'You don't know much about tree trimming, do you?' Timmy Gavigan said in a teasing tone. Then he gulped more oxygen.

She said, 'Why did you go see the doctor's brother?'

'I didn't. Didn't have to. I met him right outside the clinic – I forget the damn name.'

'The Durkos Medical Center.'

'Sounds right.' Timmy Gavigan paused, and his free hand moved to his throat. When the pain passed, he continued. 'Outside the clinic, I saw this guy hacking on the black olive trees. Asked him if he was there the day Vicky disappeared, if he saw anything unusual. Naturally he says no. After, I ask his name and he tells me George Graveline. So like the genius I am, I say: You related to the doctor? He says yeah, and that's about it.'

'George Graveline.' Christina Marks wrote the name down.

Timmy Gavigan lifted his head and eyed the notebook. 'Tree trimmer,' he said. 'Make sure you put that down.'

'Tell me what it means, please.'

'No, you ask Mick.'

She said, 'What makes you so sure I'll see him?'

'Wild hunch.'

Then Timmy Gavigan said something that Christina Marks couldn't quite hear. She leaned over and asked him, in a whisper, to repeat it.

'I said, you sure are beautiful.' He winked once, then closed his eyes slowly. 'Thanks for holding my hand,' he said.

And then he let go.

Whenever there was a bombing in Dade County, somebody in the Central Office would call Sergeant Al García for help, mainly because García was Cuban and it was automatically assumed that the bombing was in some way related to exile politics. García had left orders that he was not to be bothered about bombings unless somebody actually died, since a dead body was the customary prerequisite of homicide investigation. He also sent detailed memorandums explaining that Cubans were not the only ones who tried to bomb each other in South Florida, and he listed all the mob and labour and otherwise non-Cuban bombings over the last ten years. Nobody at the Central Office paid much attention to García's pleadings, and they still summoned him over the most chickenshit of explosions.

This is what happened when Dr Rudy Graveline's black Jaguar sedan blew up. García was about to tell the dispatcher to piss off, until he heard the name of the complainant. Then, fifteen minutes behind the fire trucks, he drove straight to Whispering Palms.

What had happened was: Rudy had gone to the airport to pick up a potentially important patient, a world-famous actress who had awakened one morning in her Bel Air mansion, glanced at herself naked in the mirror, and burst into tears. She got Dr Graveline's name from a friend of a friend of Parnell Roberts's poolboy, and called to tell the surgeon that she was flying to Miami for an emergency consultation. Because of the actress's fame and wealth (most of it accumulated during a messy divorce from one of the Los Angeles Dodgers), Rudy agreed to meet the woman at the airport and give a personal tour of Whispering Palms. He was double-parked in front of the Pan Am terminal when he first noticed the beat-up old Chrysler pull in behind him, its rear end sticking into traffic. Rudy noticed the car again on his way back to the beach – the actress yammering away about the practical joke she once played on Richard Chamberlain while they were shooting some mini-series; Rudy with a worried eye on the rear-view, because the Imperial was right there, on his bumper.

The other car disappeared somewhere on Alton

Road, and Rudy didn't think about it again until he and the actress walked out of Whispering Palms; Rudy with a friendly hand on her elbow, she with a fistful of glossy surgery brochures. The Imperial was parked right across from Rudy's special reserved slot. The same big man was behind the wheel. The actress didn't know anything was wrong until the man got out of the Chrysler and whistled at a yellow cab, which was conveniently parked under a big ficus tree at the north end of the lot. When the taxi pulled up, the man from the Imperial opened the back door and told the actress to get in. He said the cabbie would take her straight to the hotel. She said she wasn't staying in any *hotel*, that she'd rented a villa in Golden Beach where Eric Clapton once lived; the big man said fine, the cabbie knew the way.

Finally the actress got in, the taxi drove off, and it was just the stranger and Rudy Graveline alone in the parking lot. When the man introduced himself, Rudy tried very hard not to act terrified. Mick Stranahan said that he wasn't yet certain why Dr Graveline was trying to have him killed, but that it was a very bad idea, overall. Dr Graveline replied that he didn't know what on earth the man was talking about. Then Mick Stranahan walked across the parking lot, got in his Chrysler, turned on the ignition, placed a coconut on the accelerator, got out of the car, reached through the driver's window and slipped it into Drive. Then he jumped out of the way and watched the Imperial plough directly into the rear of Dr Rudy Graveline's black Jaguar sedan. The impact, plus the three jugs of gasoline that Mick Stranahan had strategically positioned in the Jaguar's trunk, caused the automobile to explode in a most spectacular way.

When Rudy Graveline recounted this story to Detective Sergeant Al García, he left out two details – the name of the man who did it, and the reason.

'He never said why?' said Al García, all eyebrows.

'Not a word,' lied Dr Graveline. 'He just destroyed my car and walked away. The man was obviously deranged.'

García grunted and folded his arms. Smoke was still rising from the Jag, which was covered with foam from the firetrucks. Rudy acted forlorn about the car, but García knew the truth. The only reason the asshole even bothered with the police was for the insurance company.

The detective said, 'You don't know the guy who did this?'

'Never saw him before.'

'That's not what I asked.'

Rudy said, 'Sergeant, I don't know what you mean.'

García was tempted to come out and ask the surgeon if it were true that he was trying to bump off Mick Stranahan, like Stranahan had said. That was a fun question, the kind García loved to ask, but the timing wasn't right. For now, he wanted Rudy Graveline to think of him as a big, dumb cop, not a threat.

'A purely random attack,' García mused.

'It would appear so,' Rudy said.

'And you say the man was short and wiry?'

'Yes,' Rudy said.

'How short?'

'Maybe five one,' Rudy said. 'And he was black.'

'How black?'

'Very black,' the doctor said. 'Black as my tyres.'

Al García dropped to a crouch and shone his

149

flashlight on the front hub of the molten Jag. 'Michelins,' he noted. 'The man was as black as Michelins.'

'Yes, and he spoke no English.'

'Really? What language was it?'

'Creole,' Rudy Graveline said. 'I'm pretty sure.'

García rubbed his chin. 'So what we've got in the way of an arsonist,' he said, 'is a malnourished Haitian midget.'

Rudy frowned. 'No,' he said seriously, 'he was taller than that.'

García said the man apparently had picked the trunk lock in order to put the containers of gasoline inside the doctor's car. 'That shows some thinking,' the detective said.

'Could still be crazy,' Rudy said. 'Crazy people can surprise you.'

One tow truck driver put the hooks on what was left of Rudy's black Jaguar. Another contemplated the remains of the Chrysler Imperial, which García kept referring to as 'that ugly piece of elephant shit'. His hatred for Chryslers went back to his patrol days.

Lennie Goldberg, a detective from Intelligence, came up and said, 'So, what do you think, Al? Think it was Cubans?'

'No, Lennie, I think it was the Shining Path. Or maybe the freaking Red Brigade.' It took Lennie Goldberg a couple of beats to catch on. Irritably García said, 'Would you stop this shit about the Cubans? This was a routine car bomb, OK? No politics, no Castro, no CIA. No fucking Cubans, got it?'

'Jeez, Al, I was just asking.' Lennie thought García was getting very touchy on the subject.

'Use your head, Lennie.' García pointed at the wreck.

'This look like an act of international terrorism? Or does it look like some dirtball in a junker went nuts?'

Lennie said, 'Could be either, Al. With bombings, sometimes you got to look closely for the symbolism. Maybe there's a message in this. Aren't Jaguars manufactured in Britain? Maybe this is the IRA.'

García groaned. A message, for Christ's sake. And symbolism! This is what happens when you put a moron in the intelligence unit: he gets even dumber.

A uniformed cop handed Rudy Graveline a copy of the police report. The doctor folded it carefully with three creases, like a letter, and placed it in the inside pocket of his jacket.

Al García turned his back on Lennie Goldberg and said to Rudy, 'Don't worry, we'll find the guy.'

'You will?'

'No sweat,' said García, noticing how uncomfortable Rudy seemed. 'We'll run the VIN number on the Chrysler and come up with our Haitian dwarf, or whatever.'

'Probably a stolen vehicle,' Rudy remarked.

'Probably not,' said Al García. *Vehicle?* Now the guy was doing Jack Webb. García said: 'No, sir, this definitely was a premeditated act, the act of a violent and unstable perpetrator. We'll do our best to solve it, Doctor, you've got my word.'

'Really, it's not that big a deal.'

'Oh, it is to us,' García said. 'It is indeed a big deal.'

'Well, I know you're awfully busy.'

'Oh, not too busy for something like this,' García said in the heartiest of tones. 'The firebombing of a prominent physician – are you kidding? Starting now, Dr Graveline, your case is a priority one.'

García was having a ball, acting so damn gung ho; the doctor looked wan and dyspeptic.

The detective said, 'You'll be hearing back from me real soon.'

'I will?' said Rudy Graveline.

Reynaldo Flemm had been in a dark funk since his clandestine visit to Whispering Palms. Dr Graveline had lanced his ego; this, without knowing Reynaldo's true identity or the magnitude of his fame. Three days had passed, and Flemm had scarcely been able to peek out the door of his Key Biscayne hotel room. He had virtually stopped eating most solid food, resorting to a diet of protein cereal and lemon Gatorade. Every time Christina Marks knocked, Reynaldo would call out that he was in the bathroom, sick to his stomach, which was almost true. He couldn't tear himself away from the mirror. The surgeon's dire assessment of Reynaldo's nose – 'two sizes too large for your face' – was savage by itself, but the casual criticism of his weight was paralysing.

Flemm was examining himself naked in the mirror when Christina came to the door again.

'I'm sick,' he called out.

'Ray, this is stupid,' Christina scolded from the hallway. She didn't know about his trip to the clinic. 'We've got to talk about Maggie,' she said.

There was the sound of drawers being opened and closed, and maybe a closet. For a moment Christina thought he might be getting ready to emerge.

'Ray?'

'What about Maggie?' he said. Now it sounded like

he was inches from the door. 'Didn't you straighten out that shit about *20/20?*'

Christina said, 'That's what we have to talk about. Fifteen thousand is ludicrous. Let me in, Ray.'

'I'm not well.'

'Open the damn door or I'm calling New York.'

'No, Chris, I'm not at my best.'

'Ray, I've seen you at your best, and it's not all that great. Let me in, or I start kicking.' And she did. Reynaldo Flemm couldn't believe it, the damn door was jumping off its hinges.

'Hey, stop!' he cried, and opened it just a crack.

Christina saw that he wore a towel around his waist, and nothing else. A bright green pair of elastic cycling shorts lay on the floor.

'Hawaii?' Christina said. 'You told that bimbette we'd send her to Hawaii?'

Reynaldo said, 'What choice did I have? You want to lose this story?'

'Yes,' Christina said, 'this story is serious trouble, Ray. I want to pack up and go home.'

'And give it to ABC? Are you nuts?' He opened the door a little more. 'We're getting so close.'

Christina tried to bait him. 'How about we fly up to Spartanburg tomorrow? Do the biker segment, like we planned?'

Reynaldo loved to do motorcycle gangs, since they almost always attacked him while the tape was rolling. The Spartanburg story had a sex-slavery angle as well, but Flemm still didn't bite.

'That'll wait,' he said.

Christina checked both ways to make sure no one

was coming down the hall. 'You heard about Chloe Simpkins?'

Reynaldo Flemm shook his head. 'I haven't seen the news,' he admitted, 'in a couple of days.'

'Well, she's dead,' Christina said. 'Murdered.'

'Oh, God.'

'Out by the stilt houses.'

'No shit? What an opener.'

'Forget it, Ray, it's a mess.' She shouldered her way into his room. He sat down on the bed, his knees pressed together under the towel. A tape measure was coiled in his left hand. 'What's that for?' Christina asked, pointing.

'Nothing,' Flemm said. He wasn't about to tell her that he had been measuring his nose in the mirror. In fact he had been taking the precise dimensions of all his facial features, to compare proportions.

He said, 'When is Chloe's funeral? Let's get Willie and shoot the stand-up there.'

'Forget it.' She explained how the cops would probably be looking for them anyway, to ask about the five hundred dollars. In its worst light, somebody might say that they contributed to Chloe's death, put her up to something dangerous.

'But we didn't,' Reynaldo Flemm whined. 'All we got from her was Stranahan's location, and barely that. A house in the bay, she said. A house with a windmill. Easiest five bills that woman ever made.'

Christina said, 'Like I said, it's a big mess. It's time to pull out. Tell Maggie to go fly her kite for Hugh Downs.'

'Let's wait a couple more days.' He couldn't stand the idea of giving up; he hadn't gotten beat up once on this whole assignment.

'Wait for what?' Christina said testily.

'So I can think. I can't think when I'm sick.'

She resisted the temptation to state the obvious. 'What exactly is the matter?'

'Nothing I care to talk about,' Flemm said.

'Ah, one of those male-type problems.'

'Fuck you.'

As she was leaving, Christina asked when he would be coming out of his hotel room to face the real world. 'When I'm good and ready,' Flemm replied defensively.

'Take your time, Ray. Tomorrow's interview is off.'

'You cancelled it – why?'

'It cancelled itself. The man died.'

Flemm gasped. 'Another murder!'

'No, Ray, it wasn't murder.' Christina waved good-bye. 'Sorry to disappoint you.'

'That's OK,' he said, sounding like a man on the mend, 'we can always fudge it.'

TWELVE

After Timmy Gavigan's funeral, García offered Mick Stranahan a ride back to the marina.

'I noticed you came by cab,' the detective said.

'Al, you got eyes like a hawk.'

'So where's your car?'

Stranahan said, 'I guess somebody stole it.'

It was a nice funeral, although Timmy Gavigan would have made fun of it. The chief stood up and said some good things, and afterwards some cops young enough to be Timmy's grandchildren shot off a twenty-one gun salute and accidentally hit a power transformer, leaving half of Coconut Grove with no electricity. Stranahan had worn a pressed pair of jeans, a charcoal sports jacket, brown loafers and no socks. It was the best outfit he owned; he'd thrown out all his neckties when he moved to the stilt house. Stranahan caught himself sniffling a little toward the end of the service. He made a mental note to clip the obit from the newspaper and glue it in Timmy Gavigan's scrapbook, the way he promised. Then he would mail the scrapbook up to Boston, where Timmy's daughters lived.

Driving back out the Rickenbacker Causeway, García was saying, 'Didn't you have an old Chrysler? Funny thing, we got one of those shitheaps in a fire the other night. Somebody filed off the VIN numbers, so we can't trace the damn thing – maybe it's yours, huh?'

'Maybe,' said Mick Stranahan, 'but you keep it. The block was cracked. I was ready to junk it anyway.'

García drummed his fingers on the steering wheel, which meant he was running out of patience.

'Hey, Mick?'

'What?'

'Did you blow up that asshole's Jag?'

Stranahan stared out at the bay and said, 'Who?'

'The doctor. The one who wants to kill you.'

'Oh.'

Something was not right with this guy, García thought. Maybe the funeral had put him in a mood, maybe it was something else.

'We're getting into an area,' the detective said, 'that makes me very nervous. You listening, *chico*?'

Stranahan pretended to be watching some topless girl on a sailboard.

García said, 'You want to play Charlie Bronson, OK, but let me tell you how serious this is getting. Forget the doctor for a second.'

'Yeah, how? He's trying to kill me.'

'Well, chill on that for a minute and think about this: Murdock and Salazar got assigned to Chloe's murder. Do I have to spell it out, or you want me to stop the car so you can go ahead and puke?'

'Jesus,' said Mick Stranahan.

Detectives John Murdock and Joe Salazar had been tight with the late Judge Raleigh Goomer, the one Stranahan had shot. Murdock and Salazar had been in on the bond fixings, part of the A-team. They were not Mick Stranahan's biggest fans.

'How the hell did they get the case?'

'Luck of the draw,' García said. 'Nothing I could do without making it worse.'

Stranahan slammed a fist on the dashboard. He was damn tired of all this bad news.

García said, 'So they come out here to do a canvass, right? Talk to people at the boat ramp, the restaurant, anyone who might have seen your ex on the night she croaked. They come back with statements from two waitresses and a gas attendant, and guess who they say was with Chloe? You, Blue Eyes.'

'That's a goddamn lie, Al.'

'You're right. I know it's a lie because I drove out here the next day on my lunch hour and talked to these same people myself. On my lunch hour! Show them two mugs, including yours, and strike out. O for ten. So Frick and Frack are lying. I don't know what I can do about it yet – it's a tricky situation, them sticking together on their story.' García took a cigar from his breast pocket. Wrapper and all, he jammed it in the corner of his mouth. 'I'm telling you this so you know how goddamn serious it's getting, and maybe you'll quit this crazy car-bombing shit and give me a chance to do my job. How about it?'

Absently, Stranahan said, 'This is the worst year of my life, and it's only the seventeenth of January.'

García chewed the cellophane off the cigar. 'I don't know why I even bother to tell you anything,' he grumbled. 'You're acting like a damn zombie.'

The detective made the turn into the marina with a screech of the tyres. Stranahan pointed toward the slip where his aluminium skiff was tied up, and García parked right across from it. He kept the engine running.

Stranahan tried to open the door, but García had it locked with a button on the driver's side.

The detective punched the lighter knob in the dashboard and said, 'Don't you have anything else you want to ask? Think real hard, Mick.'

Stranahan reached across and earnestly shook García's hand. 'Thanks for everything, Al. I mean it.'

'Hey, are we having the same conversation? What the fuck is the matter with you?'

Stranahan said, 'It's been a depressing week.'

'Don't you even want to know what the waitresses and the pump jockey really said? About the guy with Chloe?'

'What guy?'

García clapped his hands. 'Good, I got your attention. Excellent!' He pulled the lighter from the dash and fired up the cigar.

'What guy?' Stranahan asked again.

Making the most of the moment, García took his notebook from his jacket and read aloud: 'White male, early thirties, approximately seven feet tall, two hundred fifty pounds, freckled, balding—'

'Holy shit.'

'—appeared to be wearing fright make-up, or possibly some type of Halloween mask. The waitresses couldn't agree on what, but they all said basically the same thing about the face. Said it looked like somebody dragged it across a cheese grater.'

Mick Stranahan couldn't recall putting anybody in jail who matched that remarkable description. He asked García if he had any leads.

'We're busy calling the circuses to see who's escaped

lately,' the detective said sarcastically. 'I swear, I don't know why I tell you anything.'

He pushed the button to unlock the doors. 'We'll be in touch,' he said to Stranahan, waving him out of the police car. 'And stay away from the damn doctor, OK?'

'You bet,' said Mick Stranahan. All he could think of was: *Seven feet tall*. Poor Chloe.

Dr Rudy Graveline now accepted the possibility that his world was imploding, and that he must prepare for the worst. Bitterly he thought of all the crises he had survived, all the professional setbacks, the lawsuits, the peer review hearings, the hospital expulsions, the hasty relocations from one jurisdiction to another. There was the time he augmented the breasts of a two-hundred-pound woman who had wanted a reduction instead; the time he nearly liposuctioned a man's gall bladder right out of his abdomen; the time he mistakenly severed a construction worker's left ear while removing a dime-sized cyst – Rudy Graveline had survived all these. He believed he'd found safe haven in South Florida; having figured out the system, and how to beat it, he was sure he had it made. And suddenly a botched nose job had come back to spoil it all. It didn't seem fair.

Rudy sat at his desk and leafed dispiritedly through the most recent bank statements. The Whispering Palms surgical complex was raking in money, but the overhead was high and the mortgage was a killer. Rudy had not been able to siphon off nearly as much as he had hoped. Once his secret plan had been to retire in four years with six million put away; it now seemed likely that he would be forced to get out much sooner, and with much less.

Having already been banned from practising medicine in California and New York – by far the most lucrative markets for a plastic surgeon – Rudy Graveline's thoughts now turned to the cosmopolitan cities of South America, a new frontier of vanity, sun-baked and ripe with wrinkles; a place where a Harvard medical degree still counted for something. Riffling through his CDs, he wondered if it was too late to weasel out of the Old Cypress Towers project: get liquid and get gone.

He was studying a map of Brazil when Heather Chappell, the famous actress, came into the office. She wore the pink terrycloth robe and bath slippers that Whispering Palms provided to all its VIP guests. Heather's lipstick was candy apple, her skin had a caramel tan, and her frosted blonde hair was thick and freshly brushed. She was a perfectly beautiful thirty-year-old woman who, for reasons unfathomable, despised her own body. A dream patient, as far as Rudy Graveline was concerned.

She sat in a low-backed leather chair and said, 'I've had it with the spa. Let's talk about my operation.'

Rudy said, 'I wanted you to unwind for a couple days, that's all.'

'It's been a couple days.'

'But aren't you more relaxed?'

'Not really,' Heather said. 'Your masseur, what's-his-name—'

'Niles?'

'Yeah, Niles. He tried to cornhole me yesterday. Aside from that, I've been bored to tears.'

Rudy smiled with practised politeness. 'But you've had a chance to think about the different procedures.'

'I didn't need to think about anything, Dr Graveline. I

was ready the first night off the plane. Have you been dodging me?'

'Of course not.'

'I heard your car got blown up.' She said it in a schoolgirl's voice, like it was gossip she'd picked up in study hall.

Rudy tried to neutralize his inflection. 'There was an accident,' he said. 'Very minor.'

'The night I came, wasn't it? That hunk in the parking lot, the guy who put me in the taxi. What's going on with him?'

Rudy ignored the question. 'I can schedule the surgery for tomorrow,' he said.

'Fine, but I want you to do it,' Heather said. 'You personally.'

'Of course,' Rudy said. He'd stay in the OR until they put her under, then he'd head for the back nine at Doral. Let one of the young hotshots do the knife work.

'What did you decide?' he asked her.

Heather stood up and stepped out of the slippers. Then she let the robe drop to the carpet. 'You tell me,' she said.

Rudy's mouth went dry at the sight of her.

'Well,' he said. 'Let's see.' The problem was, she didn't need any surgery. Her figure, like her face, was sensational. Her tan breasts were firm and large, not the least bit droopy. Her tummy was tight and flat as an iron. There wasn't an ounce of fat, a trace of a stretch mark, the slenderest serpentine shadow of a spider vein – not on her thighs, her legs, not anywhere. Nothing was out of proportion. Naked, Heather looked like an 'after', not a 'before'.

Rudy was really going to have to scramble on this

one. He put on his glasses and said, 'Come over here, Miss Chappell, let me take a closer look.'

She walked over and, to his stupefaction, climbed up on the onyx desk, her bare feet squeaking on the slick black surface. Standing, she vamped a movie pose – one hand on her hip, the other fluffing her hair. As Rudy's eyes travelled up those long legs, he nearly toppled over backwards in his chair.

'The nose, obviously,' Heather said.

'Yes,' said Rudy, thinking: She has a great straight nose. What the hell am I going to do?

'And the breasts,' Heather said, taking one in each hand and studying them. Like she was in the produce section, checking out the grapefruits.

Bravely Rudy asked, 'Would you like them larger or smaller?'

Heather glared at him. 'Bigger, of course! And brand new nipples.'

Jesus, Rudy muttered under his breath. 'Miss Chappell,' he said, 'I wouldn't advise new nipples. There could be serious complications and, really, it isn't necessary.' Little pink rosebuds, that's what her nipples looked like. Why, Rudy wondered, would she ever want new ones?

In a pouty voice, Heather said all right, leave the nipples. Then she pivoted on the desktop and patted her right thigh. 'I want two inches off here.'

'That much?' Rudy was sweating. He didn't see it, plain and simple. Two inches of what?

'Stand up,' Heather told him. 'Look here.'

He did, he looked hard. His chin was about three inches from her pubic bone. 'Two inches,' Heather repeated, turning to show him the other thigh, 'from both sides.'

'As you wish,' the doctor said. What the hell, he'd be on the golf course anyway. Let the whizz-kids figure it out.

Heather dropped to her knees on the desk, so the two of them were nearly face to face. 'And I want my eyelids done,' she said, pointing with a long cranberry finger-nail, 'and my neck, too. You said no scars, remember?'

'Don't worry,' Rudy assured her.

'Good,' Heather said. 'Anything else?'

'Not that I can see.'

'How about my butt?' She spun around on the desk, showing it to Rudy; looking over one shoulder, waiting for his professional opinion.

'Well,' said Rudy, running his fingers along the soft round curves.

'Hey,' said Heather, 'easy there.' She squirmed around to face him. 'Are you getting worked up?'

Rudy Graveline said, 'Of course not.' But he was. He couldn't figure it out, either; all the thousands of female bodies he got to see and feel. This was no ordinary lust, this was something fresh and wondrous. Maybe it was the way she bossed him around.

'I saw you in *Fevers of the Heart*,' Rudy said, idiotically. He had rented the cassette for a pool party. 'You were quite good, especially the scene on the horse.'

'Sit down,' Heather told him, and he did. She was bare-assed on the desk, legs swinging mischievously on either side of him. He put a clammy hand on each knee. 'Maybe now's a good time to talk about money,' she said.

For Rudy Graveline, the ultimate test of sobriety. In

his entire career he had never traded sex for his surgical services, never even discounted. Money was money, pussy was pussy – a credo he drilled into his sure-handed young assistants. Some things in life you just don't give away.

To Heather Chappell, he said, 'I'm afraid it's going to be expensive.'

'Is it?' She swung one leg up and propped her foot on his right shoulder.

'All these procedures at once, yes, I'm afraid so.'

'How much, Dr Graveline?'

Up came the other leg, and Rudy was scissored.

'Come here a second,' Heather said.

Rudy Graveline was torn between the thing he loved most and the thing he needed most: sex and money. The warm feel of Heather's bare heels on his shoulders was like the weight of the world. And heaven, too.

Her toes tickled his ears. 'I said, come here.'

'Where?' Rudy peeped, reaching out.

'God, are you blind?'

Chemo bought an Ingram sub-machine-gun to go with his .22 pistol. He got it from a man who had come to the club one night with a bunch of Jamaicans. The man himself was not a Jamaican; he was from Colombia. Chemo found this out when he stopped him at the door and told him he couldn't come inside the Gay Bidet with a machine-gun.

'But this is Miami,' the man had said with a Spanish accent.

'I've got my orders,' Chemo said.

The man agreed to let Chemo take the gun while he

and his pals went inside, which turned out to be a smart thing. As the band was playing a song called *Suck Till You're Sore*, a local skinhead gang went into a slam-dancing frenzy, and fights broke out all over the place. The Jamaicans took off, but the Colombian stayed behind to do battle. At one point he produced a pocket knife and tried to surgically remove the swastika tattoo off the proud but hairless chest of a teenaged skinhead. The band took a much-needed break while the Beach police rushed in for the arrests. Later, when Chemo spotted the Colombian in the back of the squad car, he tapped on the window and asked about the Ingram. The Colombian said keep it and Chemo said thanks, and slipped a twenty-dollar bill through the crack of the window.

The thing Chemo liked best about the Ingram was the shoulder strap. He put it on and showed it to his boss, Freddie, who said, 'Get the fuck outta here with that thing!'

The next day, January eighteenth, Chemo got up early and drove out to Key Biscayne. He knew it would be unwise to go to the same marina where he had taken Chloe, so he looked around for another boat place. He found one near the Marine Stadium, where they race the big Budweiser speedboats. At first a kid with badly bleached hair tried to rent him a twenty-foot Dusky for a hundred and ten dollars a day, plus a hundred and fifty security deposit. Chemo didn't have that kind of money.

'Got a credit card?' the kid asked.

'No,' said Chemo. 'What about that thing over there?'

'That's a jet ski,' the kid said.

It was designed like a waterbug with handlebars. You

drove it like a motorcycle, only standing up. This one was yellow, with the word *Kawasaki* on the front.

'You don't want to try it,' the kid with yellow hair said.

'Why not?'

'Because,' the kid said, laughing, 'you're too tall, man. Hit a wake, it'll snap your spine.'

Chemo figured the guy was just trying to talk him into renting something bigger, something he didn't need.

'How much is the jet ski?' he said.

'Twenty an hour, but you got to sign a waiver.' The kid was thinking that, as tall as this guy is, he doesn't look healthy enough to ride a jet ski; he looks kind of tapped-out and sickly, like he's been hanging from the wall of some dungeon for a couple months. The kid was thinking maybe he ought to ask if the guy knew how to swim, just in case.

Chemo handed him two twenties.

The kid said, 'I'll still need a deposit.'

Chemo said he didn't have any more money. The kid said he'd take Chemo's wristwatch, but Chemo said no, he didn't want to give it up. It was a Heuer diving watch, silver and gold links, made in Switzerland. Chemo had swiped it off a young architect who was overdosing in the men's room at the club. While the jerk was lying there in the stall, trying to swallow his tongue, Chemo grabbed his wrist and replaced the Heuer with his own thirty-dollar Seiko with the fake alligator band.

'No jet ski without a deposit,' said the kid with yellow hair.

'How about a gun?' Chemo said.

'What kind?'

Chemo showed him the .22 and the kid said OK,

since it was a Beretta he'd hang onto it. He stuck it in the front of his chinos and led Chemo to the jet ski. He showed Chemo how the choke and the throttle worked, and tossed him a bright red life vest.

'You can change in the shed,' the kid said.

'Change?'

'You got a swimsuit, right?' The kid hopped back on the dock and gave Chemo the keys. 'Man, you don't want to ride these things in heavy pants.'

'I guess not,' said Chemo, unbuckling his trousers.

A shrimper named Joey agreed to take Christina Marks anywhere she wanted. When she gave him a hundred-dollar bill, Joey looked at it and said, 'Where you going, Havana?'

'Stiltsville,' Christina said, climbing into the pungent shrimp boat. 'And I need a favour.'

'You bet,' said Joey, tossing off the ropes.

'After you drop me off, I need you to stay close. Just in case.'

Joey aimed the bow down the canal, toward the mouth of Norris Cut. 'In case what?' he asked.

'In case the man I'm going to see doesn't want me to stay.'

Joey grinned and said, 'I can't imagine that. Here, you want a beer?'

He motored down the ocean side of Key Biscayne in amiable silence. Christina stood next to him at the wheel, guardedly watching the swarm of hungry sea-gulls that wailed and dove behind the stern. When the shrimp boat passed the Cape Florida lighthouse at the tip of the island, Christina saw the stilt houses to the south.

'Which one?' Joey shouted over the engines. When Christina pointed, Joey smiled and gave her a crusty wink.

'What's that mean?'

'Him,' Joey said. 'Why didn't you say so?'

They were maybe two hundred yards off the radio towers and making the wide turn into the channel when Joey nudged Christina Marks and pointed with his chin. Up ahead, something swift and yellow was crossing one of the tidal flats, bouncing severely in the choppy water. It was an odd, gumdrop-shaped craft, and a tall pale figure appeared to be standing in the middle, holding on with both arms.

Joey eased back on the throttle to give way.

'I hate those fool things,' he said. 'Damn tourists don't know where the hell they're going.'

They watched it cross from the starboard side, no more than thirty yards ahead of them. Joey frowned and said, 'I'll be goddamned.' He snatched a rag from his tool box and wiped the salty film from the shrimp boat's windshield.

'Look,' he said to Christina. 'Now you've seen it all.'

The tall pale man driving the jet ski was nude except for his soggy Jockey shorts.

And black sunglasses.

And a gleaming wristwatch.

And an Ingram .45 sub-machine-gun strapped on his bare shoulder.

Christina Marks was astonished. 'What do you suppose he's doing out here with *that*?'

'Whatever the hell he wants,' said Joey the shrimper.

THIRTEEN

Earlier that day, Tina and two of her girlfriends had appeared at the stilt house in a borrowed Bayliner Capri. They saw Mick Stranahan sleeping on the roof beneath the windmill, the Remington shotgun at his side.

Tina's friends were alarmed. They voted to stay in the boat while Tina went up on the dock and approached the house.

'Richie wants me back,' she called to Stranahan.

He sat up and rubbed his eyes. 'What?'

'I said, Richie wants me back. I wanted you to be the first to know.'

'Why?' Stranahan said, his voice thick.

'So you could change my mind.'

Stranahan noticed that a seagull had crapped all over the shotgun while he was asleep. 'Damn,' he said under his breath. He took a black bandanna from the pocket of his jeans and wiped the gunstock.

'Well?' came Tina's voice from below. 'You going to change my mind or not?'

'How?'

'Sleep with me.'

'I already did,' Stranahan said.

'You know what I mean.'

'Go back to Richie,' Stranahan advised. 'If he hits you again, file charges.'

'Why are you so afraid?'

Stranahan slid butt-first down the grainy slope of the roof, to a spot from which Tina was visible in her tiny tangerine thong swimsuit.

'We've been over this,' Stranahan said to her.

'But I don't want to marry you,' she said. 'I promise. Even if you ask me afterwards, I'll say no – no matter how great it was. Besides, I'm not a waitress. You said all the others were waitresses.'

He groaned and said, 'Tina, I'm sorry. It just won't work.'

Now she looked angry. One of the other girls in the Bayliner turned on the radio and Tina snapped at her, told her to shut off the damn music. 'How do you know it won't work?' she said to Stranahan.

'I'm too old.'

'Bullshit.'

'And you're too young.'

'Double bullshit.'

'OK,' he said. 'Then name the Beatles.'

'What?' Tina forced a caustic laugh. 'Are you serious?'

'Dead serious,' Stranahan said, addressing her from the edge of the roof. 'If you can name all the Beatles, I'll make love to you right now.'

'I don't believe this,' Tina said. 'The fucking Beatles.'

Stranahan had done the math in his head: she was nineteen, which meant she had been born the same year that the band broke up.

'Well, there's Paul,' Tina said.

'Last name?'

'Come on!'

'Let's hear it.'

'McCartney, OK? I don't believe this.'

Stranahan said, 'Go on, you're doing fine.'

'Ringo,' Tina said. 'Ringo Starr. The drummer with the nose.'

'Good.'

'And then there's the guy who died. Lennon.'

'First name?'

'I know his son is Julian.'

'His son doesn't count.'

Tina said, 'Yeah, well, you're an asshole. It's *John*. John Lennon.'

Stranahan nodded appreciatively. 'Three down, one to go. You're doing great.'

Tina folded her arms and tried to think of the last Beatle. Her lips were pursed in a most appealing way, but Stranahan stayed on the roof. 'I'll give you a hint,' he said to Tina. 'Lead guitar.'

She looked up at him, triumph shining in her grey eyes. 'Harrison,' she declared. 'Keith Harrison!'

Muttering, Stranahan crabbed back up to his vantage beneath the legs of the windmill. Tina said some sharp things, all of which he deserved, and then got on the boat with her friends and headed back across the bay toward Dinner Key and, presumably, Richie.

Joey the shrimper spat over the transom and said, 'Well, there's your boy.'

Christina Marks frowned. Mick Stranahan lay naked in the shape of a T on the roof of the house. His tan legs were straight, and each arm was extended. He had a bandanna pulled down over his eyes to shield them from the white rays of the sun. Christina Marks thought he looked like the victim of a Turkish firing squad.

'He looks like Christ,' said Joey. 'Don't you think he looks like Christ? Christ without a beard, I mean.'

'Take me up to the house,' Christina said. 'Do you have a horn on this thing?'

'Hell, he knows we're here.'

'He's sleeping.'

'No, ma'am,' Joey said. 'You're wrong.' But he sounded the horn anyway. Mick Stranahan didn't stir.

Joey idled the shrimp boat closer. The tide was up plenty high, rushing sibilantly under the pilings of the house. Clutching a brown grocery bag, Christina stepped up on the dock and waved the shrimper away.

'Thanks very much.'

Joey said, 'You be sure to tell him what we saw. About that big freak on the water scooter.'

She nodded.

'Tell him first thing,' Joey said. He pulled back on the throttle and the old diesel moaned into reverse. The engine farted an odious cloud of blue smoke that enveloped Christina Marks. She coughed all the way up the stairs.

When she got to the main deck, Stranahan was sitting on the edge of the roof, legs dangling.

'What's in the bag?'

'Cold cuts, wine, cheese. I thought you might be hungry.'

'This how they do it in New York?'

The sack was heavy, but Christina didn't put it down. She held it like a baby, with both arms, but not too tightly. She didn't want him to think it was a chore. 'What are you talking about?'

'The wine and cheese,' Stranahan said. 'There's a sense of ceremony about it. Maybe it's necessary where you come from, but not here.'

'Fuck you,' said Christina Marks. 'I'm on expense account, hotshot.'

Stranahan smiled. 'I forgot.' He hopped off the roof and landed like a cat. She followed him into the house and watched him slip into blue jean cutoffs, no underwear. She put the bag on the kitchen counter and he went to work, fixing lunch. From the refrigerator he got some pickles and a half pound of big winter shrimp, still in the shell.

As he opened the wine, he said, 'Let's get right to it: you've heard something.'

'Yes,' Christina said. 'But first: you won't believe what we just saw. A man with a machine-gun, on one of those water-jet things.'

'Where?'

She motioned with her chin. 'Not even a mile from here.'

'What did he look like?'

Christina described him. Stranahan popped the cork.

'I guess we better eat fast,' he said. He was glad he'd brought the shotgun down from the roof after Tina and her friends had left, when he went to find a fresh bandanna. Subconsciously he glanced at the Remington, propped barrel-up in the corner of the same wall with the stuffed marlin head.

Christina peeled a shrimp, dipped it tail-first into a plastic thimble of cocktail sauce. 'Are you going to tell me who he is, the man in the underwear?'

'I don't know,' Stranahan said. 'I honestly don't. Now tell me what else.'

This would be the most difficult part. She said, 'I went to see your friend Tim Gavigan at the hospital.'

'Oh.'

'I was there when he died.'

Stranahan cut himself three fat slices of cheddar. 'Extreme unction,' he said. 'Too bad you're not a priest.'

'He wanted me to tell you something. Something he remembered about the Vicky Barletta case.'

With a mouthful of cheese, Stranahan said, 'Tell me you didn't take that asshole up to the VA. Flemm – you didn't let him have a crack at Timmy in that condition, did you?'

'Of course not,' she said sharply. 'Now listen: Tim Gavigan remembered that the plastic surgeon has a brother. George Graveline. He saw him working outside the clinic.'

'Doing what?' Stranahan asked.

'This is what Tim wanted me to tell you. The guy is a tree trimmer. He said you'd know what that means. He was going on about Hoffa and dead bodies.'

Stranahan laughed. 'Yeah, he's right. It's perfect.'

Impatiently Christina said, 'You want to fill me in?'

Stranahan chomped on a pickle. 'You know what a wood chipper is? It's like a king-sized sideways Cuisinart, except they use it to shred wood. Tree companies tow them around like a U-Haul. Throw the biggest branches down this steel chute and they come out sawdust and barbecue chips.'

'Now I get it,' Christina said.

'Something can pulverize a mahogany tree, think of what it could do to a human body.'

'I'd rather not.'

'There was a famous murder case up in New Jersey, they had everything but the corpse. The corpse was ground up in a wood chipper so basically all they found was splinters of human bone – not enough for a good forensic ID. Finally somebody found a molar, and the tooth had a gold filling. That's how they made the case.'

Christina was still thinking about bone splinters.

'At any rate,' Stranahan said, 'it's a helluva good lead. Hurry now, finish up.' He wedged the cork into the half-empty wine bottle and started wrapping the leftover cold cuts and cheese in wax paper. Christina was reaching for one last shrimp when he snatched the dish away and put it in the refrigerator.

'Hey!'

'I said hurry.'

She noticed how deliberately he was moving, and it struck her that something was happening. 'What is it, Mick?'

'You mean you don't hear it?'

Christina said no.

'Just listen,' he said, and before she knew it the stilt house was shuttered, and the door closed, and the two of them were alone in the corner of the bedroom, sitting on the wooden floor. At first the only sound Christina Marks heard was the two of them breathing, and then came some scratching noises that Stranahan said were seagulls up on the roof. Finally, when she leaned her head against the plywood wall, she detected a far-away hum. The longer she listened, the more distinct it became. The pitch of the motor was too weak to be an aeroplane and too high to be much of a boat.

'Jesus, it's him,' she said with a tremble.

Stranahan acknowledged the fact with a frown. 'You know,' he said, 'this used to be a pretty good neighbourhood.'

Chemo wondered about the Ingram, about the effects of salt spray on the firing mechanism. He didn't know much about machine-guns, but he suspected that it was best not to get them wet. The ride out to Stiltsville had been wetter than he'd planned.

He parked the jet ski beneath one of the other stilt houses to wait for the shrimp boat to leave Mick Stranahan's place. He saw a good-looking woman in a white cottony top and tan safari shorts hop off the shrimp boat and go upstairs, so Chemo began to work her into the scenario. He didn't know if she was a wife or a girlfriend or what, but it didn't matter. She was there, and she had to die. End of story.

Chemo prised open a toolshed and found a rag for the Ingram. Carefully he wiped off the moisture and salt. The gun looked fine, but there was only one way to be sure. He took an aluminium mop handle from the shed and busted the padlock off the door of the house. Once inside, he quickly found a target: an old convertible sofa, its flowered fabric showing traces of mould and mildew. Chemo shut the door to trap the noise. Then he knelt in front of the sofa, put the Ingram to his shoulder and squeezed off three rounds. Dainty puffs of white fuzz and dust rose with the impact of each bullet. Chemo lowered the gun and carefully examined the .45-calibre holes in the cushions.

Now he was ready. He slung the gun strap over his shoulder and pulled his soggy Jockey shorts up snugly on his waist. He was about to go when he thought of something. Quickly he moved through the house, opening doors until he found a bathroom.

At the sink Chemo took off his sunglasses and put his face to the mirror. With a forefinger he tested the tiny pink patch of flesh that Dr Rudy Graveline had derma-braded. The patch no longer stung; in fact, it seemed to be coming along nicely. Chemo was extremely pleased, and ventured forth in bright spirits.

Someplace, maybe it was *Reader's Digest*, he had read that salt water actually expedited the healing process.

'Don't move,' Mick Stranahan whispered.

'I wasn't planning on it.'

'Unless I tell you.'

From the hum of the engine, Christina Marks guessed that the jet ski was very close: no more than thirty yards.

Stranahan held the shotgun across his knees. She looked at his hands and noticed they were steady. Hers were shaking like an old drunk's.

'Do you have a plan?' she asked.

'Basically, my plan is to stay alive.'

'Are you going to shoot him?'

Stranahan looked at her as if she were five years old. 'Now what do you think? *Of course* I'm going to shoot him. I intend to blow the motherfucker's head off, unless you've got some objection.'

'Just asking,' Christina said.

*

Chemo was thinking: Damn Japanese.

Whoever designed these jet skis must have been a frigging dwarf.

His back was killing him; he had to hunch over like a washerwoman to reach the handlebars. Every time he hit a wave, the gun strap slipped off his bony shoulder. A couple times he thought for sure he'd lost the Ingram, or at least broken it. Damn Japanese.

As he approached Stranahan's stilt house, Chemo started thinking something else. He had already factored the girl into the scenario, figured he'd shoot her first and get it over with. But then he realized he had another problem: surely she had seen him ski past the shrimp boat, probably noticed the machine-gun, probably told Stranahan.

Who had probably put it together.

So Chemo anticipated a fight. Screw the element of surprise; the damn jet scooter was as loud as a Harley. Stranahan could hear him coming two miles away.

But where was he?

Chemo circled the stilt house slowly, eventually riding the curl of his own wake. The windows were down, the door shut. No sign of life, except for a pair of ratty-looking gulls on the roof.

A thin smile of understanding came to his lips. Of course – the man was waiting inside. A little ambush action.

Chemo coasted the jet ski up to the dock and stepped off lightly. He took the Ingram off his shoulder and held it in front of him as he went up the stairs, thinking: Where's the logical place for Stranahan to be waiting? In a corner, of course.

He was pleased to find that the wooden deck went

around Stranahan's entire house. Walking cautiously on storklike legs, Chemo approached the south-west corner first. Calmly he fired one shot, waist level, through the wall. He repeated the same procedure at each of the other corners, then sat on the rail of the deck and waited. When nothing happened after three minutes, he walked up to the front door and fired twice more.

Then he went in.

Christina Marks was not aware that Stranahan had been hit until she felt something warm on her bare arm. She opened her mouth to scream but Stranahan covered it with his hand and motioned for her to be quiet. She saw that his eyes were watering from the pain of the bullet wound. He removed his hand from her mouth and pointed at his left shoulder. Christina nodded but didn't look.

They heard three more gunshots, each in a different part of the house. Then came a silence that lasted a few agonizing minutes. Finally Stranahan rose to his feet with the shotgun cradled in his right arm. The left side of his body was numb and wet with blood; in the twilight of the shuttered house, he looked two-tone.

From the floor Christina watched him move. He pressed his back to the wall and edged toward the front of the house. The next shots made Christina shut her eyes. When she opened them she saw two perfect holes through the front door; twin sunbeams, sharp as lasers, perforated the shadows. Beneath the light shafts, Mick Stranahan lay prone on his belly, elbows braced on the wooden floor. He was aiming at the front door when Chemo opened it.

Stranahan's shotgun was a Remington 1100, a semi-automatic twelve-gauge, an excellent bird gun that holds up to five shells. Later, when Stranahan measured the distance from the door to where he had lain, he would marvel at how any human being with two good eyes could miss a seven-foot target at a distance of only nineteen feet four inches. The fact that Stranahan was bleeding to death at the time was not, in his view, a mitigating excuse.

In truth, it was the shock of the intruder's appearance that had caused Stranahan to hesitate – the sight of this gaunt, pellucid, frizzle-haired freak with a moonscape face that could stop a freight train.

So Stranahan had stared for a nanosecond when he should have squeezed the trigger. For someone who looked so sickly, Chemo moved deceptively fast. As he dove out of the doorway, the first blast from the Remington sprinkled its rain of birdshot into the bay.

'Shit,' Stranahan said, struggling to his feet. On his way toward the door he slipped on his own blood and went down again, his right cheek slamming hard on the floor; this, just as Chemo craned around the corner and fired a messy burst from the Ingram. Rolling in a sticky mess, Stranahan shot back.

Chemo slammed the door from the outside, plunging the house into darkness once more.

Stranahan heard the man running on the outside deck, following the apron around the house. Stranahan took aim through the walls. He imagined that the man was a rising quail, and he led accordingly. The first blast tore a softball-sized hole in the wall of the living room. The second punched out the shutter in the kitchen. The third and final shot was followed by a grunt and a splash outside.

'Christina!' Stranahan shouted. 'Quick, help me up.'

But when she got there, biting back tears, crawling on bare knees, he had already passed out.

Chemo landed on his back in the water. He kicked his legs just to make sure he wasn't paralysed; other than a few splinters in his scalp, he seemed to be fine. He figured that the birdshot must have missed him, that the concussion so close to his head was what threw him off balance.

Instinctively he held the Ingram high out of the water with his right hand, and paddled furiously with his left. He knew he had to make it under cover of the house before Stranahan came out; otherwise he'd be a sitting duck. Chemo saw that the machine-gun was dripping, so he figured it must have gotten dunked in the fall. Would it still fire? And how many rounds were left? He had lost count.

These were his concerns as he made for the pilings beneath the stilt house. Progress was maddeningly slow; by paddling with only one hand, Chemo tended to move himself in a frothy circle. In frustration he paddled more frenetically, a tactic that decreased the perimeter of his route but brought him no closer to safety. He expected at any second to see Stranahan burst onto the deck with the shotgun.

Beneath Chemo there appeared in the water a long grey-blue shadow, which hung there as if frozen in glass. It was Stranahan's silent companion, Liza, awakened from its afternoon siesta by the wild commotion.

A barracuda this age is a creature of sublime instinct and flawless precision, an eating machine more calculating and efficient than any shark in the ocean. Over time the great barracuda had come to associate human activity with feeding; its impulses had been tuned by Stranahan's evening pinfish ritual. As Chemo struggled in the shallows, the barracuda was on full alert, its cold eyes trained upward in anticipation. The blue-veined legs that kicked impotently at its head, the spastic thrashing – these posed no threat.

Something else had caught its attention: the familiar rhythmic glint of stunned prey on the water's surface. The barracuda struck with primitive abandon, streaking up from the deep, slashing, then boring back toward the pilings.

There, beneath the house, the great fish flared its crimson gills in a darkening sulk. What it had mistaken for an easy meal of silver pinfish turned out to be no such thing, and the barracuda spat ignominiously through its fangs.

It was a testimony to sturdy Swiss craftsmanship that the Heuer diving watch was still ticking when it came to rest on the bottom. Its stainless silver and gold links glistened against Chemo's pale severed hand, which reached up from the turtle grass like some lost piece of mannequin.

FOURTEEN

On Washington Avenue there was a small shop that sold artificial limbs. Dr Rudy Graveline went there on his lunch hour and purchased four different models of prosthetic hands. He paid cash and made sure to get a receipt.

Later, back at Whispering Palms, he arranged the artificial hands in an attractive row on the top of his onyx desk.

'What about this one?' he asked Chemo.

'It's a beaut,' Chemo said trenchantly, 'except I've already got one on *that* arm.'

'Sorry.' Rudy Graveline picked up another. 'Then look here – state-of-the-art technology. Four weeks of therapy, you can deal blackjack with this baby.'

'Wrong colour,' Chemo remarked.

Rudy glanced at the artificial hand and thought: Of course it's the wrong colour, they're *all* the wrong damn colour. 'It's a tough match,' the doctor said. 'I looked for the palest one they had.'

'I hate them all,' Chemo said. 'Why does it have to be a hand, anyway?'

'You didn't like the mechanical hooks,' Rudy Graveline reminded him. 'Talk about advanced, you could load a gun, even type with those things. But you said no.'

'Damn right I said no.'

Rudy put down the prosthesis and said: 'I wish you wouldn't take that tone with me. I'm doing the best I can.'

'Oh, yeah.'

'Look, didn't I advise you to see a specialist?'

'And didn't I advise you, you're crazy? The cops'll be hunting all over.'

'All right,' Rudy said in a calming voice. 'Let's not argue.'

It had been three weeks since Chemo had shown up behind Whispering Palms on a blood-streaked water scooter – a vision that Dr Rudy Graveline would carry with him for the rest of his life. It had happened during an afternoon consult with Mrs Carla Crumworthy, heiress to the Crumworthy panty-shield fortune. She had come to complain about the collagen injections that Rudy Graveline had administered to give her full, sensual lips, which is just what every rheumatoid seventy-one-year-old woman needs. Mrs Crumworthy had lamented that the results were nothing like she had hoped, that she now resembled one of those Ubangi tribal women from the *National Geographic*, the ones with the ceramic platters in their mouths. And, in truth, Dr Rudy Graveline was concerned about what had happened, because Mrs Crumworthy's lips had indeed grown bulbous and unwieldy and hard as cobblestones. As he examined her (keeping his doubts to himself), Rudy wondered if maybe he had injected too much collagen, or not enough, or if maybe he'd zapped it into the wrong spots. Whatever the cause, the result was undeniable: Mrs Carla Crumworthy looked like a duck wearing mauve lipstick. A malpractice jury could have a ball with this one.

Dr Graveline had been whisking through his trusty Rolodex, searching for a kind-hearted colleague, when Mrs Crumworthy suddenly rose to her feet and shrieked. Pointing out the picture window toward Biscayne Bay, the old woman had blubbered in terror, her huge misshapen lips slapping together in wet percussion. Rudy had no idea what she was trying to say.

He spun around and looked out the window.

The yellow jet ski lay on its side, adrift in the bay. Somehow Chemo had dragged himself, soaking wet and stark naked, over the ledge of the seawall behind the clinic. He didn't look well enough to be dead. His grey shoulders shivered violently in the sunshine, and his eyes flickered vaguely through puffy purple slits. Chemo swung the bloody stump to show Dr Graveline what had happened to his left hand. He pointed gamely at the elastic wrist tourniquet that he had fashioned from his Jockey shorts, and Rudy would later concede that it had probably saved his life.

Mrs Carla Crumworthy was quickly ushered to a private recovery suite and oversedated, while Rudy and two young assistant surgeons led Chemo to an operating room. The assistants argued that he belonged at a real trauma centre in a real hospital, but Chemo adamantly refused. This left the doctors with no choice but to operate or let him bleed to death.

Gently discouraged from participating in the surgery, Rudy had been content to let the young fellows work unimpeded. He spent the time making idle conversation with the woozy Chemo, who had rejected a general anaesthetic in favour of an old-fashioned intravenous jolt of Demerol.

Since that evening, Chemo's post-op recovery had progressed swiftly and in relative luxury, with the entire staff of Whispering Palms instructed to accommodate his every wish. Rudy Graveline himself was exceedingly attentive, as he needed Chemo's loyalty now more than ever. He had hoped that the killer's spirits would improve at the prospect of reconstructing his abbreviated left arm.

'A new hand,' Rudy said, 'would be a major step back to a normal life.'

'I never had a normal life,' Chemo pointed out. Sure, he would miss the hand, but he was more pissed off about losing the expensive wristwatch.

'What are my other options?' Chemo asked.

'What do you mean?'

'I mean, besides these things.' He waved his stump contemptuously at the artificial hands.

'Well,' Rudy said, 'frankly, I'm out of ideas.' He gathered the prostheses from his desk and put them back in the box. 'I told you, this isn't my field,' he said to Chemo.

'You keep trying to dump me off on some other surgeon, but it won't work. It's you or nobody.'

'I appreciate your confidence,' Rudy said. He leaned forward in his chair and put on his glasses. 'Can I ask, what's that on your face?'

Chemo said, 'It's Wite-Out.'

After a careful pause, Dr Graveline said, 'Can I ask—'

'I thought I might go out to the club later. I wanted to cover up these darn patches.'

Out of pity Rudy had agreed to dermabrade several more one-inch squares along Chemo's chin.

'You covered them with Wite-Out?'

Chemo said, 'Your secretary loaned me a bottle. The colour's just right.'

Rudy cleared his throat. 'It's not so good for your skin. Please, let me prescribe a mild cosmetic ointment.'

'Forget it,' said Chemo. 'This'll do fine. Now what about a new thing for my arm?' With his right hand he gestured at the bandaged limb.

Rudy folded his hands in his lap, a relaxed gesture that damn near exuded professional confidence. 'As I said before, we've gone over most of the conventional options.'

Chemo said, 'I don't like therapy. I want something easy to use, something practical.'

'I see,' said Rudy Graveline.

'And durable, too.'

'Of course.'

'Also, I don't want people to stare.'

Rudy thought: Beautiful. A seven-foot, one-handed geek with Wite-Out painted on his face, and he's worried about people staring.

'So what do you think?' Chemo pressed.

'I think,' said Dr Rudy Graveline, 'we've got to use our imaginations.'

Detective John Murdock bent his squat, porky frame over the rail of the hospital bed and said, 'Wake up, fuckwad.'

Which was pretty much his standard greeting.

Mick Stranahan did not open his eyes.

'Get out of here,' said Christina Marks.

Detective Joe Salazar lit a Camel and said, 'You don't look like a nurse. Since when do nurses wear blue jeans?'

'Good point,' said John Murdock. 'I think you're the one should get out of here.'

'Yeah,' said Joe Salazar. 'We got official business with this man.' Salazar was as short as his partner, only built like a stop sign. Flat, florid face stuck on a pipestem body.

'Now I know who you are,' Christina said. 'You must be Murdock and Salazar, the crooked cops.'

Stranahan nearly busted out laughing, but he pressed his eyes closed, trying to look asleep.

'I see what we got here,' said Murdock. 'What we got here is some kinda Lily Tomlin.'

'Sure,' said Joe Salazar, though he didn't know who his partner was talking about. He assumed it was somebody they'd arrested together. 'Sure,' he chimed in, 'a regular Lily Thomas.'

Christina Marks said, 'The man's asleep, so why don't you come back another time?'

'And why don't you go change your tampon or something?' snapped John Murdock. 'We've got business here.'

'We got questions,' Joe Salazar added. When he took the Camel cigarette out of his mouth, Christina noticed, the end was all soggy and mulched.

She said, 'I was there when it happened, if you want to ask me about it.'

Salazar had brought a Xerox of the marine patrol incident report. He took it out of his jacket, unfolded it, ran a sticky brown finger down the page until he came to the box marked Witnesses. 'So you're Initial C. Marks?'

'Yes,' Christina said.

'We've been looking all over Dade County for you. Two, three weeks we've been looking.'

'I changed hotels,' she said. She had moved from Key Biscayne over to the Grove, to be closer to Mercy Hospital.

John Murdock, the senior of the two detectives, took a chair from the corner, twirled it around, and sat down straddling it.

'Just like in the movies,' Christina said. 'You think better, sitting with your legs like that?'

Murdock glowered. 'What suppose we just throw your tight little ass in the women's annexe for a night or two, would you enjoy that? Just you and all the hookers, maybe a lesbo or two.'

'Teach you some manners,' Joe Salazar said, 'and that's not all.'

Christina smiled coolly. 'And here I thought you boys wanted a friendly chat. Maybe I'll just call hospital security and tell them what's going on up here. After that, maybe I'll call the newspapers.'

Mick Stranahan was thinking: She'd better be careful. These guys aren't nearly as dumb as they look.

Murdock said, 'One time we booked a big lesbo looked just like Kris Kristofferson. I'm not kidding, we're talking major facial hair. And mean as a bobcat.'

'Resisting with violence, two counts,' Salazar recalled. 'On top of the murder.'

'Manslaughter,' John Murdock cut in. 'Actually, womanslaughter, if there is such a thing. Jesus, what a mess. I can't even think about it, so close to lunch.'

'Involved a fire hose,' Salazar said.

'I said enough,' Murdock protested. 'Anyhow, I think she's still in the annexe. The one who looks like Kristofferson. I think she runs the drama group.'

Salazar said, 'You like the theatre, Miss Marks?'

'Sure,' Christina said, 'but mainly I like television. You guys ever been on TV? Maybe you've heard of the Reynaldo Flemm show.'

'Yeah,' Joe Salazar said, excitedly. 'One time I saw him get his ass pounded by a bunch of Teamsters. In slow motion, too.'

'*That* asshole,' Murdock muttered.

'We finally agree,' Christina said. 'Unfortunately, he happens to be my boss. We're in town taping a big story.'

The two detectives glanced at one another, trying to decide on a plan without saying it. Salazar stalled by lighting up another Camel.

Lying in bed listening, Mick Stranahan figured they'd back off now, just to be safe. Neither of these jokers wanted to see his own face on primetime TV.

Murdock said, 'So tell us what happened.' Salazar stood in the empty corner, resting his fat head against the wall.

Christina said, 'You've got photographic memories, or maybe you'd prefer to take some notes?' Murdock motioned to his partner, who angrily stubbed out his cigarette and dug a worn spiral notebook from his jacket.

She began with what she had seen from the wheelhouse of Joey's shrimp boat – the tall man toting a machine-gun on the jet scooter. She told the detectives about how Stranahan had battened down the stilt house, and how the man had started shooting into the corners. She told them how Stranahan had been wounded in the shoulder, and how he had fired back with a shotgun until he passed out. She told them she had heard a splash outside, then a terrible cry; ten, maybe fifteen minutes later she'd heard somebody rev up the jet ski, but she was too scared to go to a window. Only when the engine was a faint whine in the distance did she peer through the bullet holes in the front door to see if the gunman had gone. She told the detectives how she had half-carried Stranahan down the stairs to where his skiff was docked, and how she had hand-cranked the outboard by herself. She told them how he had groggily pointed across the bay and said there was a big hospital on the mainland, and by the time they got to Mercy there was so much blood in the bottom of the skiff that she was bailing with a coffee mug.

After Christina had finished, Detective John Murdock said, 'That's quite a story. I bet *Argosy* magazine would go for a story like that.'

Joe Salazar leafed through his notebook and said, 'I think I missed something, lady. I think I missed the part where you explained why you're at Stranahan's house in the first place. Maybe you could repeat it.'

Murdock said, 'Yeah, I missed that, too.'

'I'd be happy to tell you why I was there,' Christina said. 'Mr Flemm wanted Mr Stranahan to be interviewed for an upcoming broadcast, but Mr Stranahan declined. I went to his house in the hopes of changing his mind.'

'I'll bet,' Salazar said.

'Joe, be nice,' said his partner. 'Tell me, Miss Marks, why'd you want to interview some dweeb PI? I mean, he's nobody. Hasn't been with the State Attorney for years.'

From his phoney coma Stranahan wondered how far Christina Marks would go. Not too far, he hoped.

'The interview involved a story we were working on, and that's all I can say.'

Murdock said, 'Gee, I hope it didn't concern a murder.'

'I really can't—'

'Because murder is our main concern. Me and Joe.'

Christina Marks said, 'I've co-operated as much as I can.'

'And you've been an absolute peach about it,' said Murdock. 'Fact, I almost forgot why we came in the first place.'

'Yeah,' said Detective Joe Salazar, 'the questions we got, you can't really answer. Thanks just the same.'

Murdock slid the chair back to the corner. 'See, we need to talk to Rip Van Rambo here. So I think you'd better go.' He smiled for the first time. 'And I apologize for that wisecrack about the Kotex. Not very professional, I admit.'

'It was tampons,' Joe Salazar said.

'Whatever.'

Christina Marks said, 'I'm not leaving this room. This man is recovering from a serious gunshot wound and you shouldn't disturb him.'

'We spoke to his doctor—'

'You're lying.'

'OK, we put in a call. The guy never called back.'

Salazar walked up to the hospital bed and said, 'He don't look so bad. Anyway, three weeks is plenty of time. Wake him up, Johnny.'

'Have it your way,' Christina said. She got a legal pad from her shoulder bag, uncapped a felt-tip pen, and sat down, poised to write.

'Now what the hell are you doing?' Salazar said.

'Forget about her,' Murdock said. He leaned close to Stranahan's face and sang, 'Mi-ick? Mick, buddy? Rise and shine.'

Stranahan growled sleepily, blowing a mouthful of stale, hot breath directly into Murdock's face.

'Holy Christ,' the detective said, turning away.

Salazar said, 'Johnny, I swear he's awake.' He cupped his hand at Stranahan's ear and shouted: '*Hey, fuck-wood, you awake?*'

'Knock it off,' Christina said.

'I know how you can tell,' Salazar went on. 'Grab his dick. If he's asleep, he won't do nothing. If he's awake he'll jump ten feet out of this frigging bed.'

Murdock said, 'Aw, you're crazy.'

'You think he'd let one of us grab his schlong if he was wide awake? I'm telling you, Johnny, it's a sure way to find out.'

'OK, you do it.'

'Nuh-uh, we flip a coin.'

'Screw you, Joe. I ain't touching the man's privates. The country doesn't pay me enough.'

Stranahan was lying there, thinking: Thattaboy, Johnny, stick to the book.

From the corner Christina said, 'Lay a finger on him, I'll see that Mr Stranahan sues the living hell out of both of you. When he wakes up.'

'Not that old line,' Salazar said with a laugh.

She said, 'Beat the shit out of some jerk on the street, that's one thing. Grab a man's sexual organs while he's lying unconscious in a hospital bed – try to get the union worked up about *that*. You guys just kiss your pensions goodbye.'

Murdock shot Christina Marks a bitter look. 'When he wakes up, you be sure to tell him something. Tell him we know he drowned his ex-wife, so don't be surprised if we show up in Stiltsville with a waterproof warrant. Tell him he'd be smart to sell that old house, too, case a storm blows it down while he's off at Raiford.'

With secretarial indifference, Christina jotted every word on the legal pad. Murdock snorted and stalked out the door. Joe Salazar followed two steps behind, pocketing his own notebook, fumbling for a fresh Camel.

'Lady,' he said out the side of his mouth, 'you got to learn some respect for authority.'

That weekend, a notorious punk band called the Fudge Packers was playing the Gay Bidet. Freddie didn't like them at all. There were fights every night; the skinheads, the Latin Kings, the 34th Street Players. This is what Freddie couldn't understand: why the spooks and spics even showed up for a band like this. Usually they had better taste. The Fudge Packers were simply dreadful – four frigging bass guitars, now what the hell kind of music was that? No wonder everybody was fighting: take their minds off the noise.

Since Chemo had disappeared, Freddie had hired a new head bouncer named Eugene, guy used to play in the World Football League. Eugene was all right, big as a garbage dumpster, but he couldn't seem to get people's attention the way Chemo did. Also, he was slow.

Sometimes it took him five minutes to get down off the stage and pound heads in the crowd. By comparison Chemo had moved like a cat.

Freddie also was worried about Eugene's pro-labour leanings. One week at the Gay Bidet and already he was complaining about how loud the music was, could they please turn it down? You're kidding, Freddie had said, turn it down? But Eugene said damn right, his eardrums were fucking killing him. He said if his ears kept hurting he might go deaf and have to file a workman's comp, and Freddie said what's that? Then Eugene started going on about all his football injuries and, later, some shit that had happened to him working construction down in Homestead. He told Freddie about how the unions always took care of him, about how one time he was laid up for six weeks with a serious groin pull and never missed a paycheque. Not one.

Freddie could scarcely believe such a story. To him it sounded like something out of Communist Russia. He was delighted the night Chemo came back to work.

'Eugene, you're fired,' Freddie said. 'Go pull your groin someplace else.'

'What?' said Eugene, cocking his head and leaning closer.

'Don't pull that deaf shit with me,' Freddie warned. 'Now get lost.'

On his way out of Freddie's office, Eugene sized up his towering replacement. 'Man, what happened to you?'

'Gardening accident,' Chemo replied. Eugene grimaced sympathetically and said goodbye.

Freddie turned to Chemo. 'Thank God you're back. I'm afraid to ask.'

'Go ahead. Ask.'

'I don't think so,' Freddie said. 'Just tell me, you OK?'

Chemo nodded. 'Fine. The new band sounds like vomit.'

'Yeah, I know,' Freddie said. 'Geez, you should see the crowd. Be careful in there.'

'I'm ready for them,' Chemo said, hoisting his left arm to show Freddie the new device. He and Dr Rudy Graveline had found it on sale at a True Value hardware store.

'Wow,' said Freddie, staring.

'I got it rigged special for a six-volt battery,' Chemo explained. He patted the bulge under his arm. 'Strap it on with an Ace bandage. Only weighs about nine pounds.'

'Neat,' said Freddie, thinking: Sweet Jesus, this can't be what I think it is.

A short length of anodized aluminium piping protruded from the padding over Chemo's amputation. Bolted to the end of the pipe was a red saucer-sized disc made of hard plastic. Coiled tightly on a stem beneath the disc was a short length of eighty-pound monofilament fishing line.

Freddie said, 'OK, now I'm gonna ask.'

'It's a Weed Whacker,' Chemo said. 'See?'

FIFTEEN

George Graveline was sun-tanned and gnarled and sinewy, with breadloaf arms and wide black Elvis sideburns. The perfect tree trimmer.

George was not at all jealous of his younger brother, the plastic surgeon. Rudy deserved all the fine things in life, George reasoned, because Rudy had gone to college for what seemed like eternity. In George's view, no amount of worldly riches was worth sitting in a stuffy classroom for years at a stretch. Besides, he loved his job as a tree trimmer. He loved the smell of sawdust and fresh sap, and he loved gassing yellow jacket nests; he loved the whole damn outdoors. Even Florida winters could get miserably hot, but a person could adjust. George Graveline had a motto by which he faithfully lived: *Always park in the shade.*

He did not often see his wealthy brother, but that was all right. Dr Rudy was a busy man, and for that matter so was George. In Miami a good tree trimmer always had his hands full: year-round growth, no real seasons, no time for rest. Mainly you had your black olives and your common ficus tree, but the big problem there wasn't the branches so much as the roots. A twenty-year-old ficus had a root system could swallow the New York subway. Digging out a big ficus was a bitch. Then you had your exotics: the Australian pines, the mela-leucas, and those God-forsaken Brazilian pepper trees, which most people mistakenly called a holly. Things grew like fungus, but George loved them because the roots weren't so bad and a couple good men could rip one out of the ground, no sweat. His favourite, though, was when people wanted their Brazilian pepper trees trimmed. Invariably these were customers new to Florida, novice suburbanites who didn't have the heart or the brains to actually *kill* a living tree. So they'd ask George Graveline to please just trim it back a little, and George would say sure, no problem, knowing that in three months it'd shoot out even bushier than before and strangle their precious hibiscus as sure as a coathanger. No denying there was damn good money in the pepper-tree racket.

On the morning of February tenth, George Graveline and his crew were chopping a row of Australian pines off Krome Avenue to make room for a new medium-security federal prison. George and his men were not exactly busting their humps, since it was a government contract and nobody ever came by to check. George was parked in the shade, as usual, eating a roast-beef hoagie and drinking a tall Budweiser. The driver's door of the truck was open and the radio was on a country music station, though the only time you could hear the tunes was between the grinding roars of the wood chipper, which was hooked to the bumper of George Graveline's truck. The intermittent screech of the machine didn't disturb George at all; he had grown accustomed to hearing only fragments of Merle Haggard on the radio and to letting his imagination fill in the musical gaps.

Just as he finished the sandwich, George glanced in

the rear-view and noticed a big blond man with one arm in a sling. The man wore blue jeans, boots, and a flannel shirt with the left sleeve cut away. He was standing next to the wood chipper, watching George's crew chief toss pine stumps into the steel maw.

George swung out of the truck and said, 'Hey, not so close.'

The man obligingly took a step backward. 'That's some machine.' He gestured at the wood chipper. 'Looks brand new.'

'Had her a couple years,' George Graveline said. 'You looking for work?'

'Naw,' the man said, 'not with this bum wing. Actually I was looking for the boss. George Graveline.'

George wiped the hoagie juice off his hands. 'That's me,' he said.

The crew chief heaved another pine limb into the chipper. The visitor waited for the buzzing to stop, then he said, 'George, my name is Mick Stranahan.'

'Howdy, Mick.' George stuck out his right hand. Stranahan shook it.

'George, we don't know each other, but I feel like I can talk to you. Man to man.'

'Sure.'

'It's about your little brother.'

'Rudolph?' Warily George folded his big arms.

'Yes, George,' Stranahan said. 'See, Rudy's been trying to kill me lately.'

'Huh?'

'Can you believe it? First he hires some mobster to do the hit, now he's got the world's tallest white man with the world's worst case of acne. I don't know what to tell you, but frankly it's got me a little pissed off.' Stranahan looked down at his sling. 'This is from a .45-calibre machine-gun. Honestly, George, wouldn't you be upset, too?'

George Graveline rolled the tip of his tongue around the insides of his cheeks, like he was probing for a lost wad of Red Man. The crew chief automatically kept loading hunks of pine into the wood chipper, which spat them out the chute as splinters and sawdust. Stranahan motioned to George that they should go sit in the truck and talk privately, where it was more quiet.

Stranahan settled in on the passenger side and turned down the country music. George said, 'Look, mister, I don't know who you are but—'

'I told you who I am.'

'Your name is all you said.'

'I'm a private investigator, George, if that helps. A few years back I worked for the State Attorney. On murder cases, mostly.'

George didn't blink, just stared like a toad. Stranahan got a feeling that the man was about to punch him.

'Before you do anything incredibly stupid, George, listen for a second.'

George leaned out the door of the truck and hollered for the crew chief to take lunch. The whine of the wood chipper died, and suddenly the two men were drenched in silence.

'Thank you,' Stranahan said.

'So talk.'

'On March twelfth, 1986, your brother performed an operation on a young woman named Victoria Barletta. Something terrible happened, George, and she died on the operating table.'

'No way.'

'Your brother Rudy panicked. He'd already been in a shitload of trouble over his state medical licence – and killing a patient, well, that's totally unacceptable. Even in Florida. I think Rudy was just plain scared.'

George Graveline said, 'You're full of it.'

'The case came through my office as an abduction-possible-homicide. Everybody assumed the girl was snatched from a bus bench in front of your brother's clinic because that's what he told us. But now, George, new information has come to light.'

'What kind of information?'

'The most damaging kind,' Mick Stranahan said. 'And for some reason, your brother thinks that I am the one who's got it. But I'm not, George.'

'So I'll tell him to leave you alone.'

'That's very considerate, George, but I'm afraid it's not so simple. Things have gotten out of hand. I mean, look at my damn shoulder.'

'Mmmm,' said George Graveline.

Stranahan said, 'Getting back to the young woman. Her body was never found, not a trace. That's highly unusual.'

'It is?'

'Yes, it is.'

'So?'

'So, you wouldn't happen to know anything about what happened, would you?'

George said, 'You got some nerve.'

'Yes, I suppose I do. But how about answering the question?'

'How about this,' said George Graveline, reaching for Mick Stranahan's throat.

With his good arm Stranahan intercepted George's

toad-eyed lunge. He seized one of the tree-trimmer's stubby thumbs and twisted it clean out of the socket. It made a faintly audible pop, like a bottle of flat champagne. George merely squeaked as the colour flooded from his face. Stranahan let go of the limp purple thumb, and George pinched it between his knees, trying to squeeze away the pain.

'Boy, I'm really sorry,' Stranahan said.

George grabbed at himself and gasped, 'You get out of here!'

'Don't you want to hear the rest of my theory, the one I'm going to tell the cops? About how you tossed that poor girl's body into the wood chipper just to save your brother's butt?'

'Go on,' George Graveline cried, 'before I shoot you myself.'

Mick Stranahan got out of George's truck, shut the door and leaned in through the open window. 'I think you're overreacting,' he said to the tree trimmer. 'I really do.'

'Eat shit,' George replied, wheezing.

'Fine,' Stranahan said. 'I just hope you're not this rude to the police.'

Christina Marks was dreading her reunion with Reynaldo Flemm. They met at twelve-thirty in the lobby of the Sonesta.

She said, 'You've done something to your hair.'

'I let it grow,' Flemm said self-consciously. 'Where've you been, anyway? What's the big secret?'

Christina couldn't get over the way he looked. She circled him twice, staring.

'Ray, nobody's hair grows that fast.'

'It's been a couple weeks.'

'But it's all the way to your shoulders.'

'So what?'

'And it's so yellow.'

'Blond, goddammit.'

'And so . . . kinky.'

Stiffly, Reynaldo Flemm said, 'It was time for a new look.'

Christina Marks fingered his locks and said, 'It's a bloody wig.'

'Thank you, Agatha Christie.'

'Don't get sore,' she said. 'I kind of like it.'

'Really?'

Despairing of his physical appearance since his visit to Whispering Palms, Reynaldo Flemm had flown back to New York and consulted a famous colorologist, who had advised him that blond hair would make him look ten years younger. Then a make-up man at ABC had told Reynaldo that long hair would make his nose look thinner, while *kinked* long hair would take twenty pounds off his waist on camera.

Armed with this expert advice, Reynaldo had sought out Tina Turner's wig stylist, who was booked solid but happy to recommend a promising young protégé in the SoHo district. The young stylist's name was Leo, and he pretended to recognize Reynaldo Flemm from television, which was all the salesmanship he needed. Reynaldo told Leo the basics of what he wanted, and Leo led him to a seven-hundred-dollar wig that looked freshly hacked off the scalp of Robert Plant, the rock singer. Or possibly Dyan Cannon.

Reynaldo didn't care. It was precisely the look he was after.

'I do kind of like it,' Christina Marks said, 'only we've got to do something about the Puerto Rican moustache.'

Flemm said, 'The moustache stays. I've had it since my first local Emmy.' He put his hands on her shoulders. 'Now, suppose you tell me what the hell's been going on.'

Christina hadn't talked to Reynaldo since the day Mick Stranahan was shot, and then she had told him next to nothing. She had called from the emergency room at Mercy Hospital, and said something serious had happened. Reynaldo had asked if she were hurt, and Christina said no. Then Reynaldo had asked what was so damn serious, and she said it would have to wait for a few weeks, that the police were involved and the whole Barletta story would blow up if they didn't lay low. She had promised to get back to him in a few days, but all she did was leave a message in Reynaldo's box at the hotel. The message had begged him to be patient, and Reynaldo had thought what the hell and gone back to Manhattan to hunt for some new hair.

'So,' he said to Christina, 'let's hear it.'

'Over here,' she said, and led him to a booth in the hotel coffee shop. She waited until he'd stuffed a biscuit in his mouth before telling him about the shooting.

'Theesus!' Flemm exclaimed, spitting crumbs. He looked as if he were about to cry, and in fact he was. 'You got shot at? Really?'

Christina nodded uneasily.

'With a machine-gun? Honest to God?' Plaintively he added, 'Was it an Uzi?'

'I'm not sure, Ray.'

Christina knew his heart was breaking; Reynaldo had been waiting his entire broadcast career for an experience like that. Once he had drunkenly confided to Christina that his secret dream was to be shot in the thigh – live on national television. Not a life-threatening wound, just enough to make him go down. 'I'm tired of getting beat up,' he had told Christina that night. 'I want to break some new ground.' In Reynaldo's secret dream, the TV camera would jiggle at the sound of gunshots, then pan dramatically to focus on his prone and bloodsplattered form sprawled on the street. In the dream, Reynaldo would be clutching his microphone, bravely continuing to broadcast while paramedics worked feverishly to save his life. The last clip, as Reynaldo dreamed it, was close-up of his famous face: the lantern jaw clenched in agony, a grimace showcasing his luxurious capped teeth. Then the trademark sign-off: *'This is Reynaldo Flemm, reporting In Your Face!'* – just as the ambulance doors swung shut.

'I can't believe this,' Reynaldo moaned over his breakfast. 'Producers aren't supposed to get shot, the talent is.'

Christina Marks sipped a three-dollar orange juice. 'In the first place, Ray, I wasn't the one who got shot—'

'Yeah, but—'

'In the second place, you would've pissed your pants if you'd been there. This is no longer fun and games, Ray. Somebody is trying to murder Stranahan. Probably the same goon who killed his ex-wife.'

Flemm was still pouting. 'Why didn't you tell me you were going out to Stiltsville?'

206

'You were locked in your room, remember? Measuring your body parts.' Christina patted his arm. 'Have some more marmalade.'

Worriedly, Reynaldo asked, 'Does this mean you get to do the stand-up? I mean, since you eyewitnessed the shooting and not me.'

'Ray, I have absolutely no interest in doing a stand-up. I don't want to be on camera.'

'You mean it?' His voice dripped with relief. Pathetic, Christina thought; the man is pathetic.

Clearing his throat, Reynaldo Flemm said, 'I've got some bad news of my own, Chris.'

Christina dabbed her lips with the corner of the napkin. 'Does it involve your trip to New York?'

Flemm nodded yes.

'And, perhaps, Maggie Gonzalez?'

'I'm afraid so,' he said.

'She's missing again, isn't she, Ray?'

Flemm said, 'We had a dinner set up at the Palm.'

'And she never showed.'

'Right,' he said.

'Was this before or after you wired her the fifteen thousand?' Christina asked.

'Hey, I'm not stupid. I only sent half.'

'Shit.' Christina drummed her fingernails on the table.

Reynaldo Flemm sighed and turned away. Absently he ran a hand through his new golden tendrils. 'I'm sorry,' he said finally. 'You still want to dump this story?'

'No,' Christina said. 'No, I don't.'

*

Mick Stranahan looked through mug shots all morning, knowing he would never find the killer's face.

'Look anyway,' said Al García.

Stranahan flipped to another page. 'Is it my imagination,' he said, 'or are these assholes getting uglier every year?'

'I've noticed that, too,' García said.

'Speaking of which, I got a friendly visit from Murdock and Salazar at the hospital.' Stranahan told García what had happened.

'I'll report it to IA, if you want,' García said.

IA was Internal Affairs, where detectives Murdock and Salazar probably had files as thick as the Dade County Yellow Pages.

'Don't push it,' said Stranahan. 'I just wanted you to know what they're up to.'

'Pricks,' García grunted. 'I'll think of something.'

'I thought you had clout.'

'Clout? All I got is a ten-cent commendation and a gimp arm, same as you. Only mine came from a sawed-off.'

'I'm impressed,' said Mick Stranahan. He closed the mug book and pushed it across the table. 'He's not in here, Al. You got one for circus freaks?'

'That bad, huh?'

Stranahan said, 'Bad's not the word.' It wasn't.

'Want to try a composite? Let me call one of the artists.'

'No, that's all right,' Stranahan said. 'I wouldn't know where to start. Al, you wouldn't believe this guy.'

The detective gnawed the tip off a cigar. 'He's got to be the same geek who did Chloe. Thing is, I got witnesses saw them out at the marina having a drink, chatting like the best of friends. How do you figure that?'

'She always had great taste in men.' Stranahan stood up, gingerly testing the strap of his sling.

'Where are you going?'

'I'm off to do a B-and-E.'

'Now don't say shit like that.'

'It's true, Al.'

'I'm not believing this. Tell me you're bullshitting, Mick.'

'If it makes you feel better.'

'And call me,' García said in a low voice, 'if you turn up something good.'

At half-past three, Mick Stranahan broke into Maggie Gonzalez's duplex for the second time. The first thing he did was play back the tape on the answering machine. There were messages from numerous relatives, all demanding to know why Maggie had missed her cousin Gloria's baby shower. The only message that Mick Stranahan found interesting was from the Essex House hotel in downtown New York. A nasal female clerk requested that Miss Gonzalez contact them immediately about a forty-three-dollar dry-cleaning bill, which Maggie had forgotten to pay before checking out. The Essex House clerk had efficiently left the time and date of the phone message: January twenty-eighth at ten o'clock in the morning.

The next thing Mick Stranahan did was to sift through a big stack of Maggie's mail until he found the most recent Visa card bill, which he opened and studied at her kitchen table. That Maggie was spending somebody else's money in Manhattan was obvious: she had used her personal credit card only twice. One entry was $35.50 at Ticketron, probably for a Broadway show; the other charge was from a clothing shop for $179.40, more than Maggie was probably carrying in cash at the time. The clothing store was in the Plaza Hotel; the transaction was dated February first.

Mick Stranahan was getting ready to leave the duplex when Maggie's telephone rang twice, then clicked over to the machine. He listened as a man came on the line. Stranahan thought he recognized the voice, but he wasn't certain. He had only spoken with the man once.

The voice on the machine said: 'Maggie, it's me. I tried the Essex but they said you checked out . . . Look, we've really got to talk. In person. Call me at the office right away, collect. Wherever you are, OK? Thanks.'

As the man gave the number, Stranahan copied it in pencil on the Formica counter. After the caller hung up, Stranahan dialled 411 and asked for the listing of the Whispering Palms Spa and Surgery Center in Bal Harbour. A recording gave the main number as 555–7600. The phone number left by Maggie's male caller was 555–7602.

Rudy Graveline, Stranahan thought, calling on his office line.

The next number Stranahan dialled was 1–212–555–1212. Information for Manhattan. He got the number of the Plaza, dialled the main desk, and asked for Miss Maggie Gonzalez's room. A woman picked up on the fourth ring.

'Is this Miss Gonzalez?' Stranahan asked, trying to mimic a Brooklyn accent.

'Yes, it is.'

'This is the concierge downstairs.' Like there was an *upstairs* concierge. 'We were just wondering if you had any dry cleaning you needed done this evening.'

'What are you talking about? I'm still waiting for those three dresses I sent out Sunday,' Maggie said, not pleasantly.

'Oh, I'm very sorry,' Mick Stranahan said. 'I'll see to it immediately.'

Then he hung up, grabbed the white pages off the kitchen counter, and looked up the number for Delta Airlines.

SIXTEEN

On his way to Miami International, Mick Stranahan stopped at his brother-in-law's law office. Kipper Garth was on the speaker phone, piecing out a slip-and-fall to one of the Brickell Avenue buzzards.

Mick Stranahan walked in and said, 'The files?'

Kipper Garth motioned to a wine-coloured chair and put a finger to his waxy lips. 'So, Chuckie,' he said to the speaker phone, 'what're you thinking?'

'Thinking maybe two hundred if we settle,' said the voice on the other end.

'Two hundred!' Kipper exclaimed. 'Chuckie, you're nuts. The woman tripped over her own damn dachshund.'

'Kip, they'll settle,' the other lawyer said. 'It's the biggest grocery chain in Florida, they always settle. Besides, the dog croaked – that's fifty grand right there for mental anguish.'

'But dogs aren't even allowed in the store, Chuckie. If it was somebody else's dachshund she tripped on, then we'd really have something. But this was her own fault.'

Sardonic laughter crackled over the speaker box. 'Kip, buddy, you're not thinking like a litigator,' the voice said. 'I went to the supermarket myself and guess what: no signs!'

'What do you mean?'

'I mean no No Dogs Allowed-type signs. Not a one posted in Spanish. So how was our poor Consuela to know?'

'Chuckie, you're beautiful,' said Kipper Garth. 'If that ain't negligence—'

'Two hundred thou,' Chuckie said, 'that's my guess. We'll split sixty-forty.'

'Nope,' Kipper Garth said, staring coldly at the speaker box. 'Half-and-half. Same as always.'

'Excuse me.' It was Mick Stranahan. Kipper Garth frowned and shook his head; not now, not when he was closing the deal.

The voice on the phone said: 'Kip, who's that? You got somebody there?'

'Relax, Chuckie, it's just me,' Stranahan said to the box. 'You know – Kipper's heroin connection? I just dropped by with a briefcase full of Mexican brown. Can I pencil you in for a kilo?'

Frantically Kipper Garth jabbed two fingers at the phone buttons. The line went dead and the speaker box hummed the dial tone. 'You're fucking crazy,' he said to Mick Stranahan.

'I've got a plane to catch, Jocko. Where are the Graveline files?'

'You're crazy,' Kipper Garth said again, trying to stay calm. He buzzed for a secretary, who lugged in three thick brown office folders.

'There's a conference room where you can read this shit in private.'

Mick Stranahan said, 'No, this is fine.' With Kipper Garth stewing, Stranahan skimmed quickly through the files on Rudy Graveline. It was worse than he thought – or better, depending on one's point of view.

'Seventeen complaints to the state board,' Stranahan marvelled.

'Yeah, but no action,' Kipper Garth noted. 'Not even a reprimand.'

Stranahan looked up, lifting one of the files. 'Jocko, this is a gold mine.'

'Well, Mick, I'm glad I could help. Now, if you don't mind, it's getting late and I've got a few calls to make.'

Stranahan said, 'You don't understand, I wanted this stuff for you, not me.'

Peevishly Kipper Garth glanced at his wristwatch. 'You're right, Mick, I *don't* understand. What the hell do I want with Graveline's files?'

'Names, Jocko.' Stranahan opened the top folder and riffled the pages dramatically. 'You got seventeen names, seventeen leads on a silver platter. You got Mrs Susan Jacoby and her boobs that don't match. You got Mr Robert Mears with his left eye that won't close and his right eye that won't open. You got, let's see, Julia Kelly with a shnoz that looks like a Phillips screwdriver – Jesus, you see the Polaroid of that thing? What else? Oh, you got Ken Martinez and his lopsided scrotum . . .'

Kipper Garth waved his arms. 'Mick, that's enough! What would I want with all this crap?'

'I figured you'll need it, Jocko.'

'For what?'

'For suing Doctor Rudy Graveline.'

'Very funny,' Kipper Garth said. 'I told you, the man's in my yacht club. Besides, he's been sued before.'

'Sue him again,' Mick Stranahan said. 'Sue the mother like he's never been sued before.'

'He'd settle out. Doctors always settle.'

'Don't let him. Don't settle for anything. Not for ten million dollars. Sign up one of these poor misfortunate souls and go to the frigging wall.'

Kipper Garth stood up and adjusted his necktie, suddenly on his way to some important meeting. 'I can't help you, Mick. Get yourself another lawyer.'

'You don't do this favour for me,' said Stranahan, 'and I'll go tell Katie about your trip to Steamboat next month with Inga or Olga or whatever the hell her name is, I got it written down here somewhere. And for future reference, Jocko, don't ever put your ski bunny's plane tickets on American Express. I know it's convenient and all, but it's very, very risky. I mean, with the computers they got these days, I can pull out your goddamned seat assignments – 5A and 5B, I think it is.'

All Kipper Garth could say was: 'How'd you do that?'

'I told you before, I'm still plugged in.' A travel agent in Coral Gables who owed him one. It was so damn easy Stranahan couldn't bear to tell his brother-in-law.

'What's the point of all this?' Kipper Garth asked.

'Never mind, just do it. Sue the asshole.'

The lawyer lifted his pinstriped coat off the back of the chair and checked it for wrinkles. 'Mick, let me shop this round and get back to you.'

'No, Jocko. No referrals. You do this one all by yourself.'

The lawyer sagged as if struck by a brick.

'You heard me right,' Stranahan said.

'Mick, please.' It was a pitiable peep. 'Mick, I don't do this sort of thing.'

'Sure you do. I see the billboards all over town.'

Kipper Garth nibbled on a thumbnail to mask the spastic twitching of his upper lip. The thought of actually going to court had pitched him into a cold sweat. A fresh droplet made a shiny trail from the furrow of his forehead to the tip of his well-tanned nose.

'I don't know,' he said, 'it's been so long.'

'Aw, it's easy,' Stranahan said. 'One of your paralegals can draw up the complaint. That'll get the ball rolling.' With a thud he stacked the Graveline files on Kipper Garth's desk; the lawyer eyed the pile as if it were nitroglycerine.

'A gold mine,' Stranahan said encouragingly. 'I'll check back in a few days.'

'Mick?'

'Relax. All you've got to do is go down to the courthouse and sue.'

Wanly, Kipper Garth said, 'I don't have to win, do I?'

'Of course not,' Stranahan said, patting his arm. 'It'll never get that far.'

Dr Rudy Graveline lived in a palatial three-storey house on northern Biscayne Bay. The house had Doric pillars, two spiral staircases, and more imported marble than the entire downtown art museum. The house had absolutely no business being on Miami Beach, but in fairness it looked no more silly or out of place than any of the other garish mansions. The house was on the same palm-lined avenue where two of the Bee Gees lived, which meant that Rudy had been forced to pay about a hundred thousand more than the property was worth. For the first few years, the women whom Rudy dated were impressed to be in the Bee Gees' neighbourhood, but lately the star value had worn off and Rudy had quit mentioning it.

It was Heather Chappell, the actress, who brought it up first.

'I think Barry lives around here,' she said as they were driving back to Rudy's house after dinner at the Forge.

'Barry who?' Rudy asked, his mind off somewhere.

'Barry Gibb. The singer. *Staying alive, staying alive, ooh, ooh, ooh.*'

As much as he loved Heather, Rudy wished she wouldn't try to sing.

'You know Barry personally?' he asked.

'Oh sure. All the guys.'

'That's Barry's place there,' Rudy Graveline said, pointing. 'And Robin lives right here.'

'Let's stop over,' Heather said, touching his knee. 'It'll be fun.'

Rudy said no, he didn't know the guys all that well. Besides, he never really liked their music, especially that disco shit. Immediately Heather sank into a deep pout, which she heroically maintained all the way back to Rudy's house, up the stairs, all the way to his bedroom. There she peeled off her dress and panties and lay face down on the king-sized bed. Every few minutes she would raise her cheek off the satin pillow and sigh disconsolately, until Rudy couldn't stand it any more.

'Are you mad at me?' he asked. He was in his boxer shorts, standing in the closet where he had hung his suit. 'Heather, are you angry?'

'No.'

'Yes, you are. Did I say something wrong? If I did, I'm sorry.' He was blubbering like a jerk, all because he wanted to get laid in the worst way. The sight of

Heather's perfect bare bottom – the one she wanted contoured – was driving him mad.

In a tiny voice she said, 'I love the Bee Gees.'

'I'm sorry,' Rudy said. He sat on the corner of the bed and stroked her peachlike rump. 'I liked their early stuff, I really did.'

Heather said, 'I loved the disco, Rudy. It just about killed me when disco died.'

'I'm sorry I said anything.'

'You ever made love to disco music?'

Rudy thought: What is happening to my life?

'Do you have any Village People tapes?' Heather asked, giving him a quick saucy look over the shoulder. 'There's a song on their first album, I swear, I could fuck all night to it.'

Rudy Graveline was nothing if not resourceful. He found the Village People tape in the discount bin of an all-night record store across from the University of Miami campus in Coral Gables. He sped home, popped the cassette into the modular sound system, cranked up the woofers, and jogged up the spiral staircase to the bedroom.

Heather said, 'Not here.' She took him by the hand and led him downstairs. 'The fireplace,' she whispered.

'It's seventy-eight degrees,' Rudy remarked, kicking off his underwear.

'It's not the fire,' Heather said, 'it's the marble.'

One of the selling points of the big house was an oversized fireplace constructed of polished Italian marble. Fireplaces were considered a cosy novelty in South Florida, but Rudy had never used his, since he was afraid the expensive black marble would blister in the heat.

Heather crawled in and got on her back. She had the most amazing smile on her face. 'Oh, Rudy, it's so cold.' She lifted her buttocks off the marble and slapped them down; the squeak made her giggle.

Rudy stood there, naked and limp, staring like an idiot. 'We could get hurt,' he said. He was thinking of what the marble would do to his elbows and kneecaps.

'Don't be such a geezer,' Heather said, hoisting her hips and wiggling them in his face. She rolled over and pointed to the twin smudges of condensation on the black stone. 'Look,' she said. 'Just like fingerprints.'

'Sort of,' Rudy Graveline mumbled.

She said, 'I must be hot, huh?'

'I guess so,' Rudy said. His skull was ready to split; the voices of the Village People reverberated in the fireplace like mortar fire.

'Oh, God,' Heather moaned.

'What is it?' Rudy asked.

'The song. That's my song.' She squeaked to her knees and seized him ferociously around the waist. 'Come on down here,' she said. 'Let's dance.'

In order to prolong his tumescence, Dr Rudy Graveline had trained himself to think of anything but sex while he was having sex. Most times he concentrated on his unit trusts and tax shelters, which were complicated enough to keep orgasm at bay for a good ten to fifteen minutes. Tonight, though, he concentrated on something different. Rudy Graveline was thinking of his daunting predicament – of Victoria Barletta and the up-coming television documentary about her death; of Mick

Stranahan, still alive and menacing; of Maggie Gonzalez, spending his money somewhere in New York.

More often than not, Rudy found he could ruminate with startling clarity during the throes of sexual intercourse. He had arrived at many crucial life decisions in such moments – the clutter of the day and the pressure from his patients seemed to vanish in a crystal vacuum, a mystic physical void that permitted Rudy to concentrate on his problems in a new light and from a new angle.

And so it was that – even with Heather Chappell clawing his shoulders and screaming disco drivel into his ear, even with the flue vent clanging in the chimney above his head, and even with his knees grinding mercilessly on the cold Italian marble – Rudy was able to focus on the most important crisis of his life. Both pain and pleasure dissipated; it was as if he were alone, alert and sensitized, in a cool dark chamber. Rudy thought about everything that had happened so far, and then about what he must do now. It wasn't a bad plan. There was, however, one loose end.

Rudy snapped out of his cognitive trance when Heather cried, 'Enough already!'

'What?'

'I said you can stop now, OK? This isn't a damn rodeo.' She was all out of breath. Her chest was slick with sweat.

Rudy quit moving.

'What were you thinking of?' Heather asked.

'Nothing.'

'Did you come?'

'Sure,' Rudy lied.

'You were thinking of some other girl, weren't you?'

'No, I wasn't.' Another lie.

He had been thinking of Maggie Gonzalez, and how he should have killed her two months ago.

The next day at noon, George Graveline arrived at the Whispering Palms surgery clinic and demanded to see his brother, said it was an emergency. When Rudy heard the story, he agreed.

The two men were talking in hushed, worried tones when Chemo showed up an hour later.

'So what's the big rush?' he said.

'Sit down,' Rudy Graveline told him.

Chemo was dressed in a tan safari outfit, the kind Jim Fowler wore on the *Wild Kingdom* television show.

Rudy said, 'George, this is a friend of mine. He's working for me on this matter.'

Chemo raised his eyebrows. 'Happened to your thumb?' he said to George.

'Car door.' Rudy's brother did not wish to share that painful detail of his encounter with Mick Stranahan.

George Graveline had a few questions of his own for the tall stranger, but he held them. Valiantly he tried not to stare at Chemo's complexion, which George assessed as some tragic human strain of Dutch elm disease. What finally drew the tree trimmer's attention away from Chemo's face was the colourful Macy's shopping bag in which Chemo concealed his newly extended left arm.

'Had an accident,' Chemo explained. 'I'm only wearing this until I get a customized cover.' He pulled the shopping bag off the Weed Whacker. George Graveline recognized it immediately – the lightweight household model.

'Hey, that thing work?'

'You bet,' Chemo said. He probed under his arm until he found the toggle switch that jolted the Weed Whacker to life. It sounded like a blender without the top on.

George grinned and clapped his hands.

'That's enough,' Rudy said sharply.

'No, watch,' said Chemo. He ambled to the corner of the office where Rudy kept a beautiful potted rubber plant.

'Oh no,' the doctor said, but it was too late. Gleefully Chemo chopped the rubber plant into slaw.

'Yeah!' said George Graveline.

Rudy leaned over and whispered, 'Don't encourage him. He's a dangerous fellow.'

Basking in the attention, Chemo left the Weed Whacker unsheathed. He sat down next to the two men and said, 'Let's hear the big news.'

'Mick Stranahan visited George yesterday,' Rudy said. 'Apparently the bastard's not giving up.'

'What'd he say?'

'All kinds of crazy shit,' George said.

Rudy had warned his brother not to tell Chemo about Victoria Barletta or the wood chipper or Stranahan's specific accusation about what had happened to the body.

Rudy twirled his eyeglasses and said: 'I don't understand why Stranahan is so damn hard to kill.'

'Least we know he's out of the hospital,' Chemo said brightly. 'I'll get right on it.'

'Not just yet,' Rudy said. He turned to his brother. 'George, could I speak to him alone, please?'

George Graveline nodded amiably at Chemo on his

way out the door. 'Listen, you ever need work,' he said, 'I could use you and that, uh . . .'

'Prosthesis,' Chemo said. 'Thanks, but I don't think so.'

When they were alone, Rudy opened the top drawer of his desk and handed Chemo a large brown envelope. Inside the envelope were an eight-by-ten photograph, two thousand dollars in traveller's cheques, and an airline ticket. The person in the picture was a handsome, sharp-featured woman with brown eyes and brown hair; her name was printed in block letters on the back of the photograph. The plane ticket was round-trip, Miami to LaGuardia and back.

Chemo said, 'Is this what I think it is?'

'Another job,' Dr Rudy Graveline said.

'It'll cost you.'

'I'm prepared for that.'

'Same as the Stranahan deal,' Chemo said.

'Twenty treatments? You don't *need* twenty more treatments. Your face'll be done in two months.'

'I'm not talking about dermabrasion,' Chemo said. 'I'm talking about my ears.'

Rudy thought: Dear God, will it never end? 'Your ears,' he said to Chemo, 'are the last things that need surgical attention.'

'The hell is that supposed to mean?'

'Nothing, nothing. All I'm saying is, once we finish the dermabrasions you'll look as good as new. I honestly don't believe you'll want to touch a thing, that's how good your face is going to look.'

Chemo said, 'My ears stick out too far and you know it. You want me to do this hit, you'll fix the damn things.'

'Fine,' Rudy Graveline sighed, 'fine.' There was nothing wrong with the man's ears, only what was between them.

Chemo tucked the envelope into his armpit and bagged up the Weed Whacker. 'Oh yeah, one more thing. I'm out of that stuff for my face.'

'What stuff?'

'You know,' Chemo said, 'the Wite-Out.'

Rudy Graveline found a small bottle in his desk and tossed it to Chemo, who slipped it into the breast pocket of his Jim Fowler safari jacket. 'Call you from New York,' he said.

'Yes,' said Rudy wearily. 'By all means.'

SEVENTEEN

Christina Marks slipped out of the first-class cabin while Reynaldo Flemm was autographing a cocktail napkin for a flight attendant. The flight attendant had mistaken the newly bewigged Reynaldo for David Lee Roth, the rock singer. The Puerto Rican moustache looked odd with all that blond hair, but the flight attendant assumed it was meant as a humorous disguise.

Mick Stranahan was sitting in coach, a stack of outdoors magazines on the seat next to him. He saw Christina coming down the aisle and smiled. 'My shadow.'

'I'm not following you,' she said.

'Yes, you are. But that's all right.' He moved the magazines and motioned her to sit down.

'You look very nice.' It was the first time he had seen her in a dress. 'Some coincidence, that you and the anchorman got the same flight as I did.'

Christina said, 'He's not an anchorman. And no, it's not a coincidence that we're on the same plane. Ray thinks it is, but it's not.'

'Ray thinks it is, huh? So this was your idea, following me.'

'Relax,' Christina said. Ever since the shooting she had stayed close; at first she rationalized it as a journalist's

225

instinct – the Barletta story kept coming back to Stranahan, didn't it? But then she had found herself sleeping some nights at the hospital, where nothing newsworthy was likely to happen; sitting in the corner and watching him in the hospital bed, long after it was obvious he would make a full recovery. Christina couldn't deny she was attracted to him, and worried about him. She also had a feeling he was moderately crazy.

Stranahan said, 'So you guys are going to trail me all around New York. A regular tag team, you and Ray.'

'Ray will be busy,' Christina said, 'on other projects.'

The jetliner dipped slightly, and a shaft of sunlight caught the side of her face, forcing her to look away. For the first time Stranahan noticed a sprinkling of light freckles on her nose and cheeks; cinnamon freckles, the kind that children have.

'Did I ever thank you for saving my life?' he asked.

'Yes, you did.'

'Well, thanks again.' He poured some honey-roasted peanuts into the palm of her hand. 'Why are you following me?'

'I'm not,' she said.

'If it's only to juice up your damn TV show, then I'm going to get angry.'

Christina said, 'It's not that.'

'You want to keep an eye on me.'

'You're an interesting man. You make things happen.'

Stranahan popped a peanut and said, 'That's a good one.'

Christina Marks softened her tone. 'I'll help you find her.'

'Find who?'

'Maggie Gonzalez.'

'Who said she was lost? Besides, you got her on tape, right? The whole sordid story.'

'Not yet,' Christina admitted.

Stranahan laughed caustically. 'Oh brother,' he said.

'Listen, I got a trail of bills she's been sending up to the office. Between the two of us, we could find her in a day. Besides, I think she'll talk to me. The whole sordid story, on tape – like you said.'

Stranahan didn't mention that he already knew where Maggie Gonzalez was staying, and that he was totally confident that he could persuade her to talk.

'You're the most helpful woman I ever met,' he said to Christina Marks. 'So unselfish, too. If I didn't know better, I'd think maybe you were hunting for Maggie because she beat you and the anchorman out of some serious dough.'

Christina said, 'I liked you better unconscious.'

Stranahan chuckled and took her hand. He didn't let go like she thought he would, he just held it. Once, when the plane hit some turbulence, Christina jumped nervously. Without looking up from his *Field & Stream*, Stranahan gave her hand a squeeze. It was more comforting than suggestive, but it made Christina flush.

She retreated to the role of professional interviewer. 'So,' she said, 'tell me about yourself.'

'You first,' Stranahan said; a brief smile, then back to the magazine.

Oddly, she found herself talking – talking so openly that she sounded like one of those video-dating tapes: Let's see, I'm thirty-four years old, divorced, born in Richmond, went to the University of Missouri journalism school, lettered on the swim team, graduated magna, got my first decent news job with the ABC affiliate in St Louis, then three years at WBBM in Chicago until I met Ray at the Gacy trial and he offered me an assistant producer's job, and here I am. Now it's your turn, Mick.'

'Pardon?'

'Your turn,' Christina Marks said. 'That's my life story, now let's hear yours.'

Stranahan closed the magazine and centred it on his lap. He said, 'My life story is this; I've killed five men, and I've been married five times.'

Christina slowly pulled her hand away.

'Which scares you more?' Mick Stranahan said.

When Dade County Commissioner Roberto Pepsical broke the news to The Others (that is, the other crooked commissioners), they all had the same reactions: Nope, sorry, too late.

Dr Rudy Graveline had offered major bucks to rezone prime green space for the Old Cypress Towers project, and the commissioners had gone ahead and done it. They couldn't very well put it back on the agenda and reverse the vote – not without arousing the interest of those goddamned newspaper reporters. Besides, a deal was a deal. Furthermore, The Others wanted to know about the promised twenty-five thousand dollar bribe: specifically, where was it? Was Rudy holding out? One commissioner even suggested that a new vote to rescind the zoning and scrap the project could be obtained only by doubling the original payoff.

Roberto Pepsical was fairly sure that Dr Rudy Graveline would not pay twice for essentially the same act of corruption. In addition, Roberto didn't feel like explaining to the doctor that if Old Cypress Towers were to expire on the drawing board, so would a plethora of other hidden gratuities that would have winged their way into the commissioners' secret accounts. From downtown bankers to the zoning lawyers to the code inspectors, payoffs traditionally trickled upward to the commissioners. The ripple effect of killing a project as large as Rudy's was calamitous, bribery-wise.

Roberto hated being the middleman when the stakes got this high. By nature he was slow, inattentive, and somewhat easily confused. He hadn't taken notes during Rudy's late-night phone call, and maybe he should have. This much he remembered clearly: the doctor had said that he'd changed his mind about Old Cypress Towers, that he'd decided to move his money out of the country instead. When Roberto protested, the doctor told him there'd been all kinds of trouble, serious trouble – specifically, that hinky old surgical case he'd mentioned that day at lunch. The proverbial doo-doo was getting ready to hit the proverbial fan, Rudy had said; somebody was out to ruin him. He told Roberto Pepsical to pass along his most profound apologies to The Others, but there was no other course for the doctor to take. Since his problem wasn't going away, Old Cypress Towers would.

The solution was so obvious that even Roberto grasped it immediately. The apartment project could be rescued, and so could the commissioners' bribes. Once Roberto learned that Dr Rudy Graveline's problem had a name, he began checking with his connections at the Metro-Dade Police Department.

Which led him straight to detectives John Murdock and Joe Salazar.

Roberto considered the mission of such significance that he took the radical step of skipping his normal two-hour lunch to stop by the police station for a personal visit. He found both detectives at their desks. They were eating hot Cuban sandwiches and cleaning their revolvers. It was the first time Roberto had ever seen Gulden's mustard on a .357.

'You're sure,' said the commissioner, 'that this man is a murder suspect?'

'Yep,' said John Murdock.

'Number one suspect,' added Joe Salazar.

Roberto said, 'So you're going to arrest him?'

'Of course,' Salazar said.

'Eventually,' said Murdock.

'The sooner the better,' Roberto said.

John Murdock glanced at Joe Salazar. Then he looked at Roberto and said, 'Commissioner, if you've got any information about this man . . .'

'He's been giving a friend of mine a hard time, that's all. A good friend of mine.' Roberto knew better than to mention Rudy Graveline's name, and John Murdock knew better than to ask.

Joe Salazar said, 'It's a crime to threaten a person. Did Stranahan make a threat?'

'Nothing you could prove,' Roberto said. 'Look, I'd appreciate it if you guys would keep me posted.'

'Absolutely,' John Murdock promised. He wiped the food off his gun and shoved it back in the shoulder holster.

'This is very important,' Roberto Pepsical said. 'Extremely important.'

Murdock said, 'Don't worry, we'll nail the fuckwad.'

'Yeah,' said Joe Salazar. 'It's only a matter of time.'

'Not much time, I hope.'

'We'll do what we can, Commissioner.'

'There might even be a promotion in it.'

'Oh boy, a promotion,' said John Murdock. 'Joey, you hear that? A promotion!' The detective burped at the commissioner and said, 'How about some green instead?'

Roberto Pepsical winced as if a hornet had buzzed into his ear. 'Jesus, are you saying—'

'Money,' said Joe Salazar, chomping a pickle. 'He means money.'

'Let me get this straight: you guys want a bribe for solving a murder?'

'No,' Murdock said, 'just for making the arrest.'

'I can't believe this.'

'Sure you can,' Joe Salazar said. 'Your friend wants Stranahan out of the way, right? The county jail, that's fucking out of the way.'

Roberto buried his rubbery chin in his hands. 'Money,' he murmured.

'I don't know what you guys call it over at Government Center, but around here we call it a bonus.' John Murdock grinned at the county commissioner. 'What *do* you guys call it?'

To Roberto it seemed reckless to be discussing a payoff in the middle of a detective squad room. He felt like passing gas.

In a low voice he said to John Murdock, 'All right, we'll work something out.'

'Good.'

The commissioner stood up. He was about to reach

out and shake their hands, but he changed his mind. 'Look, we never had this meeting,' he said to the two detectives.

'Of course not,' John Murdock agreed.

Joe Salazar said, 'Hey, you can trust us.'

About as far as I can spit, thought Robert Pepsical.

Three days before Mick Stranahan, Christina Marks, and Reynaldo Flemm arrived in Manhattan, and four days before the man called Chemo showed up, Maggie Gonzalez walked into a video-rental shop on West 52nd Street and asked to make a tape. She gave the shop clerk seventy-five dollars cash, and he led her to 'the studio', a narrow backroom panelled with cheap brown cork. The studio reeked of Lysol. On the floor was a stained grey mattress and a bright clump of used Kleenex, which, at Maggie's insistence, the clerk removed. A Sony video camera was mounted on an aluminium tripod at one end of the room; behind it, on another stem, was a small bank of lights. The clerk opened a metal folding chair and placed it eight feet in front of the lens.

Maggie sat down, opened her purse and unfolded some notes she had printed on Plaza stationery. While she read them to herself, the clerk was making impatient chewing-gum noises in his cheeks, like he had better things to do. Finally Maggie told him to start the tape, and a tiny red light twinkled over the Sony's cold black eye.

Maggie was all set to begin when she noticed the clerk hovering motionless in the darkest corner, a cockroach trying to blend into the cork. She told the guy to get lost, waited until the door slammed, then took a breath and addressed the camera.

'My name is Maggie Orestes Gonzalez,' she said. 'On the twelfth of March, 1986, I was a witness to the killing of a young woman named Victoria Barletta . . .'

The taping took fourteen minutes. Afterwards Maggie got two extra copies made at twenty dollars each. On the way back to the hotel she stopped at a branch of the Merchant Bank and rented a safe-deposit box, where she left the two extra videotapes. She took the original up to her room at the Plaza, and placed it in the nightstand, under the room-service menu.

The very next day Maggie Gonzalez took a cab to the office of Dr Leonard Leaper on the corner of 50th Street and Lexington. Dr Leaper was a nationally renowned and internationally published plastic surgeon; Maggie had read up on him in the journals. 'You have a decent reputation,' she told Dr Leaper. 'I hope it's not just hype.' Her experiences in Dr Rudy Graveline's surgical suite had taught her to be exceedingly careful when choosing a physician.

Neutrally Dr Leaper said, 'What can I do for you, young lady?'

'The works,' Maggie replied.

'The works?'

'I want a bleph, a lift, and I want the hump taken out of this nose. Also, I want you to trim the septum so it looks like this.' With a finger she repositioned the tip of her nose at a perky, Sandy Duncan-type angle. 'See?'

Dr Leaper nodded.

'I'm a nurse,' Maggie said. 'I used to work for a plastic surgeon.'

'I figured something like that,' Dr Leaper said. 'Why do you want these operations?'

'None of your business.'

Dr Leaper said, 'Miss Gonzalez, if indeed you worked for a surgeon then you understand I've got to ask some personal questions. There are good reasons for elective cosmetic surgery and bad reasons, good candidates and poor candidates. Some patients believe it will solve all their problems, and of course it won't—'

'Cut the crap,' Maggie said, 'and take my word: surgery will definitely solve my problem.'

'Which is?'

'None of your business.'

Dr Leaper stood up. 'Then I'm afraid I can't help.'

'You guys are all alike,' Maggie complained.

'No, we're not,' Dr Leaper said. 'That's why you're here. You wanted somebody good.'

His composure was maddening. Maggie said, 'All right – will you do the surgery if I tell you the reason?'

'If it's a good one,' the doctor replied.

She said, 'I need a new face.'

'Why?'

'Because I am about to . . . testify against someone.'

Dr Leaper said, 'Can you tell me more?'

'It's a serious matter, and I expect he'll send someone to find me before it's over. I don't want to be found.'

Dr Leaper said, 'But surgery can only do so much—'

'Look, I've seen hundreds of cases, and I know good results from bad results. I also know the limitations of the procedures. You just do the nose, the neck, the eyes, maybe a plastic implant in the chin . . . and let me and Lady Clairol do the rest. I guarantee the bastard won't recognize me.'

Dr Leaper locked his hands. In a grave voice he said, 'Let me understand: you're a witness in a criminal matter?'

'Undoubtedly,' Maggie said. 'A homicide, to be exact.'

'Oh, dear.'

'And I must testify, Doctor.' The word *testify* was a stretch, but it wasn't far from the truth. 'It's the right thing for me to do,' Maggie asserted.

'Yes,' said Dr Leaper, without conviction.

'So, you see why I need your help.'

The surgeon sighed. 'Why should I believe you?'

Maggie said, 'Why should I lie? If it weren't an emergency, don't you think I would have had this done a long time ago, when I could've got a deal on the fees?'

'I suppose so.'

'Please, Doctor. It's not vanity, it's survival. Do my face, you'll be saving a life.'

Dr Leaper opened his schedule book. 'I've got a lipo tomorrow at two, but I'm going to bump him for you. Don't eat or drink anything after midnight—'

'I know the routine,' Maggie Gonzalez said ebulliently. 'Thank you very much.'

'It's all right.'

'One more thing.'

'Yes?' said Dr Leaper, cocking one grey eyebrow.

'I was wondering if there's any chance of a professional discount? I mean, since I *am* a nurse.'

Mick Stranahan stood on the kerb outside LaGuardia Airport and watched Reynaldo Flemm climb into a long black limousine. The limo driver, holding the door, eyed

Reynaldo's new hair and looked to Christina Marks for a clue. She said something quietly to the driver, then waved goodbye to Reynaldo in the back seat. Through the smoked grey window Stranahan thought he saw Flemm shoot him a bitter look as the limo pulled away.

'I don't like this place,' Stranahan muttered, his breath frosty.

'What places *do* you like?' Christina asked.

'Old Rhodes Key. That's one place you won't see frozen spit on the sidewalk. Fact, you won't even see a sidewalk.'

'You old curmudgeon.' Christina said it much too sarcastically for Stranahan. 'Come on, let's get a cab.'

Her apartment was off 72nd Street on the Upper East Side. Third floor, one bedroom with a small kitchen and a garden patio scarcely big enough for a Norway rat. The furniture was low and modern: glass, chrome, and sharp angles. One of those sofas you put together like a jigsaw puzzle. Potted plants occupied three of the four corners in the living room. On the main wall hung a vast and frenetic abstract painting.

Stranahan took a step back and studied it. 'Boy, I don't know,' he said.

From the bedroom came Christina's voice. 'You like it?'

'Not really,' Stranahan said.

When Christina walked out, he saw that she had changed to blue jeans and a navy pullover sweater. She stood next to him in front of the painting and said, 'It's supposed to be springtime. Spring in the city.'

'Looks like an Amoco station on fire.'

'Thank you,' Christina said, 'Such a sensitive man.'

Stranahan shrugged. 'Let's go. I gotta check in.'

'Why don't you stay here?' She gave it a beat. 'On the sectional.'

'The sectional? I don't think so.'

'It's safer than a hotel, Mick.'

'I'm not so sure.'

Christina said, 'Don't flatter yourself.'

'It's not me I was thinking of. Believe it or not.'

'Sorry. Please stay.'

'The Great Reynaldo will not be pleased.'

'All the more reason,' Christina said.

They ate a late lunch at a small Italian restaurant three blocks from Christina's apartment. She ordered a pasta salad and Perrier, while Stranahan had spaghetti and meatballs and two beers. Then they took a taxi to the Plaza Hotel.

'She's here?' Christina asked, once in the lobby and again in the elevator.

Stranahan knocked repeatedly on the door to Maggie Gonzalez's room, but no one answered. Maggie was in bed, coasting through a codeine dreamland with a brand new face that she had not yet seen. The sound of Mick Stranahan's knocking was but a muffled drumbeat in her delicious pharmaceutical fog, and Maggie paid it no attention. It would be hours before the drumming returned, and by then she would be conscious enough to stumble toward the door.

Her big mistake had been to call Dr Rudy Graveline four days earlier when she had gotten the message on her machine in Miami. Curiosity had triumphed over common sense; Maggie had been dying for an update on the Stranahan situation. She needed to stay close to

Rudy, but not too close. It was a dicey act. She wanted the doctor to believe that they were on the same side, his side. She also wanted to keep the expense money coming.

The phone call, though, had been peculiar. At first Dr Graveline had seemed relieved to hear her voice. But the more questions Maggie had asked – about Stranahan, the TV people, the money situation – the more remote the doctor had become, his voice getting tighter and colder on the other end. Finally Rudy had said that something had come up in the office, could he call her right back? Certainly, Maggie had said and – stupidly, it turned out – had given Rudy the phone number at the hotel. Days later the doctor still had not called back, and Maggie wondered why in the hell he had tried to reach her in the first place.

The answer was simple.

On the thirteenth of February, the man known as Chemo got off a Pan Am flight from Miami to New York. He wore a dusty broad-brimmed hat pulled down tightly to shadow his igneous face, a calfskin golf-bag cover snapped over his left arm to conceal the prosthesis, a pea-green woollen overcoat to protect against the winter wind, and heavy rubber-soled shoes to combat the famous New York City slush. He also had in his possession a Rapala fishing knife, the phone number of a man in Queens who would sell him a gun, and a slip of prescription paper on which were written these words in Dr Rudy Graveline's spastic scrawl: 'Plaza Hotel, Rm. 966.'

EIGHTEEN

When they returned from the Plaza to the apartment, Mick Stranahan said to Christina Marks: 'Sure you want a killer sleeping on the sectional?'

'Do you snore?'

'I'm serious.'

'Me, too.' From a closet she got a flannel sheet, a blanket, and two pillows. 'I've got a space heater that works, sometimes,' she said.

'No, this is fine.' Stranahan pulled off his shoes, turned on Letterman and stretched out on the sofa, which he had rearranged to contain his legs. He heard the shower running in the bathroom. After a few minutes Christina came out in a cloud of steam and sat down at the kitchen table. Her cheeks were flushed from the hot water. She wore a short blue robe, and her hair was wet. Stranahan could tell she'd brushed it out.

'We'll try again first thing in the morning,' he said.

'What?'

'Maggie's room at the hotel.'

'Oh, right.' She looked distracted.

He sat up and said, 'Come sit here.'

'I don't think so,' Christina said.

Stranahan could tell she had the radar up. He said, 'I must've scared you on the plane.'

'No, you didn't.' She wanted to ask about everything, his life; he was trying to make it easier and not doing so well.

'You didn't scare me,' Christina said again. 'If you did, I wouldn't let you stay.' But he had, and she did. That worried her even more.

Stranahan picked up the remote control and turned off the television. He heard sirens passing on the street outside and wished he were home, asleep on the bay.

When Christina spoke again, she didn't sound like a seasoned professional interviewer. She said, 'Five men?'

Stranahan was glad she'd started with the killings. The marriages would be harder to justify.

'Are we off the record?'

She hesitated, then said yes.

'The men I killed,' he began, 'would have killed me first. You'll just have to take my word.' Deep down, he wasn't sure about Thomas Henry Thomas, the fried-chicken robber. That one was a toss-up.

'What was it like?' Christina asked.

'Horrible.'

She waited for the details; often men like Stranahan wanted to tell about it. Or needed to.

But all he said was: 'Horrible, really. No fun at all.'

She said. 'You regret any of them?'

'Nope.'

She had one elbow propped on the table, knuckles pressed to her cheek. The only sound was the hissing of the radiator pipes, warming up. Stranahan peeled off his T-shirt and put it in a neat pile with his other clothes.

'I'll get a hotel room tomorrow.'

'No, you won't,' she said. 'I'm not frightened.'

'You haven't heard about my wives.'

She laughed softly. 'Five already at your age. You must be going for the record.'

Stranahan lay back, hands locked behind his head. 'I fall in love with waitresses. I can't help it.'

'You're kidding.'

'Don't be a snob. They were all smarter than I was. Even Chloe.'

Christina said, 'If you don't mind me saying so, she seemed a very cold woman.'

He groaned at the memory.

'What about the others, what were they like?'

'I loved them all, for a time. Then one day I didn't.'

Christina said, 'Doesn't sound like love.'

'Boy, are you wrong.' He smiled to himself.

'Mick, you regret any of them?'

'Nope.'

The radiator popped. The warmth of it made Stranahan sleepy, and he yawned.

'What about lovers?' Christina asked – a question sure to jolt him awake. 'All waitresses, no exceptions?'

'Oh, I've made some exceptions.' He scratched his head and pretended there were so many he had to add them up. 'Let's see, there was a lady probate lawyer. And an architect . . . make that two architects. Separately, of course. And an engineer for Pratt Whitney up in West Palm. An honest-to-God rocket scientist.'

'Really?'

'Yeah, really. And they were all dumber than I was.' Stranahan pulled the blanket up to his neck and closed his eyes. 'Goodnight, Christina.'

'Goodnight, Mick.' She turned off the lights, returned

to the kitchen table, and sat in the grey darkness for an hour, watching him sleep.

When Maggie Gonzalez heard the knocking again, she got out of bed and weaved toward the noise. With outstretched arms she staved off menacing walls, door-knobs, and lampshades, but barely. She navigated through a wet gauze, her vision fuzzed by painkillers. When she opened the door, she found herself staring at the breast of a pea-green woollen overcoat. She tilted her throbbing head, one notch at a time, until she found the man's face.

'Uh,' she said.

'Jesus H. Christ,' said Chemo, shoving her back in the room, kicking the door shut behind him, savagely cursing his own rotten luck. The woman was wrapped from forehead to throat in white surgical tape – a fucking mummy! He took the photograph from his overcoat and handed it to Maggie Gonzalez.

'Is that you?' he demanded.

'No.' The answer came from parchment lips, whispering through a slit in the bandages. 'No, it's not me.'

Chemo could tell that the woman was woozy. He told her to sit down before she fell down.

'It's you, isn't it? You're Maggie Gonzalez.'

She said, 'You're making a big mistake.'

'Shut up.' He took off his broad-brimmed hat and threw it on the bed. Through the peepholes in the bandage, Maggie was able to get a good look at the man's remarkable face.

She said, 'My God, what happened to you?'

'Shut the fuck up.'

Chemo unbuttoned his overcoat, heaved it over a chair, and paced. The trip was turning into a débâcle. First the man in Queens had sold him a rusty Colt .38 with only two bullets. Later, on the subway, he had been forced to flee a group of elderly Amish in the fear that they might recognize him from his previous life. And now this – confusion. While Chemo was reasonably sure that the bandaged woman was Maggie Gonzalez, he didn't want to screw up and kill the wrong person. Dr Graveline would never understand.

'Who are you?' Maggie said thickly. 'Who sent you?'

'You ask too many questions.'

'Please, I don't feel very well.'

Chemo took the Colt from the waistband of his pants and pointed it at the bandaged tip of her new nose. 'Your name's Maggie Gonzalez, isn't it?'

At the sight of the pistol, she leaned forward and vomited all over Chemo's rubber-soled winter shoes.

'Jesus H. Christ,' he moaned and bolted for the bathroom.

'I'm sorry,' Maggie called after him. 'You scared me, that's all.'

When Chemo came back, the shoes were off his feet and the gun was back in his pants. He was wiping his mouth with the corner of a towel.

'I'm really sorry,' Maggie said again.

Chemo shook his head disgustedly. He sat down on the corner of the bed. To Maggie his legs seemed as long as circus stilts.

'You're supposed to kill me?'

'Yep,' Chemo said. With the towel he wiped a fleck of puke off her nightgown.

Blearily she studied him and said, 'You've had some dermabrasion.'

'So?'

'So how come just little patches – why not more?'

'My doctor said that would be risky.'

'Your doctor's full of it,' Maggie said.

'And I guess you're an expert or something.'

'I'm a nurse, but you probably know that.'

Chemo said, 'No, I didn't.' Dr Graveline hadn't told him a thing.

Maggie went on, 'I used to work for a plastic surgeon down in Miami. A butcher with a capital B.'

Subconsciously Chemo's fingers felt for the tender spots on his chin. He was almost afraid to ask.

'This surgeon,' he said to Maggie, 'what was his name?'

'Graveline,' she said. 'Rudy Graveline. Personally, I wouldn't let him trim a hangnail.'

Lugubriously Chemo closed his bulbous red eyes. Through the codeine, Maggie thought he resembled a giant nuclear-radiated salamander, straight from a monster movie.

'How about this,' he said. 'I'll tell you what happened to my face if you tell me what happened to yours.'

It was Chemo's idea to have breakfast in Central Park. He figured there'd be so many other freaks that no one would notice them. As it turned out, Maggie's Tut-like facial shell drew more than a few stares. Chemo tugged his hat down tightly and said, 'You should've worn a scarf.'

They were sitting near Columbus Circle on a bench.

Chemo had bought a box of raisin bagels with cream cheese. Maggie said her stomach felt much better but, because of the surgical tape, she was able to fit only small pieces of bagel into her mouth. It was a sloppy process, but two fat squirrels showed up to claim the crumbs.

Chemo was saying, 'Your nose, your chin, your eyelids – Christ, no wonder you hurt.' He took out her picture and looked at it appraisingly. 'Too bad,' he said.

'What's that supposed to mean?'

'I mean, you were a pretty lady.'

'Maybe I still am,' Maggie said. 'Maybe prettier.'

Chemo put the photograph back in his coat. 'Maybe,' he said.

'You're going to make me cry and then everything'll sting.'

He said, 'Knock it off.'

'Don't you think I feel bad enough?' Maggie said. 'I get a whole new face – and for what! A month from now and you'd never have recognized me. I could've sat in your lap on the subway and you wouldn't know who I was.'

Chemo thought he heard sniffling behind the bandages. 'Don't fucking cry,' he said. 'Don't be a baby.'

'I don't understand why Rudy sent you,' Maggie whined.

'To kill you, what else?'

'But why now? Nothing's happened yet.'

Chemo frowned and said, 'Keep it down.' The pink patches on his chin tingled in the cold air and made him think about Rudy Graveline. Butcher with a capital B, Maggie had said. Chemo wanted to know more.

A thin young Moonie in worn corduroys came up to

the park bench and held out a bundle of red and white carnations. 'Be happy,' the kid said to Maggie. 'Five dollars.'

'Get lost,' Chemo said.

'Four dollars,' said the Moonie. 'Be happy.'

Chemo pulled the calfskin cover off his Weed Whacker and flicked the underarm toggle for the battery pack. The Moonie gaped as Chemo calmly chopped the bright carnations to confetti.

'Be gone, Hop-sing,' Chemo said, and the Moonie ran away. Chemo recloaked the Weed Whacker and turned to Maggie. 'Tell me why the doctor wants you dead.'

It took her several moments to recover from what she had seen. Finally she said, 'Well, it's a long story.'

'I got all day,' Chemo said. 'Unless you got tickets to *Phantom* or something.'

'Can we go for a walk?'

'No,' Chemo said sharply. 'Remember?' He had thrown his vomit-covered shoes and socks out the ninth-floor window of Maggie's room at the Plaza. Now he was sitting in bare feet in Central Park on a forty-degree February morning. He wiggled his long bluish toes and said to Maggie Gonzalez: 'So talk.'

She did. She told Chemo all about the death of Victoria Barletta. It was a slightly shorter recital than she'd put on the videotape, but it was no less shocking.

'You're making this up,' Chemo said.

'I'm not either.'

'He killed this girl with a nose job?'

Maggie nodded. 'I was there.'

'Jesus H. Christ.'

'It was an accident.'

'That's even worse,' Chemo said. He tore off his hat and threw it on the sidewalk, spooking the squirrels. 'This is the same maniac who's working on my face. I can't fucking stand it!'

By way of consolation, Maggie said: 'Dermabrasion is a much simpler procedure.'

'Yeah, tell me about simple procedures.' Chemo couldn't believe the lousy luck he had with doctors. He said, 'So what does all this have to do with him wanting you dead?'

Maggie told Chemo about Reynaldo Flemm's TV investigation (without mentioning that she had been the tipster), told how she had warned Rudy about Mick Stranahan, the investigator. She was careful to make it sound as if Stranahan was the whistle-blower.

'Now it's starting to make sense,' Chemo said. 'Graveline wants me to kill *him*, too.' He held up the arm-mounted Weed Whacker. 'He's the prick that cost me this hand.'

'Rudy can't afford any witnesses,' Maggie explained, 'or any publicity. Not only would they yank his medical licence, he'd go to jail. Now do you understand?'

Do I ever, thought Chemo.

The white mask that was Maggie's face asked: 'Are you still going to kill me?'

'We'll see,' Chemo replied. 'I'm sorting things out.'

'How much is that cheap bastard paying you?'

Chemo plucked his rumpled hat off the sidewalk. 'I'd rather not say,' he muttered, clearly embarrassed. No way would he let that butcher fuck with his ears. Not now.

*

Christina Marks and Mick Stranahan got to the Plaza Hotel shortly before ten. From the lobby Stranahan called Maggie's room and got no answer. Christina followed him into the elevator and, as they rode to the ninth floor, she watched him remove a small serrated blade from his wallet.

'Master key,' he said.

'Mick, no. I could get fired.'

'Then wait downstairs.'

But she didn't. She watched him pick the lock on Maggie's door, then slipped into the room behind him. She said nothing and scarcely moved while he checked the bathroom and the closets to see if they were alone.

'Mick, come here.'

On the bedstand were two prescription bottles, a plastic bedpan, and a pink-splotched surgical compress. Stranahan glanced at the pills: Tylenol No. 3 and Darvocet. The bottle of Darvocets had not yet been opened. A professional business card lay next to the telephone on Maggie's nightstand. Stranahan chuckled drily when he read what was on the card:

Leonard R. Leaper, M.D.
Certified by the American Board of Plastic Surgery
Office: 555–6600 Nights and Emergencies: 555–6677

'How nice,' Christina remarked. 'She took our money and got a facelift.'

Stranahan said, 'Something's not right. She ought to be in bed.'

'Maybe she went for brunch at the Four Seasons.'

He shook his head. 'These scrips are only two days old, so that's when she had the surgery. She's still got to be swollen up like a mango. Would you go out in public looking like that?'

'Depends on how much dope I ate.'

'No,' Stranahan said, scanning the room, 'something's not right. She ought to be here.'

'What do you want to do?'

Stranahan said they should go downstairs and wait in the lobby; in her condition, Maggie shouldn't be hard to spot. 'But first,' he said, 'let's really go through this place.'

Christina went to the dresser. Under a pile of Maggie's bras and panties she found three new flowered bikinis, the price tags from the Plaza Shops still attached. Maggie was definitely getting ready for Maui.

'Oh, Miss Marks,' Stranahan sang out. 'Lookie here.'

It was a video cassette in a brown plastic sleeve. The sleeve was marked with a sticker from Midtown Studio Productions.

Stranahan tossed Christina the tape. She tossed it back.

'We can't take that, it's larceny.'

He said, 'It's not larceny to take something you already own.'

'What do you mean?'

'If this is what I think it is, you've paid for it already. The Barletta story, remember?'

'We don't know that. Could be anything – home movies, maybe.'

Stranahan smiled and stuffed the cassette into his coat. 'Only one way to find out.'

'No,' Christina said.

'Look, you got a VCR at your place. Let's go watch the tape. If I'm wrong, then I'll bring it back myself.'

'Oh, I see. Just sneak in, put it back where you got it, tidy up the place.'

'Yeah, if I'm wrong. If it turns out to be Jane Fonda or something. But I don't think so.'

Christina Marks knew better; it was madness, of course. She could lose her job, blow a perfectly good career if they were caught. But, then again, this hadn't turned out to be the typical Reynaldo Flemm exposé. She had damn near gotten machine-gunned over this one, so what the hell.

Grudgingly she said, 'Is it Beta or VHS?'

Stranahan gave her a hug.

Then they heard the key in the door.

The two couples said nothing for the first few seconds, just stared. Mick Stranahan and Christina Marks had the most to contemplate: a woman wrapped in tape, and a beanpole assassin with one arm down to his knees.

Maggie Gonzalez was the first to speak: 'It's him.'

'Who?' Chemo asked. He had never seen Stranahan up close, not even at the stilt house.

'Him,' Maggie repeated through the bandages. 'What're you doing in my room?'

'Hello, Maggie,' Stranahan said, 'assuming it's you under there. It's sure been a long time.'

'And you!' Maggie grunted, pointing at Christina Marks.

'Hi, again,' said Christina. 'I thought you'd be in Hawaii by now.'

Chemo said, 'I guess everybody's old pals except me.' He pulled the .38 out of his overcoat. 'Nobody move.'

'Another one who watches too much TV,' Stranahan whispered to Christina.

Chemo blinked angrily. 'I don't like you one bit.'

'I assumed as much from the fact you keep trying to kill me.' Stranahan had seen some bizarros in his day, but this one took the cake. He looked like Fred Munster with bulimia. One eye on the gun, Stranahan asked, 'Do you have a name?'

'No,' Chemo said.

'Good. Makes for a cheaper tombstone.'

Chemo told Maggie to close the door, but Maggie didn't move. The sight of the pistol had made her nauseated all over again, and she was desperately trying to keep down her breakfast bagels.

'What's the matter now?' Chemo snapped.

'She doesn't look so hot,' Christina said.

'And who the fuck are you, Florence Nightingale?'

'What happened to your arm?' Christina asked him. A cool customer she was; Stranahan admired her poise.

Chemo got the impression that he was losing control, which made no sense, since he was the one with the pistol. 'Shut up, all of you,' he said, 'while I kill Mr Stranahan here. *Finally.*'

At these words, Maggie Gonzalez upchucked gloriously all over Chemo's gun arm. Given his general translucence, it was impossible to tell if Chemo blanched. He did, however, wobble perceptibly.

Mick Stranahan stepped forward and punched him ferociously in the Adam's apple. The man went down like a seven-foot Tinkertoy, but did not release his grip on the gun. Maggie backed up and screamed, a primal wail that poured from the hole in her bandage and filled the hallway. Stranahan decided there was no time to finish the job. He pushed Christina Marks through the doorway and told her to go for the elevator. Gagging and spitting blood, Chemo rolled out of his foetal curl and took a wild shot at Christina as she ran down the hall. The bullet twanged impotently off a fire extinguisher and was ultimately stopped by the opulent Plaza wallpaper.

Before Chemo could fire again, Stranahan stomped on his wrist, still slippery from Maggie's used bagels. Chemo would not let go of the gun. With a growl he swung his refurbished left arm like a fungo bat across his body. It caught Stranahan in the soft crease behind the knee and brought him down. The two men wrestled for the pistol while Maggie howled and clawed chimplike at her swaddled head.

It was a clumsy fight. Tangled in the killer's gangliness, Stranahan could not shield himself from a clubbing by Chemo's oversized left arm. Whatever it was – and it wasn't a human fist – it hurt like hell. His skull chiming, Stranahan tried to break free.

Suddenly he felt the dull barrel of the .38 against his throat. He flinched when he heard the click, but nothing else followed. No flash, no explosion, no smell. The bullet, Chemo's second and only remaining round, was a dud. Chemo couldn't believe it – that asshole in Queens had screwed him royal.

Stranahan squirmed loose, stood up, and saw that they had attracted an audience. All along the corridor, doors were cracked open, some more than others. Under Maggie's keening he could hear excited voices. Somebody was calling the police.

Stranahan groped at his coat to make sure that the videotape was still in his pocket, kicked Chemo once in the groin (or where he estimated that the giant's groin might be), then jogged down the hallway.

Christina Marks was considerate enough to hold the elevator.

NINETEEN

Dr Rudy Graveline was a fellow who distrusted chance and prided himself on preparation, but he had not planned a love affair with a Hollywood star. Heather Chappell was a distraction – a fragrant, gorgeous, elusive, spoiled, sulky bitch of a distraction. He couldn't get enough of her. Rudy had come to crave the tunnel of clear thinking that enveloped him while making love to Heather; it was like a sharp cool drug. She screwed him absolutely numb, left him aching and drained and utterly in focus with his predicament.

For a while he kept cooking up lame excuses for postponing Heather's elaborate cosmetic surgery – knowing it would put her out of action for weeks. Sex with Heather had become a crucial component of Rudy Graveline's daily regimen; like a long-distance runner, he had fallen into a physical rhythm that he could not afford to break. TV people were after him, his medical career was in jeopardy, a homicide rap was on the horizon – and salvation depended on a crooked halfwit politician and a one-armed, seven-foot hit man. Rudy needed to stay razor-sharp until the crisis was over, and Heather had become vital to his clarity.

He treated her like a queen and it seemed to work. Heather's initial urgency to schedule the surgery had subsided during the day-long shopping sprees, the four-star meals, the midnight yacht cruises up and down the Intracoastal. In recent days, though, she again had begun to press Rudy not only about the date for the operations, but the cost. She was dropping broad hints to the effect that for all her bedroom labours she deserved a special discount, and Rudy found himself weakening on the subject. Finally, one night, she waited until he was inside her to bring up the money again, and Rudy breathlessly agreed to knock forty per cent off the usual fee. Afterwards he was furious at himself, and blamed his moment of weakness on stress and mental fatigue.

Deep down, the doctor knew better: he was trapped. While he dreaded the prospect of Heather Chappell's surgery, he feared that she would leave him if he didn't agree to do it. He probably would have done it for free. He had become addicted to her body – a radiantly perfect body that she now wanted him to *improve*. The task would have posed a career challenge for the most skilful of plastic surgeons; for a hack like Rudy Graveline, it was flat-out impossible. Naturally he planned to let his assistants do it.

Until Heather dropped another surprise.

'My agent says I should tape the operation, love.'

Rudy said, 'You're kidding.'

'Just to be on the safe side.'

'What, you don't trust me?'

'Sure I do,' Heather said. 'It's my damn agent, is all. She says since my looks are everything, my whole career, I should be careful, legal-wise. I guess she wants to make sure nothing goes wrong—'

Rudy sprung out of bed, hands on his hips. 'Look, I told you these operations are not necessary at all.'

'And I told you, I'm sick of doing sitcoms and *Hollywood Squares*. I need to get back in the movies, hon, and that means I need a new look. That's why I came down here.'

Rudy Graveline had never tried to talk anyone out of surgery before, so he was forced to improvise. By and large it was not such a terrible speech. He said, 'God was very good to you, Heather. I have patients who'd give fifty grand to look half as beautiful as you look; teenagers who'd kill for that nose you want me to chisel, housewives who'd trade their first-born child for tits like yours—'

'Rudolph,' Heather said, 'save it.'

He tried to pull up his underwear but the elastic snagged on heavily bandaged kneecaps, the product of the disco tryst in the fireplace.

'I am appalled,' Rudy was huffing, 'at the idea of videotaping in my surgical suite.' In truth he wasn't appalled so much as afraid: a video camera meant he couldn't hand over to the other surgeons and duck out to the golf course. He'd have to perform every procedure himself, just as Heather had demanded. You couldn't drug a damn camera; it wouldn't miss a stitch.

'This just isn't done,' Rudy protested.

'Oh, it is, too,' Heather said. 'I see stuff like that on PBS all the time. Once I saw them put a baboon heart inside a human baby. They showed the whole thing.'

'It isn't done *here*,' Rudy said.

Heather sat up, making sure that the bedsheets slipped off the slope of her breasts. 'Fine, Rudolph,' she said. 'If that's the way you want it, I'll fly back to

California tonight. There's only about a dozen first-rate surgeons in Beverly Hills that would give anything to do me.'

The ice in her voice surprised him, though it shouldn't have. 'All right,' he said, pulling on his robe, 'we'll video the surgery. Maybe Robin Leach can use a clip on his show.'

Heather let the wisecrack pass; she was focused on business. She asked Rudy Graveline for a date they could begin.

'A week,' he said. He had to clear his mind a few more times. In another week he also would have heard something definite from Chemo, or maybe Roberto Pepsical.

'And we're not doing all this at once,' he added. 'You've got the liposuction, the breast augmentation, the rhinoplasty, the eyelids, and the rhytidectomy – that's a lot of surgery, Heather.'

'Yes, Rudolph.' She had won and she knew it.

'I think we'll start with the nose and see how you do.'

'Or how *you* do,' Heather said.

Rudy had a queasy feeling that she wasn't kidding.

The executive producer of *In Your Face* was a man known to Reynaldo Flemm only as Mr Dover. Mr Dover was in charge of the budget. Upon Reynaldo's return to New York, he found a message taped to his office door. Mr Dover wanted to see him right away.

Immediately Reynaldo called the apartment of Christina Marks, but hung up when Mick Stranahan answered the phone. Reynaldo was fiercely jealous; beyond that, he didn't think it was fair that he should have to face Mr Dover alone. Christina was the producer, she knew where all the money went. Reynaldo was merely the talent, and the talent never knew anything.

When he arrived at Mr Dover's office, the secretary did not recognize him. 'The music division is on the third floor,' she said, scarcely making eye contact.

Reynaldo riffled his new hair and said, 'It's me.'

'Oh, hi, Ray.'

'What do you think?'

The secretary said, 'It's a dynamite disguise.'

'It's not a disguise.'

'Oh.'

'I wanted a new look,' he explained.

'Why?' asked the secretary.

Reynaldo couldn't tell her the truth – that a rude plastic surgeon told him he had a fat waist and a big honker – so he said: 'Demographics.'

The secretary looked at him blankly.

'Market surveys,' he went on. 'We're going for some younger viewers.'

'Oh, I see,' the secretary said.

'Long hair is making quite a comeback.'

'I didn't know,' she said, trying to be polite. 'Is that real, Ray?'

'Well, no. Not yet.'

'I'll tell Mr Dover you're here.'

Mr Dover was a short man with an accountant's pinched demeanour, a fish-belly complexion, tiny black eyes, and the slick, sloping forehead of a killer whale. Mr Dover wore expensive dark suits and yuppie suspenders that, Reynaldo suspected, needed adjustment.

'Ray, what can you tell me about this Florida project?' Mr Dover never wasted time with small talk.

'It's heavy,' Reynaldo replied.

'Heavy.'

'Very heavy.' Reynaldo noticed his expense vouchers stacked in a neat pile on the corner of Mr Dover's desk. This worried him, so he said, 'My producer was almost murdered.'

'I see.'

'With a machine-gun,' Reynaldo added.

Mr Dover pursed his lips. 'Why?'

'Because we're getting close to cracking this story.'

'You're getting close to cracking my budget, Ray.'

'This is an important project.'

Mr Dover said, 'A network wouldn't blink twice, Ray, but we're not one of the networks. My job is to watch the bottom line.'

Indignantly Reynaldo thought: *I eat twits like you for breakfast.* He was good at thinking tough thoughts.

'Investigations cost money,' he said tersely.

With shiny fingernails Mr Dover leafed through the receipts on his desk until he found the one he wanted. 'Jambala's House of Hair,' he said. 'Seven hundred and seventeen dollars.'

Reynaldo blushed and ground his caps. Christina should be here for this; she'd know how to handle this jerk.

Mr Dover continued: 'I don't intend to interfere, nor do I intend to let these extravagances go on for ever. As I understand it, the programme is due to air next month.'

'All the spots have been sold,' Reynaldo said. 'They've been sold for six months.' He couldn't resist.

'Yes, well I suggest you try not to spend all that

advertising revenue before the broadcast date – just in case it doesn't work out.'

'And when hasn't it worked out?'

Reynaldo regretted the words almost instantly, for Mr Dover was only too happy to refresh his memory. There was the time Flemm claimed to have discovered the wreckage of Amelia Earhart's aeroplane (it turned out to be a crop duster in New Zealand); the time he claimed to have an exclusive interview with the second gunman from Dealey Plaza (who, it later turned out, was barely seven years old on the day of the Kennedy assassination); the time he uncovered a Congressional call-girl ring (only to be caught boffing two of the ladies in a mop closet at the Rayburn Building). These fiascos each resulted in a cancelled broadcast, snide blurbs in the press, and great sums of lost revenue, which Mr Dover could recall to the penny.

'Ancient history,' Reynaldo Flemm said defensively.

Unspoken was the fact that no such embarrassments had happened since Christina Marks had been hired. Every show had been finished on time, on budget. Reynaldo did not appreciate the connection, but Mr Dover did.

'You understand my concern,' he said. 'How much longer do you anticipate being down in Miami?'

'Two weeks. We'll be editing.' Sounded good, anyway.

'So, shall we say, one more trip?'

'That ought to do it,' Reynaldo agreed.

'Excellent.' Mr Dover straightened the stack of Reynaldo's expense receipts, lining up all the little corners in perfect angles. 'By the way, Miss Marks wasn't harmed, was she?'

'No, just scared shitless. She's not used to getting shot at.' As if he was.

'Did they catch this person?'

'Nope,' Reynaldo said, hard-bitten, like he wasn't too surprised.

'My,' said Mr Dover. He hoped that Christina Marks was paid up on her medical plan and death benefits.

'I told you it was heavy,' Reynaldo said, rising. 'But it'll be worth it, I promise.'

'Good,' said Mr Dover. 'I can't wait.'

Reynaldo was three steps toward the door when Mr Dover said, 'Ray?'

'Yeah.'

'Forgive me, but I was just noticing.'

'That's all right.' He'd been wondering how long it would take the twerp to mention something about the hair.

But from behind the desk Mr Dover smiled wickedly and patted his midsection. 'You've put on a pound or three, haven't you, Ray?'

In the elevator Reynaldo angrily tore off his seven-hundred-dollar wig and hurled it into a corner, where it lay like a dead Pekinese. He took the limo back to his apartment, stripped off his clothes, and stood naked for a long time in front of the bedroom mirror.

Reynaldo decided that Dr Graveline was right: his nose was too large. And his belly had thickened.

He pivoted to the left, then to the right, then back to the left. He sucked in his breath. He flexed. He locked his knuckles behind his head and tightened his stomach muscles, but his belly did not disappear.

In the mirror Reynaldo saw a body that was neither flabby nor lean: an average body for an average forty-year-old man. He saw a face that was neither dashing nor weak: small darting eyes balanced by a strong, heavy jaw, with a nose to match. He concluded that his instincts about preserving the moustache were sound: when Reynaldo covered his hairy upper lip with a bare finger, his nose assumed even greater prominence.

Of course, something radical had to be done. Confidence was the essence of Reynaldo's camera presence, the core of his masculine appeal. If he were unhappy with himself or insecure about his appearance, it would show up on his face like a bad rash. The whole country would see it.

Standing alone at the mirror, Reynaldo hatched a plan that would solve his personal dilemma and wrap up the Barletta story simultaneously. It was a bold plan because it would not include Christina Marks. Reynaldo Flemm would serve as his own producer and would tell Christina nothing, just as she had told him nothing for two entire weeks after the shooting in Stiltsville.

The shooting. Still it galled him, the sour irony that *she* would be the one to get the glory – after all his years on the streets. To have his producer nearly assassinated while he dozed on the massage table at the Sonesta was the lowest moment in Reynaldo's professional career. He had to atone.

In the past he had always counted on Christina to worry about the actual nuts-and-bolts journalism of the programme. It was Christina who did the reporting, blocked out the interviews, arranged for the climactic confrontations – she even wrote the scripts. Reynaldo Flemm was hopelessly bored by detail, research, and the rigours of fact checking. He was an action guy, and he saved his energy for when the tape was rolling. Whereas Christina had filled three legal pads with notes, ideas, and questions about Victoria Barletta's death, Reynaldo cared about one thing only: who could they get on tape? Rudy Graveline was the big enchilada, and certainly Victoria's still-grieving mother was a solid bet. Mick Stranahan had been another obvious choice – the embarrassed investigator, admitting four years later that he had overlooked the prime suspect, the doctor himself.

But the Stranahan move had backfired, and nearly made a news-industry martyr of Christina Marks. Fine, thought Reynaldo, go ahead and have your fling. Meanwhile Willie and I will be kicking some serious quack ass.

Every time Dr Rudy Graveline got a phone call from New York or New Jersey, he assumed it was the mob. The mob had generously put him through Harvard Medical School, and in return Rudy occasionally extended his professional courtesies to mob guys, their friends or family. It was Rudy himself who had redone the face of Tony (the Eel) Traviola, the hit man who later washed up dead on Cape Florida beach with a marlin hole through his sternum. Fortunately for Rudy, most mob fugitives were squeamish about surgery, so he wound up doing mainly their wives, daughters, and mistresses. Noses, mostly, with the occasional face-lift.

That's the kind of call Rudy expected when his secretary told him that New York was on the line.

'Yes?'

'Hello, Doctor Graveline.'

The voice did not belong to Curly Eyebrows or any of his cousins.

'Who is this?'

'Johnny LeTigre, remember me?'

'Of course.' The hinky male stripper. Rudy said, 'What are you doing in New York?'

'I had a gig in the Village, but I'm on my way back to Miami.' This was Reynaldo Flemm's idea of being fast on his feet. He said, 'Look, I've been thinking about what you said that day at the clinic.'

Rudy Graveline could not remember exactly what he had said. 'Yes?'

'About my nose and my abdomen.'

Then it came back to Rudy. 'Your nose and abdomen, yes, I remember.'

'You were right,' Reynaldo went on. 'We don't always see ourselves the way other people do.'

Rudy was thinking: Get to the damn point.

'I'd like for you to do my nose,' Reynaldo declared.

'All right.'

'And my middle – what's that operation called?'

'Suction-assisted lipectomy,' Rudy said.

'Yeah, that's it. How much'd that set me back?'

Rudy recalled that this was a man who offered ten grand to have a mole removed from his buttocks.

'Fifteen thousand,' Rudy said.

'Geez!' said the voice from New York.

'But that's if I perform the procedures myself,' Rudy explained. 'Keep in mind, I've got several very competent associates who could handle your case for, oh, half as much.'

The way that Rudy backed off on the word *competent* was no accident, but Reynaldo Flemm didn't need a sell job. Quickly he said. 'No, I definitely want you. Fifteen it is. But I need the work done this week.'

'Out of the question.' Rudy would be immersed in preparation for the Heather Chappell marathon.

'Next week at the latest,' Reynaldo pressed.

'Let me see what I can do. By the way, Mr LeTigre, what is the status of your mole?'

Reynaldo had almost forgotten about the ruse that originally had gained his entry to Whispering Palms. Again he had to wing it. 'You won't believe this,' he said to Dr Rudy Graveline, 'but the damn thing fell off.'

'Are you certain?'

'Swear to God, one morning I'm standing in the shower and I turn around and it's gone. Gone! I found it lying there in the bed. Just fell off, like an acorn or something.'

'Hmmm,' Rudy said. The guy was a flake, but who cared.

'I threw it away, is that OK?'

'The mole?'

'Yeah, I thought about saving it in the freezer, maybe having some tests run. But then I figured what the hell and I tossed it in the trash.'

'It was probably quite harmless,' Rudy Graveline said, dying to hang up.

'So I'll call you when I get back to Miami.'

'Fine,' said the doctor. 'Have a safe trip, Mr LeTigre.'

Reynaldo Flemm was beaming when he put down the phone. This would be something. Maybe even better than getting shot on the air.

TWENTY

Maggie Gonzalez said: 'Tell me about your hand.'

'Shut up,' Chemo grumbled. He was driving around Queens, trying to find the sonofabitch who had sold him the bad bullets.

'Please,' Maggie said. 'I am a nurse.'

'Too bad you're not a magician, because that's what it's gonna take to make my hand come back. A fish got it.'

At a stop light he rolled down the window and called to a group of black teenagers. He asked where he could locate a man named Donnie Blue, and the teenagers told Chemo to go blow himself. 'Shit,' he said, stomping on the accelerator.

Maggie asked, 'Was it a shark that did it?'

'Do I look like Jacques Cousteau? I don't know what the hell it was – some big fish. The subject is closed.'

By now Maggie was reasonably confident that he wasn't going to kill her. He would have done it already, most conveniently during the scuffle back at the Plaza. Instead he had grabbed her waist and hustled her down the fire exit, taking four steps at a time. Considering the mayhem on the ninth floor, it was a miracle they got out of the place without being stopped. The lobby was full of uniformed cops waiting for elevators, but nobody looked twice at the Fun Couple of the Year.

As Chemo drove, Maggie said, 'What about your face?'

'Look who's talking.'

'Really, what's happened?'

Chemo said, 'You always this shy with strangers? Jesus H. Christ.'

'I'm sorry,' she said. 'Professional curiosity, I guess. Besides, you promised to tell me.'

'Do the words *none of your fucking business* mean anything?'

From behind the bandages a chilly voice said, 'You don't have to be crude. Swearing doesn't impress me.'

Chemo found the street corner where he had purchased the rusty Colt .38 and the dead bullets, but there was no sign of Donnie Blue. Every enquiry was met by open derision, and Chemo's hopes for a refund began to fade.

As he circled the neighbourhood Maggie said, 'You're so quiet.'

'I'm thinking.'

'Me, too.'

'I'm thinking I was seriously gypped by your doctor pal.' Chemo didn't want to admit that he had agreed to murder two people in exchange for a discount on minor plastic surgery.

'If I had known about this dead girl—'

'Vicky Barletta.'

'Right,' Chemo said. 'If I had known that, I would have jacked my price. Jacked it way the hell up.'

'And who could blame you,' Maggie said.

'Graveline never told me he killed a girl.'

They were heading out the highway toward La-Guardia. Maggie assumed there were travel plans.

She said, 'Rudy's a very wealthy man.'

'Sure, he's a doctor.'

'I can ruin him. That's why he wanted me dead.'

'Sure, you're a witness,' Chemo said.

Something dismissive in his tone alarmed her once again. She said, 'Killing me won't solve anything now.'

Chemo's forehead crinkled where an eyebrow should have been. 'It won't?'

Maggie shook her head from side to side in dramatic emphasis. 'I made my own tape. A videotape, at a place in Manhattan. Everything's on it, everything I saw that day.'

Chemo wasn't as rattled as she thought he might be, in fact, his mouth curled into a dry smile. His lips looked like two pink snails crawling up a sidewalk.

'A video,' he mused.

Maggie teased it along. 'You have any idea what that bastard would pay for it?'

'Yes,' Chemo said. 'Yes, I think I do.'

At the airport, Maggie told Chemo she had to make a phone call. To eavesdrop he squeezed inside the same booth, his chin digging into the top of her head. She dialled the number of Dr Leonard Leaper and informed the service that she had to leave town for a while, but that the doctor should not be concerned.

'I already told him I was a witness in a murder,' Maggie explained to Chemo. 'If what happened at the hotel turns up in the newspapers, he'll think I was kidnapped.'

'But you were,' Chemo pointed out.

'Oh, not really.'

'Yes, *really*.' Chemo didn't care for her casual attitude; just who did she take him for?

Maggie said: 'Know what I think? I think we could be partners.'

They got in line at the Pan Am counter, surrounded by a typical Miami-bound contingent – old geezers with tubas for sinuses; shiny young hustlers in thin gold chains; huge hollow-eyed families that looked like they'd staggered out of a Sally Struthers telethon. Chemo and Maggie fit right in.

He told her, 'I only got one plane ticket.'

She smiled and stroked her handbag, which had not left her arm since their breakfast in Central Park. 'I've got a Visa card,' she said brightly. 'Where we headed?'

'Me, I'm going back to Florida.'

'Not like that, you're not. They've got rules against bare feet, I'm sure.'

'Hell,' Chemo said, and loped off to locate some cheap shoes. He came back wearing fuzzy brown bath-room slippers, size 14, purchased at one of the airport gift shops. Maggie was saving him a spot at the ticket counter. She had already arranged for him to get an aisle seat (because of his long legs), and she would be next to him.

Later, waiting in the boarding area, Maggie asked Chemo if his name was Rogelio Luz Sanchez.

'Oh sure.'

'That's what it says on your ticket.'

'Well, there you are,' Chemo said. He couldn't even *pronounce* Rogelio Luz Sanchez – some alias cooked up by Rudy Graveline, the dumb shit. Chemo looked about as Hispanic as Larry Bird.

After they took their seats on the aeroplane, Maggie leaned close and asked, 'So, can I call you Rogelio? I mean, I've got to call you *something*.'

Chemo's hooded lids blinked twice very slowly. 'The more you talk, the more I want to spackle the holes in that fucking mask.'

Maggie emitted a reedy, birdlike noise.

'I think we can do business,' Chemo said, 'but only on two conditions. One, don't ask any more personal questions, is that clear? Two, don't ever puke on me again.'

'I said I was sorry.'

The plane had started to taxi and Chemo raised his voice to be heard over the engines. 'Once I get some decent bullets I'll be using that gun, and God help you if you toss your cookies when I do.'

Maggie said, 'I'll do better next time.'

One of the flight attendants came by and asked Maggie if she needed a special meal because of her medical condition, and Maggie remarked that she wasn't feeling particularly well. She said the coach section was so crowded and stuffy that she was having trouble breathing. The next thing Chemo knew, they were sitting up in first class and sipping red wine. Having noticed his disability, the friendly flight attendant was carefully cutting Chemo's surf-and-turf into bite-sized pieces. Chemo glanced at Maggie and felt guilt about coming down so hard.

'That was a slick move,' he said, the closest he would come to a compliment. 'I never rode up here before.'

Maggie exhibited no surprise at this bit of news. Her eyes looked sad and moist behind the white husk.

Chemo said, 'You still want to be partners?'

She nodded. Carefully she aimed a forkful of lobster for the damp hole beneath her nostrils in the surgical bandage.

'Graveline's gonna scream when he learns about your videotape,' Chemo said with a chuckle. 'Where is it, anyway?'

When Maggie finished chewing, she said, 'I've got three copies.'

'Good thinking.'

'Two of them are locked up at a bank. The third one, the original tape, that's for Rudy. That's how we get his attention.'

Chemo smiled a yellow smile. 'I like it.'

'You won't like this part,' Maggie said. 'Stranahan swiped the tape from the hotel room. We can't show it to Rudy until we get it back.'

'Hell,' Chemo said. This was terrible – Mick Stranahan and that TV bitch loose with the blackmail goodies. Just terrible. He said, 'I've got to get them before they get to Graveline, otherwise we're blown out of the water. He'll be on the first flight to Panama and we'll be holding our weenies.'

From Maggie came a muffled, disapproving noise.

'It's just an expression,' Chemo said. 'Lighten up, for Chrissakes.'

After the flight attendants removed the meal trays, Chemo lowered the seat back and stretched his endless legs. Almost to himself, he said, 'I don't like this Stranahan guy one bit. When we get to Miami, we hit the ground running.'

'Yes,' Maggie agreed, easing into the partnership, 'we've got to get the tape.'

'That, too,' said Chemo, tugging his hat down over his eyes.

*

The news of gunshots and a possible kidnapping at the Plaza Hotel rated five paragraphs in the *Daily News*, a page of photos in the *Post* and nothing in the *Times*. That morning New York detectives queried a teletype to the Metro-Dade Police Department stating that the victim of the abduction was believed to be a Miami woman named Margaret Orestes Gonzalez, a guest at the hotel. The police teletype described her assailant as a white male, age unknown, with possible burn scars on his face and a height of either six foot four or eight foot two, depending on which witness you believed. The teletype further noted that a Rapala fishing knife found on the carpet outside the victim's room was traced to a shipment that recently had been sold to a retail establishment known as Bubba's Bait and Cold Beer, on Dixie Highway in South Miami. Most significantly, a partial thumb-print lifted from the blade of the knife was identified as belonging to one Blondell Wayne Tatum, age thirty-eight, six foot nine, one hundred and eighty-one pounds. Mr Tatum, it seemed, was wanted in the state of Pennsylvania for the robbery-at-pitchfork of a Chemical Bank, and for the first-degree murder of Dr Kyle Kloppner, an elderly dermatologist. Tatum was to be considered armed and dangerous. Under AKAs, the police bulletin listed one: Chemo.

'Chemo?' Sergeant Al García read the teletype again, then pulled it off the bulletin board and took it to the Xerox machine. By the time he got back, a new teletype had been posted in its place.

This one was even more interesting, and García's cigar bobbed excitedly as he read it.

The new teletype advised Metro-Dade police to disregard the kidnap query. Miss Margaret Gonzalez had phoned the New York authorities to assure them that she was in no danger, and to explain that the disturbance at the Plaza Hotel was merely a dispute between herself and a male companion she had met in a bar.

Maggie had hung up before detectives could ask if the male companion was Mr Blondell Wayne Tatum.

Commissioner Roberto Pepiscal arranged to meet the two crooked detectives at a strip joint off LeJeune Road, not far from the airport. Roberto got there early and drank three strong vodka tonics to give him the courage to say what he'd been told to say. He figured he was so far over his head that being drunk couldn't make it any worse.

Dutifully the commissioner had carried Detective Murdock's proposal to Dr Rudy Graveline, and now he had returned with the doctor's reply. It occurred to Roberto, even as a naked woman with gold teeth delivered a fourth vodka, that the role of an elected public servant was no longer a distinguished one. He found himself surrounded by ruthless and untrustworthy people – nobody played a straight game any more. In Miami, corruption had become a sport of the masses. Roberto had been doing it for years, of course, but jerks like Salazar and Murdock and even Graveline – they were nothing but dilettantes. Moochers. They didn't know when to back off. The word *enough* was not in their vocabulary. Roberto hated the idea that his future depended on such men.

The crooked cops showed up just as the nude Amazonian mud-wrestling match began on stage. 'Very nice place,' Detective John Murdock said to the commissioner. 'Is that your daughter up there?'

Joe Salazar said, 'The one on the right, she even looks like you. Except I think you got bigger knockers.'

Roberto Pepsical flushed. He was sensitive about his weight. 'You're really funny,' he said to the detectives. 'Both of you should've been comedians instead of cops. You should've been Lawrence and Hardy.'

Murdock smirked. 'Lawrence and Hardy, huh? I think the commissioner has been drinking.'

Salazar said, 'Maybe we hurt his feelings.'

The vodka was supposed to make Roberto Pepsical cool and brave; instead it was making him hot and dizzy. He started to tell the detectives what Rudy Graveline had said, but he couldn't hear himself speak over the exhortations of the wrestling fans. Finally Murdock seized him by the arm and led him to the restroom. Joe Salazar followed them in and locked the door.

'What's all this for?' Roberto said, belching in woozy fear. He thought the detectives were going to beat him up.

Murdock took him by the shoulders and pinned him to the condom machine. He said, 'Joe and I don't like this joint. It's noisy, it's dirty, it's a shitty fucking joint to hold a serious conversation. We are offended, Commissioner, by what we see taking place on the stage out there – naked young females with wet mud all over their twats. You shouldn't have invited us here.'

Joe Salazar said, 'That's right. Just so you know, I'm a devoted Catholic.'

'I'm sorry,' said Roberto Pepsical. 'It was the darkest place I could think of on short notice. Next time we'll meet at St Mary's.'

Someone knocked on the restroom and Murdock told him to go away if he valued his testicles. Then he said to Roberto: 'What is it you wanted to tell us?'

'It's a message from my friend. The one with the problem I told you about—'

'The problem named Stranahan?'

'Yes. He says five thousand each.'

'Fine,' said John Murdock.

'Really?'

'Long as it's cash.'

Salazar added, 'Not in sequence. And not bank-wrapped.'

'Certainly,' Roberto Pepsical said. Now came the part that made his throat go dry.

'There's one part of the plan that my friend wants to change,' he said. 'He says it's no good just arresting this man and putting him in jail. He says this fellow has a big mouth and a vivid imagination.' Those were Rudy's exact words; Roberto was proud of himself for remembering.

Joe Salazar idly tested the knobs on the condom machine and said, 'So you got a better idea, right?'

'Well . . .' Roberto said.

Murdock loosened his grip on the commissioner and straightened his jacket. 'You're not the idea man, are you? I mean, it was your idea to meet at this pussy parlour.' He walked over to the urinal and unzipped his trousers. 'Joe and I will think of something. We're idea-type guys.'

Salazar said, 'For instance, supposing we get a warrant to arrest the suspect for the murder of his former wife. Supposing we proceed to his residence and duly identify ourselves as sworn police officers. And supposing the suspect attempts to flee.'

'Or resists with violence,' Murdock hypothesized.

'Yeah, the manual is clear,' Salazar said.

Murdock shook himself off and zipped up. 'In a circumstance such as that, we could use deadly force.'

'I imagine you could,' said Roberto Pepsical, sober as a choirboy.

The three of them stood there in the restroom, sweating under the hot bare bulb. Salazar examined a package of flamingo-pink rubbers that he had shaken loose from the vending machine.

Finally Murdock said, 'Tell your friend it sounds fine, except for the price. Make it ten apiece, not five.'

'Ten,' Roberto repeated, though he was not at all surprised. To close the deal, he sighed audibly.

'Come on,' said Joe Salazar, unlocking the door. 'We're missing the fingerpaint contest.'

Over the whine of the outboard Luis Córdova shouted: 'There's no point in stopping.'

Mick Stranahan nodded. Under ceramic skies, Biscayne Bay unfolded in a dozen shifting hues of blue. It was a fine, cloudless morning: seventy degrees, and a northern breeze at their backs. Luis Córdova slowed the patrol boat a few hundred yards from the stilt house. He leaned down and said: 'They tore the place up pretty bad, Mick.'

'You sure it was cops?'

'Yeah, two of them. Not uniformed guys, though. And they had one of the sheriff boats.'

Stranahan knew who it was: Murdock and Salazar.

'Those goons from the hospital,' said Christina Marks. She stood next to Luis Córdova at the steering console, behind the Plexiglas windshield. She wore a red windbreaker, baggy knit pants, and high-top tennis shoes.

From a distance Stranahan could see that the door to his house had been left open, which meant it had probably been looted and vandalized. What the kids didn't wreck, the seagulls would. Stranahan stared for a few moments, then said: 'Let's go, Luis.'

The trip to Old Rhodes Key took thirty-five minutes in a light, nudging sea. Christina got excited when they passed a school of porpoises off Elliott Key, but Stranahan showed no interest. He was thinking about the videotape they had watched at Christina's apartment – Maggie Gonzalez, describing the death of Vicky Barletta. Twice they had watched it. It made him mad but he wasn't sure why. He had heard of worse things, seen worse things. Yet there was something about a doctor doing it, getting away with it, that made Stranahan furious.

When they reached the island, Luis Córdova dropped them at a sagging dock that belonged to an old Bahamian conch fisherman named Cartwright. Cartwright had been told they were coming.

'I got the place ready,' he told Mick Stranahan. 'By the way, it's good to see you, my friend.'

Stranahan gave him a hug. Cartwright was eighty years old. His hair was like cotton fuzz and his skin was the colour of hot tar. He had Old Rhodes Key largely to himself and seldom entertained, but he had happily made an exception for his old friend. Years ago Stranahan had done Cartwright a considerable favour.

'White man tried to burn me out,' he told Christina Marks. 'Mick took care of things.'

Stranahan hoisted the duffel bags over his shoulders and trudged toward the house. He said, 'Some asshole developer wanted Cartwright's land but Cartwright didn't want to sell. Things got sticky.'

The conch fisherman cut in: 'I tell the story better. The man offered me one hunnert towsind dollars to move off the island and when I says no thanks, brother, he had some peoples pour gasoline all on my house. Luckily it rain like hell. Mick got this man arrested and dey put him in the big jail up Miami. That's the God's truth.'

'Good for Mick,' Christina said. Naturally she had assumed that Stranahan had killed the man.

'Asshole got six years and did fifteen months. He's out already.' Stranahan laughed acidly.

'That I didn't know,' Cartwright said thoughtfully.

'Don't worry, he won't ever come back to this place.'

'You don't tink so?'

'No, Cartwright, I promise he won't. I had a long talk with the man. I believe he moved to California.'

'Very fine,' Cartwright said with obvious relief.

House was a charitable description for where the old fisherman lived: bare cinderblock walls on a concrete foundation; no doors in the doorways, no glass in the windows; a roof woven from dried palm fronds.

'Dry as a bone,' Cartwright said to Christina. 'I know it don't look like much, but you be dry inside here.'

Gamely she said, 'I'll be fine.'

Stranahan winked at Cartwright. 'City girl,' he said.

Christina jabbed Stranahan in the ribs. 'And you're Daniel Boone, I suppose. Well, fuck you both. I can handle myself.'

Cartwright's eyes grew wide.

'Sorry,' Christina said.

'Don't be,' Cartwright said with a booming laugh. 'I love it. I love the sound of a womanly voice out here.'

For lunch he fixed fresh lobster in a conch salad. Afterwards he gathered some clothes in a plastic garbage bag, told Mick goodbye and headed slowly down to the dock.

Christina said, 'Where's he going?'

'To the mainland,' Stranahan replied. 'He's got a grandson in Florida City he hasn't seen in a while.'

From where they sat, they could see Cartwright's wooden skiff motoring westward across the bay; the old man had one hand on the stem of the throttle, the other shielding his eyes from the low winter sun.

Christina turned to Stranahan. 'You arranged it this way.'

'He's a nice guy. He doesn't deserve any trouble.'

'You really think they'll find us all the way out here?'

'Yep,' Stranahan said. He was counting on it.

TWENTY-ONE

The clerical staff of Kipper Garth's law office was abuzz: clients – real live clients – were coming in for a meeting. Most of the secretaries had never seen any of Kipper Garth's clients because he generally did not allow them to visit. Normally all contact took place over the telephone, since Kipper Garth's practice was built exclusively on referrals to other lawyers. The rumour this day (and an incredible one, at that) was that Kipper Garth was going to handle a malpractice case all by himself; one of the senior paralegals had been vaguely instructed to prepare a complaint for civil court. The women who worked Kipper Garth's phone bank figured that it must be a spectacularly egregious case if their boss would tackle it solo, for his fear of going to court was well known. Kipper Garth's staff couldn't wait to get a look at the new clients.

They arrived at eleven sharp, a man and a woman. The clerks, secretaries, and paralegals were startled: it was an unremarkable couple in their mid-thirties. The man was medium-build and ordinary-looking, the woman had long ash-blonde hair and a nice figure. Neither displayed any obvious scars, mutilations, or crippling deformities. Kipper Garth's staff was baffled –

the hushed wagering shifted back and forth between psychiatric aberration and sexual dysfunction.

Both guesses were wrong. The problem of John and Marie Nordstrom was far more peculiar.

Kipper Garth greeted them crisply at the door and led them to two high-backed easy chairs positioned in front of his desk. The lawyer was extremely nervous and hoped it didn't show. He hoped he would ask the right questions.

'Mr Nordstrom,' he began, 'I'd like to review some of the material in the state files.'

Nordstrom looked around the elegant office and said: 'Are we the only ones?'

'What do you mean?'

'Are we the only ones to sue? Over the phone you said a whole bunch of his patients were suing.'

Kipper Garth tugged restlessly at the sleeves of his coat. 'Well, we've been talking to several others with strong cases. I'm sure they'll come around. Meanwhile you and your wife expressed an interest—'

'But not alone,' John Nordstrom said. 'We don't want to be the only ones.' His wife reached across and touched his arm. 'Let's listen to him,' she said. 'It can't hurt.'

Kipper Garth waited for the moment of tension to pass. It didn't. He motioned toward the walnut credenza behind his desk. 'See all those files, Mr Nordstrom? Patients of Dr Rudy Graveline. Most of them have suffered more than you and your wife. Much more.'

Nordstrom said, 'So what's your point?'

'The point is, Mr Nordstrom, a monster is loose. Graveline is still in business. On a good day his clinic takes in a hundred grand in surgical fees. One hundred grand! And every patient walks in there thinking that Dr Graveline is one brilliant surgeon, and some of them find out the hard way that he's not. He's a putz.'

Mrs Nordstrom said: 'You don't have to tell us.'

Kipper Garth leaned forward and, ministerially, folded his hands. 'For me, this case isn't about money.' He sounded so damn earnest that he almost believed himself. 'It isn't about money, it's about morality. And conscience. And concern for one's fellow man. I don't know about you folks, but my stomach churns when I think how a beast like Rudolph Graveline is allowed to continue to destroy the lives of innocent, trusting people.' Kipper Garth swivelled his chair slowly and gestured again at the stacks of files. 'Look at all these victims – men and women just like yourselves. And to think that the state of Florida has done nothing to stop this beast. It makes me nauseous.'

'Me, too,' said Mrs Nordstrom.

'My mission,' continued Kipper Garth, 'is to find someone with the courage to go after this man. Shut him down. Bring to light his incompetence so that no one else will have to suffer. The place to do that is the courtroom.'

John Nordstrom sniffed. 'Don't tell me the sonofa-bitch's never been sued before.'

Kipper Garth smiled. 'Oh yes. Yes, indeed, Dr Grave-line has been sued before. But he's always escaped the glare of publicity and the scrutiny of his peers. How? By settling the cases out of court. He buys his way out, never goes to trial. This time he won't get off so lightly, Mr Nordstrom. This time, with your permission, I want to take him to the wall. I want to go all the way. I'm talking about a trial.'

It was a damn mellifluous speech for a man accustomed to bellowing at a speaker box. If not moved, the Nordstroms were at least impressed. A self-satisfied Kipper Garth wondered if he could ever be so smooth in front of a jury.

Marie Nordstrom said: 'In person you look much younger than on your billboards.'

The lawyer acknowledged the remark with a slight bow.

Mrs Nordstrom nudged her husband. 'Go ahead, tell him what happened.'

'It's all in the file,' John Nordstrom said.

'I'd like to hear it again,' Kipper Garth said, 'in your own words.' He pressed a button on the telephone console, and a stenographer with a portable machine entered the office. She was followed by a sombre-looking paralegal wielding a long yellow pad. Mutely they took positions on either side of Kipper Garth. Nordstrom scanned the trio warily.

His wife said: 'It's a little embarrassing for us, that's all.'

'I understand,' Kipper Garth said. 'We'll take our time.'

Nordstrom shot a narrow look at his wife. 'You start,' he said.

Calmly she straightened in the chair and cleared her throat. 'Two years ago, I went to Dr Graveline for a routine breast augmentation. He came highly recommended.'

'Your manicurist,' John Nordstrom interjected, 'a real expert.'

Kipper Garth raised a tanned hand. 'Please.'

Marie Nordstrom continued: 'I insisted that Dr

Graveline himself do the surgery. Looking back on it, I would've been better off with one of the other fellows at the clinic – anyway, the surgery was performed on a Thursday. Within a week it was obvious that something was very wrong.'

Kipper Garth said, 'How did you know?'

'Well, the new breasts were quite . . . hard.'

'Try concrete,' John Nordstrom said.

His wife went on: 'They were extremely round and tight. Too tight. I mean, they didn't even bounce.'

A true professional, Kipper Garth never let his eyes wander below Mrs Nordstrom's neckline.

She said: 'When I saw Dr Graveline again, he assured me that this was normal for cases like mine. He had a name for it and everything.'

'Capsular contracture,' said the paralegal, without looking up from her notes.

'That's it,' Mrs Nordstrom said. 'Dr Graveline told me everything would be fine in a month or two. He said they'd be soft as little pillows.'

'And?'

'And we waited, just like he told us. In the meantime, of course, John kept wanting to try them out.'

'Hey,' Nordstrom said, 'I paid for the damn things.'

'I understand,' said Kipper Garth. 'So you made love to your wife?'

Nordstrom's cheeks reddened. 'You know the rest.'

With his chin Kipper Garth pointed toward the stenographer and the paralegal, both absorbed in transcribing the incident. Nordstrom sighed and said, 'Yeah, I made love to my wife. Or tried to.'

'That's when the accident happened between John

and my breasts,' continued Mrs Nordstrom. 'I'm not sure if it was the left one or the right one that got him.'

Nordstrom muttered, 'I'm not sure, either. It was a big hard boob, that's all I knew.'

Kipper Garth said, 'And it actually put your eye out?'

John Nordstrom nodded darkly.

His wife said: 'Technically they called it a detached retina. We didn't know it was so serious right away. John's eye got all swollen and then there was some bleeding. When his vision didn't come back after a few days, we went to a specialist . . . but it was already too late.'

Gently Kipper Garth said, 'I noticed that you told the ophthalmic surgeon a slightly different story. You told him you were poked by a Christmas tree branch.'

Nordstrom glared, with his good eye, at the lawyer. 'What the hell would *you* have told him – that you were blinded by a tit?'

'It must have been difficult,' Kipper Garth said, his voice rich with sympathy. 'And this was your right eye, according to the file.'

'Yeah,' said Nordstrom, pointing.

'They gave him a glass one,' his wife added. 'You can hardly tell.'

'*I* can sure as hell tell,' Nordstrom said.

Kipper Garth asked: 'Did it affect your work?'

'Are you kidding? I lost my job.'

'Really?' The lawyer suppressed a grin of delight, but mentally tacked a couple more zeros to the pain-and-suffering demand.

Mrs Nordstrom said: 'John was an air-traffic controller. You can well imagine the problems.'

'Yeah, and the jokes,' Nordstrom said bitterly.

Kipper Garth leaned back and locked his hands across his vest. 'Folks, how does ten million sound?'

Nordstrom snorted. 'Come off it.'

'We get the right jury, we can probably do twelve.'

'Twelve million dollars – no shit?'

'No shit,' said Kipper Garth. 'Mrs Nordstrom, I need to ask you something. Did this, uh, condition with your breasts ever improve?'

She glanced down at her chest. 'Not much.'

'Not much is right,' said her husband. 'Take my word, they're like goddamn bocci balls.'

The guy would be poison as a witness, Kipper Garth decided; the jury would hate his guts. No wonder other lawyers had balked at taking the case. Kipper Garth thanked the Nordstroms for their time and showed them to the door. He promised to get back to them in a few days with some important papers to review.

After the couple had gone, Kipper Garth ordered the stenographer to transcribe the interview and make a half-dozen copies. Then he told the paralegal to type up a malpractice complaint against Dr Rudy Graveline and the Whispering Palms Spa and Surgery Center.

'Can you handle that?' Kipper Garth asked.

'I think so,' the paralegal said, coolly.

'And afterwards go down to the courthouse and do . . . whatever it is needs to be done.'

'We'll go together,' the paralegal said. 'You might as well learn your way around.'

Kipper Garth agreed pensively. If only his ski bunny knew what their dalliance had cost him. That his black-mailer was his own frigging brother-in-law compounded the humiliation. 'One more question,' Kipper Garth said to his paralegal. 'After we file the lawsuit, then what?'

'We wait,' she replied.

The lawyer giggled with relief. 'That's all?'

'Sure, we wait and see what happens,' the paralegal said. 'It's just like dropping a bomb.'

'I see,' said Kipper Garth. Just what he needed in his life. A bomb.

Freddie was napping in his office at the Gay Bidet when one of the ticket girls stuck her head in the doorway and said there was a man wanted to see him. Right away Freddie didn't like the looks of the guy, and would have taken him for a cop except that cops don't dress so good. The other thing Freddie didn't like about the guy was the way he kept looking around the place with his nose twitching up in the air like a swamp rabbit, like there was something about the place that really stunk. Freddie didn't appreciate that.

'This isn't what I expected,' the man said.

'The fuck you expect, Regine's?' Boldly Freddie took the offensive.

'This isn't a gay bar?' the man asked. 'I assumed from the name . . .'

Freddie said, 'I didn't name the place, pal. All I know is, it rhymes. That doesn't automatically make it no fruit bar. Now state your business or beat it.'

'I need to see one of your bouncers.'

'What for?'

The man said, 'I'm his doctor.'

'He sick?'

'I don't know until I see him,' said Rudy Graveline.

Freddie was sceptical. Maybe the guy was a doctor,

maybe not; these days everybody was wearing white silk suits.

'Which of my security personnel you want to see?' asked Freddie.

'He's quite a big man.'

'They're all big, mister. I don't hire no munchkins.'

'This one is extremely tall and thin. His face is heavily scarred, and he's missing his left hand.'

'Don't know him,' Freddie said, playing it safe. In case the guy was a clever bail bondsman or an undercover cop with a wardrobe budget.

Rudy said: 'But he told me he works here.'

Freddie shook his head and made sucking sounds through his front teeth. 'I have a large staff, mister, and turnover to match. Not everybody can take the noise.' He jerked a brown thumb toward the fibreboard wall, which was vibrating from the music on the other side.

'Sounds like an excellent band,' Rudy said lamely.

'Cathy and the Catheters,' Freddie reported with a shrug. 'Queen of slut rock, all the way from London.' He pushed himself to his feet and stretched. 'Sorry I can't help you, mister—'

At that instant the ticket girl flung open the door and told Freddie that a terrible fight had broken out and he better come quick. Rudy Graveline was huffing at Freddie's heels by the time a path had been cleared to the front of the stage. There a gang of anorexic Nazi skinheads had taken on a gang of flabby redneck bikers in a dispute over tattoos – specifically, whose was the baddest. The battle had been joined by a cadre of heavy-set bouncers, each sporting a pink Gay Bidet T-shirt with the word *SECURITY* stencilled on the back. The vicious fighting seemed only to inspire more volume from the band and more random slam-dancing from the other punkers.

Towering above the mêlée was Chemo himself, his T-shirt ragged and bloody, and a look of baleful concentration on his face. Even through the blinding strobes, Rudy Graveline could see that the Weed Whacker attached to Chemo's stub was unsheathed and fully operative; the monofilament cutter was spinning so rapidly that it appeared transparent and harmless, like a hologram. In horror Rudy watched Chemo lower the buzzing device into the tangle of humanity – the ensuing screams rose plangently over the music. As if by pre-arrangement, the other bouncers backed off and let Chemo work, while Freddie supervised from atop an overturned amplifier.

The fighting subsided quickly. Splints and bandages were handed out to fallen bikers and skinheads alike, while the band took a break. An expression of fatherly admiration in his shoe-button eyes, Freddie patted Chemo on the shoulder, then disappeared backstage. Rudy Graveline worked his way through the sweaty crowd, stepping over the wounded and semiconscious until he reached Chemo's side.

'Well, that was amazing,' Rudy said.

Chemo glanced down at him and scowled. 'Fucking battery died. I hope that's it for the night.'

The surgeon said, 'We really need to talk.'

'Yes,' Chemo agreed. 'We sure do.'

As soon as Chemo and Rudy went backstage, they ran into Freddie, Cathy, and two of the Catheters sharing some hash in a glass pipe. Through a puff of blue smoke Freddie said to Chemo: 'This jerkoff claimed he's your doctor.'

'Was,' Chemo said. 'Can we use the dressing room?'

'Anything you want,' Freddie said.

'Watch out for my python,' Cathy cautioned.

The dressing room was not what Rudy had expected. There was a folding card table, an old-fashioned coat rack, a blue velour sofa, a jagged triangle of broken mirror on the wall and, in one corner, an Igloo cooler full of Heinekens. On the naked floor was a low flat cage made from plywood and chicken wire in which resided a nine-foot Burmese python, the signature of Cathy's big encore.

Rudy Graveline took a chair at the card table while Chemo stretched out on the whorehouse sofa.

Rudy said: 'I was worried when you didn't call from New York. What happened?'

Chemo ran a whitish tongue across his lips. 'Aren't you even going to ask about my face, how it's healing?'

The doctor seemed impatient. 'It looks fine from here. It looks like the dermabrasion is taking nicely.'

'As if you'd know.'

Rudy's mouth twitched. 'Now what is that supposed to mean?'

'It means you're a fucking menace to society. I'm getting myself another doctor – Maggie's picking one out for me.'

Rudy Graveline felt the back of his neck go damp. It wasn't as if he had not expected problems with Chemo – that was the reason for choosing Roberto Pepsical and his crooked cops as a contingency. But it was merely failure, not betrayal, that Rudy had anticipated from his homicidal stork.

'Maggie?' the doctor said. 'Maggie Gonzalez?'

'Yeah, that's the one. We had a long talk, she told me some things.'

'Talking to her wasn't the plan,' Rudy said.

'Yeah, well, the plan has been changed.' Chemo reached into the Igloo cooler and got a beer. He twisted off the cap, tilted the bottle to his lips, and glowered at the doctor the whole time he gulped it down. Then he belched once and said: 'You tried to gyp me.'

Rudy said, 'That's simply not true.'

'You didn't tell me the stakes. You didn't tell me about the Barletta girl.'

The colour washed from Rudy's face. Stonily he stared into his own lap. Suddenly his silk Armani seemed as hot and heavy as an army blanket.

Chemo rolled the empty Heineken bottle across the bare terrazzo floor until it clanked to rest against the snake cage. The sleek green python flicked its tongue once, then went back to sleep.

Chemo said, 'And all this time, I thought you knew what the fuck you were doing. I trusted you with my own face.' He laughed harshly and burped again. 'Jesus H. Christ, I bet your own family won't let you carve the bird on Thanksgiving, am I right?'

In a thin, abraded voice, Rudy Graveline said: 'So Maggie is still alive.'

'Yeah, and she's going to stay that way as long as I say so.' Chemo swung his spidery legs off the sofa and sat up, straight as a lodgepole. 'Because if anything should happen to her, you are going to be instantly famous. I'm talking TV, Dr Frankenstein.'

By now Rudy was having difficulty catching his breath.

Chemo went on. 'Your nurse is a smart girl. She made

three videotapes for insurance. Two of them are locked up safe and sound in New York. The other . . . well, you'd better pray that I find it before it finds you.'

'Go do it.' Rudy's voice was toneless and weak.

'Naturally this will be very expensive.'

'Whatever you need,' the doctor croaked. This was a scenario he had never foreseen, something beyond his worst screaming nightmares.

'I didn't realize plastic surgeons made so much dough,' Chemo remarked. 'Maggie was telling me.'

'The overhead,' Rudy said, fumbling, 'is sky-high.'

'Well, yours just got higher by seven feet.' Chemo produced a small aerosol can of WD-40 and began lubricating the rotor mechanism of the Weed Whacker. Without glancing up from his chore, he said, 'By the way, Frankenstein, you're getting off easy. Last time a doctor screwed me over, I broke his frigging neck.'

In his mental catacomb Rudy clearly heard the snap of the old dermatologist's spine, watched as the electrolysis needle fell from the old man's lifeless hand and clattered on the office floor.

As soon as he regained his composure, Rudy asked, 'Who's got the missing tape?'

'Oh, take a wild guess.' There was amusement in Chemo's dry tone.

'Shit,' said Rudy Graveline.

'My sentiments exactly.'

TWENTY-TWO

Reynaldo Flemm hadn't even finished explaining the plan before Willie, the cameraman, interrupted. 'What about Christina?' he asked. 'What does she say?'

'Christina is tied up on another project.'

Willie eyed him sceptically. 'What project?'

'That's not important.'

Willie didn't give up; he was accustomed to Reynaldo treating him like hired help. 'She in New York?'

Reynaldo said, 'She could be in New Delhi for all I care. Point is, I'm producing the Barletta segment. Get used to it, buddy.'

Willie settled back to sip his Planter's punch and enjoy the rosy tropical dusk. They had a deck table facing the ocean at an outdoor bar, not far from the Sonesta on Key Biscayne. Reynaldo Flemm was nursing a Perrier, so Willie was confident of having the upper hand. Reynaldo was the only person he knew who blabbed more when he was sober than when he was drunk. Right now Reynaldo was blabbing about his secret plan to force Dr Rudy Graveline to confess in front of the television camera. It was the most ludicrous scheme that Willie had ever heard, the sort of thing he'd love to watch, not shoot.

After a decent interval, Willie put his rum drink on the table and said: 'Who's blocking out the interview?'

'Me.'

'The questions, too?'

Reynaldo Flemm reddened.

Willie said, 'Shouldn't we run this puppy by the lawyers? I think we got serious trespass problems.'

'Ha,' Reynaldo scoffed.

Sure, Willie thought sourly, go ahead and laugh. I'm the one who always gets tossed in the squad car. I'm the one gets blamed when the cops bang up the camera.

Reynaldo Flemm said, 'Let me worry about the legalities, Willie. The question is: can you do it?'

'Sure, I can do it.'

'You won't need extra lights?'

Willie shook his head. 'Plenty of light,' he said. 'Getting the sound is where I see the problem.'

'I was wondering about that, too. I can't very well wear the wireless.'

Willie chuckled in agreement. 'No, not hardly.'

Reynaldo said, 'You'll think of something, you always do. Actually, I prefer the hand-held.'

'I know,' Willie said. Reynaldo disliked the tiny cordless clip-on microphones; he favoured the old baton-style mikes that you held in your hand – the kind you could thrust in some crooked politician's face and make him pee his pants. Christina Marks called it Reynaldo's 'phallic attachment'. She postulated that, in Reynaldo's mind, the microphone had become a substitute for his penis.

As Willie recalled, Reynaldo didn't think much of Christina's theory.

He said to Willie: 'This'll be hairy, but we've done it before. We're a good team.'

'Yeah,' said Willie, half-heartedly draining his glass. Some team. The basic plan never changed: get Reynaldo beat up. *Now remember,* he used to tell Willie, *we got to live up to the name of the show. Stick it right in his motherloving face, really piss him off.* Willie had it down to an art: he'd poke the TV camera directly at the subject's nose, the guy would push the camera away and tear off in a fury after Reynaldo Flemm. *Now remember,* Reynaldo would coach, *when he shoves you, jiggle the camera like you were really shaken up. Make the picture super jerky looking, the way they do on* Sixty Minutes. If by chance the interview subject lunged after Willie instead of Reynaldo, Willie had standing orders to halt taping, shield the camera and defend himself – in that order. Invariably the person doing the pummelling got tired of banging his fists on a bulky, galvanized Sony and redirected his antagonism toward the arrogant puss of Reynaldo Flemm. *It's me they're tuning in to see,* Reynaldo would say, *I'm the talent here.* But if the beating became too severe or if Reynaldo got outnumbered, Willie's job then was to stow the camera (carefully) and start swinging away. Many times he had felt like a rodeo clown, diverting Reynaldo's enraged attackers until Reynaldo could escape, usually by locking himself in the camera van. The van was where, at Reynaldo's insistence, Christina Marks waited during ambush interviews. Reynaldo maintained that this was for her own safety, but in reality he worried that if something happened to her, it might end up on tape and steal his thunder.

Reflecting upon all this, Willie orderd another

Planter's punch. This time he asked the waitress for more dark rum on the top. He said to Reynaldo, 'What makes you think this doctor guy'll break?'

'I've met him. He's weak.'

'That's what you said about Larkey McBuffum.'

Larkey McBuffum was a crooked Chicago pharmacist who had been selling steroid-pills to junior high school football players. When Reynaldo and Willie had burst into Larkey's drug store to confront him, the old man had maced Willie square in the eyes with an aerosol can of spermicidal birth-control foam.

'I'm telling you, the surgeon's a wimp,' Reynaldo was saying. 'Put a mike in his face and he'll crack like a fucking Triscuit.'

'I'll stay close on him,' Willie said.

'Not too close,' Reynaldo Flemm cautioned. 'You gotta be ready to pull back and get us both in the shot, right before it happens.'

Willie stirred the dark rum with his little finger. 'You mean, when he slugs you?'

'Of course,' Reynaldo said curtly. 'Christ, you ought to know the drill by now. *Of course* when he slugs me.'

'Will that be,' Willie asked playfully, 'before or after the big confession?'

Reynaldo gnawed on this one a few seconds before giving up. 'Just get it, that's all,' he said stiffly. 'Whenever it happens, get every bloody second on tape. Understand?'

Willie nodded. Sometimes he wished he were still freelancing for the networks. A coup in Haiti was a picnic compared to this.

*

The Pennsylvania State Police were happy to wire a photograph of Blondell Wayne Tatum to Sergeant Al García at the Metro-Dade Police Department. García was disappointed, for the photograph was practically useless. It had been taken more than twenty years earlier by a feature photographer for a small rural newspaper. At the time, the paper was running a five-part series on how the Amish sect was coping with the social pressures of the twentieth century. Blondell Wayne Tatum was one of several teenaged Amish youths who were photographed while playing catch with a small pumpkin. Of the group, Blondell Wayne Tatum was the only one wearing a brand-new Rawlings outfielder's mitt.

For purposes of criminal identification, the facsimile of the newspaper picture was insufficient. García knew that the man named Chemo no longer wore a scraggly pubescent beard, and that he since had suffered devastating facial trauma as a result of a freak dermatology accident. Armed with these revisions, García enlisted the help of a police sketch artist named Paula Downs. He tacked the newspaper picture on Paula's easel and said: 'Third one from the left.'

Paula slipped on her eyeglasses, but that wasn't enough. She took a photographer's loupe and peered closely at the picture. 'Stringbean,' she said. 'Sixteen, maybe seventeen years old.'

García said: 'Make him thirty-eight now. Six foot nine, one hundred eighty pounds.'

'No sweat,' Paula said.

'And lose the beard.'

'Let's hope so. Yuk.'

With an unwrapped cigar, García tapped on the photograph. 'Here's the hard part, babe. A few years ago this turkey had a bad accident, got his face all fried up.'

'Burns?'

'Yup.'

'What kind – gas or chemical?'

'Electrolysis.'

Paula peered at the detective over the rim of her spectacles and said, 'That's very humorous, Al.'

'I swear. Got it straight from the Pennsylvania cops.'

'Hmmmm.' Paula chewed on the eraser of her pencil as she contemplated the photograph.

Al García described Chemo's face to Paula the way that Mick Stranahan had described it to him. As García spoke, the artist began to draw a freehand composite. She held the pencil at a mild angle and swept it in light clean ovals across the onionskin paper. First came the high forehead, the sharp chin, then the cheekbones and the puffy blowfish eyes and the thin cruel lips. Before long, the gangly young Amish kid with the baseball mitt became a serious-looking felon.

Paula got up and said, 'Be right back.' Moments later she returned with a salt shaker from the cafeteria. She lifted the onionskin and copiously sprinkled salt on the drawing pad. With the heel of her left hand she spread the grains evenly. After replacing the onionskin that bore Chemo's likeness, Paula selected a stubby fat pencil with a soft grey lead. She held it flat to the paper, as if it were a hunk of charcoal, and began a gentle tracing motion across the drawing. Instantly the underlying salt crystals came into relief. García smiled: the effect was perfect. It gave Chemo's portrait a harsh granular complexion, just as Mick Stranahan had described.

'You're a genius,' García told Paula Downs.

She handed him the finished composite. 'You get some winners, Al.'

He went to the Xerox room and made a half-dozen copies of the sketch. He stuck one in John Murdock's mailbox. On the back of Murdock's copy García had printed the name Blondell Wayne Tatum, the AKA, and the date of birth. Then García had written: 'This is your guy for the Simpkins case!!!!'

Murdock, he knew, would not appreciate the help.

García spent the rest of the afternoon on Key Biscayne, showing Chemo's composite to dock boys, bartenders, and cocktail waitresses at Sunday's-on-the-Bay. By four o'clock the detective had three positive IDs saying that the man in the drawing was the same one who had been drinking with Chloe Simpkins Stranahan on the evening she died.

Now Al García was a happy man. When he got back to police headquarters, he called a florist and ordered a dozen long-stemmed roses for Paula Downs. While he was on the phone, he noticed a small UPS parcel on his desk. García tore it open with his free hand.

Inside was a videotape in a plastic sleeve. On the sleeve was a scrap of paper, attached with Scotch tape. A note.

'I told you so. Regards, Mick.'

García took the videotape to the police audio room, where a couple of the vice guys were screening the very latest in bestiality *vérité*. García told them to beat it and plugged Stranahan's tape into a VHS recorder. He watched it twice. The second time, he stubbed out his cigar and took notes.

Then he went searching for Murdock and Salazar.

In the detective room, nobody seemed to know where they were. García didn't like the looks of things.

The copy of Paula's sketch of Blondell Wayne Tatum lay crumpled next to an empty Doritos bag on John Murdock's desk. 'Asshole,' García hissed. He didn't care who heard him. He pawed through the rest of Murdock's debris until he found a pink message slip. The message was from the secretary of Circuit Judge Cassie B. Ireland.

García groaned. Cassie Ireland had been a devoted golfing partner of the late and terminally crooked Judge Raleigh Goomer. Cassie himself was known to have serious problems with drinking and long weekends in Las Vegas. The problems were in the area of chronic inability to afford either vice.

The message to Detective John Murdock from Judge Cassie Ireland's secretary said: 'Warrant's ready.'

Al García used Murdock's desk phone to call the judge's chambers. He told the secretary who he was. Not surprisingly, the judge was gone for the day. Gone straight to the tiki bar at the Airport Hilton, García thought.

To the judge's secretary he said, 'There's been a little mix-up down here. Did Detective Murdock ask Judge Ireland to sign a warrant?'

'Sure did,' chirped the secretary. 'I've still got the paperwork right here. John and his partner came by and picked it up yesterday morning.'

Al García figured he might as well ask, just to make sure. 'Can you tell me the name on the warrant?'

'Mick Stranahan,' the secretary replied. 'First-degree murder.'

Christina Marks found the darkness exciting. As she floated naked on her back, the warm water touched her everyplace. Sometimes she stood up and curled her toes in the cool, rough sand, to see how deep it was. A few yards away, Mick Stranahan broke the surface with a swoosh, a glistening blond sea creature. He sounded like a porpoise when he blew the air from his lungs.

'This is nice,' Christina called to him.

'No hot showers on the key,' he said. 'No shower, period. Cartwright is a no-frills guy.'

'I said it's nice. I mean it.'

Stranahan swam closer and rose to his feet. The water came up to his navel. In the light from a quarter moon Christina could make out the fresh bullet scar on his shoulder; it looked like a smear of pink grease. She found herself staring – he was different out here on the water. Not the same man whom she had seen in the hospital or at her apartment. On the island he seemed larger and more feral, yet also more serene.

'It's so peaceful,' Christina said. They were swimming on a marly bonefish flat, forty yards from Cartwright's dock.

'I'm glad you can relax,' Stranahan said. 'Most women would be jittery, having been shot at twice by a total stranger.'

Christina laughed easily, closed her eyes and let the wavelets tickle her neck. Mick was right; she ought to be a nervous wreck by now. But she wasn't.

'Maybe I'm losing my mind,' she said to the stars. She heard a soft splash as he went under again. Seconds later something cool brushed against her ankle, and she smiled. 'All right, mister, no funny business.'

From a surprising distance came his voice: 'Sorry to disappoint you, but that wasn't me.'

'Oh no.' Christina rolled over and kicked hard for the

deep channel, but she didn't get far. Like a torpedo he came up beneath her and slid one arm under her hips, the other around her chest. As he lifted her briskly out of the water, she let out a small cry.

'Easy,' Stranahan said, laughing. 'It was only a baby bonnet shark – I saw it.'

He was standing waist-deep on the flat, holding her like an armful of firewood. 'Relax,' he said. 'They don't eat bigshot TV producers.'

Christina turned in his arms and held him around the neck. 'Is it gone?' she asked.

'It's gone. Want me to put you down?'

'Not really, no.'

In the moonlight he could see enough of her eyes to know what she was thinking. He kissed her on the mouth.

She thought: This is crazy. I love it.

Stranahan kissed her again, longer than the first time.

'A little salty,' she said, 'but otherwise very nice.' Christina let her hands wander. 'Say there, what happened to your jeans?'

'I guess they came off in the undertow.'

'What undertow?' She started kissing him up and down the neck; giggling, nipping, using the tip of her tongue. She could feel the goose flesh rise on his shoulders.

'There really *was* a shark,' he said.

'I believe you. Now take me back to the island. Immediately.'

Stranahan said, 'Not right this minute.'

'You mean we're going to do it out here?'

'Why not?'

'Standing up?'

'Why not?'

'Because of the sharks. You said so yourself.'

Stranahan said. 'You'll be safe, just put your legs around me.'

'Nice try.'

He kissed her again. This was a good one. Christina wrapped her legs around his naked hips.

Stranahan stopped kissing long enough to catch his breath and say, 'I almost forgot. Can you name the Beatles?'

'Not right this minute.'

'Yes, now. Please.'

'You're a damn lunatic.'

'I know,' he said.

Christina pressed so close and so hard that water sluiced up between her breasts and splashed him on the chin. 'That's what you get,' she said. Then, nose to nose: 'John, Paul, George, and Ringo.'

'You're terrific.'

'And don't forget Pete Best.'

'I think I love you,' Stranahan said.

Later he caught a small grouper from the dock, and fried it for dinner over an open fire. They ate on the ocean side of the island, under a stand of young palms. Stranahan used a pair of old lobster traps for tables. The temperature had dropped into the low seventies with a sturdy breeze. Christina wore a tartan flannel shirt, baggy grey workout trousers, and running shoes. Stranahan wore jeans, sneakers, and a University of Miami sweatshirt. Tucked in the waist of his jeans was a Smith .38 he had borrowed from Luis Córdova.

Stranahan was reasonably certain that he would not have to fire it.

Christina was on her second cup of coffee when she said, 'I've been a pretty good sport about all this, don't you agree?'

'Sure.' He had his eyes on the far away lights of a tramp freighter ploughing south in the Gulf Stream.

Christina said, 'I know I've asked before, but I'm going to try again: what the hell are we doing out here?'

'I thought you liked this place.'

'I love it, Mick, but I still don't understand.'

'We can't go back to the stilt house. Not yet, anyway.'

'But why come here?' She was nearly out of patience with the mystery.

'Because I needed a place where something could happen, and no one would see it. Or hear it.'

'Mick—'

'There's no other way.' He stood up and poured out the cold dregs of his coffee, which splattered against the bare serrated coral. He noticed that the tide was slipping out. 'There's no other way to deal with people like this,' he said.

Christina turned to him. 'You don't understand. I can't do this, I can't be a part of this.'

'You wanted to come along.'

'To observe. To report. To get the story.'

Stranahan's laugh carried all the way to Hawk Channel. 'Story?'

She knew how silly it sounded, and was. Willie had the television cameras, and Reynaldo Flemm had Willie. Reynaldo . . . another macho head case. He had sounded so odd when she phoned from the mainland; his voice terse and icy, his laugh thin and ironic. He was cooking up something, although he denied it to Christina. Even when she told him about the wild incident at the Plaza, about how she had almost been shot *again*, Reynaldo's reaction was strangely muted and unreadable. When she had called again two hours later from a pay booth at the marina, the secretary in New York told Christina that Reynaldo had already left for the airport. The secretary went on to report, in a snitchy tone, that Reynaldo had withdrawn fifteen thousand dollars from the emergency weekend travel account – the account normally reserved for commercial airline disasters, killer earthquakes, political assassinations, and other breaking news events. Christina Marks could not imagine what Reynaldo intended to do with fifteen grand, but she assumed it would be a memorable folly.

And there she was in Florida: no camera, no crew, no star. So she had boarded the marine patrol boat with Mick Stranahan and Luis Córdova.

Standing in the moonglow, watching the tide lick the coral under her feet, Christina said again: 'I can't be a part of this.'

Stranahan put an arm around her. It reminded Christina of the hugs her father sometimes gave her when she was a child and something sad had made her cry. A gesture that said he was sorry, but nothing could be done; sometimes the world was not such a good place.

'Mick, let's just go to the police.'

'These *are* the police. Remember?'

She looked at his face, searching the shadows for his expression. 'So that's who you're waiting for.'

'Sure. Who'd you think?'

Christina pretended to slap herself on the forehead.

'Oh, silly me – I thought it might be that huge skinny freak who keeps trying to shoot us.'

Stranahan shook his head. 'Him, we don't wait for.'

'Mick, this still isn't right.'

But the hug was finished, and so was the discussion. 'There's a lantern back at the house,' he told her. 'I want you to take a walk around the island. A long walk, OK?'

TWENTY-THREE

Joe Salazar said, 'You got to steer yesterday.'

'For Christ's sake,' mumbled Murdock.

'Come on, Johnny, it's my turn.'

They were gassing up the boat at Crandon Marina on Key Biscayne. It was the sheriff's department's boat, a nineteen-foot Aquasport with a forest-green police stripe down the front. It was the same boat that the two detectives had borrowed the day before. The sergeant in charge of the marine division had not wanted to loan the boat to Murdock or Salazar because it was obvious that neither knew how to navigate. The sergeant wondered if they even knew how to swim. Both men were wearing new khaki deck shorts that revealed pale legs, chubby legs that had seldom been touched by salt or sunlight: landlubber's legs. The sergeant had surrendered the Aquasport only when John Murdock flashed the murder warrant and said the suspect had been spotted on a house way out in Stiltsville. The sergeant had asked why they weren't taking any backups along, since there was room on the boat, but Murdock hadn't seemed to hear the question.

When the two detectives had returned to the dock a few hours later, the sergeant had been pleasantly surprised to find no major structural damage to the

Aquasport or its drive shaft. But when Murdock and Salazar in their stupid khakis showed up again the following afternoon, the sergeant wondered how long their luck would hold out on the water.

'Go ahead and drive,' Murdock grumped at the gas dock. 'I don't give a shit.'

Joe Salazar took a stance behind the steering console. He tried not to gloat. Then it occurred to him: 'Where do we look now?'

The day before, Stranahan's stilt house had been empty. They had torn the rooms apart for clues to his whereabouts, found none, and departed in frustration. The whole way back, Murdock had complained about how the shoulder holster was chafing through his mesh tank top. Twice they had run the boat aground on bonefish flats, and both times Murdock had forced Salazar to hop out in the mud and push. For this, if for nothing else, Salazar figured that he deserved to be the captain today.

Murdock said: 'I tell you where we look. We look in every goddamn stilt house on the bay.'

'Yeah, like a regular canvass.'

'Door to door, except by boat. You know the fuckwad's out there somewhere.'

Joe Salazar felt better now that they had a plan. He paid the dock attendant for the gasoline, cranked up the big Evinrude on the back of the Aquasport, and aimed the bow toward Bear Cut. Or tried. The boat didn't want to move.

The dock attendant snickered. 'Helps to untie it,' he said, pointing with one of his bright white sneakers.

Sheepishly Joe Salazar unhitched the lines off the bow

and stern and shoved off. John Murdock said, 'What a wiseass that guy was. Didn't he see we had guns?'

'Sure he did,' Salazar replied, steering tentatively toward the channel.

'This town is gone to shit,' Murdock said, spitting over the gunwale, 'when a guy with a gun has to put up with that kind of bull.'

'Everybody's a wiseass,' Joe Salazar agreed. Nervously he was watching a grey outboard coming in the other direction along the opposite side of the channel. The boat had a blue police light mounted in the centre. A young Latin man in a grey uniform stood behind the windshield. He waved to them: the world-weary wave of one cop to another.

'What do I do?' Salazar asked.

'Try waving back,' said Murdock.

Salazar did. The man in the grey boat changed his course and idled toward them.

'Grouper trooper,' John Murdock whispered. Salazar nodded as if he knew what his partner was talking about. He didn't. He also didn't know how to stop the Aquasport. Every time he pulled down on the throttle, the engine jolted into reverse. When he pushed the lever the other way, the boat would shudder and shoot forward. Backward, forward, backward again. The big Evinrude sounded like it was about to blow up. Joe Salazar could tell that Murdock was seething.

'Try neutral,' the young marine patrolman called. 'Move the throttle sideways till it clicks.'

Salazar did as he was told, and it worked.

'Thanks!' he called back.

Under his breath, Murdock said: 'Yeah, thanks for making us look like a couple of jerkoffs.'

The marine patrol boat coasted up on the port side of the Aquasport. The young officer introduced himself as Luis Córdova. He asked where the two detectives were headed, and if he could help. Joe Salazar told him they were going to Stiltsville to serve a murder warrant.

'Only one guy lives out there that I know of,' Luis Córdova said.

Murdock said: 'That's the guy we want.'

'Mick Stranahan?'

'You know him?'

'I know where he lives,' said Luis Córdova, 'but he's not there now. I saw him only yesterday.'

'Where?' blurted Joe Salazar. 'Was he alone?'

'Yeah, he was alone. Sitting on the conch dock down at Old Rhodes Key.'

Murdock said, 'Where the hell's that?'

'South of Elliott.'

'Where the hell's Elliott?'

The marine patrolman said, 'Why don't you guys just wait a few hours and follow me down? The tide won't be right until dusk. Besides, you might need some extra muscle with this guy.'

'No. Thanks anyway.' John Murdock's tone left no chance for discussion. 'But we could use a map, if you got one.'

Luis Córdova disappeared briefly behind the steering console. When he stood up again, he was smiling. 'Just happened to have an extra,' he said.

A half-hour out of the marina, Joe Salazar said to his partner: 'Maybe we should've asked what he meant about the tides.'

The Aquasport was stuck hard on another mud flat, this one a mile south of Soldier Key. John Murdock cracked open his third can of beer and said: 'You're the one wanted to drive.'

Salazar leaned over the side of the boat and studied the situation. He decided there was no point in getting out to push. 'It's only six inches deep,' he said, a child-like marvel in his voice. 'On the map it sure looked like plenty of water, didn't it?'

Murdock said, 'If you're a starfish, it's plenty of water. If you're a boat, it's a goddamn beach. Another thing. I told you to get three bags of ice. Look how fast this shit is melting.' He kicked angrily at the cooler.

Joe Salazar continued to stare at the shallow gin-clear water. 'I think the tide's coming in,' he said hopefully.

'Swell,' said Murdock. 'That means it's only what? – another four, five hours in the mud. Fanfuckingtastic. By then it'll be good and dark, too.'

Salazar pointed out that the police boat was equipped with excellent lights. 'Once we get off the flat, it's a clean shot down to the island. Deep water the whole trip.'

He had never seen his partner so jumpy and short-tempered. Normally John Murdock was the picture of a cool tough cop, but Salazar had watched a change come over him beginning the night they took the down payment from Commissioner Roberto Pepsical. Five thousand cash, each. Five more when it was done. To persuade the detectives that he was not the booze-swilling letch that he had appeared to be at the nudie joint, the commissioner had arranged the payoff meeting to take place in one of the empty confessionals at St Mary's Catholic Church in Little Havana. The con-fessional was dimly lit and no bigger than a broom closet; the three conspirators had to stand sideways to fit. It had been a dozen years since Joe Salazar had stepped inside a confessional and not much had changed. The place reeked of damp linen and guilt, just as he remembered. He and Murdock stuffed the cash in their jackets and bolted out the door together, nearly trampling a quartet of slow-footed nuns. Commissioner Roberto Pepsical stayed alone in the confessional and recited three Hail Marys. He figured it couldn't hurt.

Back in the car, John Murdock had not displayed the crude and cocky ebullience that usually followed the taking of a hefty bribe; rather, his mood had been taciturn and apprehensive. It had stayed that way for two days.

Now with the boat stuck fast on the bonefish flat, Murdock sulked alone in the stern, glaring at the slow crawl of the incoming tide. Joe Salazar lit a Camel and settled in for a long, tense afternoon. He didn't feel so well himself, but at least he knew why. This was the biggest job they'd ever done, and the dirtiest. By a mile.

In fact, the tides would not have mattered if either of the two detectives had known how to read a marine chart. Even at dead low, there was plenty of water from Cape Florida all the way to Old Rhodes Key. All you had to do was follow the channels, which were plainly marked on Luis Córdova's map.

Mick Stranahan knew that Murdock and Salazar would run the boat aground. He also knew that it would be night-time before they could float free, and that they would make the rest of the trip at a snail's pace, fearful of repeating the mishap.

He and Luis Córdova had talked this part out. Together they had calculated that the two detectives would reach the island between nine and midnight, provided they didn't hit the shoal off Boca Chita and shear the prop off the Evinrude. Luis had offered to tail the Aquasport at a discreet distance, but Stranahan told him no. He didn't want the marine patrolman anywhere near Old Rhodes Key when it happened. If Luis was there, he'd want to do it by the book. Wait for the assholes to make their move, then try to arrest them. Stranahan knew it would never work that way – they'd try to kill Luis, too. And even if Luis was as sharp as Stranahan thought, it would be a mess for him afterwards. An automatic suspension, a grand jury, his name all over the newspapers. No way, Stranahan told him, no hero stuff. Just give them the map and get lost.

Besides, Stranahan already had his hands full with Christina Marks on the island.

'I don't want to go for a walk,' she said. 'Grandmothers and widows go for walks. I'm staying here with you.'

'So you can take notes, or what?' He handed her a Coleman lantern. The jumpy white light made their shadows clash on the cinderblock walls. Stranahan said, 'You're not a reporter any more, you're a goddamn witness.'

She said, 'Is this your idea of pillow talk? Half an hour ago we were making love, and now I'm a "goddamn witness". You ever thought of writing poetry, Mick?'

He was down on one knee, pulling items from one of the duffel bags. Without looking up, he said, 'You said you couldn't be a part of this, I'm trying to accommodate you. As for the afterglow, you want to waltz in the moonlight, we'll do that later. Right now there's a pair of bad cops on their way out here to shoot me.'

'You don't know that.'

'Yeah, you're right,' Stranahan said. 'They're probably just collecting Toys for Tots. Now go.'

He stood up. In the lantern light, Christina saw that his arms were full: binoculars, a poplin windbreaker, a pair of corduroys, an Orioles cap, a fishing knife, and a round spool of some kind.

She said, 'It's not for the damn TV show that I want to stay. I'm scared for you. I don't know why – since you're being such a prick – but I'm worried about you, I admit it.'

When Stranahan spoke again, the acid was gone from his voice. 'Look, if you stay . . . if you were to see something, they'd make you testify. Forget reporter's privilege and First Amendment – doesn't count for a damn thing in a situation like this. If you witness a crime, Chris, they put you under oath. You don't want that.'

'Neither do you.'

He smiled drily. She had him on that one. It was true: he didn't want any witnesses. 'You've had enough excitement,' he told her. 'Twice I've nearly gotten you killed. If I were you, I'd take that as a hint.'

Christina said, 'What if you're wrong about them, Mick? What if they only want to ask more questions? Even if they're coming to arrest you, you can't just—'

'Go,' he said. Later he would explain that these cops were buddies of the late Judge Raleigh Goomer, and that what they wanted from Mick Stranahan was payback. Asking questions was not at all what they had in mind.

'Take the path I showed you. Follow the shoreline about half-way down the island and you'll come to a clearing. You'll see some plastic milk crates, an empty oil drum, an old camp fire hole. Wait there for me.'

Christina gave him a frozen look, but he didn't feel it. His mind was in overdrive, long gone.

'There's some fruit and candy bars in the Tupperware,' he said. 'But don't feed the racoons, they bite like hell.'

She was twenty yards down the path when she heard him call, 'Hey, Chris, you forgot the bug spray.'

She shook her head and kept walking.

Fifteen minutes later, when Stranahan was sure she was gone, he carried his things down to Cartwright's dock. There he lit another lantern and hung it on a nail in one of the pilings. Then he pulled off his sneakers, kicked out of his jeans, and slid naked into the cool flowing tides.

For Joe Salazar, it was a moment of quiet triumph at the helm. 'By God, we did it.'

John Murdock made a snide chuckle. 'Yeah, we found it,' he said. 'The Atlantic fucking Ocean. A regular needle in a haystack, Joe. And all it took was three hours of dry humping these islands.'

Salazar didn't let the sarcasm dampen his new found confidence. The passage through Sand Cut had been hairy; even at a slow speed, navigating the swift serpentine channel at night was an accomplishment worth savouring. Murdock knew it, too; not once had he tried to take the wheel.

'So this is the famous Elliott Key.' Murdock scratched

his sunburned cheeks. The Aquasport idled half a mile offshore, rocking in a brisk chop. The beer was long gone, the ice melted. In the cool breeze Murdock had slipped into a tan leather jacket, the one he always wore to work; it looked ridiculous over his khaki shorts. Dismally he slapped at his pink shins, where a horsefly was eating supper.

Joe Salazar held the chart on his lap, a flashlight in his right hand. With the other hand he pointed: 'Like I said, Johnny, from here it's a straight nine-mile run to Rhodes. Twelve feet of water the whole way.'

Murdock said, 'So let's go, Señor Columbus. Maybe we can make it before Christmas.' He readjusted his shoulder holster for the umpteenth time.

Salazar hesitated. 'Once we get there, what exactly is the plan?'

'Get that goddamn flashlight out of my face.' Murdock's eyelids were swollen and purple. Too much sun, too much beer. It worried Salazar; he wanted his partner to be sharp.

'The plan is simple,' Murdock said. 'We arrive with bells on – sirens, lights, the works. We yell for Stranahan to come out with his hands up. Go ahead with the whole bit – serve the warrant, do the Miranda, all that shit. Then we shoot him like he was trying to get away.'

'Do we cuff him first?'

'Now, how would that look? No, we don't cuff him first. Jesus Christ.' Murdock spat into the water, He'd been spitting all afternoon. Salazar hoped this wasn't a new habit.

Murdock said, 'See, Joe, we shoot him in the back. That way it looks like he's running away. Then we get on this boat radio, if one of us can figure out how to use the goddamn thing, and call for air rescue.'

'Which'll take for ever to get here.'

'Exactly. But then we're covered, procedure-wise.'

It sounded like a solid plan, with only one serious variable. Joe Salazar decided to put the variable out of his mind. He stowed the flashlight, reclaimed his post at the wheel of the police boat and steered a true course for Old Rhodes Key.

A straight line through open seas. No sweat.

The channel that leads from the ocean to the cut of Old Rhodes Key is called Caesar Creek. It is deep and fairly broad, and well charted with lighted markers. For this Joe Salazar was profoundly thankful. Having mastered the balky throttle, he guided the Aquasport in at half-speed, with John Murdock standing (or trying to) in the bow. Murdock cupped his hands around his eyes to block the peripheral light; he was peering at the island, searching for signs of Mick Stranahan. Two hundred yards from the mouth of the cut, Salazar killed the engine and joined his chubby partner on the front of the boat.

'There he is!' Murdock's breathing was raspy, excited.

Salazar squinted into the night. 'Yeah, Johnny, sitting under that light on the dock.'

They could see the lantern and, in its white penumbra, the figure of a man with his legs hanging over the planks. The figure wore a baseball cap, a tan jacket, and long pants. From the angle of the cap, the man's head appeared to be down, chin resting on his chest.

'Dumb fuckwad's asleep.' Murdock's laugh was high and brittle. He already had his pistol out.

'Then I guess we better do it,' Salazar said.

'By all means.' Murdock dropped to a crouch.

They had tested the blue lights and siren on the way down, so Salazar knew where the switches were. He flipped them simultaneously, then turned the ignition key. As the Evinrude growled to life, Salazar put all his weight to the throttle.

Gun in hand, John Murdock clung awkwardly to the bow rail as the Aquasport planed off and raced toward the narrow inlet. The wind spiked Murdock's hair and flattened his cheeks. His teeth were bared in a wolfish expression that might have passed for a grin.

As the boat got closer, Joe Salazar expected Mick Stranahan to wake up at any moment and look in their direction – but the man didn't move.

A half-mile away, sitting on a milk crate under some trees, Christina Marks heard the police siren. With a shiver she closed her eyes and waited for the sound of gunfire.

They could have come one of several ways. The most likely was the oceanside route, following Caesar Creek into the slender fork between tiny Hurricane Key and Old Rhodes. This was the easiest way to Cartwright's dock.

But a westward approach, out of Biscayne Bay, would leave more options and offer more cover. They could come around Adams Key, or circle the Rubicons and sneak through the grassy flats behind Totten. But that would be a tricky and perilous passage, almost unthinkable for someone who had never made the trip.

Not at night, Stranahan decided, not these guys.

He had gambled that they would come by the ocean.

In the water he had carried only the knife and the spool. Four times he made the swim between Old Rhodes and Hurricane Key; not a long swim, but enervating against a strong outbound current. After pulling himself up on Cartwright's dock for the last time, Stranahan had rubbed the cold ache from his legs and arms. It had taken a long time to catch his breath.

Then he pulled on some dry clothes, got the .38 that Luis Córdova had loaned him, and sat down to wait.

The spool in Stranahan's duffel had contained five hundred yards of a thick plastic monofilament. The line was calibrated to a tensile strength of one hundred and twenty pounds, for it was designed to withstand the deep-water surges of giant marlin and bluefin tuna. It was the strongest fishing line manufactured in the world, tournament quality. For further advantage it was lightly tinted a charcoal grey, which made it practically invisible underwater.

Even out of the water, the line was sometimes impossible to see.

At night, for instance. Stretched across a mangrove creek.

Undoubtedly John Murdock never saw it.

He was squatting toad-like on the front of the boat, training his .357 at the figure on the dock as they made their approach. Under Joe Salazar's hand, the Aquasport was moving at exactly forty-two miles per hour.

Mick Stranahan had strung three taut vectors between the islands. The lines were fastened to the trunks of trees and crossed the water at varying heights. The lowest of the lines was snapped immediately by the bow of the speeding police boat. The other two garrotted John Murdock in the belly and the neck, respectively.

Joe Salazar, in the bewildering final millisecond of his life, watched his partner thrown backwards, bug-eyed and gurgling, smashed to the deck by unseen hands. Then the same spectral claw seized Salazar by the throat, chopped him off his feet, bounced his over-ripe skull off the howling Evinrude and twanged him directly into the creek.

The noise made by the fishing line when it snapped on Joe Salazar's neck was very much like that of a gunshot.

Christina Marks ran all the way back to Cartwright's dock. Along the way she dropped the Coleman lantern, hissing, on some rocks. But she kept running. When she got there, Caesar Creek was black and calm. She saw no boat, no sign of intruders.

On the dock, the familiar figure of a man in a baseball cap slouched beneath another lantern, this one glowing brightly.

'Mick, what happened?'

Then Christina realized that it wasn't a man at all, but a scarecrow wearing Stranahan's poplin jacket and long corduroys. The body of the scarecrow was stuffed with palm leaves and dried seaweed. The head was a green coconut. The baseball cap fit like a charm.

TWENTY-FOUR

The Aquasport wedged itself deep in the mangroves on Totten Key. The engine was dead, but the prop was still twirling when Mick Stranahan got there. Barefoot, he monkeyed through the slick rubbery branches until he could see over the side of the battered boat. In his right hand he held Luis Córdova's .38.

He didn't need it. Detective John Murdock wasn't dead, but he would be soon. He lay motionless on the deck, his knees drawn up in pain. Blackish blood oozed from his nose. Only one eye was open, rhythmically illuminated by the strobing blue police light. Cracked but still flashing, the light dangled from a nest of loose wires on the console. It looked like a fancy electric Christmas ornament.

Stranahan felt his stomach shrink to a knot. He put the pistol in his jeans and swung his legs over the gunwale. 'John?'

Murdock's eye blinked, and he grunted weakly.

Stranahan said, 'Try to take it easy.' Like the guy had a choice. 'One quick question, I've got to ask. You fellows were going to kill me, weren't you?'

'Damn right,' rasped the dying detective.

'Yeah, that's what I thought. I can't believe you're still sore about Judge Goomer.'

Murdock managed a bloody grin and said, 'You dumb fuckwad.'

Stranahan leaned forward and brushed a horsefly off Murdock's forehead. 'But if it wasn't revenge for the judge, then why pull something like this?' Silence gave him the answer. 'Don't tell me somebody paid you.'

Murdock nodded, or tried. His neck wasn't working so well; it looked about twice as long as it was supposed to be.

Stranahan said, 'You took money for this? From who?'

'Eat me,' Murdock replied.

'It was probably the doctor,' Stranahan speculated. 'Or a go-between. That would make more sense.'

Murdock's reply came out as a dank rattle. Mick Stranahan sighed. Queasiness at the sight of Murdock had given way to emotional exhaustion.

'John, it's some kind of city, isn't it? All I wanted out here was some peace and solitude. I was through with all this crap.'

Murdock gave a hateful moan, but Stranahan needed to talk. 'Here I'm minding my own business, feeding the fish, not bothering a soul, when some guy shows up to murder me. At my very own house, John, in the middle of the bay! All because some goddamn doctor thinks I'm going to break open a case that's so old it's mildewed.'

The dying Murdock seemed hypnotized by the flashing blue light. It was ticking much faster than his own heart. One of the detective's hands began to crawl like an addled blue crab, tracking circles on the blood-slickened deck.

Stranahan said, 'I know it hurts, John, but there's nothing I can do.'

In a slack voice Murdock said, 'Fuck you, shithead.' Then his eye closed for the last time.

Mick Stranahan and Christina Marks were waiting when Luis Córdova pulled up to the dock at nine sharp the next morning.

'Where to?' he asked Stranahan.

'I'd like to go back to my house, Luis.'

'Not me,' said Christina Marks. 'Take me to Key Biscayne. The marina is fine.'

Stranahan said, 'I guess that means you still don't want to marry me.'

'Not in a million years,' Christina said. 'Not in your wildest dreams.'

Stranahan turned to Luis Córdova. 'She didn't get much sleep. The accommodations were a bit too . . . rustic.'

'I understand,' said the marine patrolman. 'But, otherwise, a quiet night?'

'Fairly quiet,' Stranahan said.

The morning was sunny and cool. The bay had a light washboard ripple that made the patrol boat seem to fly. As they passed the Ragged Keys, Stranahan nudged Luis Córdova and pointed to the white-blue sky. 'Choppers!' he shouted over the engine noise. Christina Marks saw them, too: three Coast Guard rescue helicopters, chugging south at a thousand feet.

Without glancing from the wheel, Luis Córdova said, 'There's a boat overdue from Crandon. Two cops.'

'No shit?'

'They found a body this morning floating off Broad Creek. Homicide man named Salazar.'

'What happened?'

'Drowned,' yelled Luis Córdova. 'Who knows how.'

Christina Marks listened to the two men going back and forth. She wasn't sure how much Luis Córdova knew, but it was more than Stranahan would ever tell her. She felt angry and insulted and left out.

When they arrived at the stilt house, Stranahan took out the Smith .38 and returned it to Luis. The marine patrolman was relieved to see that it had not been fired.

Stranahan hoisted two of the duffel bags and hopped off the patrol boat.

From the dock he said, 'Take care, Chris.' He wanted to say more, but it was the wrong time. She was still fuming about last night, furious because he wouldn't tell her what had happened. She had kicked the coconut head off the scarecrow, that's how mad she had gotten. It was at that moment he'd asked her to marry him. Her reply had been succinct, to say the least.

Now she turned away coldly and said to Luis Córdova: 'Can we get going, please.'

Stranahan waved them off and trudged up the steps to inspect the looted house. The first thing he saw on the floor was the big marlin head; the tape on the fractured bill had been torn off in the fall. Stranahan stepped over the stuffed fish and went to the bedroom to check for the shotgun. It was still wedged up in the box spring where he had hidden it.

The whole place was a mess all right, depressing but not irreparable. Stranahan was glad, in a way, to have such a large chore ahead of him. Take his mind off Murdock and Salazar and Old Rhodes Key. And Christina Marks, too.

She was the first woman he had loved who had ever said no to marriage. It was quite a feeling.

Luis Córdova came back to the stilt house as Mick Stranahan was finishing lunch. There was a burly new passenger on the boat: Sergeant Al García.

Stranahan greeted them at the door and said, 'Two Cubans with guns is never good news.'

Luis Córdova said, 'Al is working the dead cops.'

'Cops plural?' Stranahan's eyebrows arched.

García sat down heavily on one of the barstools. 'Yeah, we found Johnny Murdock inside the boat. The boat was up in a frigging tree.'

'Where?' Stranahan asked impassively.

'Not far from where you and your lady friend went camping last night.' García patted his pockets and cursed. He was out of cigars. He took out a pack of Camels and lit one half-heartedly. He glanced up at the beakless marlin hanging from a new nail on the wall.

Luis Córdova said, 'I told Al about how I gave you a lift down to the island after your house got trashed.'

Stranahan wasn't upset. If asked, Luis would tell the truth about what he saw, what he knew for a fact. Most likely he had already told García about loaning the two detectives a map of the bay. Nothing strange about that.

'You hear anything funny last night?' Al García asked. 'By the way, where's the girl?'

'I don't know,' Stranahan said.

'What about last night?'

'A boat went by about eleven. Maybe a little later. Sounded like an outboard. What the hell happened, Al – somebody do these guys?'

García was puffing hard on the cigarette, and blowing circles of smoke, like he did with his stogies. 'Way it looks,' he said, 'they were going wide open. Missed the channel completely.'

'You said the boat was in a tree.'

'That's how fast the bozos were going. Way it looks, Salazar got thrown, hit his head. He drowned right away but the tide took him south.'

'Broad Creek,' Luis Córdova said. 'A mullet man found the body.'

García went on: 'Murdock stayed in the boat, but it didn't save him. We're talking major head trauma. The medical examiner thinks a mangrove branch or something snapped his neck. Same with Salazar. Figures it happened when they hit the trees.'

'Wide open?'

Luis Córdova said, 'The throttle was all the way down. You got to be nuts to run that creek wide open at night.'

'Or amazingly stupid,' Stranahan said. 'Let me guess who they were looking for.'

García nodded. 'You're on some roll, Mick. A regular archangel of death, you are. First your ex, now Murdock and Salazar. I'm noticing that bad things happen to people who fuck with you. Seems to be a pattern going way back.'

Stranahan said, 'I can't help it these jerks don't know how to drive a boat.'

Luis Córdova said, 'It was an accident, that's all.'

'I just find it interesting,' said Al García. 'Maybe the word is ironic, I don't know. Anyway, you're right, Mick. The two boys were coming to pay you a visit. They kept it real quiet around the shop, too. I can only guess why.' He reached in his jacket and took out a soggy white piece of paper. The paper was folded three times, pamphlet sized.

García showed it to Stranahan. 'We found this in Salazar's back pocket.'

Stranahan knew what it was. He'd seen a thousand just like it. The word *warrant* was still legible in the standard judicial calligraphy. As he handed it back to García, Stranahan wondered whether he was about to be arrested.

'What is this?' he asked.

'Garbage,' García replied. He crumped the sodden document in his right hand and lobbed it out a window into the water.

Stranahan smiled. 'You liked the videotape.'

'Obviously,' said the detective.

At the Holiday Inn where they got a room, Maggie Gonzalez was going through the Yellow Pages column by column, telling Chemo which plastic surgeons were good enough to finish the dermabrasion treatments on his face; some of the names were new to her, but others she remembered from her nursing days. Chemo was stooped in front of the bathroom mirror, picking laconically at the patches left on his chin by Dr Rudy Graveline.

Out of the side of his mouth, Chemo said, 'Fucker's not returning my calls.'

'It's early,' Maggie said. 'Rudy sleeps late on his day off.'

'I want to see some cash. Today.'

'Don't worry.'

'The sooner I get the money, the sooner I can take

care of this.' Meaning his skin. In the mirror, Chemo could see Maggie's expression – at least, as much of it as the bandages revealed – and something that resembled genuine sympathy in her eyes. Not pity, sympathy.

She was the first woman who had ever looked at him that way. Certainly she seemed sincere about helping him find a new plastic surgeon. Chemo thought: She's either a truly devoted nurse or a sneaky little actress.

Maggie ripped a page of physicians from the phone book and said off-handedly, 'How much are we hitting him for?'

'A million dollars,' Chemo said. His sluglike lips quivered into a smile. 'You said he's loaded.'

'Yeah, he's also cheap.'

'A minute ago you said don't worry.'

'Oh, he'll pay. Rudy's cheap, but he's also a coward. All I'm saying is, he'll try to play coy at first. That's his style.'

'Coy?' Chemo thought: What in the fuck is she talking about? 'I wouldn't know about coy,' he said. 'I got a Weed Whacker strapped to my arm.'

Maggie said, 'Hey, I'm on your side. I'm just telling you, he can be stubborn when he wants.'

'You know what I think? I think you're in this for more than the money. I think you want to see a show.'

Maggie's brown eyes narrowed above the gauze. 'Don't be ridiculous.'

'Yeah,' Chemo said, 'I think you'd enjoy it if the boys got nasty with each other. I think you've got your heart set on blood.'

He was beaming as if he had just discovered the secret of the universe.

*

Dr Rudy Graveline stared at the vaulted ceiling and contemplated his pitiable existence. Chemo had turned blackmailer. Maggie Gonzalez, the bitch, was still alive. So was Mick Stranahan. And somewhere out there a television crew was lurking, waiting to grill him about Victoria Barletta.

Aside from that, life was peachy.

When the phone rang, Rudy pulled the bedsheet up to his chin. He had a feeling it was more bad news.

'Answer it,' Heather Chappell's muffled command came from beneath a pillow. 'Answer the damn thing.'

Rudy reached out from the covers and seized the receiver fiercely, as if it were the neck of a cobra. The grim gassy voice on the other end of the line belonged to Commissioner Roberto Pepsical.

'You see the news on TV?'

'No,' Rudy said. 'But I got the paper here somewhere.'

'There's a story about two policemen who died.'

'Yeah, so?'

'In a boat accident,' Roberto said.

'Cut to the punch line, Bobby.'

'Those were the guys.'

'What guys?' asked Rudy. Next to him, Heather mumbled irritably and wrapped the pillow tightly around her ears.

'The guys I told you about. *My* guys.'

'Shit,' said Rudy.

Heather looked up raggedly and said: 'Do you mind? I'm trying to sleep.'

Rudy told Roberto that he would call him right back from another phone. He put on a robe and hurried down the hall to his den, where he shut the door.

Numbly he dialled Roberto's private number, the one reserved for bagmen and lobbyists.

'Let me make sure I understand,' Rudy said. 'You were using police officers as hit men?'

'They promised it would be a cinch.'

'And now they're dead.' Rudy was well beyond the normal threshold of surprise. He had become conditioned to expect the worst. He said, 'What about the money – can I get it back?'

Roberto Pepsical couldn't believe the nerve of this cheapskate. 'No, you can't get it back. I paid them. They're dead. You want the money back, go ask their widows.'

The commissioner's tone had become impatient and firm. It made Rudy nervous; the fat pig should have been apologizing all over himself.

Rudy said, 'All right, then, can you get somebody else to do it?'

'Do what?'

'Do Stranahan. The offer's still open.'

Roberto laughed scornfully on the other end; Rudy was baffled by this change of attitude.

'Listen to me,' the commissioner said. 'The deal's off, for ever. Two dead cops is major trouble, Doctor, and you just better hope nobody finds out what they were up to.'

Rudy Graveline wanted to drop the subject and crawl back to bed. 'Fine, Bobby,' he said. 'From now on, we never even met. Goodbye.'

'Not so fast.'

Oh brother, Rudy thought, here we go.

Roberto said, 'I talked to The Others. They still want the original twenty-five.'

'That's absurd. Cypress Towers is history, Bobby. I'm through with it. Tell your pals they get zippo.'

'But you got your zoning.'

'I don't need the damn zoning,' Rudy protested. 'They can have it back, understand? Peddle it to some other dupe.'

Roberto's voice carried no trace of understanding, no patience for a compromise. 'Twenty-five was the price of each vote. You agreed. Now The Others want their money.'

'Don't you ever get sick of being an errand boy?'

'It's my money, too,' Roberto said soberly. 'But yeah, I do get sick of being an errand boy. I get sick of dealing with cheap scuzzbuckets like you. When it comes to paying up, doctors are the fucking worst.'

'Hey,' Rudy said, 'it doesn't grow on trees.'

'A deal is a deal.'

In a way, Roberto was glad that Dr Graveline was being such a prick. It felt good to be the one to drop the hammer for a change. He said, 'You got two business days to cover me and The Others.'

'What?' Rudy bleated.

'Two days, I'm calling my banker in the Caymans and having him read me the balance of my account. If it's not heavier by twenty-five, you're toast.'

Rudy thought: This can't be the same man, not the way he's talking to me.

Roberto Pepsical went on, detached, businesslike: 'Me and The Others got this idea that we – meaning the county – should start certifying all private surgical clinics. Have your own testing, licence hearings, bi-monthly inspections, that sort of thing. It's our feeling that the general public needs to be protected.'

'Protected?' Rudy said feebly.

'From quacks and such. Don't you agree?'

Rudy thought: The whole world has turned upside down.

'Most clinics won't have anything to worry about,' Roberto said brightly, 'once they're brought up to county standards.'

'Bobby, you're a bastard.'

After Rudy Graveline slammed down the phone, his hand was shaking. It wouldn't stop.

At the breakfast table, Heather stared at Rudy's trembling fingers and said, 'I sure don't like the looks of that.'

'Muscle spasms,' he said. 'It'll go away.'

'My surgery is tomorrow,' Heather said.

'I'm aware of that, darling.'

They had spent the better part of the morning discussing breast implants. Heather had collected testimonials from all her Hollywood actress friends who ever had boob jobs. Some of them favoured the Porex line of soft silicone implants, others liked the McGhan Biocell 100, and still others swore by the Replicon. Heather herself was leaning toward the Silastic II Teardrop model, because they came with a five-year written warranty.

'Maybe I better check with my agent,' she said.

'Why?' Rudy asked peevishly.

'This is my body we're talking about. My career.'

'All right,' Rudy said. 'Call your agent. What do I know? I'm just the surgeon.' He took the newspaper to the bathroom and sat down on the john. Ten minutes later, Heather knocked lightly on the door.

'It's too early on the coast,' she said. 'Melody's not in the office.'

'Thanks for the bulletin.'

'But a man called for you.'

Rudy folded the newspaper across his lap and braced his chin in his hands. 'Who was it, Heather?'

'He didn't give his name. Just said he was a patient.'

'That certainly narrows it down.'

'He said he came up with a number. I think he was talking about money.'

Crazy Chemo. It had to be. 'What did you tell him?' Rudy asked through the door.

'I told him you were unavailable at the moment. He didn't sound like he believed me.'

'Gee, I can't imagine,' said Rudy.

'He said he'll come by the clinic later.'

'Splendid.' He could hear her breathing at the door. 'Heather, is there something else?'

'Yes, there was a man out front. A process server from the courthouse.'

Rudy felt himself pucker at both ends.

Heather said, 'He rang the bell about a dozen times, but I wouldn't open the door. Finally, he went away.'

'Good girl,' Rudy said. He sprang off the toilet, elated. He flung open the bathroom door, carried Heather into the shower, and turned on the water, steamy hot. Then he got down on his bare knees and began kissing her silky, perfect thighs.

'This is our last day,' she said in a whisper, 'before the operation.'

Rudy stopped kissing and looked up, the shower

stream hitting him squarely in the nostrils. Through the droplets he could see the woman of his dreams squeezing her perfect breasts in her perfect hands. With a playful laugh, she said, 'Say so long to these little guys.'

God, Rudy thought, what am I doing? The irony was wicked. All the rich geezers and chunky bimbos he had conned into plastic surgery, patients with no chance of transforming their looks or improving their lives – now he finds one with a body and face that are absolutely flawless, perfect, classic, and she's begging for the knife.

A crime against nature, Rudy thought; and he, the instrument of that crime.

He stood up and made reckless love to Heather right there in the shower. She braced one foot on the bath faucet, the other on the soap dish, but Rudy was too lost in his own locomotions to appreciate the artistry of her balance.

The faster he went, the easier it was to concentrate. His mind emptied of Chemo and Roberto and Stranahan and Maggie. Before long Rudy Graveline was able to focus without distraction on his immediate crisis: the blonde angel under the shower, and what she had planned for the next day.

Before long, an idea came to Rudy. It came to him with such brilliant ferocity that he mistook it for an orgasm.

Heather Chappell didn't particularly care what it was, as long as it was over. The hot water had run out, and she was freezing the orbs of her perfect bottom against the clammy bathroom tiles.

TWENTY-FIVE

Mick Stranahan asked Al García to wait in the car while he went to see Kipper Garth. The law office was a chorus of beeping telephones as Stranahan made his way through the labyrinth of modular desks. The secretaries didn't bother to try to stop him. They could tell he wasn't a client.

Inside his personal sanctum, Kipper Garth sat in a familiar pose, waiting for an important call. He was tapping a Number 2 pencil and scowling at the speaker box. 'I did exactly what you wanted,' he said to Stranahan. 'See for yourself.'

The Nordstroms' malpractice complaint was clipped in a thin brown file on the corner of Kipper Garth's desk. He had been waiting all day for the moment to show his brother-in-law how well he had done. He handed Stranahan the file and said, 'Go ahead, it's all there.'

Stranahan remained standing while he read the lawsuit. 'This is very impressive,' he said, half-way down the second page. 'Maybe Katie's right, maybe you do have some genuine talent.'

Kipper Garth accepted the compliment with a cocky no-sweat shrug. Stranahan resisted the impulse to enquire which bright young paralegal had composed the document, since the author could not possibly be his brother-in-law.

'This really happened?' Stranahan asked. 'The man lost an eye to a . . .'

'Hooter,' Kipper Garth said. 'His wife's hooter, fortunately. Means we can automatically double the pain-and-suffering.'

Stranahan was trying to imagine a jury's reaction to such a mishap. The case would never get that far, but it was still fun to think about.

'Has Dr Graveline been served?'

'Not yet,' Kipper Garth reported. 'He's ducked us so far, but that's fine. We've got a guy staking out the medical clinic, he'll grab him on the way in or out. The lawsuit's bad enough, but your man will go ape when he finds out we've got a depo scheduled already.'

'Excellent,' Stranahan said.

'He'll get it postponed, of course.'

'It doesn't matter. The whole idea is to keep the heat on. That's why I brought this.' Stranahan handed Kipper Garth a page of nine names, neatly typed.

'The witness list,' Stranahan explained. 'I want you to file it with the court as soon as possible.'

Skimming it, Kipper Garth said, 'This is highly unusual.'

'How would you know?'

'It *is*, dammit. Nobody gives up their witnesses so early in the case.'

'You do,' said Mick Stranahan. 'As of now.'

'I don't get it.'

'Heat, Jocko, remember? Send one of the clerks down to the courthouse and put this list in the Nordstrom file.

You might even courier a copy over to Graveline's place, just for laughs.'

Kipper Garth noticed that all but one of the names on the witness list belonged to other doctors – specifically, plastic and reconstructive surgeons: experts who would presumably testify to Rudy Graveline's shocking incompetence in the post-op treatment of Mrs Nordstrom's encapsulated breast implants.

'Not bad,' said Kipper Garth, 'but who's this one?' With a glossy fingernail he tapped the last name on the list.

'That's a former nurse,' Stranahan said.

'Disgruntled?'

'You might say that.'

'And about what,' said Kipper Garth, 'is she prepared to testify?'

'The defendant's competence,' Stranahan replied, 'or lack thereof.'

Kipper Garth stroked a chromium sideburn. 'Witness-wise, I think we're better off sticking with these hotshot surgeons.'

'Graveline won't give a shit about them. The nurse's name is what will get his attention. Trust me.'

With feigned authority, the lawyer remarked that testimony from an embittered ex-employee wouldn't carry much weight in court.

'We're not going to court,' Stranahan reminded him. 'Not for malpractice, anyway. Maybe for a murder.'

'You're losing me again,' Kipper Garth admitted.

'Stay lost,' said Stranahan.

George Graveline's tree-trimming truck was parked off Crandon Boulevard in a lush tropical hammock.

Button-woods, gumbo limbo, and mahogany trees – plenty of shade for George Graveline's truck. The county had hired him to rip out the old trees to make space for some tennis courts. Before long a restaurant would spring up next to the tennis courts and, after that, a major resort hotel. The people who would run the restaurant and the hotel would receive the use of the public property for practically nothing, thanks to their pals on the county commission. In return, the commissioners would receive a certain secret percentage of the refreshment concessions. And the voters would have brand-new tennis courts, whether they wanted them or not.

George Graveline's role in this civic endeavour was small, but he went at it with uncharacteristic zest. In the first two hours he and his men cleared two full acres of virgin woods. Afterwards George Graveline sat down in the truck cab to rest, while his workers tossed the uprooted trees one at a time into the automatic wood chipper.

All at once the noise died away. George Graveline opened his eyes. He could hear his foreman talking to an unfamiliar voice behind the truck. George stuck his head out the window and saw a stocky Cuban guy in a brown suit. The Cuban guy had a thick moustache and a fat unlit cigar in one corner of his mouth.

'What can I do for you?' George Graveline asked.

The Cuban guy reached in his coat and pulled out a gold police badge. As he walked up to the truck, he could see George Graveline's Adam's apple sliding up and down.

Al García introduced himself and said he wanted to ask a few questions.

George Graveline said, 'You got a warrant?'

The detective smiled. 'I don't need a warrant, chico.'

'You don't?'

García shook his head. 'Nope. Here, take a look at this.' He showed George Graveline the police composite of Blondell Wayne Tatum, the man known as Chemo. 'Ever see this bird before?'

'No, sir,' said the tree trimmer, but his expression gave it away. He looked away too quickly from the drawing; anyone else would have stared.

García said, 'This is a friend of your brother's.'

'I don't think so.'

'No?' García shifted the cigar to the other side of his mouth. 'Well, that's good to know. Because this man's a killer, and I can't think of one good reason why he'd be hanging out with a famous plastic surgeon.'

George Graveline said, 'Me neither.' He turned on the radio and twirled the tuner knob back and forth, pretending to look for his favourite country station. García could sense the guy was about to wet his pants.

The detective said, 'I'm not the first homicide man you ever met, am I?'

'Sure. What do you mean?'

'Hell, it was four years ago,' García said. 'You probably don't even remember. It was outside your brother's office, the place he had before he moved over to the beach.'

With a fat brown finger George Graveline scratched his neck. He scrunched his eyebrows, as if trying to recall.

García said: 'Detective's name was Timmy Gavigan. Skinny Irish guy, red hair, about so big. He stopped to chat with you for a couple minutes.'

'No, I surely don't remember,' George said, guardedly.

'I'll tell you exactly when it was – it was right after that college girl disappeared,' García said. 'Victoria Barletta was her name. Surely you remember. There must've been cops all over the place.'

'Oh yeah.' Slowly it was coming back to George; that's what he wanted the cop to think.

'She was one of your brother's patients, the Barletta girl.'

'Right,' said George Graveline, nodding. 'I remember how upset Rudolph was.'

'But you don't remember talking to Detective Gavigan?'

'I talked to lots of people.'

García said, 'The reason I mention it, Timmy remembered you.'

'Yeah, so?'

'You know, he never solved that damn case. The Barletta girl, after all these years. And now he's dead, Timmy is.' García stepped to the rear of the truck. Casually he put one foot on the bumper, near the hitch of the wood chipper. George Graveline opened the door of the truck and leaned out to keep an eye on the Cuban detective.

The two men were alone. George's workers had wandered off to find a cool place to eat lunch and smoke some weed; it was hard to unwind with a cop hanging around.

Curiously Al García bent over the wood chipper and peered at a decal on the engine mount. The decal was in the cartoon likeness of a friendly racoon. 'Brush Bandit – is that the name of this mother?'

'That's right,' said George Graveline.

'How does it work exactly?'

George motioned sullenly. 'You throw the wood into that hole and it comes out here, in the back of the truck. All grinded up.'

García whistled over his cigar. 'Must be some nasty blade.'

'It's a big one, yessir.'

García took his foot off the truck bumper. He held up the drawing of Chemo one more time. 'You see this guy, I want you to call us right away.'

'Surely,' said George Graveline. The detective gave him a business card. The tree trimmer glanced at it, decided it was authentic, slipped it into the back pocket of his jeans.

'And warn your brother,' García said. 'Just in case the guy shows up.'

'You betcha,' said George Graveline.

Back in the unmarked county car, parked a half-mile down the boulevard at the Key Biscayne fire station, Mick Stranahan said: 'So how'd it go?'

'Just like we figured,' García replied. '*Nada.*'

'What do you think of Timmy's theory? About how they got rid of the body?'

'If the doctor really killed her then, yeah, it's possible. That's quite a machine brother George has got himself.'

Stranahan said, 'Too bad brother George won't flip.'

García rolled up the windows and turned on the air-conditioning to cool off. He knew what Stranahan was thinking and he was right: brother George could blow the whole thing wide open. If Maggie were dead or gone, the videotape alone would not be enough for an indictment. They would definitely need George Graveline to talk about Vicky Barletta.

'I'm going for some fresh air,' Stranahan said. 'Why don't you meet me back here in about an hour?'

García said, 'Where the hell you off to?'

Stranahan got out of the car. 'For a walk, do you mind? Go get some coffee or flan or something.'

'Mick, don't do anything stupid. It's too nice a day for being stupid.'

'Hey, it's a lovely day.' Stranahan slammed the car door and crossed the boulevard at a trot.

'Shit,' García muttered. *Mierda!*

He drove down to the Oasis restaurant and ordered a cup of over-powering Cuban coffee. Then he ordered another.

George Graveline was still alone when Mick Stranahan got there. He was leaning against the truck fender, staring at his logger boots. He looked up at Stranahan, straightened, and said, 'You put that damn cop on my ass.'

'Good morning, George,' said Stranahan. 'It's certainly nice to see you again.'

'Fuck you, you hear?'

'Are we having a bad day? What is it – cramps?'

George Graveline was one of those big, slow guys who squint when they get angry. He was squinting now. Methodically he clenched and unclenched his fists, as if he were practising isometrics.

Stranahan said, 'George, I've still got that problem I told you about last time. Your brother's still got some goon trying to murder me. I'm really at the end of my rope.'

'You got that right.'

'My guess,' continued Stranahan, 'is that you and Rudy had a brotherly talk after last time. My guess is that you know exactly where I can locate this goony hit man.'

'Screw you,' said George Graveline. He kicked the switch on the wood chipper and the motor growled to life.

Stranahan said, 'Aw, what'd you do that for? How'm I supposed to hear you over all that damn racket?'

George Graveline lunged with both arms raised stiff in fury, a Frankenstein monster with Elvis jowls. He was clawing for Stranahan's neck. Stranahan ducked the grab and punched George Graveline hard under the heart. When the tree trimmer didn't fall, Stranahan punched him twice in the testicles. This time George went down.

Stranahan placed his right foot on the husky man's neck and applied the pressure slowly, shifting his weight from heel to toe. By reflex George's hands were riveted to his swollen scrotum. He was helpless to fight back. He made a noise like a tractor tyre going flat.

'I can't believe you did that,' Stranahan muttered. 'Isn't it possible to have a civilized conversation in this town without somebody trying to kill you?'

It was a rhetorical question but George Graveline couldn't hear it over the wood chipper, anyway. Stranahan leaned over and shouted: 'Where's the goon?'

George did not answer promptly, so Stranahan added more weight on the Adam's apple. George was not squinting any more; both eyes were quite large.

'Where is he?' Stranahan repeated.

When George's lips started moving, Stranahan let up. The voice that came out of the tree trimmer's mouth had a fuzzy electronic quality. Stranahan knelt to hear it.

'Works on the beach,' said George Graveline.

'Can we be more specific?'

'At a club.'

'What club, George? There's lots of nightclubs on Miami Beach.'

George blinked and said, 'Gay Bidet.' Now it was done, he thought. His brother Rudy was a goner.

'Thank you, George,' said Stranahan. He removed his shoe from the tree trimmer's throat. 'This is a good start. I'm very encouraged. Now let's talk about Vicky Barletta.'

George Graveline lay there with his head in the moist dirt, his groin throbbing. He lay there worrying about his brother the doctor, about what horrible things would happen to him all because of George's big mouth. Rudy had confided in him, trusted him, and now George had let his brother down. Lying there dejectedly, he decided that no matter how much pain was inflicted upon him, he wasn't going to tell Mick Stranahan what had happened to that college girl. Rudy had made a mistake, everybody makes mistakes. Why, one time George himself got a work order mixed up and cut down a whole row of fifty-foot royal palms, when it was mangy old Brazilians he was supposed to chop. Still, they didn't put him in jail or anything, just made him pay a fine. Hundred bucks a tree, something like that. Why should a doctor be treated any different? As he reflected upon Rudy's turbulent medical career, George Graveline removed one of his hands from his swollen scrotum. The free hand happened to settle on a hunk of fresh-cut mahogany concealed by his left leg. The wood was heavy, the bark coarse and dry. George closed his fingers around it. It felt pretty good.

Still kneeling, Mick Stranahan nudged George Graveline's shoulder and said, 'Penny for your thoughts.'

And George hit him square on the back of the skull.

Stranahan didn't see the blow, and at first he thought he'd been shot. He heard a man shouting and what sounded like an ambulance. The rescue scene played vividly in his imagination. He waited to feel the paramedics' hands ripping open his shirt. He waited for the cold clap of the stethoscope on his chest, for the sting of the IV needle in his arm. He waited for the childlike sensation of being lifted onto the stretcher.

None of this came, yet the sound of the ambulance siren would not go away. In his crashing sleep, Stranahan grew angry. Where were the goddamn EMTs? A man's been shot here!

Then, blessedly, he felt someone lifting him. Lifting him under the arms, someone strong. It hurt, oh, God, how it hurt, but that was all right – at least they had come. But then he was falling again, falling or dying, he couldn't be sure. And in his crashing sleep he heard the moan of the siren rise to such a pitch that he wanted to cover his ears and scream for it to stop, please God.

And it did stop.

Somebody shut off the wood chipper.

Stranahan awoke to the odd hollow silence that follows a sharp echo. His eardrums fluttered. The air smelled pungently of cordite. He found himself on his knees, weaving, a drunk waiting for communication. His shirt was damp, his pulse rabbity. He checked himself and saw he was mistaken, he hadn't been shot. There was no ambulance, either, just the tree truck.

Al García sat on the bumper. His gun was in his right hand, which hung heavily at his side. He was as pale as a flounder.

There was no sign of George Graveline anywhere.

'You all right?' Stranahan asked.

'No,' said the detective.

'Where's the tree man?'

With the gun García pointed toward the bin of the tree truck, where the wood chipper had spit what bone and jelly was left of George Graveline.

After he had tried to feed Mick Stranahan into the maw.

And Al García had shot him twice in the back.

And the impact of the bullets had slammed him face-forward down the throat of the tree-eating machine.

TWENTY-SIX

Chemo got the Bonneville out of the garage and drove out to Whispering Palms, but the receptionist said that Dr Graveline wasn't there. Noticing the dramatic topography of Chemo's face, the receptionist told him she could try the doctor at home for an emergency. Chemo said thanks, anyway.

After leaving the clinic, he walked around to the side of the building where the employees parked. Dr Graveline's spiffy new Jaguar XJ-6 was parked in its space. This was the Jaguar that the doctor had purchased immediately after Mick Stranahan had blown up his other one. The sedan was a rich shade of red; candy apple, Chemo guessed, though the Jaguar people probably had a fancier name for it. The windows of the car were tinted grey so that you couldn't see inside. Chemo assumed that Dr Graveline had a burglar alarm wired on the thing, so he was careful not to touch the doors or the hood.

He ambled to the rear of the clinic, by the water, and peeked through the bay window into Rudy's private office. There was the doctor, yakking on the phone. Chemo was annoyed; it was rude of Graveline to be ducking him this way. Rude, hell. It was just plain stupid.

When Chemo turned the corner of the building, he saw a short man in an ill-fitting grey suit standing next to Rudy's car. The man wore dull brown shoes and black-rimmed eyeglasses. He looked to be in his mid-fifties. Chemo walked up to him and said, 'Are you looking for Graveline?'

The man in the black-rimmed glasses appraised Chemo skittishly and said, 'Are you him?'

'Fuck no. But this is his car.'

'They told me he wasn't here.'

'They lied,' Chemo said. 'Hard to believe, isn't it?'

The man opened a brown billfold to reveal a cheap-looking badge. 'I work for the county,' he said. 'I'm trying to serve some papers on the doctor. I been trying two, three days.'

Chemo said, 'See that side door? You wait there, he'll be out soon. It's almost five o'clock.'

'Thanks,' said the process server. He went over and stood, idiotically, by the side entrance to the clinic. He clutched the court papers rolled up in one hand, as if he were going to swat the doctor when he came out.

Chemo slipped the calfskin sheath off the Weed Whacker and turned his attention to Rudy's new Jaguar. He chose as his starting place the left front fender.

Initially it was slow going – those British sure knew how to paint an automobile. At first the Weed Whacker inflicted only pale stripes on the deep red enamel. Chemo tried lowering the device closer to the fender and bracing it in position with his good arm. It took fifteen minutes for the powerful lawn cutter to work its way down to the base steel of the sedan. Chemo moved its buzzing head back and forth in a sweeping motion to enlarge the scar.

From his waiting post outside the clinic door, the process server watched the odd ceremony with rapt fascination. Finally he could stand it no longer, and shouted at Chemo.

Chemo turned away from the Jaguar and looked at the man in the black-rimmed glasses. He flicked the toggle switch to turn off the Weed Whacker, then cupped his right hand to his ear.

The man said, 'What are you doing with that thing?'

'Therapy,' Chemo answered. 'Doctor's orders.'

Like many surgeons, Dr Rudy Graveline was a compulsive man, supremely organized but hopelessly anal retentive. The day after the disturbing phone call from Commissioner Roberto Pepsical, Rudy meticulously wrote out a list of all his career-threatening problems. By virtue of the scope of his extortion, Roberto Pepsical was promoted to the number three spot, behind Mick Stranahan and Chemo. Rudy studied the list closely. In the larger context of a possible murder indictment, Roberto Pepsical was chickenshit. Expensive chickenshit, but chickenshit just the same.

Rudy Graveline dialled the number in New Jersey and waited for Curly Eyebrows to come on the line.

'Jeez, I told you not to call me here. Let me get to a better phone.' The man hung up, and Rudy waited. Ten minutes later the man called back.

'Lemme guess, your problem's got worse.'

'Yes,' said Rudy.

'That local talent you hired, he wasn't by himself after all.'

'He was,' Rudy said, 'but not now.'

349

'That's pretty funny.' Curly Eyebrows laughed flatulently. Somewhere in the background a car blasted its horn. The man said, 'You rich guys are something else. Always trying to do it on the cheap.'

'Well, I need another favour,' Rudy said.

'Such as what?'

'Remember the hunting accident a few years ago?'

Curly Eyebrows said, 'Sure. That doctor. The one was giving you a hard time.'

The man in New Jersey didn't remember the name of the dead doctor, but Rudy Graveline certainly did. It was Kenneth Greer, one of his former partners at the Durkos Center. The one who figured out what had happened to Victoria Barletta. The one who was trying to blackmail him.

'That was a cinch,' said Curly Eyebrows. 'I wish they all could be hunters. Every deer season we could clean up the Gambinos that way. Hunting accidents.'

The man in New Jersey had an itch – on the line Rudy Graveline heard the disgusting sound of fat fingers scratching hairy flesh. He tried not to think about it.

'Somebody new is giving me a hard time,' the doctor said. 'I don't know if you can help, but I thought I'd give it a shot.'

'I'm listening.'

'It's the Dade County Commission,' Rudy said. 'I need somebody to kill them. Can you arrange it?'

'Wait a minute—'

'All of them,' Rudy said, evenly.

'Excuse me, Doc, but you're fucking crazy. Don't call me no more.'

'Please,' Rudy said. 'Five of them are shaking me

down for twenty-five grand each. The trouble is, I don't know which five. So my idea is to kill all nine.'

Curly Eyebrows grunted. 'You got me confused.'

Patiently Rudy explained how the bribe system worked, how each commissioner arranged for four crooked colleagues to go along on each controversial vote. Rudy told the man in New Jersey about the Old Cypress Towers project, about how the commissioners were trying to pinch him for the zoning decision he no longer needed.

'Hey, a deal is a deal,' Curly Eyebrows said unsympathetically. 'Seems to me you got yourself in a tight situation.' Now it sounded like he was picking his teeth with a comb.

Rudy said, 'You won't help?'

'Won't. Can't. Wouldn't.' The man coughed violently, then spit. 'Much as the idea appeals to me personally – killing off an entire county commission – it'd be bad for business.'

'It was just an idea,' Rudy said. 'I'm sorry I bothered you.'

'Want some free advice?'

'Why not.'

Curly Eyebrows said, 'Who's the point man in this deal? You gotta know his name, at least.'

'I do.'

'Good. I suggest something happens to the bastard. Something awful bad. This could be a lesson to the other eight pricks, you understand?'

Rudy Graveline said yes, he understood.

'Trust me,' said the man in New Jersey. 'I been in this end of it for a long time. Sort of thing makes an impression, especially dealing with your mayors and aldermen and those types. These are not exactly tough guys.'

'I suppose not.' Rudy cleared his throat. 'Listen, that's a very good idea. Just do one of them.'

'That's my advice,' said the man in New Jersey.

'Could you arrange it?'

'Shit, I ain't risking my boys on some lowlife county pol. No way. Talent's too hard to come by these days – you found that out yourself.'

Rudy recalled the newspaper story about Tony the Eel, washed up dead on the Cape Florida beach. 'I still feel bad about that fellow last month,' the doctor said.

'Hey, it happens.'

'But still,' said Rudy morosely.

'You ought to get out of Florida,' advised Curly Eyebrows. 'I been telling all my friends, it's not like the old days. Fuck the pretty beaches, Doc, them Cubans are crazy. They're not like you and me. And then there's the Jews and the Haitians, Christ!'

'Times change,' said Rudy.

'I was reading up on it, some article about stress. Florida is like the worst fucking place in America for stressing out, besides Vegas. I'm not making this up.'

Dispiritedly, Rudy Graveline said, 'It seems like everybody wants a piece of my hide.'

'Ain't it the fucking truth.'

'I swear, I'm not a violent person by nature.'

'Costa Rica,' said the man in New Jersey. 'Think about it.'

Commissioner Roberto Pepsical got to the church fifteen minutes early and scouted the aisles: a bag lady snoozing on the third pew, but that was it. To kill time Roberto lit a whole row of devotional candles. Afterwards he fished through his pocket change and dropped a Canadian dime in the coin box.

When the doctor arrived, Roberto waddled briskly to the back of the church. Rudy Graveline was wearing a tan sports jacket and dark, loose-fitting pants and a brown striped necktie. He looked about as calm as a rat in a snake hole. In his right hand was a black Samsonite suitcase. Wordlessly Roberto brushed past him and entered one of the dark confessionals. Rudy waited about three minutes, checked over both shoulders, opened the door, and went in.

'God,' he exclaimed.

'He's here somewhere.' The commissioner chuckled at his own joke.

Rudy had never been inside a confession booth before. It was smaller and gloomier than he had imagined; the only light was a tiny amber bulb plugged into a wall socket.

Roberto had planted his fat ass on the kneeling cushion with his back to the screen. Rudy checked to make sure there wasn't a priest on the other side, listening. Priests could be awful quiet when they wanted.

'Remember,' the commissioner said, raising a finger. 'Whisper.'

Right, Rudy thought, like I was going to belt out a Gershwin tune. 'Of all the screwy places to do this,' he said.

'It's quiet,' Roberto Pepsical said. 'And very safe.'

'And very small,' Rudy added. 'You had anchovies for dinner, didn't you?'

'There are no secrets here,' said Roberto.

With difficulty, Rudy wedged himself and the Samsonite next to the commissioner on the kneeling bench. Roberto's body heat bathed both of them in a warm acrid fog, and Rudy wondered how long the oxygen would hold out. He had never heard of anyone suffocating in confession; on the other hand, that was exactly the sort of incident the Catholics would cover up.

'You ready?' Roberto asked with a wink. 'What's that in your pocket?'

'Unfortunately, that's a subpoena. Some creep got me on the way out of the clinic tonight.' Rudy had been in such a hurry that he hadn't even looked at the court papers; he was somewhat accustomed to getting sued.

Roberto said, 'No wonder you're in such a lousy mood.'

'It's not that so much as what happened to my new car. It got vandalized – actually, scoured is the word for it.'

'The Jag? That's terrible.'

'Oh, it's been a splendid day,' Rudy said. 'Absolutely splendid.'

'Getting back to the money . . .'

'I've got it right here.' The doctor opened the suitcase across both their laps, and the confessional was filled with the sharp scent of new money. Rudy Graveline was overwhelmed – it really did *smell*. Roberto picked up a brick of hundred-dollar bills. 'I thought I said twenties.'

'Yeah, and I would've needed a bloody U-Haul.'

Roberto Pepsical snapped off the bank wrapper and counted out ten thousand dollars on the floor between his feet. Then he added up the other bundles in the suitcase to make sure the total came to one twenty-five.

Grinning, he held up one of the loose hundreds. 'I

don't see many of these. Whose picture is that – Eisenhower's?'

'No,' said Rudy, stonily.

'What'd the bank say? About you taking all these big bills.'

'Nothing,' Rudy said. 'This is Miami, Bobby.'

'Yeah, I guess.' Ebulliently the commissioner restacked the cash bundles and packed them in the Samsonite. He scooped up the loose ten thousand dollars and shoved the thick wad into the pockets of his suit. 'This was a smart thing you did.'

Rudy said, 'I'm not so sure.'

'You know that plan I told you about . . . about licensing the medical clinics and all that? Me and The Others, we decided to drop the whole thing. We figure that doctors like you got enough rules and regulations as it is.'

'Glad to hear it,' said Rudy Graveline. He wished he had brought some Certs. Roberto could use a whole roll.

'How about a drink?' the commissioner asked. 'We could stop at the Versailles, get a couple pitchers of *sangría*.'

'Yum.'

'Hey, it's my treat.'

'Thanks,' said the doctor, 'but first you know what I'd like to do? I'd like to say a prayer. I'd like to thank the Lord that this problem with Cypress Towers is finally over.'

Roberto shrugged. 'Go ahead.'

'Is it all right, Bobby? I mean, since I'm not Catholic.'

'No problem.' The commissioner grunted to his feet, turned around in the booth and got to his knees. The cushion squeaked under his weight. 'Do like this,' he said.

Rudy Graveline, who was slimmer, had an easier time with the turnaround manoeuvre. With the suitcase propped between them, the two men knelt side by side, facing the grated screen through which confessions were heard.

'So pray,' Roberto Pepsical said. 'I'll wait till you're done. Fact, I might even do a couple Hail Marys myself, long as I'm here.'

Rudy shut his eyes, bowed his head, and pretended to say a prayer.

Roberto nudged him. 'I don't mean to tell you what to do,' he said, 'but in here it's not proper to pray with your hands in your pockets.'

'Of course,' said Rudy, 'I'm sorry.'

He took his right hand from his pants and placed it on Roberto's doughy shoulder. It was too dark for the commissioner to see the hypodermic syringe.

'Hail Mary,' Roberto said, 'full of grace, the Lord is with thee. Blessed ar-ow!'

The commissioner pawed helplessly at the needle sticking from his jacket at the crook of the elbow. Considering Rudy's general clumsiness with injections, it was a minor miracle that he hit the commissioner's antecubital vein on the first try. Roberto Pepsical hugged the doctor desperately, a panting bear, but already the deadly potassium was streaming toward the valves of his fat clotty heart.

Within a minute the seizure killed him, mimicking the symptoms of a routine infarction so perfectly that the commissioner's relatives would never challenge the autopsy.

Rudy removed the spent syringe, retrieved the loose cash from Roberto's pocket, picked up the black suitcase, and slipped out of the stuffy confessional. The air in the church seemed positively alpine, and he paused to breathe it deeply.

In the back row, an elderly Cuban couple turned at the sound of his footsteps on the terrazzo. Rudy nodded solemnly. He hoped they didn't notice how badly his legs were shaking. He faced the altar and tried to smile like a man whose soul had been cleansed of all sin.

The old Cuban woman raised a bent finger to her forehead and made the sign of the cross. Rudy worried about Catholic protocol and wondered if he was expected to reply. He didn't know how to make the sign of the cross, but he put down the suitcase and gave it a gallant try. With a forefinger he touched his brow, his breast, his right shoulder, his left shoulder, his navel, then his brow again.

'Live long and prosper,' he said to the old woman and walked out the doors of the church.

When he got home, Rudy Graveline went upstairs to see Heather Chappell. He sat next to the bed and took her hand. She blinked moistly over the edge of the bandages.

Rudy kissed her knuckles and said, 'How are you feeling?'

'I don't know about you,' Heather said, 'but I'm feeling a hundred years old.'

'That's to be expected. You had quite a day.'

'You sure it went OK?'

'Beautifully,' Rudy said.

'The nose, too?'

'A masterpiece.'

'But I don't remember a thing.'

The reason Heather couldn't remember the surgery was because there had been no surgery. Rudy had drugged her copiously the night before and kept her drugged the whole day. Heather had lain unconscious for seven hours, whacked out on world-class pharmaceutical narcotics. By the time she awoke, she felt like she'd been sleeping for a month. Her hips, her breasts, her neck, and her nose were all snugly and expertly bandaged, but no scalpel had touched her fine California flesh. Rudy hoped to persuade Heather that the surgery was a glowing success; the absence of scars, a testament to his wizardry. Obviously he had weeks of bogus post-operative counselling ahead of him.

'Can I see the video?' she asked from the bed.

'Later,' Rudy promised. 'When you're up to snuff.'

He had ordered (by FedEx) a series of surgical training cassettes from a medical school in California. Now it was simply a matter of editing the tapes into a plausible sequence. Gowned, masked, and anaesthetized on the operating table, all patients looked pretty much alike to a camera. Meanwhile, all you ever saw of the surgeon was his gloved hands; Heather would never know that the doctor on the videotape was not her lover.

She said, 'It's incredible, Rudolph, but I don't feel any pain.'

'It's the medication,' he said. 'The first few days, we keep you pretty high.'

Heather giggled. 'Eight miles high?'

'Nine,' said Rudy Graveline, 'at least.'

He tucked her hand beneath the sheets and picked up something from the bedstand. 'Look what I've got.'

She squinted through the fuzz of the drugs. 'Red and blue and white,' she said dreamily.

'Plane tickets,' Rudy said. 'I'm taking you on a trip.'

'Really?'

'To Costa Rica. The climate is ideal for your recovery.'

'For how long?'

Rudy said, 'A month or two, maybe longer. As long as it takes, darling.'

'But I'm supposed to do a *Password* with Jack Klugman.'

'Out of the question,' said Rudy. 'You're in no condition for that type of stress. Now get some sleep.'

'What's that noise?' she asked, lifting her head.

'The doorbell, sweetheart. Lie still now.'

'Costa Rica,' Heather murmured. 'Where's that, anyhow?'

Rudy kissed her on the forehead and told her he loved her.

'Yeah,' she said. 'I know.'

Whoever was at the door was punching the button like it was a jukebox. Rudy hurried down the stairs and checked through the glass peephole.

Chemo signalled mirthlessly back at him.

'Shit.' Rudy sighed, thought of his Jaguar, and opened the door.

'Why did you destroy my car?'

'Teach you some manners,' Chemo said. Another bandaged woman stood at his side.

'Maggie?' Rudy Graveline said. 'Is that you?'

Chemo led her by the hand into the big house. He found the living room and made himself comfortable in an antique rocking chair. Maggie Gonzalez sat on a white leather sofa. Her eyes, which were Rudy's only clue to her mood, seemed cold and hostile.

Chemo said, 'Getting jerked around is not my favourite thing. I ought to just kill you.'

'What good would that do?' Rudy said. He stepped closer to Maggie and asked, 'Who did your face?'

'Leaper,' she said.

'Leonard Leaper? Up in New York? I heard he's good – mind if I look?'

'Yes,' she said, recoiling. 'Rogelio, make him get away!'

'Rogelio?' Rudy looked quizzically at Chemo.

'It's your fucking fault,' he said. 'That's the name you put on the tickets. Now leave her alone.' Chemo stopped rocking. He eyed Rudy Graveline as if he were a palmetto bug.

The surgeon sat near Maggie on the white leather sofa and said to Chemo, 'So how're the dermabrasions healing?'

Self-consciously the killer's hand went to his chin. 'All of a sudden you're concerned about my face. Now that you're afraid.'

'Well, you look good,' Rudy persisted. 'Really, it's a thousand per cent improvement.'

'Jesus H. Christ.'

Irritably Maggie said, 'Let's get to the point, OK? I want to get out of here.'

'The money,' Chemo said to the doctor. 'We decided on one million, even.'

'For what!' Rudy was trying to stay cool, but his tone was trenchant.

Chemo started rocking again. 'For everything,' he said. 'For Maggie's videotape. For Stranahan. For stopping that TV show about the dead girl. That's worth a million dollars. In fact, the more I think about it, I'd say it's worth two.'

Rudy folded his arms and said, 'You do everything you just said, and I'll gladly give you a million dollars. As of now, you get nothing but expenses because you haven't done a damn thing but stir up trouble.'

'That's not true,' Maggie snapped.

'We've been busy,' Chemo added. 'We got a big surprise.'

Rudy said, 'I've got a big surprise, too. A malpractice suit. And guess whose name is on the witness list?'

He jerked an accusing thumb at Maggie, who said, 'That's news to me.'

Rudy went on. 'Some fellow named Nordstrom. Lost his eye in some freak accident and now it's all my fault.'

Maggie said, 'I never heard of a Nordstrom.'

'Well, your name is right there in the file. Witness for the plaintiff. Why should I pay you people a dime?'

'All the more reason,' Chemo said. 'I believe it's called hush money.'

'No,' said the doctor, 'that's not the way it goes.'

Chemo stood up from the rocker. He took two large steps across the living room and punched Rudy Graveline solidly in the gut. The doctor collapsed in a gagging heap on the Persian carpet. Chemo turned him over with one foot. Then he cranked up the Weed Whacker.

'Oh God,' cried Rudy, raising his hands to shield his eyes. Quickly Maggie moved out of the way, her facial bandages crinkled in trepidation.

'I got a new battery,' Chemo said. 'A Die-Hard. Watch this.'

He started weed-whacking Rudy's fine clothes. First

he shredded the shirt and tie, then he tried trimming the curly brown hair on Rudy's chest. The doctor yelped pitiably as nasty pink striations appeared beneath his nipples.

Chemo was working the machine toward Rudy's pubic zone when he spied something inside the tattered lining of the surgeon's tan coat. He turned off the Weed Whacker and leaned down for a closer look.

With his good hand Chemo reached into the silky entrails of Rudy's jacket and retrieved the severed corner of a one-hundred-dollar bill. Excitedly he probed around until he found more: handfuls, blessedly unshredded.

Chemo spread the money on the coffee table, beneath which Rudy thrashed and moaned impotently. The stricken surgeon observed the accounting firsthand, gazing up through the frosted glass. As the cash grew to cover the table, Rudy's face hardened into a mask of abject disbelief. On his way back from the church he had meant to stop at the clinic and return the money to the drop safe. Now it was too late.

'Count it,' Chemo said to Maggie.

Excitedly she riffled through the bills. 'Nine thousand two hundred,' she reported. 'The rest is all chopped up.'

Chemo dragged Dr Graveline from under the coffee table. 'Why you carrying this much cash?' he said. 'Don't tell me the Jag dealer won't take credit cards.' His moist salamander eyes settled on the black Samsonite, which Rudy had stupidly left in the middle of the hallway.

Rudy sniffed miserably as he watched Chemo kick open the suitcase and crouch down to count the rest of the money. 'Well, well,' said the killer.

'What are you going to do with it?' the doctor asked.

'Gee, I think we'll give it to the United Way. Or maybe Jerry's Kids.' Chemo walked over to Rudy and poked his bare belly with the warm head of the Weed Whacker. 'What the hell you think we're going to do with it? We're gonna spend it, and then we're gonna come back for more.'

After they had gone, Dr Rudy Graveline sprawled on the rumpled Persian carpet for a long time, thinking: This is what a Harvard education has gotten me – extorted, beaten, stripped, scandalized, and chopped up like an artichoke. The doctor's fingers gingerly explored the tumescent stripes that crisscrossed his chest and abdomen. If it didn't sting so much, the sight would be almost comical.

It occurred to Rudy Graveline that Chemo and Maggie had forgotten to tell him their big secret, whatever it was they had done, whatever spectacular felony they had committed to earn this first garnishment.

And it occurred to Rudy that he wasn't all that curious. In fact, he was somewhat relieved not to know.

TWENTY-SEVEN

The man from the medical examiner's office took one look in the back of the tree truck and said: 'Mmmm, lasagna.'

'That's very funny,' said Al García. 'You oughta go on the Carson show. Do a whole routine on stiffs.'

The man from the medical examiner's office said, 'Al, you gotta admit—'

'I told you what happened.'

'—but you gotta admit, there's a humorous aspect.'

Coroners made Al García jumpy; they always got so cheery when somebody came up with a fresh way to die.

The detective said, 'If you think it's funny, fine. You're the one's gotta do the autopsy.'

'First I'll need a casserole dish.'

'Hilarious,' said García. 'Absolutely hilarious.'

The man from the medical examiner's office told him to lighten up, said everybody needs a break in the monotony, no matter what line of work. 'I get tired of gunshot wounds,' the coroner said. 'It's like a damn assembly line down there. GSW head, GSW thorax, GSW neck – it gets old, Al.'

García said, 'Listen, go ahead, make your jokes. But I need you to keep this one outta the papers.'

'Good luck.'

The detective knew it wouldn't be easy to keep the

lid on George Graveline's death. Seven squad cars, an ambulance, and a body wagon – even in Miami, that'll draw a crowd. The gawkers were being held behind yellow police ribbons strung along Crandon Boulevard. Soon the minicams would arrive, and the minicams could zoom in for close-ups.

'I need a day or two,' García said. 'No press, and no next of kin.'

The man from the medical examiner's office shrugged. 'It'll take at least that long to make the ID considering what's left. I figure we'll have to go dental.'

'Whatever.'

'I'll need to impound the truck,' the coroner said. 'And this fancy toothpick machine.'

García said he would have them both towed downtown.

The coroner stuck his head into the maw of the wood chipper and examined the blood-smeared blades. 'There ought to be bullet fragments,' he said, 'somewhere in this mess.'

García said, 'Hey, Sherlock, I told you what happened. I shot the asshole, OK? My gun, my bullets.'

'Al, don't take all the fun out of it.' The man from the medical examiner's office reached into the blades of the wood chipper and carefully plucked out an item that the untrained eye would have misidentified as a common black woolly-bear caterpillar.

The coroner held it up for Al García to see.

The detective frowned. 'What, do I get a prize or something? It's a sideburn, for Chrissakes.'

'Very good,' said the coroner.

García flicked the soggy nub of his cigar into the bushes and went looking for George Graveline's crew of tree trimmers. There were three of them sitting sombrely in the back seat of a county patrol car. Al García got in front, on the passenger side. He turned around and spoke to them through the cage. The men's clothes smelled like pot. García asked if any of them had seen what had happened, and to a one they answered no, they'd been on their lunch break. The officers from Internal Review had asked the same thing.

'If you didn't see anything,' García said, 'then you don't have much to tell the reporters, right?'

In unison the tree trimmers shook their heads.

'Including the name of the alleged victim, right?'

The tree trimmers agreed.

'This is damned serious,' said García. 'I don't believe you boys would purposely obstruct a homicide investigation, would you?'

The tree trimmers promised not to say a word to the media. Al García asked a uniformed cop to give the men a lift home, so they wouldn't have to walk past the minicams on their way to the bus stop.

By this time, the ambulance was backing out, empty. García knocked on the driver's window. 'Where's the guy you were working on?'

'Blunt head wound?'

'Right. Big blond guy.'

'Took off,' said the ambulance driver. 'Gobbled three Darvocets and said so long. Wouldn't even let us wrap him.'

García cursed and bearishly swatted at a fresh-cut buttonwood branch.

The ambulance driver said, 'You see him, be sure and tell him he oughta go get a skull X-ray.'

'You know what you'd find?' García said. 'Shit for brains, that's what.'

Reynaldo Flemm picked up an attractive young woman at a nightclub called Biscayne Baby in Coconut Grove. He took her to his room at the Grand Bay Hotel and asked her to wait while he ran the water in the Roman tub. Still insecure about his impugned physique, Reynaldo didn't want the young woman to see him naked in the bright light. He lowered himself into the bath, covered the vital areas with suds, double-checked himself in the mirrors, then called for the young woman to join him. She came in the bathroom, stripped, and climbed casually into the deep tub. When Reynaldo tickled her armpits with his toes, the young woman politely pushed his legs away.

'So, what do you do?' he asked.

'I told you, I'm a legal secretary.'

'Oh, yeah.' When Reynaldo got semi-blitzed on screwdrivers, his short-term memory tended to vapour-lock. 'You probably recognize me,' he said to the young woman.

'I told you already – no.'

Reynaldo said, 'Normally my hair's black. I coloured it this way for a reason.'

He had revived the Johnny LeTigre go-go dancer disguise for his confrontation with Dr Rudy Graveline. He had dyed his hair brown and slicked it straight back with a wet comb. He looked like a Mediterranean sponge diver.

'Imagine me with black hair,' he said to the legal

secretary, who flicked a soap bubble off her nose and said no, she still wouldn't recognize him.

He said, 'You get TV, right? I'm Reynaldo Flemm.'

'Yeah?'

'From *In Your Face*.'

'Oh, sure.'

'Ever seen it?'

'No,' said the secretary, 'but I don't watch all that much television.' She was trying to be nice. 'I think I've seen your commercials,' she said.

Flemm shrunk lower in the tub.

'Is it, like, a game show?' the woman asked.

'No, it's a news show. I'm an investigative reporter.'

'Like that guy on *Sixty Minutes*?'

Reynaldo bowed his head. Feeling guilty, the secretary slid across the tub and climbed on his lap. She said, 'Hey, I believe you.'

'Thanks a bunch.'

She felt a little sorry for him; he seemed so small and wounded among the bubbles. She said, 'You certainly look like you could be on television.'

'I *am* on fucking television. I've got my own show.'

The woman said, 'OK, whatever.'

'I could loan you a tape – you got a VCR?'

The secretary told him to hush. She put her lips to his ear and said, 'Why don't we try it right here?'

Reynaldo half-heartedly slipped one arm around her waist and began kissing her breasts. They were perfectly lovely breasts, but Reynaldo's heart wasn't in it. After a few moments the woman said, 'You're not really in the mood, huh?'

'I *was*.'

'I'm sorry. Here, let me do your back.'

Reynaldo's buttocks squeaked as he turned around in the tub so the secretary could scrub him. He watched her in the mirror; her hands felt wondrously soothing. Eventually he closed his eyes.

'There you go,' she said, kneading his shoulder blades. 'My great big TV star.'

Reynaldo found he was getting excited again. He touched himself, underwater, just to make sure. He was smiling until he opened his eyes and saw something new in the mirror.

A man standing in the doorway. The man with the tarpon gaff.

'Sorry to interrupt,' said Mick Stranahan.

The woman squealed and dove for a towel. Reynaldo Flemm groped for floating suds to cover his withering erection.

'I was looking for Christina,' Stranahan said. He walked up to the Roman tub with the gaff held under one arm, like a riding crop. 'She's not in her hotel room.'

'How'd you find me?' Reynaldo's voice was reedy and taut, definitely not an anchorman's voice.

'Miami is not one of the world's all-time great hotel towns,' Stranahan said. 'Hotshot celebrities like you always end up in the Grove. But tell me: why's Christina still registered out at Key Biscayne?'

Nervously the secretary said, 'Who's Christina?'

Stranahan said: 'Ray, I asked you a question.' He poked the fish gaff under the suds and scraped the point across the bottom of the tub. The steel screeched ominously against the ceramic. Reynaldo Flemm drew up his knees and sloshed protectively into a corner.

'Chris doesn't know I'm here,' he said. 'I ditched her.'

Stranahan told the legal secretary to get dressed and

go home. He waited until she was gone from the bathroom before he spoke again.

'I checked Christina's room at the Sonesta. She hasn't been there for two days.'

Reynaldo said, 'What're you going to do to me?' He couldn't take his eyes off the tarpon gaff. Wrapping his arms around his knees, he said, 'Don't hurt me.'

'For Christ's sake.'

'I mean it!'

'Are you crying?' Stranahan couldn't believe it – another dumb twit overreacting. 'Just tell me about Christina. Her notebooks were still in the room, and so was her purse. Any ideas?'

'Uuunnngggh.' The pink of Flemm's tongue showed between his front teeth. It was a cowering, poodle-like expression, amplified by trembling lips and liquid eyes.

'Settle down,' said Stranahan. His head felt like it was full of wet cement. The Darvocets had barely put a ripple in the pain. What a shitty day.

He said, 'You haven't seen her?'

Violently Reynaldo shook his head no.

They heard a door slam – the secretary, making tracks. Stranahan used the gaff to pull the plug in the Roman tub. Wordlessly he watched the soapy water drain, leaving Reynaldo bare and shrivelled and flecked with suds.

'What's with the hairdo?' Stranahan asked.

Reynaldo composed himself and said, 'For a show.'

Stranahan tossed him a towel. He said, 'I know what you're doing. You're acting Christina out of the Barletta story. I saw your notes on the table.'

Flemm reddened. It had taken him three hours to come up with ten questions for Dr Rudy Graveline.

Carefully he had printed the questions on a fresh legal pad, the way Christina Marks always did. He had spent the better part of the afternoon trying to memorize them before calling it quits and heading over to Biscayne Baby for some action.

'I don't care about your show,' Stranahan said, 'but I care about Christina.'

'Me, too.'

'It looked like somebody pushed his way into her hotel room. There was a handprint on the door.'

Reynaldo said, 'Well, it wasn't mine.'

'Stand up,' Stranahan told him.

Flemm wrapped himself into the towel as he stood up in the tub. Stranahan measured him with his eyes. 'I believe you,' he said. He went back to the living room to wait for Reynaldo to dry off and get dressed.

When Flemm came out, wearing an absurd muscle shirt and tight jeans, Stranahan said, 'When are you going to see the doctor?'

'Soon,' Reynaldo replied. Then, blustery: 'None of your business.' He felt so much tougher with a shirt on.

Stranahan said, 'If you wait, you'll have a better story.'

Reynaldo rolled his eyes – how many times had he heard that one! 'No way,' he said. The snide pomposity had returned to his voice.

'Ray, I'm only going to warn you once. If something's happened to Christina because of you, or if you do something that brings her any harm, you're done. And I'm not talking about your precious TV career.'

Flemm said, 'You sound pretty tough, long as you've got that hook.'

Stranahan tossed the tarpon gaff at Reynaldo and said, 'There – see if it works for you, too.'

Reynaldo quickly dropped it on the carpet. As a rule he didn't fight with crazy people unless cameras were rolling. Otherwise, what was the point?

'I hope you find her,' Reynaldo said.

Stranahan stood to leave. 'You better pray that I do.'

At the Gay Bidet, Freddie didn't even bother to get up from the desk to introduce himself. 'I'm gonna tell you the same as I told that Cuban cop, which is nothing. I got a policy not to talk about employees, past or present.'

Stranahan said, 'But you know the man I'm asking about.'

'Maybe, maybe not.'

'Is he here?'

'Ditto,' said Freddie. 'Now get the fuck gone.'

'Actually, I'm going to look around.'

'Oh, you are?' Freddie said. 'Like hell.' He punched a black buzzer under the desk. The door opened and Stranahan momentarily was drowned by the vocal stylings of the Fabulous Foreskins, performing their opening set.

The man who entered Freddie's office was a short muscular Oriental. He wore a pink Gay Bidet security T-shirt, stretched to the limit.

Freddie said, 'Wong, please get this dog turd out of my sight.'

Stranahan waved the tarpon gaff and its sinister glint caused Wong to hesitate. Disdainfully Freddie glowered at the bouncer and said, 'What happened to all that kung fu shit?'

Wong's chest began to swell.

Stranahan said, 'I've had a lousy day, and I'm really in no mood. You like having a liquor licence?'

Freddie said, 'What're you talkin' about, do I like it?'

'Because you oughta enjoy it tonight, while you can. If you don't answer my questions, here's what happens to you and this toilet bowl of a nightclub: first thing tomorrow, six nasty bastards from Alcohol and Beverage come by and shut your ass down. Why? Because you lied when you got your liquor licence, Freddie. You got a felony record in Illinois and Georgia, and you lied about that. Also, you've been serving to minors, big time. Also, your bartender just tried to sell me two grammes of Peruvian. You want, I can keep going.'

Freddie said, 'Don't bother.' He instructed Wong to get lost. When they were alone again, he said to Stranahan, 'That rap in Atlanta was no good.'

'So you're not a pimp. Excellent. The beverage guys will be very impressed, Freddie. Be sure to tell them you're not a pimp, no matter what the FBI computer says.'

'What the fuck is it you want?'

'Just tell me where I can find my tall, cool friend. The one with the face.'

Freddie said, 'Truth is, I don't know. He took off a couple days ago. Picked up his paycheque and quit. Tried to give me back the T-shirt, the dumb fuck – like somebody else would wear the damn thing. I told him to keep it for a souvenir.'

'Did he say where he was going?' Stranahan asked.

'Nope. He had two broads with him, you figure it

out.' Freddie flashed a mouthful of nubby yellow teeth. 'Creature from the Black Lagoon, and still he gets more poon than me.'

'What did the women look like?' Stranahan asked.

'One, I couldn't tell. Her face was all busted up, cuts and bruises and Band-Aids. He must've beat the hell out of her for something. The other was a brunette, good-looking, on the thin side. Not humungous titties but nice pointy ones.'

Stranahan couldn't decide whether it was Freddie or the music that was aggravating his headache. 'The thin one – was she wearing blue jeans?'

Freddie said he didn't remember.

'Did they say anything?'

'Nope, not a word.'

'Did he have a gun?'

Freddie laughed again. 'Man, he doesn't need a gun. He has that whirly thing on his arm.' Freddie told Stranahan what the thing was and how the man known as Chemo would use it.

'You're kidding.'

'Like hell,' said Freddie. 'Guy was the best goddamn bouncer I ever had.'

Stranahan handed the club owner a fifty-dollar bill and the phone number of the bait shop at the marina. 'This is in case he comes back. You call me before you call the cops.'

Freddie pocketed the money. Reflectively he said: 'Freak like that with two broads, man, it just proves there's no God.'

'We'll see,' said Stranahan.

TWENTY-EIGHT

Chemo's first instinct was to haul ass with the doctor's cash, which was more than he would see in a couple of Amish lifetimes. Forget about the Stranahan hit, just blow town. Maggie Gonzalez told him, don't be such a small-timer, remember what we've got here: a surgeon on the hook. A money machine, for God's sake. Maggie assured him that a million, even two million, was doable. There wasn't anything that Rudy Graveline wouldn't give to save his medical licence.

Goosing the Bonneville along Biscayne Boulevard, Chemo said, 'What I've got now, I could get my face patched and still have enough for a year in Barbados. Maybe even get some real hair – those plug deals they stick in your scalp. I read somewhere that's what they did to Elton John.'

'Sure,' Maggie said. 'I know some doctors who do hair.'

She was trying to play Chemo the way she had played all her men, but it wasn't easy. Beyond his desire for a clear complexion, she had yet to discover what motivated him. While Chemo appreciated money, he hardly displayed the proper lust for it. As for sex, he expressed no interest whatsoever. Maggie chose to believe that he was deterred by her bruises and bandages; once the facelift had healed, her powers of seduction would return. Then the only obstacle would be a logistical one: what would you do with the Weed Whacker under the sheets?

As Chemo pulled up on the Holiday Inn at 125th Street, Maggie said, 'If it would make you feel better, we could move to a nicer hotel.'

'What would make me feel better,' Chemo said, 'is for you to give me the keys to the suitcase.' He turned off the ignition and held out his right hand.

Maggie said, 'You think I'm dumb enough to try and rip you off?'

'Yes,' said Chemo, reaching for her purse. 'Plenty dumb enough.'

Christina Marks heard the door open and prayed it was the maid. It wasn't.

The lights came on and Chemo loomed incuriously over the bed. He checked the knots at Christina's wrists and ankles, while Maggie stalked into the bathroom and slammed the door.

After Chemo removed the towel from her mouth, Christina said, 'What's the matter with her?'

'She thinks I don't trust her. She's right.'

'For what it's worth,' Christina said, 'she already conned my boss out of a bundle.'

'I'll keep that in mind.' Chemo sat on the corner of the bed, counting the cash that he had taken from Dr Rudy Graveline's pockets. Counting wasn't easy with only one hand. Christina watched inquisitively. After he was finished, Chemo put five thousand in the suitcase with the rest of the haul; forty-two hundred went down the heels of his boots. He slid the suitcase under the bed.

'How original,' Christina said.

'Shut up.'

'Could you untie me, please? I have to pee.'

'Jesus H. Christ.'

'You want me to wet the bed?' she said. 'Ruin all your cash?'

Chemo got Maggie out of the bathroom and made her help undo the knots. They had bound Christina to the bed frame with nylon clothesline. Once freed, she rubbed her wrists and sat up stiffly.

'Go do your business,' Chemo said. Then, to Maggie: 'Stay with her.'

Christina said, 'I can't pee with somebody watching.'

'What?'

'She's right,' Maggie said. 'I'm the same way. I'll just wait outside the door.'

'No, do what I told you,' Chemo said.

'There's no window in there,' Christina said. 'What'm I going to do, escape down the toilet?'

When she came out of the bathroom, Chemo was standing by the door. He led her back to the bed, made her lie down, then tied her again – another tedious chore, one-handed.

'No gag this time,' Christina requested. 'I promise not to scream.'

'But you'll talk,' said Chemo. 'That's even worse.'

Since the morning he had kidnapped her from the hotel on Key Biscayne, Chemo had said practically nothing to Christina Marks. Nor had he menaced or abused her in any sense – it was as if he knew that the mere sight of him, close up, was daunting enough. Christina had spied the butt of a revolver in Chemo's baggy pants pocket, but he had never pulled it; this was a big improvement over the two previous encounters, when he had nearly shot her.

She said, 'I just want to know why you're doing this, what exactly you want.'

He acted as if he never heard her. Maggie handed Christina a small cup of Pepsi.

'Don't let her drink too much,' Chemo cautioned. 'She'll be going to the head all night.'

He turned on the television set and grimaced: pro basketball – the Lakers and the Pistons. Chemo hated basketball. At six foot nine, he had spent his entire adulthood explaining to rude strangers that no, he didn't play pro basketball. Once a myopic Celtics fan had mistaken him for Kevin McHale and demanded an autograph; Chemo had savagely bitten the man on the shoulder, like a horse.

He began switching channels until he found an old *Miami Vice*. He turned up the volume and scooted his chair closer to the tube. He envied Don Johnson's three-day stubble; it looked rugged and manly. Chemo himself had not shaved, for obvious reasons, since the electrolysis accident.

He turned to Maggie and asked, 'Can they do hair plugs on your chin, too?'

'Oh, I'm sure,' she said, though in fact she had never heard of such a procedure.

Pinned to the bed like a butterfly, Christina said, 'Before long, somebody's going to be looking for me.'

Chemo snorted. 'That's the general idea.' Didn't these women ever shut up? Didn't they appreciate his potential for violence?

Maggie sat next to Christina and said, 'We need to get a message to your boyfriend.'

'Who – Stranahan? He's not my boyfriend.'

'Still, I doubt if he wants to see you get hurt.'

Christina appraised herself – strapped to a bed, squirming in her underwear – and imagined what Reynaldo Flemm would say if he came crashing through the door. For once she'd be happy to see the stupid sonofabitch, but she knew there was no possibility of such a rescue. If Mick couldn't find her, Ray didn't have a prayer.

'If it's that videotape you're after, I don't know where it is—'

'But surely your boyfriend does,' said Maggie.

Chemo pointed at the television. 'Hey, lookie there!' On the screen, Detective Sonny Crockett was chasing a drug smuggler through Stiltsville in a speedboat. This was the first time Christina had seen Chemo smile. It was a harrowing experience.

Maggie said, 'So how do you get in touch with him?'

'Mick? I don't know. There's no phone out there. Any time I wanted to see him, I rented a boat.'

A commercial came on the television, and Chemo turned to the women. 'Jesus, I don't want to go back to that house – enough of that shit. I want him to come see me. And he will, soon as he knows I've got you.'

In her most lovelorn voice, Christina said to Maggie, 'I really don't think Mick cares one way or the other.'

'You better hope he does,' said Chemo. He pressed the towel firmly into Christina's mouth and turned back to watch the rest of the show.

On the morning of February eighteenth, the last day of Kipper Garth's law career, he filed a motion with the

Circuit Court of Dade County in the cause of Nord-strom v. Graveline, Whispering Palms, *et al*.

The motion requested an emergency court order freezing all the assets of Dr Rudy Graveline, including bank accounts, certificates of deposit, stock portfolios, municipal bonds, Keogh funds, Individual Retirement Accounts, and real estate holdings. Submitted to the judge with Kipper Garth's motion was an affidavit from the Beachcomber Travel Agency stating that, on the previous day, one Rudolph Graveline had purchased two first-class aeroplane tickets to San José, Costa Rica. In the plea (composed entirely by Mick Stranahan and one of the paralegals), Kipper Garth asserted that it was Dr Graveline's intention to flee the United States permanently.

Normally, a request involving a defendant's assets would have resulted in a full-blown hearing and, most likely, a denial of the motion. But Kipper Garth's position (and thus the Nordstroms') was buttressed by a discreet phone call from Mick Stranahan to the judge, whom Stranahan had known since his days as a young prosecutor in the DUI division. After a brief reminiscence, Stranahan told the judge the true reason for his call; that Dr Rudy Graveline was a prime suspect in an unsolved four-year-old abduction case that might or might not be a homicide. Stranahan assured his friend that, rather than face the court, the surgeon would take his dough and make a run for it.

The judge granted the emergency order shortly after nine o'clock in the morning. Kipper Garth was astonished at his own success; he never dreamed litigation could be so damn easy. He fantasized a day when he could get out of the referral racket altogether, when he would be known and revered throughout Miami as a master trial attorney. Kipper Garth liked the billboards, though. However high he might soar among the eagles of Brickell Avenue, the billboards definitely had to stay . . .

At ten forty-five, Rudy Graveline arrived at his bank in Bal Harbour and asked to make a wire transfer of $250,000 from his personal account to a new account in Panama. He also requested $60,000 in US currency and traveller's cheques. The young bank officer who was assisting Rudy Graveline left his office for several minutes. When he returned, one of the bank's vice presidents stood solemnly at his side.

Rudy took the news badly.

First he wept, which was merely embarrassing. Then he became enraged and hysterical and, finally, incoherent. He staggered, keening, into the bank lobby, at which point two enormous security guards were summoned to escort the surgeon from the premises.

By the time they deposited Rudy in the parking lot, he had settled himself and stopped crying.

Until one of the bank guards had pointed at the fender of the car and said, 'The hell happened to your Jag, brother?'

Perhaps it was the euphoria of a legal triumph, or perhaps it was simple prurient curiosity that impelled Kipper Garth to drop by the Nordstrom household during his lunch hour. The address was in Morningside, a pleasant old neighbourhood of bleached stucco houses located a few blocks off the seediest stretch of Biscayne Boulevard.

Marie Nordstrom was surprised to see Kipper Garth, but she welcomed him warmly at the door, led him to the Florida room, and offered him a cup of coffee. She wore electric-blue Lycra body tights, and her ash-blonde hair was pulled back in a girlish ponytail. Kipper couldn't take his eyes off the subject of litigation, her breasts. The exercise outfit left nothing to the imagination; these were the merriest-looking breasts that Kipper Garth had ever seen. It was difficult to think of them as weapons.

'John's not here,' Mrs Nordstrom said. 'He got a job interview over at the jai-alai fronton. You take cream?'

Kipper Garth took cream. Mrs Nordstrom placed the coffee pot on a glass tray. Kipper Garth made space for her on the sofa, but she moved to a love seat, facing him from across the coffee table.

Kipper Garth said, 'I just wanted to bring you up to date on the malpractice case.' Matter-of-factly he told Mrs Nordstrom about the emergency court order to freeze Dr Graveline's assets.

'What exactly does that mean?'

'It means his money won't be going anywhere, even if he does.'

Mrs Nordstrom was not receiving the news as exuberantly as Kipper Garth had hoped; apparently she could not appreciate the difficulty of what he had done.

'John and I were talking just last night,' she said. 'The idea of going to trial . . . I don't know, Mr Garth. This has been so embarrassing for both of us.'

'We're in it now, Mrs Nordstrom. There's no turning back.' Kipper Garth tried to suppress the exasperation in his voice: here Rudy Graveline was on the ropes and suddenly the plaintiffs want to back out.

'Maybe the doctor would be willing to settle the case,' ventured Mrs Nordstrom.

Kipper Garth put down the coffee cup with a clack and folded his arms. 'Oh, I'm sure he would. I'm sure he'd be delighted to settle. That's exactly why we won't hear of it. Not yet.'

'But John says—'

'Trust me,' the lawyer said. He paused and lowered his eyes. 'Forgive me for saying so, Mrs Nordstrom, but settling this case would be very selfish on your part.'

She looked startled at the word.

Kipper Garth went on: 'Think of all the patients this man has harmed. This *alleged* surgeon. If we don't stop him, nobody will. If you settle the case, Mrs Nordstrom, the butchery will continue. You and your husband will be wealthy, yes, but Rudy Graveline's butchery will continue. At his instruction, the court file will be sealed and his reputation preserved. Again. Is that really what you want?'

Kipper Garth had listened intently to his own words, and was impressed by what he had heard; he was getting damn good at oratory.

A few awkward moments passed and Mrs Nordstrom said, 'They've got an opening for a coach over at the jai-alai. John used to play in college, he was terrific. He even went to Spain one summer and trained with the Basques.'

Kipper Garth had never heard of a Scandinavian jai-alai coach, but his knowledge of the sport was limited. Oozing sincerity, he told Mrs Nordstrom that he hoped her husband got the job.

She said, 'Thing is, he can't tell anybody about his eye. They'd never hire him.'

'Why not?'

'Too dangerous,' Mrs Nordstrom said. 'The ball they use is like a rock. A *pelota* it's called. John says it goes like a hundred sixty miles an hour off those walls.'

Kipper Garth finished his coffee. 'I've never been to a jai-alai game.' He hoped she would take the hint and change the conversation.

'If you're playing, it helps to have two good eyes,' Mrs Nordstrom explained. 'For depth perception.'

'I think I understand.'

'John says they won't let him coach if they find out about the accident.'

Now Kipper Garth got the picture. 'That's why you want to settle the lawsuit, isn't it?'

Mrs Nordstrom said yes, they were worried about publicity. 'John says the papers and the TV will go crazy with a story like this.'

Kipper thought: John is absolutely right.

'But you're a victim, Mrs Nordstrom. You have the right to be compensated for this terrible event in your life. It says so in the Constitution.'

'John says they let cameras in the courtrooms. Is that true?'

'Yes, but let's not get carried away—'

'If it were your wife, would you want the whole world to see her tits on the six o'clock news?' Her tone was prideful and indignant.

'I'll speak to the judge, Mrs Nordstrom. Please don't be upset. I know you've been through hell already.' But Kipper Garth was excited by the idea of TV cameras in the courtroom – it would be better than billboards!

Marie Nordstrom was trying not to cry and doing stolidly. She said, 'I blame that damn Reagan. He hadn't busted up the union, John'd still have his job in the flight tower.'

Kipper Garth said, 'Leave it to me and the two of you will be set for life. John won't need a job.'

Mrs Nordstrom wistfully gazed at the two sturdy, silicon-enhanced, Lycra-covered cones on her chest. 'They say contractures are easy to fix, but I don't know.'

Kipper Garth circled the coffee table and joined her on the love seat. He put an unpractised arm around her shoulders. 'For what it's worth,' he said, 'they *look* spectacular.'

'Thank you,' she whispered, 'but you just don't know – how could you?'

Kipper Garth removed the silk handkerchief from his breast pocket and gave it to Mrs Nordstrom, who sounded like the SS *Norway* when she blew her nose.

'Know what I think?' said Kipper Garth. 'I think you should let me feel them.'

Mrs Nordstrom straightened and gave a stern sniffle.

The lawyer said: 'The only way I can begin to understand, the only way I can convey the magnitude of this tragedy to a jury, is if I can experience it myself.'

'Wait a minute – you want to feel my boobs?'

'I'm your lawyer, Mrs Nordstrom.'

She eyed him doubtfully.

'If it were a burn case, I'd have to see the scar. Dismemberment, paraplegia, same goes.'

'Looking is one thing, Mr Garth. Touching is something else.'

'With all respect, Mrs Nordstrom, your husband is going to make a lousy witness in this case. He's going to come across as a selfish prick. Remember what he said

that day in my office? Bocci balls, Mrs Nordstrom. He
said your breasts were hard as bocci balls. This is not the
testimony of a sensitive, caring spouse.'

She said, 'You'd be bitter, too, if it was your eye that
got poked out.'

'Granted. But let me try to come up with a more
gentle description of your condition. Please, Mrs
Nordstrom.'

'All right, but I won't take my clothes off.'

'Of course not!'

She slid a little closer on the love seat. 'Give me your
hands,' she said. 'There you go.'

'Wow,' said Kipper Garth.

'What'd I tell you?'

'I had no idea.'

'You can let go now,' Mrs Nordstrom said.

'Just a second.'

But one second turned into ten seconds, and ten
seconds turned into thirty, which was plenty of time for
John Nordstrom to enter the house and size up the
scene. Without a word he loaded up the wicker *cesta*
and hurled a goatskin jai-alai ball at the slimy lawyer
who was feeling up his wife. The first shot sailed wide to
the left and shattered a jalousie window. The second
shot dimpled the arm of the love seat with a flat *thunk*.
It was then that Kipper Garth released his grip on Marie
Nordstrom's astoundingly stalwart breasts and made a
vain break for the back door. Whether the lawyer fully
comprehended his ethical crisis or fled on sheer animal
instinct would never be known. John Nordstrom's third
and final jai-alai shot struck the occipital seam of Kipper
Garth's skull. He was unconscious by the time his silvery
head smacked the floor.

'Ha!' Nordstrom exclaimed.

'I take it you got the job,' said his wife.

Willie the cameraman said they had two ways to go; they could crash the place or sneak one in.

Reynaldo Flemm said: 'Crash it.'

'Think of the timing,' Willie said. 'The timing's got to be flawless. We've never tried anything like this.' Willie was leaning toward trying a hidden camera.

Reynaldo said: 'Crash it. There's no security, it's a goddamn medical clinic. Who's gonna stop you, the nurse?'

Willie said he didn't like the plan; too many holes. 'What if the guy makes a run for it? What if he calls the police?'

Reynaldo said: 'Where's he gonna go, Willie? That's the beauty of this thing. The sonofabitch can't run away, and he knows it. Not with the tape rolling. They got laws.'

'Jesus,' Willie said, 'I don't like it. We've got to have a signal, you and me.'

'Don't worry,' Reynaldo said, 'we'll have a signal.'

'But what about the interview?' Willie asked. It was another way of bringing up Christina Marks.

'I wrote my own questions,' Reynaldo said sharply. 'Ball busters, too. You just wait.'

'OK,' Willie said. 'I'll be ready.'

'Seven sharp,' Reynaldo said. 'I can't believe you're so nervous – this isn't the Crips and Bloods, man, it's a candyass doctor. He'll go to pieces, I guarantee it. True confessions, you just wait.'

'Seven sharp,' Willie said. 'See you then.'

After the cameraman had gone, Reynaldo Flemm called the Whispering Palms Spa and Surgery Center to confirm the appointment for Johnny LeTigre. To his surprise, the secretary put him through directly to Dr Graveline.

'We still on for tomorrow morning?'

'Certainly,' the surgeon said. He sounded distracted, subdued. 'Remember: nothing to eat or drink after midnight.'

'Right.'

'I thought we'd start with the rhinoplasty and go on to the liposuction.'

'Fine by me,' said Reynaldo Flemm. That's exactly how he had planned it, the nose job first.

'Mr LeTigre, I had a question regarding the fee . . .'

'Fifteen thousand is what we agreed on.'

'Correct,' said Rudy Graveline, 'but I just wanted to make sure – you said something about cash?'

'Yeah, that's right. I got cash.'

'And you'll have it with you tomorrow?'

'You bet.' Reynaldo couldn't believe this jerk. Probably grosses two million a year, and here he is drooling over a lousy fifteen grand. It was true what they said about doctors being such cheap bastards.

'Anything else I need to remember?'

'Just take plenty of fluids,' Rudy said mechanically, 'but nothing after midnight.'

'I'll be a good boy,' Reynaldo Flemm promised. 'See you tomorrow.'

TWENTY-NINE

The wind kicked up overnight, whistled through the planks of the house, slapped the shutters against the walls. Mick Stranahan climbed naked to the roof and lay down with the shotgun at his right side. The bay was noisy and black, hissing through the pilings beneath the house. Above, the clouds rolled past in churning grey clots, celestial dust devils tumbling across a low sky. As always, Stranahan lay facing away from the city, where the halogen crime lights stained an otherwise lovely horizon. On nights such as this, Stranahan regarded the city as a malignancy and its sickly orange aura as a vast misty bubble of pustular gas. The downtown skyline, which had seemed to sprout overnight in a burst of civic priapism, struck Stranahan as a crass but impressive prop, an elaborate movie set. Half the new Miami skyscrapers had been built with coke money and existed largely as an inside joke, a mirage to please the banks and the Internal Revenue Service and the chamber of commerce. Everyone liked to say that the skyline was a monument to local prosperity, but Stranahan recognized it was a tribute to the anonymous genius of Latin American money launderers. In any case, it was nothing he wished to contemplate from the top of his stilt house. Nor was the view south of downtown any kinder, a throbbing congealment from Coconut Grove to the Gables to South Miami and beyond. Looking westward on a clearer evening, Stranahan would have fixed on the newest coastal landmark: a sheer ten-storey cliff of refuse known as Mount Trashmore. Having run out of rural locations in which to conceal its waste, Dade County had erected a towering fetid landfill along the shore of Biscayne Bay. Stranahan could not decide which sight was more offensive, the city skyline or the mountain of garbage. The turkey buzzards, equally ambivalent, commuted regularly from one site to the other.

Stranahan was always grateful for a clean ocean breeze. He sprawled on the eastern slope of the roof, facing the Atlantic. A DC-10 took off from Miami International and passed over Stiltsville, rattling the windmill on Stranahan's house. He wondered what it would be like to wake up and find the city vaporized, the skies clear and silent, the shoreline lush and virginal! He would have loved to live here at the turn of the century, when nature owned the upper hand.

The cool wind tickled the hair on his chest and legs. Stranahan tasted salt on his lips and closed his eyes. One of his ex-wives, he couldn't remember which, had told him he ought to move to Alaska and become a hermit. You're such an old grump, she had said, not even the grizzly bears'd put up with you. Now Stranahan recalled which wife had said this: Donna, his second. She had eventually grown tired of all his negativity. Every big city has crime, she had said. Every big city has corruption. Look at New York, she had said. Look at Chicago. Those are great goddamn cities, Mick, you gotta admit. Like so many cocktail waitresses, Donna steadfastly refused to give up on humanity. She believed that the good people of the world outnumbered the bad, and she got the tips to prove it. After the divorce, she had enrolled in night school and earned her Florida real estate licence; Stranahan had heard she'd moved to Jacksonville and was going great guns in the waterfront condo market. Bleakly it occurred to him that all his former wives (even Chloe, who had nailed a CPA for a husband) had gone on to greater achievements after the divorce. It was as if being married to Stranahan had made each of them realize how much of the real world they were missing.

He thought of Christina Marks. How did he get mixed up with such a serious woman? Unlike the others he had loved and married, Christina avidly pursued that which was evil and squalid and polluted. Her job was to expose it. There was not a wisp of true innocence about her, not a trace of cheery waitress-type optimism . . . yet something powerful attracted him. Maybe because she slogged through the same moral swamps. Crooked cops, crooked lawyers, crooked doctors, crooked ex-wives, even crooked tree trimmers – these were the spawn of the city bog.

Stranahan's fingers found the stock of the shotgun, and he moved it closer. Soon he fell asleep, and he dreamed that Victoria Barletta was alive. He dreamed that he met her one night in the Rathskellar on the University of Miami campus. She was working behind the bar, wearing a pink butterfly bandage across the bridge of her nose. Stranahan ordered a beer and a cheeseburger medium, and asked her if she wanted to get married. She said sure.

*

The boat woke him up. It was a familiar yellow skiff with a big outboard. Stranahan saw it a mile away, trimmed up, running the flats. He smiled – the bonefish guide, his friend. With all the low dirty clouds it was difficult to estimate the time, but Stranahan figured the sun had been up no more than two hours. He dropped from the roof, stowed the Remington inside the house, and pulled on a pair of jeans so as not to startle the guide's customers, who were quite a pair. The man was sixty-five, maybe older, obese and grey, with skin like rice parchment; the woman was twenty-five tops, tall, dark blonde, wearing bright coral lip gloss and a gold choker necklace.

The guide climbed up to the stilt house and said, 'Mick, take a good look. Fucking lipstick on a day like this.'

From the skiff, tied up below, Stranahan could hear the couple arguing about the weather. The woman wanted to go back, since there wasn't any sun for a decent tan. The old man said no, he'd paid his money and by God they would fish.

Stranahan said to his friend, 'You've got the patience of Job.'

The guide shook his head. 'A killer mortgage is what I've got. Here, this is for you.'

It was an envelope with Stranahan's name printed in block letters on the outside. 'Woman with two black eyes told me to give it to you,' the guide said. 'Cuban girl, not bad looking, either. She offered me a hundred bucks.'

'Hope you took it.'

'I held out for two,' the guide said.

Stranahan folded the envelope in half and tucked it in the back pocket of his jeans.

The guide said, 'You in some trouble?'

'Just business.'

'Mick, you don't have a business.'

Stranahan grinned darkly. 'True enough.' He knew what his friend was thinking: single guy, cosy house on the water, a good boat for fishing, a monthly disability cheque from the state – how could anybody fuck up a sweet deal like that?

'I heard some asshole shot hell out of the place.'

'Yeah.' Stranahan pointed to a sheet of fresh plywood on the door. The plywood covered two of Chemo's bullet holes. 'I've got to get some red paint,' Stranahan said.

The guide said, 'Forget the house, what about your shoulder?'

'It's fine,' Stranahan said.

'Don't worry, it was Luis who told me.'

'No problem. You want some coffee?'

'Naw.' The bonefish guide jerked a thumb in the direction of his skiff. 'This old fart, he's on the board of some steel company up north. That's his secretary.'

'God bless him.'

The guide said, 'Last time they went fishing, I swear, she strips off the bottom of her bathing suit. Not the top, Mick, the bottom part. All day long, flashing her bush in my face. Said she was trying to bleach out her hair. Here I'm poling like a maniac after these goddamn fish, and she's turning somersaults in front of the boat, trying to keep her bush in the sun.'

Stranahan said, 'I don't know how you put up with it.'

'So today there's no sunshine and of course she's throwin' a fit. Meanwhile the old fart says all he wants is a world-record bonefish on fly. That's all. Mick, I'm too old for this shit.' The guide pulled on his cap so tightly that it crimped the tops of his ears. Lugubriously he descended the stairs to the dock.

'Good luck,' Stranahan said. Under the circumstances, it sounded ridiculous.

The guide untied the yellow skiff and hopped in. Before starting the engine, he looked up at Stranahan and said, 'I'll be out here tomorrow, even if the weather's bad. The next day, too.'

Stranahan nodded; it was good to know. 'Thanks, Captain,' he said.

After the skiff was gone, Stranahan returned to the top of the house and took the envelope out of his pocket. He opened it calmly because he knew what it was and who it was from. He'd been waiting for it.

The message said: 'We've got your girlfriend. No cops!'

And it gave a telephone number.

Mick Stranahan memorized the number, crumpled the paper, and tossed it off the roof into the milky waves. 'Somebody's been watching too much television,' he said.

That afternoon, Mick Stranahan received another disturbing message. It was delivered by Luis Córdova, the young marine patrol officer. He gave Stranahan a lift by boat from Stiltsville to the Crandon Marina, where Stranahan got a cab to his sister Kate's house in Gables-by-the-Sea.

Sergeant Al García was fidgeting on the front terrace. Over his J. C. Penney suit he was wearing what appeared to be an authentic London Fog trenchcoat. Stranahan knew that García was upset because he was smoking those damn Camels again. Even before Stranahan could finish paying the cabbie, García was charging down the driveway, blue smoke streaming from his nostrils like one of those cartoon bulls.

'So,' the detective said, 'Luis fill you in?'

Stranahan said yes, he knew that Kipper Garth had been gravely injured in a domestic dispute.

García blocked his path up the drive. 'By a client, Mick. Imagine that.'

'I didn't know the client, Al.'

'Name of Nordstrom, John Nordstrom.' García was working the sodden nub of the Camel the same way he worked the cigars, from one side of his mouth to the other. Stranahan found it extremely distracting.

'According to the wife,' García said, 'the assailant returned home unexpectedly and found your brother-in-law, the almost deceased—'

'Thank you, Al.'

'—found the almost deceased fondling his wife. Whereupon the assailant attempted to strike the almost deceased at least three times with *pelotas*. That's a jai-alai ball, Mick. The third shot struck your brother-in-law at the base of the skull, rendering him unconscious.'

'The dumb shit. How's Kate?'

'Puzzled,' García said. 'But then, aren't we all?'

'I want to see her.' Stranahan sidestepped the detective and made for the front door. His sister was standing by the bay window of the Florida room and staring out at Kipper Garth's sailboat, the *Pain-and-Suffering*, which was rocking placidly at the dock behind the house. Stranahan gave Kate a hug and kissed her on the forehead.

She sniffed and said, 'Did they tell you?'

'Yes, Kate.'

'That he was groping a client – did they tell you?'

Stranahan said, 'That's the woman's story.'

Kate gave a bitter chuckle. 'And you don't believe it? Come on, Mick, *I* believe it. Kipper was a pig, let's face it. You were right, I was wrong.'

Stranahan didn't know what to say. 'He had some good qualities.' Jesus, how stupid. '*Has* some good qualities, I mean.'

'The doctors say it's fifty-fifty, but I'm ready for the worst. Kipper's not a fighter.'

'He might surprise you,' Stranahan said without conviction.

'Mick, just so you know – I was aware of what he was up to. Some of the excuses, God, you should have heard them. Late nights, weekends, trips to God knows where. I pretended to believe him because . . . because I like this life, Mick. The house . . . this great yard. I mean, it sounds selfish, but it felt *good* here. Safe. This is a wonderful neighbourhood.'

'Katie, I'm sorry.'

'Neighbourhoods like this are hard to find, Mick. You know, we've only been burglarized twice in four years. That's not bad for Miami.'

'Not at all,' Stranahan said.

'See, I had to weigh these things every time I thought

about leaving.' Kate put a hand on his arm and said, 'You know about all his fooling around.'

'Not everything.'

'Thanks for not mentioning it.' She was sincere.

Stranahan felt like a complete shit, which he was. 'This is my fault,' he said. 'I told Kipper to take this case. I *made* him take it.'

'How?' she asked. 'And why?'

'Whatever you're thinking, it's even worse. I can't tell you the details, Kate, because there's going to be trouble and I want you clear of it. But you ought to know that I'm the one who got Kipper involved.'

'But you're not the one who played grab-the-tittie with your client. *He* did.' She turned back to the big window and folded her arms. 'It's so . . . tacky.'

'Yes,' Stranahan agreed. 'Tacky's the word.'

When he came out of the house, García was waiting.

'Wasn't that courteous of me, not barging in and making a big Cuban scene in front of your sister?'

'Al, you're a fucking prince among men.'

'Know why I'm wearing this trenchcoat? It's brand new, by the way. I hadda go to another funeral: Bobby Pepsical, the county commissioner. Dropped dead in confession.'

'Good place for it. He was a stone crook.'

'Course he was, Mick. But I got a feeling he didn't get his penance.'

'Why not?'

'Because there wasn't a priest in there. Bobby's confessing to an empty closet – that's pretty weird, huh? Anyway, they make a bunch of us go to the fucking funeral, because of who he was. That's why I've got the new coat. It was raining.'

Stranahan said, 'How was it? Did they screw him into the ground? That's about how crooked he was.'

'I know, but Christ, have some respect for the dead.' García rubbed his temples like he was massaging a cramp. 'See, this is what's got me so agitated, Mick. Ever since I got into this thing with you and the doctor, so many people are dying. Dying weird, too. There's your ex, and Murdock and Salazar – another funeral! Then the business with that goddamn homicidal tree man. So after all that, here I am standing in the rain, watching them plant some scuzzbucket politician who croaks on his knees in an empty confessional, and my frigging beeper goes off. Lieutenant says some big-shot lawyer got beaned by a jai-alai ball and could be a homicide any second. A jai-alai ball! On top of which the big-shot lawyer turns out to be *your* brother-in-law. It's like a nightmare of weirdness!'

'It's been a bad month,' Stranahan conceded.

'Yeah, it sure has. So what about these Nordstroms?'

'I didn't know them, I told you.'

García lit up another cigarette and Stranahan made a face. 'Know why I'm smoking these things? Because I'm agitated. I get agitated whenever I get jerked around, and I hate to waste a good cigar on agitation.'

Stranahan said, 'Can you please not blow it in my face? That's all I ask.'

The detective took the cigarette out of his mouth and held it behind his back. 'There, you happy? Now help me out, Mick. The assailant's wife, she says Kipper Garth phones her out of the blue and asks if she wants to sue – guess who – Rudy Graveline! Since he's the quack who gave her the encapsulated whatchama-callits.'

'If that's what she says, fine.'

'But lawyers aren't supposed to solicit.'

'Al, this is Miami.'

García took a quick drag and hid the Camel again. 'My theory is you somehow got your sleazy, almost-deceased brother-in-law to sue Graveline, just to bust his balls. Shake things up. Maybe flush the giant Mr Blondell Tatum out of his fugitive gutter. I don't expect you to open up your heart, Mick, but just tell me this: did it work? Because if it did, you're a fucking genius and I apologize for all the shitty things I've been saying about you in my sleep.'

'Did what work?'

García grinned venomously. 'I thought we were buddies.'

'Al, I'm not going to shut you out,' Stranahan said. 'For God's sake, you saved my life.'

'Aw, shucks, you remembered.'

Stranahan said: 'Which one do you want, Al? The freaky hit man or the doctor?'

'Both.'

'No, I'm sorry.'

'Hey, I could arrest your ass right now. Obstruction, tampering, I'd think of something.'

'And I'd be out in an hour.'

García's jaw tightened for a moment and he turned away, stewing. When he turned back, he seemed more amused than angry.

'The problem is, Mick, you're too smart. You know the system too damn well. You know there's only so much I can get away with.'

'Believe me, we're on the same side.'

'I know, *chico*, that's what scares me.'

'So, which of these bastards do you want for yourself – the surgeon or the geek?'

'Don't rush me, Mick.'

THIRTY

Early on the morning of February nineteenth, Reynaldo Flemm, the famous Shock Television journalist, arrived at the Whispering Palms Spa and Surgery Center for the most sensational interview of his sensational career. A sleepy receptionist collected the $15,000 cash and counted it twice; if she was surprised by the size of the surgeon's fee, she didn't show it. The receptionist handed Reynaldo Flemm two photocopied consent forms, one for a rhinoplasty and one for a suction-assisted lipectomy. Reynaldo skimmed the paperwork and extravagantly signed as 'Johnny LeTigre'.

Then he sat down to wait for his moment. On a buff-coloured wall hung a laminated carving of one of Rudy Graveline's pet sayings: TO IMPROVE ONE'S SELF, IMPROVE ONE'S FACE. That wasn't Reynaldo's favourite Rudyism. His favourite was framed in quilted Norman Rockwell-style letters above the water fountain: VANITY IS BEAUTIFUL. That's the one Reynaldo had told Willie about. Be sure to get a quick shot on your way in, he had told him. What for? Willie had asked. For the irony, Reynaldo Flemm had exclaimed. For the irony! Reynaldo was proud of himself for thinking up that camera shot; usually Christina Marks was in charge of finding irony.

Soon an indifferent young nurse summoned Reynaldo to a chilly examining room and instructed him to empty his bladder, a tedious endeavour that took fifteen minutes and produced scarcely an ounce. Reynaldo Flemm was a very nervous man. In his professional life he had been beaten by Teamsters, goosed by white supremacists, clubbed by Mafia torpedoes, pistol-whipped by Bandito bikers, and kicked in the groin by the Pro-Life Posse. But he had never undergone surgery. Not even a wart removal.

Flemm stiffly removed his clothes and pulled off his high top Air Jordans. He changed into a baby-blue paper gown that hung to his knees. The nurse gave him a silly paper cap to cover his silly dyed hair, and paper shoe covers for his bare feet.

A nurse anaesthetist came out of nowhere, brusquely flipped up the tail of Reynaldo's gown and stuck a needle in his hip. The hypodermic contained a drug called Robinul, which dries up the mouth by inhibiting oral secretions. Next the nurse seized Reynaldo's left arm, swabbed it, and stuck it cleanly with an IV needle that dripped into his veins a lactated solution of five per cent dextrose and, later, assorted powerful sedatives.

The anaesthetist then led Reynaldo Flemm and his IV apparatus into Suite F, one of four ultramodern surgical theatres at Whispering Palms. She asked him to lie on his back and, as he stretched out on the icy steel, Reynaldo frantically tried to remember the ten searing questions he had prepared for the ambush of Dr Rudy Graveline.

One, did you kill Victoria Barletta on March 12, 1986?

Two, why would one of your former nurses say that you did?

Three, isn't it true that you've repeatedly gotten into trouble for careless and incompetent surgery?

Four, how do you explain . . .

Explain?

Explain this strap on my fucking legs!

'Please quiet down, Mr LeTigre.'

And my arms! What've you done to my arms? I can't move my goddamn arms!

'Try to relax. Think pleasant thoughts.'

Wait, wait, wait, wait, wait!

'You ought to be feeling a little drowsy.'

This is wrong. This is not right. I read up on this. I got a fucking pamphlet. You're supposed to tape my eyes, not my arms. What are you smiling at, you dumb twat? Lemme talk to the doctor! Where's the doctor? Jesus Christ, that's cold. What are you *doing* down there!

'Good morning, Mr LeTigre.'

Doctor, thank God you're here! Listen good now: these Nazi nurse bitches are making a terrible mistake. I don't wanna general, I wanna local. Just pull the IV, OK? I'll be fine, just pull the tubes before I pass out.

'John, we're having a little trouble understanding you.'

No shit, Sherlock, my tongue's so dry you could light a match on it. Please yank the needles, I can't think with these damn needles. And make 'em quit fooling around with me down there. Christ, it's cold! What're they doing!

'I assumed they told you – there's been a change of

plans. I've decided to do the lipectomy first, then the rhinoplasty. It'll be easier that way.'

No no no, you gotta do the nose first. Do the fucking nose.

'You should try to relax, John. Here, hold still, we're going to give you another injection.'

No no no no no no no.

'That didn't hurt a bit, did it?'

I wanna ask I gotta ask right now . . .

'Go ahead, push the Sublimaze.'

Did you kill . . .?

'What did he say?'

Is it true you killed . . .?

'This guy looks sort of familiar.'

Did you . . . kill Victoria . . . Principal?

'Victoria Principal! Boy, is he whacked out.'

Well did you?

'Where's the mask? Start the Forane. Give him the mask.'

Willie hadn't slept much, fretting about Reynaldo's big plan. He had tried to call Christina Marks in New York, but the office said she was in Miami. But where? Reynaldo's plan was the craziest thing Willie had ever heard, starting with the signal. Willie needed a signal to know when to come crashing into the operating room with the camera. The best that Reynaldo could come up with was a scream. Willie would be in the waiting room. Reynaldo would scream.

'What exactly will you scream?' Willie had asked.

'I'll scream: WILLIE!'

Willie thought Reynaldo was joking. He wasn't.

'What about the other patients in the waiting room? I mean, here I am with a TV camera and a sound pack – what do I tell these people?'

'Tell 'em you're from PBS,' Reynaldo had said. 'Nobody hassles PBS.'

The shot that Reynaldo Flemm most fervently wanted was this: himself prone, prepped, cloaked in blue, preferably in the early stages of rhinoplasty and preferably bloody. That was the good thing about a nose job, you could ask for a local. Most plastic surgeons want their rhinoplasty patients to be all the way zonked, but you could get it done with a local and a mild IV if you could stand a little pain. Reynaldo Flemm had no doubt he could stand it.

Willie would burst like a fullback into the operating room, tape rolling, toss the baton mike to Reynaldo on the table, Reynaldo would poke it in Rudy Graveline's face and pop the questions. Bam bam bam. The nurses and scrub techs would drop whatever they were doing and run, leaving the hapless surgeon to dissolve, alone, before the camera's eye.

Wait'll he realizes who I am, Reynaldo had chortled. Be sure you go extra tight on his face.

Willie had said he needed a soundman, but Reynaldo said no, out of the question; this was to be a streamlined attack.

Willie had said all right, then we need a better signal. Just screaming isn't good enough, he had said. What if somebody else starts screaming first, some other patient?

'Who else would scream your name?' Reynaldo had asked in a caustic tone. 'Listen to what I'm saying.'

The plan was bold and outrageous, Willie had to admit. No doubt it would cause a national sensation, stir up all the TV critics, not to mention Johnny Carson's gag writers. There would be a large amount of cynical speculation among Ray's colleagues that what he really wanted out of this caper was a free nose job – a theory that occurred even to Willie as he listened to Reynaldo map out the big ambush. The possibility of coast-to-coast media ridicule was no deterrent; the man seemed to relish being maligned as a hack and a clown and a shameless egomaniac. He said they were jealous, that's what they were. What other broadcast journalist in America had the guts to go under the knife just to get an interview? Mike Wallace? Not in a million years, the arrogant old prune. Bill Moyers? That liberal pussy would faint if he got a hangnail!

Yeah, Willie had said, it's quite a plan.

Brilliant, Reynaldo had crowed. Try brilliant.

However inspired, the plan's success depended on several crucial factors, not the least of which was the premise that Reynaldo Flemm would be conscious for the interview.

Although the surgical procedure known as liposuction, or fat sucking, was developed in France, it has achieved its greatest mass-market popularity in the United States. It is now the most common cosmetic procedure performed by plastic surgeons in the country, with more than a hundred thousand operations every year. The mortality rate for suction-assisted lipectomy is relatively low, about one death for every ten thousand patients. The odds of complications – which include blood clots, fat embolisms, chronic numbness, and severe bruising – increase considerably if the surgeon performing the liposuction has had little or no training in the procedure. Rudy Graveline fell decisively into this category – a doctor who had taken up liposuction for the simple reason that it was exceedingly lucrative. No state law or licensing board or medical review committee required Rudy to study liposuction first, or become proficient, or even be tested on his surgical competence before trying it. The same libertarian standards applied to rhinoplastics or haemorrhoidectomies or even brain surgery: Rudy Graveline was a licensed physician, and legally that meant he could try any damn thing he wanted.

He did not give two hoots about certification by the American Board of Plastic Surgery, or the American Academy of Facial Plastic and Reconstructive Surgery, or the American Society of Plastic and Reconstructive Surgeons. What were a couple more snotty plaques on the wall? His patients could not care less. They were rich and vain and impatient. In some exclusive South Florida circles, Rudy's name carried the glossy imprimatur of a Gucci or de la Renta. The lacquered old crones at La Gorce or the Biltmore would point at each other's shiny chins and taut necks and sculpted eyelids and ask, not in a whisper but a haughty bray, 'Is that a Graveline?'

Rudy was a designer surgeon. To have *him* suck your fat was an honour, a social plum, a mark (literally) of status. Only a boor, white trash or worse, would ever question the man's techniques or complain about the results.

Ironically, most of the surgeons who worked for Rudy Graveline at Whispering Palms were completely qualified to do suction lipectomies; they had actually trained for it – studied, observed, practised. While Rudy admired their dedication, he thought they were overdoing things – after all, how difficult could such an operation really be? The fat itself was abundantly easy to find. Suck it out, close 'em up, next case! Big deal.

To be on the safe side, Rudy read two journal articles about liposuction and ordered an instructional video cassette for $26.95 from a medical supply firm in Chicago. The journal articles turned out to be dense and fairly boring, but the video was an inspiration. Rudy came away convinced that any fool doctor with half a brain could vacuum fat with no problem.

The typical lipectomy patient was not a grotesque hypertensive blimp, but – like Johnny LeTigre – a healthy person of relatively normal stature and weight. The object of their complaint was medically mundane – bumper-car hips, droopy buttocks, gelantinous thighs, or old-fashioned 'love handles' at the waist. Properly performed, liposuction would remove contour. Improperly performed, the surgery would leave a patient lumpy and lopsided and looking for a lawyer.

On the morning of Reynaldo Flemm's undercover mission, nothing as sinister as a premonition caused Rudy Graveline to change his mind about doing the nose job first. What changed the doctor's mind, as usual, was money. Because a lipectomy usually required general anaesthesia, it was more labour-intensive (and costly) than a simple rhinoplasty. Rudy figured the sooner he could get done with the heavy stuff, the sooner he could get the anaesthetist and her gas machine off the clock. He could do the rhino later with intravenous sedation, which was much cheaper.

That Rudy Graveline could still worry about overhead at this point, with his career crumbling, was a tribute both to his power of concentration and his ingrained devotion to profit.

He grabbed a gloveful of Reynaldo Flemm's belly roll and gave a little squeeze. Paydirt. Fat city.

Rudy selected a Number 15 blade and made a one-quarter inch incision in Reynaldo's navel. Through this convenient aperture Rudy inserted the cannula, a long tubular instrument that resembled in structure the nose of an anteater. Rudy rammed the blunt snout of the cannula into the soft meat of Reynaldo's abdomen, then scraped the instrument back and forth to break up the tissue. With his right foot the surgeon tapped a floor pedal that activated the suction machine, which vac-uumed the fat particles through small holes in the tip of the cannula, down a long clear plastic tube to a glass bottle.

Within moments, the first yellow glops appeared.

Johnny LeTigre's spare tyre!

Soon he would be a new man.

In the waiting room, Willie got to talking with some of the other patients. There was a charter-boat captain with a skin cancer the size of a toad on his forehead. There was a dancer from the Miami ballet who was getting her buttocks suctioned for the second time in as many years. There was a silver-haired Nicaraguan man whom Willie had often seen on television – one of the Contra leaders – who was getting his eyelids done for eighteen hundred dollars. He said the CIA was picking up the tab.

The one Willie liked best was a red-haired stripper

from the Solid Gold club up in Lauderdale. She was getting new boobs, of course, but she was also having a tattoo removed from her left thigh. When the stripper heard that Willie was from PBS, she asked if she could be in his documentary and hiked up her corduroy mini-skirt to show off the tattoo. The tattoo depicted a green reticulated snake eating itself. Willie said, in a compli-mentary way, that he had never seen anything like it. He made sure to get the stripper's phone number so that he could call her about the imaginary programme.

The hour passed without a peep from Reynaldo Flemm, and Willie began to get jittery. Reynaldo had said give it to nine o'clock before you freak, and now it was nine o'clock. The halls of Whispering Palms were quiet enough that Willie was certain he would have heard a scream. He asked the ballet dancer, who had been here before, how far it was from the waiting area to the operating room.

'Which operating room?' she replied. 'They've got four.'

'Shit,' said Willie. 'Four?'

This was shocking news. Reynaldo Flemm had made it sound like there was only one operating room, and that he would be easy to find. More worried than ever, Willie decided to make his move. He hoisted the Betacam to his shoulder, checked the mike and the cables and the belt pack and the battery levels, turned on the Frezzi light (which caused the other patients to mutter and shield their eyes), and went prowling through the corridors in search of Reynaldo Flemm.

*

When the telephone on the wall started tweeting, Dr Rudy Graveline glanced up from Johnny LeTigre's gut and said: 'Whoever it is, I'm not here.'

The circulating nurse picked up the phone, listened for several moments, then turned to the doctor. 'It's Ginny at the front desk. There's a man with a minicam running all over the place.'

Rudy's surgical mask puckered. 'Tell her to call the police . . . No! Wait—' Oh Jesus. Stay calm. Stay extremely calm.

'He just crashed in on Dr Kloppner in Suite D.'

Rudy grunted unhappily. 'What does he want? Did he say what he wants?'

'He's looking for you. Should I tell Ginny to call the cops or what?'

The nurse-anaesthetist interrupted: 'Let's not do anything until we finish up here. Let's close up this patient and get him off the table.'

'She's right,' Rudy said. 'She's absolutely right. We're almost done here.'

'Take your time,' the anaesthetist said with an edge of concern. Under optimum conditions, Rudy Graveline scared the daylights out of her. Under stress, there was no telling how dangerous he could be.

He said, 'What're we looking at here?'

'One more pocket, maybe two hundred ccs.'

'Let's do it, OK?'

The wall phone started tweeting again.

'Screw it,' said Rudy. 'Let it go.'

He gripped the cannula like a carving knife, scraping frenetically at the last stubborn colony of fat inside Reynaldo's midriff. The suction machine hummed

411

contentedly as it filled the glass jar with gobs of unwanted pudge.

'One more minute and we're done,' Rudy said.

Then the doors opened and an awesome white light bathed the operating room. The beam was brighter and hotter than the surgical lights, and it shone from the top of a camera, which sat like a second head on the shoulder of a man. A man who had no business in Rudy Graveline's operating room.

The man with the camera cried out: 'Ray!'

Rudy said, 'Get out of here this minute.'

'Are you Dr Graveline?'

Rudy's hand continued to work on Reynaldo Flemm's belly. 'Yes, I'm Dr Graveline. But there's nobody named Ray here. Now get out before I phone the police.'

But the man with the camera on his shoulder shuffled closer, scorching the operating team with his fierce, hot light. The anaesthetist, the scrub nurse, the circulating nurse, even Rudy flinched from the glare. The camera-headed man approached the table and zoomed in on the sleeping patient's face, which was partially concealed by a plastic oxygen mask. The voice behind the camera said, 'Yeah, that's him!'

'Who?' Rudy said, rattled. 'That's Ray?'

'Reynaldo Flemm!'

The scrub nurse said: 'I told you he looked familiar.'

Again Rudy asked: 'Who? Reynaldo who?'

'That guy from the TV.'

'This has gone far enough,' Rudy declared, fighting panic. 'You better . . . just get the hell out of my operating room.'

Willie pushed forward. 'Ray, wake up! It's me!'

'He can't wake up, you asshole. He's gassed to the gills. Now turn off that spotlight and get lost.'

The scope of the journalistic emergency struck Willie at once. Reynaldo was unconscious. Christina was gone. The tape was rolling. The batteries were running out.

Willie thought: It's up to me now.

The baton microphone, Ray's favourite, the one Willie was supposed to toss to him at the moment of ambush, was tucked in Willie's left armpit. Grunting, contorting, shifting the weight of the Betacam on his shoulder, Willie was able to retrieve the mike with his right hand. In an uncanny imitation of Reynaldo Flemm, Willie thrust it toward the face of the surgeon.

Above the surgical mask, Rudy Graveline's eyes grew wide and fearful. He stared at the microphone as if it were the barrel of a Mauser. From behind the metallic hulk of the minicam, the voice asked: 'Did you kill Victoria Barletta?'

A bullet could not have struck Rudy Graveline as savagely as those words.

His spine became rigid.

The pupils of his eyes shrunk to pinpricks.

His muscles cramped, one by one, starting in the toes. His right hand, the one that the held the cannula, the one buried deep in the livid folds of Reynaldo Flemm's freshly vacuumed tummy – his right hand twisted into a spastic nerveless talon.

With panic welling in her voice, the anaesthetist said: 'All right, that's it!'

'Almost done,' the surgeon said hoarsely.

'No, that's enough!'

But Dr Rudy Graveline was determined to finish the operation. To quit would be an admission of . . .

something. Composure – that's what they taught you at Harvard. Above all, a physician must be composed. In times of crisis, patients and staff relied on a surgeon to be cool, calm, and composed. Even if the man lying on the operating table turned out to be... Reynaldo Flemm, the notorious undercover TV reporter! That would explain the woozy babbling while he was going under – the jerkoff wasn't talking about Victoria Principal, the actress. He was talking about Victoria Barletta, she of the fateful nose job.

The pain of the muscle cramps was so fierce that it brought viscous tears to Rudy Graveline's eyes. He forced himself to continue. He lowered his right shoulder into the rhythm of the liposuction, back and forth in a lumberjack motion, harder and harder.

Again, the faceless voice from behind the TV camera: 'Did you kill that girl?'

The black eye of the beast peered closer, revolving clockwise in its socket – Willie, remembering Ray's instructions to zoom tight on Rudy's face. The surgeon stomped on the suction pedal as if he were squashing a centipede. The motor thrummed. The tube twitched. The glass jar filled.

Time to stop.

Time to stop.

But Dr Rudy Graveline did not stop.

He kept on poking and sucking ... the long hungry snout of the mechanical anteater slurping through the pit of Reynaldo's abdomen ... down, down, down through the fascia and the muscle ... snorkelling past the intestines, nipping at the transverse colon ... down, down, down the magic anteater burrowed.

Until it glomped the aorta.

And the plastic tube coming out of Reynaldo's navel suddenly turned bright red.

The jar at the other end turned red.

Even the doctor's arm turned red.

Willie watched it all through the camera's eye. The whole place, turning red.

THIRTY-ONE

The first thing Chemo bought with Rudy's money was a portable phone for the Bonneville. No sooner was it out of the box than Maggie Gonzalez remarked, 'This stupid toy is worth more than the car.'

Chemo said, 'I need a private line. You'll see.'

They were driving back to the Holiday Inn after spending the morning at the office of Dr George Ginger, the plastic surgeon. Maggie knew Dr Ginger from his early days as one of Rudy's more competent underlings at the Durkos Center. She trusted George's skill and his discretion. He could be maddeningly slow, and he had terrible breath, but technically he was about as good as cosmetic surgeons come.

Chemo had prefaced the visit to Dr Ginger with this warning to Maggie: 'If he messes up my face, I'll kill him on the spot. And then I'll kill you.'

The second thing that Chemo had bought with Rudy's money was a box of bullets for the rusty Colt .38. Brand new rounds, Federals. The good stuff.

Maggie had said, 'You're going into this with the wrong attitude.'

Chemo frowned. 'I've had rotten luck with doctors.'

'I know, I know.'

'I don't even like this guy's name, George Ginger.

Sounds like a fag name to me.' Then he had checked the chambers on the Colt and slipped it into his pants.

'You're hopeless,' Maggie had said. 'I don't know why I even bother.'

'Because otherwise I'll shoot you.'

Fortunately the dermabrasion went smoothly. Dr George Ginger had never seen a burn case quite like Chemo's, but he wisely refrained from enquiry. Once, when Chemo wasn't looking, the surgeon snuck a peek at the cumbersome prosthesis attached to the patient's left arm. An avid gardener, Dr Ginger recognized the Weed Whacker instantly, but resisted the impulse to pry.

The sanding procedure took about two hours, and Chemo endured stoically, without so much as a whimper. When it was over, he no longer looked as if someone had glued Rice Krispies all over his face. Rather, he looked as if he had been dragged for five miles behind a speeding dump truck.

His forehead, his cheeks, his nose, his chin all glowed with a raw, pink, oozing sheen. The speckled damage of the errant electrolysis needle had been scraped away for ever, but now it was up to Chemo to grow a new skin. While he might never enjoy the radiant peachy complexion of, say, a Christie Brinkley, at least he would be able to stroll through an airport or a supermarket or a public park without causing small children to cringe behind their mothers' skirts. Chemo conceded that this alone would be a vast improvement, socially.

Before leaving the office, Maggie Gonzalez had asked Dr George Ginger to remove her sutures and inspect the progress of her New York facelift. He reported – with toxic breath – that everything was healing nicely, and gave Maggie a make-up mirror to look for herself. She was pleased by what she saw: the angry purple bruises were fading shadows under the eyes, and the incision scars had shrunk to tender rosy lines. She was especially delighted with her perky new nose.

Dr Ginger studied the still-swollen promontory from several angles and nodded knowingly. 'The Sandy Duncan.'

Maggie smiled. 'Exactly!'

Popping a codeine Tylenol, Chemo said, 'Who the fuck is Sandy Duncan?'

In the Bonneville, on the way back to the motel, Chemo remarked, 'Three grand seems like a lot for what he did.'

'All he did was make you look human again,' Maggie said. 'Three grand was a bargain, if you ask me. Besides, he even gave a professional discount – fifteen per cent off because I'm a nurse.'

As he steered, Chemo kept leaning toward the middle of the seat to check himself in the rear-view. It was difficult to judge the result of the dermabrasion, since his face was slathered in a glue-coloured ointment. 'I don't know,' he said. 'It's still pretty broken out.'

Maggie thought: Broken out? It's seeping, for God's sake. 'You heard what the doctor said. Give it a couple weeks to heal.' With that she leaned over and commandeered the rear-view to examine her own refurbished features.

A beep-beep noise came chirping out of the dashboard; the car phone. With a simian arm Chemo reached into the glove compartment and snatched it on the second ring.

With well-acted nonchalance, he wedged the receiver between his ear and his left shoulder. Maggie thought it looked ridiculous to be riding in a junker like this and talking on a fancy car phone. Embarrassed, she scooted lower in the seat.

'Hello,' Chemo said into the phone.

'Hello, Funny Face.' It was Mick Stranahan. 'I got your message.'

'Yeah?'

'Yeah.'

'And?'

'And you said to call, so I am.'

Chemo was puzzled at Stranahan's insulting tone of voice. The man ought to be scared. Desperate. Begging. At least polite.

Chemo said, 'I got your lady friend.'

'Yeah, yeah, I read the note.'

'So, you're waiting to hear my demands.'

'No,' said Stranahan. 'I'm waiting to hear you sing the fucking aria from *Madame Butterfly* . . . *Of course* I want to hear your demands.'

'Christ, you're in a shitty mood.'

'I can barely hear you,' Stranahan complained. 'Don't tell me you got one of those yuppie Mattel car phones.'

'It's a Panasonic,' Chemo said, sharply.

Maggie looked over at him with an impatient expression, as if to say: Get on with it.

As he braked for a stop light, the phone slipped from Chemo's ear. He took his good hand off the wheel to grab for it.

'Hell!' The receiver was gooey with the antibiotic ointment from his cheeks.

Stranahan's voice cracked through the static. 'Now what's the matter?'

'Nothing. Not a damn thing.' Chemo carefully

propped the receiver on his shoulder. 'Look, here's the deal. You want to see your lady friend alive, meet me at the marina at midnight tonight.'

'Fuck you.'

'Huh?'

'That means no, Funny Face. No marina. I know what you want and you can have it. Me for her, right?'

'Right.' Chemo figured there was no sense trying to bullshit this guy.

'It's a deal,' Stranahan said, 'but I'm not going anywhere. You come to me.'

'Where are you now?'

'I'm at a pay phone on Bayshore Drive, but I won't be here long.'

Impatiently Chemo said, 'So where's the meet?'

'My place.'

'That house? No fucking way.'

''Fraid so.'

The car phone started sliding again. Chemo groped frantically for it, and the Bonneville began to weave off the road. Maggie reached over and steadied the wheel.

Chemo got a grip on the receiver and snarled into it: 'You hear what I said? No way am I going back to that damn stilt house.'

'Yes, you are. You'll be getting another call with more information.'

'Tell me now!'

'I can't,' Stranahan said.

'I'll kill the Marks girl, I swear.'

'You're not quite that stupid, are you?'

The hot flush of anger made Chemo's face sting even worse. He said, 'We'll talk about this later. What time you gonna call?'

'Oh, not me,' Mick Stranahan said. 'I won't be the one calling back.'

'Then who?' Chemo demanded.

But the line had gone dead.

Willie played the videotape for his friend at WTVJ, the NBC affiliate in Miami. Willie's friend was sufficiently impressed by the blood on his shirt to let him use one of the editing rooms. 'You gotta see this,' Willie said.

He punched the tape into the machine and sat back to chew on his knuckles. He felt like an orphan. No Christina, no Reynaldo. He knew he should call New York, but he didn't know what to say or who to tell.

Willie's friend, who was a local news producer, pointed to the monitor. 'Where's that?' he asked.

'Surgery clinic over in Bal Harbour. That's the waiting room.'

The friend said. 'You were portable?'

'Right. Solo the whole way.'

'So where's Flemm? That doesn't look like him.'

'No, that's somebody else.' The monitor showed an operating room where a tall bald doctor was hunched over a chubby female patient. The bald doctor was gesticulating angrily at the camera and barking for a nurse to call the authorities. 'I don't know who that was,' Willie said. 'Wrong room.'

'Now you're back in the hallway, walking. People are yelling, covering their faces.'

'Yeah, but here it comes,' Willie said, leaning forwards. 'Bingo. That's Ray on the table.'

'Jeez, what're they doing?'

'I don't know.'

'It looks like a goddamn Caesarean.'

Willie said, 'Yeah, but it was supposed to be a nose job.'

'Go on!'

The audio portion of the tape grew louder.

'Yeah, that's him!'

'Who? That's Ray?'

'Reynaldo Flemm.'

'I told you he looked familiar.'

'Who? Reynaldo who?'

'That guy from the TV.'

'This has gone far enough . . .'

When the frame filled with Reynaldo Flemm's gaping muzzled face, Willie's friend hit the Pause button and said, 'Fucker never looked better.'

'You know him?'

'I knew him back from Philadelphia. Back when he was still Ray Fleming.'

'You're kidding,' Willie said.

'No, man, that's his real name. Raymond Fleming. Then he got on this bi-ethnic kick . . . "Reynaldo Flemm" – half Latin, half Eastern bloc. Told everybody in the business that his mother was a Cuban refugee and his father was with the Yugoslavian Resistance. Shit, I laugh about it but that's when his career really took off.'

Willie said, 'Romania. What he told me, his old man was with the Romanian Underground.'

'His old man sold Whirlpools in Larchmont, I know for a fact. Let's see the rest.'

Willie pressed the Fast Forward and squeaked the tape past the part when he confronted Dr Rudy Graveline about Victoria Barletta; he didn't want his producer friend to hear the dead woman's name, on the off-chance that the story could be salvaged. Willie slowed the tape to normal speed just as he zoomed in on the doctor's quavering eyes.

'Boris Karloff,' said Willie's friend.

'Watch.'

The camera angle widened to show Rudy Graveline feverishly toiling over Reynaldo's belly. Then came a mist of blood, and one of the nurses began shouting for the surgeon to stop.

'Geez,' said Willie's friend, looking slightly queasy. 'What's happening?'

The doctor abruptly wheeled from the operating table to confront the camera directly. In his bloody right hand was a wicked-looking instrument connected to a long plastic tube. The device was making an audible slurp-slurp noise.

'*Your turn, fat boy!*'

Willie's friend gestured at the monitor and said: 'He called you fat boy?'

'Watch!'

On the screen, the surgeon lunged forward with the pointy slurp-slurping device. There was a cry, a dull clunk. Then the picture got jerky and went grey.

Willie pressed the Stop button. 'I hauled ass,' he explained to his friend. 'He came at me with that sucking . . . *thing*, so I took off.'

'Don't blame you, man. But what about Ray?'

Willie took the videotape out of the editing console. 'That's what got me scared. I get in the van and take off, right? Stop at the nearest phone booth and call this clinic. Whispering Palms is the name.'

'Yeah, I've heard of it.'

'So I call. Don't say who I am. I ask about Reynaldo

Flemm. I say he's my brother. I'm s'posed to pick him up after the operation. Ask can I come by and get him. Nurse gets on the line and wants to know what's going on. She wants to know how come Ray was using a phoney name when he checks in at the place. Johnny Tiger, some shit like that. I tell her I haven't got the faintest – maybe he was embarrassed, didn't want his nose job to turn up in the gossip columns. Then she says, well, he's not here. She says the doctor, this Rudy Graveline, the nurse says he drove Ray to Mount Sinai. She says she's not allowed to say anything more on the phone. So I haul ass over to Emergency at Sinai and guess what? No Ray anywhere. Fact there's nothing but strokes and heart attacks. No Reynaldo Flemm!'

Willie's friend said, 'This is too fucking weird. Even for Miami.'

'Best part is, now I gotta call New York and break the news.'

'Oh, man.'

Willie said, 'Maybe I'll ship the tape first.'

'Might as well,' agreed the producer. 'What about Ray? Think he's all right?'

'No,' said Willie. 'You want the truth, I'd be fucking amazed if he was all right.'

The nurses had wanted to call 911, but Rudy Graveline had said no, there wasn't time. I'll take him myself, Rudy had said. He had run to the parking lot (stopping only at the front desk to pick up Reynaldo's $15,000), got the Jag and pulled up at the staff entrance.

Back in the operating suite, the anaesthetist had said: 'Everything's going flat.'

'Then hurry, goddammit!'

They had gotten Reynaldo on a gurney and wheeled him to Rudy's car and bundled him in the passenger seat. The scrub nurse even tried to hook up the safety belt.

'Oh, forget it,' Rudy had said.

'But it's a law.'

'Go back to work!' Rudy had commanded. The Jaguar had peeled rubber on its way out.

Naturally he had no intention of driving to Mount Sinai Hospital. What was the point? Rudy glanced at the man in the passenger seat and still did not recognize him from television. True, Reynaldo Flemm was not at his telegenic best. His eyes were half-closed, his mouth was half-open, and his skin was the colour of bad veal.

He was also exsanguinating all over Rudy's fine leather seats and burled walnut door panels. 'Great,' Rudy muttered. 'What else.' As the surgeon sped south on Alton Road, he took out the portable telephone and called his brother's tree company.

'George Graveline, please. It's an emergency.'

'Uh, he's not here.'

'This is his brother. Where's he working today?'

The line clicked. Rudy thought he had been cut off. Then a lady from an answering service came on and asked him to leave his number. Rudy hollered, but she wouldn't budge. Finally he surrendered the number and hung up.

He thought: I must find George and his wood-chipping machine. This is very dicey, driving around Miami Beach in a $47,000 sedan with a dead TV star in the front seat. *Bleeding* on the front seat.

The car phone beeped and Rudy grabbed at it in frantic optimism. 'George!'

'No, Dr Graveline.'

'Who's this?'

'Sergeant García, Metro Homicide. You probably don't remember, but we met that night the mysterious midget Haitian blew up your car.'

Rudy's heart was pounding. Should he hang up? Did the cops know about Flemm already? But how – the nurses? Maybe that moron with the minicam!

Al García said: 'I got some bad news about your brother George.'

Rudy's mind was racing. The detective's words didn't register. 'What – could you give me that again?'

'I said I got bad news about George. He's dead.'

Rudy's foot came off the accelerator. He was coasting now, trying to think. Which way? Where?

García went on: 'He tried to kill a man and I had to shoot him. Internal Review has the full report, so I suggest you talk to them.'

Nothing.

'Doctor? You there?'

'Yuh.'

No questions, nothing.

'The way it went down, I had no choice.'

Rudy said dully, 'I understand.' He was thinking: It's awful about George, yes, but what am I going to do with this dead person in my Jaguar?

García could sense that something strange was going on at the end of the line. He said, 'Look, I know it's a bad time, but we've got to talk about a homicide. A homicide that may involve you and your brother. I'd like to come over to the clinic as soon as possible.'

'Make it tomorrow,' Rudy said.

'It's about Victoria Barletta.'

'I'm eager to help in any way I can. Come see me tomorrow.' The surgeon sounded like a zombie. A heavily sedated zombie. If there was a realm beyond sheer panic, Rudy Graveline had entered it.

'Doctor, it really can't wait—'

'For heaven's sake, Sergeant, give me some time. I just found out my brother's dead, I need to make the arrangements.'

'To be blunt,' García said, 'as far as George goes, there's not a whole lot left to arrange.'

'Call me tomorrow,' Rudy Graveline said curtly. Then he threw the car phone out the window.

When the phone rang again in the Bonneville, Chemo gloated at Maggie Gonzalez. 'I told you this would come in handy.'

'Quit picking at your face.'

'It itches like hell.'

'Leave it be!' Maggie scolded. 'You want it to get infected? Do you?'

On the other end of the phone was Rudy Graveline. He sounded worse than suicidal.

Chemo said, 'Hey, Doc, you in your car? I'm in mine.'

He felt like the king of the universe.

'No, I'm home,' Rudy said. 'We have a major problem.'

'What's this *we* stuff? I don't have a problem. I got a hundred-twenty odd grand, a brand new face, a brand new car phone. Life's looking better every day.'

Rudy said, 'I'm delighted for you, I really am.'

'You don't sound too damn delighted.'

'He got Heather.' The doctor choked out the words.

'Who's Heather?' Chemo said.

'My . . . I can't believe . . . when I got home, she was gone. He took her away.'

Maggie asked who was on the line and Chemo whispered the doctor's name. 'All right,' he said to Rudy, 'you better tell me what's up.'

Suddenly Rudy Graveline remembered what Curly Eyebrows had warned him about cellular phones, about how private conversations sometimes could be picked up on outside frequencies. In his quickening state of emotional deterioration, Rudy clearly envisioned – as if it were real – some nosy Coral Gables housewife overhearing his felonious litany on her Anna toaster oven.

'Come to my house,' he instructed Chemo.

'I can't, I'm waiting on a call.'

'This is it.'

'What? You mean this is the phone call he—'

'Yes,' Rudy said. 'Get out here as fast as you can. We're going on a boat ride.'

'Jesus H. Christ.'

THIRTY-TWO

Maggie and Chemo left Christina Marks tied up in the trunk of the Bonneville, which was parked in Rudy Graveline's flagstone driveway. Miserable as she was, Christina didn't worry about suffocating inside the car; there were so many rust holes, she could actually feel a breeze.

For an hour Maggie and Chemo sat on the white leather sofa in Rudy's living room and listened to the doleful story of how he had come home to find his lover, his baby doll, his sweetie pie, his Venus, his sugar bunny, his pumpkin, his blonde California sunbeam missing from the bedroom.

They took turns studying the kidnap note, which said:

'Ahoy! You're invited to a Party!'

On the front of the note was a cartoon pelican in a sailor's cap. On the inside was a hand-drawn chart of Stiltsville. Chemo and Rudy grimly agreed that something had to be done permanently about Mick Stranahan.

Chemo asked about the fresh dark drops on the foyer, and Rudy said that it wasn't Heather's blood but someone else's. In chokes and sighs he told them about the mishap at the clinic with Reynaldo Flemm. Maggie

Gonzalez listened to the gruesome account with amazement; she had never dreamed her modest extortion scheme would come to this.

'So where is he?' she asked.

'In there,' Rudy replied. 'The Sub-Zero.'

Chemo said, 'The what? What're you talking about?'

Rudy led them to the kitchen and pointed at the cabinet-sized refrigerator. 'The Sub-Zero,' he said.

Maggie noticed that the aluminium freezer trays had been stacked on the counter, along with a half-dozen Lean Cuisines and three pints of chocolate Häagen-Dazs.

Chemo said, 'That's a big fridge, all right.' He opened the door and there was Reynaldo Flemm, upright and frosty as a Jell-O pop.

'It was the only way he could fit,' explained Rudy. 'See, I had to tear out the damn ice maker.'

Chemo said, 'He sure looks different on TV.' Chemo propped open the refrigerator door with one knee; the cold air made his face feel better.

Maggie said nothing. This wasn't part of the plan. She was trying to think of a way to sneak out of Rudy's house and run. Go back to the motel room, grab the black Samsonite, and disappear for about five years.

Chemo closed the freezer door. He pointed to more brownish spots on the bone-coloured tile and said, 'If you got a mop, she can clean that up.'

'Wait a second,' Maggie said. 'Do I look like a maid?'

'You're gonna look like a cabbage if you don't do what I say.' Balefully Chemo brandished the Weed Whacker.

Maggie recalled the savage thrashing of Rudy Graveline and said, 'All right, put that stupid thing away.'

While Maggie mopped, Rudy moped. He seemed shattered, listless, inconsolable. He needed to think; he needed the soothing rhythm of athletic copulation, the sweet crystal tunnel of clarity that only Heather's loins could give him.

The day had begun with such promise!

Up before dawn to pack their bags. And the airline tickets – he had placed them in Heather's purse while she slept. He would drive to the clinic, perform the operation on the male go-go dancer, collect the fifteen grand, and come home for Heather. Then it was off to the airport! Fifteen thousand was plenty for starters – a month or two in Costa Rica in a nice apartment. Time enough for Rudy's Panamanian lawyer to liquidate the offshore trusts. After that, Rudy and Heather could breathe again. Get themselves some land up in the mountains. Split-level ranch house on the side of a hill. A stable, too; she loved to ride. Rudy envisioned himself opening a new surgery clinic; he had even packed his laminated Harvard diploma, pillowing it tenderly in the suitcase among his silk socks and designer underwear. San José was crawling with wealthy expatriates and aspiring international jet-setters. An American plastic surgeon would be welcomed vivaciously.

Now, disaster. Heather – fair, nubile, perfectly apportioned Heather – had been snatched from her sick bed.

'We need a boat,' Rudy Graveline croaked. 'For tonight.'

Chemo said, 'Yeah, a big one. If I'm going back to that damn house I want to stay dry. See if you can find us a Scarab thirty-eight.'

'Are you nuts?'

'Just like they had on *Miami Vice*.'

'You *are* nuts. Who's going to drive it?' Rudy stared pointedly at the unwieldy garden tool attached to Chemo's left arm. 'You?'

'Yeah, me. Just get on the phone, see what you can do. We've gotta move before the cops show up.'

Rudy looked stricken by the mention of police.

'Well, Jesus,' Chemo said, 'you got a dead man in your fridge. This is a problem.'

Maggie was rinsing the mop in the kitchen sink. She said, 'I've got an idea about that. You might not like it, but it's worth a try.'

Rudy shrugged wearily. 'Let's hear it.'

'I used to work for a surgeon who knew this guy . . . this guy who would buy certain things.'

'Surely you're not suggesting—'

'It's up to you,' Maggie said. 'I mean, Dr Graveline, you've got yourself a situation here.'

'Yeah,' said Chemo. 'Your ice cream is melting.'

The man's name was Kimbler, and his office was in Miami's hospital district; a storefront operation on 12th Street, a purse-snatcher's jog from Jackson Hospital or the Medical Examiner's Office. The magnetic sign on the door of the office said: 'International Bio-Medical Exports, Inc.' The storefront window was tinted dark blue and was obscured by galvanized burglar mesh.

Kimbler was waiting for them when they arrived – Rudy, Chemo, Maggie, and Christina. Chemo had the Colt .38 in his pants pocket, pointed at Christina the whole time. He had wanted to leave her in the trunk of the Bonneville, but there was not enough room.

Kimbler was a rangy thin-haired man with tortoise-shell glasses and a buzzard's-beak nose. The office was lighted like a stockroom, with cheap egg-carton overheads. Rows of grey steel shelves covered both walls. The shelves were lined with old-fashioned Mason jars, and preserved in the Mason jars were assorted human body parts: ears, eyeballs, feet, hands, fingers, toes, small organs, large organs.

Chemo looked around and, under his breath, said, 'What the fuck.'

Kimbler gazed with equal wonderment at Chemo, who was truly a sight – his freshly sanded face glistening with Neosporin ointment, his extenuated left arm cloaked with its calfskin golf-bag cover, his radish-patch scalp, his handsome Jim Fowler safari jacket. Kimbler examined Chemo as if he were a prized future specimen.

'This is some hobby you got,' Chemo said, picking up a jar of gall bladders. 'This is better than baseball cards.'

Kimbler said, 'I've got the proper permits, I assure you.'

Maggie explained that Kimbler sold human tissue to foreign medical schools. She said it was perfectly legal.

'The items come from legitimate sources,' Kimbler added. 'Hospitals. Pathology labs.'

Items. Christina was nauseated at the concept. Or maybe it was just the sweet dead smell of the place.

Kimbler said, 'It may sound ghoulish, but I provide a much-needed service. These items, discarded organs and such, they would otherwise go to waste. Be thrown away. Flushed. Incinerated. Overseas medical schools are in great need of clinical teaching aids – the students are extremely grateful. You should see some of the letters.'

'No thanks,' Chemo said. 'What's a schlong go for these days?'

'Pardon me?'

Maggie cut in: 'Mr Kimbler, we appreciate you seeing us on short notice. We have an unusual problem.'

Kimbler peered theatrically over the tops of his glasses. A slight smile came to his lips. 'I assumed as much.'

Maggie went on, 'What we have is an entire . . . *item*.'

'I see.'

'It's a pauper-type situation. Very sad – no family, no funds for a decent burial. We're not even sure who he is.'

Christina could scarcely contain herself. She had gotten a quick glimpse of a body as they angled it into the trunk of the Bonneville. A young man; that much she could tell.

Kimbler said to Maggie: 'What can you tell me of the circumstances? The manner of death, for instance.'

She said, 'An indigent case, like I told you. Emergency surgery for appendicitis.' She pointed at Rudy. 'Ask him, he's the doctor.'

Rudy Graveline was stupefied. He scrambled to catch up with Maggie's yarn. 'I was doing . . . he had a chronic heart condition. Bad arrhythmia. He should've said something before the operation, but he didn't.'

Kimbler pursed his lips. 'You're a surgeon?'

'Yes.' Rudy wasn't dressed like a surgeon. He was wearing Topsiders, tan cotton pants, and a Bean crewneck pull-over. He was dressed for a boat ride. 'Here, wait.' He took out his wallet and showed Kimbler an ID card from the Dade County Medical Society. Kimbler seemed satisfied.

'I realize this is out of the ordinary,' Maggie said.

'Yes, well, let's have a look.'

Chemo pinched Christina by the elbow and said, 'We'll wait here.' He handed Maggie the keys to the Bonneville. She and Rudy led the man named Kimbler to the car, which was parked in a city lot two blocks away.

When Maggie opened the trunk, Rudy turned away. Kimbler adjusted his glasses and craned over the corpse as if he were studying the brush strokes on a fine painting. 'Hmmmmm,' he said. 'Hmmmmmm.'

Rudy edged closer to block the view of the trunk, in case any pedestrians got curious. His concern was groundless, for no one gave the trio a second look; half the people in Miami did their business out of car trunks.

Kimbler seemed impressed by what he saw. 'I don't get many whole cadavers,' he remarked. 'Certainly not of this quality.'

'We tried to locate a next of kin,' Rudy said, 'but for some reason the patient had given us a phoney name.'

Kimbler chuckled. 'Probably had a very good reason. Probably a criminal of some type.'

'Every place we called was a dead end,' Rudy said, lamely embellishing the lie.

Maggie stepped in to help. 'We were going to turn him over to the county, but it seemed like such a waste.'

'Oh, yes,' said Kimbler. 'The shortage of good cadavers . . . by good, I mean white and well-nourished. Most of the schools I deal with – for instance, one place in Dominica, they had only two cadavers for a class of sixty medical students. Tell me how those kids are ever going to learn gross anatomy.'

Rudy started to say something but thought better of it.

The whole deal was illegal as hell, no doubt about

it. But what choice did he have? For the first time in his anal-retentive, hyper-compulsive professional life he had lost control of events. He had surrendered himself to the squalid street instincts of Chemo and Maggie Gonzalez.

Kimbler was saying, 'Two measly cadavers, both dysenteries. Weighed about ninety pounds each. For sixty students! And this is not so unusual in some of these poor countries. There's a med school on Guadeloupe, the best they could do was monkey skeletons. To help out I shipped down two hearts and maybe a half-dozen lungs, but it's not the same as having whole human bodies.'

Shrewd haggler that she was, Maggie had heard enough. Slowly she closed, but did not lock, the rusty trunk of the Bonneville; Reynaldo Flemm had begun to thaw.

'So,' she said, 'you're obviously interested.'

'Yes,' said Kimbler. 'How does eight hundred sound?'

'Make it nine,' said Maggie.

Kimbler frowned irritably. 'Eight-fifty is pushing it.'

'Eight seventy-five. Cash.'

Kimbler still wore a frown, but he was nodding. 'All right. Eight seventy-five it is.'

Rudy Graveline was confused. 'You're paying *us*?'

'Of course,' Kimbler replied. He studied Rudy doubtfully. 'Just so there's no question later, you *are* a medical doctor? I mean, your state licence is current. Not that you need to sign anything, but it's good to know.'

'Yes,' Rudy sighed. 'Yes, I'm a doctor. My licence is up to date.' As if it mattered. If all went as planned, he'd be gone from the country by this time tomorrow. He and Heather, together on a mountaintop in Costa Rica.

The man named Kimbler tapped cheerfully on the

trunk of the Bonneville. 'All right, then. Why don't you pull around back of the office. Let's get this item on ice straightaway.'

Mick Stranahan brought Heather Chappell a mug of hot chocolate. She pulled the blanket snugly around her shoulders and said, 'Thanks, I'm so damn cold.'

He asked how she was feeling.

'Beat up,' she replied. 'Especially after that boat ride.'

'Sorry,' Stranahan said. 'I know it's rough as hell – there's a front moving through so we got a big westerly tonight.'

Heather sipped tentatively at the chocolate. The kidnapper, whoever he was, watched her impassively from a wicker barstool. He wore blue jeans, deck shoes, a pale yellow cotton shirt and a poplin windbreaker. To Heather the man looked strong, but not particularly mean.

In the middle of the living room was a card table, covered by an oilskin cloth. On the table was a red Sears Craftsman toolbox. The kidnapper had been carrying it when he broke into Dr Graveline's house.

Heather nodded towards the toolbox and said, 'What's in there?'

'Just some stuff I borrowed from Rudy.'

The furniture looked like it came from the Salvation Army, but still there was a spartan cosiness about the place, especially with the soft sounds of moving water. Heather said, 'I like your house.'

'The neighbourhood's not what it used to be.'

'What kind of fish is that on the wall?'

'It's a blue marlin. The bill broke off, I've got to get it fixed.'

Heather said, 'Did you catch it yourself?'

'No.' Stranahan smiled. 'I'm no Hemingway.'

'I read for *Islands in the Stream*. With George C. Scott – did you see it?'

Stranahan said no, he hadn't.

'I didn't get the part, anyway,' said Heather. 'I forget now who played the wife. George C. Scott was Hemingway, and there was lots of fishing.'

The beakless marlin stared down from the wall. Stranahan said, 'It used to be paradise out here.'

Heather nodded; she could picture it. 'What're you going to do with me?'

'Not much,' said Stranahan.

'I remember you,' she said. 'From the surgery clinic. That night in the parking lot, you put me in the cab. The night Rudolph's car caught fire.'

'My name is Mick.'

Being a famous actress, Heather didn't customarily introduce herself. This time she felt like she had to.

Stranahan said, 'The reason I asked how you're feeling is this.' He held up three pill bottles and gave them a rattle. 'These were on the nightstand by your bed. Young Dr Rudy was keeping you loaded.'

'Painkillers, probably. See, I just had surgery.'

'Not painkillers,' Stranahan said. 'Seconal 100s. Industrial strength, enough to put down an elephant.'

'What . . . why would he do that?'

Stranahan got off the barstool and walked over to Heather Chappell. In his right hand was a small pair of scissors. He knelt down in front of her and told her not to move.

'Oh, God,' she said.

'Be still.'

Carefully he clipped the bandages off her face. Heather expected the salty cool air to sting the incisions, but she felt nothing but an itchy sensation.

Stranahan said, 'I want to show you something.' He went to the bathroom and came back with a hand mirror. Heather studied herself for several moments.

In a puzzled voice she said, 'There's no marks.'

'Nope. No scars, no bruises, no swelling.'

'Rudolph said ... See, he mentioned something about microsurgery. Lasers, I think he said. He said the scars would be so small—'

'Bullshit.' Stranahan handed her the scissors. She gripped them in her right hand like a pistol.

'I'm going in the other room for a little while,' he said. 'Call me when you're done and I'll explain as much as I can.'

Ten minutes later Heather was pounding on the bedroom door. She had cut off the remaining bandages and phoney surgical dressings. She was standing there naked, striped with gummy adhesive, and crying softly. Stranahan bundled her in the blanket and sat her on the bed.

'He was s'posed to do my boobs,' she said. 'And my hips. My nose, eyelids ... everything.'

'Well, he lied,' said Stranahan.

'Please, I wanna go back to LA.'

'Maybe tomorrow.'

'What's going on?' Heather cried. 'Can I use your phone, I've got to call my manager. Please?'

'Sorry,' said Stranahan. 'No telephone. No ship-to-shore. No fax. The weather's turned to shit, so we're stuck for the night.'

'But I'm s'posed to do a *Password* with Jack Klugman. God, what day is it?'

Stranahan said: 'Can I ask you something? You're a beautiful girl – you get points for that, OK – but how could you be so fucking dumb?'

Heather stopped crying instantly, gulped down her sobs. No man had ever talked to her this way. Well, wait; Patrick Duffy had, once. She was playing a debutante on *Dallas* and she forgot one lousy line. One out of seventeen! But later at least Patrick Duffy had said he was sorry for blowing his stack.

Mick Stranahan said, 'To trust yourself to a hack like Graveline, Jesus, it's pathetic. And for what? Half an inch off your hips. A polyurethane dimple in your chin. Plastic bags inside your breasts. Think about it: a hundred years from now, your coffin cracks open and there's nothing inside but two little bags of silicone. No flesh, no bones, everything's turned to ashes except for your boobs. They're bionic. Eternal!'

In a small voice Heather said, 'But everybody does it.'

Stranahan tore off the blanket, and for the first time Heather was truly afraid. He told her to stand up.

'Look at yourself.'

Diffidently she lowered her eyes.

'There's not a thing wrong with you,' Stranahan said. 'Tell me what's wrong with you.'

The wind shook the shutters, and shafts of cold air sliced the room. Heather shivered, sat down, and put her hands over her nipples. Stranahan folded his arms as if he were awaiting something: an explanation.

'You're a man, I don't expect you to understand.' She wondered if he would try to touch her in some way.

'Vanity I understand,' Stranahan said. 'Men are experts on the subject.' He picked the blanket off the floor. Indifferently he draped it across her lap. 'I think there's some warm clothes in one of the drawers.'

He found a grey sweatsuit with a hood and a pair of men's woollen socks. Hurriedly Heather got dressed. 'Just tell me,' she said, still trembling, 'why did Rudolph lie about this? I can't get over it – why didn't he do the operation?'

'I guess he was scared. In case you didn't notice, he's crazy about you. He probably couldn't bear the thought of something going wrong in surgery. It's been known to happen.'

'But I paid him,' Heather said. 'I wrote the bastard a personal cheque.'

'Stop it, you're breaking my heart.'

Heather glared at him.

'Look,' said Stranahan, 'I've seen his Visa bill. Swanky restaurants, designer clothes, a diamond here and there – you made out pretty well. Did he mention he was going to fly you away on a tropical vacation?'

'I remember him saying something about Costa Rica, of all places.'

'Yeah, well, don't worry. The trip's off. Rudy's had a minor setback.'

Heather said, 'So tell me what's going on.'

'Just consider yourself damn lucky.'

'Why? What are you talking about?'

'Rudy killed a young woman just like you. No, I take that back – she wasn't just like you, she was innocent. And he killed her with a nose job.'

Heather Chappell cringed. Unconsciously her hand went to her face.

'That's what this is about,' Stranahan said. 'You don't believe me, ask him yourself. He's on his way.'

'Here?'

'That's right. To save you and to kill me.'

'Rudolph? No way.'

'You don't know him like I do, Heather.'

Stranahan went from room to room, turning off the lights. Heather followed, saying nothing. She didn't want to be left alone, even by him. Carrying a Coleman lantern, Stranahan led her out of the stilt house and helped her climb to the roof. The windmill whistled and thrummed over their heads.

Heather said, 'God, this wind is really getting nasty.'

'Sure is.'

'What kind of gun is that?'

'A shotgun, Heather.'

'I can't believe Rudolph is coming all the way out here on a night like this.'

'Yep.'

'What's the shotgun for?'

'For looks,' said Stranahan. 'Mostly.'

THIRTY-THREE

Al García was feeling slightly guilty about lying to Mick Stranahan until Luis Córdova's patrol boat conked out. Now Luis was hanging over the transom, poking around the lower unit; García stood next to him, aiming a big waterproof spotlight and cursing into the salt spray.

García thought: I hate boats. Car breaks down, you just walk away from it. With a damn boat, you're stuck.

They were adrift about half a mile west of the Sea-quarium. It was pitch black and ferociously choppy. A chilly north-westerly wind cut through García's plastic windbreaker and made him wish he had waited until dawn, as he had promised Stranahan.

It did not take Luis Córdova long to discover the problem with the engine. 'It's the prop,' he said.

'What about it?'

'It's gone,' said Luis Córdova.

'We hit something?'

'No, it just fell off. Somebody monkeyed with the pin.'

García considered this for a moment. 'Does he know where you keep the boat?'

'Sure,' said Luis Córdova.

'Shit.'

'I better get on the radio and see if we can get help.'

Al García stowed the spotlight, sat down at the console and lit a cigarette. He said, 'That bastard. He didn't trust us.'

Luis Córdova said, 'We need a new prop or a different boat. Either way, it's going to take a couple hours.'

'Do what you can.' To the south García heard the sound of another boat on the bay; Luis Córdova heard it, too – the hull slapping heavily on the waves. The hum of the engine receded as the craft moved further away. They knew exactly where it was going.

'Goddamn,' said García.

'You really think he did this?'

'I got no doubt. The bastard didn't trust us.'

'I can't imagine why,' said Luis Córdova, reaching for the radio.

Driving across the causeway to the marina, Chemo kept thinking about the stilt house and the monster fish that had eaten off his hand. As hard as he tried, he could not conceal his trepidation about going back.

When he saw the boat that Rudy Graveline had rented, Chemo nearly called off the expedition. 'What a piece of shit,' he said.

It was a twenty-one-foot outboard, tubby and slow, with an old sixty-horse Merc. A cheap hotel rental, designed for abuse by tourists.

Chemo said, 'I'm not believing this.'

'At this hour I was lucky to find anything,' said Rudy.

Maggie Gonzalez said, 'Let's just get it over with.' She

got in the boat first, followed by Rudy, then Christina Marks.

Chemo stood on the pier, peering across the bay toward the amber glow of the city. 'It's blowing like a fucking typhoon,' he said. He really did not want to go.

'Come on,' Rudy said. He was frantic about Heather; more precisely, he was frantic about what he would have to do to get her back. He had a feeling that Chemo didn't give a damn one way or another, as long as Mick Stranahan got killed.

As Chemo was unhitching the bow rope, Christina Marks said, 'This is really a bad idea.'

'Shut up,' said Chemo.

'I mean it. You three ought to get away while you can.'

'I said shut up.'

Maggie said, 'She might be right. This guy, he's not exactly a stable person.'

Chemo dumped awkwardly into the boat and started the engine. 'What, you want to spend the rest of your life in jail? You think he's gonna forget about everything and let us ride off into the sunset?'

Rudy Graveline shivered. 'All I want is Heather.'

Christina said, 'Don't worry, Mick won't hurt her.'

'Who gives a shit,' said Chemo, gunning the throttle with his good hand.

By the time they made it to Stiltsville, Chemo felt like his face was aflame. The rental boat rode like a washtub, each wave slopping over the gunwale and splashing spray against the raw flesh of his cheeks. The salt stung like cold acid. Chemo soon ran out of profanities. Rudy

Graveline was no help, nor were the women; they were all soaking wet, queasy, and glum.

As he made a wide weekend-sailor's turn into the Biscayne Channel, Chemo slowed down and pointed with the Weed Whacker. 'What the fuck?' he said. 'Look at that.'

Across the bonefish flats, Stranahan's stilt house was lit up like a used-car lot. Lanterns hung off every piling, and swung eerily in the wind. The brown shutters were propped open and there was music, too, fading in and out with each gust.

Christina Marks laughed to herself. 'The Beatles,' she said. He was playing 'Happiness Is a Warm Gun'.

Chemo snorted. 'What, he's trying to be cute?'

'No,' Christina said. 'Not him.'

Maggie Gonzalez swept a whip of wet hair out of her face. 'He's nuts, obviously.'

'And we're not?' Rudy said. He got the binoculars and tried to spot Heather Chappell on the stilt house. He could see no sign of life, human or otherwise. He counted a dozen camp lanterns aglow.

The sight of the place brought back dreadful memories for Chemo. Too clearly he could see the broken rail where he had fallen to the water that day of the ill-fated jet ski assault. He wondered about the fierce fish, whatever it was, dwelling beneath the stilt house. Inwardly he speculated about its nocturnal feeding habits.

Maggie said, 'How are we going to handle this?'

Rudy looked at her sternly. 'We don't do anything until Heather's safe in this boat.'

Chemo grabbed Christina's arm and pulled her to the console. 'Stand here, next to me,' he said. 'Real close, in case your jerkoff boyfriend gets any ideas.' He pressed the barrel of the Colt .38 to her right breast. With the stem of the Weed Whacker he steadied the wheel.

As the boat bucked and struggled across the shallow bank toward Mick Stranahan's house, Christina Marks accepted the probability that she would not live through the next few moments. 'For the record,' she said, 'he's *not* my boyfriend.'

Maggie nudged her with an elbow and whispered. 'You could've done worse.'

Chemo stopped the boat ten yards from the dock.

The stereo had died. The only sound was the thrum of the windmill and the chalkboard squeak of the Colemans, swinging in the gusts. The house scorched the sky with its watery brightness; a white torch in the blackest middle of nowhere. Christina wondered: Where did he get so many bloody lanterns?

Chemo looked down at Rudy Graveline. 'Well? You're the one who got the invitation.'

Rudy nodded grimly. On rubbery legs he made his way to the bow of the boat; the rough, wet ride had drubbed all the nattiness out of his L. L. Bean wardrobe. The doctor cupped both hands to his mouth and called out Stranahan's name.

Nothing.

He glanced back at Chemo, who shrugged. The .38 was still aimed at Christina Marks.

Next Rudy called Heather's name and was surprised to get a reply.

'Up here!' Her voice came from the roof, where it was darker.

'Come on down,' Rudy said excitedly.

'No, I don't think so.'

'Are you all right?'

'I'm fine,' said Heather. 'No thanks to you.'

Chemo made a sour face at Rudy. 'Now what?'

'Don't look at me,' the doctor said.

Chemo called out to Heather: 'We're here to save you. What's your fucking problem?'

Suddenly Heather appeared on the roof. For balance she held onto the base of the windmill. She was wearing a grey sweatsuit with a hood. 'My problem? Ask him.' She pulled the hood off her head, and Rudy Graveline saw that the bandages were gone.

'Damn,' he said.

'Let's hear it,' Chemo muttered.

'I was supposed to do some surgery, but I didn't. She thought – see, I told her I did it.'

Maggie Gonzalez said, 'You're right. Everybody out here is crazy.'

'I paid you, you bastard!' Heather shouted.

'Please, I can explain,' Rudy pleaded.

Chemo was disgusted. 'This is some beautiful moment. She doesn't want to be rescued, she hates your damn guts.'

Heather disappeared from the roof. A few moments later she emerged, still alone, on the deck of the stilt house. Rudy Graveline tossed her the bow rope and she wrapped it around one of the dock cleats. The surgeon stepped out of the boat and tried to give her a hug, but Heather backed up and said, 'Don't you touch me.'

'Where's Stranahan?' Chemo demanded.

'He's around here somewhere,' Heather said.

'Can he hear us?'

'I'm sure.'

Chemo's eyes swept back and forth across the house, the deck, the roof. Every time he glanced at the water he thought of the terrible fish and how swiftly it had happened before. His knuckles were blue on the grip of the pistol.

A voice said: 'Look here.'

Chemo spun around. The voice had come from beneath the stilt house, somewhere in the pilings, where the tide hissed.

Mick Stranahan said: 'Drop the gun.'

'Or what?' Chemo snarled.

'Or I'll blow your new face off.'

Chemo saw an orange flash, and instantly the lantern nearest his hand exploded. Maggie shrieked and Christina squirmed from Chemo's one-armed clasp. On the deck of the house, Rudy Graveline dropped to his belly and covered his head.

Chemo stood alone with his lousy pistol. His ears were roaring. Shards of hot glass stuck to his scalp. He thought: That damn shotgun again.

When the echo from the gunfire faded, Stranahan's voice said: 'That's buckshot, Mr Tatum. In case you were wondering.'

Chemo's face was killing him. He contemplated the damage that a point-blank shotgun blast would do to his complexion, then tossed the Colt .38 into the bay. Perhaps a deal could be struck; even after splurging on the car phone, there was still plenty of money to go around.

Stranahan ordered Chemo to get out of the boat. 'Carefully.'

'No shit.'

'Remember what happened last time with the 'cuda.'

'So that's what it was.' Chemo remembered seeing pictures of barracudas in sports magazines. What he remembered most were the incredible teeth. 'Jesus H. Christ,' he said.

Stranahan didn't mention that the big barracuda was long gone – off to deeper water to wait out the cold. Probably laid up in Fowey Rocks.

Chemo moved with crab-like deliberation, one gangly limb at a time. Between the rocking of the boat and the lopsided weight of his prosthesis, he found it difficult to balance on the slippery gunwale. Maggie Gonzalez came up from behind and helped boost him to the dock. Chemo looked surprised.

'Thanks,' he said.

From under the house, Stranahan's voice: 'All right, Heather, get in the boat.'

'Wait a second,' said Rudy.

'Don't worry, she'll be all right.'

'Heather, don't!' Rudy was thinking about that night in the fireplace, and that morning in the shower. And about Costa Rica.

'Hands off,' said Heather, stepping into the boat.

By now Christina Marks had figured out the plan. She said, 'Mick, I want to stay.'

'Ah, you changed your mind.'

'What—'

'You want to get married after all?'

The words hung in the night like the mischievous cry of a gull. Then, from under the stilt house, laughter. 'Everything's just a story to you,' Stranahan said. 'Even me.'

Christina said, 'That's not true.' No one seemed particularly moved by her sincerity.

'Don't worry about it,' Stranahan said. 'I'll still love you, no matter what.'

Rudy cautiously got to his feet and stood next to Chemo. In the flickering lantern glow, Chemo looked more waxen than ever. He seemed hypnotized, his puffy blowfish eyes fixed on the surging murky waves.

Heather said, 'Should I untie the boat now?'

'Not just yet,' Stranahan called back. 'Check Maggie's jacket, would you?'

Maggie Gonzalez was wearing a man's navy pea jacket. When Heather reached for the pockets, Maggie pushed her arm away.

There was a metallic clunking noise under the house: Stranahan, emerging from his sniper hole. Quickly he clambered out of the aluminium skiff, over the top of the water tank, pulling himself one-handed to the deck of the house. His visitors got a good long look at the Remington.

'Maggie, be a good girl,' Stranahan said. 'Let's see what you've got.'

Christina took one side of the coat and Heather took the other. 'Keys,' Christina announced, holding them up for Stranahan to see. One was a tiny silver luggage key, the other was from a room at the Holiday Inn.

Chemo blinked sullenly and patted at his pants. 'Jesus H. Christ,' he said. 'The bitch picked my pockets.'

He couldn't believe it: Maggie had lifted the keys while helping him out of the boat! She planned to sneak back to the motel and steal all the money.

'I know how you feel,' Stranahan said to Chemo. He reached into the boat and plucked the keys from

Christina's hand. He put them in the front pocket of his jeans.

'What now?' Rudy whined, to anyone who might have a clue.

Chemo's right hand crept to his left armpit and found the toggle switch for the battery pack. The Weed Whacker buzzed, stalled once, then came to life.

Stranahan said, 'I'm impressed, I admit it.' He aimed the Remington at Chemo's head and told him not to move.

Chemo paid no attention. He took two giraffe-like steps across the dock and, with a vengeful groan, dove into the stern of the boat after Maggie. They all went down in a noisy tangle – Chemo, Maggie, Heather and Christina – the boat listing precariously against the pilings.

Mick Stranahan and Rudy Graveline watched the mêlée from the lower deck of the stilt house. One woman's scream, piercing and feline, rose above the uproar.

'Do something!' the doctor cried.

'All right,' said Stranahan.

Later, Stranahan gathered all the lanterns and brought them inside. Rudy Graveline lay in his undershorts on the bed; he was handcuffed spread-eagle to the bedposts. Chemo was unconscious on the bare floor, folded into a corner. With the shutters latched, the lanterns made the bedroom as bright as a television studio.

Rudy said, 'Are they gone?'

'They'll be fine. The tide's running out.'

'I'm not sure if Heather can swim.'

'The boat won't sink. They'll all be fine.'

Rudy noticed fresh blood on Stranahan's forehead, where he had been grazed by the Weed Whacker. 'You want me to look at that?'

'No,' Stranahan said acidly. 'No, I don't.' He left the bedroom and returned with the red Sears Craftsman toolbox. 'Look what I've got,' he said to Rudy.

Rudy craned to see. Stranahan opened the toolbox and began to unpack. 'Recognize any of this stuff?'

'Yes, of course . . . what're you doing?'

'Before we get started, there's something I ought to tell you. The cops have Maggie's videotape, so they know about what you did to Vicky Barletta. Whether they can convict you is another matter. I mean, Maggie is not exactly a prize witness. In fact, she'd probably change her story again for about twenty-five cents.'

Rudy Graveline swallowed his panic. He was trying to figure out what Stranahan wanted and how to give it to him. Rudy could only assume that, deep down, Stranahan must be no different than the others: Maggie, Bobby Pepsical, or even Chemo. Surely Stranahan had a scam, an angle. Surely it involved money.

Stranahan went out again and returned with the folding card table. He placed it in the centre of the room, covered with the oilskin cloth.

'What is it?' the doctor said. 'What do you want?'

'I want you to show me what happened.'

'I don't understand.'

'To Vicky Barletta. Show me what went wrong.' He began placing items from the toolbox on the card table.

'You're insane,' said Rudy Graveline. It seemed the obvious conclusion.

'Well, if you don't help,' Stranahan said, 'I'll just have

to wing it.' He tore open a package of sterile gloves and put them on. Cheerily he flexed the latex fingers in front of Rudy's face.

The surgeon stared back, aghast.

Stranahan said, 'Don't worry, I did some reading up on this. Look here, I got the Marcaine, plenty of cotton, skin hooks, a whole set of new blades.'

From the toolbox he selected a pair of doll-sized surgical scissors and began trimming the hairs in Rudy Graveline's nose.

'Aw, no!' Rudy said, thrashing against the bedposts.

'Hold still.'

Next Stranahan scrubbed the surgeon's face thoroughly with Hibiclens soap.

Rudy's eyes began to water. 'What about some anaesthesia?' he bleated.

'Oh yeah,' said Stranahan. 'I almost forgot.'

Chemo awoke and rolled over with a thonk, the Weed Whacker bouncing on the floor planks. He sat up slowly, groping under his shirt. The battery sling was gone; the Weed Whacker was dead.

'Ah!' said Mick Stranahan. 'The lovely Nurse Tatum.'

A knot burned on the back of Chemo's head, where Stranahan had clubbed him with the butt of the Remington. Teetering to his feet, the first thing Chemo focused upon was Dr Rudy Graveline – cuffed half-naked to the bed. His eyes were taped shut and a frayed old beach towel had been tucked around his neck. A menacing tong-like contraption lay poised near the surgeon's face: a speculum, designed for spreading the nostrils. It sounded like something Moe would have used on Curly.

Stranahan stood at a small table cluttered with tubes and gauze and rows of sharp stainless-steel instruments. In one corner of the table was a heavy grey textbook, opened to the middle.

'What the fuck?' said Chemo. His voice was foggy and asthmatic.

Stranahan handed him a sterile glove. 'I need your help,' he said.

'No, not him,' objected Rudy, from the bed.

'This is where we are,' Stranahan said to Chemo. 'We've got his nose numb and packed. Got the eyes taped to keep out the blood. Got plenty of sponges – I'm sorry, you look confused.'

'Yeah, you could say that.' Scraggles of hair rose on the nape of Chemo's scalp. His stomach heaved against his ribs. He wanted out – but where was the goddamn shotgun?

'Put the glove on,' Stranahan told him.

'What for?'

'The doctor doesn't want to talk about what happened to Victoria Barletta – she died during an operation exactly like this. I know it's been four years, and Dr Graveline's had hundreds of patients since then. But my idea was that we might be able to refresh his memory by re-enacting the Barletta case. Right here.'

Rudy fidgeted against the handcuffs.

Chemo said, 'For Christ's sake, just tell him what he wants to hear.'

'There's nothing to tell,' said Rudy. By now he was fairly certain that Stranahan was bluffing. Already Stranahan had skipped several fundamental steps in the rhinoplasty. He had not attempted to file the bony dorsum, for example. Nor had he tried to make any incisions inside of Rudy's nostrils. This led Rudy to believe that Stranahan wasn't serious about doing a homemade nose job, that he was merely trying to frighten the doctor into a cheap confession.

To Chemo, of course, the makeshift surgical suite was a gulag of horrors. One glimpse of Rudy, blindfolded and splayed like a pullet on a bed, convinced Chemo that Mick Stranahan was monstrously deranged.

Stranahan was running a forefinger down a page of the surgical text. 'Apparently this is the most critical part of the operation – fracturing the nasal bones on both sides of the septum. This is very, very delicate.' He handed Chemo a small steel mallet and said, 'Don't worry, I've been reading up on this.'

Chemo tested the weight of the mallet in his hand. 'This isn't funny,' he said.

'Is it supposed to be? We're talking about a young woman's death.'

'Probably it was an accident,' Chemo said. He gestured derisively at Rudy Graveline. 'The guy's a putz, he probably just fucked up.'

'But you weren't there. You don't know.'

Chemo turned to Rudy. 'Tell him, you asshole.'

Rudy shook his head. 'I'm an excellent surgeon,' he insisted.

Stranahan foraged through the toolbox until he found the proper instrument.

'What's that, a chisel?' Chemo said.

'Very good,' Stranahan said. 'Actually, it's called an osteotome. A Storz number four. But basically, yeah, it's just a chisel. Look here.'

He leaned over the bed and pinched the bridge of Rudy Graveline's nose. With the other hand he gingerly slipped the osteotome into the surgeon's right nostril, aligning the instrument lengthwise along the septum. 'Now, Mr Tatum, I'll hold this steady while you give it a slight tap—'

'Nuggghhh,' Rudy protested. The dull pressure of the chisel reawakened the fear that Stranahan was really going to do it.

'Did you say something?' Stranahan asked.

'You were right,' the surgeon said. His voice came out in a wheeze. 'About the Barletta girl.'

'You killed her?'

'I didn't mean to, I swear to God.' Between the pinch of Stranahan's fingers and the poke of the osteotome, Rudy Graveline talked like he had a terrible cold.

He said, 'What happened was, I let go of her nose. It was . . . terrible luck. I let go just when the nurse hit the chisel, so—'

'So it went all the way up.'

'Yes. The radio was on, I lost my concentration. The Lakers and the Sonics. I didn't do it on purpose.'

Stranahan said, 'And afterwards you got your brother to destroy the body.'

'Uh-huh.' Rudy couldn't nod very well with the Number 4 osteotome up his nostril.

'And what about my assistant?' Stranahan glanced over at Chemo. 'You hired him to kill me, right?'

Rudy's Adam's apple hopped up and down like a scalded toad. Sightless, he imagined the scene by what he could hear: the plink of the instruments, the two men breathing, the wind and the waves shaking the house, or so it seemed.

Stranahan said, 'Look, I know it's true. I'd just like to hear the terms of the deal.'

Rudy felt the chisel nudge the bony plate between the eye sockets, deep in his face. He was, understandably, reluctant to give Mick Stranahan the full truth – that the price on his head was to be paid in discount dermatological treatments.

Rudy said, 'It was sort of a trade.'

'This I gotta hear.'

'Tell him,' Rudy said blindly to Chemo. 'Tell him the arrangement with the dermabrasion, tell—'

Chemo reacted partly out of fear of incrimination and partly out of embarrassment. He let out a feral grunt and swung the mallet with all his strength. It was a clean blow to the butt of the osteotome, precisely the right spot.

Only much too hard. So hard that it knocked the chisel out of Stranahan's hand.

So hard that the instrument disappeared entirely, as if inhaled by Rudy Graveline's nose.

So hard that the point of the chisel punched through the brittle plate of the ethmoid bone and penetrated Rudy Graveline's brain.

The hapless surgeon shuddered, kicked his left leg, and went limp. 'Damn,' said Stranahan, jerking his hand away from the blood.

This he hadn't planned. Stranahan had anticipated having to kill Chemo, at some point, because of the man's stubborn disposition to violence. He had figured that Chemo would grab for the shotgun or maybe a kitchen knife, something dumb and obvious; then it would be over. But the doctor, alive and indictable, Stranahan had promised to Al García.

He looked up from the body and glared at Chemo. 'You happy now?'

Chemo was already moving for the door, wielding the mallet and neutered Weed Whacker as twin bludgeons, warning Stranahan not to follow. Stranahan could hear the seven-foot killer clomping through the darkened house, then out on the wooden deck, then down the stairs toward the water.

When Stranahan heard the man coming back, he retrieved the Remington from under the bed and waited.

Chemo was panting as he ducked through the doorway. 'The fuck did you do to your boat?'

'I shot a hole in it,' Stranahan said.

'Then how do we get off this goddamn place?'

'Swim.'

Chemo's lips curled. He glowered at the bulky lawn appliance strapped to the stump of his arm. He could unfasten it, certainly, but how far would he get? Paddling with one arm at night, in these treacherous waters! And what about his face – it would be excruciating, the stringent salt water scouring his fresh abrasions. Yet there was no other way out. It would be lunacy to stay.

Stranahan lowered the gun and said, 'Here, I think this belongs to you.'

He took something out of his jacket and held it up, so the gold and silver links caught the flash of the lantern lights. Chemo's knees went to rubber when he saw what it was.

The Swiss diving watch. The one he lost to the barracuda.

'Still ticking,' said Mick Stranahan.

THIRTY-FOUR

At dawn the cold front arrived under a foggy purple brow, and the wind swung dramatically to the north. The waves off the Atlantic turned swollen and foamy, nudging the boat even further from the shore of Cape Florida. The tide was still creeping out.

The women were weary of shouting and waving for help, but they tried once more when a red needlenose speedboat rounded the point of the island. The driver of the speedboat noticed the commotion and cautiously slowed to approach the other craft. A young woman in a lemon cotton pullover sat beside him.

She stood up and called out: 'What's the matter?'

Christina Marks waved back. 'Engine trouble! We need a tow to the marina.'

The driver, a young muscular Latin, edged the speedboat closer. He offered to come aboard and take a look at the motor.

'Don't bother,' said Christina. 'The gas line is cut.'

'How'd that happen?' The young man couldn't imagine.

It was a strange scene so early on a cold morning: three women alone on rough water. The one, a slender brunette, looked pissed off about something. The blonde in a sweatsuit was unsteady, maybe seasick.

Then there was a Cuban woman, attractive except for an angry-looking bald patch on the crown of her head.

'You all right?' the young man asked.

The Cuban woman nodded brusquely. 'How about giving us a lift?'

The young man in the speedboat turned to his companion and quietly said, 'Tina, I don't know. Something's fucked up here.'

'We've got to help,' the young woman said. 'I mean, we can't just leave them.'

'There'll be other boats.'

Christina Marks said, 'At least can we borrow your radio? Something happened out here.' She motioned toward the distant stilt houses.

'What was it?' said Tina, alarmed.

Maggie Gonzalez, who had prison to consider, said firmly: 'Nothing happened. She's drunk out of her mind.'

And Heather Chappell, who had her career to consider, said: 'We were s'posed to meet some guys for a party. The boat broke down, that's all.'

Christina's eyes went from Heather to Maggie. She felt like crying, and then she felt like laughing. She was as helpless and amused as she could be. So much for sisterhood.

'I know how that goes,' Tina was saying, 'with parties.'

Heather said, 'Please, I don't feel so hot. We've been drifting for hours.' Her face looked familiar, but Tina wasn't sure.

The Cuban woman with the bald patch said, 'Do you have an extra soda?'

'Sure,' said Tina. 'Ritchie, throw them a rope.'

*

Sergeant Al García bent over the rail and got rid of his breakfast muffins.

'I thought you were a big fisherman,' needled Luis Córdova. 'Who was it told me you won some fishing tournament.'

'That was different.' García wiped his moustache with the sleeve of the windbreaker. 'That was on a goddamn lake.'

The journey out to Stiltsville had been murderously rough. That was García's excuse for getting sick – the boat ride, not what they had found inside the house.

Luis Córdova chucked him on the arm. 'Anyway, you feel better now.'

The detective nodded. He was still smouldering about the patrol boat, about how it had taken three hours to get a new pin for the prop. Three crucial hours, it turned out.

'Where's Wilt?' García asked.

'Inside. Pouting.'

The man known as Chemo was standing up, his right arm suspended over his head. Luis Córdova had hand-cuffed him to the overhead water pipes in the kitchen. As a security precaution, the Weed Whacker had been unstrapped from the stump of Chemo's left arm. Trailing black and red cables, the yard clipper lay on the kitchen bar.

Luis Córdova pointed at the monofilament coil on the rotor. 'See that – human hair,' he said to Al García. 'Long hair, too; a brunette. Probably a woman's.'

García turned to the killer. 'Hey, Wilt, you a barber?'

'Fuck you.' Chemo blinked neutrally.

'He says that a lot,' said Luis Córdova. 'It's one of

his favourite things. All during the Miranda, he kept saying it.'

Al García walked over to Chemo and said, 'You're aware that there's a dead doctor in the bedroom?'

'Fuck you.'

'See,' said Luis Córdova. 'That's all he knows.'

'Well, at least he knows *something*.' García groped in his pocket and came out with a wrinkled handkerchief. He put the handkerchief to his face and returned to the scene in the bedroom. He came out a few minutes later and said, 'That's very unpleasant.'

'Sure is,' agreed Luis Córdova.

'Mr Tatum, since you're not talking, you might as well listen.' García arranged himself on one of the wicker barstools and stuck a cigar in his mouth. He didn't light it.

He said, 'Here's what's happened. You and the doctor have a serious business disagreement. You lure the dumb bastard out here and try to torture some dough out of him. But somehow you screw it up – you kill him.'

Chemo reddened. 'Horse shit,' he said.

Luis Córdova looked pleased. 'Progress,' he said to García. 'We're making progress.'

Chemo clenched his fist, causing the handcuff to rattle against the rusty pipe. He said, 'You know damn well who it was.'

'Who?' García raised the palms of his hands. 'Where is the mystery man?'

'Fuck you,' Chemo said.

'What I can't figure out,' said the detective, 'is why you didn't take off. After all this mess, why'd you stay on the house? Hell, *chico*, all you had to do was jump.'

Chemo lowered his head. His cheeks felt hot and prickly; a sign of healing, he hoped.

'Maybe he can't swim,' suggested Luis Córdova.

'Maybe he's scared,' García said.

Chemo said nothing. He closed his eyes and concentrated on the soothing sounds of freedom; the wind and the waves and the gulls, and the ticking of his waterproof wristwatch.

Al García waited until he was outside to light up the cigar. He turned a shoulder to the wind and cupped the match in his hand.

'I called for the chopper,' said Luis Córdova. 'And a guy from the ME.'

'Gives us what, maybe half an hour?'

'Maybe,' said the young marine patrolman. 'We got time to check the other houses. Wilt's not going anywhere.'

García tried to blow a smoke ring, but the wind sucked it away. The cusp of the front had pushed through, and the sky over Biscayne Bay was clearing. The first sunlight broke out of the haze in slanted golden shafts that fastened to the water like quartz, lighting up the flats.

'I see why you love it out here,' García said.

Luis Córdova smiled. 'Some days it's like a painting.'

'Where do you think he went?'

'Mick? He might be dead. Guy that size could probably take him. Dump the body off the house.'

García gnawed sceptically at the end of the cigar. 'It's possible. Or he could've got away. Don't forget, he had that pump gun.'

'His skiff's sunk,' Luis Córdova noted. 'Somebody blasted a hole in the bottom.'

'Weird,' said Al García. 'But if I had to guess, I'd say he probably wasn't around when all this happened. I'd say he got off the house.'

'Maybe.'

'Whatever happened out here, it was between Tatum and the doctor. Maybe it was money, maybe it was something to do with surgery. Christ, you notice that guy's arm?'

'His face, too,' said Luis Córdova. 'What you're saying makes sense. Just looking at him, he's not the type to file a lawsuit.'

'But doing it with a hammer, that's cold.' García puffed his cheeks as if to whistle. 'On the other hand, your victim ain't exactly Marcus Welby . . . whatever. It all fits.'

That was the main thing.

A small boat, a sleek yellow outboard, came speeding across the bonefish flats. It was headed south on a line toward Soldier Key. García watched the boat intently, walked around the house to keep it in view.

'Don't worry, I know him,' said Luis Córdova. 'He's a fishing guide.'

'Wonder why he's out here alone.'

'Maybe his clients didn't show. That happens when it blows hard – these rubes'll chicken out at the dock. Meanwhile it turns into a nice day.'

Just south of Stiltsville, the yellow skiff angled off the flats and stopped in a deep blue channel. The guide took out a rod and casted a bait over the side. Then he sat down to wait.

'See?' said Luis Córdova. 'He's just snapper fishing.'

García was squinting against the sun. 'Luis, you see something else out there?'

'Whereabouts?'

The detective pointed. 'I'd say a quarter mile. Something in the water, between us and that island.'

Luis Córdova raised one hand to block the glare. With the other hand he adjusted his sunglasses. 'Yeah, now I see it,' he said. 'Swimming on top. Looks like a big turtle.'

'Yeah?'

'Grandpa loggerhead. Or maybe it's a porpoise. You want me to get the binoculars?'

'No, that's OK.' García turned around and leaned his back against the wooden rail. He was grinning broadly, the stogie bobbing under his moustache. 'I've never seen a porpoise before, except for the Seaquarium.'

'Well, there's still a few wild ones out here,' Luis Córdova said. 'If that's what it was.'

'That's what it was,' said Al García. 'I'm sure of it.'

He tapped the ashes off the cigar and watched them swirl and scatter in the sea breeze. 'Come on,' he said, 'let's go see if Wilt's learned any new words.'

EPILOGUE

BLONDELL WAYNE TATUM, also known as Chemo, pleaded guilty in Dade Circuit Court to the murders of Dr Rudy Graveline and Chloe Simpkins Stranahan. He later was extradited to Pennsylvania, where he confessed to the unsolved slaying of Dr Gunther MacLeish, a semi-retired dermatologist and pioneer in the use of electrolysis to remove unwanted facial hair. Because of his physical handicap, and because of favourable testimony from sympathetic Amish elders, Tatum received a relatively lenient sentence of three seventeen-year terms, to be served concurrently. He is now a trusty in charge of the winter vegetable garden at the Union Correctional Institution at Raiford, Florida.

MAGGIE ORESTES GONZALEZ pleaded no contest to one count of obstruction for lying to investigators after Victoria Barletta's death. She received a six-month suspended sentence, but was ordered to serve one hundred hours of community service as a volunteer nurse at the Dade County Stockade, where she was taken hostage and killed during a food-related riot.

HEATHER CHAPPELL continued to appear in numerous television shows, including *Matlock, L.A.*

Law and *Murder, She Wrote*. Barely five months after Dr Rudy Graveline's death, Heather quietly entered an exclusive West Hollywood surgical clinic and underwent a breast augmentation, a blepharoplasty, a rhinoplasty, a complete rhytidectomy, a chin implant, and suction lipectomies of the thighs, abdomen, and buttocks. Soon afterward, Heather's movie career was revived when she was offered – and accepted – the role of Triana, a Klingon prostitute, in *Star Trek VII: The Betrayal of Spock*.

KIPPER GARTH never fully recovered from his *pelota* injuries and retired from the law. His lucrative personal injury practice was purchased by a prominent Miami Beach firm, which sought – and received – permission to retain the use of Kipper Garth's name and likeness in all future advertising and promotion.

The Dade County Grand Jury refused to indict JOHN NORDSTROM for assaulting his lawyer. Nordstrom and his wife pursued their malpractice claim against the Whispering Palms Spa and Surgery Center and eventually settled out of court for $315,000, forty per cent of which went straight to their new attorney.

MARIE NORDSTROM'S contractured breast implants were repaired in a simple out-patient procedure performed by Dr George Ginger. The operation took only ninety minutes and was a complete success.

The seat held on the County Commission by ROBERTO PEPSICAL was filled by his younger brother, Charlie. The zoning rights to the Old Cypress

Towers project were eventually picked up by a group of wealthy South American investors. Ignoring protests from environmentalists and local home owners, the developers paved over the ballpark and playground to construct a thirty-three-storey luxury condominium tower, with a chic roof-top night-club called Freddie's. Nine weeks after it opened, the entire building was seized by the Drug Enforcement Administration in a money-laundering probe that was code-named 'Operation Piranha'.

The popular television show *In Your Face* was cancelled after the disappearance and presumed death of its star, REYNALDO FLEMM. The programme's executive producers soon announced that a $25,000 scholarship in Reynaldo's name would be awarded to the Columbia University School of Journalism, from which, ironically, he had been twice expelled.

Exporter J. W. KIMBLER received a personal letter from the vice-chancellor of the Leeward Islands Medical University in Guadeloupe. The note said: 'Thank you for your most recent shipment, which has become the highlight of our spring semester. On behalf of the faculty and of the future surgeons who study here, accept my deepest gratitude for a superior product.'

For his dramatic videotaped footage of Reynaldo Flemm's cosmetic surgery, cameraman WILLIE VELASQUEZ was offered – and accepted – his own news-documentary programme on the Fox Television Network. *Eyewitness Undercover!* premiered in the 8 p.m. time slot on Thursdays, and in four major markets decisively beat out *The Cosby Show* in both the Nielsens and Arbitrons.

CHRISTINA MARKS declined an offer to become a producer for Willie's new programme. Instead, she left television and took a job as an assistant city editor at the *Miami Herald*, and with it a pay cut of approximately $135,000. Soon after moving to Miami, she purchased a second-hand Boston Whaler and a nautical chart of South Biscayne Bay.

The parents of Victoria Barletta were puzzled to receive, via UPS, a black Samsonite suitcase containing approximately $118,400 in cash. A letter accompanying the money described it as a gift from the estate of Dr Rudy Graveline. The letter was signed by a retired investigator named MICK STRANAHAN and bore no return address.